T0277222

Of SEA and SMOKE

Books by Gillian Bronte Adams

The Songkeeper Chronicles
Orphan's Song
Songkeeper
Song of Leira

The Fireborn Epic
Of Fire and Ash
Of Sea and Smoke
Of Dawn and Embers

Out of Darkness Rising

# of SEA and SMOKE

THE FIREBORN EPIC
BOOK TWO

GILLIAN BRONTE ADAMS

Published by Enclave Publishing, an imprint of Oasis Family Media, LLC

Carol Stream, Illinois, USA.
www.enclavepublishing.com

ISBN: 979-8-88605-078-3 (hardback)
ISBN: 979-8-88605-079-0 (printed softcover)
ISBN: 979-8-88605-081-3 (ebook)

Cover design by Darco Tomic
Typesetting and jacket design by Jamie Foley, www.JamieFoley.com
Map and illustrations by Gerralt Landman, www.DimensionDoor.nl

Printed in the United States of America.

This one is for Brynne,
whom I have always looked up to,
the Delmar to my Rafi.

SABEE-SAÃ

LANGEE RIVER

WASTES OF ELIAM

CHOTH TERRITORY

CHIZNOWITH ARENAS

CETMUR

ISKIL MOUNTAINS

KALAMI

URDE

OLD NADAA

THE EMPIRE OF NADAAR

CENTRAL TERRITORIES

TEHORRA PEAK
NON MOUNTAINS
THE GORGE
QUE TERRITORIES
MAH JUNGLE
ZORRAD
DAGMUR
THE ALON COAST
SOLDONIA
THE ISLAND EMPIRE OF CANTHOR
DIMENSION DOOR

PROLOGUE: SEA-DEMONS

"Run, Rafi," Delmar gasped, and Rafi ran, wincing as his bare feet pounded the earth, soles cut and bruised and weeping with sores. Sores still marked his wrists and ankles, too, though it had been three weeks since he'd been freed from his manacles. His wounds stung in the raw wind gusting in off the sea, just visible in glimpses through the foliage to their right.

But he ran on, until Delmar finally called the halt, and then he collapsed at the base of a saga tree, exhausted, but still wary enough to avoid the poisonous sap oozing from each thorny knot. Tilting his head back to gulp for air, he eyed the pink fruits bobbing from the springy, arching branches, and he was suddenly so hungry, he felt dizzy.

Climbing the spiky trunk was out of the question, but if Delmar boosted him onto his shoulders, he might be able to snatch a few.

He licked his dry lips. "Del?"

Delmar blinked the sweat from his eyes and tracked his gaze. "No, not ripe yet. Too risky."

He was probably right. He usually was. Poison not only bled from the saga's trunk but lurked in the rinds of unripe fruit—most potent in the palest, petering out as the rind darkened to crimson, until they were finally safe to eat. These wouldn't kill them, but they might make them sick. Too great a risk when *he* was on their heels.

Once, Rafi had found Delmar's persistent rightness annoying. That was before they'd spent three years imprisoned together beneath the earth. Without sun or moon to mark the days, or even consistent meals to mark the time, Delmar had been his only constant.

Always there. Always steady. Always right.

Delmar was his brother, yes, but also his prince, and Rafi would follow him to the ends of the earth.

So when Delmar's heaving chest slowed, and he pushed back to his feet, strong and sturdy and determined to set forth again, Rafi shoved down his own prickling weariness and his aching hunger, and he gripped Delmar's hand and shot up beside him. And when Delmar ran, he ran too.

Side by side, step by step, breath by breath.

The jungle seemed to blur around them and time with it. His feet felt like stones bound to the ends of his legs. He staggered, weaving clumsily from side to side with each step, and though he had never been drunk, he guessed it must feel something like this.

Something like drifting, mind and body, in different directions.

Then Delmar was there, steadying him. Delmar, who ran on with his head high, the glow of sunset a fire in his eyes. Delmar, who still looked the prince, despite his tattered trousers and the shredded tunic flapping open to expose his scratched and bitten chest.

Rafi couldn't remember their father's face anymore, only the hints of it he saw in Delmar's heavy brow and in the set of his mouth—strong, proud, even a tinge cruel, if you didn't know him. Didn't know to wait and watch for the softening of his eyes and the crinkling lines that blossomed around them whenever he unveiled his kindly, kingly smile.

"Come on, brother. You can do it. You can keep going."

And whether it was the strength of conviction in Delmar's voice, or the calloused hand holding him up, or just the knowledge that slowing down meant giving up with the Emperor's Stone-eye on their trail, Rafi dug deep into his failing reserves and kept running.

"Sleep, Rafi," Delmar murmured softly, and Rafi tried.

Stretched out in the damp jungle loam, he tried, but he couldn't. His mind was too alert, his senses too heightened. When he flopped onto his back, vines and leaves canopied high above him, the ocean of moon-washed sky even higher, he felt exposed without ceiling or walls to shelter him from the host of things crawling, rustling, hooting, and yowling through the night. When he rolled to his stomach, arms under his head, one ear pressed to the earth, he could hear his heart thudding against the soil, and it sounded like footsteps, running, running, running.

On and on and on without end.

"Rafi . . . *sleep*."

Delmar was only a shadow at the base of a neefwa tree, one long leg outstretched, the other bent, yet Rafi knew his brother's eyes gleamed restlessly, alert for signs of pursuit. It was so every time they halted—Delmar still awake when Rafi fell asleep and awake again when Rafi awoke.

Did he ever rest?

Rafi sat up. "What about you?"

Delmar shifted, stretching out both legs. "Sleep? Sleep is for mortals. I have given it up."

"Probably for the best." Rafi smiled slyly. "Who could sleep once you start rumbling?"

Delmar gave a quiet laugh. "You sound like her, you know? Mother."

Rafi's stomach twisted. When the cell door had first clanged shut behind them, leaving them sprawled in the filth littering the floor, shock had given way slowly to horror. To anger and to grief. Which, as days turned into months, became despair. Delmar had broken free of it first, and he had towed Rafi with him, telling him fiercely, "We are not this, brother. We do not give up quietly. We do not fade into the dark. We are Tetrani. We cannot forget. Not who did this. Not what they deserve. Not where we came from. Not who we are. We must remember."

That word had been a rolling drumbeat, a throbbing pulse.

REMEMBER. REMEMBER. REMEMBER.

Delmar's voice turned wistful now. "She was always complaining about Father's snoring. Even lodged a formal grievance one morning over a pot of seaweed tea. Called us three as witnesses—you, me, and—" He bit off the end, for even he had trouble speaking her name.

Cira, their little sister, lost along with their parents.

Not to illness, no matter what the imperial court claimed. But to poison. Or so Delmar believed, and who was Rafi to doubt him?

"He denied it, claimed she was dreaming. She insisted no one could dream over such a roaring, and on they went." Delmar hesitated. "Do you . . . do you remember, Rafi?"

There it was. The question.

With that question as their net, they had cast for memories each day in their cell, drawing them all, big and small and shining with detail, from the briny expanse of the past.

Rafi closed his eyes, too ashamed to look at his brother, even in the dark. "I . . . I can't even see their faces anymore, Del. I try, but it's like looking at them through water."

Colors muddled. Features blurred. Lost in his hazed memory.

Silence seeped between them in the wake of his confession, and the noises of the night rushed to fill the void. Rafi wished he'd bitten his tongue instead.

Then grasses rustled, and Delmar eased down beside him, and Rafi gratefully shifted over to make room. There, at last, with his spine pressed against Delmar's—as they had slept for years on the single mildewed straw mat in that cramped cell—he started to drift off to sleep.

But not before he heard Delmar whisper, "Sometimes, I wish I didn't see them so clearly."

"—up, Rafi." Delmar spoke low and urgently into his ear.

Rafi bolted to his feet, then swayed dizzily, disoriented by the sunlight bathing earth, leaves, and vines. It was bright. Too bright. They had overslept, lost half a day of running, of distance from *him*.

Gut sinking, he turned to Delmar. "Del, I—"

Delmar clamped one hand over his mouth and tugged him down behind a tigertooth shrub. "He's here, Rafi. He's caught up."

Needles prickled Rafi's skin. "Sahak?"

Delmar released his grip and nodded toward a thick cluster of towering neefwa trees forming a wall across the wild undergrowth of the Mah. Scarlet, orange, and gold flashed between the trunks, spreading out to surround them, and over the crackle of trampled plants sounded the faint clinking of mail and rattling of chariot wheels.

Delmar swiped at his mouth, hand scraping over the stubble on his chin. His shoulders, ribs, and spine formed sharp ridges beneath his shredded tunic. Built like their father, he'd always been the strong one. Sturdy limbs, broad chest, and corded muscle. Even on their worst days in the dungeon, he had seemed unshakable. But after a few weeks on the run, he seemed to be wasting away, until only raw bones and sinew remained—something for the Emperor's Stone-eye who hunted them to gnaw at, chew up, and spit back out.

Now, he looked almost as frail and frightened as Rafi felt.

"What do we do, Del?"

Delmar set his jaw. "We run."

Soldiers burst from the thicket, and Delmar took off, and Rafi tore after him.

A voice—familiar—shouted for them to halt.

Wind catching in his teeth, Rafi raced after Delmar. Normally, they ran side by side, but today, no matter how hard he pushed, he could not close the gap between them. Delmar set a grueling pace to leave their armored pursuers behind, and maybe, Rafi couldn't help but think, to punish him for insisting that Delmar rest and causing them both to oversleep.

If they were caught now, it would be his fault.

That fear thrust him onward through slapping leaves and grasping vines and raking thorns. Over soggy ground that spattered mud and tree roots that tripped and bruised. Maybe Rafi should have expected to find the jungle itself in league with their foes, for when the empire of Nadaar seized a land, it claimed its very soul. But surely the Mah was old enough to recall a time before the imperial interlopers arrived. Shouldn't it be on their side?

Or did it see them as interlopers too?

He shook free of the dizzying spiral of thoughts. "Del?"

"Save your breath, Rafi, and run."

"Sorry, Del," Rafi mumbled through cracked lips. "I can't . . . go on."

His vision swam, and he curled over his knees in the fog creeping across the mountainside. Misty droplets cooled his flushed forehead, and he shivered, though his whole body burned like a fire was spreading beneath his skin. He twisted his head and could make out Delmar standing over him with the sun only a bloody sliver behind him as it sank beyond the peak. His brother gazed back the way they had come, tattered tunic flapping in the breeze that sighed across the bald slope, across oozing stumps and muddy ruts left by a recent deforesting. The breeze carried the sting of salt blown off the Alon coast, and if he held his breath, Rafi could hear the roar of the sea around the next curve and far, far below. Even closer came clanking armor and thudding boots.

They were done for. Or at least, he was.

Delmar rested one calloused hand on Rafi's shoulder, and now all he could see were his brother's feet, just as battered and wounded and filthy as his. "Catch your breath. You'll be fine in a minute."

Rafi would sooner see the sky fall than disappoint Delmar.

It had been three days since Sahak had nearly caught them sleeping. Three days of staggering doggedly onward, smothered by exhaustion, and strung out on the fear of hearing soldiers in every rustle, seeing knives in every flash of movement. Three days that had ground them down to exposed bones and raw nerves and failing flesh.

He coughed and spat. "I've got nothing left. I can't . . . keep running."

"What you can't do is quit. We're Tetrani. We don't give up."

That might be true of Delmar, but never of Rafi. He had always been the unreliable son, the mischievous prince, the foolish younger brother, ever quicker with his wit than his fists. "I do. You go, Del. Go on without me."

"Go on without you?" Delmar seized the front of Rafi's tunic and hauled him to his feet. "Too tired to run, but not to make jokes, is that it? Because you know I'm not leaving you behind."

Mere inches separated them now, and Rafi couldn't help but see the exhaustion that dulled his brother's eyes.

Oh, Ches-Shu, Delmar was close to cracking too.

He had always been strong for Rafi. Maybe, just this once, Delmar needed someone to be strong for him. "You got me," he heard himself saying. "Just a joke."

Convincing his legs, though, that would be the trick.

With a grunt, Delmar wedged his shoulder under Rafi's arm, holding him up. "Good, because we are not dying today, Rafi." His voice rang with defiance, and so did each step as they staggered on, arm in arm, scaling the steep slope above the deforested section, weaving around jumbled boulders, and ducking under vine-choked trees with roots pulling free of the soil. They pressed on, while the light dimmed to a murky gray, until they stumbled around a bend and found their path blocked by sheer cliffs ahead and a long drop-off to their left.

"No," Delmar breathed, reeling to a stop. "No, no, no."

Rafi's legs gave out, and his arm slipped from his brother's shoulder as Delmar scrambled to the edge overlooking the howling ocean below. A long thin shriek quavered on the air until the wind shredded it and scattered the echoes. Gooseflesh shivered up Rafi's arms. He had heard such a cry only once before, but his mother had been Alonque by birth, and she had told him tales of the creatures that haunted the coast.

"Rafi . . . look."

The wind strangled Delmar's voice, stripping it of emotion, so Rafi didn't know what to expect as he dragged himself close enough to peer over that dizzying drop. Shimmering four-legged forms darted in and out of the cresting waves far, far below, rushing in on each swell, surging high on seafoam, and diving down again into the troughs beneath. One reared back its head, flinging its thick, twisted mane, and let out a keening shriek that seemed to rend flesh from bone and stab deeper and deeper still.

"Are those . . . sea-demons?"

"The ledge." Delmar crouched beside him, pointing. "See?"

Rafi blinked and tracked his finger to the narrow shelf of rock sticking out from the cliffside nearly fifteen feet below. Carpeted with moss and a few stubborn shrubs, it was barely two feet wide, and it was all that stood between them and the tossing, churning sea. Just the sight of that drop made his parched throat tighten.

One wrong move, and they could fall.

Could fall and fall forever.

"Come on." Showing no sign of fear, Delmar flung himself onto his stomach, chest sticking out over the plunge, then reached a hand toward Rafi. "I'll lower you down."

Down there?

His body reacted even before the words sank in. He fell back, scrabbling, trying to get as far from the drop as possible. But the look of desperation and of disappointment on Delmar's face broke through his panic, and he stopped.

"This is it, Rafi. This is our escape."

"I-I can't . . ."

"Yes, you can, and you will, for me." Delmar seized his wrist and brought his forehead to touch Rafi's. The slow and steady throb of his brother's pulse, and the certainty in his eyes, seemed to pull Rafi forward like a riptide towing him out to sea, until his filthy, battered feet slipped past the edge and dangled over the drop into oncoming darkness.

He sucked in a shaky breath, then another, and still couldn't get enough air.

"Look at me," Delmar said, and Rafi did, catching the shimmer of a tear welling in the corner of his eye. It was a rare thing for his brother, and it startled Rafi enough that he couldn't even react as Delmar shoved him over the side.

He fell, choking on a scream.

Then jerked to a stop at the end of Delmar's grip.

The world swung sickeningly beneath Rafi's feet as voices broke out overhead, one distinct above the rest. Sahak. Too late. "Pull me up, Del." He tried to swing his other arm up, to latch on with both hands. "Pull me up!"

They couldn't be taken like this, helpless, exposed, unable to fight back.

Delmar grunted, face darkened from the strain, then slowly shook his head, and the cold churn of nausea that washed over Rafi had nothing to do with the height and everything to do with the look in his brother's eyes. Not sorrow. Not fear. But anguish.

"Del . . . Del . . . please . . ."

"I'm sorry, Rafi."

With a wrench and a twist of his arm, Delmar let go.

Rafi plummeted like a stone toward the dark and turbulent waters. But the impact came sooner than expected. His feet struck something and slipped off, toppling his body forward and slamming his head against the cliff face.

The burst of pain blinded him.

Once, on a dare, he had tried to dive with Delmar to the bottom of the sound outside Cetmur, clinging to his brother as an anchor to sink deeper than he could have managed on his own. He'd swum down until his chest burned, his ears throbbed, and his vision blurred, and he had to kick and thrash and fight his way back to the surface before he drowned.

Rafi fought like that toward consciousness now. He reached sluggishly to his head, and his fingers came back sticky and wet. Eerie shrieks sounded below, and his senses reeled as he came fully alert, sprawled on the ledge, with half his body hanging over the brink.

He shoved away from the drop, flinging his back against the rock wall, chest heaving in sharp gasps, tunic fluttering in the wind. His skull felt like it was about to split. Gravel pelted the top of his head, dislodged from above, and he craned his neck to see Delmar lurch into view on the cliff's edge, clutching one arm to his side.

His brother's name formed on his lips, but Delmar was speaking. "Rafi? I left him to die. He couldn't keep up. Slowed me down. Too weak and feverish. I doubt he'll last the night."

Rafi tried to call up, to explain that he had tried, that he hadn't meant to fail him, but his vision blurred, and his mind seemed to skim through time like a stone skipping across a pond, because when his senses returned, it wasn't his brother he heard, but Sahak. Then something shot out over the edge, flashing in the dying light, and dropped toward the sea, and Delmar . . . Delmar plunged with it. He fell clumsily, unlike himself. His feet struck the mossy ledge and slipped off, but his arms latched on, slamming his chest against the edge.

He raised his chin to meet Rafi's eyes. "Run, brother," he whispered. "Run!"

Then he shuddered and blood spilled down his chin, and Rafi's gaze dropped to the twin blades buried in Delmar's chest. *No!* Rafi flung a hand out but only felt his brother's slick wrist sliding through his fingers. Something ripped across his palm, gouging a hot line all the way to his thumb. His grip flew open, and Delmar tumbled into darkness, his cry trailing off.

Run, Rafi. Run. Those were Delmar's dying words. His final command.

But Rafi couldn't move as footsteps crunched above and the gilded toes of Sahak's boots appeared on the cliff's edge. Rafi could see the glint of the baldric of knives slung across his chest and the smug twist of his lips as he gazed out over the drop where Delmar had fallen into the gnashing teeth of the sea.

If he shifted, if he looked down, he would see Rafi.

But he turned, with a clank of chain mail, and dismissed his soldiers with a barked command, and Rafi was alone with his tears as shivers racked his body. The only sounds were the wailing wind and the weeping waves and the screaming beasts below. He waited until the coming of the sun, then he stood on legs that no longer shook, turned his back on the drop, climbed to the top of the cliff, and ran. He ran, and he kept on running, and he never once slowed long enough to wonder what might happen if he stopped.

ONE: RAFI

Clouds darken and the storm may not break,
but where smoke gathers, fire awaits.
- Alonque saying

Rafi awoke to the smell of smoke. Not the comforting scent of woodsmoke or the sweetly spiced aroma of Saffa's cooking fires, but a sharper, wilder tang that coiled down his nostrils, clawed into his throat, and whispered to him of danger.

Was that the ghost speaking to him again?

Disoriented, he jolted up, clutching at the hammock's webbed sides. His left hand twinged in pain, startling his gaze down to the brownish stains smearing the ragged bandage knotted around his palm—the one on his thigh, too, though that wound was still oozing. Ches-Shu take Sahak and all his wicked blades. Raucous snoring jarred Rafi from his thoughts. Cradling his left hand to his chest, he blinked through the hazy dawn light spilling over the thicket of hammocks strung across the crew's quarters to where Moc sprawled in the closest, scarred head thrown back, long limbs spilling over the sides, calloused feet brushing the deck each time the ship rocked.

Rafi couldn't imagine sleeping with such easy abandon. Yet, somehow, despite his injuries—or maybe because of them—he'd managed to sleep through the night with the giant Alonque snoring like a thunderstorm beside him. He still felt like he waded through a heavy fog. Only slowly did the rest of his senses catch up.

Voices filtered from above. Bare feet thumped nearby.

The cords of that strange webbed hammock thrummed beneath

him, and beyond the surrounding bulkheads, the sea moaned. Closer, a high-pitched scream shivered through the ribs of the ship, and prickles broke out across his neck and spine as he caught a whiff of that smoke again.

"Moc," he whispered. "Do you smell that?"

Moc grunted and rolled over. His hammock creaked and groaned in complaint, straining under his bulk. His snoring resumed. Stretching out his good leg, Rafi kicked at his friend's bundled form. Instead of jostling Moc, that just made Rafi's own hammock wobble and sway, but luckily it lacked the wild, twisting action of the one he'd slept in—and fallen out of—for two years in Torva's hut. Oddly enough, he actually *missed* that ornery thing.

"Moc!" Rafi raised his voice. "Wake up!"

But Moc just grumbled and snored on.

So Rafi pitched his voice lower instead, enticingly. "Breakfast, Moc. Rice cakes and simba wedges and fried saga crisps, still dripping from the oil." His own stomach started rumbling at that, but the ploy worked.

Moc cracked an eye open and mumbled, voice thick with sleep, "Is Saffa cooking?"

Rafi understood the awe in his tone. Saffa's cooking could roust a rebel from his hammock like nothing else, and it deserved its near mythical reputation. No one used spices and sauces quite like Saffa, creating flavors that fed both nostalgia and novelty. Of course, Saffa was far away, safe in the headquarters of the Que Revolution, so he ignored the question and slid gingerly from his hammock, careful to land on his good leg. "Smoke, Moc. Do you smell it?"

"Don't smell food, that's for sure." Moc yawned and scratched his stomach. "So who's cooking then, cousin, and are they burning the saga crisps?"

Shaking his head, Rafi limped toward the companionway, chasing the smoke topside.

"What?" Moc called after him. "No one likes burnt crisps!"

Grumbled complaints shushed Moc as Rafi squeezed past three other dozing, cocooned forms who must have rotated off the night watch. Drained by his aquatic confrontation with Sahak, not to mention the strain of his wounds, Rafi had collapsed straight into his hammock last night and slept like a felled log since. Given all this talk of food, he hoped someone had thought about breakfast, otherwise he would have to scrape something together himself that would make Saffa proud. Or at least not disappointed. Seaweed tea and fried saga crisps sounded like a decent start.

But would a foreign ship have such supplies? What exactly did they eat in Soldonia?

He surfaced through the hatch into a hustle of activity. A brisk, salty breeze whipped the mist around him, ruffling his tattered trousers and stinging his numerous scabbed-over cuts. Elder Gordu barked orders from the helm that sent the fisherfolk scurrying to scale the rigging. Under his direction, the villagers of Zorrad seemed to have taken to sailing with ease, though the foreign vessel, with its tall mast and snapping sails and decks raised fore and aft, was a far cry from the simple oared crafts they'd used to ply their trade before.

"Out of the way!" someone shouted, rushing past with a coiled line.

Rafi dodged, knocked against a tethered barrel, and tripped against it, hampered by his wounded leg. He caught himself face-to-face with old Hanu, who slouched behind the barrel with a large, floppy hat shadowing his thin face. Hanu raised a crooked finger to his lips, tugged the hat down, and continued snoozing, conveniently hidden from Gordu's sight.

Still up to his old tricks. Nice to know some things didn't change.

Straightening, Rafi caught a scowl from Gordu clear across the deck and smiled pleasantly in return. Some people were as fond of scowling as he was of smiling, and who was he to deny them such a simple pleasure? Hanu could sleep. Moc could snore. Gordu could scowl. What did Nahiki care?

That stray thought jarred him from his complacency.

Nahiki was no more. He had made his choice. He was Rafi Tetrani, an identity with roots, no longer free to drift and let drift, and that meant learning to make his stand.

Gordu raised one eyebrow, jabbing a finger at Rafi, but something closer to hand snagged his attention. "Sev!" Gordu had a voice like a water buffalo and the lungs to match, which had been wasted in the fishing village but here meant the whole ship could hear his commands. "Get that boat secured. Don't want it sliding across my deck."

Ducking around the mast, Rafi came upon Sev and a handful of others midship, lowering a boat, hull up, beside the large central hatch. Water slicked the boat's sides and spattered their feet.

He recognized several who had been on Nef's team the day before, sent inland as a distraction, so the ship must have reached the rendezvous point and launched the boat to retrieve them, all while he'd still been sleeping.

"You got salt in those ears?" Gordu bellowed.

"Working on it," Sev yelled back, then muttered, "you great blowhard!" At his nod, the others tossed lines over the boat, and he knotted them off, then tugged the tail end twice.

The ship shuddered and seemed to skip across the waves.

Rafi flung out his arms to balance himself. That was odd. It almost felt like . . . like what he'd done to the longboat full of royal guards, twisting through the water atop his sea-demon colt, churning and striking and leaping, until it seemed he wielded the sea itself against Sahak. He stumbled to the port rail and searched until he spotted a familiar dappled shape with bright blue eyes cutting through the swell alongside.

Ghost haunting him still.

His lips tugged into a relieved grin. Of course, he'd been too exhausted last night to wonder if the colt would follow once released into the sea, but recalling yesterday's wild, exhilarating dive, and the strength of Ghost's surging form while he clung to his soft, white, rippling mane, he breathed easier knowing Ghost had chosen to stay. For Saffa's cala root crackers, probably, but also, maybe, for him.

Cresting a wave, the colt tossed his mane and squealed before diving again. His movements seemed playful rather than threatening. Rafi doubted the colt was to blame for whatever was—

The ship trembled again, and the planks groaned under Rafi's feet.

Muttered cursing drew his focus back to Sev, whose knots had slipped, allowing the boat to skid forward and crunch against the rail. Waving off Gordu's shouting, Sev dropped to his knees and struggled to wrestle the boat and ropes back into place. He jammed his thumb and yanked his hand back, shaking blood from his split nail. "Ches-Shu!"

"Here!" Rafi limped over. "Let me help."

Sev's head shot up, and his initial scowl faded. "Oh, it's you."

"Me," Rafi said lightly, "who happens to be a master at tying knots, whereas you have always been all thumbs."

"It's not me. It's those cursed beasts, rioting below." He punctuated each word with a tug that made the boat scrape across the deck, then flicked his gaze up briefly to meet Rafi's. "Having those creatures so close . . . it's bad luck, for certain."

Rafi eyed the weathered planks beneath his feet, only a thin barrier separating them from their unexpected cargo. A stiff gust caught him across the face, bringing another whiff of that wild and tangy smoke. Standing shirtless in his bloodstained, salt-stiff trousers, he felt gooseflesh prickling his arms, though the breeze wasn't cold. Could all of this—the strange smoke, the bizarre way the ship moved—be *their* doing? He'd barely begun to understand what Ghost could do. How could he comprehend these far stranger beasts of fire and wings and stone?

He shook off his concern for now. "Still, want a hand?"

Sev's lips twisted wryly. "Depends. Which one are you offering?"

Rafi noted Sev's glance to his bandaged left hand and wriggled his right instead. "The good one, of course." Ironic, since he was left-handed. But Sahak had stabbed his left hand, so until it healed—and Ches-Shu grant it did—his right would have to suffice.

"I'll take my chances alone, thanks." Sev bent over his work again, tying off a haphazard string of knots sure to drive Gordu to wrath—chancy, indeed—while Rafi scanned the deck for Nef. It was always a good idea to keep an eye on that python in the grass, and besides, it would be helpful to know if he had discovered anything about Sahak's operations while ashore. Between the newly constructed harbor, the contingents of royal guards, and this unprecedented shipload of steeds from Soldonia, Sahak was clearly up to something, and that never boded well for anyone but Sahak.

Nahiki would have pretended not to care. Rafi had to.

"You see where Nef went, once you got back?"

Sev pushed up to his feet, inspecting his split thumbnail. "Didn't come."

"He didn't make the rendezvous point?"

"Took off after your cousin to shadow him." Sev's voice took on an edge, and Rafi wasn't sure whether it was the mention of Sahak, or because Nef had made an even worse first impression on Sev than he had on Rafi—whom he'd first threatened, then attempted to kill.

"So you just left him?"

"Left who?" Moc thumped up alongside, yawning and scratching the dark, puckered scar that marked the side of his head. It had still been red and freshly scabbed when they'd first met. Rafi had never asked about it, but he'd gathered that Nef had been involved somehow.

"Nef," Rafi said. "He took off after Sahak, and they let him go."

Sev set his jaw in that belligerent expression Rafi knew too well. "No one let him go. Your friend—"

"He's not my—" Rafi clamped his teeth and stared out toward the distant shore, visible through a gap in the mist as a thin strip of white sand trapped between the encroaching blue of the ocean and the creeping green of the jungle. Nef might not be a friend, but leaving him felt too much like running, and he'd done enough of that to last a lifetime.

He half expected the ghost to disagree and urge him to flee, but the voice had fallen strangely quiet recently. Could he even recall the last time he'd heard the ghost speak? He found the silence troubling. "We just shouldn't have left him."

Maybe if he'd stood with Delmar long ago, he wouldn't be plagued by nightmares whenever he closed his eyes. It was worse now that Sahak had told him his brother had survived the fall, only to die in agony later. Alone.

"Maybe." Moc shrugged. "But Nef can handle himself, and once his mind is fixed, there's no changing it. He is tough as a kaava and twice as prickly. You know this."

"Besides, he was gone before I arrived," Sev said, then added, "not that I would have stopped him. We must seize every chance if we are to save her."

His tone dared Rafi to disagree, but he couldn't.

He had six days until he met with Sahak to trade their stolen cargo for the hostages of Zorrad, including Sev's wife, Kaya. But if six years had not prepared him to face his brother's killer, six days were unlikely to help. They needed every advantage they could get. He rubbed the back of his neck. "I know, and I swear, I will make it right. All of it."

The words sounded strange coming from his lips, but it wasn't the first time he'd remade himself and become someone new—just the first time he sounded like his brother.

Sev searched his face, brow furrowing. "You really aren't him, are you?"

"Who? Rafi?" If only. Rafi offered a thin smile. "Sadly, I have the scars to prove it."

"No. Nahiki." With that baffling remark, Sev rounded the mast and strode away.

Watching him go, Rafi asked, "You think that's good or bad, Moc?"

Moc just clapped him on the shoulder. "Come. We must see to those fried saga crisps. You were right about that smoke. Someone is burning something."

"Moc, no one is—" Rafi broke off as a crash sounded in the hold below, where the steeds were housed, and cold sluiced through his gut. If anything happened to them . . .

He shoved toward the stern, passing the mainmast and the ten Soldonian sailors trussed at its base. He ignored their sullen stares, catching alternately at the rigging and rail to limit the strain on his wounded leg. He reached the helm where Gordu stood with his burly arms knotted over his chest, listening to one of the fisherfolk who gestured with one hand and gripped a wriggling nine-year-old boy with the other.

Iakki, face set like a thunderstorm, which made him look surprisingly like Sev.

"I caught him," the fisherman, Aruk, was saying. There was no hint of the roguish smile he was notorious for using to charm fresh rice cakes and cups of seaweed tea from the women of Zorrad—that smile, along with the dark waves of his hair, barely salted with gray, and his skill with the pan flute he wore strung on a cord about his neck, meant he was regarded, apparently, as quite a catch. "He was trying to sneak below and wreak havoc among the demon-steeds."

Iakki glared up at his accuser. "Was not!"

"I saw you with my own two eyes." Aruk matched him stare for stare, though one of his eyes was watering and already swelling shut. Never one to come quietly, Iakki.

"I weren't wreaking no havoc. I don't even know what that is!"

"Trouble," Gordu said. "Havoc means trouble, which might as well be your first name."

"Oh." Iakki sounded mollified, even pleased. "Well, I was just looking."

Beside Rafi, Moc barked out a deep laugh. "Like you just looked at Hald's goats?"

"I only teased them a little."

"They started fainting anytime anyone came near them!"

"Yeah." Iakki's eyes gleamed, and Rafi couldn't help snorting in amusement, which drew the boy's attention. "Nahiki?" Iakki wrenched free and dove into him, forcing his weight back onto his injured leg.

Ches-Shu, that hurt. He made quite the cautionary tale these days, a warning for anyone mad enough to join the Que Revolution or cross the Emperor's Stone-eye.

"So," Gordu grunted, eying Rafi balefully and using the flapping tail of his shirt to wipe the sweat from his bald skull. "You've decided to grace us with your presence at last." He jabbed a thick finger at Rafi's chest. "Something is wrong with those steeds of yours."

His manner instantly set Rafi on edge, which meant his own voice emerged with a deliberate lightness. Old instincts. Mildly annoying humor and subtle sarcasm had been his only recourse to deflect the cruelty of his long-ago jailers.

"*Something* is very vague. Could you be more specific?"

Gordu's chest swelled. "This is no time for jokes, Tetrani's son. We face a disaster."

Which was the best time for jokes. How else could you hope to distract death with a grin so you could slip past without being caught? Rafi should know. He'd evaded death a half dozen times already, give or take. But as he squared off with the village elder, he was struck by the wrinkles that sagged under the man's eyes, and how his muscular bulk, which had once strained the seams of his vest, now seemed swallowed by the folds of his threadbare shirt.

Sighing, he looked at Iakki. "Did you set off the demon-steeds?"

"No, honest, I didn't. Just wanted to take a peek, but I didn't even get the hatch open before *he*"—Iakki flung an arm back toward Aruk—"swooped in and grabbed me."

Aruk shrugged. "He was messing with the hatch. Something set them off."

Gordu's thick eyebrows drew together. "It is Ches-Shu, mark my words. We have displeased her by ferrying demon-steeds across her domain." His deep rumble dropped deeper still. "She will not be appeased until this taint has left her waters, for good."

Sea-demons were aquatic beasts, so they actually lived in Ches-Shu's domain, but Rafi doubted pointing that out would help. "So, as soon as we reach the smuggler's cove then?"

The elder harrumphed. "*If* we reach it."

The ship shuddered again, as if in response to Gordu's dire prediction, then pitched and heaved, tossing them all off-balance. Rafi fetched up against the wheel and heard muffled thuds as the others hit the rail or deck. His vision blurred, and he shook his head, convinced his senses were failing him as the world seemed to tip further over.

No, oh, Ches-Shu, *no*. Not the world. The *ship*.

TWO: CERIDWEN

These are the breeds of the solborn:
riveren swift, earthhewn strong, shadowers silent, seabloods fierce,
stormers intrepid, fireborn zealous, dawnlings radiant.
- Wisdom of the Horsemasters

Chaos and ruin spread around Ceridwen like a shock wave. With a twitch of her reins, she drew Mindar out of the *firestorm* seconds before his flames burned out, feeling his hooves catch, stride faltering, as he stumbled in exhaustion. White smoke dribbled from his nostrils, whisked to shreds by his next breath. She rubbed the knuckles of her rein hand on his neck in appreciation, for he had cleared a space around her, Nadaarian soldiers and treacherous Soldonian warriors alike fleeing before his wrath. She had a moment to breathe.

To slick the sweat from her eyes and the blood from her blade.

To study the field of battle and make sense of the pandemonium she had unleashed when she sabotaged Rhodri's rigged negotiations with the Nadaari. The deal he had struck would have secured his own throne while subjecting the kingdom of Soldonia to foreign rule. More than that, to the Dominion of Murloch, the ruthless god of Nadaar, who thirsted ever for conquest. Now, everywhere, solborn screamed and raged, chariots drawn by stone-eye tigers rattled and clattered, and warriors slew and were slain, bled and fell and were trampled underhoof.

"Do you see him?" she demanded, rising in her stirrups as Finnian te Donal, soundless upon his shadower, seemed to materialize at her side out of the shreds of dissipating smoke. From the smudges of soot dusting his nose and cheekbones, and from the steady stream of copper-fletched arrows that had guarded her back, she knew he'd never been far from her flank.

Unseen. Unheard. But there all the same.

Even now, with the effects of his ghosting fading, with his dark hair falling across his face, the scruff of a beard shadowing his jaw, and his gray cloak gusting behind him as he shook his head without needing to ask whom she meant, he seemed less a man and more a creature of falling leaves and woodsmoke. Once that had unnerved her. But now, she trusted it as she trusted the ferocity of the steed dancing beneath her and the unwavering heft of the sabre in her own right hand as she turned her gaze back to the surging tide of combat, to the tumult of steeds and riders crashing and clashing on all sides.

"Where are you?" she murmured, flexing that hand to work the feeling back into gloved fingers numbed from the shock of striking blow after blow against wood, steel, and bone.

"I think we're winning."

Finnian's voice was thick. With smoke. With relief.

But she couldn't share that relief, for they had not won. Not yet. Here and there, distinct clusters formed amidst the crushing throng and moved against the flow of combat. Not fighting for her or the Nadaari, neither for the kingdom nor against it, but fighting simply to break free. She recognized the billowing black banner of Harnoth flying over one mass, while nearby, Gimleal's heavily armored earthhewn grouped into a solid square. Even now, with so much at stake and the truth laid bare, still they refused to commit hoof or blade?

Sparks dripped from Mindar's mane, triggered by her anger. She smothered them, conserving his rekindling fire for the fight, and tossed her reins to Finnian. "Here! Hold him."

"What are you . . ." He trailed off as she pushed herself up, wincing slightly at the strain in her wounded shoulder, to get a knee and then a boot on the seat of her saddle. "*Shades*, Ceridwen, you do realize you're making yourself a target for every Ardon archer on the field?"

"Let us hope they lack your skill, then."

"Oh, and the Nadaari too?"

She couldn't resist a grin. "We both know they are no match for you." She patted Mindar's neck and stood up straight, balancing with her sabre still in hand. Mindar snorted out dusky smoke and shifted nervously, disquieted by Finnian's agitation. On an ordinary day, a calm day, she would trust him to stand still under a loose rein—and her own skill to retake her seat and reclaim her reins if he did not—but not on a day like today, a day of smoke and vengeance, a day when his blood was up and boiling with the furor of battle. Like hers.

Standing on the saddle like a captain on the prow of a ship, she scanned the waves of warriors and steeds shifting around her: seabloods and riveren, fireborn and earthhewn, shadowers visible only momentarily before ghosting again in the dust stirred by the wings of stormers hurtling overhead. And then, through a fleeting break in the frenzied stream, in a glimpse of a blood-red steed and a banner of gold and green, she finally spotted her quarry.

"Rhodri."

On her tongue, that name was the snap of a blade striking edge on edge. It was a sound she would excise from the world along with all the harm he had wrought.

"Ceridwen!" Finnian barked, and she jerked toward his voice.

An arrow sailed past her chest, scarcely a finger-width away. It would have struck her cuirass if she hadn't moved, maybe even struck flesh, and with the wound in her left shoulder throbbing even now from the strain of the day's exertion, it was all too easy to imagine the flare of pain from another arrow burrowing deep into her chest, her spine, her throat. She eased back down into the saddle and reached for her reins.

Finnian withheld them. "Pull out one more stitch, Ceridwen, and so help me . . ."

She rolled her spurs lightly across Mindar's sides, cuing a tiny spurt of flame, startling the shadower and forcing Finnian to release her reins to control his own steed. She gathered them up, readying to ride as pockets of fighting soldiers and mounted warriors began to spill back into the gap Mindar had cleared. "We have him. He's up against a wall of Craddock's earthhewn—"

"Craddock has joined the fight?"

"Hardly, but Rhodri must either break through or push around, which will slow him." She caught Finnian's gaze. "We must ride now, if we would take him."

Only one quarry mattered today, and he knew it as well as she.

If the Nadaari fled this battle, they could not get far on foot with all the war-hosts thundering in pursuit. But if Rhodri fled across the River Tain, he could be safe in his own lands before the end of the day, and there he could lead her on a wild chase, elusive as a dawnling, before she managed to snare him in battle again.

Rather than questioning her resolve, Finnian simply lifted his horn to his lips and cocked an eyebrow, awaiting permission. Old instincts tugged her to press onward now, without delay. But she'd tried riding alone before, and that had failed. She had determined to do things differently. So she nodded and, as three clear blasts rang out over the tumult, urged Mindar forward, trampling a Nadaarian soldier before he could ram his spear into the flank of a familiar dusky riveren whose rider wielded an overlong spear and wore a helm tilted jauntily atop his head.

Or maybe, as she recognized both steed and spear, simply too large for him.

"Liam?" She checked her steed alongside him, blade up, scanning for threats. "What are you doing here in the thick of it? You were supposed to stay back in the rear."

"Sticking with you. You did tell me to. Said you'd look after me."

Startled, she glanced over to find him grinning cheekily, wholly unabashed at being caught disobeying her orders. "That was one time. Not a standing command for every battle."

He shrugged and straightened his helm with a brush of his spear arm, righting it atop his unruly brown hair, before it abruptly slid askew again. It was far too big for him, and therefore, more hindrance than help in combat where any distraction—

Movement flickered in her peripheral vision.

A wisp of gray. A glint of steel. Not Finnian.

Any distraction, like Liam was to her, could be deadly.

But hers were a firerider's reflexes, honed to react to the slightest spark, and no steed could spin so swiftly, nor flare to speed so rapidly, as a fireborn. She whirled Mindar and, with a touch of the spurs, unleashed a quick blast toward the charging Ardon shadowrider. The burst did its trick, forcing the shadowrider to throw up his blade arm to shield his face, baring his side for her strike. He collapsed against the shadower's neck as his steed ran on, and the battle swallowed him.

This was why she had wanted Liam to stay back. He was too eager, too thoughtless, and too much of a concern when she should be focused on bringing down Rhodri. She wheeled Mindar to tell him so and nearly rammed her steed chest-first into a second shadower. The rider's blade quavered inches from her throat, ice sharp and deadly, then slipped from his grasp as he toppled from the saddle and crashed to the ground inches from her fireborn's coallike hooves. Unhorsed by a powerful thrust from Liam's spear.

The lad hauled his spear from the corpse, his helm now tilted over one eye. "Finnian said I could tail him today."

Ceridwen eyed Finnian as he slid silently alongside, face turned away, watching for danger, steering with his legs to keep both hands upon bow and string. His movements were swift and smooth as the wind that swirled the hem of his cloak and ruffled his hair. "Oh, he did, did he?"

"Sure he did. Said one back-rider wasn't enough to look out for you."

"The words were 'keep up with,' not 'look out for,'" Finnian corrected, keen eyes still focused away, "and I spoke them to Markham. If I'd known you were skulking around eavesdropping, Liam te Harkin, I wouldn't have promised to teach you scouting." He flicked a glance toward Ceridwen that was no doubt meant to be apologetic.

The lad did tend to interpret facts by the light of his own candle.

But it did not matter, not with Rhodri out there. She could sense her warriors amassing around her, drawn by Finnian's horn call.

She urged Mindar forward. "Lose the helm, Liam, and fall in."

"Aunt Iona told me to stop losing it—" he began, then broke off at a cough from Finnian, tugged the helm from his head, and tossed it over his shoulder.

"And what do I keep telling you?" Finnian asked patiently.

"I know, I know. Fight first. Talk later."

"That'll be the day." Nold laughed, jogging into file on his earthhewn. He offered Ceridwen a crisp salute that contrasted oddly with his laughing eyes and crooked grin. "I wager a full flask of fine Ardon vintage the lad can't hold his tongue for more than a breath. Any takers?"

Liam scoffed. "Fight now, Nold. Wager later."

"You see? Couldn't even wait for takers!"

Ceridwen almost rode on and left them. This was no time for jesting. This was a time for action. Swift, decisive, and deadly. She could feel the heat blooming within Mindar's ribcage, feel the strength coursing through his limbs, feel him pulling against the reins, yearning to be unleashed. To launch like an arrow from a bow and slice through her enemies, straight for Rhodri's heart. But there was too much at stake. Too many in her way.

So she aimed Mindar for the sky and summoned another burst of flame.

Sparks rained down, startling her companions into silence. She twisted to face Nold through the flickering cascade and swept her sabre toward where she'd last seen Rhodri. "He's there, Nold. Ripe for the taking. Clear me a path to him."

"Aye, my queen." Gone was the grin, but his salute was no less crisp.

His earthhewn rumbled forward and gradually picked up speed to ram a path through the fray. Ceridwen plunged after him, trailed by Finnian and Liam, and with flame and blade, she beat back any who tried to bar her way. But not all sought to hinder her. Riders swept up alongside, mustering again to her horn, some bearing the black badge of the Outriders or the flaming symbol of Lochrann. Even a few of Telweg's seabloods and Eagan's shadower kill-squads folded in around her. Propelled by fury, carried by momentum, they advanced until the crushing weight of the embattled forces surrounding them forced them to slow.

Ceridwen called for flame again, but the ground shivered, then bucked, throwing Mindar off his stride. Snorting, he tossed his head, sending a spike of pain through her left shoulder. Gritting her teeth, she glanced up as Kassa tor Bronwen and her earthhewn tore past, widening the path and opening a clear shot, at last, to Rhodri. She spied him straight ahead, wreathed in smoke atop his blazing steed, embroiled in combat with a mass of seabloods led by none other than Telweg herself, Cenyon's war-chief.

Sights and sounds blurred around her as her focus narrowed to Rhodri alone.

He burned like a star fallen to earth, so fierce she could not look away. Once, long ago, they had trained together. Now, she considered the warrior he had become and felt an undeniable stirring of awe. Skill and ferocity defined his every move, every cut of his blade. His posture in the saddle was perfection. Spine straight. Precise lines from head to shoulders to seat to heels. Exact angles between. Riding had always felt natural to her. It was a thing of feeling, of listening, of hearkening to the wild and untamable rhythm that beat at the heart of your steed and simply falling into step. But Rhodri had focused most upon correct technique, and now he seemed master of it, and of his steed, Vakhar.

Commanded by cues so subtle even she could not see them, the fireborn seemed an extension of Rhodri. Marked by the same restrained fury, a deadly thing held steadfastly in check, like his own calm, quiet voice, until at last released.

Rhodri spun unexpectedly into a crisply executed *firestorm*, and flames blurred into a searing swirl of fulgent red all around him. Shrieking seabloods drew back like a wave. They could not withstand such an inferno. But she could.

She offered slack and Mindar surged forward, lunging into each stride.

Then over the thunderous noise of battle, gongs crashed and fell still. Horns rang out in their wake. Singly, one after another, rising from every corner of the plain. Something shifted subtly in the flow of the battle. Immersed as Ceridwen was in the grit and grind of it, she couldn't see what had changed, but she could feel it. Mindar sensed it, too, judging by how his muscles coiled beneath her and tiny ribbons of flame streamed off his mane.

"I don't like this." Finnian's warning hummed in her ears. "Something is wrong."

She was barely a hundred strides from closing with Rhodri when one final horn call sang out a deep and brassy note. Rhodri straightened abruptly from delivering a killing blow, blade dripping onto the crumpled form of the searider fallen at his feet, and looked over his shoulder, eastward across the plains. Toward Rysinger. He stabbed his sabre toward the sky, then whirled his steed at the head of his warriors and fled.

He *fled*?

Wings throbbed overhead, and a familiar stormer with iridescent blue-black wings swooped past so low, Ceridwen had to duck beneath its hooves. She reined Mindar to a stuttering halt, only dimly aware of the riders coursing past her, while Finnian came to a stop at her side, dust and cloak swirling around him. The stormer landed, stumbling, and flared its wings to slow before whirling back to face them.

"*Shades*, tal Vern, you nearly—"

Ceridwen cut Finnian off with an upraised hand. Something was very wrong.

Iona shoved back the fur-lined hood of her quilted gambeson. Wisps of brown hair clung to her damp forehead. "It's Rysinger. Rhodri delayed us upon the field, diverted our focus, while his forces in the city opened the gates and allowed the Nadaari to march into the fortress." Her voice cracked. "Ceridwen, Rysinger has fallen."

Ceridwen broke free of the fray and left the battle behind, warriors thundering at her heels. It was a race now, and while Rhodri and his forces had a strong head start, she would not let him reach the fortress. She spared only a glance for Finnian, whose form began to blur before her eyes as his shadower, racing neck and neck with Mindar, ghosted in the smoke and heat that poured off her fireborn. She sank low, demanding more speed, more heat, and more flame, with every muscle, every nerve, and every fiber of her being concentrated on communicating that need to her steed. Mindar blazed in answer, lunging forcefully into each stride.

They crested a rise, and the final stretch sprawled before them with Rysinger standing at the end atop a shallow plateau, like a crown awaiting the victor. But smoke hung over the outer walls, flames raged in pockets within, and beyond the deep fosse and the drawbridge, Nadaar's scarlet-and-orange banner flew atop the great house.

The sight stole her breath.

The great stronghold, Soldonia's final defense, fallen in a single battle—for there had been a battle, futile though it may have been. Rhodri might have left traitors within with orders to surrender to the Nadaari, but the smoke declared that some within the fortress had resisted. Some had remained true to their kingdom, and they had fought desperately and perished valiantly. And somehow, she had allowed it to happen.

She could have sworn the Nadaari were fully engrossed in the conflict, but she'd been focused upon Rhodri, convinced he posed the greatest threat. A part of her believed it still. He had probably set the fall of Rysinger in motion even before selecting the plain for his negotiations. Out away from the fortress, where the rise and fall of the ground could conceal the movement of armies. She had used the terrain herself to get her warriors into position. She should have foreseen this, and she might have, if she had thought of Rysinger as Rhodri's.

He *was* the greatest threat. The Nadaari outnumbered her forces, controlled the coast, and were backed by the full might of an empire, yet Rhodri struck a wedge through the heart of her kingdom, dividing the war-chiefs when they should unite to drive out the invaders.

No longer.

More, she demanded, and still more Mindar gave.

Stretched low, his speed increased until he skimmed over the earth like a wildfire fed by gusting winds. His mane and tail ignited with a *whoosh*. She didn't bother extinguishing him now, only reached up with her blade hand and tugged her hood down further to shield her eyes from flying sparks.

"Steady, Ceridwen!" Iona's voice rang overhead, and beating wings pulsed in her ears. Sometime in the course of their run, she must have taken flight. She soared now over Ceridwen's right shoulder, nocking an arrow to her bow. "You'll leave them all behind!"

She already had. She could no longer sense Finnian directly at her side. He would be furious. Markham, too, when he found out.

"Reckless, ill-tamed, and volatile," he'd mutter before downing a swig of ale and pointedly not offering her the flask. "Just like your steed."

Still, she had carved off more than half the distance separating her from Rhodri's force. She could hear the heaving breaths of the Ardon steeds, could taste the dirt stirred by their passage, still hanging in the air. She was close. Just not close enough. Ahead, they swept beneath the shadow of Rysinger's wall, and half the force vanished—shadowriders, like the ones that had nearly killed her the last time she rode off alone. But Vakhar blazed in the center, like a torch.

"Ceridwen!" Iona warned. "The gates!"

What of them? She tore her eyes from Rhodri to the towering gates that pierced Rysinger's outer wall and felt a thrill of excitement. The gates were closed. Had the Nadaari decided to abandon their would-be puppet king to his fate?

But Rhodri did not slacken pace. He charged straight for the gate.

"Fall back! Fall back!" Iona shouted. "Ceridwen!"

The strange note of panic in her voice shattered Ceridwen's single-minded focus. Iona never issued commands, not to her. So, why—

She saw it. Soldiers crowded the parapets flanking the gates, maneuvering something into place. Something hulking and deadly, with sharp angles and bowed arms.

Ceridwen dug her heel sharply into Mindar's side, and he cut to the right, a bolt as long as a spear stabbing the earth where he had been. Iona banked to evade another one whistling by. Ceridwen was no expert in war machines, but surely it was impossible to reload so fast.

One glance confirmed her thought: three more ballistae lined the wall, readying to fire.

Part of Ceridwen longed to stand her ground, to rear Mindar's head toward the sky and destroy any bolts flung her way. But she could not hope to catch them all, and she was not alone now. Iona soared above, and Finnian and the others were racing up behind. She could not lead them to their deaths. However much it might surprise the other war-chiefs to hear it—Glyndwr especially—reckless defiance was not her only aim.

Not this time, at least.

"Flames take you, Rhodri," she swore through gritted teeth, slowing

Mindar and spinning him into a turn so sharp her left boot dragged in the dust. Still, she couldn't resist looking back as she retreated out of reach. She watched the gates crack wide just in time for Rhodri and his traitors to pour inside, and then slam shut again, locking him within and her without.

Bolts struck nearby with a *crack* and a puff of dust.

Truly, she thought grimly as Iona alighted, and together they rode to rejoin the others, the Nadaari *did* lack Finnian's aim. She said as much when she reached him, and he wearily shook his head as he fell in beside her, checking himself from running a hand through his hair—a habit his still-healing head wound denied him. That pinched look in his forehead meant she would hear more of this later, but all he said was, "So that's why you're still not dead."

"Though not, it seems, for lack of trying," a familiar voice added, and the massed warriors parted to reveal the Cenyon war-chief, Telweg tal Anor, seated atop her dappled seablood. "I trust you do not intend to make such narrow brushes with death a habit, Ceridwen tal Desmond. It is an unseemly quality in a queen."

Never before had Telweg openly acknowledged her thus.

Not just as a war-chief. But as heir to the throne and declared queen.

Ceridwen fingered the thick gold band of her father's signet ring upon her finger, then forced herself to straighten, stubbornly ignoring the ache in her shoulder and the exhaustion that threatened to crash over her, now that the need for action was gone. "On the contrary," she said, dry throat stinging, "no queen who shrinks from death can ask such sacrifice of her people."

And today, many of her people had made such a sacrifice.

Telweg only sniffed, though her expression seemed to thaw slightly. "Come then. The field is ours, the fortress theirs, and though the battle is ended, the war must be won, and for that, we will need our queen to survive long enough to attend her own oath-taking ceremony."

THREE: JAKIM

Where Aodh's hand leads, a Scroll shall follow.
- The Precepts of the Scrolls

Jakim contemplated throwing himself off the back of his captor's steed. It wouldn't be the first time he'd taken a hard fall. He had tumbled out of a mango tree, slipped from a ship's mast into the sea, and once, tripped down a flight of ornately carved stairs in his third master's house. The tree had been the result of his own distracted clumsiness, the mast had been toppled during an attack, and he had not tripped so much as he had *been* tripped by another slave.

But this would be the first time he'd take a fall on purpose. Despite the thick clods of earth flung up by the creature's devouring stride as it sped over ground broken and scarred by the fury of men and of armies, despite the thunder of hooves tearing up rapidly behind, he would work himself up to it. One second more, one more breathless prayer, and he would pry his numb fingers from their grip on the saddle and fling himself outward, bound wrists and all.

Hoping, trusting, *begging* Aodh's hand to catch him.

But the rest of the fleeing war-host overtook them too soon, and amidst the mass of a thousand steeds jostling, kicking, and running, he dared not leap. Not even when they seemed to be running headlong toward a collision with the shuttered fortress gates, nor when the gates opened at the last possible moment, and they poured inside and slowed gradually, coming to a ragged, shuddering halt. Then the gates of the fortress slammed shut behind them, cutting him off from Ceridwen's forces and any hope of rescue. Or escape.

With a snap and a twang, war machines fired above.

Jakim ducked instinctively, throat seizing as he recalled dying, strangled by the engineer's killing fog. His abrupt movement smacked his forehead against his captor's armored back, earning him a scowl from the thin man—or at least, he interpreted that sharp head turn as a scowl, but since his captor wore the visor of his helm down, he couldn't actually make out his expression. Or his features. Only a flicker of movement behind the eye-slit.

The projectiles didn't land inside the fortress, though.

Gingerly raising his head, Jakim spied the ballistae on the wall tops, firing out upon the mounted warriors outside, then the horde of snorting, stamping steeds around him moved forward again, parting a sea of soldiers in the scarlet and orange of Nadaar. Most stood in ranks, facing the outer wall, spears planted beside them, but some sat or sprawled, wounded or dying or dead, waiting for healers to cart them away. Beyond them still others were scattered like cast-off leaves, bearing no armor and few weapons, forgotten in the dirt. Those would be the civilians, the common folk, slaughtered when the fortress was seized.

Up a winding path they rode, deeper into the fortress, and the air grew thicker with the reek of smoke and of despair, until Jakim's throat stung with it. Crossing a drawbridge over a deep ditch, they passed under a portcullis, skirted a ramshackle Sanctuary engulfed in flames, traversed an open grassy space spotted with patches of brown, then drew up before the wide stone steps to an enormous manor. Rhodri rode his coppery steed to the foot of the stairs and seemed to halt reluctantly, gaze lifted to the double doors guarded by a bristling line of soldiers and six pairs of stone-eye tigers. He sat for a long moment, unmoving, then drew his steed halfway about, scanning the throng of his followers for something. Or someone.

His gaze skipped over Jakim and his captor, then stilled.

Out of the saddle in an instant, he cut through their ranks like a blade, and the gap widening around him allowed Jakim to see who held his focus. It was her. Astra tor Telweg. Wisps of dark hair clinging to her face, she sat atop a quivering steed whose silvery coat was stained with blood. Shoulders bowed under battered armor, trident held low at her side. Rhodri clasped her hand to his chest, and she pressed her forehead against his.

It made Jakim fidget uncomfortably, for these two, who had so ruthlessly betrayed their own king, schemed with the invaders of their nation, and slaughtered innocents in cold blood, clearly cared more for one another than his brothers had ever cared for him.

The saddle lurched abruptly as his captor dismounted, then reached up to haul him down by the collar of his tunic. The sleeve rode up the man's arm, exposing a strip of skin on the inside of his wrist and the curled edges of a fading blue mark.

Jakim fixated on it, pulse rising in his throat. Was that a . . . Scroll marking?

His captor yanked him down, and Jakim landed awkwardly, shoving his bound hands forward to steady himself. His elbow struck something with a metallic clank, and his guard cursed in a hoarse voice that was not quite so deep as he'd expected.

"Shades take the clumsy oaf. What did I do to be saddled with him?"

A warrior to their left snorted. "Must be your charming personality, Ineth."

His captor's grumbled response drifted past Jakim's ears without taking roost as his eyes fell on the bodies strewn across the lowest manor steps. Was that a flicker of movement? Someone still living, still bleeding, still in need of the help that the seal inked on his crown, covered by a fresh growth of hair, compelled him to give. Before he could think twice, he stumbled forward, heedless of the startled curses that rang out behind. He knelt over the closest form, the one he thought he had seen move, and watched as a groaning gasp made the bloodstained tunic rise and fall. The old man's watering eyes stared unseeing at the sky, and a trickle of blood trailed down his chin.

He hovered still on the border between life and death.

One of his venerable age should never fall to violence. He should have passed in his sleep with all the members of his tribe there to witness his gathering into Aodh's hand. Jakim could offer no healing, only comfort, so whispering the truths of Aodh, he gripped the old man's bony hand with his bound ones and felt the fingers twitch, drawing his focus down. A knife, barely as long as Jakim's palm, lay half buried beneath him.

Jakim stared at it, pulse quickening. Could he . . .?

Something cracked across his shoulder blades, startling a cry from his lips. Out of the corner of his eye, he glimpsed the flat of a sword being drawn back for another strike, and he reacted, cupping the knife bctween his palms and shoving it up his sleeve where the blade rested cool against the inside of his forearm. Then he raiscd his bound hands in surrender.

With a snort of disgust, the man hauled him to his feet.

Jakim pivoted to face his captor and found that *she* had removed her helmet, exposing salted gray hair escaping a loose braid and a pinched face marked by harsh lines that formed a perpetual scowl. It probably shouldn't have surprised him so—there had been as many Soldonian women as men among Ceridwen's riders—but she could have been his grandmother.

Only far more wiry. Tougher, too, like boiled leather.

With the markings of a Scroll—the holy writ—inked into her skin.

Mindful of the blade concealed up his right sleeve, he twisted his left wrist, revealing the first line of script on his own forearm. "May Aodh hold you in his hand," he said, offering the traditional greeting of the Scrolls and relishing the rich, warm, rolling sounds of his mother tongue, Eliami, which was spoken in all the Sanctuaries. "I sought only to bring him peace."

Her eyes narrowed, and her scowl deepened, and she gave no sign of understanding or recognition. Could he have mistaken what he'd seen on her wrist?

What were the odds he'd stumble across a Scroll here, among his enemies?

Aodh have mercy but he was getting desperate, grasping for signs, aching to see some evidence that turning back hadn't been a mistake. That delaying his return home and his oath to offer peace to his brothers, delaying even the sacred charge he had inherited from Enok and the other Scrolls as the sole survivor of their mission, had been Aodh's will. That the searing glow that flooded his vision of late whenever he closed his eyes and the half-forgotten snatches of whispered words that echoed in his dreams meant something.

He had felt a brief thrill of comprehension out on the plain when Ceridwen appeared upon her flaming steed, but then the battle had broken out, and he'd been hauled, jostled and jolting like a sack of potatoes on the back of his captor's steed, here. Out of sight. Out of reach.

But not, he prayed, out of hope.

Swallowing, he lowered his bound hands, tucking his right arm against his ribs to stabilize the hidden knife. His captor prodded him roughly back toward her steed. Groaning hinges rang out above as the manor entrance opened, revealing the priest Nahrog standing within, torchlight flickering at his back and casting aglow the fluttering hems of his silken robes. Nahrog raised his chin and disappeared within.

"Come, Ineth," Rhodri called as he climbed the steps with Astra, voice ringing steadily out over the ragged breathing of lathered steeds and weary riders. "And bring the Scroll."

Tsemarc Izhar picked his way through a ruin. Crimson cloak trailing over ash and charred debris, he skirted toppled thrones and splintered beams fallen in a sprawl from the ceiling beside a central hearth filled with dark, pitted rocks that glowed with a molten heat. He did not look up when they entered behind Nahrog, only prodded at a singed parchment with his sword, dragging it across the flagstones until he could trap the edge under his boot, splaying it flat for reading.

This, Jakim realized, was the same dark wood and dark stone hall where he had denounced Rhodri as a traitor, only to watch Rhodri turn the accusation on Ceridwen instead. Something crunched under his heel, and he sidestepped, accidentally kicking an abandoned goblet, sending it rolling and clinking across the floor.

His captor hauled him back into line as Rhodri and Astra halted before the tsemarc, who stood alone, aside from the priest, while they were accompanied by ten warriors with weapons gripped tightly at their sides.

"This, I believe, is yours," Izhar said in Nadaarian, stabbing the parchment and offering it to Rhodri, then letting it slip from the tip of his blade. It fluttered to the floor between them, covered in a scrawl of text in the sweeping Soldonian style where letters flowed into words which flowed into sentences, defying easy comprehension.

"It is," Rhodri acknowledged quietly in the same tongue, "as is this fortress. You shelter here upon my sufferance. Were it not for my warriors who died to seize control of the gates and guide your forces in by secret ways, they would all have been massacred upon the plain."

"This fortress belongs to the empire now, and so do you."

"That wasn't our agreement."

"Neither was allowing the king's daughter to wrest control of the war-hosts."

The rasping edge to the tsemarc's voice was a warning, like the rumble of a stone-eye tiger or the hiss of a snake before it struck. It made Jakim's hackles rise, made him glad for the knife pressed cold and flat against his arm—not that he could draw it easily with his hands bound, or know how to wield it if he did.

Rhodri offered a strained smile. "For a moment there, with my men dying outside, it almost seemed as though you weren't planning to open the gates."

Izhar didn't flinch at the veiled accusation. "For a moment, I almost didn't."

They eyed one another in silence, and Jakim couldn't help fidgeting uneasily, then Rhodri turned deliberately and righted the closest throne, guiding Astra over to sit. One hand resting on her shoulder, he again met the tsemarc's gaze, but when he spoke, it was no longer in Nadaarian but Soldonian. "Scroll, you will translate my words."

So that was why he was here?

A tool to be used and discarded again in their struggle for power?

Ineth shoved Jakim forward, jostling his arms, causing the knife to slip farther down his sleeve. It pricked the inside of his elbow, then slid down into the sagging lower seam of his sleeve, where it hung, weighing down the cloth. It seemed such an obvious bulk there, dangling against his arm, that Jakim froze as the tsemarc's piercing gaze fixed upon him, certain that he would see it. That they all would.

His impulsive decision to steal the knife felt even more foolish now. What exactly was he hoping to do? Cut his bonds and make a run for it in a fortress crowded with enemy soldiers? He certainly wasn't planning to *stab* anyone.

"Speak, Scroll," rasped Ineth. "Lest you swallow your tongue."

He licked his lips and did *not* swallow and dutifully explained his role. Izhar's eyes flashed with coldness, but he did not object. Or notice the knife.

Rhodri spoke first. "The engineer sends his regards."

It was an opening attack, a show of strength questing for weakness. Izhar, of course, displayed none. "Khilamook's promises have worn as thin as yours."

Out of habit, Jakim began to translate the tsemarc's response, but Rhodri cut him off, answering once more in Soldonian. "His manuscripts seem promising enough, and with his designs recovered, he is eager to continue building—for you, for me, he does not seem to care which."

"I did not need his designs to seize control of your fortress." Izhar stepped up onto the elevated platform that supported the one throne yet standing—an ornate one with a flaming horse head carved into its crest—and planted a booted foot on the seat. "Take my advice, son of Soldonia, and rid yourself of the engineer while you yet can. His uses, such as they were, are long since spent, and you will soon weary of his scheming."

His tone implied that the same could be said of Rhodri.

Rhodri answered in Nadaarian, freeing Jakim of any need to translate. "Matters may not have gone according to plan today, but we still have recourse. Ceridwen is a live coal kicked from the fire. Wherever she lands, dissension will flare. Mark my words. I know her. It will not be long before she sets the war-chiefs at odds and they come clamoring for me. The kingdom—"

"Kingdom?" Izhar shook his head. "Your kingdom has fallen, little king."

With one shove of his booted foot, he sent the throne toppling down into the hearth. Sparks gusted up, and flames licked at the carved crest. Rhodri started forward, then stopped.

"You would not be here without me." His voice resonated the way the sky throbs before a storm. "I swept clear the path before your feet.

Cast down my own king. Without my sacrifices, you would have spent a thousand lives for every step you took into this land—"

"Such," Nahrog growled from behind, "is your due service to Murloch. No more. Consider your life your reward, son of Soldonia, and live, that you may serve him still."

That, finally, seemed to shatter Rhodri's defenses.

"But," he faltered, "the kingdom . . .?"

Izhar stared implacably down at him. "Soldonia is a kingdom no more."

The door shut with a resounding thud, and Rhodri strode off down the passage, thunder in his steps. Jakim started to follow, but Ineth abruptly seized his elbow and flung him back against the wall, her sword wedged under his chin.

She held out her hand, expression hard. "Give it to me."

The knife. It had to be. Oh, Aodh, she *had* seen.

But if there was one thing his years as a slave had taught him, it was never to answer a question that had not been asked outright. "Give what?" Not a lie, only a deflection, though he doubted such a justification would have satisfied Scrollmaster Gedron.

"You know what, Scroll. Now hand it over, or—"

Ineth turned as a blow echoed farther down the hall. It was only Rhodri slamming his fist against the dark, paneled wall. Astra swept up beside him, graceful and deadly as an icy breeze, and in the silence of the corridor, the murmur of their voices reached Jakim.

"Were I Ceridwen"—Rhodri's was metal grating on stone—"I would blaze in on Vakhar and sear the satisfaction off Izhar's face."

"But you are not Ceridwen, are you? You master your passions, suffering no bit, no tether, no hand upon the reins, save your own."

Her voice, strangely, reminded Jakim of his sister Siba—strangely, because Siba was one of the warmest people he'd ever known, while the blood in Astra's veins ran colder than an entire tangle of sosswyrms. He would sooner receive comfort from a snake.

The blade at his throat twisted, digging into his skin. "The knife, Scroll."

His mouth went dry. One look at Ineth's eyes, hard and unblinking, and he knew she could kill him easily, and no one would care.

What use was the knife to him? Trapped as he was by walls and a host of warriors?

In the end, his eyes betrayed him, flicking unconsciously toward his right sleeve, and hers narrowed in response. She seized the sleeve, and with one swift yank, she ripped it away.

The knife clanked at his feet.

"I wasn't going to attack anyone," he offered weakly, feeling sick. Somehow losing the knife just felt like losing all over again. "I am a Scroll of Aodh."

"You think that means anything to me?" Her voice bit like steel.

Jakim shook his head. He'd added that last bit more for himself—a reminder that his hope rested in Aodh's hands. Stooping, Ineth snatched the knife from the floor and shoved it in her belt, then motioned him on with a sharp twitch of her head down the corridor, toward the waiting warriors.

She did not sheathe her own blade.

Spine prickling, Jakim shuffled down the hallway.

"So"—he overheard Astra say as he neared—"what will you do?"

"Seize the reins, Astra. Seize the reins." Standing tall, Rhodri settled his hand on the sabre belted at his waist, and his warriors seemed to unconsciously mimic his stance as he addressed them. "We are not meant to war caged behind walls. We are masters of the solborn. Muster the war-host. We ride out to maintain the fight."

Some faces reflected his determination. Others, concern or doubt.

But only Ineth, coming up behind Jakim, dared give voice. "You know we will follow you anywhere, my lord, but the gates will be watched. Should the war-chiefs unite against us, under Ceridwen's banner or not, we will be outmatched."

Rhodri smiled grimly. "Have a little faith, Ineth."

FOUR: RAFI

Ches-Shu smiles, and the sea glistens with the light of her laughter.
She frowns, and the sea churns with her wrath.
- Alonque teaching

The ship yawned over on one side, tackle creaking, planks groaning, sails going slack, the ocean itself rushing up to swallow them whole. Rafi sucked in a panicked breath. Sure, he'd survived a drowning attempt and could last underwater far longer than the average man—even an Alonque—but it was hard to ignore the bone-chilling inevitability of that slow tilt toward the sea and death.

Still nothing? Rafi thought toward the ghost. *Not even a goodbye?*

Gordu staggered up and wrestled the helm away, easing the steep angle of the ship. Sweat trickled down his cheeks as he strained against the combined forces of ship, sail, and sea to correct for their lean. "You see? Ches-Shu will not smile upon us so long as those cursed beasts are in the hold."

Spine-tingling shrieks reverberated below.

Something hit with a resounding *crack* that shook the deck. Once. Twice. It struck up a rhythmic pounding like a shutter flapping in a storm.

Rafi's pulse throbbed in his throat. "This . . . isn't Ches-Shu's doing."

"No, it's not." Sev lurched up to the group, wiping blood from his lip with the back of his hand. "It's those demon-steeds. What's wrong with them?"

Iakki backed away, hands raised. "I didn't do nothing, I swear."

Sev shot him a withering glare. "Not you. Rafi. What's stirred them up?"

"Me? How should I know?"

"How should—" Sev's voice cracked, and he shook his head. "Ches-Shu! You tamed one, didn't you? You're supposed to be the expert. So do something. Fix this!"

Iakki's eyes pleaded with him. Gordu raised a thick eyebrow.

Below, the pounding increased until it sounded like all-out war raging beneath their feet. Ships were built to withstand the force of wind and waves but not fire and stone. These demon-steeds were wholly unnatural forces. Who knew what damage they could unleash?

Rafi scrubbed his hand across his face. Ches-Shu, he was in over his head. Taming Ghost had been more mishap than anything else and certainly hadn't prepared him for wading into whatever riot was unfolding below, but Sev was right. He'd gotten them into this mess, and the demon-steeds were his responsibility, if only because he was the sole man aboard who'd ever handled one . . .

Or was he?

Someone had managed to get them all the way here, hadn't they?

He pivoted toward the huddle of captives roped to the mainmast, some with their heads hanging despondently, others with necks arched in defiance. "Moc, you get ready to open the hatch so we can check on those steeds. Sev, come with me. We're going to go make friends."

Sev tracked his gaze and heaved a sigh. "Sure, we stole their ship, but let's be friends."

Rafi clapped him bracingly on the back and started away, but Gordu seized his forearm. "Whatever you do, Tetrani's son, do it *fast*. Wood cannot long withstand such pounding."

Smiling was an art form. Rafi had learned that from his mother. You could say a lot with the shape of your smile, whether you let it blossom in your eyes or confined it below, whether you twitched your lips up or drew them wide, or more often in his mother's case, indulged in a wry twist capable of hinting at mystery, merriment, or mockery, depending.

He did not unleash her smile today.

It was a smile best held in reserve, a hidden weapon.

Instead, the smile he gave the ten Soldonian sailors trussed hand and foot and secured to the mast was open and genuine and withheld nothing. It creased the corners of his eyes, wrinkled his nose, and stretched wide. *Trust me,* that smile said, *you want us to be friends.* Unfortunately, judging by the ten glowering faces staring up at him, it didn't seem to be doing much good.

Still, Rafi was nothing if not persistent. "You may have noticed the commotion." This, he said with a straight face, though the cacophony was growing deafening, and Moc hadn't even opened the hatch yet. "Our friends below appear displeased with their accommodations." He studied the various expressions on the captives' faces. Most he'd expected—hostility, confusion, fear, anger. But on one, boredom? Curious. "I'd like to make them, and you, comfortable—preferably not at the bottom of the sea, if you catch my drift. Not that I'm threatening you. I'm asking for your help. We're all trapped on this ship, and I think you know what will happen if those demon-steeds riot."

Sev stepped up beside him. "Do you . . . think they understand Nadaarian?"

One of the captives let out a muffled snort—a bearded man with a hooked nose and blue eyes that simmered with hate.

Rafi squatted before him. "You understand me. You can help us."

The man met his gaze and deliberately looked away.

Oh, he clearly understood, and just as clearly did not intend to help.

"Nahiki," Moc called from where he stood over the enormous hatch that opened into the central hold. His voice had gone strangely quiet, lacking its usual boisterous resonance. "You should see this."

Rafi smelled it before he saw it. One whiff of the scent—acrid and thick with a fierce, wild tang—and he knew it was what he'd been smelling since he awoke. Danger. "No." He sprinted the half dozen strides and dropped beside the hatch. Wisps of smoke leaked from the seams. The thin tendrils dispersed in the sea breeze and melted into the misty gray of the morning.

He yanked on the knotted latch before remembering he'd stowed the knife stolen from Sahak so it rested against the small of his back. He freed it and sliced the rope, then bent to heave the hatch open. It was heavy enough that he needed both hands, and he grimaced as he tried to lift it, wounds protesting. But Moc's burly fist settled over the ring, and Rafi stepped aside. With a grunt, Moc heaved the hatch up—wood creaking, hinges groaning—flung it back, and let it fall open against the deck with a bang.

Smoke billowed from the opening.

Damp, cloying smoke that crawled down his throat and drove him, coughing, to his knees, eyes stinging as he tried to see through the murky haze below. Shrieks rang in his ears. Flames climbed one of the walls, throwing off a spotty illumination that reflected strangely off charred ropes, broken barriers, dark planks underhoof, and the whirling shapes darting and lunging in panic.

One massive steed rose on its hindquarters, frayed ropes dangling from its churning forelegs, eyes rimmed with white, then it dropped again, and its stony hooves struck with a snap like lightning. Spray shot up around its legs, and ripples spread across the dark surface. Not the decking, Rafi realized, but water that had seeped in through cracks and pooled in the hold.

The sea had invaded their ship.

"Ches-Shu, Cael, and Cihana Three!" Moc cursed. "We're sinking."

Sinking, yes, but also on fire, and from the sound of that ominous creaking and snapping, splitting apart at the seams. Rafi rounded on the sailors. "See? The ship is in danger. Tell us what to do. How to fix it." Oh, Ches-Shu, let there be a way to fix it.

Without the ship, without the steeds, he had no way to bargain with Sahak.

Several of the sailors shifted nervously, and one muttered something in his foreign tongue.

But the bearded sailor just cracked an unpleasant smile and spat on the deck. "Once the bottle is shattered," he said in fluent Nadaarian, "stuffing the cork back in does no good."

Sev loomed over him, expression dark. "You're saying the ship is doomed?"

"The ship. The steeds. You. You are all of you dead."

"You too," Rafi pointed out. "If the ship sinks, we'll all drown together."

"Good," the sailor said grimly.

Sev's voice dropped to a growl. "Do you want to die?"

"Better to die than see solborn in the hands of the unworthy." His jaw jutted in a steely determination that reminded Rafi of Nef. "You only waste what little time you have left."

Was all the world full of idealists and fanatics?

Sev drew back his fist, but Rafi towed him away, past Moc who still stood over the central hold, hand raised to his scarred head, looking stunned. Doubtless the sailor was right, and they were all doomed, but Rafi wasn't willing to concede the ship as lost. Delmar would never have given up so easily, so neither would he. Releasing Sev, he dragged in another breath of smoke-tinged air, then half limped, half jogged back to the helm where Aruk now braced Gordu as he clung stubbornly to the wheel.

"How soon will we reach the smuggler's cove?" Rafi asked.

Surely, it wasn't too much to hope that they could reach it before the ship fell apart beneath their feet, but the moment Gordu's eyes met his, he knew, even before the words left the elder's lips. "Not soon enough."

FIVE: CERIDWEN

It was upon the scorched banks of the River Tain that the war-chiefs cast down their blades and formed of them a conqueror's crown for Uthold the Bold, naming him the first king of Soldonia.
– Soldonian lore

The oath-taking ceremony would take place upon the battlefield, Telweg told her, upon ground drenched in the blood of warriors and their steeds and the invaders who had come to claim their land. It felt fitting somehow, in the worst sense, since Ceridwen stood to inherit the throne because of the deaths of her brother and her father. And because of the blood she had spilled to defend this kingdom and the blood she would yet spill to ensure its survival.

She knelt on the edge of the field and peeled off her gloves to scrub away the filth of the fight, using water from her half empty skin. It ran warm and red through her fingers. She rinsed her hands, shook off the droplets, then tugged off the sweaty crimson scarf that concealed the *kasar* brand on her forehead so she could wash her face. Her eyes still stung from ash and dirt, so she bathed them too. Closed them and tipped her head back, relishing the breeze that whisked over her. She listened as warriors moved across the plain, some collecting the wounded and the dead, others mustering for the ceremony.

Soon, Telweg had said. *Soon.*

That word had been a knife slicing across her skin. Why, she could not say. She had fought hoof and blade for so long to reach this moment, yet now, it all seemed to be happening too fast. Racing out of control, like a steed with the bit caught between its teeth.

Behind, Mindar gave an uneasy snort. Someone approached.

She'd left him ground-tied to graze at her back and had laid her sabre before her—both within easy reach. Steadily, she lowered her hand to the sabre's hilt.

"Too late," Markham drawled. "You're already dead."

The weathered Outrider Apex slouched beside her steed, the bandaged stump of his left arm still bound to his chest in a sling. That and the sweat beading on his forehead were the only signs of the lingering weakness that had forced him to sit out this battle, guiding tactics from behind the lines with Finnian's wolfhound, Cù, keeping watch. "Or you should be," he added, "after that stunt you pulled today. Racing headlong into ballista fire?" He snorted. "Only you, tal Desmond. Only you."

"Finnian told on me, I see."

"Te Donal? No. Tal Vern this time." He ignored the lanky, flea-bitten gray shadower mare that ambled up beside him, neck craned to one side to avoid treading on its trailing reins.

Ceridwen blinked. "Is that . . .?"

"The fool beast? Aye."

"Shouldn't you tend to it?"

He eyed her flatly. "I did tend to it, left it tied up, in fact, a ways from here, but the fool thing untied itself, because it doesn't know when to let well enough alone, like a certain person I could name." Snuffling softly, nostrils flared, the mare extended her neck toward his hand, and he begrudgingly allowed her to smell it. "Good thing you've more than one rider watching your back. One is hardly up to the task, especially given how distracted te Donal seems of late—and don't look so sand-blasted pleased with yourself, tal Desmond. That's hardly something to be proud of."

Ceridwen couldn't hide her smile but nodded to steer his attention toward the mare. She had an ungainly look about her, with a wide barrel of a chest, legs disproportionately long for her body, and ears that seemed fixed in opposite directions. "I take it she doesn't have a name yet?"

"Sure she does, it's Fool Beast."

"Come, Markham, a real name."

"Only name that suits her, the way she constantly chomps that bit and scrapes against every tree we pass. I swear she jogs like she's trying to break my spine and turns like a barge drifting in a current." He shook his shaggy head. "She's a sand-blasted idiot."

Or just not Feara, Markham's old steed who had been slain in battle.

Ceridwen's gaze strayed to Mindar, who slouched with one hip cocked and his head drooping so close to the ground that the little wisp of smoke that puffed from his nostrils with each breath fluttered the grass. She could not imagine losing him. To spend so many years bonded with one steed until you began to think and move and react as one, only to be forced to begin anew with another—could riding ever feel right again?

Stifling a groan, Markham lowered himself down, stretched his long legs out, propping one booted foot on the other, then fumbled one-handed with the clasp of his cloak.

Ceridwen eyed him. "Shouldn't you be resting?"

"Rest is for the dead. Life is strife and striving."

"You nearly did die, Markham."

"More reason not to waste another flaming breath."

His words stirred something dormant and frozen within her. She too had sensed the long dark of death approaching, and sometimes at night, when she closed her eyes, she felt an echo of that cold blossoming inside her chest, stealing the breath from her lungs, clamping tightly around her throat, until the tension in her limbs as she tried to thrash and couldn't, finally startled her from sleep before it could swallow her whole. Did Markham feel that too?

She would never ask. She did not dare.

She could not bear such weakness, not even before him. She was a warrior and a firerider—and soon, a queen. She could not fear death when it came for her, not if she was to face it with defiance, as had the ancient warriors, and so sear her mark upon the legends.

The clasp finally sprang, and Markham tossed her the cloak. "Here. Dry off."

She took it, for her own clothes were soaked through with sweat from the battle. She sensed Markham's scrutiny as she dried her damp face and hands, then sought to tame the wisps that had escaped her braid. "Telweg left little time for washing."

"Shouldn't have bothered. You cut a fearsome figure. Made a statement, like all of this." He gestured toward the mounted warriors massing on the plain before Rysinger, forming up in blocks by chiefdom and Outrider *ayed*, not for battle, but for her.

Only a few banners could be seen on the field: the rich brown of Craignorm with a sliding shadower silhouetted against a pale moon; the fiery crimson of Lochrann with its fireborn depicted mid-*firestorm*; and the sea blue of Cenyon with its surging seablood cresting a wave. If this was a statement, Ceridwen wondered what, exactly, it was intended to say. "What of the other war-chiefs? Glyndwr, Ormond, Craddock?"

"Withdrew to lick their wounds. Hunkered down on opposite ends of the plain, like they did in their own chiefdoms after Idolas." Markham scratched his grizzled beard. "But you wedged a boulder in the streambed the moment you flamed in and halted negotiations, declared war on Rhodri. There's no going back, tal Desmond. Not for you. Not for them. They know it, the stiff-necked fools, and still they fight the bit."

Ceridwen raised an eyebrow. "So that's what this is. You would capitalize on victory to establish the throne and display strength to force them to a decision: swear to me and the crown or align with traitors . . ."

"And foreswear the kingdom itself, aye."

"So this was your idea then?"

His teeth flashed in his familiar sardonic grin. "Sure, if you don't count the dozens of other battlefield coronations strewn throughout Soldonia's history." He patted down his belt and pockets, then frowned. "Spare an invalid's legs, will you, and fetch my flask from my saddlebags?"

"Oh, so you're an invalid now, are you?"

"When it suits me. Fool Beast trod on my toes earlier."

Ceridwen tossed his cloak into his lap. The mare perked one long ear toward her as she rummaged through first one saddlebag then the other. She did not find the flask, but she did uncover something else, something thin and circular and metal. It was a circlet of deep, burnished gold, unornamented, save for a dark firerock set in the center, claimed, she had no doubt from its hue, from the crater of

Koltar. It did not burn now, but one breath from Mindar would set it alight upon her forehead, while the sol-breath that transformed her into a firerider would shield her from its radiant heat until the glow faded. She drew it forth and turned to Markham, holding it in both hands.

Grinning wolfishly, Markham lowered his flask from his lips, confirming her suspicions—this was what he had truly meant her to find. He flourished the crimson scarf dangling between his fingers. The scarf she had removed earlier. Her hand flew to the raised lines of the scar on her forehead. She had revealed it occasionally on accident, or at times had chosen to display it in defiance. She had never forgotten that it was uncovered, exposed simply as a part of who she was.

She reached instinctively for the scarf, but Markham shook his head. "Time to leave the scarf behind," he said, sole eye glistening. "Time for you to rise, Ceridwen tal Desmond. Rise and ride again."

How often had she heard those words before, back in those early days of struggle in the Outriders, when she had tasted dust between her teeth more often than the wind, and failure far more often than success? But falling, Markham had always insisted, wasn't failing, so long as you got back up off the ground, set boot to stirrup, and mounted up again.

Past Markham, she spied Iona and Finnian approaching with long, measured strides, leading their steeds by the reins, displaying an unfamiliar solemnity.

Soon, Telweg had said. Or perhaps now.

Ceridwen's throat tightened, and with a strange burn of panic in her chest, she looked back to the circlet, then to her Apex, to the man who had found her shattered and taught her how to remake herself, who had plunged her into the fire again and again so she might become tempered steel. "Will it work, Markham?"

Could she do this? Become this?

Would the war-chiefs ever see past the *kasar* on her skin?

Markham snorted softly, almost fondly. "You always did struggle to see beyond your own shadow. Look up, tal Desmond, and blink the grit from your eyes. You are the Fireborn now. Nothing else matters." He spoke with a certainty and a conviction that warmed her through and through. She might struggle to believe it, but he did not.

He rose awkwardly, the arm bound to his chest confusing his balance, but he shoved his free hand out to ward off help.

Finnian, coming up, ignored it, and hauled him to his feet. "*Shades*, Markham, and you say I'm stubborn."

"You are, flames take you," Markham growled, wrenching free and shaking out his overcoat. He plucked the circlet from Ceridwen and set it on her head, then stepped back to eye her appraisingly. It sat higher on her forehead than the scarf had, and though she could tell by feel that it was not thick enough to fully conceal the brand, the smile that spread across his face bore only the glow of pride. He turned and stalked off with the shadower nosing at his heels, but not before Ceridwen caught the shimmer of a tear welling in his one eye.

"Ceridwen," Iona said, beaming, "they're ready for you."

"No, Iona," declared Finnian, gathering up Mindar's reins and holding them out toward Ceridwen. "I don't think they are." She took the reins and could feel Mindar's eagerness in their tautness, then looked up to find a glint of admiration in Finnian's dark gaze. "But they need you nonetheless, Fireborn. We all do."

So it was that Ceridwen tal Desmond rode out onto the plain with her brand uncovered, still clad in the stain of battle and wreathed in the smoke of her fiery steed, to pledge her oath to the seven chiefdoms of Soldonia as their queen. Neck arched proudly, Mindar pranced and stamped and snorted wisps of flame, while overhead, the banner of Lochrann, with its spinning fireborn enveloped in fire, snapped and crackled like a gusting blaze. Iona bore it aloft today, riding at her heels beside Finnian.

The chieftains of Lochrann, her own chiefdom, bowed as she passed, weapons fisted forward in salute. Kassa tor Bronwen added a sweeping bow and a broad grin, then elbowed her broad-shouldered and red-haired brother, Ballard, to do the same. Yianna tal Rorych's wrinkled cheeks glistened with tears. The last in line, a tall man with brown hair tied back loosely, and a thin smile like an unstrung bow, was a stranger to her, though she knew who he must be: Callum te Orin, who had been wounded at Idolas and unable to answer her muster until now. Pressing one hand to his chest, he dipped his head as she passed, and at some cue she could not see, so did his stormer, stretching one leg forward and going down on one knee with its wings extended in imitation of a bow.

But it was the absences in their ranks that lodged like a barbed arrow in Ceridwen's mind as she rode on and her chieftains fell in behind: Gavin, her cousin, slain by Rhodri and Astra's betrayal; and Doogan, flames take him, too cowardly to answer the call to war; and Forrold, the seventh chieftain, who had fallen without an heir and whose holdings she must reassign.

She reached for her blade, thumb falling into the groove worn smooth along the nose of the horse-head pommel, and rubbed it slowly, steadying herself as she neared the massed war-hosts. Horns blared, and as one, the assembled riders dismounted, landing with a solid crunching of boots on earth, then stepped up beside their steeds' heads.

Only the war-chiefs remained mounted and advanced to meet her.

On the right, Telweg, war-chief of Cenyon, seemed as rigid and imposing atop her dappled blue seablood as the white stone columns of Tel Renaair, while on the left, Eagan, war-chief of Craignorm, seemed wholly at ease atop his rangy shadower, with his shoulders thrown back and a sharp smile on his face. In the center, Markham—flames kiss him, dear Markham—who was as powerful as any war-chief as the Apex over all the Outriders, sat unusually straight and stiff upon his borrowed steed. He had even taken a comb to his disheveled hair, set aside his overcoat, and oiled his weathered gear until it gleamed richly. For her.

That was almost enough that she could overlook the absence of the others. Of the remaining three, she had hoped Ormond would come, at least.

Could he truly believe she was worse than imperial occupation?

Markham caught her gaze, and the glint in his steely eye was a clarion reminder to rise, as his voice rang out, "Hail, Ceridwen, war-chief of—"

"Hold, te Hoard," a raspy voice broke in. "Hold!"

Glyndwr, war-chief of Harnoth, trotted up, mounted on a stormer whose thick coat, feathered fetlocks, and wings were all such a pale gray, it seemed pure white, while its mane and tail were like wisps of cloud strung across the sky. Its leather barding creaked with each step, and the old war-chief posted stiffly, almost clumsily, no longer the practiced rider he had once been. Still, Ceridwen noted, as he halted between her and Markham, he no longer seemed the withered husk she had seen on that fateful night when he had declared Rhodri the heir to the throne instead of her. His cheeks were ruddy. His eyes bright. His hands firm upon the reins.

"This," Glyndwr declared with startling strength, "is a task for the regent."

Markham looked to her before nodding to the war-chief, but before Glyndwr could resume the ceremony, Ceridwen raised her fist, demanding silence. She ignored the whispers and the shocked glances, even ignored Telweg's raised eyebrow, and cued Mindar forward so she could speak to Glyndwr alone.

The aged war-chief regarded her through hooded eyes.

She dipped her head in respect for who he had been—advisor to her father, mentor to her brother, and once, her defender, even if he had come to regret it. "You yielded the title of regent when you delivered the kingdom to Rhodri. You take it up again to deliver the kingdom to me?"

"I consider my office, like your father's, yet unfulfilled."

"You have made it clear what you think of me. So why are you here?"

He placed his gnarled hand on her forearm, his eyes searching deep into hers. "I am here, Ceridwen tal Desmond, because I have been proved wrong once to my shame and the detriment of the kingdom. And yet I find that I would have you prove me wrong again. Not to shame but to relief and restoration. Can you do this?"

It was more fair than she had anticipated.

"I can, and I will." She flexed her fingers around her hilt and slid the sabre free just slightly, marking it an oath only he would see. "I so swear."

"Prove this and Harnoth will swear to you. But for now"—his voice cracked as he raised it—"it is my duty as regent of Soldonia, to pronounce you, Ceridwen tal Desmond, war-chief of Lochrann—"

"Our Fireborn," shouted someone in the war-host.

She could not be certain, but it sounded like Nold.

Glyndwr's expression soured slightly at the interruption. "Queen of Soldonia."

Ceridwen raised her sabre as Glyndwr guided her through the words of the ancient oath-taking ritual and held it aloft as Telweg and Eagan swore to her, and she to them. She met Liam's eyes in the second row and caught his wink. Then she lowered her blade at last and settled it in her scabbard with a faint click, and suddenly the plain rang with shouts and blared horns and wild spurts of flame aimed into the sky, and the rolling, rumbling stamp of a thousand, thousand hooves as her people welcomed her as their queen.

SIX: RAFI

He who beats at waves to change the tide will not long stay afloat.
- Alonque saying

Steal a ship. That had been his brilliant idea. Sounded simple enough. Sail the ship to safety—seemed even simpler. Bend the sails to catch the wind, man the helm to aim for their destination. What could possibly go wrong?

Rafi grabbed onto the rail as the ship shuddered. Gordu would insist that the question itself provided the answer, for only a fool would tempt Ches-Shu, goddess of the sea and mistress of fate, with talk of possibilities. Now the ship was sinking, taking with it all hope of freeing the hostage villagers of Zorrad from Sahak. Not to mention that fainter, more desperate wish of providing the Que Revolution with the weapons they needed to win this war against the empire: the mighty demon-steeds.

Voices swirled around him: cries of alarms, demands for solutions.

Rafi blocked them all out, closed his eyes, and envisioned himself cutting through the ocean depths on Ghost's back, surging upward to burst forth in a spray of foam, his head flung back and his arms outstretched as he soared over a cresting wave. It was the closest he'd ever come to tasting true freedom.

Run, Rafi, came the whisper, so soft he couldn't be sure whether it was his own inner voice or the ghost's.

No. His fingers dug into the rail he was gripping.

Straightening, he sought to emulate the air of command Delmar had always worn with such ease, whether clad in the garb of a prince or the rags of a prisoner. It was in the stance and voice, Rafi thought, and maybe the eyes too. He turned to find them all clustered around the helm—Gordu, Sev, Moc, Iakki, and Aruk. "Elder Gordu, is the ship maneuverable?"

Yes, that sounded like Delmar. Calm. Firm. In control.

Still wrestling with the helm, Gordu grunted. "If Ches-Shu smiles upon us, and if the leaks are slow, and if the rudder lines are secure, and if those beasts—"

"Yes or no?"

"Maybe, if—"

"Good, then run us aground."

Gordu's eyes snapped up. "Aground?"

It was, without a doubt, a horrible idea. It was also, equally undeniably, a day for horrible ideas, and more than worth it to see Gordu's shocked expression. Rafi nodded confidently. "Or as close to shore as possible before the ship sinks. Sev, launch the boats and get the villagers aboard. Moc and Aruk, you load the captives—"

"What for?" Sev asked. "They want to sink. I say we let them."

"No one gets left behind, Sev. No one."

"And just what are you going to do?" Gordu demanded, eyes dark with suspicion.

Oh, just save the ship and, barring that, its cargo. "I'll handle the rest."

Gordu shook his head and started bellowing orders to the villagers to tie this off or move that. Rafi still expected the others to disagree, to call out the absurdity of the idea, or hopefully, suggest something better, something less reliant upon him, but they were all still looking to him, awaiting his command. Wood crunched below, and the ship lurched again.

Panic eddied in Rafi's chest. They were running out of time.

In the end, all of life was running, wasn't it? Running to. Running from. Running out.

Swallowing, he summoned Delmar's voice once more. "Go. Go!"

It was a voice made for command, so it made sense that they listened. But he still felt a tinge of surprise, even unease, as Moc and Aruk made for the sailors; as Sev stomped off toward the fishing boats, calling for help; and as Gordu fought to bring the ship around, aiming for shore. Delmar had been a leader born and bred, whereas he had always just been Rafi, just the younger brother. The mischief-maker. The jester and juggler and twister of words. Until Delmar fell and Rafi endured the long dark of the night alone, and somehow the person who stumbled out into the ensuing dawn wasn't anyone he recognized anymore.

"Nahiki . . . did I do this?" Iakki raised wide eyes to him.

"No, cousin. I did." Rafi squeezed the boy's shoulders, then aimed him on his way. "Go help Sev with the boats. Hurry. Last one there is a turtle's egg."

Iakki grinned, revealing his broken front tooth, tossed a salute, and ran off. Watching him go, Rafi dared hope Ches-Shu had a kindly fate in store for the boy. With a nod to Gordu, he fetched the rope halter he'd removed from Ghost before setting him loose. Looping the halter over his shoulder, he leaned over the rail and whistled for the sea-demon.

Once, trusting the frisking colt would hear.

Twice, hoping the wild creature would answer his call.

He pursed his lips a third time, but before he could whistle again, a long whiskery nose and dusky blue neck broke the surface. Rafi exhaled at the sight. Nickering, Ghost tossed his head and the water frothed white around his churning legs. Clutching the rigging with his good hand, Rafi climbed onto the rail and immediately felt his stomach lurch, cold sweat speckling his forehead.

It wasn't that he minded heights so much as the idea of falling—or jumping—from them. Prying his fingers from the rigging, he sucked in a sharp breath, and for the second time in as many days, dove over the side.

Salt water broke around him, stinging his many cuts. The shock of it propelled him back to the surface, where the flow of the sea shifted as Ghost swept in alongside him. Rafi caught hold of the colt's seaweed-wrapped mane and drew himself astride the dark scales tracing Ghost's spine.

Calves hugging ribs. Heels hanging loose below.

So quickly, the art of riding had become natural to him.

He leaned forward, cheek pressed flat against Ghost's neck, and eased the halter from his shoulder. With both hands, he drew the halter up and around Ghost's head, settling one loop on his nose and one behind his inquisitive ears. Straightening, he drew the third loop down Ghost's neck to serve as reins. Ghost coiled with anticipation beneath him.

Not yet, Rafi thought, ruffling the colt's mane. *Not yet*.

Clumsily, he drew Ghost in a wide arc, curving back to approach the ship from the stern. Somehow, he had to help drive the ship ashore. He'd witnessed Ghost's ability to summon a wave before. Could Rafi also summon one on command? He'd acted without thought when he'd charged Sahak's longboat. He'd been furious and desperate and somewhere along the way, instinct had taken over, guiding him and the colt.

Ches-Shu grant he was so lucky today.

Rafi gave the colt his head, and Ghost sprang forth like a dam released. Pulsing strides propelled them toward the ship. Rafi squinted through the streaming water as they surged faster and faster toward the barnacled hull. Seconds from impact, he dropped the reins, flinging his arms wide then sweeping them forward, as if to shove the sea with them.

Nothing happened. No surge from the deeps. No clashing cataclysmic force.

Ghost twisted into a dive and passed under the ship so close that Rafi felt the keel tug at his hair as they circled around again.

Once more, Ghost poured himself out in the approach. Once more, Rafi flung out every ounce of will to convey his intent to the steed . . . and to the sea.

Once more they plunged under the ship at the last second.

And still nothing. Ches-Shu, why couldn't he figure this out?

Because you are Rafi, that's why. Not Delmar. You could never be him.

It was Sahak's cruel voice in his ears, chasing Rafi all the way to the surface to replenish his dwindling air. One breath now sustained him far longer than it should, but eventually, even he needed to breathe. So he twisted Ghost into a climbing spiral and burst out through the spray into glaring sunlight.

The mist had burned off until no shreds remained to soften the stark reality of their plight. Rafi let Ghost circle slowly. The ship wallowed from trough to trough, crawling ponderously on its course. Sev had launched the fishing boats, but not to flee. Taut lines connected the boats to the ship's prow, and both villagers and captive sailors alike bent to their oars, towing the struggling vessel behind, just like when they'd stolen it from Sahak's secret harbor.

It was a relief to know this did not all rest on his shoulders.

He spun Ghost and submerged again, circling wide behind the ship. With the stern straight ahead, he halted just below the surface and closed his eyes, drifting, feeling the swell of the waves building behind and rocking over him.

Shh, shh, shh, the sea sang. As he had sung to the colt. As his mother had sung to him.

He sank low and hummed Ghost forward, slowly at first, then faster, building in speed like a cresting wave. Vibrations coursing along the colt's ribs told Rafi that Ghost was keening in response, pitch climbing higher and higher as he extended his long neck and stretched his jaws wide to let out a shriek.

The sound pulsed through the water.

Ripples shot out in all directions and dissipated.

The ocean shifted, welling up around them in a wave that broke and surged into a racing current. It swept them along, caught the ship by the stern, and propelled it ahead of them. Rafi let out a muffled whoop as they chased after. They overtook the ship when the current petered out, and Ghost shot under the keel again.

The wake tugged at Rafi, and he felt his grip on the colt's slick hide slipping. He slid sideways and clutched at Ghost, squeezing harder with his legs. Ghost jolted, then with a wrench of his spine, kicked his hind legs up, flinging Rafi over his head.

Rafi tumbled head over heels before coming to a stop.

Oh, Ches-Shu, that was embarrassing. Ghost nuzzled curiously at his arm, not at all apologetic for sending him flying. He swiveled to face the colt, but a disturbance in the water caught his eye.

Ahead, a dark shape dropped below the surface and hung limp.

It was a body. It wasn't moving. Rafi's gut twisted. What if the wave he had summoned had thrown someone from the boats? He acted on instinct, swinging onto the colt and surging forward.

Closer, he could identify the body as one of the villagers. Vendak.

He was a short, bowlegged man with a flair for cooking, who'd forever been concocting new delicacies for the fisher tribe to enjoy. Now, he floated, mouth open, eyes gaping, frozen in shock. Dead. Clouds of blood bloomed around his chest, trailing from wounds. Stab wounds.

Rafi's pulse throbbed in his own healing injuries. Sahak.

Whispering an Alonque farewell over Vendak, he surfaced into chaos. Shouts and screams rained down from the fishing boats. Oars thudded and splintered. Fists pounded and struck flesh. He searched for a glimpse of his cousin—a figure in a priest's robe, a tsemarc's breastplate, and an assassin's baldric of blades—or for the company of royal guards who followed him, clad in gleaming mail with white plumes cresting their helms.

It took him a moment to recognize the actual threat: the Soldonian sailors.

Wielding their oars, stolen knives, and fists, they fought with a ferocity that reminded Rafi of the wild steeds in the hold of the ship. They clashed with the villagers, pummeling them, and were close to overwhelming them in one boat. Rafi spotted Moc in the center, with his hands raised, shouting for calm.

One of the sailors bashed an oar into his head.

Moc dropped flat and disappeared from view. He did not get back up. Another sailor sprang forward with a knife, slashing Aruk's arm.

Rafi stooped low over Ghost's neck and hummed in his ear. The colt's taut muscles coiled, and his churning hooves lashed the sea to froth. Rafi held him back until he sensed a shriek building in the colt's throat. It burst in a wail, and Ghost sprang forward, charging for the boat, and the sea glided with him, sweeping him up alongside in a foaming wave. It was only a small thing compared to the swell that had carried the ship, yet it crashed into the boat, flinging it sideways. Half the combatants tumbled to their knees; the others stood in shocked amazement. Aruk tipped over into the sea, arms flailing.

He could swim. He would be fine.

Stares widened as Ghost reared up beside the boat, spray flying from his hooves. "Peace!" Rafi shouted, which struck him as ironic.

"Or I'll capsize the boat and leave you all to swim ashore." Possibly that threat would have been more effective if he'd tipped one of the Soldonians overboard instead of one of his own. He'd never been particularly good at threats.

Still, they drew back. Discarded oars clattered. Garbled muttering caught his ears.

He brought Ghost's right flank alongside, stretching to see past a bearded Soldonian who still gripped a lowered oar. "Moc? How are you, cousin?"

Only a groan came in response, then burly fingers gripped the edge near the stern, and Moc managed to hook his chin and one forearm over. "Feels like I've got a dozen demon-steeds kicking around inside my skull, but otherwise, never better, cousin."

Good old Moc. Sturdy and reliable as the jungle itself.

"I know the feeling—" Rafi cut off as Ghost snorted and pricked his ears, alert.

Shadows shifted in his peripheral vision, lunging for him. No time to think, he acted on instincts trained by Moc and flung up his arm to catch the brunt of the blow, but it cracked against his skull. Pain blazed behind his eyes, blinding him.

Someone crashed into him, smashing the wind from his lungs. Strong fingers seized his throat and dragged him from Ghost's back, down into the sea. He forced his chin up to snare one final gasp of air before the water swallowed him.

Down he sank, too stunned to struggle.

Strangely, the whisper that filled his mind did not belong to the ghost, but to Kaya. *You know the stories, Nahiki.* She sounded faintly amused. *Caught by the throat. Dragged below. Surely you saw it coming?*

Kaya was a born storyteller, one of the best in the village. Such tales she'd spun for him and Sev on moonlit nights sprawled out on the sand, with the humming sea and the whispering leaves for accompaniment. Of stars that wept and moons that died, of inhuman creatures lurking in the deep and winged leviathans that ravaged from the sky, and of unsuspecting fisherfolk who were caught by the throat and dragged to their deaths by . . . sea-demons.

He had scoffed then. He wasn't scoffing now.

But his attacker was no sea-demon. Only a man.

Someone born to land who needed air to breathe, just like him. Or maybe even more. With the thought came revelation: one gasp was all he'd managed to snag, but for him, one gasp was enough. Enough to fight back. Enough to outlast any other swimmer. Rafi kicked, lashed out with his elbows, and managed to twist in his attacker's grip until they faced one another. It was the bearded Soldonian sailor with the hooked nose and the hate-filled eyes, the man who had chosen to die rather than help Rafi save his crew.

One hand still squeezing his throat, the sailor drew the other fist back, but Moc's training aided Rafi. He dropped his chin, and the fist smashed into his forehead instead of his nose.

A silent howl escaped the sailor, but he didn't let go.

Rafi dug at the grip on his throat, expecting it to weaken as the sailor's own instincts for self-preservation sent him kicking for the surface. But the sailor bore down instead and hooked one leg behind his knee, wrestling him into a stranglehold. Panic sparked inside him. Not even the Alonque could dive so long.

Ches-Shu, if this sailor was somehow like him . . .

He wouldn't be able to outlast him.

Rafi didn't think, didn't hesitate, just whistled into the sea. The sound warbled oddly in his ears, distorted by the shifting currents. It was a waste of breath, maybe, but worth it if he succeeded in summoning Ghost. He whistled again, then accidentally blocked a punch with his teeth. Tasted copper on his tongue. Shook his head to dismiss the fuzziness.

Blood . . . in the water . . . dangerous.

Something enormous loomed overhead, its shadow falling across him like a chill piercing to his core. Still locked with the sailor, he peered up, expecting a scadtha, not the barnacle-crusted hull of the ship foundering above. His foe seized upon his distraction, kicked upward, and slammed him against the hull. Something sliced into his shoulder.

In his mind's eye, Sahak sent knives spinning to stab his flesh.

Energy boiled through Rafi, infusing his limbs with the speed of a striking scadtha and the ferocity of a netted sea-demon, until he broke free. Smashed the dazed sailor against the ship's bottom, heard an ominous *snap*, and drew back in a trail of bubbles.

He watched, stunned, as cracks widened and beams splintered and the hull itself burst open, disgorging an enormous, muscled boulder of a gray steed that crashed into the sailor. Its hooves struck him, left him bent and broken, sinking to the ocean floor. Dead.

Rafi dropped low, certain he would be next.

But rippling muscles and striking limbs propelled the steed to the surface. It did not cut through the sea with Ghost's graceful finesse. It left a trail of froth and blood behind as it battled for shore, but it had clawed out from the belly of the ship. It would survive. What of the others? A pinch in Rafi's side warned that his air was running low, but he had to see.

Gripping one side of the breach, he peered in. He glimpsed a blur of motion and threw himself aside as a speckled shape shot out, then another and another. Sea-demons, five of them, with streaming manes, glistening scales, and hides of dappled gray, trailing frayed rope halters and hobbles. When no more emerged, he slipped in with the water gushing to fill the hold. He brushed against something large and soft wedged against the hole and glanced down as he swept over it, catching faint details in the illumination from the open hatch overhead. Coppery coat. Black nose.

One of the fire-demons had drowned.

Beside it, wings blanketing its form, one of the sky-demons. Also dead.

Floating, Rafi peered through the murky water. Two more limp steeds sprawled in splintered stalls, halters bound to submerged rings, tied down until they'd drowned. But farther in, shadowy shapes moved, and hooves still churned. Some still lived, protected by the slope of the listing ship which must have left them space to breathe.

His lungs were burning now, so he kicked upward and surfaced with a gasp into a rapidly diminishing space of air. Rising water slapped at his chin. He swiveled, getting his bearings.

Heads flung back, five demon-steeds strained against their leads, nostrils flared, eyes white-ringed. The rest were gone. Ches-Shu grant they weren't all dead. Rafi doubted Sahak would take corpses in exchange without offering corpses in return. He lunged toward the closest steed, narrowly evading its flashing teeth and hooves.

Staying just out of reach, he eased alongside it and hummed softly. His fingers brushed its knotted lead, noted how swollen and stiff the fibers were—no chance of working it loose, not with the ship sinking so fast. He needed something sharp. His hand went instinctively to the blade in the back of his belt before he realized what he was doing.

Ches-Shu. He was the greatest fool alive.

How long had he grappled that sailor without once thinking of the knife?

He severed the rope with a single slice, and the wild-eyed steed spun away. Rafi dove behind the stall to avoid its tossing head. Surfaced and sliced through the next lead and the next. Until all the steeds were loose in the hold. But they were still trapped in the ship.

Rafi bobbed up on a swell and grazed his head on the tilted ceiling. He eased along the side of the ship toward the hatch, careful to stay away from the frenzied steeds. He could swim out through the breach in the hull or wait until the water rose enough that he could grip the edge of the hatch and climb out onto the deck, but the steeds couldn't. These were not sea-demons eager to brave the unknown deeps.

Frantic as they were, how could he coax them to follow him anywhere?

"Ches-Shu!" he swore aloud, splashing a fist into the rushing flood.

His ears were so full of the roar of the invading sea and the desperate efforts of the snorting steeds to stay alive, he almost ignored the faint and muffled sound of a human cry. Just the ghost, he thought, just a memory. Only it was coming from within the hold, and there could only be one person left aboard.

"Gordu?"

Something thumped and the cry came again. He followed the sound to a wooden ramp wedged at an angle against the ship's side in time to see Gordu's bald head slip under the rising water.

"Hold on!" Rafi submerged and squeezed into the gap behind the ramp. It had fallen on Gordu's lower leg, pinning him in a half-sitting position. Rafi tried to wedge his fingers into the crack between the ramp and the deck but couldn't get a good grip. He planted his feet and shoved up instead, throwing his shoulder against the plank. Gordu roared in pain as Rafi shifted the plank, freeing the foot. They broke the surface together. The water had risen enough now that standing flat-footed on the upper slope of the deck, groaning under the ramp's weight, left Rafi's mouth and nose underwater.

He motioned for Gordu to get clear so he could drop the ramp.

"Up. Up!" Gordu shouted, splashing as he tried to get his footing.

Baffled, Rafi blinked from the ramp to the hatch where Gordu pointed. On the top edge of the ramp, another board extended at an angle, forming a ledge. Suddenly he understood. This was their way out. Gordu's thick hands gripped alongside his, and together they heaved, catching the hooked end on the edge of the hatch, securing it in place. Hooves struck the ramp and tore up onto the deck with a clatter. The steeds were free.

Gordu collapsed back into the water with a groan.

"Come on." Rafi floundered toward him, exhausted. "Come on, old Gordy. Got to get out still." He shoved his shoulder under the elder's arm, towed him around the ramp, and struggled up and onto the deck before his own limbs failed him.

Below, the ship gave a final groan. Rafi held Gordu tightly as the ship sank into the waves beneath them. Before the rushing sea swept over his head, he thought he heard a familiar, throaty nicker.

SEVEN: CERIDWEN

*It was in the troubled years following the first Nadaarian invasion
and the third Rhiakki incursion that Talien of the Mountains mustered
a band of elite warriors from all seven chiefdoms to keep watch upon
the borders, and thus, the Outriders were born.*
- Soldonian lore

R ysinger blazed in the night with the flames of a thousand
torches that reflected off the forest of spearpoints, helmets, and
breastplates lining the walls, enough to leave the war-chiefs stunned,
even without the latest count from the stormrider flyover Markham
had ordered. The force that had seized the fortress was far larger than
reports had claimed, nearly twice the size of the force they had faced
upon the plain today, which they had been told comprised the full
strength of the Nadaarian division that had marched south from Idolas
months before.

Of course, those reports had come from Ardon. From Rhodri.

Every time Ceridwen thought she knew the full extent of Rhodri's
treachery, she uncovered depths deeper still. Standing now, overlooking
the conquered fortress with Finnian, a silent but watchful presence
at her back, she gripped the hilt of her sabre, not trying to quell her
anger but to preserve it, like Mindar's flame, for the fight she knew was
yet to come.

"They make a fine target of themselves with their arrogant display,"
Telweg observed, speaking quietly so as not to disturb Markham's
drawling delivery of the scouts' full report for the war-chiefs. In true
Soldonian fashion, the revels following Ceridwen's coronation had

lasted only as long as the feasting, and as soon as the spits were picked clean, flasks drained, and fires burned down to embers, the war-meet had begun instead. They stood now atop the final rise before Rysinger, their war-camps nestled in the depression behind. "One *ayed* of stormriders with quivers to spare," she declared, "and they might regret their hubris . . ."

Ceridwen could not deny the truth of her words. It was arrogant indeed to reveal their defenses, their numbers, even expose their soldiers to attack, for she could dispatch stormriders on a strafing run as easily as a scouting mission. But it was an arrogance born of truth, as the speed with which they had claimed the fortress proved. So many soldiers, and yet . . .

She swung toward Markham. "What about war machines?"

He fixed her with a scorching stare. "Counting the ones that nearly killed you? Five ballistae, all mounted on the outer wall."

Only ballistae? And only five? "No mangonels?"

Markham only downed a swig from his flask in answer, and Telweg eyed her curiously. "What are you thinking? It is possible they have yet to construct the rest."

Ceridwen shook her head, instinctively seeing the likeliest scenario as clearly as pieces splayed out upon a battle map. "Or the rest are with the main column, still crawling across Lochrann. We've tracked how slowly it moves, burdened by its sheer size and supplies, but this force attacked rapidly. Even if they faced no resistance in Ardon, they covered ground at a surprising pace for infantry." Markham winked at her, and she knew he had seen it too. "They could not have done so with carts laden with dismantled war machines."

"Which means they cannot employ them here to defend Rysinger," Telweg said. "We should attack swiftly, retake the fortress—"

"Retake it how?" Glyndwr demanded. "Or have you forgotten that Rysinger was built to withstand a solborn assault?"

"Why did they take Rysinger, do ye think?"

The unexpected nature of the question caught Ceridwen off guard—the others, too, it seemed, as all eyes turned to Eagan, who crouched off to one side, turning a knife over in his fingers. His dark hair had been thrust back from his sharp face, and the glow of the torch in

Glyndwr's hand lit the twin hilts of the blades strapped to his back. "We call it the last stronghold, the final defense, but it's not, is it? They took it in a day. For what?"

"Classic imperial invasion tactics," Markham drawled. "Seize key cities, ports, and strongholds. Sink their claws into the bones of a nation and suck the marrow dry."

"But what does Rysinger gain them?" Eagan pressed. "Sure, it's demoralizing t' see their tattered banner flying over the great house, but only Nadaar with its grand cities an' its infantry would see taking Rysinger as claiming Soldonia's seat of power." He gestured toward the masses of grazing steeds scattered across the shallow basin surrounding the war-camps, each with a team of night riders to watch and shield them from attack. "Our true seat of power is divided among a hundred thousand saddles on a hundred thousand steeds, whereas they . . ."

"Possess only the earth beneath their feet," Ceridwen murmured, catching Telweg's eye. With such words, she had convinced Telweg to support her plan to cut the Nadaari off from the coast and strand them inland. Could that goal finally be within reach?

"'Twas the war machines that carried the day at Idolas," Eagan continued, shoving stiffly to his feet. "Now that the engineer has been captured an' can no longer supply the Nadaari with more deadly designs, I say we leave them t' rot in Rysinger and ride out t' destroy the rest of his contraptions instead. Remove the advantage, before we meet them in pitched battle again."

It was strikingly similar to the plan Astra had suggested before betraying Gavin and his family to their doom. In Ceridwen's mind, it was not war machines but treachery that had cost them the battle of Idolas—and continued to cost them now.

Markham tossed back another swallow. "It's clever enough, Fox, only there's one flaw in your scheme. We don't have the engineer. You want him, you'll find him in there." He tipped his flask toward the distant hulk of the fortress. "Rhodri took him, though whether Rhodri or the tsemarc has him makes scant difference to us now. So we must focus on securing allies of our own." He gave Ceridwen a sharp glance. "If not from within, from without."

She held her tongue in check with difficulty.

He had spoken of this before, but it irked her that he would raise it tonight without warning her first. She was barely queen of a splintered nation and yet somehow must convince others to stand with them in this fight? How, when some of her own war-chiefs refused her?

Telweg turned to him. "You speak of renewing the old alliances?"

"With Hurron? Mabassi?" A cough rattled Glyndwr's chest. "Those have been derelict for years. We have had more recent dealings with Rhiakkor—"

Eagan snorted. "There is no Rhiakkor."

"Of course there is. We trade with—"

"With the Rhiakki tribes, but Rhiakkor hasn't existed as a unified nation in ninety years." In the flickering torchlight, Eagan's ever-changing Rhiakki eyes looked as black as tar. "Not since Teague the Steadfast dropped a mountain on their chief's head."

"Ending their southward incursion. What would you have had her do instead? Allowed the Rhiakki to overrun the kingdom?"

"Ye mean as ye did with the Nadaari?"

Ceridwen stifled a groan as that pitched the war-chiefs into a quarrel. Weariness clung to her shoulders like a cloak. Her arrow wound burned. She stifled a wince as she tried to rotate her arm into a more comfortable position.

"I warned you about those stitches." Finnian's voice drifted to her.

She rolled her eyes and covertly glanced back at his cloaked form, Cù, his wolfhound, seated at his side. It was comforting to have him at her back in times like these, so long as he wasn't nagging at her or disagreeing with her. Or threatening to have Cù sit on her.

A burst of laughter drew her focus to the closest fire in the basin, where if Ceridwen read the scene correctly, Liam had taken his tale-telling to a whole new level and was singlehandedly reenacting the entire battle, to his audience's delight. On the far side of the fire, Nold strummed a mandolin, serenading a smiling Kassa, who wore red flowers in her dark braid, and the gleam in his eyes—like the flames that burned eternal at the heart of the craters—completely transformed his lean face as she pressed a kiss to his lips.

Nold sat back, grinning, then shot to his feet. Kassa tilted her head curiously, and he strummed a rapid sequence, then kicked out his heels.

She waved him off, but she couldn't conceal her smile.

That seemed the only answer Nold needed. His crooked grin deepened, and he leaned over his mandolin as he strummed a wild and racing tune that reminded Ceridwen of frisky foals tossing their heads, throwing out their heels, and tearing across open pasture. Still playing, Nold began to dance a jig. Kassa flung her head back with a laugh, then leaped to her feet and joined him.

Finnian brushed Ceridwen's good shoulder.

She started at the touch and found Markham scowling at her. He jerked his chin toward the war-chiefs who, flames take their stubborn hides, were still arguing. She knew what he wanted of her. He would have her seize the reins, as though she were a horsemaster and they but ill-tamed, untrained, and volatile steeds.

Doubtless he was right. He usually was.

She stepped up to Glyndwr and took the torch from his hand, then tossed it at their feet, throwing up a burst of sparks that silenced them all. "New oaths have been sworn today, and soon, new alliances must be forged, but first, it is time old oaths were fulfilled." She leveled her gaze on Telweg. "Cenyon has suffered from this invasion long enough. We will help you retake the coast."

Telweg's lips parted in disbelief, but Ceridwen forged on. "One-third of our combined force will reclaim the coastal paths and control of our ports, while the second rides to reinforce the Outrider *ayed* tailing the main column in Lochrann—with the sole purpose of targeting the war machines. Once they succeed, they are to herd the column into Rysinger."

"Into Rysinger?" Glyndwr repeated, brow furrowing.

"Penned in with the rest, while the final third of our forces camps outside."

Eagan's smile spread slowly, but Glyndwr looked aghast. "But what of our kin trapped inside? We cannot simply abandon them to the Nadaari."

It was a valid point, and Ceridwen berated herself for not seeing it sooner.

She had witnessed the results of invasion in Lochrann firsthand. She had watched Finnian comfort the grieving while she burned the dead, and with hand to blade, she had sworn that help would come. Markham caught her eyes and shook his head, no doubt reading the resolve in her expression as clearly as she read the disapproval in his.

"Perhaps . . . we are fortunate Rhodri is there to shield them from harm," Glyndwr said in a voice that quavered like reeds in the wind, and perhaps he was truly as feeble and withered as she had recalled, for surely, no man of reason could think that.

Eagan barked out a harsh laugh. "*Shades*, Glyndwr, he's not our man on the inside. He's a flaming traitor. He murdered our own. Sided with the invaders. He's the enemy."

"I am aware," Glyndwr snapped. "I merely find it unlikely that Rhodri would harm innocents—not in Rysinger, of all places. He grew up there, did he not?"

Reasoning fled.

Blood seethed in her veins.

She saw her father fall again at Idolas, the pyre ignite around Fiona and her sons, and the life fade from Gavin's eyes as she arrived too late to save him. Dimly, she was aware of Finnian's steadying grip on her shoulder. When she spoke, her voice came thick with ash. "Tell that to the children slaughtered at Soras Ford."

The war-chief blinked at her, the whites of his eyes stark in the dying torchlight, and she turned away, suddenly weary beyond measure, and stalked off without a second look.

Markham's voice rose behind, dismissing the others.

Ceridwen halted on the outskirts of the small fire where Liam now sprawled beside his aunt while Hab stirred the charred and lumpy contents of a stew pot. Kassa sat with her head tipped back and eyes closed, the sheen of tears on her cheeks but a smile on her lips, listening as Nold whistled and strummed a sweetly sad and lilting melody.

They all seemed so peaceful, so at ease, while all within her was chaos, sorrow, and war. She should be planning a rescue, not resting. She started to turn away.

"You done skulking out there?" Iona's cheery voice rang out. "Don't let Hab's cooking scare you off, even if it is better suited for fireborn than men."

Hab grumbled something unintelligible.

Liam's head shot up. "Who's skulking, Aunt?"

Iona tugged off her boots, tossed them aside, and rubbed her feet. "Never you mind, lad. What have I told you about listening in?"

"I wasn't listening in. You was shouting in my ear!" Liam finally spied Ceridwen. "Oh, you just missed it! My reenactment of the battle, I mean. Suppose I could do it again, though, just for you, you know—"

Groans arose at this threat of a repeat performance.

Ceridwen smiled and settled down beside Iona. She sensed Finnian behind her and reached back to yank him down by his cloak. He resisted until she shot him a glare, and then grudgingly crouched down, bow gripped horizontally in front of him.

"Stubborn," she whispered.

"You're one to talk."

Cù flopped between them, setting his chin on Ceridwen's knee. She gently laid her hand on top of his misshapen head and felt him sink against her, relaxing under her touch. Out of the corner of her eye she caught a hint of a smile on Finnian's lips as he thumbed his bowstring then drew out a small lump of beeswax and ran it down the cord. Wrapping a leather string twice around the cord, he slid it down, pressing the wax deep into the twisted strands and scraping the excess away.

"Right then." Liam got to his feet. "Now that you're settled, I—"

"Can listen while someone else tells a tale for once." Nold passed his mandolin off to Kassa, then stood and hefted a laden sack. "Gather around, one and all, for the tragic tale of young Liam the Stone-Eye Killer and his travails."

Grinning curiously, Liam lowered himself back to the ground.

"Young Liam was a fierce warrior who wielded a long spear and told longer tales—sadly, many of them untrue. He had a smile that could charm a kiss from the sun, a tongue that could talk any foe to death, and a voice like a burbling brook."

"Hang on! Burbling?"

"*Yet* for all his . . . gifts . . . he had one flaw. His head was too small. Sort of funny looking, too, with too-big ears and a—" A cough from Iona redirected Nold. "Right. Head. Too small. So small, in fact, that he couldn't for the life of him keep a helm on his head, which made his fair aunt fairly sick with worry. Why, he lost three helms in one month and—"

"Three?" Finnian raised an eyebrow. "I thought it was four."

Nold didn't break stride. "Four helms in one month—and that last helm, which admittedly wobbled so distractingly it nearly got him speared by a shadowrider, his queen ordered him to toss aside in the midst of battle, leaving him without protection when she then decided to rain sparks down on his head, and on the heads of his handsome friends." He tossed Ceridwen a pointed look before resuming his tale. "Singed and helmless, our poor young hero was left without recourse as he—oh, but what's this?" Holding up the sack as if he'd just discovered it in his hand, Nold reached in and drew out a helm.

It gleamed with a fresh polish, and so did Liam's grin as Nold stepped over to him and tugged the helm down over his unruly hair where it sat securely.

"What do you think?" Nold asked, rapping a knuckle against it.

"It fits!" Liam shook his head to test it. "Snugly. Comfortable too."

"You can thank Nold for that," Finnian said, looking up, and the gleam in his eyes told Ceridwen that he'd been in on it too. Though when Iona promptly stood and planted a kiss on Nold's cheek, she decided to keep that observation to herself. "He sewed a padding for the inside to make it fit. If you're going to learn scouting from me and ride anywhere near this one"—his gaze flicked briefly to Ceridwen—"you'll want a good helm."

"But . . ." Liam looked confused. "What about the tragic part of this tragic tale?"

"Oh, that?" Nold grinned mischievously. "Well, tragically, the helm did nothing whatsoever to curtail our young hero's talkativeness, and sadly, one night, he was smothered by persons unknown who were desperate for a full night's sleep. Come on then," he added, rapidly moving on, "let's see you test it out. Jump. Spin. Dance a jig."

Without being prompted, Kassa swung the mandolin back into Nold's hands. He strummed out a rapid, driving melody that sent Liam darting to snatch his spear so he could plant it and kick his heels higher, then turn to drag his aunt, Iona, into the dance.

The helm managed to stay on his head throughout.

Ceridwen leaned back. With the heat of the fire skimming her cheeks and Finnian's nearness a comfortable warmth in her chest, she could almost allow herself to relax. She closed her eyes. Sometimes life was war and anguish and pain, but sometimes it was also music and laughter and companionship by the fireside after the battle.

She could embrace one as well as the other, couldn't she?

Something tapped the toe of her boot.

She opened her eyes to see Finnian leaning toward her, a small smile on his lips. "Careful, tal Desmond, you look almost happy. What were you thinking just now?"

Oh, *shades*, her breath caught in her throat. There was something about the way that smile creased his eyes that made her feel alive as she only ever felt racing the wind atop her fiery steed. When the surge of motion caused all the world to fall away until all she heard was the sound of his hooves and all she felt was the strength of his stride and all she saw was the horizon almost within reach.

What was she thinking? Nothing she could speak aloud.

So she sprang to her feet instead. "That the night is still young."

"And you're off to seek trouble in it?"

"Most certainly, te Donal. Are you coming?"

His smile deepened. "Wouldn't miss it for the world."

EIGHT: CERIDWEN & JAKIM

The duty of the Outriders is threefold: bring peace to the wilds,
ward off external threats, and shield the native solborn herds
from exploitation and foreign hunters.
– Code of the Outriders

Stars breached the darkness above as Ceridwen and Finnian wandered into the night. Sometimes they walked, her boots thudding, her spurs jingling faintly, his steps falling cloaked and unheard. Sometimes they rode, shadower and fireborn matched stride for stride. Sometimes they talked, and sometimes they lapsed into comfortable, companionable silence.

Even then, in the quiet, Ceridwen did not allow herself to think.

She simply moved, simply lived, simply breathed, letting instinct guide her—onward, ever onward—until she sensed Finnian's steps slowing, his backward glances growing more pronounced.

Until his voice broke across the hushed velvet of the moonlit night. "Where, exactly, are we going?"

The question drew her back to herself, to an awareness of where her wandering feet had taken her, across the empty plain covered in rustling grasses, skirting the camps of the various war-chiefs, and now rounding the eastern side of the fortress of Rysinger where the farthest stretches of the Gauroth range tumbled down in spurs and folds.

Suddenly, she knew where she was headed.

She drew upon her reins, and her fireborn came, snorting softly. Setting boot to stirrup, she looked at Finnian over the seat of her saddle. "Once, when I was young, my father told us the story of Ingold, the first earthrider who ruled from Rysinger, long ago, before Soldonia was a kingdom."

Finnian looked curious. "I have never heard of her."

"She awoke, one day, to find Rysinger surrounded by foes." Ceridwen swung astride her steed and waited for Finnian to mount his, then rode forward at a gentle lope. "By a force so vast, it stretched to the horizon. She knew that she could not win, but she flamed her warriors to courage with a speech, then disappeared within while they held the outer walls against clouds of harrying stormers until the attackers retreated with the setting sun.

"Earthriders charged the gates with the dawn, and once again, Ingold rallied the defenders, commanding them to dismantle the old Keep, which was built of stones carved from mountain-root to reinforce the gate, and then she again disappeared. All the long day, they built onto the barricade, while the earthhewn charged again and again without breaking through. But when the next sunrise revealed smoke hanging low and thick on the eastern horizon, the courage of the defenders failed them. They confronted Ingold, demanded to know where she was going, what she was doing, why she kept leaving them to fight alone."

"Can you blame them?" Finnian remarked. "I would have done the same."

Of that Ceridwen had no doubt. He had confronted her often enough, challenged what he perceived as recklessness, yet still rode willingly at her back when she held to her decision.

"Ingold told them she needed more time. So once again, they held the wall while she went below. My father broke off the tale then and called Rhodri to join me and Bair. He took us below the fortress into a rough-hewn cavern. Ingold had carved it out with her steed." Some of the awe Ceridwen had felt upon seeing that work for the first time seeped into her voice. Finnian might not understand it, for shadowers were a subtle breed, but most of the solborn could be blunt instruments, and earthhewn and fireborn alike tended to destroy with abandon. True mastery came not in rock-breaking displays, but in restraint.

"He asked us," she added, "what we thought it was for."

"And what did you say?"

She could no longer see him or his shadower at her side, for both had melted into the dark of the night-washed grasses, but she could sense the tension in his voice over the humming of cicadas. They were very near the walls of Rysinger now, near to her enemies and her goal, so she slowed Mindar to a walk. So close, an errant spark might draw arrows upon them.

"I said that Ingold sought to undermine the fortress, so if it was taken, it could be collapsed from within, burying the living and the dead."

He whistled softly. "So, you were a firestorm even then?"

She heard in his voice a trace of the strange, distant look she had seen in her father's eyes when she'd said it. "Bair thought it an attempt at escape, a way out for everyone inside."

"I agree with him."

"Of course you do."

"So what was the answer? How did the story end?"

"Sadly, how else?" Most of the old stories did. Glory and death so often rode in step. "She was slain as she emerged from the fortress that night, cut down by some of her own warriors who were desperate to surrender, so we can never truly know what she intended."

"Which makes for a fascinating story but doesn't explain what we're doing here."

"This is where my father took us next. There's a crevice ahead, connected to a natural system of caves that runs below Rysinger. If Ingold had managed to tunnel through to them . . ."

"So Bair was right? She intended to create an escape?"

"Maybe." Ceridwen halted Mindar on the stony rim of a gully that ran toward Rysinger. "But Rhodri offered a different theory. He felt that Ingold dug the cavern not to die, or to escape, but to—"

Somewhere in the gully, a dislodged stone clacked and clattered.

Ceridwen smothered the sparks that sprang to life in Mindar's mane and eased her sabre from her scabbard. Not to die, no. Or to escape. But to bring the fight to her enemies on her own terms.

Whenever a thunderstorm loomed over the sea in Kerrikar, the entire island stilled. Wildlife retreating, bees quieting, the air itself hovering close and thick until the rain struck with a force that set all the trees dancing in the howling wind. Jakim felt a similar hush coursing through Rysinger now as warriors streamed into Rhodri's wake and refugees emerged from the shadows, clutching satchels and baskets and children's hands, and they all moved on together in a gathering tide. On the outward side of the path, closest to the gates, soldiers of Nadaar rose as they neared, discarding whetstones and oil rags and gripping spears to ward off attack.

But Rhodri was not heading for the gates.

He led the way down a ramp carved into the ditch that encircled the wall of the inner fortress, and there, concealed beneath the drawbridge, was a tunnel. A way out. Jakim sat up higher behind Ineth and spied soldiers guarding the tunnel, blocking the way with shields interlocked, torches and spears bristling between them.

Rhodri rode right up to the formation before halting, his steed snorting sparks that skipped harmlessly over their shields. "Stand aside," he commanded in Nadaarian. "I will not ask again."

Boots scuffed. Weapons shifted. The line remained.

Jakim's skin tingled as Rhodri drew his fireborn back a step, and its head dropped low, dragging in a breath that he could almost hear sizzling in the air. Suddenly, a harsh voice rang out among the soldiers. "Hold your fire!" It was a voice like scraping metal or grinding stones, recognizable even before Nahrog the priest shoved through the shield wall, the chains of his service that ran from his wrists to his neck clanking with each deliberate stride. Grounding his spear with a thud, he raised his baleful expression to Rhodri.

Ineth tensed and reached for the blade slung at her side.

"Do not think, priest," Rhodri said in a quiet, measured voice, "that I will not kill you where you stand. Vakhar longs to rage, and only my will restrains him."

Nahrog didn't flinch, only slowly, deliberately, turned to address the soldiers, exposing his back to the fireborn. "Hear me. They ride upon the will of Murloch, and none shall hinder them. The Voice has spoken. Let them pass."

That, Jakim certainly hadn't expected.

Ineth either, apparently, for she released a breath but not her blade as the priest's command took effect. Shields shifted, spears lowered, and the soldiers drew back, allowing the warriors and refugees amassed behind Rhodri to begin to flow past him into the tunnel and on until the darkness swallowed them.

Rhodri brought his steed one step closer to Nahrog. "The tsemarc will not look kindly upon your interference here, priest."

"The tsemarc will do as the tsemarc wills. I ride with you."

"Ride with me? You trampled upon our agreement and told me to be grateful I yet live. Convince me to let you continue to do the same, creature of Murloch."

Nahrog's lip curled. "Your betrothed will speak for me."

Confusion etched on his brow, Rhodri shifted to view Astra, but she forestalled any questions with a gentle touch to his arm. "Later, my love. Just think how useful he may be to us." She lowered her voice then. "The tsemarc may have the emperor's ear, but there are other powers at work within the empire. We need not win this fight alone."

"Later," Rhodri repeated in a tone that made it a promise, then turned to the priest. "We travel at speed. One of my riders can—"

"No need." Nahrog flicked a hand, and an attendant emerged from behind the soldiers, guiding a tiger and chariot. Despite his bulk and flowing robes, the priest sprang easily aboard, slid his spear through a pair of rings mounted on the inside, and seized the reins in both hands. He snapped the ends against the tiger's back as Rhodri spurred his steed forward.

"You should recall, my lord," Ineth said in Soldonian, urging her steed up alongside Rhodri's, "that the engineer's plans for the tunnel were carried out. We should be cautious."

Which sounded ominous enough to Jakim.

But then Nahrog demanded to know what her words meant.

"It means, *priest*," Rhodri answered darkly, "that you should be wary of antagonizing me and sparking open flame from my steed. Very wary."

So, on they rode, with only the weak glow of a few hooded lanterns held aloft on scattered spears to light their path through the lurking dark. Hooves clopped on stone. Tack creaked, and weapons clanked faintly. Snorted breaths rang out harshly, echoing off the walls, but none of the riders spoke, and soon, Jakim found the oppressive cloak of silence suffocated even his thoughts. Occasionally sparks pierced the inky gloom but were smothered so hastily that whatever traps the engineer had designed did not ignite. Yet.

Stars finally broke the dark above as they emerged from the tunnel, and Jakim breathed freely again as the wind that forever roamed this rugged country once more drifted across his face. No longer tinged with smoke or the reek of battle, it carried to him only the faintly musty scent of countless steeds and the metallic tang of oil and rust from the armor of countless riders, and for a brief moment, as it gusted and shifted, a taste of fetid dampness. Was there rain sweeping in?

Or just water nearby? A lake, or maybe a river?

Nahrog broke the silence. "Something is wrong. There should be guards."

Ceridwen tried to still her breathing as warriors streamed from a crevice in the earth not a hundred strides away. Pulse still racing from the scuffle, blood spattering from the tip of her blade, she rubbed her rein hand across Mindar's neck and whispered calming words, so soft none but he could hear.

Tonight, one spark could kill, not just her but Finnian too.

He had dismounted to retrieve his arrows from the corpses of the Nadaarian guards they had discovered and was now ghosted like his steed. Probably crouched with arrow to string, watching intently while the riders streamed past. Only a few paces away, a Nadaarian voice rumbled a warning into the night, and a voice she knew all too well replied in the same tongue, "Be wary. If I know Ceridwen, she will not be far."

The blade trembled in her grip. *Rhodri.*

She had come looking for him, but *flames*, she hadn't expected to find him in the midst of making his move to bring the fight back to the war-chiefs.

"Shoot him," she breathed, knowing Finnian would hear, for his senses were as sharp and attuned as those of his wolfhound. "Shoot him, Finnian."

His hushed response came startlingly close beside her—even now, after being paired for so many months in battle, the way his bond silenced his movements still unnerved her. "Ceridwen—"

"Shoot him now."

"They're not alone, Ceridwen."

The hooded lanterns drifted toward the ragged edges of the force, and she understood what his enhanced vision had enabled him to see. There were people there, marching all along the outskirts—not warriors but refugees, escaping the fall of Rysinger with the clothes on their backs and the children in their arms. They were *her* people, and Rhodri had gotten them out.

Something gently nudged her arm. Finnian's bow. "You see?"

"I see." She could not order him to fire, not without a clear shot. She could only watch, helpless, as Rhodri himself moved on with the rest, angling southward. From that direction, he could attack any of the war-chiefs, or take her own forces from the flank.

Ormond would be at risk first, then Telweg.

Then her own patrol, gathered for song and tale around the fire.

No. She would not let Rhodri escape, nor would she let Iona, Liam, and the others come to harm. She whispered for Finnian to mount and a moment later, his shadower brushed alongside her. "*Shades*, Ceridwen, how did you know they'd be here?"

"Because I know Rhodri," she said simply.

As he, apparently, knew her.

"Go, Finnian. You must ride and muster the hosts."

"While you do what?"

"Seek trouble, what else? I will tail them, see where they go."

"You do realize Sif is better suited to that task. They won't see or hear me."

"But they will see *me* if I race back to camp like a torch in the night."

She spoke quickly, hoping to quell all arguments at once. "You know how Mindar runs, how it stokes his flames. They will know they've been seen, and all advantage will be lost."

He shook his head. "Markham will have my hide if I leave you again."

Tightening her reins, Ceridwen felt Mindar quiver with anticipation. "Go, te Donal, and tell him your queen commanded it."

She sensed rather than saw his reluctant salute, and then he was gone, his absence a swirl of emptiness at her side. Setting her jaw, she rode after Rhodri.

NINE: RAFI

He who already drowns beneath the waves has no fear of storm clouds.
– Alonque saying

Ghost's hooves struck the surf, and Rafi slid off his back to run, allowing Gordu to slump over the colt's neck. His bare feet struck sand—the crisp, white sand of an unfamiliar beach now speckled with the waterlogged forms of the boat crews, sprawled out flat like debris thrown ashore. They huddled in clumps, nursing wounds or wandering aimlessly in circles. Rafi drew up short as several villagers crowded around, slowing Ghost with one hand on the lead.

Oh . . . Ches-Shu . . . they were alive.

He sank to his knees, dimly aware that Aruk and old Hanu were seeing to Gordu, lowering him to the sand. The weight of all Rafi had just done—summoning a wave to propel the ship, fighting the sailor, freeing the steeds and Gordu from the hold—left him utterly drained.

Whiskers tickled his ear, and he brushed Ghost's head away before the colt could start nibbling at his hair. Wearily, he patted the colt's neck. "Cala root crackers, Ghost. Buckets of them. Soon as we return to the rebel camp. You've earned it."

More than earned it. Ghost had saved him again.

He'd shown up moments after the ship went under. None too soon. Rafi had been all but spent, his wounded leg seized in a cramp, struggling to support both his weight and Gordu's. Given his increased lung capacity, it would have been ironic to have drowned in the end, too exhausted to swim. Even so, Gordu had eyed the colt askance, reluctant to climb on the unlucky beast, until Rafi had gasped out, "Ches-Shu! It's the demon or drowning, take your pick!"

Splashing and snorting drew Rafi's head up, and he blinked against the sting of salt and sand clinging to his eyelashes. Steeds charged ashore past him and fanned out across the beach, shying away from the villagers. Some with wings, some with mottled hides, some speckled with scales in dull, earthy tones. Far more steeds than he had released from the hold, and none looked like Ghost, though he'd seen several like him fleeing the sinking ship.

"How . . ." Rafi trailed off, awed at the sight.

"I'm not entirely useless, Tetrani's son." Gordu's voice was weak and thin. Moisture beaded on his upper lip, and his thick arms trembled as he supported himself in a half-sitting position while Aruk and Hanu hovered over him, inspecting his injured foot.

"You got them out?" It finally sank in. "The ramp?"

"See"—Gordu shook his head—"that's the problem with you young spawnlings." His voice strengthened. He always did love giving a lecture. "You never consider the current before taking the plunge. Stood to reason the Soldonians had some plan for off-loading their cargo. So while you were off kicking up a storm, I found that ramp lashed to the deck, and climbed down to cut 'em loose. Worked, too, until the ship tipped, and the ramp near about crushed me."

"I thought you didn't like demon-steeds."

Gordu shot him a glowering look. "Don't like you either, but that—" He hissed in pain as old Hanu prodded his foot. "Careful!"

Hanu nodded sagely. "Nothing for it, I'm afraid."

"Nothing for what? What are you chattering about?"

Hanu ignored him, twisting to yell over his shoulder. "Anybody got a knife? Knife? Anybody?" He reached a gnarled hand toward Gordu's shoulder and patted it lightly. "Don't worry. Once we cut it off, you'll be right as rain."

Gordu slapped his hand away. "Don't touch me, you old barnacle."

"Don't snap at me, old crab." Beneath his wide-brimmed hat, Hanu's eyes twinkled. "Just trying to save your life."

Rafi surveyed the injury. Gordu's foot was swollen, certainly, and already bruising, but there weren't any bones protruding from the skin. He opened his mouth to say so when Hanu tipped his hat up and winked at him.

Rafi couldn't resist. "Hmm, yes, I see what you mean—"

Gordu shot him a withering look.

"—but maybe try splinting and bandaging first?"

"Nahiki!" Moc loped up, apparently none the worse for having an oar broken over his head, and flung a sturdy arm around Rafi's neck. It was like being hit with a log—affectionately, of course. "Cousin, that was some stunt you pulled back there."

"You know me—all about the crazy stunts. How is everyone?"

"Couple knife wounds, broken ribs, sore skulls. We lost two—"

"Vendak and Korb." Aruk's voice dropped respectfully. "May Ches-Shu cradle them in her ever-loving embrace."

Rafi rubbed the base of his skull. "And the sailors?"

"Dead, mostly. Two wounded. Sev told Yorg to sit on them."

Yorg was almost as brawny as Gordu and about twenty years younger. If anyone could intimidate captives into behaving, it was him. "Good choice."

Moc grunted in agreement. "They won't be going anywhere."

Rafi eyed him. "You mean he is literally sitting on them, don't you. Not just watching to make sure they don't run away?"

"Of course. Why else would I say it?" Moc thumbed over his shoulder to where Yorg could indeed be seen sitting atop two forms in the sand, thick arms crossed over his broad chest.

Why, indeed. Good old, straightforward, dependable Moc.

"Would you just use it, you stubborn old crab?" Hanu demanded, pulling his ragged brown shirt up over his head and shaking it toward Gordu. "Here it is. Take it. Take it!"

Gordu dashed it aside. "Get it out of my face."

"It's not for your face. It's for your foot."

"You're not bandaging my foot with that. You never bathe!"

"I do too. I take a dip in the sea every new moon."

"Yes, but you leave your clothes on shore, so they never get washed." Gordu jabbed a finger at Aruk instead. "What about your shirt?"

"Mine?" Aruk drew back. "It's . . . wet." Not to mention expensive, judging by that ruffled collar and delicate weave. He'd always preferred fine things. "We need dry bandages," he asserted confidently. "Surely someone has something we can use."

Rafi eyed his own bare chest and tattered trousers.

Moc gripped the collar of his own shirt and yanked it off, ripped it straight down the middle, and tossed it to Aruk, exposing a ropey mass of scars covering his broad back. Were those cane marks? "Here. Use this." He gripped Rafi's elbow. "Come, Nahiki. It looks like trouble is brewing."

Rafi turned to see Sev marching furiously toward them, backed by a cluster of villagers, one or two clutching oars as weapons. He had a sinking feeling that he knew who they were planning to attack.

"What now, Rafi?" Sev flung his arms wide. "We are stranded. No ship. No steeds. What will we trade to your cousin now?"

"Come on, Sev." Rafi pointed to the loose clusters of horses scattered along the beach. "We have the steeds." Or some of them, at least. Sahak would no doubt balk at receiving less than he had lost, but that was a problem for later. Once they all dried off, calmed down, and had a bite to eat.

"Do we?" Sev shoved closer. "You can just whistle them all to heel, can you?"

"Well, not exactly—"

Others voiced their frustration. "I just want my Ada back!"

"Should have known better than to trust a Tetrani."

Rafi tried to speak and found his voice drowned out as the villagers closed around him. They had come when Sev called for help and agreed to rob Sahak willingly enough, but grudges, it seemed, had not been forgotten, and he had not been forgiven.

One of the villagers jabbed his chest with a stiff finger. "He wants you, doesn't he? The Emperor's Stone-eye? Maybe we trade you instead."

Moc cracked his knuckles. "I wouldn't try it if I were you."

"Oh, wouldn't you?" The man squared up to fight, though Moc towered over him.

Sev shouldered between the two. "Didn't work, Tibbs. If Rafi says he can fix it, we should at least hear his plan." His gaze flicked to Rafi and away again. "I owe him that much."

Rafi stifled a twinge of shame.

"Sev knows the way of it." Gordu shoved aside Aruk who was still bandaging his foot and propped himself up so his scowl could reach them all equally. "We've courted Ches-Shu all our lives. We know how to be dashed down by waves and pick ourselves up again. So bandage your wounds, scavenge what you can from the wreckage, and then do what Nahiki tells you to, because without him and those cursed steeds, none of us will see our families again. Got it?"

Grudging mumbles of assent rose, and all eyes shifted to Rafi.

Rafi drew in a sharp breath, but before he could speak, Sev took off in a sprint, down the beach toward the demon-steeds. While they'd been distracted, Iakki had scaled a neefwa tree sprouting from the sand and now dangled from a sagging branch over the enormous gray steed that had smashed through the ship's hull. Oh, Ches-Shu, *no.*

Sev pounded toward him. "Get down!"

Poor choice of words. It was practically an invitation.

Iakki dropped onto the horse's broad back. The creature's hide quivered as if trying to twitch away an annoying fly, then it stamped a hoof, and ripples swam across the sand. Grabbing onto its mane, Iakki hunched low. When nothing happened, he relaxed, flinging his arms wide with a triumphant grin just as Sev rushed up to grab him.

The steed bolted forward a step and swung around to face Sev. Iakki didn't stand a chance. The sharp motion sent him sailing, and he crashed face-first into the sand. Startled, the horse whirled and plunged through the demon-steeds, scattering them like a flock of feeding gulls before a wave.

Some took off down the beach at a run. Others spun and crashed into the jungle. Within moments, they were gone, vanished into the thick of the Mah, leaving only crushed plants and a slow drift of swirling sand in their wake.

Ghost loosed a keening scream and broke into a jog. Rafi lunged and only just managed to snatch his lead as he passed, bringing him to a stamping halt.

"Ches-Shu, Cael, and Cihana," Moc breathed out. "What now?"

Sick with dread, Rafi turned to see the villagers standing aghast. What now? *We die,* a mournful voice whispered in his head. *We die, our families die, our friends die, Sahak finds us and kills us all. Just like Delmar.*

Ghost tossed his head, and Rafi itched to climb astride him and dive back into the sea—back into the deeps, where all was cold and still, and there were no voices demanding answers he could not give. Only wild, breathless freedom. Instead, he squared his shoulders like a prince should, like Delmar always had. "We find them, that's what. We split up and track them down. Meet back here in a day. Moc, you handle the beach. I'll take the jungle."

"Sure." Moc nodded uncertainly. "And the boy?"

"Iakki?" Rafi watched Sev march back, hauling Iakki by one arm. Clearly none the worse for his tumble, the boy was scowling darkly at the back of his brother's head. "Oh, believe me, I won't let him out of my sight."

TEN: CERIDWEN

She who would join the Outriders must first ride the gauntlet,
passing between two rows of riders with scabbarded blades,
blunted spears, and striking hooves, and emerge undaunted.
- Code of the Outriders

Stealth was not in a fireborn's nature. They breathed and sparks stung the sky. They moved, and charred hoofmarks scarred the earth. They flamed, and all the world felt their inferno. When Ceridwen first joined the Outriders, brand raw and heart even more so, yet neither as raw as her steed who sparked at every shifting leaf, Markham had insisted she learn control. So the first time Mindar flamed out of turn, he hauled her from her bedroll in the dead of night and dragged her off to complete the rigorous Shadower Run. Riding up a pitch-black gully with shadowrider archers lining the rim, armed with blunted arrows, scanning for any hint of a spark.

One flare of flame and the arrows hissed toward her.

Some thumped her, some her steed, causing a fiery burst that drew even more arrows. She'd sprinted and finished the course bloodied and bruised, only to find Markham waiting at the end, sighting down a black-shafted bolt that caught her squarely in the chest of her cuirass and sent her tumbling backward from the saddle.

Winded, gasping, watching her wildborn kick his way back down the gully, she'd complained that it was a training for shadowriders, not fireriders.

"So?" Markham had drawled. "You think that's an excuse to be bad at it? You think that will mean a blasted thing when your pit-spawned steed draws enemy fire upon you? Trust me, tor Nimid"—for she had gone by her mother's name then—"you'll thank me for this one day."

She and Mindar never had managed to conquer that particular test.

Not yet anyway. Ceridwen called upon every trick Markham had ever taught her now, as she rounded the mass of refugees and urged Mindar on after Rhodri's forces. She kept up a delicate interplay upon his reins, soothing him with a light, distracting touch, watching his mane for the faintest hint of a spark that would betray her. Preoccupied, it took her a moment too long to realize that the riders were pulling away as the slow-moving refugees fell behind, or no—

Off in the night, rumbling hooves picked up speed.

Rhodri had increased his pace. He was moving away from them, with their children and their wounded and their dim, hooded lanterns as a decoy for any scouts she might have out patrolling, while he . . . while he, what? She rose in her stirrups, peering at the shifting shapes ahead, trying to discern the riders' path. They seemed to be aiming slightly westward of a straight southernly course, clearly taking advantage of the rolling terrain to shield their movement from the war-chiefs. Though if they meant to strike at the camps, surely Rhodri would begin to veer eastward now instead.

It came to her then like a bolt from the sky.

He didn't mean to flank them. He meant to flee.

Twists of flame flared in Mindar's mane. Ceridwen cursed and relaxed her grip which had inadvertently tightened on the reins, kindling her flammable steed. So much for stealth. Still, Rhodri might wish to escape unnoticed, but she knew where he was headed, and she need only delay him until the muster could arrive.

And she knew just where to do it.

She gave Mindar his head, and he sprang away, carving a new path. Rhodri had swung wide toward his destination, clinging to cover, but she cut the corner to gain ground and flew like an arrow fired straight and true for the bridge over the River Rys.

A flaming signal arrow, marking their path for the war-chiefs.

Mindar leaned into each stride, snorting sparks, mane and tail igniting in a rush. Ceridwen tugged her mask up and her hood down to shield her eyes and leaned with him.

Something hissed past her ear.

She had been spotted. Without looking, she knew that some of Rhodri's archers had broken off to pursue her. Beneath her heels, Mindar poured on even more speed, shifting slightly left and right to confuse their aim. She had been shot at many times, clipped frequently, but pierced only once, weeks ago. Somehow that had changed everything. At any moment, she expected to feel the bite of steel in her flesh, and as more arrows whisked past and one snapped into her saddle, her heart pounded and her breathing shallowed.

No. No. She would not falter.

Only speed mattered now, if she would reach the crossing and claim it, so she stretched low, reins slack, demanding more, and Mindar answered. He surged forward, and his flame surged with him, until his heat was a shield about her. His hooves clattered upon stone, and she drew him to a shuddering halt in the center of the bridge.

Mindar rocked slightly, breathing hard, but the smoke that coiled from his nostrils was still black as tar. He had flame enough for what must come.

"Easy, easy," she whispered, turning him to face her foes.

Below, the River Rys carved through a hollow, roaring like a caged beast, drowning out the sounds of approach. She did not strain to hear but watched her steed instead—the way his ears flicked, his limbs quivered, his nostrils flared. Before eye could detect movement or ear sound, she felt the change in him, and she summoned his flame.

It poured from his throat in a radiant stream.

His forelegs stiffened, bracing himself. Ceridwen ducked as an arrow broke through, loosed too soon for flames to stop it. Over the flickering edges of his fire, she saw dark shapes suddenly rearing up, pulling back, or circling on the threshold of the bridge. But one merely raised his hand to shield his face and advanced into the searing wave. Rhodri.

She quieted Mindar with a twitch of her reins. "I did not think you would run, Rhodri. I did not think you a coward."

"It is called a tactical retreat," he said. "I understand if the strategic implications are beyond you. You never did seem to grasp the concept when we tested such ploys upon the game map—you, Bair, Gavin, and

I." He lingered over each name, clearly aware he poured salt onto fresh wounds.

Ceridwen sent a spurt of flame licking at his steed's hooves. "You would cross this bridge? Dismiss your warriors and come face me."

"You think to goad me into a fight?"

"Or you can wait and surrender when the war-chiefs come."

Rhodri sighed. "I need not fight you, Ceridwen. You have ever been shortsighted, your vision far too narrow. You do not watch your flank." He raised his voice. "Take her." His command sank in, and she spun Mindar to the right, rolling her spurs lightly across his sides.

In a flash, the world went up in flames.

Only a firerider, like her and like Rhodri, sheltered by both sol-breath and oiled gear, could endure such a blaze, though charging headlong into any inferno was still a risk. She expected, at the very least, to hear the clatter of arrowheads falling to the bridge as their shafts burned. But Rhodri did not attack, nor did his archers fire. He knew that all flames eventually die out, even those that burn within the heart of a fireborn. He could afford to wait.

Shadows deepened on her right.

What was it Rhodri had said? That she did not watch her *flank*.

Oh, *blazes*. A wave erupted from the river far below. It reared up, towering higher than the bridge, and within its rippling mass, lit by Mindar's fire glow, she spied the distorted shapes of masked riverriders and their steeds.

The wave crashed into her, slamming her against Mindar's neck and extinguishing his flames with a hiss. The rush nearly dragged her from the saddle, but she clung on. Pinned by the weight of the cascade, she heard the throaty hum of Ruiadh's riveren mingling with the torrent. Ormond, it seemed, had joined the fight, and not on her side.

Then the roar faded, the flood eased, and the river returned to its course.

She raised her head, dripping and exposed on the bridge, without flame to ward off the arrows she knew would follow. Swerving Mindar to the left, she charged the downstream edge, and when all she could see was open air before her, she spurred him to leap.

Soaring out over the side and down toward the river.

ELEVEN: RAFI

In the Mah, the wise tread lightly while fools dash ahead.
- Mahque saying

The jungle had barely swallowed them, its tightening jaws closing off the beach from view, when Iakki jammed his big toe into a rock, resulting in a flood of tears that only subsided when Rafi offered to let him ride Ghost. Of course, that sparked an argument with Sev, who relented only after Iakki scampered up a tree in protest. It was that or climb up after him, and Rafi thought that Sev's odds of successfully prying Iakki's fingers from a branch while also clinging to said branch were slim to say the least.

Wisely, he held his tongue.

Still, Iakki's behavior baffled Rafi. He'd always been a handful, but he seemed to be striving to reach new levels these days. Overly cheerful one moment. Obstinate the next. Not to mention sneaking off and dropping onto the back of a demon-steed without a word of warning.

Rafi didn't like to think it, but maybe Iakki had sparked the riot that destroyed the ship. He eyed the boy, who now swayed happily atop Ghost, humming tunelessly to himself, while Rafi was stuck leading the colt, limping along on his aching leg after Aruk. Sev trod along in the rear with several coils of rope slung over his shoulder, radiating irritation at the whole world.

If the whole world were named Rafi.

No familiar jungle noises met Rafi's ears. No chattering monkeys skylarking overhead. No trilling bird calls or fluttering wings darting between branches. No slither and hiss of reptiles in the underbrush. It was as though the Mah itself had been disturbed into an uneasy silence by the unexpected presence of the demon-steeds.

The damp air trapped beneath the leafy canopy made Rafi want to lie down and sleep until the skin sloughed off his bones and fed the rotting loam. It was a decidedly morbid thought, for which he could only blame his cousin, Sahak.

Sahak the assassin. Sahak the monster.

Sahak who could turn pleasant days into nightmares.

Rafi shook himself and scratched at the neckline of his borrowed Soldonian tunic that one of the villagers had found washed ashore. "Sev?" he called back softly. "Do you hear that?"

Stomp. Stomp. Pause. "Hear what? There's nothing."

"Yes, exactly."

Sigh. The stomping resumed. "If this is a joke, Rafi, I'm not in the mood."

Rafi was distracted by the sight of Aruk crouching to inspect a pile of something dark and lumpy with flies buzzing around it. Aruk broke off a woody stalk and prodded it, then raised the end to his nostrils and sniffed before flinging it away. He rose, continuing on his way.

Sev drew up alongside Rafi. "Did he just . . ."

"Yes, I believe he did," Rafi said with a flicker of amusement that turned to bafflement as he stepped over the fresh mess of manure and caught whiff of the stink. Why Aruk had felt the need to sniff it up close, he couldn't begin to guess. It wasn't exactly hard to follow the trail of trampled earth, crushed plants, and tangled vines the runaway steeds had left. And in any case, Aruk was an Alonque fisherman, attuned to the sea and sky, not a Mahque earthtender with a sense for the soil.

Sev snorted. "Look at him. Just who is he trying to impress?"

Ahead, Aruk stooped to brush the soil with his fingers, tracing the shape of a hoofmark. Only a few steps later, he paused to taste the weeping stalk of a torn leaf.

"What do you think the leaf told him?" Rafi murmured to Sev.

"That you two have clearly never spent time with Eliamite hunters and herders," Aruk called back without slackening pace or looking behind him.

Sev shot Rafi a glance and mouthed, "How could he—"

"Know what you're saying behind his back?" Aruk swiveled to face them with that same twinkling grin that had charmed all the widows of Zorrad, and more than a few wives too. "I am exceptionally perceptive, with senses sharp as a tiger's—or so said the Choth stone-eye trainers when I apprenticed among them." He plucked up a hairy yellow simba from the jungle floor and tossed it to Rafi before he resumed walking jauntily.

Food. Finally. Rafi peeled the simba and offered a ring of the pale white fruit to Sev, who looked in baffled disbelief at Aruk and then gave a muffled snort of laughter. He hadn't heard a laugh from Sev since the priests came to Zorrad. Some of the creases and scowl lines on Sev's face diminished. He looked so much like his old self that Rafi almost expected him to clap his shoulder, call him "cousin," and scheme to see him wedded before the next new moon.

"Nahiki," Iakki called, and Rafi turned to see him sprawled on Ghost's neck with his hands propping up his chin. "We stopping anytime soon?"

"Not until we find the steeds. We need them."

The boy groaned and buried his face in Ghost's mane.

"This isn't easy, you know," Sev said gruffly. "One moment, it feels like old times, and I am ashamed for turning you in. The next, I could strangle you for what you brought upon us. If we don't find those steeds, I—" He looked away, clenching his jaw.

He would what? Turn him in again? "Sahak won't snap at the same bait twice."

"You think I don't know that?" Sev rounded on Rafi, forcing him to halt. "So I must trust you, because finding those steeds, freeing Kaya, that's all that matters."

"No argument from me," Rafi said gently, "if that's what you're expecting."

"I know Nahiki would not let anything happen to Kaya, but what about Rafi Tetrani?"

"Um, Nahiki?" Iakki called, and Rafi raised a hand for him to wait.

"We're the same person, Sev. I mean, I'm both of them. I'm . . . me. Same person I've always been. Now you just know who that person was born to be."

"No, you're not. You're different, and—" Sev broke off, turning to glare at Iakki, who'd leaned over to tap his shoulder. "What, Iakki?"

"Shh! Want to scare them off again?" Iakki pointed past Aruk, who was kneeling to inspect the ground, to a thick web of vines and branches beyond. Something moved on the other side. Something that formed a dark gray blot amongst the riotous green.

Something like a demon-steed. Of the ship-destroying variety.

Not just one either. Rafi glimpsed patches of white and black as well. "We found them," he whispered, shoving the rest of the simba into his pockets.

Iakki coughed. "I found them, you mean."

"You lost them, Iakki," Sev growled. "Don't push it." Setting two fingers to his lips, he whistled like a bird to get Aruk's attention, then waved at him to get down.

Soon, they all crouched in a sweaty huddle, listening to the rustling of shrubs by whiskery noses, the tearing of leaves by crunching teeth, and the swish of long tails.

"So," Sev hissed in Rafi's ear, "now what?"

Ches-Shu take him if he knew, but saying that aloud wouldn't exactly inspire confidence. "Wait here." Still crouching, Rafi started to creep forward, but a hand snagged his wrist. Aruk.

"Tell me you're not planning to just march out there."

"Okay, I'm not planning to just—"

"You were." Aruk sounded incredulous. "I thought you were the expert. Don't you know anything? You've got to woo these things."

Rafi shrugged free of his grip. "Choth tiger tamers tell you that too?"

"Oh, please, have you ever tried to woo a tiger?"

"Have you ever tried to flirt with a sea-demon?"

"More to the point," Sev interrupted with a hint of humor, "have you ever seen Nahiki flirt? He stinks. Worse than old Hanu's raggedy clothes."

"Oh, trust me, it's simple," Aruk replied nonchalantly. "Stroll out there casually and pretend you're not interested. No eye contact. No abrupt moves." He inclined his head to Ghost. "Curiosity will bring them to you both."

That actually made a fair amount of sense.

"Okay." Rafi shrugged. "Wooing it is."

It certainly wouldn't be the strangest thing he'd done.

Once Iakki climbed down, Rafi strolled toward the demon-steeds alongside Ghost, eyes canted away. He paused when Ghost paused, advanced when he advanced. It felt a bit like a dance. One of the steeds nickered. One let out a shrill whinny. But they didn't seem threatened or even threatening, just curious. Within moments, he was surrounded by a sea of tossing manes and flashing hooves.

Terrifying and exhilarating at the same time.

Cautiously, he touched the enormous gray steed. He wasn't sure what he'd expected—the scabrousness of tree bark or perhaps the grittiness of scadtha chitin—but its coat felt more like freshly tilled earth splintered here and there with veins of rock. It lunged abruptly, and Ghost squealed and yanked his head back as its teeth clacked a hairsbreadth from his neck. The frayed end of the lead dangling beneath its whiskery chin brushed Rafi's hand. His fingers closed instinctively, and he sensed the steed's focus shift to him, eyes dark as the void of starless night. Oh. *Ches-Shu.*

Before fear could take hold, he looped his arm through Ghost's reins, shoved his hand in his pocket, and dug out a ring of the simba fruit. He held it out and hoped that this beast, too, preferred fruit to human. It huffed a damp breath, lips curling back to expose yellowed teeth. Rafi grimaced as its rough lips scraped the ring into its mouth.

Now, instinct commanded, *while it's distracted.*

He lightly pulled the trailing rope, and the stone-demon snorted but followed. Crashing broke out as most of the steeds ambled after them. Ches-Shu, what luck! He beckoned his companions out to help. Iakki held Ghost while Rafi caught the horses one at a time and passed them off to Sev and Aruk to secure to trees, until only three stragglers remained. Rafi started for them but was distracted by a yell.

Sev was doubled over beside a white-winged steed, one of its feathered hooves planted on his bare foot. He shoved, and the horse skittered sideways, blowing noisy breaths. Rafi caught Sev by the shoulders as he grabbed his foot, blood weeping from a crushed toenail.

Crashing sounded out. Hooves tore off and faded.

"No. No! Come back!" Aruk sprinted after them.

Sev clutched at Rafi's arm. "Go. Catch them. For Kaya."

Rafi felt that plea like a lightning strike down his spine. He spun to assess the damage: the three stragglers were missing, and so was Ghost. Iakki had caught Sev's winged steed but was shaking out his other hand where Ghost must have yanked free. Iakki pointed the direction they'd gone.

Rafi's feet itched to run, so he did. Ignoring the painful hitch in his stride. Ignoring the futility of his race, as if he could outrun a demon-steed. Running, he almost believed he could. Running, he felt alive. Free. He tore through the jungle, leaping logs and slapping aside branches. He caught up with Aruk and left him behind, crashing through a thicket of enormous leaves and breaking out onto the edges of the clearing beyond. He staggered to a halt, favoring his cramping leg, and cast about. But the trail was gone.

TWELVE: CERIDWEN

Only when she has proven she can rise and ride again
may she be named an Outrider.
- Code of the Outriders

Mindar plunged into the water, and it struck Ceridwen like a blow to the face, disorienting her. Her chest tightened as she was dragged down, and her lungs felt like they were being crushed as she fought to fend off panic. Then Mindar surfaced, head and forelegs flying, and she yanked the half mask beneath her chin, flung back her head, and gulped in air, clinging to her trembling steed.

Oh, *shades*, she couldn't believe he'd made that leap. He feared water nearly as much as she feared drowning. Maybe more. She could have asked for it a hundred times on another day without so much as getting him near the edge, but in the dark and confusion of the fight, thrown off by the shock of his own extinguishing, instinct had given way to training. He had spun on cue and leaped on command, and because of that, they had survived.

So far. The burn of an arrow grazing her upper arm reminded her of the danger. Shadowriders could see as well as their steeds in the dark. She was not safe here, not with archers above and her steed on the verge of panic. Not to mention Ormond's riverriders, who could be moving toward her even now, concealed by the dark and the churn of the water. She urged Mindar onward, downstream, and he struck out, head high, grunting deep in his throat, toward a curve in the bank that would shield them from arrows.

Off in the distance, a familiar brassy horn blared.

The muster had come. *Flames kiss you, Finnian.*

Rhodri's voice rang out above, calling words she could not hear, then the current strangely seemed to slacken, almost as if the river were pulling away from her in both directions. Mindar struggled on toward the bend, and then Ceridwen heard it, a roar, like all the earthhewns in Soldonia were charging downstream at once. Oh. *Flames.*

The riveren had called a flood down upon her.

She aimed Mindar straight for the bank instead of the bend to outpace the flood thundering toward them. His hooves struck the shallows, and he floundered, strength spent. Not far enough. She flung herself off his back and slogged out of the water, pulling him after her, then scrambled up the incline, boots sloshing water.

Not a moment too soon. White, frothing currents thundered downstream, crashing up along the sides of both banks, ripping shrubs from the earth, and careening onward. Mindar skittered up the bank and spun to face the river, ears pricked and quivering. He blew out sharply as the flood hissed at his hooves, and Ceridwen felt it tugging and sucking at her ankles before she managed to drag herself up beyond its reach.

Still clutching Mindar's reins, she dropped with a groan and blew out a shuddering breath. That had been close, and she was still exposed to archers, if any remained to fire, but she almost didn't care. She'd nearly had Rhodri. Now he was gone, escaped into the wilds of Ardon, taking Ormond and all his forces with him.

Motion shifted in her peripheral vision, and she froze, too slow to reach for her blade.

"Off for a midnight swim, tal Desmond?" drawled a familiar voice.

Markham. Of course. She rolled to her feet. Sparks flickered to her right, then flared, revealing the bowl and shank of a pipe and the weathered face of her Apex as he lounged over the pommel of his saddle, seemingly unconcerned at having discovered her half-drowned.

"How did you know where to find me?"

"Simple," he said around the pipe. "Just followed the chaos. You leave it in your wake, you know, like refuse washed ashore after a storm."

Or the ash left by a raging inferno.

She sniffed and spat to be rid of the river's muddy taste. "Finnian found you?"

"Finnian found me." He repeated the words deliberately. "Good to find you still breathing. It'd be a shame for your reign to be recorded in legend only as the shortest in Soldonian history. Who do you think would sit on the throne in your stead? Telweg? She cares only for the coast. Eagan? Craddock would never stand for it. Glyndwr? He watched the kingdom burn and did nothing."

"I catch your meaning, Markham."

"It's only the truth. It's oft a sore potion, I'll grant you, but worth swallowing if it keeps you alive. You owe this kingdom that. You are our queen."

First her death. Now her life.

Must she always owe the kingdom something?

A thunderous boom in the distance stole her reply. She swung around to see a roiling blast of flame falling back into a ferocious glow that burned on.

Markham stared, pipe forgotten in his mouth. "Was that—?"

Not Rysinger. Or Rhodri, doubtless already racing away across Ardon. She glanced back, orienting herself on the river and on the stars above. "It was the tunnel."

Smoke drifted over the gully, and the dull glow of flames lit a devastating scene as Ceridwen and Markham drew their steeds to a halt. Ceridwen was out of the saddle in an instant, boots crunching on shattered earth. Steeds plunged and whirled, wild-eyed with panic, while unhorsed riders stumbled away from the fall of rock that was all that remained of the tunnel. Wounded figures clutched broken limbs and raw burns.

Nearby, Kassa struggled against Nold's restraining hold, wails rising. Her boots dug divots in the dirt and her fists struck wildly, clipping his chest, his head, his cheek, but he held her fast, drawing her closer.

Oh, *flames*, what had happened here?

Still mounted, Markham started barking out commands, bringing order to the chaotic scene. She should join him. Or seek to help the injured.

A familiar figure caught her eye. Wreathed in swirling smoke, sparks clinging to the hem of his cloak, he picked himself up and swayed, nearly falling.

"Finnian!" She tore to his side and caught him against her shoulder. He blinked blearily and shook his head, disoriented, his weight falling on her. Just like the weight of her dying brother whom she'd carried, staggering, all the long, arduous way home.

She focused her mind here, now, on Finnian.

Dust clung to his lips, and raw scrapes marked the side of his face. He clutched his other arm to his side as she dragged him away, clear of the fumes, passing Kassa, who had collapsed in Nold's arms, weeping as though her heart had been torn from her chest.

Ceridwen looked to Finnian. "Ballard?"

He swallowed, then nodded.

Ballard te Bronwen was dead. Five of his scouts too.

Still streaked with soot from the explosion, Finnian hoarsely relayed the tidings to the war-chiefs gathered by torchlight in the smoke-tinged gully which sheltered them from bowshot from the walls of Rysinger. Fireriders, all six of them, Ballard and his scouts had ventured inside to determine whether they could use the tunnel to strike at the Nadaari from within. If she had not ridden first after Rhodri, Ceridwen would have done the same. But the tunnel had been rigged to collapse, crushing those inside and wounding many others thrown by the fiery blast. Watching Finnian conclude his report and then limp stiffly away, Cù trotting at his heels, Ceridwen realized how close he must have come to death. She sank onto a boulder, exhausted.

"It was the engineer, surely. Floods take him," Telweg declared, stroking the stripe of dusky blue scales that ran down her seablood's nose. Summoned from her bedroll by the disaster, she scarcely looked like herself tonight, clad in a simple tunic and cloak rather than gleaming armor, dark hair loose and unbraided. But that had not stopped her from charging across the bridge with all her seariders in futile pursuit of Rhodri. And by the time the war-hosts had mustered to the river, then regrouped after the explosion and crossed, it *had* been futile, for Rhodri had been well away across lands he knew best. Not even Glyndwr's stormrider scouts had been able to close in on his tail.

Ceridwen pried her soaked boots from her feet. Even if the engineer had devised the explosion, Rhodri had planted it. For her, not Ballard, which made the sound of Kassa's weeping all the more gut-wrenching. Occasionally, Nold's voice murmured, trying to console her. Better he left her alone. Ceridwen knew what it was to lose a brother. Words rang hollow before such grief.

She banished a vision of coal-dark eyes awash with flame, then upended her boots, emptying out a gush of water that made Mindar shy back from her side, snorting weak, white smoke that was barely visible even in the ring of torchlight. She drew her sabre and set it to air dry on the boulder. Her gear would need to be oiled eventually—the metal to keep from rusting, the leather from cracking—but she hadn't the time now.

"We have gathered the refugees you saw into our camp, offering them aid after the suffering they have endured this day," Glyndwr said, stifling a ragged cough. He sat hunched over in his saddle, cloaked in the thick, quilted gear of a stormrider. Only he and Telweg remained, Markham having excused himself to ready their forces in case the Nadaari seized upon the confusion to launch another attack. Eagan had remained in the camp lest Craddock move on the offensive, and by all reports Ormond had indeed joined Rhodri's flight. Scarce hours since her coronation, and already the chiefdoms were splintering. "They seemed grateful, indeed, that Rhodri escorted them out to safety."

Ceridwen eyed him sharply. "Rhodri used them as a distraction."

"She speaks true, Glyndwr," Telweg said, which might have been the nicest thing the woman had ever said about her. "You cannot think this absolves him of his crimes."

"No. No. *Sky's blood*, it does not." Glyndwr rubbed at the stubble on his chin. "But there is one thing I do not understand, tal Desmond. Many years, I served your father, stood at his back, followed his horn into battle, and never did he speak of a secret passage under the fortress. Yet you knew to look for Rhodri here?"

Was that suspicion she heard in his voice? Saw in his hooded eyes?

She drew Mindar closer and scratched his chin softly. He huffed, still shivering and uneasy from their soaking, and who could blame him? Water diminished him, extinguished part of who he was. How ironic that she should feel the same whenever she encountered Rhodri te Oengus. He had known her before, after all. Before the challenge with Bair. Before the traitor's brand. Before the Outriders remade her into who she was today.

"*Shades*, Markham, I'm not your son!"

Finnian's voice rang out distinctly in the night. He stood a short distance off with Markham, shoulders taut, stance combative. Ceridwen could not hear Markham's reply, but whenever he was truly angry, his voice sank low in the back of his throat, like the warning growl of a stone-eye tiger, and anyone with an ounce of sense backed down.

Sure enough, Finnian abruptly flung up his hands and stalked away.

Suddenly weary of talk, Ceridwen tugged her boots on and stood, then retrieved her sabre. "I did not know that I would find Rhodri here tonight, but I do know this: so long as he remains free, Soldonia is at risk. Ormond's support more than offsets his recent losses. Should Craddock also align with them, the nation will split. We will have a civil war on our hands, and then the Nadaari need not fight us, they need only wait until we have slaughtered each other to emerge the victor over a kingdom of corpses." Oddly, she felt no frustration, only certainty of the path ahead. With or without the other war-chiefs. "You can aid me, or stand aside, but I will ride to deal with Rhodri once and for all."

Silence bloomed after her words.

Then Glyndwr urged his stormer forward, and the creature dipped its pale gray head toward her face. Over its forelock, he met her gaze, and his expression was stern. "And Harnoth," he said, "will ride with you."

THIRTEEN: RAFI

When the jungle howls, the stone-eye does not prowl.
But when the jungle falls silent, beware—the stone-eye stalks this night.
- Choth saying

"Starting to wish we'd left these beasts to torment your cousin instead," Sev grumbled, limping stiffly up beside Rafi on the edge of the clearing, where the trail that Ghost and the other three runaways had left abruptly vanished. "Seems they deserve each other. What possessed them, do you think? To make them go in there?"

There being the Mahque treetop village nestled in the arms of a massive cluster of banyan trees ahead, and the crowd feasting, singing, and dancing beneath its sprawl. Voices chattered, drums beat, gourds rattled, and pipes wailed a song.

"Cala root crackers," Iakki said cheerfully. "What else?"

What else indeed? Still, Rafi shook his head. "We don't know that they went in there. We don't know where they went. The trail disappeared. Not even Aruk could pick it up again."

And he had circled the clearing three times trying.

Sev grunted and shifted his weight. His foot had to be killing him, but he wouldn't let on. "Speaking of, where is Aruk? Shouldn't he be finished securing those beasts by now?"

"Beasts are secured." Aruk drew up alongside, tugging at the ruffled front of his shirt, allowing the air to seep through. "At least we won't have any more runaways to chase."

Rafi couldn't help glancing back over his shoulder. "You're sure?"

"Trust me. I know knots. So, what was the plan again?"

The sun was slipping low on the horizon, its soft, golden glow bleeding across the clearing, while the strings of hanging lights swaying beneath the treetop village shone out brighter. One more day gone. One more day closer to the meeting with Sahak.

Oh, Ches-Shu, what a mess they'd gotten into.

Rafi swallowed. "It's simple. Walk in. Find out if anyone has seen anything. Walk out."

"Right." Sev grunted. "Simple."

His skepticism was understandable. It seemed to defy reason to imagine that Ghost and the other three demon-steeds would have left the seclusion of the jungle to wade into the midst of a celebration. Or if they had, that their arrival hadn't caused a stir or even a riot. But with time racing against Rafi and no trail to follow, the off chance that someone had spotted something was his only hope. So, with Sev gripping Iakki tightly by the arm, they emerged from the underbrush and melted easily into the midst of the merrymakers.

More like they were swept up by them. Caught up in a swirling tide.

Someone shoved a cup of saga wine into Rafi's hands and was gone before he could see who had done it. A woman slung a string of blood-red and tiger-striped reesha flowers around Sev's neck. He scowled and yanked the string off, but Aruk took it from his hands and blew a kiss after the woman, who laughed as she was whisked away into a dance.

"Honestly, Sev, would it actually hurt you to smile?" Aruk draped the flowers around his own neck.

Sev ignored him, wheeling around. "Hoy, Iakki! Where—" He broke off, face-to-face with the boy, who was holding a skewer of goat meat over his open mouth to catch the drops of whatever savory sauce it had been dipped in.

Iakki tore off a chunk of meat and lowered the skewer. "What?" he demanded, chewing. "I'm hungry. There's more over there if you want some."

Aruk darted off in the direction Iakki indicated, and Rafi shrugged at Sev—a little food wouldn't hurt—before following him to a table bearing enormous baskets of flatbread, platters of meat skewers, and steaming cauldrons of thick tuber and root-vegetable stews. He helped himself to a skewer, and as the spices struck his tongue, the headache that had been knocking at his temples all day started to recede.

He grabbed another as Sev came up. "Remember when I convinced you to try old Hanu's fish-leavings pie?"

"Of course I do. I was heaving for hours."

"Yeah. Well, this isn't anything like that. Trust me. Try one!"

Sev eyed the skewer, then flicked his gaze to Rafi. "Trust you, eh?" He spoke softly, and somehow that ascribed extra weight to those words. "Ches-Shu knows I've only ever wanted to." He reached for the skewer, but Iakki snatched it and ripped off a chunk of meat, pointedly looking at Rafi.

"You know what he is, Nahiki? Slower than a turtle's egg."

Disgust tinged the boy's voice, and Rafi was taken aback. Still gnawing at the skewer, Iakki grabbed for a flatbread only to knock hands with Sev, who glared and whipped it away, rolled it up, and made a point of eating it very, very slowly.

Iakki moved out of Sev's reach on the other side of Rafi, which now pinned him in the midst of the conflict.

"Oh, look, Sev," Aruk said, oblivious to the tension between the brothers. He pointed to a clump of Mahque, who lurked off to one side where their scowling expressions made them stand out like a rock in the sand. "Some of your kind. What do you suppose set them off?"

Rafi glimpsed three figures in gilded steel pushing through the crowd, and he swallowed the rest of his wine in a sudden gulp. "I don't know. Maybe those soldiers over there?"

"Should we be worried?" Aruk asked.

"Just act normal!" Rafi hissed, mostly at Sev, whose eyes narrowed dangerously as the soldiers walked past, clutching cups of saga wine and bedecked with garlands of reesha flowers.

But the soldiers didn't spare them a glance, didn't even seem to be looking for them, just enjoying the festivities. A quick scan revealed several more soldiers mingling with the tribe, even one dancing. And deep beneath the trees, planted behind a man in a long, many-colored coat, who stood on a stump with an enthralled crowd hanging on his every word, Rafi spied a standard topped with a gilded shape he knew all too well.

The snarling stone-eye tiger of the house of Korringar, the house of his father and of the usurper who had stolen his place.

"Ches-Shu!" Aruk muttered. "Nothing about this is normal."

Sev tossed his half-eaten flatbread down, as though he'd just discovered maggots crawling through it. "What kind of celebration is this?"

"The best kind, cousin—free," a whiskered tribesman answered, plucking cups of deep red wine off a table and shoving them into their hands. He wore the traditional wide, beaded Mahque belt, but his crimson tunic shone with the lustrous hue of Nadaarian silk, while the gilt edging on the sleeves and collar bore geometric patterns in the imperial style.

It was a surprising combination, to say the least. Even now, centuries after the Que tribes had been subjugated, they stubbornly rejected Nadaarian influence.

"So drink up! To our benefactor! May his root strengthen and his fruit flourish on the vine." With a wink, the tribesman drained his cup by throwing first his head back and then his shoulders, until his spine arced so far it seemed he would fall over, only with a surprisingly acrobatic twist, he lurched up again, and swiped the back of his hand across his lips.

Iakki gaped at him, full cup forgotten in his hands.

The tribesman nudged his elbow. "Go on. Drink up. That is fine Nadaarian wine you have there—" He broke off as his gaze settled on Rafi, and recognition sank like a stone in Rafi's gut. Before he could react, the man bounded forward and crushed him in a hug. "Talik! It's good to see you, cousin!"

"You, uh . . . you too."

"It's been, what, three years?"

Rafi rubbed the back of his neck. "Something like that." Inwardly, he was preoccupied with poking at the name Talik in his mind. It felt oddly threadbare to him now. He'd only used it for the few weeks he'd spent in a small Mahque village, miles from here, before the incessant restless itch had driven him to move on, tossing it and everything else he'd gained there aside.

Well, all except for one thing.

He cleared his throat. "Sev, Aruk, Iakki, this is an old friend—"

"Old friend!" An elbow dug into his ribs. "Would you listen to him? You'd think we were on death's doorstep! The name's Nahiki."

"Oh . . ." Aruk blinked twice. "Really?"

Rafi's wine cup suddenly struck him as very interesting—certainly far more interesting than the death stare now emanating from Sev's general direction as the young fisherman cleared his throat and repeated the name. "Nahiki?"

"That's the name. What am I missing? It's not *that* uncommon, I don't think."

"Oh, no," Aruk said, grinning broadly. "Surprisingly not."

Oh, he was enjoying this. What Rafi wouldn't give to be back astride Ghost in this moment, bounding over the waves a thousand miles away, with no ties to keep him from chasing that endless horizon. He shook his head, suddenly recalling their purpose in this village, the oh-so-simple plan: Walk in. Find out information. Walk out. "Well, this has been great, but we should be—"

"Drinking?" Nahiki hooked Rafi's neck and hauled him toward the wine table. "You read my mind! Can't let good wine like this go to waste, not when it's been paid for out of the imperial coffer."

Rafi twisted free. "Sorry, what now?"

Sev dropped his cup as if it were poison.

"You mean you missed my speech?" Clutching two more cups of wine, Nahiki held them out, then shrugged when no one claimed them and kept them himself. "We drink, thanks to the generosity of our esteemed benefactor, his imperial majesty, to celebrate the most joyous tidings to break forth over the land since his highness ascended to his seat."

Suddenly, everything fell into place, like Alonque beads threaded on a cord, their colors and patterns telling a story. Nadaarian wine, soldiers, even the reesha blooms, which weren't native to the Mah but grew in abundance atop the cliffs overlooking the thousand waterfalls of Cetmur.

He knew what Nahiki would say before the words left his mouth.

"Our beloved empress is with child. Soon, we will have an heir."

We had an heir, Rafi thought toward the ghost with a pang. *You.*

But the ghost gave no response—no comfort, no humor, no bitter disappointment like he'd felt when trapped in the scadtha's claws. Just like that, his uncle's coup was complete, with an heir to guarantee stability and establish the succession—the sorts of things any ruler, even a murdering usurper, might long for.

"We?" Sev demanded flatly.

"Of course." Nahiki's joviality faded slightly. "We are a part of the empire, and we are fortunate to have an emperor who would see the Que tribes taste the benefits of his rule."

"Benefits? Are you serious? Since when did bleached skulls and burned villages count as benefits?" Sev looked fit to burst through his skin, but Aruk stepped in and towed him away.

Which left Rafi alone with Iakki and a man he now scarcely recognized. "You used to sing a different song," he said, choosing his words carefully.

"Yes, well, every part of the empire thrives when we all fall in tune." Staring into his cup, Nahiki watched the wine swirl. "But I imagine your friend is tone-deaf as well as a rebel hothead. It's time the Que made the best of their situation, and with the Soldonian barbarians practically eating his troops as fast as he can send them across the sea, the emperor wants peace at home. Only a fool would refuse to drink to that, especially when the wine is so good." Nahiki winked, then, raising his cup and calling for a toast, drifted away.

Rafi lingered, feeling strangely unmoored by the conversation. When he'd first met Nahiki, he'd admired the man's carefree outlook, and the escape it had seemed to offer from the responsibility that he bore like an ankle chain, bumping and thumping behind him.

"I don't like him."

Iakki's voice jolted Rafi to the present. "Who? Nahiki?"

"You're Nahiki." His dark eyebrows were drawn tight in a scowl, but it was aimed toward the direction that Sev had stomped off earlier.

Rafi switched tracks. "So, what's going on with you and Sev?"

"Maybe I don't like him either. He's bossy."

"Always been that way. You didn't mind before."

"That was before he turned traitor. Tried to get you killed." Iakki crossed his arms. "I'm a rebel, and we don't like people who do that."

"He's not people, Iakki. He's your brother."

"Not anymore, he's not." Iakki shrugged, then grinned crookedly up at Rafi. "But you are."

Rafi felt a twinge in his chest. "Iakki, you can't—"

"You know," Iakki cut him off, one corner of his mouth quirked up in a grin, "for a second there, earlier, you looked like you'd seen a ghost."

That word rooted Rafi in their current mission. The last thing he wanted was to drive a wedge between Sev and Iakki, but their relationship was a problem for another time. The missing steeds had to be dealt with now.

"I wish. We really need to find one."

"Found it!" Aruk abruptly gripped both their arms from behind and towed them along. "Just need to catch it. Come on!"

FOURTEEN: CERIDWEN

These are the forms of battle by which solborn are commonly trained for war:
the firestorm, the thunderbolt, the noon-strike, the surge, the sundering stance,
the water-dance, and the gliding stop. Of these the firestorm, thunderbolt,
and sundering stance are of particular note.
- Wisdom of the Horsemasters

Ceridwen trailed the sounds of a knife on wood to the farthest edges of the torch glow. She found Finnian beneath a scrubby tree, long legs stretched before him, a small belt knife and his carving in hand. Cù stood over him, a shaggy mass of fur in the dark, licking the raw scrapes on his face. It struck Ceridwen as odd that Finnian, who worried so about stitches and soured wounds, would suffer it, but then she took in his slumped posture. He must be exhausted.

Wrapped in his cloak and in the deepness of night, shadows blurred the outline of his form, so he appeared less an intruder here, and more a thing of nature, of the earth. Reluctant to disturb his solitude, she stilled, but his head tipped ever so faintly in her direction, and she knew he was aware of her presence.

"Don't tell me," she said. "Another pipe to appease Markham?"

He did not look up but lifted the carving so she could see. Clearly, he had only begun to rough out the shape, but there was no mistaking the sweeping curve of a horse's head, neck, and spine. She pried off her damp gloves and flexed her hands, fingers wrinkled by the wet and stained by the tannins leaching from the leather. "You two seemed at odds."

He raised one hand and scratched at his hairline, waving Cù

off as the wolfhound started licking at his wrist too. "So perceptive, tal Desmond."

"Oh, it's back to tal Desmond, is it?"

"Let's just say Markham disapproves of how I carry out my back-rider duties."

Ceridwen flinched at the bitterness in his voice. "If it's any consolation, I approve of how you fulfill your duties, with the exception of how you sneak up behind me."

"Sure you do. Because I follow every pit-spawned idea you have."

"That certainly helps." She grinned at him, and he gestured for her to sit. Until her forces were ready to ride in the morning, there was little more she need do. Markham would implement the rest of their strategy, working with Telweg to relieve Cenyon and with Eagan to destroy the war machines currently crawling across Lochrann. Only a token force need watch the Nadaari in Rysinger and send warning to the war-hosts if they made a move. So she eased in beside Finnian, back to the tree, startling Cù aside, though he darted back in quickly to sniff at her still-damp clothes.

"Speaking of which," she began.

"Oh no." Finnian shook his head. "That is my cue to run far, far away before we wind up scaling the walls of Rysinger with knives between our teeth to assassinate the tsemarc." Sheathing his knife awkwardly with his left hand, he made as if to rise, and she tugged at his arm to stop him. He tried to mask a groan in a laugh, but she knew the sound of pain.

He had been wounded. "Stay there, I'll fetch Iona."

"No, don't go. It's nothing, really. I'm fine." He eased back, then smiled unconvincingly. "You were about to tell me your new pit-spawned idea?"

She scratched at the wolfhound's raggedy ears. "We ride after Rhodri tomorrow. With Glyndwr. He will swear to me if I can prove my worth to wear the crown. What better opportunity than this? Bringing a traitor to justice? Forestalling civil war?"

"Prove?" Finnian stared at her. "Where was he after Idolas? Who brought retribution to the Nadaari? Who unearthed the traitor he placed upon the throne?"

"That would be Jakim, the Scroll."

"The Scroll you rescued. You have proved yourself a thousand times over. If anyone has anything to prove, it is Glyndwr." Finnian shifted against the trunk, wincing.

Ceridwen eyed him. "You don't seem fine to me."

He rubbed at his temples. "I felt that blast, Ceridwen. Got thrown clear off my feet, thought my ears would burst from the ringing, but I could swear I still heard those fireriders screaming after the tunnel collapsed." He hitched himself around to meet her gaze. "All I could think was . . . what if it had been you?"

She rolled her eyes. "Oh, not you too. Markham has already scolded me once today for throwing myself into peril without thinking of the throne."

"I'm not thinking of the throne, Ceridwen."

Something in his voice sparked her senses alert. She became aware of her own pulse drumming swiftly in her veins, of the way his lashes flickered above his dark eyes, of the raw openness in his gaze and how it did not shrink back from hers. Sitting this close beside him, she could not ignore the rough hatching of scrapes reddening his cheekbone, or the raw skin visible through a singed patch in his jerkin. Her hand moved of its own accord, rising to brush across the scorched threads, and she could not shake the image that crashed into her mind.

Bair, her brother, gone in an instant.

Carved from her life in the space between one breath and the next, leaving only the specter of his presence lingering in the persistent ache in her chest. She blinked, and it was Finnian turning cold before her eyes, strength unwinding as the life bled from him like smoke.

Something brushed the side of her face.

Her hand was still on his shoulder, and when her vision focused again, she found his hand drawing back from her cheek, fingers wet with her tears. "No," he said. "Not the throne. Just . . . you."

She felt as though she stood over the molten heart of Koltar.

Battle was chaotic, thought and motion spooling together, a whirlwind of stimuli and analysis, of action and reaction blossoming out like a shock wave. But there was a moment, whenever Ceridwen unleashed the *firestorm* and spun with her steed into a vortex of radiant flame, where everything else disappeared.

Thought slowed. Uncertainty faded. Doubt eased.

There was only here, only now, only the breath parting your lips. Only momentum flinging you onward. Ceridwen felt that now as she tilted her head forward and Finnian's rose to meet hers. Then stopped, with no more than an inch between them.

"This wouldn't be another of those pit-spawned ideas, would it?"

Those words shivered through her. She drew back, aware of the closeness between them, of his knee touching hers, of the rough bark of the tree digging into her shoulder, of the sabre hilt pressing into her hip, focusing on anything, everything, to avoid the sudden, overwhelming burst of fear inside her. Out of the corner of her eye, she glimpsed a shape beyond the tree that shook itself as if stunned, then darted off, carrying a long spear. Liam.

Oh, *blazes*, what was she doing?

She shoved to her feet and staggered, blindly, away. She had not felt so vulnerable, so exposed and worthless, since Glyndwr read out her father's writ, declaring Rhodri heir instead of her. She wanted only to escape, but Finnian's long legs brought him alongside her quickly, and she could not hear the words he said, could only feel his touch as he grasped her elbow, and she rounded on him, snapping her arm away and shoving him back in one fierce motion, her chest heaving, her skin flushed with heat.

Finnian drew back, eying her askance. "Ceridwen, I didn't mean . . . it's just . . ." He let out a sharp breath and wrenched a hand through his hair. "Oh, *shades*, I'm a fool."

Somehow that cut even more deeply. "No, I am. We'll leave it at that."

His jaw tensed. "One word from you, and that's it, is it?"

She did not trust herself to speak, so she just nodded, and smothered her pain, as she always did, burying it deep under ash and dust, and though his voice chased after her as she strode away, he did not. "One moment there's something between us, and the next, you wield that crown of yours like a door, locking me out. You can't hide behind your title, Ceridwen, not with me. Not as you did behind your brand."

Stubborn, stubborn, infuriating man.

Nothing set a fireborn at odds with the world like a rainstorm. Mindar loped along with his ears pinned back, and a wild lunge in his stride that kept Ceridwen on edge, expecting him to break suddenly into a sprint or fling his heels toward the sky.

She could not tell whether her frustration fueled his, or his hers.

But the sheeting rain certainly didn't help his mood. It was the sort of downpour that soaked through an oilcloak in minutes, and hours later, showed no signs of slacking. It shrouded Ceridwen's vision and transformed her fearsome fireborn into a shivering, cringing, agitated thing, who snapped whenever Finnian's shadower drifted too close, and once, even swung around to kick. Ceridwen straightened him out with a hiss and a twitch of the reins, though from the way Finnian shot her a look she couldn't quite distinguish beneath his hood as he increased the gap between them, she wondered if he thought it had been on purpose. But with her faithful three hundred rumbling at her heels, beating their way southward across Ardon through the storm, she couldn't raise her voice loud enough to reassure him.

Mindar tossed his head, tangling the wet strands of his mane, and loosed a damp snort. Shielding her eyes, Ceridwen made out a dense cloud of winged shapes swooping down, banking before the wind. She flung up her fist, and Finnian loosed a short blast on his horn. Wind and rain muted the sound, causing her riders to come to an unsteady, jostling halt, as ahead, Glyndwr and his stormriders finally descended in a flurry of gusting rain and splattered mud.

It had taken them long enough to catch up. But between his four hundred and her three, she should have enough for what she planned.

The rush of his landing blew Glyndwr's hood back, exposing his white head to the downpour as he jogged stiffly over, far too swiftly and near for Mindar's liking. His flames were dampened, but Ceridwen still barely restrained him from sinking his teeth into the creature's hide, eliciting a scowl from the war-chief's back-rider, a rough-cut statue of a man who rode a stormer that was dark gray from ears to wingtip.

"So, tal Desmond," Glyndwr said, drawing his stormer to a halt and eying her shrewdly. "I don't suppose you know where te Oengus is headed this time?"

"Straight to a pyre, one can only hope," Iona said bluntly.

Finnian's muffled cough recalled to mind his urging to insist Glyndwr prove himself instead. Perhaps he was right—about that if nothing else. She sidestepped Mindar closer to the stormer. "What is it you would ask of me, Lord Glyndwr? Truly?"

Glyndwr sniffed. "I merely seek to understand."

"Do you doubt my resolve?" She leaned over the saddle and lowered her voice for his ears alone. "It was not I who chose writ over ring and set Rhodri in power."

He flinched, and his frown deepened. "No, you did not. Do not think I've forgotten my choice yielded the crown to Rhodri and handed him the means to destroy us. He betrayed all of us, yes, but he fooled me, and that is why I have come. This, too, I consider a task unfulfilled." His gaze lost focus, drifting past her. "So, no, Ceridwen tal Desmond, she that is the Fireborn, it is not your resolve I doubt. Merely my own judgment."

She looked into his eyes now and understood. "Then trust mine. I do not know where Rhodri went, but I have no intention of chasing after him. It is time we seize the reins and refuse to allow Rhodri to dictate our path. It is time we conquer him on our own terms."

"Then," Iona put in at her elbow, "you do have a plan?"

"Of course. I intend to launch a counterstrike of my own."

"Yes, but where, Ceridwen?"

It was the first time Finnian had spoken to her since she retreated alone into the night. She set her face forward as Mindar tossed his head. "We ride, te Donal, to Torcrest."

FIFTEEN: RAFI

To stare a man in the eyes is to lay bare his soul.
- Choth proverb

"It was right there. I swear it!" Aruk jabbed a hand toward the colorfully coated storyteller, who crouched atop his stump, the better to make faces at the children clustered at the front of his audience. One and all listened with rapt attention while his voice rose and fell in a rhythmic chant, their bodies swaying in time with his. Until with a roar, he pounced among them and snarled like a stone-eye, sending them scattering.

"Just to be clear," Rafi said, scanning the crowd, "by 'it' you do mean one of the steeds and not the Eliamite taleweaver you're pointing at?"

"That's a taleweaver?" Iakki popped up on his toes, craning to see.

Chuckling to himself, the taleweaver snapped out his coat, causing all the colors to ripple and flare, then took a seat on his stump. He restored order to his dark, curly hair and resumed his tale while the children slowly crept back into place. Iakki watched wide-eyed. So scadtha slaying and sea-demon taming meant nothing to the boy, but show him a nomadic storyteller in a colorful coat and suddenly he was impressed.

Iakki scrunched his nose. "Huh."

Or maybe not. "What?"

"Nothing. I just thought he'd be older. Gray beard. Wrinkles."

Aruk snapped his fingers in their faces. "Demon-steed!"

Shushes rose from the crowd and more than a few disapproving looks. Rafi smiled apologetically and dragged Aruk back a few paces.

"You know the idea is *not* to make a scene, right? Where do you see it? I still don't."

"Of course you don't. That's what I've been trying to tell you. It vanished. Here one moment. Gone the next. Like a puff of smoke."

Rafi frowned. "You realize 'Ghost' is just a name, right?"

"You mean unlike 'demon-steeds' which seems a fit description to me, considering all the trouble they've caused us—"

Cheers and applause drowned out the rest of Aruk's words, announcing the end of the taleweaver's story, followed by shouts of "Eshur!"—which Rafi gathered was the man's name—and clamors for another tale.

Eshur bounded atop his stump again, seized the corners of his coat, and spread his arms as he swept into a low bow, causing pleats in the fabric to flare open, revealing even more panels of color beneath. Colors in every hue imaginable under the sun—there, a stab of red brighter than any bloodfin, and there, a streak of deep foamy jade Rafi had only seen during a storm at sea, and there, a dark and dreamy purple dripping like mollusk moss across a square of jungle green. It was said that each color-panel in a taleweaver's coat depicted a story the wearer could tell, so such a colorful coat surely could only belong to a master of the art.

With his coat still extended, Eshur smiled warmly and beckoned a tiny girl from the front row. He turned slowly until she'd seen all the colors inside and out, and she finally tugged her thumb from her mouth and pointed to one. "Ah, now that is a fine choice," he said, "for it is one of my very, very favorites. It begins with a girl, you see, who looked quite a lot like you—"

"Enough children's stories!" barked a gruff female voice.

Rafi found himself shoved aside as the group of scowling Mahque that Aruk had pointed out earlier shouldered their way to the front of the crowd.

"Bunch of would-be rebels," Aruk muttered.

In the short months Rafi had spent in the rebel camp, much of his training had looked like learning to take a beating—in the spear from Moc, in the art of falling from the colt. But he had been coached in a few subtler things, including how to disguise the fact that you were carrying a weapon—like a knife or even a *chet*—under your tunic, or how to spot when someone else was. Clearly, these Mahque had received no such training. Aside from the obvious telltale lumps, some held their elbows too close to their sides, while others swung their arms too wide—nervous signs that were sure to alert any imperial soldiers, assuming those soldiers hadn't already drowned their wits in wine.

The woman who had spoken tossed back her bristling hair and squared up before Eshur's stump. "We want something else. Something real."

Eshur let the tails of his coat fall back to his sides. "Some of the truest tales I know are mistakenly deemed mere children's stories by some."

"You've come from Cetmur, haven't you? You must have some news then? Some tidings from the war across the sea?" She was clearly hinting after something specific, but the other members of her group didn't bother with such subtlety.

"Tell us about the Fireborn," one demanded.

"Yes! We want to hear about the barbarian queen."

"Is it true that one look from her can set a man ablaze?"

Scoffs and shouts rang out, but Rafi didn't hear more because Aruk suddenly gripped his shoulder and pointed toward a drooping string of lights deeper beneath the banyan trees, which were slowly being painted in darker and darker hues as night deepened. "There! See?"

Something stirred beneath the lights.

Something soft as a dream and hazy as a morning mist at sea, yet somehow simultaneously real and alive and nibbling on a fallen rind before Rafi blinked, and it was gone, vanished into the darkness again.

"Ches-Shu," he breathed.

"You see? You see!"

"I see. Or rather, I don't."

Aruk clapped Rafi's shoulder. "Come on, let's catch it and go." He hastened off toward where they'd seen the steed.

Rafi started to follow, but a tug from Iakki pulled him back.

With a snap of his coat, Eshur quieted the crowd. "I'm afraid, my friends, that I concern myself most with stories that spring from soil I myself have trod, watered by wells I have tasted." He turned back to the girl. "Now then, where were—"

"What of the Tetrani prince, then?" the woman insisted.

"You have me at a loss there," said the taleweaver with a laugh. "Not even I can tell the end of a story from the beginning, so who among us can say whether the empress will give birth to a daughter or son?"

"I don't mean the babe. I mean the old one."

Murmurs spread like waves through the crowd. Rafi tried to tug Iakki away. But the boy dug in his heels and wrenched his arm free, then pointed off to the right. "Look!"

Curiously pointed ears. Wispy, white mane. Deep blue eyes.

Ghost, it seemed, had indeed come for cala root crackers. The colt stood in the shadows behind a vacant food table, nosing its spread. Something shifted in Rafi's chest at the sight of the colt, and he felt he could breathe again. His relief lasted about half a second. Ghost stretched out his long neck and crunched down on an ishna melon, causing bowls to rattle and tipping a pitcher. It clattered loudly, but a quick glance showed all eyes wholly focused on the taleweaver, who was dissembling, quite charmingly, in an effort to regain control of the crowd. Unfortunately, atop his stump, he had a clear view of the colt.

The taleweaver's eyes widened, and he trailed off.

"Get Ghost!" Rafi hissed to Iakki, then sprang into action and up onto the stump. "Cousin!" He flung an arm around Eshur's shoulder. "It's been too long." Up close, the flecks of gray in the taleweaver's dark beard became visible, along with the tints of stone muddling the sunbaked clay of his eyes, while the laugh lines etched into his skin seemed a stark contrast to his current dismayed expression. "Oh, for Ches-Shu's sake, just smile," Rafi muttered, pasting on a grin for the benefit of the crowd. "Smile like everything is completely normal."

"Smile," Eshur repeated. "Of course." If his tone sounded a bit forced, the smile that bloomed on his face was convincing enough to make up for it, as he added, in a quieter voice, "I assume you're here to kill me."

"What? Why would you—"

"No need to deny it. I won't hold it against you, provided you permit me one more tale. Sakura and the Stone-eye is far from a worthy final performance. The tale of the god kings of Nadaar would be far more interesting, don't you think?"

"What? No, I'm not here to kill you."

"Oh? Suppose you get off my stump, then." With a twist of his arm, Eshur caught and pinned Rafi's wrist in a viselike grip that sent a jolt from stab wound to elbow and gained him complete control over the limb. Control that could break bone, dislocate joints, or steer Rafi like a puppet on a string.

Instead, Eshur used it to casually lift his arm and step free.

Rafi snagged the man's ankle with his own and tripped him, sending him tumbling off the stump before he could draw attention to Ghost, who was now circling the table at a sidestep, evading Iakki. Which left Rafi standing alone before a crowd that bore a distinct resemblance to a swollen storm cloud. He backed up a step.

Some on the fringes started to drift away, losing interest.

Rafi bounded forward again. "Wait!" Maybe interrupting the one thing that had been keeping people preoccupied had been a bad idea. "I . . . uh . . ."

"Rafi!" Sev's voice. "Catch!"

Something flew straight for his face.

Only his reflexes saved his nose. He lowered his bandaged left hand, clutching a fuzzy, yellow simba fruit. He locked eyes with Sev, who stood in the midst of that sea of discontented faces, like a beacon pointing the way. Two more simbas whistled toward him. Rafi probably could have caught both in his right hand, but where was the fun in that? So instead, he threw the one in his left hand high, caught one of the new arrivals, flipped it gently to his left, caught the other, and then ducked low in a spin before reclaiming the one he'd sent up.

Grunts of reluctant approval rose from those watching.

Grinning, Rafi began to juggle.

Remember this, Rafi . . .

It was not the voice of the ghost.

It was not real or distinct or alive.

It was only a distant echo of a memory in Rafi's ears as he sent the simba fruits dancing through the air. Teaching themselves to juggle to pass the time in their cell had been Delmar's idea, of course. Delmar had been the ember that kept on burning, refusing to be quenched, so every speck and spark of light that had brightened those imprisoned years had been his.

Only now did it strike Rafi to wonder what that had cost his brother. If constantly mining his own soul for hope to offer Rafi might have left him brittle and empty in the end.

Might have been the reason he was caught on that cliff's edge.

They had started juggling with balls of mud scraped up off the dungeon floor. Then their bowls, making a game of seeing who could lick theirs clean first from morning and evening slop. But somehow, near the end, Delmar had convinced a guard to bring them a set of real leather balls. How they had prized those, stashing them in a tiny hollow Rafi had discovered in the stone lintel over their cell door, concealing them from Sahak and the surprise shakedowns ordered to deprive them of any sense of stability.

In their rushed escape, Rafi had forgotten them there.

Maybe some other poor imprisoned soul had found them.

So deeply ensconced was Rafi in memory that when someone snatched one of the simbas from his pattern, interrupting his flow, he fully expected to see Delmar winking at him, not the taleweaver. Startled, Rafi fumbled his next throw, but Eshur caught that one, too, then simply popped it back up toward him.

He seemed to be taking this all in stride—more than that, he seemed to be enjoying it.

Rafi spun the simba back into the mix and realized as it left his hand that it wasn't a simba at all, but a used wine cup. The simba came next, lobbed gently his way, then a pipe with the bowl still warm, followed by a seashell. Not since Delmar had Rafi juggled with a partner, but within moments, he and Eshur were passing throws and trading objects like they'd been practicing together for years, much to the crowd's delight.

Finally, at Eshur's prompting, they caught the cascade and took a bow. The crowd erupted in applause, and Rafi's grin stretched wide, until he spotted the panic on Iakki's face.

Only then did he feel the tug on his trousers. Ghost stood behind him, whiskery lips quivering and thumping, trying to get at his pocket. Or rather, at the half-eaten ring of simba he'd stowed there earlier.

"By all the bright stars above," Eshur breathed, awestruck.

Startled gasps arose from the crowd, along with murmurs of *"anhana lasha,"* referring to a creature of omen. Something crashed deeper in the village. One of the wine tables had been knocked over, sending a wave of celebrants dodging back. Out of the wreckage rose a figure in a ruffled shirt, dripping red. He stood, silhouetted against a fallen torch for the briefest of moments before being yanked off his feet. Snatched, it seemed, by the night itself.

Something moved there in that darkness.

Something looming and monstrous and impossibly fast.

Even knowing what it was, Rafi's pulse stuttered as the wave of disruption spread, marking the route the invisible creature had taken. The Mahque didn't stand a chance. Some ran for *chets* and spears. Others simply fled. Shouts and screams replaced the sounds of celebration. Ghost quivered as Rafi swung up onto his back and turned to haul Iakki up too.

Then Eshur was there at his side, gripping his elbow. "Who are you?"

Two voices warred in his head.

Run, Rafi, run.

Remember this, brother.

Both Delmar. Both dead. He alone was left.

He met the taleweaver's eyes. "I am Rafi Tetrani, second son and sole surviving heir of Nement, once emperor of Nadaar."

He watched the shock bloom like a bloodstain in sand.

It was then that he did something truly insane. He couldn't say what impulse drove him to it, whether it was inspired by the allure of legend that had sparked such interest in Soldonia's barbarian queen, or the revelation that the tribes still hummed with rumors of the old Tetrani heir on the night the empire sought to commemorate the coming of the new.

"You want stories rooted in soil? I can give you one."

With a shriek, Ghost surged up into a rear, and Rafi found his voice strong. "The Tetrani prince lives," he cried, "and the demon-steeds ride with him. Down with the usurper!"

Then he spun and tore out of the village, chaos in his wake.

On the edge of the jungle, he rounded a bush and nearly crashed into Aruk, battered but alive and clinging doggedly to the shadow-demon with one hand and a dying torch with the other. "Ches-Shu!" Aruk gasped, as the steed snorted and plunged. This struck Rafi as distinctly unnerving, for the sputtering torchlight allowed only a vague impression of the beast's head, chest, and fluttering mane, while the rest simply melted into nothingness.

Not blackness. Not a dark blot against darker night, or a cloud against a starless sky. If he strained his eyes, he was almost convinced he could see trees through it.

"Ches-Shu!" Aruk gasped again, folding over his knees.

He didn't seem capable of anything else at the moment, and Rafi didn't blame him, preoccupied as he himself was with the sick feeling rising in his gut. Only one straggler out of three caught and only four days until Sahak expected to receive an entire shipload of demon-steeds, and he'd chosen that moment to announce his true identity to an entire village?

Not to mention soldiers. Soldiers who would surely come for him soon.

Jolted back to the present need, Rafi looked back at the pandemonium they'd left behind. Somehow a fire had sprung up, and shadowed shapes darted across its glow. "Sev should be—"

Rustling behind brought them all to full alert. Ghost stiffened and swung toward the sound, ears pricked. Webbed vines parted as Sev hacked through, tugging a massive brute of a steed with silver wings bound to its back. Swiping his forehead, he sighted them. "Hoy! What took you so long? Got tired of waiting and came back to see if you needed help dragging Iakki away from the food . . ." He trailed off, looking toward the growing blaze. "Oh. So, we should be running then?"

Somehow the lack of condemnation in his voice freed Rafi's tension. "Briskly walking at the very least." Back to the other recaptured steeds, then back to the beach, where, if Ches-Shu smiled on them, Moc would be waiting with the rest of the runaways and no wild adventure to relay.

SIXTEEN: JAKIM

On the truths of Aodh, a Scroll shall meditate day and night,
so they may be etched in memory as well as in flesh.
- The Precepts of the Scrolls

Jakim awoke to the patter of rain on his cheek and stared as, all around him, riders emerged from under trees and makeshift oilskin tents to ready their steeds for what would no doubt be another day of hard riding. With his limbs still aching and stiff after a whole night and a day in the saddle—or in his case, clinging behind Ineth's saddle—with few stops to rest, he wanted nothing more than to lie unmoving all day.

Or he would, that is, if he wasn't lying in a puddle.

"You're still here," said a wry voice near his feet.

He pried his cheek out of the mud to see Ineth, with her hood thrown back and rain soaking the strands of her straggly gray hair, eying him with a sort of detached curiosity. His hands were still bound, but his feet were free. He had contemplated trying to escape in the night, even started to gingerly rise to his feet, watching for sentries, when Ineth had told him to go on and try it, just to watch out for the shadowrider patrols.

Of course they had set their vanishing warriors on patrol.

And so of course, he had decided not to risk it.

He might not know why Aodh had led him here, but he doubted that purpose would be served by running headlong into an invisible sword.

"Still here." He tried for a grin. "Unless you've decided to let me go?"

She snorted and stepped over him, moving to retrieve her saddle, which she had secured for the night under an oilskin covering that seemed to offer far more protection than the cloak she'd wrapped herself in. Maybe she was just inured to such weather. Jakim couldn't help but view it as a hostile force, determined to strip flesh from bone. In Canthor, rain was a slow soaking by clouds that sat for weeks, resulting in a dampness so thick you could taste it, long after the storm finally passed. Nadaarian rain came in focused bands: first sunlight, then a rigorous downpour, then more sunlight that sparkled off every drop of water collected on every leaf. Soldonian rain seemed ruthless by comparison, lashed by that relentless wind that burrowed straight through clothing and stung exposed skin.

But Jakim did want more than just to lie here today. He wanted to sleep somewhere dry and eat food that wasn't saturated with rainwater, and he wanted to convince Ineth to untie his hands.

He picked himself up with a groan and followed Ineth to the center of the camp, where the steeds were picketed. He passed the priest, Nahrog, supervising as two attendants fended his stone-eye tiger off with spears while a third fastened its harness to the chariot. The beast was blindfolded, of course, for they were known to be unmanageable otherwise, but it still snarled and snapped, and as the spearmen stepped back, it lunged against its traces.

The chariot jolted but didn't move, wheels chocked to hold it steady.

Growling, the tiger sank back, ears pinned against its skull, as the priest approached, the chains of his service clanking. But all its ferocity drained away when the priest climbed up and seized the whip. It cowered, spine hunching, and Jakim felt sick. If he were to peer beneath the thick layers of its coat, would he find the same sort of crisscrossing scars that covered his own back?

Nahrog raised the whip. Jakim took a step forward, but a cough from Ineth stopped him. The whip cracked out, tip stinging the tiger's ear, and the beast hissed.

Jakim turned to Ineth, but she was already striding away. He reluctantly left both tiger and priest, and by the time he caught up, she had thrown her blanket and saddle up onto the back of her massive steed and was busy fastening whatever belts and straps made it stay there. She paused occasionally to run a hand over her steed's coat, which was the color of rich Mah soil, save for spiderwebbing veins of a pale sandy hue like Jakim had seen sometimes in stones.

Her sleeve slid up her right arm as she reached to adjust its bridle, and he leaned closer, hoping to see the marking he'd glimpsed before.

"What are you looking at?" she demanded, without turning.

"I . . . um . . ." Jakim cast about. "His hooves . . . are they made of stone?"

It wasn't a lie, exactly. Just another deflection, if still an honest question. He was looking at those enormous, craggy hooves now, and couldn't for the life of him tell.

"He is an earthhewn. His hooves are harder than mountain-root. So stand back and give me some room before you catch one between your teeth."

Jakim backed away and tried not to stare again. That left him standing there, fidgeting and feeling supremely useless, when he heard a voice nearby that was oddly familiar. He pivoted and saw Rhodri coming toward them, leading his steed, which seemed to have wilted slightly in the rain. The speaker, a lean, wispy man, hastened along at his side, taking two steps for every one of Rhodri's long strides.

"This wasn't how this was supposed to go," he complained.

Jakim had always had a good ear for voices, and this one, thin and wavering with an underscoring touch of arrogance, he'd definitely heard before. But where? The Nadaarian camp? Rysinger? The speaker was certainly Soldonian.

"You told me we were simply going to slip off into the night. You said nothing whatsoever about launching an offensive strike against the other war-chiefs."

Rhodri turned to call out an order to a pair of warriors, then strode on.

The speaker halted abruptly. "Come, Lord Rhodri, can you not stop one moment to speak with me? The fate of my chiefdom hangs in the balance." He wore no oilcloak or hood, and the drumming rain had plastered his hair flat over his forehead. His face struck Jakim as familiar too—though not nearly as familiar as the figure who emerged from behind him. Clad in a tapestried robe with a high collar, a thin crop of pale golden hair concealing the inked markings that declared him a scholar of the tenth order, it was the engineer, his former master, Khilamook.

Oh, Aodh have mercy.

This man had nearly killed him.

Jakim stood rooted in place as Rhodri turned back to face the speaker, halting the group a dozen paces away. "The fate of the kingdom hangs in the balance, Ormond."

"I know, and I would know what it is you mean to do."

"I mean to muster my hosts to fight, as will you."

"I have done what you asked. I kept the engineer safe for you in my war-camp. I covered your retreat across the Rys. I took out tal Desmond with a flood—"

Rhodri gave a short laugh. "You think a flood enough to halt her? Rest assured, Ormond, she is no doubt hard on our heels once more. You should speak quickly, if you must speak at all, so we may be on our way again."

"Plainly then? I have made many enemies by siding with you."

"Then you would be foolish indeed to add me to their number." He took a step closer, momentarily blocking Jakim's view of Khilamook.

Pulse hammering, Jakim turned and nearly rammed into Ineth. Her eyes narrowed, scrutinizing him, then she jerked her head for him to follow as she walked over to join the three men. For one brief moment, Jakim seriously contemplated running instead. Climbing up on top of the earthhewn, squeezing its sides, and racing away as fast as he could.

But he wouldn't get far before he was shot. Or simply fell off.

Judging by the number of warriors he'd seen passing through the camp, Jakim guessed there were dozens of other camps like this scattered throughout the woods, and somehow, he had wound up in the same one as the engineer. So, with a prayer for mercy upon his lips—or better still, justice—he walked over to face his former master.

Khilamook's gaze latched onto him at once, and the thin smile that stretched across his face felt as cold and calculating as ever. "So . . . you're still alive. I thought you might be."

That voice. Oh, Aodh, Jakim *hated* that voice.

Hearing it now, he remembered dying, each breath stinging as if he had inhaled shards of metal into his lungs. And that pain had been nothing compared to the agony of knowing that his vows would go unfulfilled because of this man.

But he had fought back. He had resisted. He had won.

So why did he feel like shrinking as Khilamook's gaze dissected him as if he were a faulty design or a device in need of tinkering? "No lingering effects?" the engineer asked. "No weakness or dizziness? No coughing up blood or . . . other things? Fascinating. Clearly, Carpaartin's work was incomplete. I shall have to run some tests once we convince these barbarians to turn over my manuscripts. Now that I have once again proved the efficacy of my designs with that fireball the other night, we have some bargaining power." He appraised Jakim. "I declare, it is such a relief to have a chance for true civilized conversation again, even if you are but a slave." On he rattled until the words hummed like a swarm of bees in Jakim's ears.

"Stop," he blurted. "Just stop."

Khilamook looked so taken aback, it was almost comical.

Or it might have been, if Jakim hadn't been trying to keep from trembling. "I'm not going to help you with anything. Ever again."

"Why? Because I'm temporarily in chains?"

Chains? Sure enough, iron manacles peeked out beneath the engineer's sleeves, and there was a warrior standing at his elbow the way Ineth stood at Jakim's.

"You're a prisoner," he breathed.

"Temporarily," the engineer repeated.

Ineth coughed loudly, and only then did Jakim realize that the war-chiefs had fallen silent and were watching them narrowly—probably because they had been speaking Canthorian.

"What did the engineer say to you?" Ineth demanded.

"Go on then," Khilamook prompted. "Translate. Only do as you usually do and emphasize the value of my inventions and what absolute imbeciles they would be not to utilize my expertise."

The engineer actually believed Jakim would do it. Would just obey, meekly, even after the man had tried to kill him. Twice. Worse, a part of Jakim, deep down inside, felt like he should. Old habits. Slave habits. They had kept him alive as a slave in Canthor, and as a captive in the Nadaarian war-camp, but they had also made him complicit.

No, he would not lie for this man again.

"He wants me to help him manipulate you," he found himself saying in Soldonian. "You cannot trust him. He speaks your tongue. He cares only for power and will use any advantage he can gain."

Rhodri folded his arms, eying Jakim with sudden interest. "What of the Nadaari? Do they comprehend his designs? Could they employ them against us?"

"They have the war machines he built."

"What of the killing fog?" Ineth asked.

Khilamook hissed a warning, but Jakim forged ahead. "No, there is none left—" He broke off as the engineer suddenly lunged at him, then pulled up short, Ineth's blade at his throat. "Without his manuscripts, he cannot make more." Jakim did not add that those manuscripts had not even been Khilamook's work in the first place, for although the engineer was practically seething with fury, there was a look of betrayal in his eyes.

"Well?" Rhodri asked, gaze slipping past Jakim.

"Your Scroll speaks true, from what I overheard." Astra swept around him to take Rhodri's arm, and beneath the hood of her cloak, Jakim caught a glint of cold, blue eyes fixed on him. "Though he didn't tell you that the engineer wants to run some sort of tests on him."

"There." Rhodri turned to Khilamook. "You see? We have your manuscripts. We can translate your tongue. We do not need you. Consider that before you make any further demands."

The engineer's face paled as it did only when he was truly furious, and he answered in Soldonian. "You think that simply because a foolish slave can speak my language, he can unlock the mysteries of my designs? Comprehend calculations too complex for the greatest scholarly minds in Canthor? But no, what do you know of such things? You are barbarians and grasp only the language of violence."

As if to reinforce his words, shouts broke out on the outskirts of camp, and Jakim felt a brief jolt of hope. Perhaps Ceridwen had caught up with them. But the shouts were not followed by the roar of battle, and at a nod from Rhodri, Ineth gave Jakim a pointed signal to stay put, then hastened to investigate. She returned a moment later, escorting four riders on steeds the color of woodsmoke. It was only misting now, so they rode with their hooded overcoats thrown back, and beneath, they all possessed the same brawny build, thick forearms, and features that seemed molded roughly from clay.

"Ondri's sons," Rhodri muttered. "What are they doing here?"

"Mustering, I imagine," Astra said with a smile. "I did summon them."

Rhodri's brow creased as she moved off to greet the newcomers. Seeming distracted, he clapped Ormond on the shoulder and sent him off with an oddly reassuring nod, considering the threats he had issued before, then dismissed Khilamook and his keeper with a curt gesture. But he barely glanced at Jakim before squaring off to face the riders.

Saddles creaked as three of them dismounted. The fourth did not.

"You missed his pyre, te Oengus," said the brother on the right, swiping the sheen of rainwater from his bald head with an already wet sleeve.

Rhodri shifted slightly. Standing behind him, Jakim couldn't help but notice the way his adjusted stance brought his hand closer to the weapon belted at his waist. "His pyre?"

"Yes, his pyre," growled the one in the middle, taller and thicker, with a heavy thatch of blond hair. "Our father is ashes, thanks to you. His steed returned, dragging his corpse, with only his wounds to tell the tale of his passing."

"We lit his pyre only yesterday," added the third, in a voice that cracked. He was even younger, Jakim guessed, than himself, though raw boned and deep chested like the others and with a mop of hair so pale it almost looked white. "And his smoke sank cold and weak for we had no songs to sing of his death."

"No songs," repeated the first, "or vows of vengeance."

Astra opened her mouth, but Rhodri spoke first, addressing the one who still sat, slouched almost disrespectfully, on his shadowy steed. "Ondri has five sons, does he not, Cormag? Where is your other brother?"

Cormag, the broadest and bulkiest of the brothers, with a beard to match, grunted, and then gave a piercing whistle. Jakim jumped despite himself as a cloaked rider and steed seemed to peel away from the shadow of a tree on Rhodri's left, holding a bow drawn and ready to fire at his chest. Ineth sprang in front of Rhodri, drawing her sword, but he waved her aside, and at a chuckle from Cormag, the bowman relaxed, and slipped the arrow back into his quiver.

He was slighter than his brothers, and slightly darker too.

It was Astra who spoke now. "Did you bring it?"

The bowman lifted his chin. "You can tell us who killed him?"

"Show it to me, and you will have your retribution, Arlen. I swear it."

He scrutinized her, then he nodded. Cormag barked out a command, and all five brothers moved off to one side. Astra started to follow, but Rhodri grasped her hand, and Jakim, "staying put" as Ineth had ordered, couldn't help overhearing.

"What is this, Astra? What did they bring for you?"

"It is nothing," she said, then as his frown deepened, clarified, "nothing but the incentive I have promised the priest in exchange for his aid. It would seem that the legends of our most mythic steeds have spread all the way to Nadaar and captured his fancy."

Rhodri stiffened at this and slipped his fingers from hers. "Why would a Murlochian priest exchange anything for something that no longer exists save in myth? There's more to this than you're saying. What aren't you telling me, Astra?"

"I intended to tell you eventually, my love—"

He started to pull away, but she grasped his forearm tightly.

"But I did not wish to raise your hopes until it was certain. Ondri's sons have something they swear will help us find one, and while the chance to see it will earn us the priest's support, my first thought was, of course, for . . . *him*."

She endowed that last word with a weight even Jakim felt.

The hope that bled across Rhodri's face then was almost as startling as the agony that chased it away. "No." He shook his head. "No, this is a distraction, nothing more. We are at war, and Ormond is our only ally against the chiefdoms that stand united behind Ceridwen. Now is not the time to go chasing after . . . after dawnlings."

He spat the word out savagely.

But the sensation it awakened within Jakim was of a pleasant warmth blossoming after winter's chill, of flowers unfurling and green roots crawling through the earth, and a faint shiver of recognition that was impossible to ignore. It stayed with him as Rhodri removed Astra's hand from his arm, then strode off, calling for his warriors to break camp.

Ineth's knife sheared through the ropes with only a slight tug of resistance, and the bonds fell from Jakim's wrists, freeing his hands. He winced as he rubbed at the raw marks beneath, where the swelling strands had bitten into his skin, but even that couldn't keep him from grinning. He had stood up to Khilamook, resisted him simply by speaking the truth as he had not dared for so many months, and that would have been enough on its own, but it had also, somehow, earned him this small taste of freedom.

"Thank you," he said, looking at Ineth, and he meant it.

She did not quite meet his eyes as she sheathed her knife with a snap and turned back to tighten her saddle, drawing in such a massive amount he was amazed it hadn't simply slid off the creature's back. "Don't go getting ahead of yourself." She gave a tug that caused the beast to flick its ears in annoyance. "There's plenty more rope to be had, so behave."

Jakim nodded absently, already reaching for his left sleeve, the word Rhodri had just spoken still humming in his veins. He peeled it back, exposing the blue lines of script inked into his brown skin. Not many yet for a Scroll, but enough for one whose vows were so newly sworn. He scanned the marks and the truths they contained, the central tenets of his faith along with quotations taken directly from the holy writ, and there, curving along the underside of his forearm, one fragment of a line chosen specifically for him by Scroll Enok.

One fragment he had never understood.

He had thought it an error of transcribing when Scroll Enok first inked the words. He'd even gone so far as to tell him. After all, who would expect an unknown foreign word to show up in the Eliamite's most sacred holy text?

Enok had insisted the quotation was true.

Surveying it now, Jakim believed him and felt the gentle tugging of Aodh's hand deep within. The fragment read: *who will not be shaken but will rise when the dawnling comes.*

He still didn't understand the words. Or why, exactly, he was here.

But maybe he didn't need to. Yet.

Snorting, the earthhewn stamped impatiently, quaking the ground directly beneath Jakim's feet and splattering his already soaked trousers with mud. Ineth scowled down at him from the saddle with an expression that declared her distaste for waiting and warned him not to make her regret freeing him and hinted that maybe she was already beginning to—which was more in a single look than she had ever said to him aloud. He slogged over to climb up, but he had scaled trees smaller than this beast, so it took some stretching and some undignified hopping, until he finally managed to wedge his foot into the stirrup and scramble up behind her.

She left him alone to his thoughts as they moved out through the rain, and as the day wore on and the clouds finally scattered, the sun tried to boil off all the moisture in the air. He found his thoughts drifting, across the landscape they traversed with such marvelous speed and across the sea and the wild Mah jungle to the deserted wastes his tribe called home. But when Siba's voice filled his mind, it was not with the familiar prophecy she had spoken over him all those years ago—*The hand of Aodh is upon you, Jakim. You will save us.*

But with a single word repeated—*dawnling, dawnling, dawnling.*

The earthhewn slowed with a jolt, and Jakim clutched at the back of the saddle to steady himself. Ineth swung out of line and trotted toward the front of the halted column as a rider skidded up on a lathered steed and slung himself from the saddle before Rhodri. Cloak spattered with mud, the man swayed, looking like he was about to pass out from exhaustion, or maybe, considering the stain seeping around the hand clutched to his side, blood loss.

"I've come, my lord, from Torcrest. We were attacked."

"When?" Rhodri demanded.

"Not three days ago. We didn't see it coming, didn't—"

The reins creaked under Rhodri's tightening grip. "She rides an ill-tamed fireborn that throws off more smoke than the entire Gauroth range. How did you not see Ceridwen coming?"

"Because it wasn't her. It wasn't the Fireborn."

No, it couldn't have been. That had been even before the incident at the bridge. Jakim saw the same calculation cross Rhodri's face before the war-chief's voice fell, softer yet deadlier than before. "Then who, flames take you, was it?"

SEVENTEEN: CERIDWEN

To unleash the full fury of the sundering stance battle form, an earthhewn
sinks deep on its hocks, accumulating strength, then rears,
keeping its forelegs tucked, and finally descends with a force that can
crack stone, shatter rocks, and cause the ground to tremble.
- Wisdom of the Horsemasters

With a resounding crash, the manor door shook and fell in. Dust shot up, casting a haze over Kassa and her earthhewn, who stood framed by the opening, before gradually dissipating, revealing darkened corridors beyond. With an effort, Ceridwen restrained herself from advancing, reserving the honor of first entry for Kassa. It was only just, for Ballard's sake. She scanned instead for signs of resistance, of life, and found nothing. The entire holding, from greensward to manor, seemed deserted, swathed in an eerie silence broken only by the flapping of the banner overhead.

Iona tapped her fingers on the haft of her bow. "Where are they?"

If this were a trap, it should have sprung by now. Something else was going on.

No sooner had Ceridwen crossed the threshold than the reek of death within became unmistakable. She tugged her half mask more securely up over her nose and mouth and breathed in its earthy scents of leather and skivva oil to combat the stench of decay. Someone gagged behind her and let out a strangled curse. Liam, she thought it, though Iona would surely scour his hide if she caught him speaking so.

"Breathe through your mouth," Finnian advised him. "You'll adjust soon enough."

Finnian moved up alongside Ceridwen, and together they ventured deeper into Torcrest, the ancestral home of Ardon's war-chiefs. She had been once before, long ago, ere the death of Rhodri's father, Oengus, had deposited him on the threshold of Rysinger as a ward to hers. She recalled a thriving manor surrounded by vineyards, where warriors sparred on the greensward and herds roamed the hills beyond. Oengus had still been hale and strong then, stout enough to leave her father in the dirt during a practice bout and challenge him to a drinking match after. Now, she stepped around a string of fallen bodies strewn along the hallway.

"Several days gone, by the look of it," Finnian observed.

She trusted his judgment. He'd always been skilled at reading signs.

Some of the fallen clung to weapons, but most did not. Clearly, this attack had been unexpected. Not until they reached the entrance to the central hall and surveyed the carnage there did Ceridwen begin to understand. Though making sense of it was another matter entirely, for there, nearly half the bodies wore the scarlets, oranges, and bright steel of the empire of Nadaar. Nold used the toe of his boot to roll one soldier over, revealing the broken Soldonian blade buried in his chest and odd yellow flecks in his sightlessly staring eyes.

One of the tribes conquered long ago by the empire had eyes like that—that much Ceridwen recalled from her childhood lessons. She had never been the natural student that Bair was, no matter how much she sought to apply herself, but it seemed she had retained more than Rhodri, or he would never have dared set himself stirrup to stirrup with the Nadaari.

"Come, Rhodri," she said under her breath. "Did no one teach you? Taunt a fireborn, and you're bound to get flamed."

"My queen." Kassa spoke quietly from within. "You should see this."

Skirting a fallen soldier, Ceridwen entered, and Kassa drew back, directing her gaze deeper into the room. Past overturned tables, sprawled bodies, and abandoned weapons. Past the central firepit with embers now cold and white, toward the far end of the hall.

Glyndwr stood there, though Ceridwen had not seen him enter, gaze fixed rigidly upward. Her boots ground to a halt as she saw what held the aged war-chief's attention. There, mounted on the wall over the high seats, like a trophy from the hunt, was an embalmed human head that bore features she knew all too well.

Her father, the king.

"Is that—" Liam broke off as Finnian silenced him.

Ceridwen's limbs seemed turned to stone, arrested by her father's vacant gaze as though by the potent stare of a stone-eye tiger. When last he had looked upon her, on her defiant return to Rysinger with tidings of the invasion, he had offered no more warmth than she saw now in those glassy, sightless eyes. But once, he had been different, hadn't he?

Calloused hands that softly set the reins in hers. Gentle voice rising and falling with the cadence of a natural storyteller, relaying tales of the warriors of old. Stern brow demanding that she never offer less than her all. It was hard to note the exact moment he had begun to change. Everything had shifted after Bair's death and her branding with the *kasar*, but like an arrow drawn slightly off the mark, her father had begun to drift away years before, moment by moment, stride by stride, until the distance that separated the king from both daughter and son had nearly engulfed them all.

Glyndwr stirred and turned away, shaking his head as he passed his wrinkled hand over his face, over the tears that shone in his eyes. "We should cut him down," he rasped, waving his back-rider forward.

"Come away, Ceridwen." Finnian gently touched her elbow. "You need not see this."

But she stood her ground, braced as if against a storm, as Glyndwr's stern-faced back-rider dragged a table over, wood grating loudly on wood, and leaped up onto it. Then he drew his blade, and all the heat seemed to drain from her body at once, leaving her breathless and trembling.

Oh, *flames*.

She felt a coward as she wheeled blindly away and strode back into the center of the room, tightening her grip until her knuckles throbbed, aware only of what lay directly before her as her senses constricted. Peripheral vision, gone. Hearing, mercifully dulled. She needed an outlet, something to claim her focus and restrain the firestorm she felt building in her chest before she lashed out at the first unfortunate soul to cross her path.

Movement caught her eye.

Liam abruptly straightened from crouching over a corpse, and cast about, clearly searching for something. Finnian gripped her by the shoulders, speaking, though his words slipped through her ears without gaining purchase. She brushed past him, intent upon Liam. Finnian had left Cù behind with Markham but since he had begun training Liam in the ways of scouting, the lad had persistently stuck closer to his heels than the wolfhound usually did.

Now, he wheeled off on his own and started down a side passage.

Rough wood rang hollowly under her boots as she followed, replacing the polished planks of the central hall. Her vision blurred in the dim passage, obscured by flashes of the ruin of Soras Ford where her cousin Fiona and her sons had been slain. Relief came as Finnian closed in behind, and she felt his presence like a steadfast tree shielding her spine. *Blazes*, what was happening to her? What was she, if not master of herself?

"Wait!" Finnian called out sharply, and her vision came back into focus.

Liam poked his head around the corner he had just rounded. "You're here—"

"What are you doing, wandering off alone?" Finnian demanded. "I agreed to train you to read signs to keep you from dashing headlong into trouble, not to—"

"Pick up a trail?" Liam jabbed his thumb over his shoulder. "Because I found one in the attacker's bodies, all leading this direction, as if they had a—"

"Had a destination to reach," Finnian finished, comprehending.

The boy nodded eagerly and beckoned them deeper into the passage. No carved reliefs adorned the walls, and no rugs concealed the scuffed floors—this was doubtless a servers' hallway, connecting the central hall with the kitchens, and the bodies they passed, lightly armed and unarmored, seemed to confirm that. Straight ahead, the passage ended abruptly in a sharp turn to the left. There hung the first tapestry Ceridwen had seen, depicting the famed shadowrider Sidra the Swift completing her most legendary assassination, worked in threads of muted silvers, blacks, and grays, with occasional vibrant splashes of crimson.

Liam leaned in close to inspect it. "Aye, this is it."

"Is what?" Finnian asked, pressing beside him.

Boots scuffed behind, and Ceridwen swung around to see Glyndwr and his back-rider hastening toward them. Breathing hard, the aged war-chief clapped her on the shoulder, conveying his readiness to press forward.

Raising his spear, Liam prodded the tapestry, and one half of it lifted, slashed raggedly down the middle. Behind it, a richly ornamented door gaped open, twisted on its hinges, a corpse in a crimson robe wedged in the opening.

"Flames kiss you, Liam," Ceridwen whispered.

He tossed a grin at her and stepped over the corpse into a room, which contrasted starkly with the austerity of the hall, with its vibrant tapestries, thick rugs, and elaborately carved furniture. Ceridwen entered next, noting that the man had fallen face up, pierced through the heart by a dagger. She sidestepped another wearing the subtly patterned leathers of a shadowrider, slumped with his spear broken beneath him, while farther in, Liam crouched over a third, who lay tangled in a rich covering that had been swept from a low bed.

"I know this man." Glyndwr stooped over the first corpse. "His name is Tormark. He was Nadaar's envoy."

Ceridwen recognized the name if not the man, who had only been stationed in Rysinger after her exile. "He was reported missing, wasn't he?"

The war-chief nodded grimly. "So Rhodri claimed."

Liam dropped suddenly, as if his legs had been cut out from under him, toppling with a cry into the grip of a pair of brawny arms that emerged from the tangled bed covering and wrapped tightly around his neck. Ceridwen sprang forward with a shout, Finnian at her side. Choking, face crimsoning, Liam grappled with the hold on his throat, shoving with his heels to gain leverage.

Between twisted folds of cloth, Ceridwen glimpsed a face, contorted with exertion. Skin seamed like the bark of an oak, deeply wrinkled eyes, a straggly gray beard.

The creak of a bowstring told her Finnian had taken aim.

"Wait!" Ceridwen pointed her sabre at the attacker's eyes.

"Release him." The eyes flicked from her blade to her face, then the arms relaxed, and Liam rolled away, coughing. But safe. "Up," she commanded the man.

He shoved up onto his elbows, and the covering slipped away from his head, revealing a matted thatch of gray hair working loose from the restraints of a thick braid.

She shoved the blade closer. "On your feet."

He spat at her boots, and a string of spittle clung to his lips. He made no move to wipe it away.

Something about him locked her in place, for the second time today.

"Ceridwen?" Finnian glanced at her, then shouldered his bow, and leaned over the man. "You heard her. Your queen commanded you to rise." He swept the covering back, exposing withered legs extending beyond the embroidered hem of a soiled bed robe.

One hand pressed to a weeping wound in his side, the man's only response was in his steely eyes, haughty expression, and defiantly tilted head.

Oh, *shades*, Ceridwen knew this man, and like everything else in this accursed place, his presence made no sense, for he should not be alive.

Glyndwr gripped the doorframe. "Oengus te Lorcan?"

Slowly, the man's eyes shifted to Glyndwr, and a seeping smile spread across his face. "In the flesh, old bear. Tell me, have you come to kill me too?"

"Your son is a traitor." Glyndwr's voice rang out as Ceridwen paced before the hearth where her father's head had hung as a gruesome trophy on the wall. The aged war-chief had claimed one of the high seats beneath and urged her to take one as well, but she could not sit still, not with her mind racing and her pulse with it. "Rhodri is a traitor. He has sided with the Nadaari who have murdered our king and invaded our country."

The words seemed to have no effect upon Oengus, who lay on a stretcher while Iona bound the wound in his side. It was only a shallow slash across his ribs, the sort a knife might make if shoved aside on the descent, and it was days old but had not soured. He was fortunate to be alive, even without considering the extremely inaccurate reports of his death.

Of course, those reports cast a sinister shadow in light of recent events. "He knows it already," she said, and caught a fleeting gleam of satisfaction in Oengus's eyes that made her blood burn. "He has known it all along, for he is no less a traitor than his son."

Glyndwr leaned to the edge of his seat. "But the attack here—"

"Merely a tightening of the reins from Rhodri's new masters." She angled her sabre at Oengus. "You were to be their pawn to keep him in check."

He had not spoken since they carried him out to the bloodstained hall, which though now emptied of bodies, still reeked of decay, so she did not expect a response. But his gaze latched onto her with an intensity that suggested he had simply been waiting for her to speak. "Tormark saw only an invalid, bound by illness. He thought me weak and helpless, and I slew him the instant he lowered his guard. You should beware, Desmond's daughter, lest the same fate befall you."

His eyes flicked pointedly past her to the empty spot over the hearth.

She tightened her grip on her hilt. "It is not my fate at stake. You will answer for your treachery."

"Treachery?" Oengus sat up partially, somehow maintaining an air of dignity despite the soiled robe that Iona had cut open so she could tend his wound. "Your own ancestor, Uthold, said nothing spreads so quickly as the poison that seeps from a rotten throne."

Glyndwr barked a laugh. "So you would have us—have me—believe that you sought to save the kingdom by yielding our very sovereignty as a nation to the empire of Nadaar? No, Oengus, I am not—"

"I sought to right a wrong," Oengus bellowed, shoving down with his arms to prop himself upright. "To me, to my Idrissa, to my son, to Desmond's."

Ceridwen's throat tightened. "Do not speak of Bair—"

"Oh, but I do not, Desmond's daughter."

Something inside Ceridwen went cold at the way he uttered those words. Idrissa was the name of Oengus's wife, that much she recalled, but the woman had died in childbirth years before she and Bair had been born. What could any of that have to do with her father? She sensed it then, his meaning, hovering on the verge of comprehension, and she shrank from it, instincts flaring, the habits of a lifetime kicking in to shield her from imminent threat.

Strike first before it was too late.

She rotated her sabre, settling the cutting edge below his jaw where it caught against his skin. How she longed to end this man for all he had unleashed, for the heaps of slain in the valley of Idolas, for her father's corpse among them. But steadying fingers gripped her forearm, and she looked up. Almost imperceptibly, Finnian shook his head. She pulled her arm away.

She was not a steed to be restrained or a thing to be tamed.

Not now. *Flames*, not ever.

She watched the shift in Oengus's eyes—a tinge of fear, a flare of fury, a wash of resignation—then she lowered her blade. "Rhodri flees, but he will not escape, because you, te Lorcan, will help me draw him out." Without turning, she addressed Finnian. "Take him away, and see that he is guarded."

Glyndwr coughed as if he were about to speak, but Ceridwen needed to cast off the suffocating stench of this place and its stifling secrets, to taste the open air again. She brushed past Iona, who was wiping bloodstains from her fingers, past Finnian and Liam, who hugged his helmet to his chest. Her pace quickened until she burst out the manor doors onto the steps.

Gusting wind greeted her, and the sun warmed her face. Kassa sat with her head resting on Nold's shoulder, his arm wrapped comfortingly around her, their fingers intertwined. Tears still moistened Kassa's cheeks, but the two of them seemed so at ease and at rest together, Ceridwen could not fathom it. She closed her eyes and forced her lungs to expand, until the faint scuff of approaching boots brought her back to alertness and drove her down toward her waiting steed.

Mindar's ears flicked at the sound of her spurs, and he snorted softly as she rested her palm on his neck, savoring the living warmth of him through her treated gloves. She scratched his crest, and he leaned in, bobbing his head.

"Ceridwen? Are you all right?"

She closed her eyes. Some part of her had known Finnian would follow, though she had hoped he would not. "I asked you to see to Oengus."

"Iona has him in hand." He rested an arm on her saddlebow, causing Mindar to flick his tail in agitation at his closeness. "We need to speak."

"We need to plan." She drew back, putting her steed between them, and reached for her saddlebags. "Bait means nothing without a trap."

"So you truly mean to do it? Take an ill old man hostage?"

"You heard him. He made his choice, as did Rhodri." Rummaging in her saddlebag, she pushed aside a bundle of food for a pot of ink and quill pen. She drew them out, along with a sodden lump of paper, spoiled, no doubt, by her time in the river.

Cursing beneath her breath, she crumpled it in her fist.

"Ceridwen." Finnian stooped his head to look her directly in the eyes, and she thought of Kassa and Nold on the steps. "I fear for you. Let me help."

"Not now, te Donal, please."

"Then when, Ceridwen? When? There will always be another battle, another challenge to conquer." He shook his head. "Always, it's the same. You never can see beyond the fight."

She snapped her saddlebags shut forcefully. "I am queen of a nation at war. If you wish to help me—" She faltered, for the message that would summon Rhodri was not one she wished to speak aloud, nor one she could entrust to just any messenger. But this was *Finnian*. Taking a deep breath, she forged ahead. "You will muster your scouts and ride to deliver my words to Rhodri."

"So, you would send me away?"

"I would merely send you."

He stood still as she relayed her message, then raked a hand through his hair and nodded woodenly. "We'll ride at once." Striding off, he called for Liam and his scouts.

Oengus was awake. Ceridwen knew it the moment she eased open the door to his concealed chamber. His breathing remained even and slow, his body motionless under the fresh coverlet Iona had placed on his bed, but she felt his baleful gaze upon her as she entered.

"You needn't feign sleep," she said and let the door close with a thud.

Oengus cracked one eye open. "How did you know?"

"You warned me to expect duplicity from you."

"Sleep is a ruse even a child can see through. I want to know how you guessed that Rhodri and I are allies. Not all fathers and their offspring see eye to eye." His eyes locked on her forehead, where the thin circlet Markham had given her did not fully cover the *kasar*.

She raised her chin. "With you alive, nothing else made sense. Otherwise, I must be willing to believe that at merely fourteen, Rhodri faked your death and unleashed a plot to undermine and eventually overthrow a reigning king, all on his own. I knew him then. He was not so cunning."

"Oh, you knew him, did you? Yet still you underestimate him." Oengus sat up without a wince, though she could see fresh staining on the bandage around his ribs, and held himself upright. "You truly think he will come for me? With what I told you?"

"You told me nothing but lies."

"Why would I lie?"

"Why would you do any of this? I have come for the truth."

His lips curled, and he leaned so close she could smell the faintly rotten odor of his breath as he enunciated each word. "I gave it." Up close his eyes burned with a feverish glow. "What more would you know, Desmond's daughter? Ask me. Ask me outright."

She should not have come.

But she could not have stayed away.

She swallowed her pride and her anger and voiced the only question she could bring herself to utter. "How did my father wrong you?"

Oengus's eyes took on a distant look. "Once, he was my dearest friend, but he held nothing so dear that he would not eventually cast it aside. You know this. You have suffered it yourself. We were just two young fools when we met Idrissa. She was the youngest daughter of a minor chieftain of Ruiadh, and your father saw her as a distraction, a passing fancy, but I . . ." His voice caught, startling her. "I was stricken. Nowhere had I seen her equal. She was as vibrant as the sun, as sweet as new wine, and wholly without guile."

"So Rhodri gets it from you, then."

His eyes flashed. "Not from me. From *him*. He wooed and won Idrissa, though his love changed like the passing of the seasons. Spring, it bloomed; summer, it ran wild; autumn, it faded. Winter saw them both wed, though not to each other, and come spring, Rhodri was born, and she was gone. Her life, her light, snuffed out, like a candle, and he was to blame."

His words ripped through Ceridwen, scattering the fog of the past. Of course her father had taken Rhodri in. Of course he had raised them all together, forever pitting the three of them against one another as if to identify the fittest to sit upon his throne. Of course he had crafted the writ to name Rhodri as his heir. But such clarity was the white-hot grinding of an arrow against bone. Undeniable, painful, and impossible to ignore.

"He knew," Oengus informed her. "But he would not admit it. He would not acknowledge wrongdoing or accept the son I was forced to claim as my own." He sagged back weakly, voice fading, and she bent to catch the words. "You know he was capable of it. You came here to confront me, a traitor, but asked only what he had done, not I."

Ceridwen tasted ash in the back of her throat. She drew herself up. "I do not need to ask what you have done, old man. I have seen it firsthand. You would speak of wrongdoing? What of the thousands of corpses left piled after the slaughter? What of the murder of innocents like my cousin's sons?" Resting her fists on the bed, she leaned over him, forcing him to confront the truth in her eyes. "They were as young as Rhodri when you named him your son. Cut down in their sleep to draw me into a trap so Rhodri could claim my head for your wall."

It was his eyes that betrayed him, darting to the side an instant before he struck, lashing out with a short blade that extended from his closed fist. She flung herself to the side. The tip scraped across her cuirass and stabbed through a gap between pauldrons, piercing her right shoulder instead of her throat. Gritting her teeth against the pain, she caught his wrist before he could withdraw it and pried open his grip, then yanked the blade from her shoulder and retaliated with a thrust that pierced the coverlet a hairsbreadth from his chest.

Oengus dragged his hooded eyes to hers and licked his cracked lips.

"You are not dead," she said, "because I am not through with you yet. Should that change, your son will not arrive in time to catch the smoke of your pyre, let alone sing of your treacherous deeds."

He spat on the floor. "You forget one thing, Desmond's daughter. My son sang me to rest a long time ago."

Ceridwen shoved out into the passage, firmly closing the door behind her, cutting off Oengus's view, then finally clenched a hand to her wound. It was not deep. She had not lost much blood, certainly not enough to explain the chill creeping over her limbs. She put her back against the wall, seeking something to steady her as the world seemed to spin.

Sheer stubbornness held her on her feet as her vision darkened.

"Steady," a raspy voice said beside her, and someone gripped her elbow. She caught only a glimpse of a fur-lined cloak draped over a gnarled hand before it raised a flask to her lips. "Here. Drink this."

One sip and oily sweetness clung to her tongue. She had been expecting the sharp tang of Markham's ale, not the cloying thickness of dark Ardon wine. It tasted of betrayal and unshed tears. She choked down a swallow and swept her hand over her mouth, finally recognizing the hovering form as Glyndwr.

"Is it poison?" she gasped.

His eyebrows rose. "This? It is a rare old vintage."

"No." She forced herself to stand up straight, still relying upon the wall for support, and held out the blade she had taken from Oengus. "This."

Where had he concealed it? This was why she had sent Finnian to see him confined, not Iona. He would not have missed it. On occasion, his suspicious nature had its merits.

Glyndwr took the blade without bothering to inspect it. "It is not poison that ails you, child. At least, not in the way you think. Come, sit." Shuffling to the side, he gestured toward the central hall.

She resisted his efforts to draw her away. "What do you mean? I would not put it past Oengus and his ilk to resort to poison."

"Poisonous words, perhaps, falling from a poisonous tongue, like the fruit of a poisonous vine." His expression grew distant, then he sighed heavily and shook his head. "I would have you know that I regret my earlier defense of Rhodri. I did not know of his involvement in your cousin's death."

Her stomach twisted. "You overheard?"

The lines of his brow deepened as he nodded. She could not stifle the sickening sense of shame that crashed over her. "Did you know? When you chose him over me?"

He raised the blade and set it in her palm. "Your father was my king and my friend, but it seems he kept much from me. Rhodri is a blight upon this world and must be eradicated, whatever the cost." He waited until she nodded, then he walked slowly down the passage toward the hall, head and shoulders bowed.

His muttered words drifted softly back to her. "Poisonous fruit, indeed."

Ceridwen waited until the faint echoes of his footsteps faded away, and the creeping haze threatening her vision was gone. She shoved away from the wall and found that she could stand. Steeling her spine, she strode out into the night.

"You're bleeding, you know."

Ceridwen startled awake, heart pounding, to find her oil rag clutched in one hand, head resting on the seat of her saddle which gleamed beneath a fresh coat of skivva oil. She instinctively reached for her blade, until the speaker's face came into focus.

Bright cheeks. Broad smile. Iona.

"Your shoulder," Iona said, gesturing. "Or did you forget?"

Ceridwen glanced down at the bloodstained rent in her tunic. Her discarded leathers were laid out to dry from oiling. She had worked late into the night, mending tack, sharpening her blade, busying herself with anything that might keep her from thinking about Oengus's words, or about Finnian and Liam and the rest of her scouts out trying to track down Rhodri.

She gingerly prodded the wound. "Not bleeding anymore."

"Were you planning to leave it to sour?" Iona shook her head. "I swear you're more trouble than Liam and both my sons put together. Don't move. I'll fetch my kit."

With that, Iona bustled away.

Ceridwen rubbed at her stinging eyes, still raw from lack of sleep, then tugged her leather chaps on and belted them in place. She reached for her jerkin as footsteps hurried up and brushed against her pot of skivva oil, still uncapped. She caught it before it tipped and hastily fitted the cap on. What had she been thinking? Leaving it unsecured? It was far too valuable to waste, particularly here in hostile territory where she must be ready to flame.

Kassa halted before her, helmet under one arm, eyes bright with a heat she knew well. She felt a jolt of that same heat shoot through her veins. "He's here, isn't he?"

"Stormriders spotted his forces coming this way, riding hard."

Ceridwen hastily saddled Mindar. "How long?"

"Maybe three hours."

She stalled with the bridle halfway over Mindar's ears, which made him snort and toss his head. Three. Rhodri must have been close when Finnian found him.

"Shall we muster archers to the wall top?"

Ceridwen shook her head, bundling oil pot and rag into her saddlebags. Something fell out as she swung the bags over Mindar's hindquarters, and she bent to retrieve it. "We have no need to defend these walls. Ready the host to ride . . ."

She trailed off as she recognized the fallen object. It was a small horse carved from wood, captured midspring with its forelimbs flying, a wildly curling mane that resembled leaping flames, and a familiar tilt to its head that made her breath catch in her throat. It was Mindar.

Chest aching, she traced the point of the ears and looked up, half expecting to see Finnian lounging against her saddle, looking at her with that warm smile of his.

But she had sent him away, and now Rhodri had come.

"Ready the host to ride?" Kassa prompted, regarding her curiously.

She tucked the carved fireborn into her saddlebags and tied off the straps. "We'll meet him in the field, on ground of our choosing." Gathering up Mindar's reins, she started up the manor steps, then paused before the shattered doors and asked, "What word of Finnian?"

The breath that lapsed before Kassa replied was time enough to conjure up images of Finnian lying slain on some forsaken hilltop, his bow broken beneath him.

"He has not yet returned."

Yet. Ceridwen braced herself upon that word and led Mindar over the wreckage of the doors. In the central hall, she plucked a cold oil lamp from a decorative stand. Hefting the lamp in her hand, she watched the sway of the viscous liquid within, then tipped it, pouring a thin stream out onto the floor before the hearth.

Shaping lines into words that formed a message.

Spurs clanking dully in the empty hall, she drew Mindar to the hearth and cued him to flame. With a *whoosh*, blue-tinged flames leaped up along the lines she had drawn, branding the message into the floor. Searing it there forever.

It ended with one word, one truth. *Brother.*

EIGHTEEN: RAFI

Come sun. Come storm. All tides shift soon enough.
- Alonque saying

Ches-Shu did not smile upon them. Or if she did, Rafi decided, it was only from some sick sense of amusement at their misfortune. He awakened after a restless, tossing sleep to find the final straggler standing inconceivably in the midst of their captive herd. But the swell of hope that filled his lungs at the sight slowly leaked out over the course of their long trek back.

Only Gordu was waiting for them on the beach when they arrived late in the afternoon, footsore and weary, cursing the string of troublesome steeds they trailed behind. Moc's crew, apparently, had not yet returned from their chase. To make matters worse, Yorg had abandoned his post, allowing the captured sailors to flee into the Mah, leaving Rafi uncertain how to prevent his shipwrecking steeds from wrecking whatever pen he eventually put them in, or from uprooting the trees where he tied them for now.

Sitting beside a pitiful fire that spat halfheartedly at a pile of driftwood, wounded foot propped on a heap of sand, Gordu eyed their dejected faces, then rolled a handful of overly ripe saltplums toward them. "Come sun. Come storm. All tides shift soon enough."

"Soon enough can't come too soon for us." Rafi eyed the small blue fruits, all of which were so bruised they'd clearly been scavenged as windfall, and selected one. He tapped his thumb against its speckled skin, and it split, juice staining his fingernail. "Of course, it would be nice if the tides stopped shifting from bad to worse to worser still and brought us some good fortune for a change, eh, Ches-Shu?" He raised his voice toward the sea that had swallowed their ship and spat them ashore, earning a glare from Gordu.

Of course, Ches-Shu and the tides did nothing of the sort.

When night fell without Moc or his crew returning, and when the morning of the fifth day dawned upon a deserted beach, and when Rafi rode all the points of the compass searching for signs of the missing steeds, he wondered if Gordu had been right, and if he had been a fool to tempt the sea. And when Moc's team finally stumbled up after dark with as many broken bones as steeds among them, Rafi knew the only one smiling upon them would be Sahak as he readied his knives to spill every last drop of blood belonging to the fisher tribe of Zorrad.

Both tides and time, it seemed, had finally run out.

Ever since Sev had betrayed him to Sahak—no, before that, ever since Rafi had looked up in the jungle and seen the face of his brother's killer for the first time in six years, something inside of him had stretched taut. Taut and taut and tauter still, until it began fraying.

Now, he was pretty sure he was about to snap.

His feet itched to run, but all the exertion of the past few days had left a throbbing ache in his wounded leg, so he limped down to the water's edge, where Ghost frolicked in the shallows, and let the wash of the sea creep across his toes. The scales speckling the colt's shimmering hide glimmered, and curls of water whisked strangely about his legs, defying the natural ebb and flow of the sea, until a dry pocket opened before him, leaving a clump of seaweed on the sand.

Ghost lunged and caught it with his teeth, simultaneously unleashing the wave that had built up behind him. It crashed down with a force that swept Rafi back a step before it receded, carrying Ghost with it.

The colt resurfaced in a burst of spray a hundred yards from shore.

"Tides shift," Rafi murmured, feeling awe and the faintest breath of a plan stirring within him at the sight. "And when they don't, we have to make them. Come sun. Come storm. And come sea-demon."

"You cannot be serious, cousin!" Moc's voice broke the sacred hush of dawn, drawing moans from the sleepers scattered like flotsam across the sand and shushes from the wakeful few clustered around the fire, where Gordu had just finished delivering a remarkably depressing summary of their current situation.

Ship, wrecked. Steeds, missing. Sahak, waiting in one more day.

Which was also, Rafi noted, depressingly accurate—never a given, considering Gordu's tendency to see a monsoon in every sun shower. Still, they'd all looked to Rafi when he'd stood, eager to hear his plan. Or, in Moc's case, to object to the opening statement. "You want to meet him alone?"

Rafi studied the faces before him as they were bathed in the glow of the sun breaking over the sea at his back. He hadn't called this meeting or chosen whom to summon but still they had come, trickling in one by one. Gordu, Moc, Aruk, Sev, even Iakki, whom no one would let out of sight. Each one looked as worn down and hollowed out as he felt, but it was Sev who drew his gaze, slouching bleary-eyed and restless, one heel thumping the sand.

Sev who above all else he owed this chance at hope.

"To be clear," Rafi said, "no one, not even his own mother, wants to meet with Sahak, but I, unfortunately, need to, and yes, I need to go alone."

"Why?" Moc's eyes narrowed. "You mean to turn yourself in?"

"And spend more quality time with my cousin's knives? No, thank you. I want to meet with him to negotiate. Nothing more."

"Just how do you plan to do that, Rafi?" Sev asked, voice tight. "The ship is wrecked, the steeds scattered. You've got no leverage, and he's got all of it. We should bring him every steed we have and beg him to be merciful."

Gordu snorted. "You ever known a stone-eye to abandon a kill?"

"No, but he's not a tiger. He's . . ."

"Human?" Rafi supplied the word. "Only in that he doesn't know everything, which is our one advantage." The others exchanged confused glances, but Gordu nodded knowingly.

"He means to bluff," Gordu explained gruffly.

"Stall," Rafi clarified. "We can't give Sahak what he wants right now, because we don't have it. But so long as he thinks we do, we can stroll in like nothing is wrong and strike a deal that buys us time."

"Bluff," Gordu repeated. "To the Emperor's blighted Stone-eye."

"I've done it before. Moc heard me." Rafi waved his bandaged hand.

Moc's smile was more of a pained grimace. "Yes, and had your screams been more convincing, maybe he would have stopped throwing knives. This cousin of yours, he is a monster. Suppose you do stall, buy time, what then?"

"Yes, what then, Rafi?" Sev hitched himself closer to the fire. "Do we scour the entire empire for the missing steeds? That could take weeks. Months."

"And once you catch them, then what?" Moc pressed. "Would you arm our enemy with the weapon that could kill the revolution?"

"Revolution be drowned!" Sev burst out. "He could kill my wife!"

Moc rubbed at the scar on his head. "I know."

"No, you don't." Sev clenched his jaw and turned to Rafi. "You want to strike a deal? How about a trade? We've got at least half the steeds now. Half for half. Save some of them."

Some of them.

Rafi felt the tension coalesce in the air like a thick sea fog, sensed the doubt seeping into every mind, and leaned forward to address it, keeping his voice steady. "And who do you think would choose which half stays behind? Not us, that's who. You think any of your loved ones would be a part of that deal, then you don't know Sahak."

Rafi did know Sahak, knew his sadistic nature.

He wouldn't put it past him to twist such a deal into his own gruesome interpretation. Half of the villagers? Break out the carving knives. How would you like them? Sliced cleanly down the middle or hacked in two?

Aruk coughed politely. "Not to be the proverbial fly in the ointment, but aren't we missing the point? Sahak may not know everything now, but I imagine he'll sense something is wrong when you show up with half the steeds he's expecting, no matter what you say to cover for it."

"He's got a point there, Tetrani's son," Gordu said.

"He has got a point . . . which is why none of the steeds are coming with me." Rafi sensed the objections coming and spoke over them. "Our hold on those steeds is the only thing keeping your families alive, so while I meet with Sahak, you'll stash them somewhere safe, and I'll stall, bluff, and lie our way to more time for us, and for Nef."

"Nef!" Moc blurted out, his expression brightening. "I'd forgotten he was still out there. Could be he's found your people."

"Could be," Gordu remarked. "Could be on his way back. Could be dead. Could be moldering into jungle loam right now."

"Nef can take care of himself. You will see."

Moc spoke with certainty, as if the idea of Nef failing were utterly absurd, and Rafi couldn't deny that his former nemesis had a certain defiant arrogance that seemed to taunt even the winds to oppose him if they dared.

Of course, Rafi had once felt that way about Delmar.

Scratching at the bristly white stubble on his chin, Gordu shifted his gaze across the beach where the sleepers were stirring, yawning, and beginning to sit up, to the hobbled steeds tied to the tree line. "Somewhere safe, huh." Only the slightest hint of inflection at the end of his sentence made it a question.

Rafi responded in like. "Smuggler's cove a walkable distance?"

"Three days north, more or less. More or less," Gordu repeated, to himself.

"So . . ." Aruk slapped his hands on his knees and glanced from one to another, eyes bright with hope. "That's settled then? We're decided?" He focused on Rafi last, and despite the presence of the village elder among them, it was clear whom he expected to answer.

Something twisted inside Rafi as all eyes shifted toward him.

He looked instead to Sev, who had gnawed his thumbnail down to the quick, who hunched over his knees drained from lack of sleep, who seemed to have aged five years in the past two days. Sev, who had befriended him and was now the worse for it. Sev, who didn't deserve any of this. "What do you say, Sev?"

Sev nodded slowly. "We'll do it your way, Rafi. Except for one thing." He drew himself up straight. "I'm coming too, and don't you dare try to stop me."

Sev, who could always be counted on to see things through.

Rafi felt a bit of Moc's pained grimace seep into his smile. "Couldn't if I wanted to, Sev. Couldn't if I wanted to."

NINETEEN: CERIDWEN

The most challenging of all battle forms is the thunderbolt.
With wings drawn back, a stormer must leap into the air with its forelegs
tucked, then kick out its hind legs with a synchronous beat of its wings.
If timed correctly, the stormer can exploit the force of the strike
to achieve flight without a lengthy run to gain speed.
- Wisdom of the Horsemasters

Standing as if he had been carved from stone, Mindar stretched his neck high, nostrils flared, ears aligned with the furious wind. Ceridwen knew the moment he sensed the approaching forces because his every muscle stiffened, and he snorted out a coil of pitch-black smoke that the wind instantly shredded into a thousand fraying strands that drifted over the water coursing before them. Rhodri and his forces were close.

It seemed he had found her message.

"What will you demand of him, my queen?" Still holding her helmet, Kassa flung her head back as the wind twisted and tugged loose wisps of her hair. "If you were to behead him here and now in exchange for his father, none would claim it unjust."

Her eyes burned with a fervor for vengeance.

It was just such a longing that had driven Ceridwen to return to the crater of Koltar after Bair's death, armed with a catch-rope and a blade and a fervor to see a flame-colored steed dead.

Ceridwen glanced over her massed warriors to the towering bluffs behind, crowded with Harnoth's host of stormriders, the cloaked figure of Glyndwr braced against the gusts atop his stormer in the forefront.

Halting on his flank, his back-rider dismounted and unceremoniously deposited Oengus atop an outcropping that jutted beyond the edge of the cliff.

He shakily propped himself up, clutching the ends of a tattered green cloth to his chest so it draped around his thin shoulders. It took her a moment to recognize Ardon's banner.

Head raised archly, Glyndwr gave Ceridwen a decisive nod.

Something stirred uneasily inside her, but before she could seek to comprehend it, Mindar tossed his head as Rhodri's force swept over the rise on the opposite side of the stream. They poured down the bank in a mass of frothing steeds and flashing steel, riders bearing the crests of Ardon and of Ruiadh, and in the center, wreathed in the smoke of his own steed, as if in a cloak made of night, was Rhodri.

Ceridwen felt a chill seep through her at the sight. Where was the fury she relied upon, the anger she trusted to carry her through?

Saddle leather creaked beside her as Iona leaned forward. "I know what it is you are about to do, Ceridwen."

"Do you?" she muttered. "Because I do not."

Iona gave her a bracing smile. "You never have been a fair judge of yourself, Fireborn. Should have let me tend that wound." This, with a nod at Ceridwen's shoulder.

"It will take more than a cut for Rhodri to defeat me."

Iona's smile broadened. "See? You do know. Ride well, Fireborn."

Closing her eyes, Ceridwen knotted her fingers in Mindar's mane. She did not seek to conjure up images of those slaughtered at Idolas or of her cousin Gavin dying just beyond her reach. She recalled instead the warmth of that fireside gathering outside Rysinger where Nold strummed his mandolin, Liam captivated them all with wild tales, and Kassa laughed with flowers in her hair, and the light she'd seen in Finnian's eyes then was a far cry from the sheen of disappointment she'd seen last night.

Mindar's mane shot up in flames. Curling tongues of fire roared to life all along his crest, and for once, Ceridwen let him rage, the heat carving a berth around her as it drove her companions back.

With her wildborn lunging into each stride, she advanced toward the stream, and Rhodri did the same. He carried himself proudly as always, the epitome of control, as Vakhar strutted to a precise halt on the edge.

Ceridwen sought her father in his features and found nothing familiar save the sense of impending judgment locked behind the storm on his brow.

"So," Rhodri said with a derisive twist to his mouth. "It has come to this, *sister?*"

She shuddered inwardly at hearing him speak a word once reserved for Bair's lips alone, and Mindar shied uncertainly. One of his hooves splashed into the stream, and steam arose around her in a hiss.

"Would you have me trade my life for his? He is not my father, Ceridwen, and you have seen what I am willing to do to my own flesh and blood. What makes you think I would yield for his sake?"

"You're here, aren't you?"

"I am here because you are. You have thwarted me long enough. It is time we end this." He spoke in his customary measured tone that somehow still rang with conviction. Almost, she believed his indifference.

But she knew him. She had seen him weep, overcome with emotion after bonding his steed, and she had seen the look in his eyes when she carried Bair back into Rysinger. He might be ruthless and calculating, but he was not utterly heartless as he would have her believe.

Nor was she. She might have used threats to draw him here, but she would not demand his surrender the way he and the Nadaari had demanded hers, with a loved one's life hanging in the balance.

Iona was right. She knew what she must do.

She drew her sabre and pointed it at Rhodri. "I did not summon you to demand your life in trade. You could willingly bend your neck before my blade, and it would not begin to undo the ruin you have unleashed."

His eyes narrowed. "Then what do you seek? Battle? Our forces could clash here and now and accomplish nothing more than self-immolation."

"Our forces need not ride at all. Only you and me." She saw understanding spark in his eyes, and the way they gleamed then reminded her of Oengus. "I challenge you to single combat, firerider upon firerider. I challenge you to the Sol-Fiere."

"And gladly, *sister*, do I accept."

Long and long ago, it was said, when Uthold first rode from the flaming craters of the east upon his magnificent fireborn mare, Itandris, the other war-chiefs had received him with a hostility that unfolded in a decade of bitter war. Until at last, Uthold challenged his chief rival to meet him in combat, firerider upon firerider, in a ritual test that came to be known as the Sol-Fiere.

Uthold had emerged from the inferno victorious, while his rival's ashes were carried from the scorched battleground and scattered downstream.

It was the setting of the Sol-Fiere that made it unique.

Her pulse thrumming with anticipation, Ceridwen adjusted her half mask and hood, then tested the lacings on the sleeves of her jerkin, watching as riverriders from both forces formed a ring around them. The stream their steeds had parted to allow her and Rhodri to enter, now swirled into a whirlpool that twisted and curled around silver-scaled legs. The deep, throaty hum of the steeds intensified, and the water shifted and swelled like a towering wave before them, forming the boundaries of the battleground.

Within the dry heart of the whirlpool, she and Rhodri would match both steed and steel, and only one would emerge the victor.

Ceridwen held her sabre low at her side and felt Mindar quiver with eagerness, smoke coiling hot and black from his nostrils. When the horn blast came, echoing off the bluffs behind, Mindar flamed first. Rushing, roaring flame poured from him in an incandescent flood that struck Rhodri full force and engulfed Vakhar.

Neither could be taken down so easily—Vakhar was a fireborn, and Rhodri bore the protection of the sol-breath, like her—but she knew what it was to face down such a blinding, ferocious stream, to feel the breath ignite in your lungs and scorch the back of your throat, to find the instinct to shrink from such a blaze ingrained so deep that years of practice had not erased it. So she drove Mindar forward, watching for Rhodri to wheel to either side to evade the grasping inferno, or to launch a counterstrike of his own.

He did neither. He stood his ground.

Through the riotous torrent of fire, swirling in yellow and orange, Rhodri appeared like a pillar of solid smoke as she closed in. Rein arm raised to shield his eyes beneath his hood, blade arm striking toward her. His blade appeared to be made of molten, white-hot gold, as it caught the firelight. Shoving Mindar away with her heel, she barely got her own blade up in time to deflect, and she felt the force of it shiver through her bones. Blade slid on blade, then sliced free as Mindar's dodge carried her away toward the swirling ring of water.

She checked him sharply and cued him into a tight inward turn around her heel, seeking to whip him around to loose flame again, but Rhodri was already there, racing up alongside on her right, towering on his taller, heavier steed. His knee locked against hers. Too close to wield her blade. She lashed out with the hilt instead. Rhodri took the hit with a grunt and caught her hilt beneath his arm, pinning it against his side.

Rising in the stirrups, he twisted to strike at her in a downward arc. Such a blow could snap her collarbone if it landed on her pauldrons, or cleave straight through into bone if it struck higher up on her shoulder.

Either could end her in this fight, if not kill her outright.

She shoved down with her heels, thrusting her weight back, prompting Mindar into a swift, sliding halt. With Rhodri's grip on her hilt, the sudden shift in momentum jerked him off balance, sending his sword strike wild, even as it threatened to yank her forward. Tightly gripping her saddle, she wrenched her arm free, blade slicing across his cuirass.

Something popped painfully in her elbow, numbing her arm.

Gritting her teeth, she let her arm fall to her side and only then noticed that the edge of her sabre glistened with blood. The focused blast Mindar had loosed earlier must have weakened Rhodri's cuirass, allowing her slice to do damage. She spun Mindar in an arc, seeking to come up on Rhodri's offside and press him against the boundary. Only once again, Rhodri was there, wheeling to meet her head-on.

Rolling her spurs, she summoned another blast.

Vakhar ignited then for the first time, thrusting his head low to unleash a deep, boiling red current that crashed into Mindar's torrent of flame before it struck. Both streams of fire flared together, throwing up radiant tendrils and pulsing waves of heat. Shaking her head to clear the sweat from her eyes, Ceridwen pressed forward into the inferno. Even beneath her treated leathers, she felt its bite, and her left arm flared with pain.

But she shoved inward, onward, refusing to yield.

The roar of Vakhar's blaze slackened slightly, and she guessed that Rhodri was backing away, seeking distance so he could pull out and attack from the flank again, without taking a direct hit from Mindar. He would not evade her so easily. Shouting the cry of the Outriders into her half mask, she urged Mindar into a rear, feeling the strength in his hindquarters as he surged up and struck with his forelegs.

Vakhar's flames abruptly cut off in a cloud of hissing steam.

Half blinded by the smog of combat, even with her vision enhanced by the sol-breath, she didn't comprehend until too late. Propelled forward by his strike, Mindar crashed head-on into the swirling wall of water, and the whirlpool swept around her. Sunlight pierced the cresting wave, so she seemed to be surrounded by rippling light on all sides, through which the shimmering shapes of riveren and their riders could only distantly be seen, but of Rhodri and Vakhar, she saw no sign. The shock seemed to have dazed her steed, but now she sensed panic uncoiling within him and knew that at any instant, he might start blindly thrashing, and she would lose any hope of calming him. She spun him out of the whirlpool in a burst of spray.

Rhodri skidded Vakhar broadside across her path.

Her senses flared at the threat, and Mindar came to a hard stop. She caught only a glimpse of Vakhar's upraised head, eyes cold and white from his soaking, of the sheen of water on Rhodri's dripping cuirass, as he lunged forward in his stirrups and slashed for her neck.

Her blade arm still hung numb at her side.

She would never raise her sabre in time. She flung herself over into her right stirrup, instinctively lifting her left arm to disrupt the strike.

White hot pain bit into her forearm.

She blinked up to find Rhodri's blade lodged in her cloven vambrace, grating on bone. It quivered as he tried to force the blow, and she groaned, but with the breadth of their horses between them, he lacked reach. He reached up to lower his mask and hood. Neither were needed now, with both steeds' fire extinguished. Clearly, he thought this battle won.

Perhaps she was just too stubborn to admit it.

"You entered the barrier on purpose," she said, teeth beginning to chatter as shock sluiced through her veins.

"You rely far too much on flame. You always did."

"You know me so well, do you?"

"Enough to know you believe you can still turn this fight around. I did not strike the final blow against our father myself, Ceridwen, but I will end you now." With a sharp motion, he withdrew the blade, wringing a gasp of pain from her lips, and urged Vakhar forward on Mindar's right, swinging again for her neck.

This, at last, was what she had been waiting for.

She had endured the agony in her left arm, all the while working the fingers of her lowered right hand, trying to shake off the numbness. Strength and feeling had returned, and she lashed upward with her sabre, catching his blade on hers and forcing it up and over, pinning his arm against his chest. She launched herself from the saddle, straight at him. Wrapping her wounded arm around Rhodri's neck, she kicked off with both legs, sending them both tumbling off the far side.

She landed on top of him, their blades still locked together, and felt him scrabbling to get his free arm under him, so she clamped her boot on his wrist and shifted to press her knee against his sternum, straining to pin him down.

A horrible, wailing cry sounded above.

Ceridwen darted a glance up to see a flailing figure clutching a ragged green flag, plummeting toward her. Instinct kicked in, and she flung herself to the side, coming to a stop with her wounded arm trapped painfully beneath her. The figure struck with a sickening thud. Using her blade hand, she shoved up into a defensive crouch as a dark gray stormer banked overhead. Not to attack, but to wheel back toward the bluff.

It was Glyndwr's back-rider.

"No!" Rhodri let out a choked cry, scrambling toward the fallen figure. Oengus te Lorcan sprawled with his gray head bent to one side, a thin trickle of blood trailing from his mouth. Seizing hold of Oengus's shoulders in his gloved hands, Rhodri bent his ear over his chest, but Ceridwen already knew.

Oengus was dead. Slain in defiance of her command.

But not, she thought, of another's. She shoved to her feet and looked to Glyndwr. He stood silhouetted on his white steed, alone atop the bluff. Coiling dust marked where the rest of Harnoth's stormriders had already vanished below the edge of the cliff. They were pulling out and leaving her and her faithful few to withstand the treacherous hosts of Ardon and Ruiadh combined. They were abandoning her warriors to die.

Glyndwr had doomed them all. Why?

The old war-chief met her gaze, neck arched proudly like a fireborn's, then bowed his head and wheeled his stormer away.

Ceridwen heard the scuff of a boot behind her an instant before Iona's warning shout rang out. She ducked and spun away, bringing her sabre up, but the force of Rhodri's enraged swing nearly snapped it from her hands. She staggered back, and he attacked, teeth bared, roaring with each wild stroke. Any one of them could have cleaved bone if they had landed, but none did. Gone was the careful precision and deliberate control that had always marked Rhodri in battle.

She had never before seen him so driven by rage, so racked with fury.

The heat pulsing through her impelled her to match his assault, deflecting his blade, evading his attacks, and slashing whenever his onslaught slackened, but she could feel herself weakening, dizzying, her reflexes slowing. Dark crimson droplets fell with startling quickness from the fingers of her gloved left hand and spattered the gravel below.

Oh, *flames*. She needed to . . . needed to . . .

With a tumultuous roar, the whirlpool fell. Water crashed back into the streambed, sweeping her from her feet. Her blade struck something and was wrenched from her grip as the current dragged her away, flinging her toward her bank of the stream. Catching her feet under her, she staggered up as the flood subsided, and emerged waterlogged and breathless into chaos.

Screams rang out from both shores as arrows hissed through the air. One of her riveren reared sideways and collapsed, a spear in its side. Its rider splashed free and buried his blade in his Ruiadh attacker, only to be trampled as the remaining riverriders engaged in a furious spray of combat. Warriors on both sides charged into the fray and met with a clash of steel in the stream, the hooves of their steeds churning the water into a bloody foam.

In the midst of the conflict, Rhodri surfaced in a mighty heave, clutching the lifeless body of his father in one arm, holding her lost blade in the other. Beyond him, Ceridwen at last sighted Mindar. The rush of returning water had startled him into flight, fleeing the seething current.

Toward the wrong bank.

He trod on his trailing reins, which yanked him to a halt.

Ceridwen dashed toward her steed, kicking up streamwater. Rhodri lunged for her but was hampered by his grip on his father, and she evaded him. She dodged a spear thrust from a passing riverrider and slowed as she neared to avoid startling Mindar. He still jolted and blew out sharply as she freed his reins from his hoof and spun to spring into the saddle.

A long horn call resounded over the clangor of the fight.

It was not a signal to retreat, nor a summons to attack, but a call for a truce. Ceridwen paused with one foot in the stirrup. Out of the midst of the warriors massed on the bank emerged five burly men clad in heavy, rugged leathers and thick shadowrider cloaks, surrounding a searider she recognized all too well.

One who had too long escaped her blade. Astra tor Telweg.

In the wake of the horn call, a hush descended over the stream. Astra lowered the horn from her lips, and the tallest of the five warriors rode forward, dragging a bound figure from a rope behind him. It was Liam. Astra prodded him with her trident, sending him sprawling before the shining hooves of her seablood. She centered the prongs over his exposed neck and deliberately drew back to strike.

Ceridwen's pulse stalled. Not Liam too.

In her mind's eye, her brother's body became cold and stiff in her arms, Gavin's head sank onto his chest, and her father was swallowed by the crush of dying steeds. The thrum of wings snapped her back into focus. A brilliant white stormer with blue and black wings dropped from the bluffs in a long dive, swooped low over the stream, and arced up over the opposite bank. Iona swiveled in the saddle to loose an arrow backward at Astra. It was a truly masterful shot, and it would have struck Astra, if she hadn't chosen that moment to spur her seablood forward, trampling Liam on the streambank.

Iona's stormer reached the top of its arc and hung, seemingly suspended in the sky, before plunging back into a dive.

Only the dive never came.

Bowstrings snapped, and Iona lurched in the saddle while the stormer shuddered and dropped sideways, one wing dipping, the other straining. The next arrow caught the stormer in the throat, and like a leaf plucked by the wind, both horse and rider fell from the sky.

Below, all five warriors lowered their bows.

They clapped one another on the back, voices ringing with a triumph that wrenched Ceridwen's heart. Liam groaned on the bank, right leg twisted and bent, Astra's trident once more menacing his throat. Ceridwen dashed the grief from her mind and flung herself into a run, forgetting her steed, forgetting her empty scabbard, forgetting all but her need to keep Liam alive.

For Iona's sake. For his own.

And for hers, for she could not watch him die.

She broke out of the stream, and all five warriors trained their bows upon her. Raising her hands, she met the cold, blue eyes of the woman who had murdered her kin. "It is not in the blood of Lochrann to beg, Astra. You know this. But my life . . . my life for his."

Still, the trident hovered over his throat.

She was so intent upon Liam, upon the sickening angle of his leg and the shock that had stolen the color from his face and made the freckles stand out upon his skin, that she didn't sense Rhodri's approach until his blade pricked her spine. Hot breath hissed in her ear. "Beg all you will, Ceridwen. You cannot bargain with what you do not possess, and your life is mine."

"Not yours, my lord," Astra declared. "His."

Rhodri drew in a sharp breath. "What does that mean?"

"It means that she may yet be worth something to us alive." With a flick of her wrist, Astra pivoted her trident away from Liam's throat, which was exactly what Ceridwen had been waiting for. She lashed back with her elbow only to feel Rhodri's boot slam into the back of her knee, driving her toward the ground. She thrust out with her wounded arm to break the fall, but it gave out on impact, toppling her onto her face.

The shock of pain nearly blinded her.

Grit clung to her lips. The taste of copper filled her mouth. Rhodri's boot pressed down on her spine. She shoved down a wave of nausea as Liam cried out and lifted her chin to see the tallest shadowrider hauling the boy over his saddle.

No. Those weren't the terms. He was supposed to be safe.

Hooves crunched closer, and Astra's voice drifted down. "His fate rests entirely in your hands, Ceridwen. One word, one threat, one ill-contrived attempt to escape, and he will suffer. You may calculate the cost. What need has he of two eyes when one will do? Two ears? Ten fingers? One tongue is harder to spare, I'll grant you, but as I recall, he is quite the talker, so perhaps it would be no great loss."

Dread leached the strength from her limbs. She bowed her head.

"You see," Astra mused, "even a fireborn can be tamed."

TWENTY: RAFI

He who would hunt with tigers must paint himself with their stripes.
- Nadaarian maxim

"*Stone-eyes can sniff out weakness, Tetrani's son.*"

With Gordu's parting words throbbing in Rafi's mind, he charged Ghost in on the surf and emerged onto the gull-haunted shore where the fisher tribe of Zorrad had once plied their trade. Once, but no more. Salt crusted the overturned hulls of two boats lying neglected and weathered where more than a dozen had once sat in a row. No smoke rose from the huts scattered among the trees, no voices carried down the jungle path to the sea, and no boats skimmed across the sparkling waves.

Were it not for the cries of the gulls, it would have been eerily silent, desolate even. With a shudder, Rafi dismounted, bare feet sinking through the warm top layer of sand to the coolness beneath. When last he had stood here, violence had raged across this beach. Slaughter unleashed by the choices he had made—to rescue the colt, slay the scadtha, stay instead of run. Of life, no sign remained but the dozens of pale, almost translucent, crabs that scuttled out of their path. Of death, only the carcass of the scadtha, scoured clean by scavengers, bleached by the sun, and slowly being swallowed by the creeping sand.

"*Stone-eyes can sniff out weakness.*"

Gordu had emphasized each word with a sharp finger jab to Rafi's chest, casting a meaningful glance toward Sev as he said it. But if it were true, and if stone-eyes truly could, Rafi worried more about himself. Even though every trace of blood had been washed back out to sea, Rafi's memories could not be so easily scrubbed clean. Here, on this beach, he had watched Torva die. Here, he had become Rafi again.

Here, for all his dreams of freedom, he had set down roots.

Choosing to meet Sahak here had been a mistake. Warily, Rafi guided Ghost forward, and the colt drifted sideways, blowing sharply, as they skirted the scadtha's carcass, startling another dozen crabs into flight. He halted halfway between the sea and the break in the trees that marked the opening of the path. Movement to his left caught his eye as Sev shoved through thick brush, scoped out the beach, then headed toward him.

Sweat ran in rivulets down Sev's face and soaked the front of his tunic as he came up, breathing hard. "It's done. Aruk's in place. Any sign of him?"

"Not yet, but he always did like to make an entrance."

More than once, in the early days of Rafi and Delmar's imprisonment, Sahak had announced his coming by scraping the flat of a knife along the wall all the way down the dungeon passage to their cell. Creepy, certainly, but most definitely memorable.

So Rafi wasn't startled when the scream started.

It shivered its way through the thick of the Mah to the beach. Not a cry of terror or even of despair. Not the eerie and unmaking shriek of a sea-demon. This was a sound of raw agony, torn unwillingly from a human throat, and Rafi felt shaken as it reverberated through his core. Such sounds had been ripped from his own throat before.

"Kaya!" Sev broke into a run, and Rafi stirred too slowly to stop him. "Wait. Sev! Wait!"

Sev barreled over the uneven surface of the sand onto the jungle path where he disappeared into the encroaching foliage. "Kaya . . . Kaya!" His shouts tore across a silence that somehow seemed louder, more terrifying, than the scream itself.

"Stone-eyes can sniff out weakness," Gordu rumbled in Rafi's mind.

"I know, I know, I know," Rafi growled, tugging Ghost behind as he threw himself after Sev. Ches-Shu take Gordu for always being right. Every curve of the trail, every dip beneath his feet, every washed-out root should have been so familiar to Rafi that he could have run it in his sleep. He had run it in the dead of night often enough. But both overgrowth and undergrowth had crept back in, and his wounded thigh caused a hitch in his stride, so his feet fell in unexpected places, until the only familiarity the run offered was the nightmare kind, where everything felt just slightly off, slightly out of step.

If he'd been thinking instead of reacting, he'd have jumped on Ghost instead of dragging the colt uselessly behind him.

Still, he always had been able to outrun Sev, who ran like a boulder tumbling downhill. Rafi managed to catch up and haul Sev back before he could dive headlong into whatever trap Sahak had planted. And it was a trap. Rafi could feel it lurking, unseen, in that hushed space, like he could sense the presence of a predator looming in the murky deeps.

Sev whirled on him. "Don't try to stop me, Rafi."

"I'm not. Just slow down."

"It could be her. It could be."

"I know, Sev. I know."

"I'm going in."

Rafi gripped Sev's shoulder and sensed the trailing edges of the net draw tight around them. "We're going in together. Just . . . carefully. Carefully into the trap, eh?"

Creeping vines speckled with bright yellow flowers carpeted the ground, crawled up trees, and drooped from every roof. Several huts still looked livable—no doubt those occupied by Gordu and the others until Sev dragged them into Rafi's ship-stealing scheme—but most had broken doors and caved-in thatching. One even tilted drunkenly on a cracked stilt, but it was the gap in the scenery that drew them forward until they halted before a pile of charred rubble.

Only a faint wisp of smoke drifted from the ashes of Sev's hut.

Sev worked his jaw and swallowed. "We . . . we were to raise our first child in that hut." Speaking those words seemed to drive the loss home, and he sagged, voice sounding hoarse. "Kaya already made space for the cradle."

"We'll build another," Rafi offered. "A better one." No answer. Silence swelled between them like a suffocating shadow. He groped for something to say to lighten the dark, like Delmar had for him. "You always did complain about the drafty floorboards."

Instantly, he knew it was the wrong thing to say.

"The floorboards, Rafi? The floorboards?"

"Ches-Shu net my tongue! I'm sorry, I—"

"Have you forgotten who put those floorboards in?" Sev twisted to face him, and Rafi realized that he was trying, painfully, for a weak smile.

Oh. "I did. Fine, then *you'll* build another, and I'll watch." Something metallic caught his eye in the middle of the rubble pile, and he bent closer to inspect it but was forced back by the residual heat. This fire had blazed fiercely and recently.

Which confirmed that Sahak was already here, watching them.

Wood creaked behind them, and Rafi's already heightened senses caught the faint scuff of a leather sole. In his mind's eye, he could see how his brother would have responded—calmly raising his head, then standing with an almost languid air to reinforce the notion that he had not been caught off guard, he could never be caught off guard, because he was, of course, in control. Ever the prince, even in chains.

Rafi thought of his unprotected back and bolted upright, startling a snort from Ghost.

Sahak emerged through the open doorway of the dilapidated hut opposite, focused on the shiny silk rag he was using to wipe the blood from his hands and knives. The contrast between the smeared stains left by his fingers and the serene expression on his face left Rafi utterly transfixed. But not Sev.

"You!" Sev made the word a bludgeon.

He lunged as he had before—chin down, fists knotted. Rafi flung out his right hand and caught him, while still looking at Sahak. He didn't miss the flick of the Stone-eye's gaze toward them, or the faintly amused twist of his lips. No longer clad in the robes of a priest or the breastplate of a tsemarc, Sahak had draped his baldric of knives over a loose tunic and trousers of common Que make.

Rafi wondered if he'd stolen them from the hut.

Sev tried to yank free, but if Rafi had gained anything from wrestling with Ghost, it was a strong grip. "Carefully," he hissed. "Remember?" However alone Sahak appeared to be, it was clearly a trick. Stone-eyes didn't just sniff out weakness, they enjoyed playing with their food. That much he knew. Teeth gritted, Sev nodded abruptly, and Rafi released him.

"Where is my wife?" Sev called out. "Where is Kaya?"

Sahak raised the knife he was cleaning to inspect the edge against the light. "Where is my ship?" He flicked his wrist and spun the blade in the air. Rafi's blood ran cold as he imagined it carving through his skin. Again.

He cleared his throat to answer. "Somewhere you'll never find it."

"Somewhere at the bottom of the ocean, you mean."

"Oh? What makes you say that?"

"Oh, Rafi, Rafi, Rafi, will you never learn?" Sahak dropped his blade, caught it with his other hand, then sheathed it in his baldric with a flourish. "I control the eyes, ears, and tongues of the entire empire. Surely you didn't imagine your trouble in that little Mahque village would go unnoticed? Unreported?"

Rafi felt Sev shift uncomfortably beside him and forced a smile. "What trouble? That was a demonstration."

"Of incompetency?"

"Of the power I now wield."

Sahak lifted his focus to him. "Do you even have my steeds?"

"They're my steeds right now, and I think I've proved that I do. Whether or not they become your steeds, well, that's why we're here, isn't it?" No sooner had the question left his lips than he recognized his mistake—asking granted Sahak control over the course of the conversation, over the negotiation he had demanded.

"No." Sahak smiled thinly. "It isn't."

Without any signal that Rafi could see, the trap sprang.

Soldiers poured from every hut and stepped out from behind every tree, surrounding them. One stepped aggressively close to Ghost, and the colt tossed his head and squealed. It was not a full-throated shriek, but it did the trick, forcing back the ring of menacing spears.

Three soldiers clanked up beside Sahak, dragging a woman with a sack over her head and her wrists bound before her.

"Kaya!" Sev cried out.

Her hooded head tilted toward him, but she did not speak. Sahak seized the back of her neck and pressed his knife point to her ribs. "This is why you're here, so let's not forget what's at stake. Tell me where my steeds are. Now."

There was no hint of humanity in Sahak's eyes, only cold steel.

"You'll find one at the lightning tree," Rafi blurted out, and felt in his soul that if he had not spoken at that exact moment, Sahak would have struck. "Where you captured me." And tortured him and threatened to feed him to a tiger.

He felt certain Sahak would remember it.

"One? This is not a game, Rafi. I am not scavenging for clues."

"And I am not playing." Rafi forced his eyes from the knife in Sahak's hand. "One is all we brought. Consider it a pledge of more to come, once we negotiate the safe return of all the hostages."

Sahak considered, then twitched his head, sending a group of soldiers crashing through the thicket toward the distant lightning tree where Sev had left the stone-demon at Gordu's suggestion. Why, the elder had pointed out, should they endure the curses of these beasts alone? Why not give the Emperor's Stone-eye a taste of what he desired? Just enough to string him along and leave a trail heavy enough for Aruk to follow. After all, why trust the burden of hope to Nef alone when they could increase their odds of finding the Stone-eye's lair?

Sahak stepped forward, shoving Kaya before him. "Power is an interesting thing, Rafi. With your sea-demon, you can do truly unimaginable things, and yet, with a single blade, I can undo you." His calculating gaze slid to Sev, and Sahak showed his teeth. "You will tell me where the steeds are right now, or I will slit this woman's throat."

He did not start a countdown. He did not need to.

"Smuggler's cove!" Sev shouted, shoving past Rafi. "I don't know exactly where, but I can find it. Up the coast. Two, maybe three days' walk."

Rafi's pulse spiked, but he kept his expression calm.

"I can take you. Please."

Sahak released the pressure on his blade, but then abruptly tightened his grip. "He's lying, isn't he? Or, no, he doesn't think he is." Sahak was practically crowing in delight. "He doesn't know, does he?"

"Doesn't know?" Sev repeated. "Doesn't know what?"

Rafi kept his gaze fixed on Sahak. "Neither of us does."

He could sense Sev gaping at him, utterly taken aback.

"Clever," Sahak said flatly. "Were it not for one minor thing: if that truly is the case, then I have no reason to keep you alive."

"Keep me? And here I thought I'd been surviving in spite of your best attempts to kill me." Rafi waved his bandaged hand. "Oh, but before you do—kill me, that is—you should know that if we don't leave here alive, the steeds will be delivered to the Que Revolution at once."

"Seriously?" Sev burst out. "The revolution?"

"That's right." Rafi spoke feverishly fast, thinking faster, wracking his brain for the right words, the right lies, to stall for time. Sweat beaded on his neck, and he became aware of a single droplet trickling down his spine, which seemed, in that moment, an unbearable distraction. "So if you want my steeds to become your steeds instead of the rebels' steeds, I can give you . . . three weeks . . . to return all the villagers safely to their homes, which should give you time to have them rebuilt, and *then*, you will get a location for the steeds." Flushed with elation at the rush of words, Rafi threw in a crooked grin. "The choice is yours."

Sahak tilted his head. "On that we agree."

Then he slashed the knife.

"No!" Rafi reached out helplessly, too far away to do anything but watch metal flash and satisfaction burn in Sahak's eyes as Kaya shuddered, then crumpled without a sound.

She fell like a thing without bones.

Gone before she struck the ground.

Rafi stood rooted. Sight came sluggishly, and understanding in patches. A blur of movement, and roaring broke through, a wordless, animal cry that resolved with a jolt into Sev's voice. Through his haze, he saw Sev collapse over Kaya's limp form, as soldiers poured from the jungle, scattered by the sudden onrush of the massive demon-steed they were leading. Their movements slowed to a crawl until they were like insects trapped in resin: the steed, veins bulging, jaws agape, throwing its head high; the handler, hauled off his feet by his grip on the lead, helmet flying from his head, shock on his face; one soldier tumbling head over heels, spear falling from his splayed hands; another flung backward from a kick in the stomach, body folded in half from the force of the impact.

And Rafi knew that he had felt this way before—caught in an eddy of time, dragged down, tossed out, plunged back again—when Delmar fell.

Not now, he thought desperately to the ghost. *Help me!*

But the ghost did not answer.

Pain in his foot jolted him out of his shock. Ghost, fixated on the other steed, had planted one hoof on his toes. Simultaneously blessing and cursing the colt, Rafi shouldered him aside and looked to Sahak. Sahak fiddled with the knife in his hands, flipping it between his fingers until the crimson that stained the blade also stained his skin. He ignored the chaotic rush to bring the stone-demon under control, an effort requiring dozens of ropes held by twice that many soldiers, and listened while a priest in vivid robes murmured in his ear, too low for Rafi to hear.

Sahak's eyes gleamed with an intensity that boded ill, but he casually sheathed his blade as he turned to Rafi. "You have your three weeks. Bring the steeds then, or don't. It's your choice whether or not I carve out the eyes, ears, and tongues of every villager from Zorrad. Starting, of course, with everyone you knew best. Oh, and that reminds me . . ." He flicked a lazy hand, and soldiers appeared at the door of the hut behind him, hauling a limp, bloody figure they tossed out onto the grass.

Wiry limbs, beaded belt, spiked black hair. Nef.

Sahak toed him over onto his back, ensuring Rafi could see the shock of bruises, the waxy skin, the raw wound where his left eye had been. "Speaking of eyes, he was using his to spy. Consider this a 'pledge of worse to come' to all the villagers should you set anyone else to follow me." He ground his foot down on Nef's ribs, drawing a coughing groan from the rebel's bloody lips. "I do believe he's still alive. How surprising." Waving his soldiers on ahead, he said over his shoulder, "Let it not be said that I am not merciful, Rafi. Hurry and you might be able to save him."

TWENTY-ONE: CERIDWEN & JAKIM

The firestorm is one of the most deadly tactics a firerider can wield.
As the fireborn spins on its haunches, the rider summons flame,
transforming steed and rider into an impenetrable, spinning ring of death.
- Wisdom of the Horsemasters

Ceridwen hit the earth hard where Rhodri's warriors dropped her and rolled onto her back. Chains snapped cold onto her wrists, jostling her wounded arm, sending a wave of agony through her. She shifted and retched into the grass, so disoriented, she could barely distinguish the taunts of the jeering voices surrounding her.

Oh, *flames*, what had she done?

Astra had paraded her before her forces before she was dragged away, and she had sensed their dismay and their anger. She had abandoned them, and the kingdom, for the sake of a single warrior. She doubted they had even needed Astra's threats to dissuade them from a rescue, and she could not blame them, for she had failed as their queen.

But it had been Liam. *Liam.* She could not have watched him die.

He landed nearby, letting out a deep moan, and she could feel the encroaching darkness towing her down, but his suffering demanded she muster her strength. So she clamped down onto her throbbing forearm and squeezed. It blazed like a live coal under her grip, and she grounded herself in that pain, using it to keep herself present, and the long seeping cold at bay.

She dragged her head up, catching the pale glint of stars through the branches overhead, and located the dark shape of the trunk where her shackles were anchored. Beyond, a limp form huddled just out of reach. She crawled toward him. "Liam?"

"My lady?" His voice was weak. "You're alive?"

Straining against her chains, she could just reach his shoulder. He tried to sit up, only to fall back with a whispered curse.

"Easy. Take it slow," she cautioned.

"It's just . . . it's just my leg."

"I'll help. On three then." Clutching his arm, she pulled as he shoved himself up again, and together they fell back against the tree.

He gasped raggedly. "Oh, *floods*, floods, I think it's broken."

Ceridwen tipped her head back, trying to stop the world from swaying. Her voice sounded oddly distant. "It needs a splint and—"

But he didn't seem to hear. "Iona . . . she fell, didn't she?"

Oh, *shades*. An ember lodged in her throat, hot and pulsing.

She couldn't speak, could only nod.

"You shouldn't have come for me. Either of you." His shoulder trembled against hers. "You should have just let me die."

"You know your aunt could never have done that. Neither could I."

He fell silent then, and Ceridwen sank back, closing her eyes. Sticky warmth crept down her arm, pooling in the fingers of her glove. She clamped the wound and held as tight as she could, though the renewed flare of pain almost made her sick. *Shades*, she was lightheaded. Shivering too. Shock or fever, she wasn't sure which.

Not that it mattered since she would soon be dead anyway.

Not dead yet, she could almost hear Finnian say, could almost see the faintly exasperated expression on his face as he shoved his hair back from his forehead.

"Finnian." Her eyes jolted open. "He was with you."

Why hadn't she thought to ask about him before?

"We were ambushed, while we were out on Rhodri's trail." His voice was thin. "Ondri's sons found us. Scattered us like so many leaves. I lost sight of him then, but we didn't stand a chance. They took me alive but ran the others down . . ." He trailed off.

But she already knew the rest. "So Finnian is dead then," she said and felt something fracture within her, felt the cracks spreading far, widening into fissures.

"Maybe. I didn't see. He might be alive."

Since when had the warrior spirits ever chosen to be so kind?

Liam swallowed, and his voice hitched in pain. "Do you think they will kill us now?"

Out in the night, dozens of fires had sprung up, surrounded by the massed shadows of warriors and their steeds. Voices rose over the low hum of untacking and of tending to wounds and weapons. It might have been her own forces making camp, were it not for the sight of the hulking stone-eye chariot planted in their midst and Rhodri dismounting to sit at the closest fire, handing both her steed and his off to an attendant.

No, the warrior spirits had never been kind, and they had even less reason to be so now. For they were said to favor only the bravest, truest, and fiercest warriors, and what was she but a dishonored daughter so tainted by the lies of her father that her own war-chief betrayed her?

What was she but a faithless queen unworthy of her people's trust?

When death came for her, she could only hope it would be swift.

"No." She moistened cracked lips. "Not yet."

Rhodri was furious. Jakim could sense his rage building, could see it in the muscle twitching in his jaw, even in the way he braced himself as he sat, shirtless before the fire, while Ineth tended his wounds. Ceridwen may have suffered the brunt of the fight that Jakim had watched unfold earlier, but she had not left Rhodri unbloodied.

His blood stained the cloth Ineth dabbed against his wounds, then plunged into the bowl of warmed water in Jakim's hands. Her forehead furrowed in concern as she wrung it out.

One particularly long gash across his ribs sliced down to the bone, and Jakim winced as Ineth peeled away a sliver of cloth stuck to the raw flesh, though Rhodri did not even flinch. He only stared relentlessly into the night, alternately clenching and flexing his fists, heedless of the raucous shouts of laughter from Ondri's sons, who clustered around him, feasting and boasting and clanking drinks to toast their victory.

But the heat of his gaze was not aimed toward Ceridwen, chained at the base of a tree, but across the camp to where Astra stood conferring with Nahrog, the priest.

Still in full armor, she shone in the firelight like a fallen star.

Ineth coughed pointedly, alerting Jakim to the fact that, in his distraction, he had raised the bowl out of her reach. He swung it back down in time to catch the wadded up cloth. Shaking her head, she threaded her needle with catgut and skillfully drew the gash closed.

Rhodri clenched the gloves he held until the leather creaked.

Ineth raised an eyebrow but did not pause her work. "Breathe, my lord."

But it was not the pain he reacted to, Jakim thought, as Astra strolled over to the fire and the sons of Ondri, arms slung over shoulders, ale sloshing from overfilled drinking horns, parted before her. The tallest brother, sporting a bandage on his thigh, refilled his horn and shoved it toward her as she passed, calling for her to join their revels. She calmly took it, raised it to shouts of approval, and drained it in a single gulp, then dropped it back into his hands.

Rhodri stood so swiftly, he upset Ineth's supplies. Several bandage rolls tumbled around Jakim's feet, and he bent to pick them up, passing them to Ineth, who stuffed them back into her satchel. He paused with his fingers on the final two rolls, darting a glance toward the tree where Ceridwen and the other captive were bound.

Before he could think twice, he slipped the bandages into his pockets and straightened, overly conscious of the theft, though no one so much as looked at him.

"Leave us," Rhodri commanded, eyes on Astra.

His voice startled the sons of Ondri from their revelry, and Arlen, who hadn't touched a drop from his horn, stood and jerked his head to the side, summoning his brothers to follow. Ineth simply crossed her arms and adjusted her stance, which seemed a dare to dismiss her, so Jakim stayed too.

Astra watched the brothers stagger away, smiling faintly. "One might consider the wisdom of being so harsh with one's allies, my love."

"One might consider that you seem to have a great many opinions on what I should or should not do . . . my love."

"Of course I do. We are one in heart, are we not?"

"But not in mind, it would seem," Rhodri replied, voice languid but sharp. "I held Ceridwen's life in my hand today, tasted sweet victory on my tongue, and you forestalled me. I would know why."

"It was the wise choice. You must trust me."

"I have trusted. I have waited and bided my time, while you have plotted and schemed and forged alliances behind my back. No longer, Astra. You will tell me what you are doing, or *sky's blood*, though you beg until your final breath, I swear you will never be queen."

"So." Astra drew out the word. "We resort to threats now, do we?"

"Threats?" Rhodri's brow furrowed, seeming conflicted. "No, not threats. Merely the truth. I will not bind myself to one I cannot trust."

"You mean as you bound yourself to the emperor? To his tsemarc?" Scorn flooded her voice. "And where has that left you? Chased out of your own fortress lest you become even more of a pawn? But there are other powers in the empire, powers with a reach you cannot even begin to imagine, and I bound myself to them so we would not find ourselves stranded afoot when your venture failed."

"Who, Astra? You spoke of a *he*. The priest, Nahrog?"

"Nahrog? He is only a spokesman. He brokered the deal."

Shoulders tense, Rhodri lowered himself back to the ground, which Ineth seemed to take as a sign she could complete her work. Muttering to herself, she cleaned the gash again and resumed her stitching, while Jakim helpfully dug out supplies from her satchel, using that as a cover to sneak a few of the leaves she'd been using to make a paste to ward off infection. Only after Ineth knotted a bandage over the wound did Rhodri speak again.

"The terms of this deal, Astra?"

"Come, my love, you should not need me to tell you."

"You would turn over a dawnling, the rarest of our steeds, to the empire."

She sighed and sat beside him. "Not just a dawnling. Solborn."

"So those words you spoke about thinking of my father, that was just to draw me in because you knew I could not resist." Rhodri leaned forward suddenly, voice low and intense. "Did you never stop to consider that solborn are the only strength we have to make them fear us? To force them to treat with us instead of seeking our outright annihilation?"

"Our bargain was for steeds not riders. They will still need our expertise. Only a Soldonian can share the sol-breath. In any case, it's done. One shipload sealed the deal."

Rhodri sat back. "In exchange for what? What did you demand in return?"

"More than you. Our pact recognizes your claim to the throne. Once he achieves power, you will not rule as a vassal or a subjugated lord of a conquered kingdom, but as a trusted ally."

"So that's it then? The deal is complete?"

"Not quite," rumbled a gravelly voice behind Jakim.

He nearly dropped the satchel he had been holding for Ineth as Nahrog emerged from the darkness. Though wearing chains that stretched from neck to wrists, somehow, the burly man had managed to come upon them as silently as a tiger stalking his prey. He had spoken in Soldonian, responding to words he should not have been able to understand, and this sudden revelation of fluency did not seem lost on Rhodri, who answered him in the same tongue.

"What more do you want, priest?" Rhodri spat.

"He does not want more, dearest. Only what was promised. But first, some privacy?" This, with a sidelong glance toward Jakim and Ineth, who stiffened and looked to Rhodri for his nod before seizing her satchel and stalking off without waiting for Jakim to follow.

Why should she? He had made no attempt to escape since she freed his hands, earning a begrudging sort of sufferance from her that seemed as close to trust as he would get. He doubted it would stretch so far as to overlook what he planned to do next.

So as soon as he was away from the fire, he checked to be sure his path was clear, then abruptly dodged around a cluster of hobbled steeds and moved furtively toward the captives instead. Ceridwen rested against the tree with her eyes shut, gripping her wounded forearm, while the boy slumped against her shoulder. Unconscious, both of them. Or maybe only asleep.

No warriors stood guard—or at least none Jakim could see as he gingerly crouched over Ceridwen and pulled out a roll of bandages.

"You do a lot of stealing for a Scroll," Ineth said behind him.

Jakim jolted, heart leaping in his chest. He fumbled the roll, and it spun from his fingers over to Ineth, who stopped it with a tap of her boot. She crossed her arms over her chest, watching him. She hadn't drawn her sword. That had to be a good sign, right?

So, sheepishly, he pulled out the second roll too. "I just . . . want to help."

Her frown deepened, then she motioned him on. Taking a deep breath, he reached cautiously for Ceridwen's arm. Her eyes shot open, and he jerked back, only to be snared by her viselike grip on his tunic. She dragged him closer, breathing raggedly.

"It's me," he murmured. "Jakim Ha'Nor."

"The . . . Scroll?" Her voice sounded weak.

"I came to bandage your wound."

She searched his face with haunted eyes, then eased her grip from his tunic. Holding up the bandage, he reached for her arm again, but she shook her head. "No," she rasped. "Liam first."

Jakim eyed the sheen of fever sweat on her brow, but, sighing, did as she asked, turning to the boy, who was watching him blearily.

"It's my leg," he said, teeth chattering. "It's broken, you see."

"I . . . I see." Swallowing, Jakim eyed the bandage roll, dug out the handful of stolen leaves, then hesitated. Aodh have mercy. He had no idea what to do.

"Something the matter there, Scroll?" Ineth asked dryly.

"I, um, don't actually know what I'm doing."

"You didn't train in healing in that Sanctuary of yours?"

"Didn't train in much at all, actually. I had just sworn my vows."

She sniffed. Something snapped close to his ear, and he looked up. Ineth considered the branch she had broken over her knee, then dropped one half beside the boy and discarded the other. She slid the knife from her belt and casually tossed it to Jakim, then scanned the ground for more branches.

"What's this for?" Jakim held the knife up as if it were a snake.

"We need to see the leg before we can set it."

Oh. That made sense. Working carefully, Jakim sliced open the trouser leg, exposing the swollen, twisted limb beneath, then moved out of Ineth's way. She motioned for him to crouch behind the boy's head. "Hold his shoulders down."

Setting the knife aside, Jakim gripped the boy's arms.

"Shoulders," Ineth snapped, and Jakim adjusted his hold, noting the way the boy's fingers dug into the ground at Ineth's prodding and the tears that sprang from his eyes as he fought to hold back a groan.

"Steady, Liam," Ceridwen said. "Steady."

She gingerly leaned across the boy's chest, adding her weight to help hold him down. Jakim didn't watch, but the ragged cry that burst from Liam told him when Ineth set the leg. When he finally looked up, she had splinted it with branches and bandages and was reaching to tie off the final knot, exposing her forearm, which was covered in intricate lines of blue script. Hundreds of them. They were faded, warped, and twisted by scars, but the shapes of the truths of Aodh had been burned into Jakim's mind even before they were inked onto his own forearms.

He would know them anywhere. He had been right. She was a Scroll.

Before he could speak, Ineth yanked her sleeve down, then stiffly stood. She stepped carefully over the boy, who was practically unconscious, and knelt beside Ceridwen. "Where's that knife, Scroll?" Abruptly, she tensed, steel flashing next to her throat.

"You mean this one?" Ceridwen demanded. She clenched the knife in a bloodied grip, supporting herself on an arm that trembled with the strain, but the blade never wavered.

"What are you doing?" Jakim exclaimed. "She's trying to help you."

"She will. She will help us escape, and so will you, whether you will it or not." She flicked her gaze to him briefly, and the suspicion in her eyes made him suddenly wary of that blade, which could just as easily turn on him. "Why are you here, Jakim? I thought you were going back to your brothers. Have you betrayed me, too, like Glyndwr? Have you been Rhodri's this whole time?"

What? "No. No, Ceridwen, I swear it."

He couldn't tell whether or not she believed him.

Ineth closed then opened her eyes. "I wondered whether you had any spark left in you, Fireborn, or whether the daughter of Cenyon had beaten it all—" She inhaled sharply as the blade pricked her skin.

Ceridwen's gaze remained on Jakim. "Can he ride?"

The boy still wasn't moving. "I don't know. Can you?"

"Of course. Always."

Ineth snorted at that. "You are half dead, even now, and in chains. And when you are caught, you know what will happen. Tor Telweg does not make idle threats."

"No," a deep, weary voice said. "She does not."

Rhodri stalked out of the night like a specter haunting a battlefield. Shoulders bare, wounds bandaged, a hollow cast to his eyes—he looked as vulnerable as he had that first night in Rysinger after his father's death, when Ceridwen had found him alone on the manor roof, crying to the stars. Of course, he'd been lying then, flames take him.

Just the sound of his voice now sent a spike through Ceridwen's chest, demolishing the facade of strength she'd been rebuilding. Her distraction cost her the knife as the woman seized her injured arm and wrenched the knife away. But rather than attacking, the woman used it to slice open the lacings binding both vambrace and sleeve so she could tend the wound. None too gently, she peeled back flesh, washed out the gash with a splash of burning liquid, then picked out the debris by the light of a torch she sent Jakim to fetch. Ceridwen still felt ashamed.

"No need to expend too much effort, Ineth," Rhodri said, shoving his fists into his trouser pockets, shoulders tense. "She needn't keep the arm. She need only stay alive to reach her destination."

Ineth just grunted and kept working, Jakim helping at her side.

Ceridwen tried to moisten her throat. "And where is that?"

"Where do you think? You are wanted in Nadaar. It seems the empire has plans for the wild Fireborn queen."

More disgust than triumph tinged his voice, but her blood still ran cold. She could think of only one reason for the empire to desire her: so her death could be a public spectacle.

She had known such might be her fate, and still . . .

"What of Liam? I traded my life for his. You should honor our bargain."

"As you honored the Sol-Fiere?" His mouth twisted into a snarl. "Tell me, Ceridwen, was it always your plan to murder my father? Or was that merely a desperate attempt to change the field once you knew you were losing?"

She shoved forward until the chains snapped tight. "How long did you have Glyndwr by the reins? Was he in league with you and the Nadaari all along?"

"He murdered my father. You think I agreed to that?"

"You killed one father. Why should you hesitate to kill another?"

Rhodri slammed his hands against the trunk and bent so close she could smell the ale on his breath as he hissed, "Oengus is the only father I claim."

Hope then. Just a spark. "So what, then? It was only a lie? To rattle me?"

He laughed, but there was no mirth in it. "You would like to think that, wouldn't you? But I needn't lie to rattle you, Ceridwen. You're going to Nadaar, and you will die there, and if you want to keep young Liam from facing his fate alongside you, you will not resist the blade that comes for your throat." He roughly seized the circlet from her head and raised his voice to Ineth. "See that the boy is bound elsewhere. Somewhere she can see him but not speak to him."

Then dropped his voice again. "Only a fool releases the catch-rope with a wildborn restrained. You, of all people, should know that, sister."

TWENTY-TWO: RAFI

Cael beams, and the mountains are warmed by her light.
She weeps and floods all the earth with her tears.
- Hanonque teaching

Sahak was gone. Gone, and Ches-Shu grant that he never return. But he had once again left the world hemorrhaging blood, and it was Rafi's task to bind up the wounds.

Sev slumped over Kaya, brow pressed to her hooded head.

Nef moaned on the ground and coughed weakly, spitting up blood.

Somebody would have to clean his wounds to forestall infection, and somebody would have to help lay Kaya to rest, and—Aruk. Sahak's parting threats drove Rafi's attention toward the splintered trail created by the stone-demon's rampage from the lightning tree where Aruk had been stationed, waiting in concealment to follow Sahak.

Somebody would have to warn him off too.

Rafi dropped Ghost's lead and crouched beside Sev. "Sev, I'm sorry but I need you. One of us has to help Nef while the other goes after Aruk and—"

"No need. I'm here." Aruk stumbled into the village as if he were being chased. "I trailed the soldiers from the lightning tree, but they came back here, and I overheard what he said, there at the end. I just couldn't risk following them, Rafi. Not with so much at stake."

"You made the right choice," Rafi said, though he couldn't escape the nagging sense that Aruk was right about the stakes but not the risk. Now that Nef would not be returning with a location and a rescue plan, they were doomed already, unless he could change their tides again.

But first, he must staunch the wounds before him.

He found the silk rag Sahak had used to clean his knife and decided it would have to do for a bandage. He folded it into padding to cover Nef's socket and suppressed a spike of alarm when the rebel didn't even stir. There was the sound of tearing cloth, and Aruk crouched, holding out a ruffled sleeve he'd torn from his shirt.

Rafi accepted it with a nod of thanks and used it to secure the padding. "Watch him, will you? Call me if he wakes. I need to help Sev with Kaya."

"It's not her." Sev sounded dazed. "It's not Kaya."

Standing required a strength Rafi didn't think he had left, but he made his way over to Sev, who sank back on his heels, tears falling down his cheeks.

"Oh, Ches-Shu, Rafi, it's not her."

"Sev," Rafi started kindly, then broke off, finally glimpsing the face Sev had uncovered, staring lifelessly up amongst the flowering vines. Not Kaya, but Yeena, her younger sister. He blinked, struggling to reconcile what he saw with the words Sahak had spoken while he'd been his captive, leading him to believe that Yeena had already died.

Now she had, and it felt like he'd failed her twice over.

Wordlessly, Rafi gathered Yeena up into his arms, carried her out to sea on Ghost, and gently entrusted her to Ches-Shu's never-ending embrace. Not for the first time, Rafi wondered what might have happened if he had run the opposite direction down the beach on that stormy, portentous night months ago. If he'd left the colt to its fate, ignored the scadtha, and embraced the place Torva had offered him as his son.

A hut, a boat, a life of his own.

Somehow those dreams felt weak and fading now, something that had belonged to the person he had been and not to the person he was learning to be. Now, he couldn't help wondering what might have happened if he'd stopped running sooner.

Watching as the rock anchor bore her down into the depths, Rafi whispered an Alonque farewell for her, and for Nahiki, then charged Ghost back over the waves and onto the shore.

Sev sat staring out over the sea and did not stir when Rafi dismounted, but Aruk looked up from the stretcher he was building using scavenged odds and ends. "What now?"

Rafi rubbed the back of his neck. "We have our three weeks. Dearly bought." He didn't add his suspicion that something else, something aside from Yeena's death and Nef's wounds, had bought them that time. Sahak had made up his mind only after his whispered conversation with that priest. Which meant he was undoubtedly up to something.

He studied the odd contraption Aruk was working on. It consisted of two poles, lashed together only at the front, forming a sort of wedge shape with the sling bound perpendicularly across them close to the open end, which struck Rafi as wildly unbalanced, not to mention cumbersome.

"How do we carry this?" he asked. "One at the front? Two at the back?"

"It's a drag-sled. Only needs one."

"Who's the unlucky hauler?"

"Not you, don't worry. We've got something bigger."

Rafi followed his glance to the colt in the shallows. "Ah, lucky us."

"Right. Lucky." Straightening, Aruk dusted off his hands and the knees of his shredded trousers, then adjusted the ruffle of his sole remaining sleeve. "So where do we go now?"

Rafi took a breath. "There was only ever one place we could go after all of this, Aruk. Only ever one place that could offer us help and hope." He looked at Sev, who still sat with his back toward them. "It's time I introduce you both to the Que Revolution."

TWENTY-THREE: JAKIM

*The weeping of the stars is not hidden from Aodh
and neither are the tears of men.*
- *Scroll Nineteen of the Holy Writ, Kerrikar Sanctuary*

"Is he truly sending them to Nadaar to be executed?"

Ineth stilled at his voice, then resumed her scrubbing, working at the blood staining the creases of her wrinkled hands and around the beds of her nails. But the pinch in her lips as she reached for the waterskin next to her boot was answer enough. He bent to get it for her. That pinch tightened in annoyance, but she held out her hands, chapped and rough with callouses, and he tugged the stopper free, then poured a stream into her cupped palms.

They stood by her earthhewn on the opposite end of the camp from the tree where Ceridwen was chained, but it would be long before he could forget the despair in her eyes when Rhodri had ordered Liam taken away. It drove him to speak again.

"Why did you do it?" he asked Ineth. "You helped me heal them. You set his leg, stitched up her wound. Why bother when they are just going to be shipped off to be killed?"

"You heard my lord Rhodri. She must reach Nadaar alive."

"To be killed," Jakim repeated, trying to catch her eye.

"This is war, young Scroll. Such things happen." Ineth shook out her hands to dry them, then took the waterskin from him and stoppered it. "You think your Fireborn would hesitate to do the same? You saw how eagerly she set a knife to my—"

"Ineth, a word."

Rhodri stood a short distance away, a dark shape on the edge of the firelight. Ineth straightened at his summons, brushing a wisp of hair from her face with the back of her hand, then slung her satchel against Jakim's chest where he caught it, awkwardly.

"Put back what you stole," she said, then strode to join the war-chief.

The low murmur of their voices reached Jakim, but he couldn't make out a word. Chest burning with frustration over his own helplessness, he dug out the unused bandages and the crushed flakes of leaves from his pocket and returned both to her satchel. He half expected to find his fingers leaving bloody prints on the rolled cloth. Ineth had done all the actual tending of wounds, but somehow, he still felt like his hands had been stained tonight.

Somewhere out there, somewhere close, was a ship that would soon sail to Nadaar, only it would not be delivering him to his brothers but Ceridwen to her death. He wanted so desperately to do something, but what? Even if he could free her and Liam from their chains, the boy couldn't walk, and she was weak from blood loss. They wouldn't get far, even with what little aid he could offer. But Ineth had Rhodri's trust. If he could just get through to her, convince her to help. She was a Scroll of Aodh, after all.

Ineth strode past and at once began tacking up her steed. "Come. We head out tonight."

"Tonight?" Jakim flipped the satchel shut. "Going where?"

"Wherever my lord Rhodri says." Her tone was curt as she snapped buckles into place and yanked down on straps. That wasn't so unusual for her, though from what Jakim had seen, she rarely took it out on her steed. Surveying the camp revealed that only a portion was stirring, small clusters here and there tacking up and gathering on the outskirts. Though the priest, Nahrog, and the sons of Ondri were among them, Astra tor Telweg was not, and neither were the two captives.

If he was going to say anything to help them, it must be now.

But Aodh have mercy, he hated confrontation.

He offered the satchel to Ineth, though she barely glanced at him as she slung it over her saddlebow. "You are a very skilled healer," he began. "Was that your chosen course of study at your Sanctuary?"

She ignored him, snatching up her reins to lead her steed away.

He needed something more. Something she could not deny.

"I saw the marking on your arms," he called after her. "The truths of Aodh. Your scrawl begins with the words, 'Aodh is compassionate.' It is one of my favorite truths." She stilled then, and Jakim felt a thrill of hope. He must be getting through to her. "You are a Scroll of Aodh, like me."

"I am not a Scroll. Not anymore."

She spoke so quietly, Jakim almost missed her words.

Even then, he couldn't make sense of them. "But you can't simply stop being a Scroll." Their vows were as indelible as the ink that marked their skin. A Scroll might fail to honor those vows or refuse to follow Aodh's hand, but that did not change who they were simply by virtue of the fact that they bore the holy writ etched upon them. Of course, knowing that hadn't prevented him from feeling unworthy of being a Scroll after the lies he had told. "It does not matter what you have done," he began, but she cut him off.

"Just because we share a few scars, you think we are the same? You think you know me?"

Jakim nodded resolutely. "Yes, I think I do. I saw the care you took with Ceridwen's wound, even after she threatened you. You were compassionate and merciful to one who is your enemy, as Aodh is. What I don't understand is how you can stand by now and—"

"Enough," she snapped, startling her steed with the anger in her voice. "You forget your place, Scroll. I am a warrior of Ardon, sworn to te Oengus's horn, and you are but a captive here. Speak again, and I will have you silenced."

It seemed an errant wind had seized control of his tongue, for Jakim, who had survived for seven years by knowing when not to speak, opened his mouth again. Which was how he wound up with a gag thrust between his teeth, slung over the saddle of a riderless steed, wrists and ankles bound to a rope under its ribcage, towed by Ineth into the night.

TWENTY-FOUR: CERIDWEN

Born of flame and searing embers, a fireborn's greatest weakness is water.
- Wisdom of the Horsemasters

They took Liam from her, hauling him away as if he were only a sack of bones for the pyre. Ceridwen managed only to catch and squeeze his hand before he was gone. They took her cuirass and chain mail too, leaving her shivering in her stained and battered leathers. Alone, she sank into fevered dreams where she wandered scorched battlefields and every corpse bore a face she knew and loved, every wound had been dealt by her own hand, and every step brought the touch of death closer to her own neck. She startled awake under the wan light of a crescent moon to the clink of tack and clank of weapons.

Somewhere deep inside her, the spark of hope flared again. Her warriors had come. With Finnian at their head.

She watched as Rhodri mounted up and thundered away with half his host. She waited, pulse thudding, for the consequences Astra had threatened. She forced herself to stay awake, eyes burning from lack of sleep, until the long hours of the dark were spent and the sun dawned rust-red in the sky, and she could not deny the truth: Rhodri had left, Finnian was gone, and her riders had not come. Her fate now rested solely in Astra's hands.

She saw Liam only from a distance over the next two days, until they were shoved together into a longboat on the shore of a sandy bay. She was seated in the stern, he in the bow, and when the longboat lurched out onto the surf toward the ship that would carry them to Nadaar, he craned his head back to toss her a wink and a cheeky grin. Seeing color in his face again caused some of the pinch in her chest to ease. But then they were hustled below into the hold where water splashed up beneath her boots and the air reeked of the sickly sweet stench of horse urine. Where she was forced to her knees and chained to an iron ring in one empty stall, while Liam, moaning in pain, was thrown into the one opposite. Where she smelled the sudden tang of damp smoke flooding the hold and spied her fireborn, muzzled tightly, his eyes dull and utterly devoid of spark. Where she could feel every sickening shift and sway of the vessel that would deliver them to their doom, and she wondered if they would even live that long when the filthy wash that kept Mindar's flame at bay also threatened soured wounds and agonizing, rotted flesh. And finally, every ounce of resolve seemed to drain from her blood.

It turned out that when Ceridwen tal Desmond gave herself up to death, it was not with shouted fury or blazing defiance, but with anguished silence.

TWENTY-FIVE: JAKIM

Aodh's hand holds all things.
- The truths of Aodh

"So they spat you out, too, slave, did they?"

No. Not him. Jakim closed his eyes with a groan at the engineer's familiar haughty tone, with its faintly nasal edge and drawling undercurrent of superiority. He couldn't feel his toes. Or his fingers. Only the pain in his ribs and the thudding pressure in his skull that no doubt came from being slung over the back of a steed like a sack for an entire day's journey.

He had tumbled limply to the ground as soon as Ineth cut the rope binding him to the steed, and he lay there still, waiting for the blood to return to his limbs so he could try to work the gag from between his teeth. Of course, that would have been considerably easier if she had bothered to cut the cords on his wrists and ankles too. To add insult to injury, she had dumped him next to the engineer, who seemed surprisingly less the worse for wear than he was.

"Can't say I'm surprised," Khilamook added. "You do have a knack for the irritating."

Wood clattered at Jakim's feet, slightly too close for comfort. He pried his head off the ground to see Ineth crouching over the pile of deadwood she had clearly just dropped. Using a hatchet, she scraped out a shallow trench, then began building a fire, while beyond, Rhodri's warriors rapidly set up camp, trying to utilize every last drop of light before the sun was fully eaten by the hills off to their left. Flint and steel rang out, and sparks ignited the kindling into a crackling flame. Wincing, Jakim managed to sit up.

"Still," Khilamook continued musingly, "I am glad to have you here, slave."

Over the dancing flames, Jakim saw Ondri's sons tear up on their steeds and dismount before approaching in a rowdy knot, scuffling with elbows digging into ribs, until a growl from Cormag, the eldest, separated them.

The engineer let out a peeved sniff. "Not talking to me now, are you? I find it very tiresome. Is it because I called you a slave? Fine then, Jakim. Satisfied?"

Hardly. But in the interest of convincing him that further conversation was pointless, Jakim turned, finally, to face the engineer and gestured with his bound hands at his gag.

Ineth chose that moment to step up to him, and Jakim looked up, hoping she might have gotten over her anger with him for confronting her about being a Scroll. But she slashed the rest of his bonds without so much as looking him in the eye, then left him to untie his own gag. Definitely still mad. It took an infuriatingly long time to work the knot loose before he managed to slip the gag from between his teeth and stretch out his sore jaw.

"Oh, you were gagged. You might have said so." Khilamook turned dismissively as Ondri's sons stomped noisily up around the fire, where they dug out dried meat rations from their belt pouches and dug in.

So far as food went, it looked about as appetizing as old leather. That didn't stop Jakim's stomach from growling or the engineer from fixating hungrily on the food.

"That your steed, Madden?" Arlen asked, nodding toward a shadower that was drifting away from the others, trailing a loose rein. He alone had remained standing with his bow held low before him in both hands, as if he were on watch.

The youngest brother looked up, a strip of dried meat clenched in his teeth, and his pale eyebrows shot up. He promptly tripped over his own enormous boots as he bolted after the steed and nearly collided with Nahrog, who was striding toward the fire in his vibrant silky robes.

Nahrog glowered after the boy, and at the bald brother who

stood and lumbered more slowly after him, then turned to find Ineth barring his path.

"He may share my fire, Ineth," Rhodri told her as he approached. He loomed over the shorter man, one hand pressing down on the hilt of his sabre. "We have an understanding, priest, do we not?"

Nahrog stared long at him, then rumbled his assent. "We do."

"You may have an understanding with the priest," Cormag said bluntly, as Nahrog took the spot Madden had vacated by the fire. "But our understanding was with tor Telweg. Why are we here when she is not?"

Rhodri stepped up to the fire's edge. "Your understanding was with me, through my betrothed. She is occupied, overseeing the muster of our forces in coordination with Lord Ormond, while you are here because we are going to hunt a dawnling."

Again, that word thrummed through Jakim, and he couldn't help leaning closer. Khilamook, too, sat up straighter, listening intently, eyes agleam with interest. But it was the taut expression on Ineth's face that truly caught Jakim's attention.

Rhodri held out a bundle wrapped in embroidered silk and reverently undid the cloth, then raised a star-shaped object, roughly the size of his palm, dangling on the end of a chain. Jakim thought it was polished stone at first. Then metal. Then something else entirely, for though it was black, it was pitted like honeycomb with gold and amber-colored crystal that flashed in the dying sunlight as it twisted and spun below his grip.

"You gave this to Astra," he said. "Do you know what it is?"

Ondri's sons exchanged glances, then Cormag grunted and answered, "It's a relic taken from a dawnling, te Oengus, or so we were told."

"You were told true, though it's the first I've seen outside of ancient drawings or descriptions in old tales passed down through the ages. Where did you get it?"

"Off a Canthorian poacher, where else?" snorted the tallest of the brothers, scratching at the bandage on his thigh.

Arlen took up the tale. "We caught him crossing into Ardon several years ago. He had sacks of fresh trophies taken from multiple steeds, so when he claimed to have used the relic to locate a dawnling herd deep in the wilds of Gimleal, my father believed him."

"Locate how?" Ineth demanded.

"He said it reacts somehow when dawnlings are near."

"Meaning what?"

Arlen's tone stiffened to match hers. "If I knew, I would tell you."

But Ineth did not draw back. "So, we're supposed to wander through the wilds of Gimleal, guided by a relic taken from some long-slain steed, waiting for it to react somehow so we can locate a herd no one has seen in centuries?"

The tallest brother bristled, but Cormag silenced him with a smack to the shoulder, while Arlen just shrugged. "You could do that. Or you could look at that cloth it was wrapped in. There are Canthorian words stitched around the edges. Tor Telweg said it was some sort of map. She was going to translate it for us."

Suddenly, Jakim understood why he and Khilamook were there, listening in on this conversation. Clearly, Rhodri already knew some of this, or he wouldn't have had two translators standing by, ready to work. He might be testing them, all of them. They would have to engage very, very carefully.

Khilamook stood. "I would be honored to offer my services."

It was so unlike the engineer to offer anything without launching a verbal or mental sparring match first that Jakim could only gape as Khilamook held out his hand, eagerly, for the cloth. "If I may?"

Rhodri let it drop, fluttering, into the waiting hand.

Handling it delicately, Khilamook spread the green silk over his palm and forearm. Even from where Jakim was sitting, he could see it was covered with intricate embroidery. A running line of text in the strangely angular yet fluid script of Canthor was stitched along the border.

"Your poacher was actually a trusted royal servant, carrying orders from high within the Canthorian court." The engineer sounded fascinated. "This instructs him to cross into Gimleal near the springs of Soltain, then travel north by northeast, following the landmarks indicated on the map. Curious, since the landmarks featured in the embroidered scene are all from Canthor: the blue trees of the Jishdrujen Forest, the glistening fields of Ish-Koleth, even the Kholar Canals."

"So we should look for a dawnling in Canthor?" Rhodri sounded skeptical.

"Sadly, no." Khilamook carefully folded the cloth and handed it back to Rhodri. "I'm saying the true map is concealed, likely encoded somewhere in the stitching."

"But you can uncover it?"

"Undoubtedly, but it will take time."

Nahrog snorted. "And let me guess: your freedom and a pile of wealth as well."

Khilamook smiled thinly. "Let us not forget my manuscripts too."

Rhodri regarded him narrowly, then swung the cloth toward Jakim. "Scroll, is what he said true?"

Jakim took a breath as all eyes fell on him. Particularly Khilamook's. He had no desire to be drawn into anything to do with the engineer, or indeed the war-chief, again. Yet, he was curious about the dawnling. About all of it.

He rose slowly and took the square of silk, which felt as cool as running water over his rough fingers. It took him a moment to decipher the flowing text that formed the stitched border before he could confirm that Khilamook's paraphrase had been accurate, then he focused on the intricate design itself. The embroidered scene centered on a four-legged creature sewn in shades of shining, almost metallic, gold and white threads, and though its arched neck and mane were clearly meant to depict a horse, it was far more sprightly and gazelle-like than Ineth's stocky earthhewn, which had legs thick as tree trunks.

He did not recognize most of the landmarks Khilamook had mentioned, but the steep, snow-tipped mountains in the background were clearly the Halarma peaks, which surrounded the emperor's summer palace, and none of it resembled anything he had seen in Soldonia.

"It is, my lord," he said to Rhodri, "as far as I can tell."

"Hear my terms then, both of you. We depart in the morning for Gimleal. Either you, engineer, or you, Scroll, must uncover the rest of the location. Whoever does shall live."

There seemed an obvious corollary to that threat.

Jakim had to ask. "And the other?"

The sun was gone now, and a gust of wind caused the flames to leap, casting a fiendish glare across Rhodri's face. "You will not want to be that other."

The fire had burned down to pale ash and glowing embers now, and still Khilamook pored over the cloth, muttering as he mentally catalogued every minute detail. Jakim was already so tired he could hardly see straight, and the dizzying array of threads and colors in the intricate design made his eyes water and his head spin. He scrubbed at his face and blew out a sigh. Khilamook might solve the mystery tonight, and there would be nothing he could do.

So, really, what was the point of trying?

"You should let me tend your wounds, my lord." Ineth lowered herself beside Rhodri and started rummaging through her satchel. They were alone now, her and Rhodri on one side of the fire, Jakim and Khilamook on the other. Nahrog had retired to his bedroll, and Ineth had banished Ondri's sons after a brotherly quarrel turned into a brawl.

Rhodri waved her off absently. "I'm fine, Ineth."

He sat, turning the relic in his hand. Tomorrow, Jakim would do his best to uncover the concealed message in the embroidery, but for now, he could no more tear his gaze away from the strange object than Rhodri could. He watched as Rhodri angled it slightly so the firelight struck dazzlingly on each unique surface and Jakim's breath caught.

"Pardon my boldness, lord, but you do not seem fine."

Jakim braced for Rhodri's biting response, but the war-chief only tilted his head.

"Just . . . look at it." There was awe in his voice, and he seemed to be speaking more to himself. "So many years of my youth spent searching for such proof, for my father. He was dying long before the world believed him gone, and I was desperate to save him. I sought out every graybeard who could tell me a tale, devoured every legend, ventured out into the wild on my own, without finding so much as a single golden hair, and now, I hold a piece of a dawnling in my hand, and it is too late for my father." He shook his head bitterly. "To think that it would take a Canthorian poacher to uncover the way to locate our sacred lost breed."

"A profane way, and a cursed one," Ineth said sternly.

"Superstition from you, Ineth? Still?"

"I don't like this, my lord. Crossing into Gimleal is dangerous. Craddock might not have sworn to Ceridwen, but he could still see our presence there as a threat."

"We shall take care that he does not know of it. Once we enter the wilds, we will be safe enough. From him, at least. Those lands are too vast for him to patrol with any regularity. How else could such a treasure as a dawnling herd go unnoticed there for so many years?"

"I don't trust that priest either."

Rhodri snorted. "You don't trust anyone. But the priest has promised me ten thousand soldiers who will march under my direct command, and until they arrive, I mean to keep him under a tight rein. Why do you think he is here with me, instead of off with Astra, intimidating that wayward colt, Ormond, into keeping his oaths?"

"If you ask me, Astra is the one in need of reining."

"I did not ask you." His tone was suddenly cold and laced with menace.

But Ineth persisted. "I know you, my lord. You would never have chosen this course if she had not backed you into it. She should remember her place—"

"No, you should. You will not speak ill of my lady again, Ineth, or flames take me, I will cast you from my service and leave you as I found you. Lost."

Closing his fist tightly around the relic, Rhodri rose to his feet.

"I only seek to serve you, my lord," Ineth said, voice thin.

His face was lost in shadow. "I know you do. Which is why I leave these two and their task to your oversight. You are the only one here I trust not to fail me."

"Never, my lord," she replied, but by the time she spoke, he was gone.

Ineth stood, then stalked over to Khilamook and snatched the cloth from him. She disappeared into the night, abandoning Jakim to the engineer's questionable mercies.

Khilamook cracked his knuckles with a satisfied sigh. "I solved it."

TWENTY-SIX: CERIDWEN

*Once dampened, the fires that blaze through a fireborn's blood
require time to reignite, and until they do, he is vulnerable.*
- Wisdom of the Horsemasters

Ceridwen dreamed of drowning. Chained, unable to move, consumed by a creeping cold that climbed her limbs and shot up her chest, then slowly scaled upward while she tipped her chin further and further back, clinging to life. One breath at a time. If her corpse was consigned to the deeps, she would be denied both release in the pyre and rebirth into legend when her closest kin voiced the hero's song, reciting the litany of her deeds to convince the warrior spirits of old to welcome her into their mighty company.

Then again, she had no kin to sing for her nor deeds worthy of song.

She woke to Liam choking out strangled sobs, and she could not help him. She could not even help herself. She curled around the burning ember that her wounded arm had become, both it and her head propped up out of the putrid pool that sloshed through the hold and soaked her leathers. Something felt different, something she fought to grasp through the dense fog of fever, something about the movement of the ship. Then anchor chains rattled against the hull, and she understood.

The ship had stopped. They had arrived.

"Liam?" Her voice grated in her throat.

He did not respond. He had not responded for a long time. She dragged her body toward the slumped figure in the opposite stall, using only the elbow of her freed right arm to crawl. When Liam had first gone silent, she had wrenched her right hand from the manacle, striving to reach him. But nothing, no force of will or blaze of strength could free her left.

Pain had defeated her when she tried, stole her consciousness.

She let her left arm stretch behind her now until the chains drew her up short. She was only able to reach Liam's uninjured foot, so she shook it, calling his name, but he did not stir. She couldn't tell if he was sleeping or unconscious or even dead. With footsteps thudding on the deck above, voices shouting in a foreign tongue, and cries of gulls keening over a hostile shore, she did not know which mercy to pray for anymore.

She drifted then and dreamed of suffocating. Of being trapped beneath a crushing weight, corpses piled above, beneath, and around her. Such was the death her father had found in the killing pits at Idolas, only each of the slain here bore the faces of her friends. Mindar sprawled beside her, eyes cold, white, lifeless. Slain not by the fall, but by a poison that seeped from her own skin, withering everything it touched, while Glyndwr's rasping voice echoed in her ears.

"Like the fruit of a poisonous vine."

It was her own thrashing that finally startled her awake, and not even the sight of Mindar standing in his stall, ears pricked upward toward the clank of armored feet, could banish the chill of that dream. She glanced at Liam and found that his head had rolled to the side, freckles stark on his sickly, pale skin. Slowly, achingly, she dragged one foot under her, then one knee, before the hatch flew open.

"Silent One Alive, what a stench. It smells like death."

Searing sunlight flooded the hold, so she could not see the speaker. His voice was smooth, his Nadaarian speech cultured and refined so she easily understood him, but his tone bore an edge of cruelty that drove her to her feet. She was Ceridwen tal Desmond, tor Nimid, born of warriors, forged in flame, and declared war-chief and queen upon the strength of her victories. If she could not face death in the saddle, at least she would not meet it on her knees.

She doggedly held herself upright beneath the blinding square of light until the speaker came into focus. Curly dark hair, mouth etched in a sneer, guards at his back.

Were they so afraid of her even now?

She tottered forward, and the chain snapped taut on her wounded arm. The sudden shock of pain crashed over her, dashing her senseless. She collapsed, and the last thing she latched onto was the amusement in his voice. "So this is Soldonia's Fireborn?"

TWENTY-SEVEN: RAFI

Even the tallest mountain may be dismantled one stone at a time.
– Hanonque saying

"Thought you said these were friends of yours?" Aruk's voice rattled, which told Rafi that the man was about to begin pacing again, and he should probably decide whether or not to pull his legs out of the way. Over the past two days, Aruk had done nothing but trek from one side of the circular hut to the other. From the barred-over window, past the trio of hammocks where Sev stared at the ceiling, on to the chained door where sunlight streamed through cracks and so did the shadows of the rebel guards stationed with spears outside.

"*Friends,*" Rafi mused, letting his head thump against the wall, "can mean so many things. Why shouldn't they be my friends just because they decided to lock us up in here, eh?" He raised his voice at the end, ensuring that it reached the guards, though he hadn't recognized either of them. It wasn't like he'd actually been a part of the revolution for very long.

Though he was beginning to wonder if he still was. So far, his return to the rebel camp had mimicked his first arrival, sack-over-the-head and all. When they were still miles from Tehorra Peak, they had found themselves netted by rebels, their hands trussed, their heads hooded. Before the burlap blocked his vision, Rafi saw Sev go completely rigid when the sack was tugged over his head, and wondered, with a pang, if he too was thinking of Yeena. One of the rebels had tried to pluck Ghost's lead from Rafi's fingers, causing the colt to plunge about, jostling Nef in the drag-sled. They left the colt to Rafi after that.

Questions had resulted only in a stony silence, jokes in the threat of gagging, so Rafi had been left to guess at their destination, until a distant roar resolved into the familiar thunder of the waterfall, piercing the three caverns of the rebel hideout.

Hustled through the gorge, where Rafi was forced to relinquish his hold on Ghost, past the waterfall pool and up the wobbly slat-and-rope staircase to the second level, where Rafi caught a whiff of roasting onions and peppers coming from Saffa's kitchen, and then up to the third where their sacks were removed seconds before they were shoved into this hut.

And here, they had sat since.

Or rather, Rafi had sat, while Sev lay still, and Aruk took up pacing.

In the end, Rafi decided to leave his legs stretched out as Aruk resumed his trek. Only two weeks had passed since Sahak had used him for target practice, and the injured muscles seemed wound tighter than Elder Gordu on tax day. Stretching felt good, and Aruk didn't even pause as he stepped over, crossed the room, turned, and stepped over again.

Back and forth. Back and forth.

One more day of this was sure to etch the man's footprints into the floor, and drive Rafi completely and utterly insane. He rubbed his eyes. He was probably being unfair to Aruk. Sev was the one who hadn't spoken to him in days. No doubt that was the true source of his frustration. It was just so unlike Sev. Ordinarily, he would have shouted up a storm by now, maybe even tried to kick a hole in the wall.

"I will fix this," Rafi whispered to himself.

So fix it, his own voice whispered back. *Like Delmar would.*

Stung by restless energy, Rafi shot to his feet and approached the door. Through the slats, he could make out the rebel guards, one sitting, the other leaning on his spear—both seemingly bored by the monotony of their duty. He rapped his good fist on the door.

Which only earned him an irritated glance from the standing rebel.

"I know you hear me! You can't ignore me forever. Let me speak to Umut."

Nothing. Not so much as a shrug. "Fine. How about Moc? Where is he? Moc! I WANT TO SPEAK TO MOC!" Pebbles clattered off the exterior side of the door. Ches-Shu, he'd been shouting and hammering both fists against the door like a complete maniac, and all he'd earned was a raw throat, more pain in his injured hand, a fistful of pebbles, and a rude gesture before the irritated guard turned his back again.

Shakily, Rafi turned to find Aruk stalled out mid-trek, and Sev sitting up, both eying him warily. "Guess that'll show them," Rafi offered weakly.

Behind him, the latch rattled, and the door creaked open.

Iakki swaggered in, sporting a blue band tied around his head, and wearing a *chet* that was much too big for him from a belt slung across his chest. He strolled up to Rafi, looked him up and down, then jerked his thumb over his shoulder. "Umut wants to see you."

"Iakki?" Sev's feet hit the ground. "When did you get here?"

"Just Nahiki," Iakki said, holding up a hand. "Umut's orders."

"What are you playing at?"

"Umut's. Orders."

"I'll give you orders, you little sea-urchin. I haven't seen you in days, and you come in spouting nonsense. Where have you been?"

Relieved to see Iakki in one piece, Rafi ignored the outburst of brotherly conflict and went to the door. He touched the slats, and the door swung open to reveal Moc talking to the two rebels a few paces away. The big Alonque clapped them on the shoulders companionably—which, coming from him, was no doubt strong enough to rattle their teeth in their skulls. Rafi felt they almost deserved it.

He shoved his fists into his pockets. "Hoy, Moc."

Moc wheeled around. "Ah, cousin, are you ready then?"

"Ready for what? We've been locked up for two days. No one will tell us anything."

"Umut summoned you. Iakki didn't say? He begged to deliver the news, so I figured, what's the harm?" Moc broke off as the clamor of voices inside the hut rose several notches, and both guards shot Rafi a scowl—as if the ruckus were somehow his fault—before latching the door and resuming their positions outside it again.

"You know," Rafi said, "I get the feeling they don't like me."

Moc shrugged noncommittally, starting off across the wide rim of the cavern, rounding the waterfall toward the natural bridge where they could look out across the gorge and into the two caverns stacked below. "Nef has many friends," Moc said at last, "and you are a Tetrani."

"Meaning what, exactly?"

"Meaning nothing you don't already know."

Rafi sighed, but it was true. Even if he had reclaimed his true name, he had originally left it behind for a reason. "Could have used you two days ago, Moc. Where have you been?"

Moc halted abruptly on the middle of the bridge. "You realize you left me with both the demon-steeds and Iakki? Getting them here in one piece was not easy, cousin."

Out here in the sunlight, Rafi noticed the stoop to Moc's shoulders and the way he stood, like a man either braced for an impact, or one who'd already been knocked clean off his feet. "But you did? Get them here in one piece?"

Moc just tipped his head toward the edge invitingly.

Rafi craned his neck so he could avoid approaching the drop-off. Verdant jungle bristled at the far end of the gorge. Closer, workers dotted both fields and cultivated orchards. Still closer—which meant that he had to inch terrifyingly near the edge to see—were sleek-brown and inky-black and dappled-gray shapes, crowded into the enclosure he had built for Ghost. Some with wings, some with stony hooves, some with scales.

The demon-steeds, here, in the hands of the revolution, at last.

He let out a breathless, disbelieving laugh. "Whoa."

"Yes." Moc's grin was exhilarated. "You will need to build a bigger enclosure, I think. I for one do not plan to chase any more runaways." He took off again down the bridge, and Rafi hesitated only a moment to marvel at the sight before loping after.

"Just me? You wouldn't . . . maybe . . . want to help?"

"You," Umut said, "are a thorn in my heel, did you know that? You gave your oath to the revolution. You broke our bread, shared our refuge, shed blood in our fight."

All of which, it seemed to Rafi, should count for something.

Like, maybe, a chance to talk it over before being locked up for two days?

Rafi had expected this to be more of an official audience. Instead, he found himself in the dim, cluttered confines of Umut's own hut, where bundled herbs dried from the ceiling, pots of ointments and tinctures were stacked on shelves, and the regalia of his office—the feathered cloak and beaked crown—hung nonchalantly from a hook beside the door, where it could be grabbed easily on the way out. He sat at a low table, cross-legged on overlapping woven rugs, facing a pair of curtained doorways that hinted at other rooms beyond. Off to his left, Umut stooped over a stone oven, salted hair bound loosely at his neck, crutch propped under one arm, steeping a pot of tea.

Pale rainflower, judging by that muted, tangy scent. It made Rafi's mouth water.

"You," Umut continued pointedly, clunking two cups down, "were to be our distraction. Plans were set in place. Then you deserted us, and you took that steed with you. So, tell me, young Tetrani, why should I trust you now?"

"Honestly? I'd have thought the demon-steeds below answer enough."

"Why? Because the 'prince lives and the demon-steeds ride with him?'" Umut fixed him with his piercing gaze, the words a direct quote.

Rumor, it seemed, could travel even faster than demon-steeds.

Rafi coughed. "Ah, so you heard about that?"

"I'm the head of the Que Revolution. Of course I heard about it. You do recall that we've been setting things in motion, important things, things that were meant to capitalize on the timely reveal that the crown prince lives, like thunder follows the lightning strike. Only you ripped that thunder right out of the sky."

"Sorry about that. It was . . . mostly an accident. But you were right," he added quickly, "about the demon-steeds, about the advantages they offer in battle." He recalled soaring over Sahak's head on a wave, drenching his cousin and leaving an entire longboat filled with royal guards swamped, incapable of pursuing the stolen ship, giving him a few moments of breathless, giddy victory. Back before the ship had imploded beneath his feet, and everything had gone to utter rot and ruin.

Umut's eyes narrowed. "You succeeded then? You trained the sea-demon for battle?"

"More or less." More like they'd figured it out together.

"How did you do it? Must make for quite the tale."

"It would have. If you'd let me tell it two days ago."

Maybe that was petty. Judging from Umut's expression, it wasn't going to earn him any favors, which was unfortunate, since he'd come to ask a big one.

"Make no mistake, Rafi Tetrani, this is war, not a game. We rebels may be few compared to the might of the empire, but we are dedicated and patient. We run minor raids, harass small garrisons, rescue those we can and mourn those we can't, all so that one day soon, we can strike hard and make it count. So tell me now and tell me true, are you in? Or are you out?"

Rafi straightened. "I'm in, and yes, the demon-steeds with me."

"Good," Umut said wryly. "Because word is already spreading fast of raids taking place in your name, Crown Prince, and rumors are not so easily tamed."

With that staggering remark, Umut splashed steaming red liquid into the cups, releasing an aromatic scent that took on a deeper, more earthy tone as he stirred in a few drops of a murky tincture. Rather than offering one to Rafi, he clutched both in one hand and deftly maneuvered to the curtained doorways, ducked into the one on the left first, emerged minus one cup, and then crossed into the one on the right.

Before the curtain trailed back into place, Rafi glimpsed a bandaged form sprawled on a cot, one bare foot sticking out from sweat-stained sheets. He caught a whiff of sickness and stale air and astringent salves.

"Nef?" he asked quietly when Umut reappeared. "How is he?"

"Resting." Umut lowered himself stiffly beside the table, stretching the stump of his missing leg before him. He'd always seemed weathered to Rafi, but resilient, like a rock outcropping that endured, resistant to the elements. But now, Rafi could almost hear the creak of his bones bowing under the weight he carried. There always had been something fatherly about the way he treated Nef, about the way he treated all of them.

Rafi had always viewed responsibility like a rock anchor, towing you down to drown you, but now he considered how it might sit like a mountain on your shoulders.

He nodded at the dangling herbs. "So, you really are a healer?"

"Wasn't always a leader. Or a rebel."

"Must be quite the tale . . ."

Umut's smile was tired. "Maybe someday you'll hear it."

The door creaked open suddenly, and Saffa shuffled in, a basket balanced on her head. Rafi grinned at the sight of the old woman and jumped up to help, but she just patted his shoulder and lowered the basket to the table with a wiry strength that contradicted her frail form. She pulled out cala root crackers, bushka beans and rice topped with roasted vegetables and goat meat, and Rafi's favorite—fried saga crisps, still glistening with hot oil. Umut reached for one, and she slapped his hand away, then slid the bowl toward Rafi.

He plucked out a fat, curling crisp from the top, blew on it, and bit through the crunchy batter to the warm, tangy fruit inside. "Saffa," he said, mouth full. "No one, not even the finest chefs in all of Cetmur, can make saga crisps like you can. One of these days, you'll have to show me how you do it."

She shook her head, looking injured, and tapped one finger against her chest.

"Come on. You know I missed you even more than your food."

Her smile crinkled her entire face as she set a bowl of thin broth on the table before Umut.

He sniffed at it suspiciously. "Is this for me?" She tilted her chin toward the curtained doorway on the right. "For Nef? He's sleeping. It'll get cold." She raised one eyebrow. "Fine. Yes. I'll warm it when he wakes."

She patted Rafi's shoulder once more, then exited.

Shoveling down bushka beans and rice, Rafi eyed Umut curiously until the rebel leader explained. "She's still angry I wouldn't allow her to see you before."

"Why was that?" Rafi asked, meeting his eye levelly.

"Consequences. You are a Tetrani. You do not think Nef is the only one who struggles to see past your blood? Many questioned my leadership when your true name became known. How much more so, do you think, when you deserted?"

"More of a disappearance, really. Maybe a minor detour."

Umut's flat stare made Rafi squirm.

"Saga crisp?" He slid the bowl forward as a peace offering, then cleared his throat when Umut didn't move to take one. "So, that's what these past two days were about? Saving face?"

"Not face. Saving the revolution."

Rafi feigned a smile. "Who knew locking me up in a hut could be so effective? Why not just throw away the key?"

Umut, luckily, ignored that suggestion, sea-blue gaze drifting past Rafi toward a woven tapestry depicting the territories of the three Que tribes. Somehow both more and less than a map, it captured the sweltering feeling of being trapped within the wild, tangled sprawl of the Mah jungle; the dizzying, rushing awe of scaling the Hanon peaks and finding the world itself splayed at your feet, the sky an infinite expanse above you; and the restless, yearning sense that when standing on the snakelike stretch of sand that formed the Alon coast, you were both nowhere and on the edge of everything.

It was also dotted with spots of color—groups of mostly orange and blue beads stuck on pins, with the occasional odd green or yellow thrown in. Marking the locations of rebel companies, maybe? Or tracking Nadaari movements?

"We call ourselves the Que, as if we were one body, and not three distinct tribes, and though I am the head of the revolution, we do not all share the same mind." Umut sounded thoughtful. "Many believe the only path to Que freedom lies in Que fighting alone—as though we did not already fail alone when the empire defeated us the first time. Choosing to rescue you and your brother six years ago nearly caused a permanent rift, and when that mission failed, the split widened."

He met Rafi's eyes, and his voice hardened. "Shortsightedness has ever been the revolution's downfall, but I have an eye for the long view. So when that means casting my weight behind a loose boulder of a Tetrani, sending him tumbling to crush our foes, I'll do it, and when that means netting said Tetrani until I'm convinced he won't become a wedge in that split or crush my own forces in his free fall, well, I'll do that, too, and I won't apologize for it."

Silence bloomed between them, dense and suffocating.

Rafi shifted uneasily. "Could we maybe consider a scenario that doesn't involve falling? You wanted a distraction to soak up attention, and I'll put my Tetrani blood to use. But I need your help, too, so I guess I'm here to make another deal."

Sensing Umut's interest sharpening, he poured all his heartfelt earnestness into his voice, until even to his own ears, his explanation sounded less like himself and more like Delmar. "I need help finding and rescuing my friends from Sahak before our time runs out, and I think you can give me that. You need an edge in this war, and with those steeds, I can give it to you. And," he added, sensing oncoming objections, "before you point out that the steeds are here and my friends are a highly risky mission away, so what do you need me for, and why should you risk it—"

"You must admit it's a fair point."

"Remember that these are our cousins who are suffering, and also that no one else has ever ridden one of the *anhana lasha* into the deeps and out again."

No one outside of Soldonia, that is. But Rafi decided not to put too fine a point on it.

The rebel leader tilted his head. "You've changed," he said simply, and the words rushed over Rafi like a whisk of sweet, summery air.

Yes, he *had* changed, and he was still changing.

He grinned. "Well, a tiger ate my shirt. Got a few new scars too. Stole this Soldonian tunic . . . and a ship. You could say," he added as an afterthought, "it's been a busy two weeks."

"You should rest up then, Tetrani," a weak, nasally voice said.

Nef sagged against the door frame to his room, damp tunic askew on his thin shoulders, a bandage covering his missing eye. "We've got a long walk to reach your friends. Wouldn't do to have us both fainting from exhaustion before we arrive."

Us, he had said. *Walk*, he had said. *Arrive*.

Words that conveyed partnership, a plan, and a destination.

Rafi didn't know whether that surprised him more or the fact that Nef had cracked a joke at his own expense. "What are you saying, Nef?"

Nef took a step, swayed, and caught the door frame again. "I'm saying your cousin is an overconfident fool. I'm saying I trailed him all the way to his den, and he was too arrogant to see the danger when he finally caught me." His mouth tightened. "I'm saying I know where he's holding your friends, and I know how we can get inside to rescue them."

Rafi strolled toward the kitchen alcoves, feeling lighter and freer than he had in weeks. Stronger, too, despite the slight tug in his stride, and despite the eyes tracking his path each step of the way. Rebels and refugees dwelled side by side in these caverns, this last hidden stronghold of the Que peoples. Though no one bothered him, he could sense the whispers spreading like ripples in the water, calling him demon-rider, Tetrani's son, and ghost.

Some viewed him with hostility. Some with outright awe.

He exchanged smiles for every scowl, nods for curious glances, and winks for the occasional wonderstruck look, mimicking the confidence that had always graced his brother's face, even if it still felt foreign on his own. Rounding the corner of the alcove, the sounds of feasting and the fog of spicy scents that forever floated on the waves of heat and steam wafted over him, awakening a deep ache that told him he was home.

Here, Gordu and the ten fisherfolk who had formed his ship-stealing turned demon-steed-transporting crew crowded around the long table on an assortment of stools, benches, and the occasional overturned barrel, while Saffa and her cooks bustled around, keeping plates and cups full. On the end closest to Rafi, Moc and Iakki stooped over the table, their heads almost touching, and occasionally one or the other would let out a shout. Several seats down, old Hanu, who hadn't touched his food, drained his cup, then Aruk's, then reached for the unattended cup in front of Sev. But Sev folded his burly arms around it and stared into its depths.

Hanu licked his lips and eyed Gordu's cup next.

"Coming through!" Jasri, one of the cooks, brushed past, carrying a jug of saga wine, still dripping from being chilled by the churn of the waterfall in the pool below. Her head was always tipped to one side, dark hair falling to conceal her scars, and Rafi found himself staring, remembering how the shine and thickness of it had first reminded him of Yeena.

Without even closing his eyes, he could see Yeena again, sinking into the depths of the sea, dark hair blooming like a sea fan around her face. Cheers erupted from Moc and Iakki, startling Rafi back to the present, where it was not Yeena's face he was staring at but Jasri's, and she was staring back. A little flustered, she paused mid-pour, jug suspended over Hanu's cup, then she tilted her chin and tossed Rafi a crooked smile.

Her smile, like her scars, she usually kept tucked away.

It was a smile that knew pain and existed not only despite it, but in spite of it. He smiled back at her and caught a bitter scowl from Sev.

Right. Rafi let out a breath. Time to fix this.

Saffa kept a special spiced vintage stashed away, reserved for moments of bitter victory or bloody defeat, both of which required something strong rather than sweet. Rafi poured two cups of it, then nudged an empty crate over to Sev and dropped beside him. "We found them, Sev. We know where they are."

Sev stared rigidly ahead, a muscle twitching in his jaw.

Rafi set the cups down, suddenly feeling a fool for bringing them, as if Sev would drink with him when he wouldn't even talk to him. Down the table, he could see that Moc and Iakki were playing a game that involved calling out patterns and tossing a set of colorful wooden dice, then smacking the top of the other player's head whenever their throw fell incorrectly. Iakki was winning. Ruthlessly. Rafi felt like he was offering his own head for the blow as he launched into an explanation of how Nef had trailed Sahak back to his base, found the villagers inside, then escaped undetected until Sahak finally caught him outside of Zorrad.

"But he convinced Sahak that he'd been planted there to shadow him, so Sahak has no clue that we know where they are. We have a plan, Sev. Or the start of one at least."

"When?" Sev's voice was taut. "How soon?"

"Soon as Nef is strong enough. We'll need him to guide us. But this is good news, don't you see? She'll be safe soon, and we won't have to search the entire empire for the missing steeds."

No sooner had the words escaped than Rafi wished to reclaim them.

Sev rounded on him, dark eyes boiling. "What do you want from me? You want me to congratulate you? You got what you wanted, Tetrani, now leave me be."

"This isn't what I wanted, Sev. I wanted to fix what's wrong. We were friends—"

"We were brothers, Rafi, and you lied to me. You lied to me once, and I tried to move past it, to go back to the way things were, but you lied to me again."

Rafi opened his mouth to object, but Sev cut him off.

"You kept the truth from me. You gave the steeds to the revolution without telling me. You brought me along to lay a false trail for the Emperor's Stone-eye, and it almost worked, and you want to know why? Because you and he have more in common than just blood." Sev lurched up from his stool, then twisted and swept both cups from the table. Crockery shattered, wine splattered, and sounds of feasting ceased, leaving Sev's voice ringing in the sudden silence. "There's nothing between us anymore. Nothing but this debt you owe, and once this is over, once Kaya is safe, you and I are through."

TWENTY-EIGHT: JAKIM

The vow of a Scroll is this: to commit oneself flesh and soul to the will of Aodh, the preservation of the holy writ, and the recovery of the lost words.
- The Precepts of the Scrolls

K hilamook had lied, of course, about deciphering the stitching. Or at least, Jakim was almost convinced that he had, though not until after spending an agonizing day waiting for the engineer to tell Rhodri and leave him to his fate. But the sun was already soaring high a full day later, and Khilamook still hadn't approached Rhodri. And when it was Khilamook's turn to study the embroidery—Ineth grudgingly made them pass it back and forth—he did it with a keen interest that did not appear to be faked.

Even so, a part of Jakim did wonder.

The engineer had spent months arguing with the Nadaari via translation, without once revealing his own fluency. He did nothing without committing fully, including deception. Never without reason, even if only according to his own twisted logic.

Jakim studied the silk cloth now, or tried to, while rocking on the back of Ineth's steed. They moved at a walk, but Jakim's head still swayed slightly with each step, which made trying to track any one thread amidst the vibrant web of colors, or any hint of variation in the intricate stitching, an exercise in frustration. To compound it, each element of the ornately stylized scene was formed of smaller elements that were in themselves miniature pictures, so the more Jakim studied it, the more there was to see. It was an incredible work of art, yet looking at it for too long made his eyes lose focus.

Sighing, he concentrated on the radiant steed, with its long delicate neck and spindly legs and what looked like a blazing star on its forehead. "Is this what a dawnling looks like?" he asked Ineth.

She didn't look back, just grunted. "Haven't seen one. No one has for years."

"Why is that? Did they all just . . . disappear?" Having watched the sons of Ondri vanish on their shadowers upon entering the shadow of a copse of trees ahead just moments earlier, it seemed a valid question, but Ineth only snorted.

"Died off. Killed off. Hunted for bones, blood, relics."

It was a particularly gruesome thought. "Why?"

"Because," came Khilamook's voice behind them, where he rode with a burly earthrider whose shoulders were even broader than the chest of his steed, "'the breath of a dawnling is life.' Or so my brother Vishna was fond of saying. He's a scholar of the ninth order and always took a particular interest in your solborn and their uses."

"Healing," Ineth clarified. "It was said that the breath of a dawnling could cure one even on the verge of death itself. But then legends say many things."

"So do rumors." Khilamook sounded almost exuberant and more engaged than Jakim had ever seen him. More genuine, too. "Nine years ago, the emperor of Canthor was a very, very sick man. He took to his deathbed, unlikely ever to rise again. Until he did. Vishna always claimed it was the heart of a dawnling that saved him. I thought it nonsense, but seeing that map . . ."

"Or not seeing it," Ineth corrected, "since you haven't uncovered it yet."

"Scoff if you must, woman, but Emperor Hikatari is now one hundred and nine years old and has been reasoning for the empire for as long as you have been alive—eighty-seven years come spring."

"As long as—what?" Ineth stiffened, then urged her steed on, leaving the engineer behind. Jakim caught only snatches of her irritated muttering as Nahrog clattered past in his chariot and started up the long slope of the hill before them. "Flames take him . . . how old does he think I am?"

Moving at this faster clip, Jakim found it impossible to concentrate on the stitching, so he tucked the cloth away into his belt. "What legends?" he asked at last.

Ineth turned her head back to look at him.

"Talking about legends before, you sounded disappointed. What legends did you mean? If you don't mind me asking," he added.

Her expression said she did. But she didn't threaten to tie him up again, which he took as a good sign. "What legends do you think?"

"You mean"—he swallowed—"the holy writ?"

She snorted. "The holy writ, the truths, the City, all of it."

Gooseflesh prickled his arms at her words. He had left the Sanctuary in Kerrikar after lying his way onto a mission bound for the wastes of Broken-Eliam, to search out the City and recover lost sections of the holy writ from its sacred walls. Of course, war had caught him up and spat him out here in Soldonia instead, in the company of this woman who had once been a Scroll.

He opened his mouth but was unsure what to say.

Partway up the hill before them, the chariot slowed, and the priest dug out his whip, cracking it to spur the struggling tiger on. It was limping slightly on its left forepaw. The day before, while the attendants were forcing it into its traces, one had stepped too close and gotten his arm mauled. The other had stabbed at the tiger with his spear until the beast let go. Jakim got a closer look at it now as they passed and could see the dark stain of dried blood on its shoulder and the dullness of its lank, neglected coat.

As Nahrog's rumbled curses faded behind them, Ineth spoke again. "I will say this, young Scroll, the only evidence I have ever seen of Aodh's so-called mercy is that man's inability to bond one of our steeds. One such as he should not be given power."

Jakim couldn't help but agree.

Shouts sounded ahead, and with a click of her tongue, Ineth cued the earthhewn to speed, quickly gaining on the front of the column. Pale hair flying back from his forehead, Madden dashed up to Rhodri and slid to a halt.

"Te Oengus," he gasped, "there's a rider ahead."

Both rider and steed were little more than a dark stain moving slowly across the floor of the grassy valley that opened before them. The slow pace seemed due to a hitch in the steed's stride—it was injured, somehow. That much Jakim could make out, though it was too far to tell more from the top of the rise where Rhodri's forces were clustered.

Ineth, however, caught her breath. "Is that . . .?"

"Aye, tor Rira, I believe it is." Rhodri straightened with grim satisfaction and pitched his voice to reach the four sons of Ondri jostling impatiently around him on their wild-eyed steeds, and Arlen, who waited, calmly, a little ways off. "I want him alive. Run him down."

Cormag gave a muffled shout, and away they sprang.

Tearing down the hill, stretched out low, the five shadowers moved silently, without the thunder of hooves or the rattling of grasses to warn of their approach. On the trail, their silence had been obscured by the sounds of every other steed. But here, watching them plunge down the slope, then fade like smoke in a gray sky as they swept through the shadow of the rise at the bottom to solidify on the other side, it both defied and terrified reason.

The strange rider suddenly drew up sharply, then spun, and urged his steed into an ungainly run. He raced eastward, back the way he'd come, where a scrubby sprawl of trees spilled from a gap in the hills, and where his shadower might vanish and lose the pursuit.

"Go," Jakim breathed, suddenly aching for someone to escape.

But the injured steed struggled to maintain its speed, and the race was over far too quickly. The shadower went down, flinging the rider over its head. He hit and rolled, and Ondri's sons descended around him like a pack of wild dogs, hiding him from view.

The rider was kneeling, restrained by two brothers, when Rhodri and Ineth reached the valley and broke through the ring. Chest heaving, dark hair littered with debris from his fall. His face was bruised, and his lip was split—as were the knuckles on the tallest brother's left fist—but he raised his chin defiantly as Rhodri dismounted and surveyed him.

"I didn't expect to take you without a fight, te Donal." Rhodri turned as the bald brother guided the injured shadower haltingly over, its mottled brown coat lathered with sweat. Frowning, he ran a hand down the creature's swollen and trembling left foreleg. "Shame. You've run her into the dust."

He upended the quiver strapped to the saddle, spilling out the few arrows left inside, and Jakim could sense the rider's frustration in the twitch of his head as Rhodri moved on toward the bow sheath. "Is it true what they say? That you're one of the finest archers in the Outriders?"

Cormag picked up one of the arrows and ran his thumb over the copper-colored fletching, then tossed it to the brother with the bloodied knuckles. "Look familiar?"

Rhodri withdrew the bow. It came out in two splintered pieces, connected by a frayed string. "It'd be hard to kill me with that."

"I'm not here you to kill you," the rider, te Donal, said. He tried to straighten, then winced, tucking his right arm protectively against his side. That shoulder didn't look right to Jakim. It sagged low, uneven with the other. Clearly, he'd been injured along with his steed. "I have a message for you from our queen."

Rhodri's eyes narrowed. "You are late in coming, then."

"That's what happens when you let your hounds"—the stranger's dark eyes flicked to the sons of Ondri surrounding him—"attack riders traveling under a flag of truce. You should—" He broke off in a groan, as the brother with the bloodied knuckles suddenly wrenched the injured arm to the side, causing him to fold over his knees.

"Brawly still hasn't forgiven you for shooting him," Cormag growled.

Rhodri grabbed the rider's dark hair, tugging his head back to reveal a face gone pale and clammy from shock. "I meant, te Donal, that you are late because your queen and I have already met in combat."

The rider's lips parted, but he did not speak.

Still, the look in his eyes seemed to satisfy Rhodri. "Your queen is dead."

The tidings seemed to drain the rider of all defiance. He went as wooden as a statue, immobile as death, and offered no resistance as Ondri's sons dragged him, stumbling, away. Jakim expected to find him stunned still when they halted for the night. Instead, he found te Donal, hands bound before him, slamming his shoulder against a tree. The impact dropped him to his knees in silent agony, while at a fire a short distance away, Ondri's sons roared in laughter.

Ineth muttered a curse beneath her breath and shot Jakim a glare, as if it were his fault for convincing her to come tend the rider's injuries. Obviously racked and trembling with pain, te Donal didn't seem to notice their approach until Ineth touched his shoulder. He flinched and tried to move away as she probed the swollen, uneven joint with her fingertips.

"Shades take you for a fool," she said. "What were you thinking? Trying to ram a dislocated shoulder back into place? You'll be lucky if you haven't made it worse."

He winced and gave her a baffled look. "Who are you?"

"Just the idiot who got herself cornered into coming down here to help you. Lie down." She slung her satchel from her shoulder and started to open it, but when he made no move to obey, she dropped it with a sigh. "Fine. Sit. But you need to relax, or this won't work. I'm assuming you do want to be able to wield a bow again."

The rider eased himself stiffly down to the base of the tree where he sat as rigidly as if he had taken root there.

"I said 'relax.'"

"I am relaxed," he said through clenched teeth.

With a dismissive sniff, Ineth motioned for Jakim to steady the man as she slowly began to manipulate his arm. Her manner might be harsh, and there was a certain no-nonsense quality to her movements, but her touch was as gentle as Siba's had ever been as she rotated the rider's arm with a grip on his elbow.

Still, the rider hissed at the pain, and Jakim could feel him shaking against his bracing hands. Jakim had been planning to wait until Ineth finished, even until she was gone, but the words spilled out of him anyway. "She's not dead."

"What?" Te Donal started to bolt upright, but at that moment Ineth twisted his arm, felling him with a groan, then a gasp, as his shoulder slipped back into place. "Ceridwen is alive?"

Ineth shot Jakim a look he couldn't quite identify, then tapped te Donal's shoulder warningly. "Try not to go ramming into any more trees." She stood creakily. "There's cloth for a sling in my satchel and tala he can chew for the pain. Pale green leaves," she added as Jakim wrinkled his forehead, "white ridges, can't mistake them."

"No, it's just . . . you didn't think to give him any before setting his shoulder?"

Her scowl dared him to go on, then she turned and walked off.

"You're the Scroll, aren't you?" Te Donal winced, raising his bound hands awkwardly to prod his shoulder, as he gently eased his arm around, testing its mobility. "The one Ceridwen told me about. What are you doing here?"

"It's a long story. But yes, I'm Jakim."

"Finnian. She truly lives?"

The hope welling in his eyes . . .

Jakim dug out cloth for a sling. Tying it as Finnian directed—one strip supporting the weight of his forearm, another securing his elbow to his side—he told him everything, about Ceridwen's battle with Rhodri, Glyndwr's betrayal, the sacrifice she had made to save Liam, and how they had both been shipped to Nadaar to be executed.

And he watched the rider's hope evaporate like water in the wastelands.

"So she is dead then," Finnian said slowly. "Or as good as. I thought Liam was already gone. When they opened fire on us, I thought . . ." His voice caught. "One moment, we were alone, and the next, my friends were falling on all sides. Then Sif caught her hoof and tumbled down a gully into a thicket, and by the time we hobbled out, there was only the slain." He trailed off as Jakim pulled out the leaves Ineth had mentioned. Pale green, the size of his thumb, with white veins and a sharp astringent scent.

Tala leaves. Or ekra, as they were called among his people. He recognized them from watching his sister, Siba, prepare her poultices.

"No." Finnian set his jaw. "No tala."

"It should help with the swelling."

"Should numb my mind too. I do know a thing or two about healing. About Rhodri too. You think I don't know why I'm still alive? He wants something from me, and I don't intend to give it to him. You can tell him that too."

Suddenly, Jakim understood the edge in his voice, the suspicion in his eyes. Like Ceridwen, he assumed that Jakim was here in Rhodri's camp of his own free will. "It's not what you think," he said quickly. "I'm a captive here, like you."

"Are you?" Finnian eyed him narrowly. "Because if I had the run of the camp, like you do, I wouldn't be here anymore."

Which was hard to argue with. Even if he overlooked the obvious obstacles that stood in his path, like trying to evade shadowrider patrols while escaping across a foreign country on foot, Jakim didn't feel the urge to run at the moment, despite Rhodri's threats. He couldn't hope to put into words for this stranger a feeling that he could barely grasp himself, yet, somehow, he knew that he was meant to be here.

Here in Soldonia. Here on this hunt for a dawnling. Here with Rhodri and Ineth, and yes, maybe Finnian. Because Aodh's hand was upon him here too.

TWENTY-NINE: CERIDWEN

Stormers, soaring overhead or swooping low for an archery attack,
expose their underside to deadly bowshot from below, while the stormer
grounded by a wing injury is hampered by their weight and easily taken.
- Wisdom of the Horsemasters

When the cascade of water tumbling before the bars of her cell abruptly stopped, Ceridwen awoke, knowing he was there, watching. She stayed motionless, old instincts warning her not to react too quickly to the gaze of a predator. But she shivered as the cold wash of fear spread over skin that had boiled with fever only a short while before.

She felt lucid now, for the first time in days, perhaps weeks.

Oh, *flames*, how did she not know how long it had been? Longer than she had expected to still be alive. Overtaken again and again by delirious dreams, she had died a thousand deaths already in her sleep, every one of them ignoble. Sometimes dragged through the streets of Cetmur behind a howling mob that clamored for her head. Sometimes felled before the emperor's throne, her blood staining the floor of his palace. More often, succumbed to the slow rot of her imprisonment, entombed in her cell and forgotten in death, even by her enemies.

Only now, with her mind infused with a cold clarity by her captor's unrelenting stare, did she survey the clean bandages on the arm bound in a sling across her chest and slowly clench her swollen, reddened fingers, knowing that they would not have bothered to heal her if that last fate was to be her end. Perhaps, today, she would find out what would.

"Silent One Alive, you truly are as stubborn as they say."

Oily amusement slicked his voice, crawled under Ceridwen's skin.

She licked her cracked lips, tasting the oddly salty spray from the waterfall, which had misted on her filthy leathers, rusted the manacles on her wrists, and chilled the pitted stone of her hollowed-out cell, then she finally turned to meet the gaze of the man leaning against the bars. He cocked his head to one side, an unpleasant smile tugging his lips, and she stared back, taking in the callouses on the fingers resting on the bars, the glint of malice in his odd, tawny-colored eyes, and the baldric slung over his chest, bristling with knives.

Several of the blades, she realized, were still streaked with blood.

Markham would have smacked her over the head with the flat of her own sabre if she ever cared so poorly for her weapons. Judging by those callouses on his hands, this man was no amateur, so either he was careless or trying to convince her he was. Surely, he did not think a bloodstain enough to unnerve her. He stared at her expectantly, waiting.

Ceridwen finally cleared her throat. "What, no guards this time?"

He had spoken to her in Nadaarian, so she answered him in the same tongue. After months of war with the Nadaari, of questioning captured soldiers and releasing them to deliver her threats, the language came far more easily to her lips than it once had.

Still, triumph seemed to burn behind his eyes, as though she had lost something by speaking. As though she had anything left to lose. "I wanted to see if the battlefield reports were true, but I must confess to being rather disappointed. You haven't spontaneously burst into flame or vanished into a cloud of smoke. Tell me"—he pressed his head forward with a smirk— "are you truly the Fireborn?"

"Tell me," she responded, "who are you?"

"Oh, you won't have heard of me, but I am called Sahak." His voice dripped with such an obvious affectation of modesty he'd clearly meant it to sound false.

She had, of course, heard of the emperor's infamous assassin, which at once gave credence to the threat of those bloodstained blades. That caused her to swallow a demand to see Liam lest she draw him into this man's strike path. She steeled any reaction from her expression. "Then, Sahak, bring me to my steed, and you will see what I am."

He stepped back from her cell with a sardonic smile. "Oh, trust me to do better than that. I'll bring you to your young friend, too. I'm told he's dying to see you." With the chill of those words still hanging over her, he reached out of her view and pulled down, and with a ratcheting and a clanking, the entire wall of bars retracted upward like a portcullis.

Ceridwen stood, fighting a rush of dizziness. Clutching her chained hands before her, she stepped down through the damp opening. She passed so close to Sahak that their shoulders brushed, and her eyes darted to the blades strapped to his chest.

"Go on," he murmured. "See if you can take one from me."

Startled, she flicked her gaze up to meet his hawklike stare. The loose sleeves of his tunic were rolled up past his elbows, and his grip on the iron lever that had opened her cell exposed the sinewy strength of his wrists and forearms. Clearly, he baited her. He would be fast—deadly fast. But even if she had trusted her reflexes, she did not know where Liam was.

So she just offered her chains. "Take these off, and I will."

Sahak's mouth twitched, and he waved her on ahead, then released the lever, dropping the bars with a clang. With a tug on a second lever, water cascaded from a seam high in the wall, falling over the cell, and collected in a trough that sloped gradually downward until it drained into a wide canal that ran lengthwise down the center of the rectangular room and out beneath an ornamented portcullis at the far end.

Ceridwen stopped, taking in the enormity and volume of the space, which rang with the chattering, splashing sound of a hundred waterfalls. Smaller cascades, like the one over her cell, streamed down the wall behind her and the one opposite, each one falling between pairs of ornate columns that sat on either side of the drainage troughs. Off to her left, one massive cascade poured over the top of a structure, shaped like a miniature mountain, built against the end wall, or perhaps carved from it. Steps were cut into both sides, and two braziers flanked the stream at the top. There at last she found the guards she expected, clad in white-plumed helms, standing beside a robed figure she took for a priest. Unlike the other priests she had encountered, his robes were a pale ash that darkened to soot at the hems, and instead of a gilded headpiece, a mask covered his face. Still, she scarcely gave priest or guards a second look, for her eyes were drawn toward the true source of light which came from an opening above.

Through it, she could see the sky, deep and vast and blue.

Somewhere, out there, the world still existed, and life persisted. She had almost forgotten that, and the sudden appearance of a trio of wildly colored birds darting over the opening on wings that flashed with gold in the sunlight made her eyes sting with unshed tears.

"What is this place?" she asked.

"This is Dagmur, temple of Murloch, and I am its high priest."

Suddenly, she knew the true purpose of those drainage troughs. Sacrificial cisterns to channel blood into the water for the god of Nadaar. Was that to be her end?

"Or it used to be anyway. Now, you could say it's something more."

She swallowed. "You do not look like a priest. Where are your chains?"

Sahak only shrugged. "I, too, am something more. Power is an interesting thing, Ceridwen tal Desmond. You can possess it. You can lose it. You can find it. You can steal it. But you cannot create it where it does not already exist. There are many powers in the world, some truer than others. Your steed for example." He pointed across the canal, past a set of enormous barred doors that she could have ridden a team of earthhewn through, and down to the right. "The true fireborn."

Oh, *flames*, she saw him. Mindar.

Muzzled, saddleless, and tied to a ring in the opposite wall, his sorrel coat dull, eyes dim. She whistled for him, her cracked lips taking two tries to produce a sound. His head shot up, and he let out a muffled nicker.

If she could just get to him . . .

But she saw no path, no bridge, no way, save swimming or reaching the steps at the end—where the guards stood. She took a step forward.

Strong fingers seized her elbow, held her fast.

"But there is a power older and stronger and deeper still, a power that has slumbered for centuries at the Center of the World. A power that is waking. The Eyes have seen it. The Ears have heard it. The Voice has spoken." Sahak's fingers dug tighter. "You have heard it, I think. The Voice."

It was not a question, and she shivered at the forced recollection.

Chilled still, months later, at the bone-shattering, flesh-rending, earth-unmaking sound that had torn through her mind after the priest she was interrogating attacked her: *Prepare yourself, woman, for the falling of all nations.*

She took a breath. "You said you would bring me to Liam."

For a moment, she feared he would strike her. His mouth wrenched into a snarl, then he summoned her to follow with a jerk of his head toward the next waterfall. He gestured dismissively toward the higher of two levers set into the stone. Were there cells like hers behind every cascade? She gripped the rough iron in her good hand and pulled down. The flow slowed to a trickle, and she ducked into the cave-like opening behind, grasping the bars to peer inside.

Liam was huddled at the back of the cell, swathed in shadow. Shoulders hunched, head down, muttering to himself. It took her a moment to realize that she didn't understand the words. He wasn't speaking Soldonian. She wasn't sure he was speaking any recognizable language at all.

"Liam?" *Shades.* "Liam, answer me."

The muttering stopped.

His head slowly tilted up, and Ceridwen froze. Oh, *flames.* Oh, fire and smoke and ash. Something was wrong with his eyes. She took an involuntary step back, struggling to grasp the utter wrongness of the thing she saw—too large, too pale, too flat—and the shift in perspective brought a sudden, piercing understanding.

She pivoted to face Sahak, anger constricting her throat. "That is not Liam."

The huddled form belonged to a full-grown man, far too broad and burly.

"Oh?" Sahak feigned surprise. "Well, that can't be right. Must be in the next one." Tossing the lever up so the cascade began again, he waved her on.

Warily now, she closed off the next waterfall and looked inside.

Nothing. The cell appeared completely empty. Silent too. She could hear the last droplets of the waterfall plopping to the floor. She started to turn back, but something hurtled against the bars and clung there, wailing wordlessly. Greasy, matted hair hung across his face, spittle stuck to his straggly beard, but it was the strange claws curving out from the center of the man's filthy palms that captured Ceridwen's attention. Mottled purple and crimson, growing out from beneath the skin. Like the one the priest had stabbed her with months ago, in Lochrann.

She stood still, though fury pounded within her, as Sahak pressed in close behind, peering over her shoulder. "Hmm, no? Not Liam either?"

His breath struck hot against her neck. He was so close.

Ceridwen closed her eyes, sensing, as she did with Mindar, the shift in Sahak's muscles before he moved, and she moved first. Whirling, she snapped her right hand out, not caring how the chains tugged her wounded arm in its sling, and snatched a blade from his baldric—or tried to. She moved first, but he moved faster. Her hand clasped only air. Whipping out of the way, he lashed out, flinging a knife that hissed past her cheek and clanged off the wall behind her. She ignored the sting and lunged for him, ducking under a slice from the blade that had suddenly appeared in his left hand.

Only it wasn't a blade, but a claw.

Not embedded in his hand but clenched like a knife.

THIRTY: RAFI

He who would conquer must be sly as a stone-eye,
tenacious as a python, and ferocious as a scadtha intent upon feeding.
- Nadaarian axiom

So, this was the Stone-eye's den.

Rafi stroked Ghost's nose, hoping to tame his own jitters. At the base of a rocky hillside, carpeted in thick foliage and crowned with neefwa trees, the ornate stone structure looked like it was on the verge of being consumed by the jungle. Vines clung to the walls, and from the ornamented facade on the face of the rectangular left wing, a stream poured out beneath the jaws of a portcullis and wrapped around the front, so the only entrance to the walled courtyard on the right wing lay across a wide stone bridge.

Guards in white-plumed helmets flanked the entrance, and a steady stream of priests in flowing scarlet robes moved about the courtyard behind them. It would be impossible to make that approach without being seen. Good thing being seen was a part of the plan.

"So," Rafi said, out loud this time, "this is the Stone-eye's den."

"What did you expect?" Nef asked, head tilted to keep him in view, due to the patch over his left eye.

"I don't know. Skulls over every door? Skeletons hanging on trees?"

That only earned him a grunt, which, oddly, felt reassuring coming from Nef. Nearby Moc let out a low, rumbling laugh. He sat on the tail of the closest supply cart with an arm slung around the shoulders of his younger brother, Lowen. Judging from the snatches Rafi caught—mostly Moc, whose hushed voice could be clearly heard ten feet away—the two seemed to be speculating about increasingly wild and implausible methods for sneaking into the temple. Everything from climbing the vines up and over the wall, to scaling the hillside from the back and dropping into the courtyard from a rope tied to a tree above, to stealing a priest's robes and simply strolling in.

Nef's eye twitched as he listened, and he cracked a thin smile.

Rafi shot him a curious glance. "They know we have a plan, right?"

"They're trying to figure out how I got in last time."

"You going to tell us then?" Lowen leaned forward, eyes bright. "Come on, one hint?"

"No." Resting one hand on the *chet* in his belt, Nef paced past them. "Off-load and take up positions, cousins. We have a stone-eye to beard in his own den."

Moc stared after him, shaking his head. "Sometimes, I think he enjoys this too much." He slapped the booted feet sticking out from the back of the cart. "What do you think?" He got no response, of course, from the bound and gagged men stacked like driftwood in the bed. "That's what I thought." He dropped to his feet and stretched, then turned and grabbed one set of ankles, towed the hapless man out, and slung him over one shoulder, then traipsed off into the jungle as if the burden he carried weighed nothing at all.

Lowen and the other rebels pitched in, emptying the cart of its unusual load.

Compared to the theft of a ship, not to mention its entire cargo of demon-steeds, waylaying a supply caravan en route to the temple and stealing their carts and teams of water buffalo had been easy, thanks to the entire company of rebels Umut had sent with them. Rafi had watched from the sidelines while the rebels swarmed the carts, overpowered the drivers, trussed them up, and tossed them in the back of their own carts. Stifling the churn of guilt in his stomach when Nef welcomed them to the revolution and thanked them for their service had been less easy—they were Mahque merchants after all, just trying to make a living—though not as difficult as keeping a straight face when one spat at Nef in response.

Nef did enjoy this all a bit much.

But Rafi couldn't shake the warning Umut had given him before they left. *"You do this raid, you take the fight to Sahak in this way, he will strike back hard. You must be ready for the consequences."*

"Ready, cousin?" Moc slapped the bed of the newly empty cart. One of six that they planned to use to smuggle Rafi and Sev in and the hostages out.

"Ready." Rafi patted Ghost's neck, then dropped the steed's lead into Lowen's waiting hand and turned to the cart where he came face-to-face with Sev. The fisherman pointedly looked away. "Oh." Rafi stepped back. "You going in this one? I can hop in the next—"

Gordu lumbered up, flapping a sweaty rag at them. "Get in the cart. Both of you."

"Shouldn't we split up?" Rafi suggested. "Less chance we'll both be caught?"

Gordu fixed him with a scowl. "One of you gets caught, we all get caught, so you two better stow your issues or—" He broke off, attention snared on the next cart over where Hanu knelt working on one of the wheels, then continued, sounding distracted. "Who's the smuggler here, anyway?"

Creak. Thump. The wheel fell off and wobbled on the ground.

Gordu threw up his hands. "Ches-Shu, Hanu. You were just supposed to loosen it!"

"Former smuggler," Rafi called after Gordu as he stomped over to Hanu. He cocked an eyebrow at Sev, who rolled his eyes and vaulted into the cart.

"Just net your tongue, Rafi, and get in."

It was the first thing he'd said to him in days.

Rafi gripped the side of their transport and sailed neatly up onto it, as if he were mounting Ghost. He flicked a farewell salute toward the colt, who was wholly engrossed in the cala root crackers Lowen was feeding him, and grinned when Ghost's blue eyes found him. He was still grinning as he crawled down into position beside Sev. The rebels piled sacks of rice all around them, and Moc tied down an oilcloth over the top.

Nef rapped twice on the side. "Moving out!"

But before they could lurch into motion, Aruk, who'd been on scouting duty, suddenly crashed out of the woods. "Soldiers. Soldiers coming!"

THIRTY-ONE: CERIDWEN

*A riveren ridden through arid lands will quickly become parched
and listless without a sufficient supply of water, while a seablood
traveling inland must be supplemented with salt or dried seaweed
to counteract the weakening effects of freshwater.*
- Wisdom of the Horsemasters

Ceridwen faltered, pulling up short, and Sahak's right hand shot out and seized her wounded forearm, giving a vicious wrench that dropped her to her knees. Dark spots circled over her vision, and she gasped as the claw hovered over her throat, expecting a killing or maiming blow.

Sahak's eyes were fevered and bright, his lips drawn tightly over bared teeth, but he did not strike.

"What did you do to them?" she demanded.

Without lifting his gaze, he smiled thinly and called, "Vishna, bring out the boy!" Seizing the chains on her wrists, he towed Ceridwen swiftly across the room, splashing through the shallows of half a dozen troughs, toward a man in a brightly embroidered, high-collared tunic who was dragging a limp form out of another cell and into the drainage trough out front.

The man bent over one side of the trough, then the other, then straightened as they approached. Puffing slightly, he used a silk rag to wipe the sheen of sweat from his shaved skull, drawing Ceridwen's eye to the swirl of gold markings that wrapped over his crown and dipped down onto his forehead. If the beaded sleeves of his robe hadn't covered his arms, she expected she'd find markings there too. He was a Canthorian and a scholar of high order.

"Vishna," Sahak said, coming up alongside the shorter man. He stood only a head taller but still towered over the scholar, who was rounding in the middle and walked with his head and shoulders stooped forward. "Is everything prepared?"

"Y-yes, I believe so." Vishna spoke Nadaarian with a harsh accent. He tugged out a wax tablet and stylus from a pouch at his belt, then stepped back, allowing Ceridwen to finally see into the trough.

Liam lay on his back in a shallow pool of water, hair floating around his head, eyes closed as if he were sleeping. With the cascade over his cell turned off, it was rapidly draining. Someone had replaced the splint and bandages on his leg, though the cloths were once again soiled with stains, and his cheeks looked gaunt, his fluttering eyelids almost translucent. Chains ran from his wrists to rings on the sides.

She took an involuntary step forward, and Sahak yanked her back, slamming her up against the column beside the open cell. Pressing the claw to her throat, he unlocked the shackle from her wounded wrist and fastened it instead to an iron ring set in the stone.

He left the shackle on her right, leaving her bound to the wall.

"Vishna?" he called over his shoulder.

"Still nothing." Vishna sounded disappointed. "No response whatsoever."

Ceridwen couldn't keep her confusion from showing. Response from whom? Liam? Slowly, Sahak moved back but stopped within her reach—if she lunged to the end of the chain and drew her left arm from its sling. He was baiting her again. His next words made that clear. "Tell me, Ceridwen tal Desmond, do you feel powerless?"

She raised her chin. "No. What do you want from me?"

"Your death, eventually. Maybe. Remains to be seen. But first, I would know of your bond with your steed. Your life has been threatened several times without sparking any reaction. Clearly you cannot communicate across a distance. So how can you control him?"

Ceridwen blinked, struggling to comprehend. "Control?"

"Your power. What binds you two together? Makes you who you are?"

"We . . . simply are."

"Don't lie to me."

Slowly, it dawned on her. He wished to know of the sol-breath. But she could not speak to him of that. It was a mystery too beautiful, too sacred to her people to betray. Nor would it aid him if she did. "Only a Soldonian can—"

"You're lying." He paced before her, fidgeting with the claw in his hand. "You Soldonians claim that only you can bond your deadly beasts, but I know a bid to grasp power when I see it. And I have seen it." Fervor tinged his voice. "I have seen a man of Nadaar ride a sea-demon with my own eyes, so don't tell me it isn't possible. Just tell me how."

"Or what? You'll kill me?"

She knew it was a mistake as soon as the words left her lips.

Sahak's smile was a gaping wound, his voice a drawn blade. "Or your friend will join those you saw in the cells." He seemed to savor the horror that flooded her eyes. "Oh, it's not an exact art, I'll grant you, so there's no telling what might become of him." He reached past her, snatching a torch from the wall. "So, she who rides the fire-demon, will you tell me, what did you become?"

She did not flinch as he lowered the flame toward her face.

She was a firerider. She did not fear flame. She had ventured on foot into the crater of Koltar, tamed a wildborn, and summoned a *firestorm* in the midst of her foes. With the sol-breath, she was more resilient to heat, less susceptible to smoke or flame.

But she was not invincible. Even upon Mindar, she was not.

She had broken before, bled before, burned before. With the torch throwing up a violent flare that licked hungrily at her skin, with the reek of singed hair suddenly all she could smell, with that grasping, vibrant glow consuming her vision, suddenly she crouched on the crater's rim with Bair in her arms, and she watched him die again.

She kicked out blindly, and the torch dropped from Sahak's hand, clattered across the damp stone, and extinguished itself with a hiss. Gasping, she folded over her knees, each breath pinching in her lungs, as if the torch had consumed all the oxygen in the room.

She couldn't seem to get enough air.

Sahak rounded on her, face a mask of fury, then stalked toward Liam.

"No. No!" Ceridwen pushed herself upright and lunged to the end of the chain. "I'll tell you what you want to know, I swear it. Oh, *blazes*, no. No!" Her voice died as Sahak leaped into the trough and crouched over Liam, fingering the claw in his hand.

Oh, Aodh, please, no.

It sprang from the very depths of her being, a wild, desperate prayer.

Shouts echoed suddenly down nearby corridors, armored footsteps clattered, and a gong crashed outside the enormous double doors. Sahak paused, expression sharp, then annoyed. He drew back his arm to strike, only to be halted by a resounding thud that rattled the doors against their hinges.

"Open up in the name of Murloch," a muffled voice called out beyond the doors, "and of His Imperial Majesty Emperor Lykier, who sits enthroned upon the Center of the World."

"Silent One Alive," Sahak cursed beneath his breath. "Now?"

But slipping the claw back into his baldric, he stood, straightened the sleeves of his tunic with a flick of his wrists, then motioned his guards to open the door. It groaned wide, and soldiers in the scarlet and crimson of Nadaar flooded inside, forming up on either side of the entrance. Someone lingered behind them on the threshold.

Sahak stepped up to the edge of the canal. "Oh, hello, *Father.*"

THIRTY-TWO: RAFI

Of all things fanged, spined, and barbed in the central territories of Nadaar,
the most toxic are these: the specter jellyfish, the scythro scorpion,
the crimson sea urchin, and the spines of the saga tree.
- Teaching of the Que tribes

Once, when Rafi was ten, his uncle, then commander of his father's charioteers, had taken him for a ride in his massive war-chariot. Gilded fore and aft, the four-wheeled platform was drawn by a team of four rare, blood-red stone-eye tigers, and it far outweighed and overshadowed the lighter, two-wheeled, single-tiger chariots Nadaari typically used in war.

"But it's not as fast, is it, uncle?" he'd asked.

"Speed isn't everything, Rafi. Sometimes the spectacle matters more."

Standing braced against the curved front with his uncle's hand on his forearms to guide him, Rafi had taken the reins and felt the restrained power surging through those mighty beasts and through the rumble of those iron-shod wheels. He'd laughed at the sheer joy of it, and his uncle had ruffled his hair and claimed he'd make a fine charioteer someday. Three weeks later, his family sickened mysteriously and died, and before their bodies were even sealed in the tomb, Lykier ascended to the throne, while Rafi and Delmar descended to the dungeons.

Rafi had not seen him since. Until now.

Staring at the temple courtyard into which that same gilded, four-wheeled chariot had disappeared, followed by fifteen smaller chariots and a full contingent of imperial guards, marching under the streamered scarlet-and-orange flag of Nadaar and snarling stone-eye sigil of House Korringar, Rafi felt like he'd taken a blow to the gut.

"Was that who I thought it was?" Moc jogged up with a spear on his shoulder. He was supposed to be directing the other rebels to assume offensive positions around the temple, so they could launch a feint attack if anything went wrong. Of course, nothing was supposed to go wrong before they got inside, let alone before they even tried.

"Ches-Shu," Hanu cursed from his driving perch.

"The Sisters Three conspire against us," Gordu muttered from the front of the cart that Rafi and Sev had been hidden in before they crawled out to watch their plans falling apart.

Sev rounded on him. "Why is he here, Rafi?"

He licked his dry lips. "I don't know. We don't exactly speak regularly."

"So what do we do now?" Aruk asked. "We're doomed, aren't we? I mean, there's no way we can sneak into a temple guarded by both royal and imperial guards, is there?"

Both royal and imperial guards . . . both . . .

Rafi scrambled up to stand on the driver's perch, ignoring Gordu's grumbling, where he could glimpse the gold-plumed helmets of the imperial guards now flanking the entrance alongside the white-plumed royal guards. "Actually, that's the only way this works." He looked down to find confused faces staring up at him. "My brother and I—"

"What brother? You have a brother?" Moc asked.

"Yes. He was the . . . crown prince."

It hurt to know that the world had forgotten Delmar so quickly.

It hurt to know that he'd tried to forget him, too, only to fail, as in so much else.

But he couldn't face that hurt right now, so he let it slick off him like water off a sea-demon's coat. "We both had guards. His were imperial, mine were royal, and sometimes, we'd use them against each other—tell one group one thing, the other something else, so we could be free to do whatever we wanted."

Nef coughed. "If the point's that you're an entitled Tetrani, we knew that already."

"My point is that we have two groups here with separate commanders and orders, not to mention a temple filled with people who aren't typically there. If we wanted a chance to move around unnoticed, we couldn't have asked for a better setup." Granted, he was probably stretching the truth a bit, but Gordu just grunted, Sev looked relieved, and Moc nodded.

"Besides," Rafi added, "we've already stolen the carts. If we don't go through with this, Sahak will find out, and the hostages will pay for it. It's now or never."

Aruk raised an eyebrow. "You can't think that'll actually work?"

Nef smiled grimly. "There's only one way to see. Let's move out."

Only once Rafi was again concealed beneath rice sacks and oilcloth as the carts rattled forward, carrying them toward either victory or certain death, did he allow himself to consider the knot of panic he felt at creeping closer, step by step, not only to his cousin, the murderer of his brother, but to his uncle, who was responsible for the death of his entire family.

"You never mentioned your brother before," Sev said, the creaking of the wheels drowning out any nuance of feeling or tone.

The cart abruptly tossed them together then jostled them apart.

"He died years ago," Rafi said, bracing himself. "Sahak killed him. Maybe I don't understand what you're going through, Sev. Not fully. But I have a better chance of guessing than most."

Loud, phlegmy coughing from Gordu warned them into silence as the cart rumbled over an uneven stone surface—the bridge, already?— and lurched to a halt. Up the line, an imperious voice demanded to know their business, and old Hanu, who drove the first cart, shouted back.

Rafi blinked trickling sweat from his eyes. Here, Gordu's smuggling wisdom would be put to the test. Gordu had suggested the order of the carts and drivers, slotting two burly rebels at the back to provide muscle if needed; Aruk next, because the man tended to fidget and scratch his neck suspiciously when nervous; then their cart third in line; Nef, wearing Hanu's floppy hat to shield his face, going second because he knew the way; while Hanu went first, because, in Gordu's words, "Two seconds of dealing with his nonsense, and they'll wave us through just to be rid of him. There's nothing so infuriating as incompetency."

To which, old Hanu had just chuckled, "Oh, go on, you old crab."

Rafi squirmed forward on his stomach and pried two sacks apart just enough that he could see what was happening over the swishing tails of the water buffalo. Hanu gestured as he argued with a tall and imposing soldier—made all the more tall and imposing by the height of his gold plume.

Other imperial guards were inspecting the carts, searching underneath, prodding the contents with their spears, even destroying several innocent rice sacks, which was a shameful waste of good food. Of course, Rafi noted, as the soldiers moved on from harassing Nef, there would be an equally shameful waste of good blood if he or Sev got skewered as well. But Gordu saved them by bursting into a fit of hacking coughs so severe the entire cart shook, and the soldiers shot him disgusted looks as they veered wide, giving his load only a cursory glance before moving on to Aruk. So the old smuggler did know some tricks after all.

What about some royal guards now, to balance out the equation?

Nef dropped from his cart, floppy hat tugged low, and appealed to the knot of white-plumed soldiers standing off to the side. Whatever he said caused one of the guards to disappear within the temple complex and return with a young man in a large apron, who walked with an odd, somewhat hesitant, somewhat loping step. He flung up his hands as if in exasperation when he saw Nef, and together all three approached the lead imperial guard, but Rafi didn't see what happened next because Sev elbowed him aside so he could take a look.

Gordu coughed violently again, then snapped his reed, prodding the water buffalo until the cart clattered forward. Only a short distance, then it swung around and backed up a few steps. It shook as Gordu climbed down. "Don't move," he warned in a low voice, which of course only made Rafi that much more desperate to break free of the cramped space, prickling with sweat and dust and the restless energy arcing across his skin.

It seemed an age before the sacks shifted overhead, and Rafi sucked in fresh air.

They crawled clumsily out, joints stiff and limbs tangled, and landed sprawling on a carpet of damp leaf litter. Gordu scowled down at them. Shaking his head, he motioned for them to hide behind the cart, which had rounded the right corner of the temple and backed close to an open doorway with barrels stacked on one side and empty crates on the other. Monkeys gamboled over the tiled roof and chickens scratched in the dirt. Tossing them each a sack, Gordu waved them toward the doorway. "Stick to the wall, and you'll be sheltered from view in the courtyard. May Ches-Shu smile on us all."

Sev clutched his sack to his chest, and Rafi slung his over his shoulder just in time to conceal his face from the imperial soldier who rounded the corner. He hurried on into the sweltering warmth of the kitchen as Gordu intercepted the man. A moment later, the elder's bellowing shouts rang out, urging the drivers to unload. Rafi stopped alongside Sev in front of three enormous stone ovens. Nef stood off to their left, facing the aproned cook who was stooped under a low, arched doorway at the top of a set of steps that descended into a storage cellar.

"What took so long?" the cook demanded, sweat beading on his high forehead. He looked as young as Lowen, but there was a hard glint in his eye. "We should have had an hour before the others showed up for supper preparations, but you're late. And on top of that the emperor and a hundred of his guards dropped in, and who knows what that means, but if we have to cook for all of them . . ." Catching sight of Rafi and Sev, he broke off his rant to point down the stairs with the lidded jar in his hands. "Sacks on the right, stacked according to content. Crates on the left. Barrels go all the way to the back, and don't spill anything, or we'll be overrun by rats as big as—"

"We'll pass it along," Nef said. "These two come with us."

"But . . ." The cook faltered. "You can't mean to go on."

Nef nodded, and Rafi and Sev deposited their sacks on the floor. A thin trickle of rice dribbled from one corner of Rafi's sack, but he nudged it under with his toe. The cook ducked past them, shaking one hand. "Didn't you hear me? The emperor of Nadaar is here. We lost our chance. You press on, we'll lose more than that." He plunked the jar down on a table and pivoted to face them. "I can't risk my neck any more than I—"

His gaze landed on Rafi, and his eyes widened. "You."

"Me?" Rafi pointed to himself, questioningly. "Do I know you?"

"His name is Iska, and he was a soldier." Nef nearly spat the word.

"Until he crossed the wrong person—which, I'll add, he's in danger of doing again—and got assigned here."

So, that was how Nef had gotten in before. He'd made a contact on the inside. Somehow, Rafi couldn't help thinking that Moc and Lowen would be disappointed to discover the truth was far less elaborate than their theories.

"Sure." The cook flung up his hands. "Tell them my name. Why not shout it from the roof while you're at it?" He hurried over to the cellar to direct Aruk and the other drivers as they tramped in, carrying the offload from the carts.

Outside, something crashed against stone, and Hanu's shouts rang out, sounding convincingly annoyed.

Gordu poked his bald head in and scowled at them. "Why are you still here? Guard's getting leery. Old Hanu's buying time with that cart wheel, but you'd best hurry."

Nef reached for the bone-handled knife in his belt, and Iska's eyes widened.

Suddenly, a knot untangled itself in Rafi's mind and he recognized the cook. "Hold on." He caught Nef's wrist, raising his voice to carry. "Iska's been far too much help to us for that. He's the one who told Sahak about the ship when I was being tortured. Without him, we wouldn't have been able to steal it or the steeds. Can you believe all he got for that was kitchen duty?"

"Lucky he didn't take your place," Nef said grimly.

Rafi eyed Iska. "You think that luck will hold once Sahak finds out who vouched for us today? I mean, the odds we'll get caught get worse the longer we're here, and we're not leaving without our friends."

"No." Sev cracked his knuckles. "Not budging."

"Fine." Iska mopped the sweat from his face. "Fine." He sprang into a frenzy of motion, shoving a giant bowl of rice at Sev, a pair of water buckets at Nef, and a tray at Rafi. "But you have to follow my lead, and we have to do this quietly."

Rafi saw Nef's grip tighten on his knife. "Sure. Quietly."

The soldier toppled like a felled tree, crashing onto his back, and Nef rode him down, clinging to the knife buried in the slit in his helm. The clatter of his armored fall resounded in the corridor while Rafi collapsed, his back against the wall, and kicked free of the suddenly limp weight of a second guard, who'd been strangling him, quite successfully, only moments before. He looked up to find Sev standing over him, gripping the broken halves of the bowl, which he'd apparently used to brain the guard, scattering rice everywhere. Sev tossed the shards aside and hauled Rafi unsteadily to his feet beside Iska, who clutched a bleeding head wound, wide-eyed with shock.

"What happened to quietly?" Iska moaned.

Nef happened, that's what. No sooner had they been challenged by the soldiers guarding the cells than he'd gone strangely wooden, which had, of course, raised first suspicion and then alarm when he suddenly lashed out without warning. Brushing rice from his clothes, Rafi watched out of the corner of his eye as Nef retrieved his blade and wiped it on his pants, then tried twice to sheathe it, before succeeding and flexing his shaking hand.

Working quickly, Nef removed the soldier's armor, piling pieces beside him. "You could stop talking," he growled, without looking up. "That would be quiet."

"Keys!" Sev rose from patting down the other soldier and jangled a large key ring. He hurried down the cramped, dark passage, checking side to side and picking up speed with each cell he passed. Cries broke out, and he rushed to grasp the waving hands suddenly reaching through the bars on the left side. "They're here!"

Rafi started after him, but a grunt from Nef stopped him. "Take that one." Nef nodded toward the other soldier. "Toss him in once you get them out."

Sev was still fumbling with the keys in the lock when Rafi dragged the unconscious guard over to the cell and deposited him before the crowd of familiar faces. Rafi clasped hands and traded grins and whispered encouragement and felt his chest swell with something that ached and sang at the same time.

"I'm getting all of you out of here," Sev promised, shoving another key in.

It clicked and turned, and Rafi breathed out a silent thanks. He hauled the door open, releasing the fisherfolk in a flood that swept past Sev into the hallway only to stall at the sight of Nef in Nadaarian armor dragging the body of a guard toward them. But with that taste of freedom, the villagers seemed to discover that they were fierce. They recoiled at the sight, but it was the coiling of a sea-demon rearing to strike.

"It's all right." Sev stepped out in front before they could rush Nef. "He's with us!"

Dropping the guard's legs, Nef straightened and silenced the villager's objections with a look, then motioned for them to follow. With Iska scouting each cross passage ahead, signaling when to move, they would make their way back to the kitchens. Rafi hung back, dragging first one guard, then the other, into the vacated cell, then locked it and ran after the others, eager to bid farewell to this wretched place for good.

An incredulous voice stopped him. "Rafi?"

It came from a cell to his right, from a lanky man with curly brown hair and eyes pale as sand. The man clutched the bars, thin face swollen and streaked with dried blood and bruises. "Oh, Aodh be praised! It's me," he added, drawing back his filthy hands and wiping them on his equally filthy tunic. "Yath Ha'Nor? You probably don't remember—"

It was that simple, unconscious gesture that rooted him in Rafi's mind.

This was the Eliamite informant that Rafi had helped rescue on his first real raid as a rebel. His first time to wield a spear in combat, to shout the Tetrani war cry in battle too. His first step to becoming who he was today.

"Yath? What are you doing here?"

Yath dabbed at a seeping cut above his right eyebrow and sagged against the bars. "Not nearly as much as I would be away from here." He gave an ironic smile that only accentuated his air of weariness. "Care to set me loose again?"

Seconds later, they were hurrying down the passage together, Rafi half supporting, half dragging Yath, who seemed barely able to stand. The sounds of strife greeted them as they neared the kitchens. Sharp voices. The *crack* of a fist on flesh.

Someone thudding to the floor.

Rafi shoved through the villagers waiting to be ushered out to the carts, where they would be concealed between stacks of empty barrels and crates, to the knot that had formed before the door. Shouldering into the center, he found Nef hauling Sev away from Iska, who lay on his back, lip bleeding.

"Go on," Rafi told the villagers. "Keep moving."

Hanu and Gordu could only attempt to "fix" the broken wheel for so long before the distraction became suspicious. And they needed to have everyone loaded before any more guards decided to investigate. Passing Yath off to Aruk, he seized Iska and dragged him over to the corner where Nef was still restraining Sev.

"What happened?"

Sev spoke through gritted teeth. "She's not here, Rafi. She's not here, and he knew it. Ches-Shu, he knew Sahak had locked her somewhere else, and he said nothing!"

It was rare that Rafi felt true anger, boiling and pulsing like a fever in his veins. He had felt it on the beach when Cortovah threatened Iakki, and he had felt it in the days after Delmar died, and he felt it now, as he rounded upon the cringing cook, felt it with such starkness that he was thankful he did not hold a spear in his hands.

Nef released Sev, who once more raised his fists, causing Iska to flinch in Rafi's grip. "Why," Nef grated out, "didn't you tell us before?"

"Because . . ." Iska swallowed, eyes darting between them. "Because it's no use. Because there's no getting in where he took her, let alone getting out, not now that the emperor and his guards are there too. Because I knew you'd refuse to listen to reason, so I—"

"Reason?" Sev caught the front of his tunic and yanked him close. "Reason be drowned, and the emperor, too, and you along with him. I just want my wife. Where is she?"

"In the heart of the temple," Iska gasped out. "Where the purification waters flow."

Rafi felt the ebb and shift of tides falling into place within him and without. "You mean the wing on the left with the canal pouring out of it?" Ches-Shu. He turned to Sev. "I know how we can get in. I know how we can save her. But we'll need a distraction."

THIRTY-THREE: CERIDWEN

To all fireriders, let Turgin the Brash give warning, for when his wrath
burned fierce and his wildborn even fiercer, he mastered neither
and was taken by flame, and his steed with him.
– Soldonian lore

Emperor Lykier strode into the temple, a massive stone-eye sauntering at his heels. Sovereign ruler of Nadaar, conqueror of nations, invader of kingdoms, he left no bloodstained footprints behind him, bore no fume or cloud of death upon him, and yet this man was responsible for the deaths of thousands of her people. Watching him stroll past soldiers who pressed their spears against their chests and bowed as one, Ceridwen longed to burn as she had never burned before, to unleash an inferno that would reduce the rock of this temple to molten slag and the bones of those within it to ash.

Even if it meant she'd burn too.

She let that feeling banish the chill in her bones, as the emperor, trailed by his tiger and a phalanx of guards, scaled the steps cut into the mountainlike structure, crossed behind the waterfall, and halted a short distance from his son. Over a tunic of gleaming gold that strained across his barrel-like chest, the wide, armored belt that curved up over his ribs gave him a martial appearance. Its embossed sigil of a snarling tiger was repeated on the gilded vambraces fastened to his forearms and the clasp of the rust-orange cloak that draped from his left shoulder, wrapped around his arm, and trailed at his heels.

His back toward her, Sahak remained unbowed, an arrogant slouch to his shoulders, a casual threat in the hand he rested on his daggers.

"You've come such a long way, Father, to show up unannounced. To what do I owe the honor of this visit?"

"You should know. You have been trying very hard to get my attention."

"Your attention? Honestly, Father, you hardly ever cross my mind."

"Is that so?" The emperor's voice bore a distinctive rasp. He stood a head taller than his son and had a burly, thickset neck that reminded Ceridwen of an earthhewn. "So claiming for yourself the barbarian queen of the nation with which we are currently at war, rather than yielding her to the court, was . . ."

"Certainly not a ploy to draw you out here." Sahak sounded amused. "Silent One Alive, you make it sound as though I planned to—how do the Alonque put it—net her? Why, Father? Concerned about Soldonian blood tainting the royal line? Or no, I forgot that's not a concern—or perhaps I should say I'm not—now that Mallell is carrying your heir."

"So you have heard the tidings."

"Why? Did you come all this way to tell me yourself? How touching." Mockery dripped from Sahak's tongue. "What do I care that your wife is with child? Or that you would pledge me to a Canthorian widow twice my years without my consent? Yes, I've heard that too."

"She is a high princess of the court, and her station is—"

"Higher than mine, yes, I know, and whose fault is that? But as I said, what do I care about your paltry political maneuvering? I have aims such that you have never dared dream of, Father. You or your tamed priests," he added as a man in fluttering robes, ornate gold headset, and chains that draped in long loops from neck to wrists stepped up beside the emperor. So tall, that although the emperor stood a head taller than his son, this priest stood head and shoulders over the emperor, and so thin that everything about him seemed sort of stretched, from his gait to his limbs to his features.

"Sahak," the priest said dryly. "Still profane as ever."

Sahak spread his arms expressively. "Abheer, you've noticed."

"That you no longer wear the robes of our order, yes. But what are robes if not an outward expression of devotion? You abandoned that long ago when you stole holy relics from the temple archive in Cetmur—"

"You mean as the priests abandoned the religion of Old Nadaar?"

Abheer raised his chin. "Those pagan heresies ended with the rise of Murloch."

"No, they ended after the days of ravaging, when the priests became a weak and failing order, driven to bury mysteries they did not understand. I look to the glory day of the past, when Nadaar was not ruled by emperors but god kings." Sahak smiled as the priest abruptly stilled, and added, "I found more than dusty relics in the archive."

For an instant, the priest seemed as taut as a drawn bowstring.

Then he shook his head. "Was it not enough for you to claim the title of high priest unearned? Must you also pervert our traditions and desecrate the temple of our master while he slumbers by twisting it to your own ends? How long do you think the Silent One will suffer you?"

"Oh, but he is not the Silent One to me. He speaks."

Abheer's smile bore the oily gleam of condescension, his eyes the yellow flecks that marked one of Choth heritage. "And has he spoken to you of the discarded cutting now taking root in the jungle? Of the threat that festers deep within the soil of our empire? Pulsing like a soured wound, sending poison out into the bloodstream."

Sahak went still. "The Voice did not tell you that."

"No, the Voice did not tell *you* that. Because you already knew."

"You do not deny it?" The emperor studied his son. "You knew my brother's son still lived, still conspired against me, and said nothing?"

"You know me, Father, I aim to disappoint."

With an abrupt flick of his hand, the emperor sent his tiger bounding past Sahak toward Ceridwen. The chain cutting into her right wrist was still stretched taut after her futile attempts to break free, and she eased back, regaining room to maneuver. Not that it would help against the massive beast tearing toward her, muscles rippling over its broad chest, enormous paws extended, teeth bared in its gaping jaw, and its eyes—

Shades, it wore no blinders.

She tried to look away, but it was too late. Creeping paralysis encased her spine in stone and claimed her senses one by one. Hearing went last, narrowing until the only sound in her ears was that of the creature's throaty breaths. She gave herself up for lost, until the sharp crack of the emperor's voice broke through, and all her senses returned in a dizzying rush.

Or almost all. She could hear, feel, see again, but she could not move, and a haze of yellow still clouded one eye. With the other, she could make out the tiger crouched before her, ears flat against its skull, tail twitching, and the emperor standing at its side. So close she could make out the leathery texture to the man's weathered skin, see the ridge where his nose had once been broken, and the calculating glint in the pale, hazel eyes he shared with his son.

So close, she could grasp him by the throat if she were not immobilized.

"So, this is she who rides the fireborn," the emperor murmured.

His gaze raked her from head to toe while a rumbling growl emanated from the tiger. Compared to the unsettling air of restrained strength, coiled quickness, and volatility that Sahak exuded, such a transparent threat awakened only anger in her. Though she strained against the tiger's hold, she could not break free, and when the emperor spoke, it was not to her. "You sabotage my efforts, seek to thwart me at every turn, and scheme ever to your own ends, which leaves me to wonder whether the festering threat the Voice spoke of is my brother's son or my own."

"Oh, but you have no son. At least, that's what you've been telling me, over and over, these past twenty-odd years. Unless, of course, you're finally feeling guilty about it. Could that be why you wish to ship me off to the Canthorian court?"

"Do not taunt me. I am your emperor."

Sahak laughed quietly, dangerously. "Considering how I killed the last one, I'm not sure what I'm supposed to take from that."

With a swift clatter of footsteps, soldiers and spears formed a bristling ring around him.

The emperor strode back to face him, leaving his tiger to menace Ceridwen. "Only this: whatever forces you think you have converted to your own ends, I have countless more. Should you wish to survive to scheme against me another day, you will deliver the barbarian queen over to me, and then you will hunt down my brother's son and bring me his bones. Or I will raze this temple right now, burying you and your high and lofty goals—"

A sudden rumbling overtook his words.

Ceridwen inwardly braced herself for the tiger to lunge, but then she felt the ground shuddering beneath her feet, saw the ripples spreading across the stream. That, incomprehensible as it seemed, was the aftereffect of an earthhewn strike. There was a crash beyond the cavern, and shouts echoed down distant halls.

"What was that?" the emperor demanded.

"That would be him now, I think. Still want to claim his bones?"

The tension in the air ignited. Commands and controlled chaos erupted across the cavernous room. Within moments, the contingent of imperial guards was marching out, escorting the emperor and his priest, while his tiger bounded after.

Without the beast's stare to hold her upright, Ceridwen collapsed to her knees. Shivering, spent, and struggling to lift her head. She could feel the cold of oblivion creeping over her, and something inside her reeled away from its approach, and something inside her didn't.

Something inside her longed for that numbness. For relief.

She watched through the matted hair falling across her face as Sahak stepped up to the edge of the canal, looking after his father. Hands twitching at his sides until those massive, ponderous doors scraped shut, then he turned slowly to meet her eyes. She watched as he dragged the claw from his baldric and stalked over to Liam, then plunged it into the boy's side. She watched, and she did nothing as Sahak straightened with a savage grin, then turned and walked unsteadily out, the temple emptying behind him, and she felt the last embers of whoever she had once been flicker inside her and die.

THIRTY-FOUR: RAFI & CERIDWEN

The man pinned beneath a stone-eye is close enough to stab out its eyes.
- Choth adage

Another tremor shook the surface of the water over Rafi's head. He sat motionless atop Ghost, who braced against the current, hooves buried in the silt that coated the canal floor. Widening ripples distorted the image of Sev, looking down to wave the all clear.

Squeezing Ghost's ribs with his calves, Rafi shot for the surface and slowed just before breaching, so both the colt's head and his emerged without a splash. Seamless, just like their exit from the temple complex with the hostages. The wagons had rolled out without a hitch, waved on by guards who were far more concerned about potential threats entering than leaving, which had freed him and Sev to embark on their second infiltration of the day. This time, smuggled in like barnacles on a boat hull, with Ghost, of course, playing the role of the boat.

He slid Ghost alongside Sev, who crouched on the brink, nerves or maybe the strain making his right leg shake. What with working their way upstream from outside the temple complex, diving beneath the portcullis to enter the left wing, and then creeping slowly along the bottom of the canal to avoid being seen while waiting for Nef and Iska to unleash Sahak's captured earthhewn as their distraction, and for his murderous uncle and cousin and all their combined guards to take the bait, they had been submerged much longer than Rafi had expected. His strange new capacity meant he wasn't even winded, but Sev had nearly been forced to rise before the coast was clear.

Sev, however, was nothing if not stubborn.

He swiped his wet face. "You'll keep watch?"

"I've got you." Rafi clapped his shoulder. "Go on. She's waiting."

Sev nodded and moved off at a crouching run over the damp stone, one hand resting on the borrowed *chet* slung through his belt, the other holding the key ring.

Rafi watched his progress toward the string of waterfalls lining the wall—each one, according to Iska, concealing a cell—then realized that he was shirking his duty as lookout. He circled Ghost slowly in the center of the canal, scanning every angle of the heart of the temple. It was just as massive and impressive as Iska had described, and it made his skin crawl. It was the stretched layout of the room, so disproportionately narrow compared to its length. It was those columns marching in pairs along either side. It was the feeling that he was trapped inside them, and at any moment, they might collapse inward and cage him, like the claws of that scadtha he'd fought so many months ago. Come to think of it, the design of the temple did seem to intentionally conjure up thoughts of those amphibious monsters with their segmented plates and their dozens upon dozens of rippling leg pairs.

Scadtha were sacred in Murlochian worship, after all.

The creak of gears and the clank of ratcheting chains drove his gaze first toward the doors—still closed—and then toward Sev, who ducked warily into a cave-like opening, where moments before, there had been a waterfall.

If Ches-Shu smiled and Iska wasn't lying, Kaya would be there.

Alive, hopefully, a cynical voice added in his head.

Ghost let out a soft, inquisitive nicker which echoed strangely off the walls. Sound undoubtedly did odd things in here with so many wet surfaces to bounce off, and so many crashing tons of water to deaden it. Only when the noise repeated in a different tone and pitch did Rafi see the copper-colored steed chained in the shadow of the wall. Its neck arched proudly, while its mane and tail hung in limp snarls. It snorted, and a weak haze of steam shot up around it.

That was a fire-demon.

He hadn't thought any had escaped the wreckage of the ship, though it had been so chaotic, he might have missed one. How had Sahak caught it?

Fixated on the other steed, Ghost tossed his head and let out a squeal.

"Shh, shh," Rafi whispered, circling the colt again, trying to steer his attention away from the fire-breathing beast. "Come on, Ghost, cala root crackers, simba fruit, saga crisps—"

He drew Ghost up short, causing the colt to rear up in the water. They were not alone in the temple. She stood on the other side of the room, though he would have sworn she wasn't there before. Her garb was foreign, battered, and stained, and she looked like a strong gust of wind might blow her over, and like it would regret it if it tried. Matted hair the color of dried blood hung across her face. Only one eye was visible beneath the sweeping strands, and it was dark and empty as the sea on a moonless night, as the void that always lurked only one step before his feet in his dreams—

Ches-Shu, as Delmar's had been in the instant before he fell.

She stood and she stared and she did not sound the alarm.

It took Rafi too long to realize why. One arm in a sling across her chest, the other chained to the wall—she was a captive then, and a foreigner. Maybe, with that hair, even Soldonian.

Sev hissed his name, and Rafi started guiltily, spinning to see him on the edge of the canal, and Kaya—dear, sweet Kaya, with her curly dark hair escaping her braid and her smile that defied the tears shining on her round cheeks—was with him. If she was surprised or even horrified to see Rafi come gliding up on a sea-demon, she didn't show it. She held out both her hands. They were cold when he took them, drawing her onto Ghost behind him. Her arms gripped his waist. Her cheek pressed between his shoulder blades.

"Go on," Sev said, hand on her shoulder. "I'll be right behind you."

Kaya nodded uncertainly, and her grip tightened reflexively as Ghost moved off. Wheeling the colt around, Rafi's eyes lingered on the captive on the opposite shore. She had sunken to her knees and bowed her head, and something about her awakened a deep, unexpected sadness inside him, and an almost inexplicable sense of loss. He didn't realize what he'd decided until he'd circled Ghost back to the canal's edge and slid off the side. "Actually, Sev, don't tell Iakki, but I think you should ride up front."

Ceridwen drifted. She felt like she was always drifting these days. Slipping back into that haze of fever and despair that had enveloped her shipboard journey, not to mention most of her time in her cell. One moment, one breath, one nightmare, constantly bleeding into the next.

So when the strange searider with the curious eyes had surfaced unexpectedly in the midst of the temple, she'd been half convinced it was a dream. Less so, when he and his companions staged their escape and dove back into the stream without a trace, for surely only the waking world was so cruel as to force air back into the lungs of a drowning soul but still leave them tied to the anchor towing them down.

Life, she thought, and undoubtedly Sahak.

With a heave and a cascade of water, the searider seized the edge of the canal and flung himself up onto the shore. His sleeveless tunic was torn slightly along the seam of one shoulder, which made it hang lopsided on his neck. He twitched his arm to adjust it. Shook loose the dark hair plastered to his forehead, scattering droplets like rain. Offered a small, companionable grin as he held out a hand.

Her gaze latched onto the iron key ring he held.

There was freedom. There was revenge. It shocked her to discover how much she could still desire such things after giving herself up for dead. But if not for her own sake, then for Liam's. Rapidly, she evaluated the threat the searider posed. He was tall and lean and looked like he could run alongside a loping steed for a league or more without losing ground. But in close quarters, in sheer ferocity alone, she wagered she could take him in a fight.

Something in his expression told her that he'd seen the calculation in her eyes. "Before you finish deciding how you're going to kill me," he said in Nadaarian, "you should know that the list of things that have tried to kill me and failed is fairly long." He waved the hand with the key ring looped around his fingers, and she could see the thick, reddened scar that cut across—or rather, through—his palm.

"Also, I'm here to set you free."

Sure he was.

She called his bluff in his own tongue. "Then toss me the keys."

He shrugged and lobbed them at her, a perfect throw. She caught the ring in her chained hand and gingerly drew the sling over her head, freeing her left arm. Ignoring the dull throb of the wound, she flexed her fingers and found them oddly tingly, almost numb. She took the ring from her chained hand, tried to grip one key between her thumb and forefinger, and nearly dropped it.

"Really, I could—"

A glare silenced the searider.

Exerting all her willpower over her trembling, near useless hand, she managed to line up one key with the lock, but it wouldn't go in. Wrong one. *Blazes.*

She tried another key, and something clanked, but it wasn't the lock. It was far too loud and resonant for that. On the far side of the room, the massive doors grated open, and Sahak walked in, deep in conversation with Vishna, a handful of guards trailing behind. The searider sprang forward, and she shoved the key into his hand. With a click, the manacle sprang from her wrist, and he caught it deftly before it could clang against the stone wall.

Shaking away the sting of the abrasions on her wrist, Ceridwen scrambled over to the trough where Liam lay, still unmoving save for the labored rise and fall of his chest. She was reaching for the chains, about to demand the key, when the searider suddenly grabbed her shoulders and hauled her to the floor.

"Get down!" His hissed warning kept her from resisting as they rolled into the trench and broke apart. She landed with her face inches from Liam's hand, while the searider crashed onto his back on Liam's chest. He lifted his head, pressed the heel of his palm to his temple, and only then seemed to notice that the trough was already occupied. "Is he dead? He looks dead."

"He's not." Or he hadn't been. "Get his chains off."

Levering himself up with one arm, the searider attacked the shackles on Liam's wrist. "We need to get out of here. Sahak's coming back this way, and I've had my fill of being used for target practice—"

"Not without Liam."

"Ah, so he's Liam, I'm Rafi, and you"—there was a soft *clank*, and he shifted to look down at her—"know how to swim, I hope?" He nodded past her down the drain to the canal.

So they would be leaving the same way he had come.

With a grunt, he shoved Liam ahead of him, and she backed down the angled trough, crawling with her bad arm, and dragging Liam by the foot with the other. Working together, they managed to move the boy a couple inches at a time, until the water slopped over her legs, then her midsection, and then she slipped fully into the canal. She swung out to the side and managed to guide Liam's limp form in as well, so the stream cocooned him and he didn't make a splash. The searider—Rafi, was it?—slid in after them, tucked into a flip underwater, and surfaced smoothly alongside.

Sahak's voice suddenly cracked off the walls, and Ceridwen knew that he had discovered her absence. Booted feet pounded into the room in response and began spreading out in all directions.

They were coming. Searching.

She thought of Mindar still chained on the opposite bank and dashed aside the pang she felt at escaping without him. They had endured so much together. But she had to save Liam first. That much, and so much more, she owed to him, and to Iona. She inhaled a deep breath, readying for the plunge, but Rafi raised a finger, signaling her to wait. Pinching Liam's nostrils closed, he blew a long, steady stream into his lungs, then motioned for her to shield the lad's nose and mouth. So she held Liam, and Rafi held her, and, diving, towed them both down.

Onrushing water enveloped her, and with the sensation of being dragged outside of her own control, came a surreal disorientation. She had dreamed so often of drowning. Now, it seemed, she would. Or was. Or maybe already had. Her muscles seized involuntarily. Her chest constricted and specks of blackness swirled across her vision.

Only her grip on Liam grounded her in reality, for she would not fail him.

She could not. That thought beat a steadying refrain in her chest, strengthening her to withstand the instinct that would send her thrashing and clawing back to the surface. They slowed, abruptly, floating over the murky streambed, and out of the greenish haze before them emerged the seablood. Slivers of refracted light glimmered off the scales spattered across the creature's crested neck and broad chest as it drew up before Rafi, stretched out its delicate head, and nuzzled, then nipped, playfully, at the searider's hand.

Just then, a shout rang out directly above them. Even though Ceridwen's hearing felt strangely distorted and muffled by the pressure of the water, she could make out the words. "Here! In the canal!"

Spears pierced the water—a foolish attack, for the current stole their force before the weapons even penetrated to a depth of their own length—but they were already speeding away on the seablood, Rafi in front, she in the back, and Liam crammed between them. So long as they were submerged and floating, the colt could carry far more than if they were running on dry land. With her legs wrapped around the colt's sides, her muscles singing as she moved in stride, she could almost forget the burn of stale air in her lungs, could almost ignore the cold prickling at the tips of her fingers.

Bright light slanted down through an opening ahead.

It was shielded by an iron grate of a portcullis that extended beneath the surface, but it was raised just enough that they could pass beneath. Beyond it, broad daylight and an endless expanse of sky. Ceridwen gripped Liam tighter, leaning in and using every trick of muscle and balance that she had learned to convey her urgency to this strange steed, and she felt its speed increase.

They were only five horse lengths away. Then four. Three.

Rumbling vibrations shook the canal and the portcullis slammed shut.

THIRTY-FIVE: RAFI & CERIDWEN

Of all predators in the central territories of Nadaar, the deadliest are these:
the sacred scadtha, the devouring python, the howling spider
which hunts in packs, the ravenous stone-eye tiger,
and the insatiable emperor upon his voracious throne.
- Teaching of the Que tribes

Ghost skidded to a stop before the massive, rusted iron grate, and Rafi braced against his withers to keep from hurtling over his head. Motes of soil and grass particles stirred by their approach drifted lazily beyond, and he wanted to shove his hands through the squares of the grate and grasp hold of the freedom that lay just beyond his reach.

So close. Always so, so close. But never close enough.

Rafi thudded his forehead against the colt's upraised neck and stifled a groan.

At least Sev and Kaya were out. Ghost's return told him that.

Sending them off alone on the colt had felt like a risk. But he'd dived with them to the bottom of the canal where they would have a straight shot out, then told Sev how to resurface once they made it past the portcullis. No sooner had he somersaulted into the canal than he'd started whistling to recall the colt and Ghost had come. And now they were both caught.

A heavy, metallic sound groaned through the water then, and Rafi felt a brief stab of hope that the portcullis might be lifting, that there might be a way out. He sensed the woman shifting to look over her shoulder and felt her tense.

The churning darkness at the inward end of the canal seemed to rip open, as if shredded by the claws of the massive creature that boiled out through the waterfall. The creature reared up like a snake, horned head tipped back, exposing twin mandibles and venomous pincers poised above the clacking, waving, clawed leg-pairs that lined each plate of its segmented form.

Of course Sahak kept a scadtha trapped in his temple.

Of course he would unleash it now.

Run, brother, echoed that tiresome, old refrain in Rafi's head as the scadtha slithered toward them with a speed that defied reason, body weaving from side to side, propelled by legs that undulated with an almost mesmeric effect.

Urgency radiated from the woman as she tightened her hold on the unconscious Liam. She hadn't flinched from the sea-demon, hadn't hesitated before springing onto his back, but from the revulsion and shock he saw in her profile now, he doubted she'd ever seen a scadtha before. Maybe she actually was from Soldonia.

He spun Ghost to face the monster, then looked back. "Go," he mouthed. He could have sworn she was about to fight him on it. "Get him out of here."

Mentioning Liam did the trick.

She shoved off the colt and struggled toward the surface with the boy. There, they would doubtless be slain or retaken. That might be preferable to being eaten by a scadtha, but it was what Sahak wanted, and Rafi ranked that as agony worse than a scadtha's bite.

So Rafi charged straight toward the monster instead.

Toward a sheen of metal he saw drifting in the water beyond.

The scadtha veered and flowed up onto the side of the canal where it skittered toward him along the wall. Submerged, this creature wasn't bound to the ordinary rules Rafi had known all his life. Then again, neither was he.

It launched itself at him, pincers extended, and Rafi twisted Ghost into a spin. They shot up and over its segmented neck, evaded one of its impossible flips, and wove away in a dizzying set of spirals as its clawed legs punched the stone where they'd been an instant before. It struck again and again and again. It got closer each time, twisting and coiling and striking with a blinding speed that rivaled Ghost's uncanny skill for channeling his own currents.

That skill alone kept them alive, adding an extra thrust to every leap, allowing them to cut in and out of twists and spins without drift or drag.

Until an upward dodge finally brought Rafi in reach of the spear he'd spotted floating, tip downward, its haft gradually drifting downstream.

He seized it, felt its weight settle into his hand.

It wasn't his harpoon. But it would do.

Gasping for air, Ceridwen pushed Liam up onto the shore of the canal and managed to drag herself out after him. She collapsed onto her back, but a spasm of coughing forced her onto her side, spitting out the brackish liquid she'd inadvertently sucked in. Past the toes of her soaked boots, the water of the canal looked like a massive storm front. Roiling and heaving and tossing up great waves, as somewhere within, Rafi faced off with that creature of nightmare.

She had heard the myths, of course. But she had not truly understood.

Shaking with exhaustion, she forced herself up on one arm. She caught sight of the soldiers spreading out along both sides of the canal, spears raised as they peered into frothing depths lashed by the twisting, shimmering shapes of man and steed and monster. One stood only thirty paces away on her left, and on her right—*flames*, boots scuffed toward her in a rush.

She shot to her feet, ducked under a spear thrust, and glimpsed the soldier's bearded scowl through the open face of his helmet. He came at her again, striking furiously as she darted backward, right, left, left, until he overextended with a deep lunge, allowing her to catch and wrap her right arm around the spear haft, and drive her left toward his unprotected face.

Her knuckles cracked his nose, but the force of the blow sent a jolt through her wounded arm. She lost control of the spear as he stumbled back, lost sight of him, too, in the haze that settled over her vision. She reeled around, suddenly realizing that she'd crossed nearly the whole width of the room, and Mindar, her reckless, glorious, inflammable steed, stood only a dozen strides away. She threw herself toward him, and his head came up, eyes settling on her. He let out a muffled nicker, lurching to the end of his chain.

It ran over the simple leather halter he wore, wrapped behind his ears, over the muzzle that prevented him from opening his jaws wide enough to breathe out flame, and ended at an iron ring in the wall. Just like hers had.

Blazes, she was a fool. How could she have forgotten the chains?

Something slammed her to the ground with a force that drove the air from her lungs. She was already gasping, so when the soldier's crushing weight settled on her, and he used the spear haft to pin her arms down, stars burst across her vision. His broken nose and bloodied teeth hovered so close she could practically taste the copper.

She smashed her head forward. But just before impact, the soldier was heaved off and slammed to the ground by another soldier with a white-plumed helmet. His blade fell in a sharp, chopping motion, then stuck fast. Ceridwen got her feet under her as the new arrival grunted and tugged his weapon free. Blood dripping from his blade, he stepped over the corpse. But he didn't attack her, just dragged the helmet off his head and tossed it aside, revealing black hair spiked into a fin and a patch over his left eye.

His lip curled slightly. "You don't look like a Kaya."

"I'm not," she said warily. "You are a friend of Rafi?"

"I'm Nef. Where's Sahak?"

"I don't know. He—"

Nef spun to the side to avoid a rush from a pair of soldiers, blocking a spear strike with his wide, heavy blade. It made an audible *crack.* He sprang between them, rapidly trading blows with one while the other broke toward Ceridwen. She got a foot under the spear her attacker had dropped and kicked it up into her hand. She had trained with lances before. But only mounted, never afoot. And never with one arm made useless.

She feinted and harried the soldier, relying on fury to counterbalance her clumsiness, until the stream behind suddenly erupted in a gigantic wave that crashed down onto the temple floor, depositing a shimmering

seablood and a writhing, hissing scadtha on their side of the canal. The
soldier's focus broke for one brief moment, and Ceridwen struck, catching
the spear head behind his knee and ripping his feet out from under him.
She wheeled around and thrust for his throat.

He threw himself to the side, straight into the path of Nef's boot. The
kick to the face laid him out cold, and Nef stepped over him.

Ceridwen scanned the temple. On the edge of the canal, Rafi spun to
face the scadtha, which coiled to spring. Both Rafi and the seablood were
bleeding—he from a long cut on his cheek, his steed from twin gashes
down the flank. Her retreat had drawn the soldiers lining the canal away
from Liam, but more flooded in through the massive doors to Mindar's
left and halted, momentarily arrested by the fight that had spilled onto
the shore. They needed a way out, and with who knew how many more
waiting beyond those doors, their only hope was raising the portcullis.

But no gears or levers flanked the opening.

"There you are," Nef growled.

She turned to see Sahak standing atop the mountainlike stone
structure, watching the unfolding conflict with an air of rapt attention.
Against the wall behind him was a complex series of wheels and levers.
Her target, undoubtedly. She tossed the spear aside—she had a better
weapon—and hastily searched the downed soldiers for a set of keys.
There. Her fingers closed around the rough metal. "We need to open the
portcullis," she said. "Escape downstream."

"Do whatever you want. I need to kill Sahak." Nef eyed the mass of
soldiers and the roiling clash between scadtha and seablood, trying to
work out a path.

Working feverishly, Ceridwen unlocked Mindar's chains, cast off his
hobbles, and eased the vicious muzzle from the raw sores on his face. He
trembled, but his breath puffed warm over her hand and heat simmered
off his skin. She looped the chain through his halter, creating makeshift
reins, and sprang onto his back. With no gloves, no saddle, she could feel
all the ridges of his spine and ribs through her battered leathers, which
only stoked her anger.

He'd been malnourished and mistreated, just like her.

But like her, he still burned.

Sparks flew from his hooves, sizzling on wet stone, as she spun him in front of Nef, cutting him off from the fray. "You want Sahak to burn, I'll clear the way. But we get the portcullis opened first."

Nef cocked his chin. "So, what, Red, I run behind you?"

Mindar snorted, fighting her restraint, and his smoke was black as char. "Trust me. You won't want to ride." With that, she tugged down her hood to shield her eyes, then gave him his head, and away he sprang. Heat stung her fingers as flames ignited along his mane, but the solbreath stole its bite, and the torrent that poured from his throat as he wove under the pressure of her heels scattered soldiers first to one side, then the other, blazing a path toward Sahak.

On the ship, Mindar's fires had been kept carefully dampened, but Sahak, greedy to uncover the secrets of their bond and convinced of his power over them, had left him dry. That would be his undoing.

She was only a few strides more from the steps, when the seablood suddenly crashed across her path, skidding on its side, sending Rafi tumbling. His spear flew from his hands. The scadtha ripped down a soldier as it charged for him, and at the sound of its many skittering legs, Mindar shied, plunging sideways until he faced the beast. The fireborn froze, limbs so taut they quivered.

Grayish blood oozed from several of the scadtha's cracked plates where hoof or spear had scored a hit. Several legs wobbled or trailed or hung uselessly. But it still raced for the kill.

"Come on!" Nef cried, already sprinting up the stairs. "Sahak's retreating!"

Rafi picked himself up, dazed. His steed scrambled up, limping, and its hooves struck Rafi's spear, spinning it away.

Ceridwen hesitated as the image of Bair's broken body flashed across her vision. And of Markham wounded, of Iona falling from the sky. Then she abandoned vengeance, and she abandoned Sahak, and she sprang with Mindar before Rafi, into the scadtha's path. Mindar drew up, poised to flame, and she could feel the fear in his quivering limbs, but he did not flee.

She waited until the creature reared back to strike, mandibles parting, pincers stretched wide, then with the cry of the Outriders upon her lips, she unleashed Mindar's inferno. Fire roared from him in a pulsing stream that shone with the radiance of a noonday sun, blazed hotter than a crater's molten core, and reduced the plate it struck to ash. This was the blaze of embers caged and stoked and raging to be free.

With an eerie shriek, the scadtha recoiled, and Mindar lowered his neck, chasing the creature with that unrelenting fire, until it collapsed to the stone. Its head struck near Rafi, who had regained his spear and thrust it into its maw. Claws twitching, chitin igniting, it shriveled in on itself, and the smoke of its burning drifted over the water.

Mindar reeled in a circle. The world was white-hot before Ceridwen's eyes, so it took her a moment to realize his entire coat was alight with tiny twists of flame. She reached to stroke his neck, to calm his ire, but the heat coming off his skin beat her hand back and bore down upon her.

"Easy, Mindar," she rasped. "Easy."

Heedless, he burned. He would not stop. Perhaps could not. And she could not stop him. Not with voice, rein, or leg. With each passing second, the glow of his conflagration seemed to pulse brighter, grow more searing, until, with a cry, she spun him over the side of the canal, and together, they crashed into the water.

Just before the current rushed over her head, and the shock of sudden cold scattered her senses, she saw the portcullis rising.

Rafi charged Ghost out of the brackish stream and away from the temple as a hail of arrows flew overhead—not aimed at him, thankfully, or he'd have been dead before it occurred to him to dodge. Moc, it seemed, had chosen to launch his feint assault, which included a flaming barricade of overturned supply carts, blocking the path across the bridge. Smoke roiled from the obstruction, and the rebel archers targeted any soldiers attempting to put it out.

It would be just Rafi's misfortune to survive a second scadtha attack only to be struck by a stray arrow from his own side, so he kept his head down while he guided the fire-demon out, using the chain he'd eased from the rider's taut fingers. She was barely conscious but still clinging to her steed with a death grip.

The Fireborn of Soldonia. Captive in Nadaar.

The shouts of the soldiers had revealed the truth, but he should have seen it sooner. What else could draw his usurping uncle from his usurped throne at the Center of the World? Certainly not a minor annoyance, such as discovering his long-lost nephew lived and was plotting against him.

No, only something with the power of legend could do that, and after witnessing that radiant blast she'd unleashed to defeat the scadtha, he almost believed the stories the villagers had begged from the taleweaver. Her fiery onslaught had disoriented the soldiers enough that he'd been able to leap Ghost into the canal and catch the thrashing fire-demon's chain, while Nef seized Liam on their way out.

As Moc loped up, spear in hand, Nef splashed past, dragging the unconscious Liam by the shoulders. He dumped him unceremoniously on the bank. "We got a backup plan for that barricade? Because we're about to lose it."

Sure enough, stone-eye tiger-drawn chariots were lining up as shouted commands brought order to the rush for buckets. Soldiers with shields formed up in front, denying the efforts of the Hanonque archers, while others passed buckets from the stream to the bridge. Soon, the flaming barricade would be reduced to a smoldering pile that the soldiers could simply kick aside.

Before pouring across the bridge to kill them all.

"Tell me we got a way to stop those chariots from crossing."

In the thick of the jungle, a tribesman could outmaneuver a chariot, but with both soldiers and tigers on their heels, not to mention their need to protect the rescued villagers Moc had sent ahead, Rafi didn't like those odds.

Moc smiled wide. "Cousins. Please. Surely you noticed how rundown this bridge is, how desperately its pylons are in need of repair? Aruk did. He was a stonemason, it seems, so he knows about such things."

Stonemason, tracker, carpenter—exactly how many skills did Aruk have?

"He also noted how disastrous a flood, or even a powerful wave, could be."

Both Moc's and Nef's gazes settled on Rafi. Oh. Ches-Shu. Rafi looked back across the stream. There, in the center before the temple's entrance, was the massive war-chariot with its four blood-red tigers, and standing poised upon the platform, his uncle.

He could have sworn he could feel his uncle's eyes lock onto him, felt the charge of recognition like a current in the air.

"Wait until they start crossing," Nef commanded.

"I'm not sure it'll even work," Rafi replied. "If I wait, I won't get to try twice."

"Then make it work, Tetrani. How many chances you think we'll get to take out the emperor? I missed my shot at Sahak. You better not miss yours."

"I won't even get one. He won't cross first, trust me."

The look on Nef's face told him he really, truly didn't.

Rafi dropped the fire-demon's chain into Moc's hand and nodded at the unconscious rider slumped against the creature's neck. The fire-demon was waterlogged and steaming now, but thankfully thoroughly extinguished. "Get her out of here. We're going to need her help."

Assuming they made it back alive.

Whirling Ghost around, he plunged back into the stream. Seconds before, the colt had been drooping with exhaustion, spent by the fight with the scadtha, but the brackish water seemed to revive him. As Rafi charged upstream, humming for Ghost to pick up speed, he sensed the moment the current shifted and moved with them. It responded far more quickly than the sea had, swelling on all sides, building up above them, until Rafi could feel the weight of it pressing down, could see the strain in his colt's strides.

Change the tides, he thought.

Ghost arced up and over in a twisting somersault, allowing Rafi one swift glimpse of the bridge where the collapsing barricade still sent off a roiling fume, preventing the charioteers from crossing. It might make him a poor rebel, but he felt only relief that he wouldn't be responsible for any casualties as Ghost leveled out and charged at the bridge, unleashing the towering wave in his wake.

The wave boiled and seethed like a thousand furious scadtha, crashed into the weakened stone pylons with a roar like thunder, and swept the bridge away.

THIRTY-SIX: JAKIM

*Before scadtha surfaced or stone-eye roamed or the first songbird sang
to greet the dawn, they were cradled in Aodh's hand.*
- Scroll Eighty-Seven of the Holy Writ, Kerrikar Sanctuary

Jakim had never gotten close enough to a stone-eye tiger to touch
one before. That was going to change tonight. Pockets bulging with
borrowed supplies, he hefted the chunk of meat he had convinced the
beast's attendants to give him and tossed it before the tiger. It landed
with a wet *thunk*, and the tiger paused its grooming, ears pricking
forward in interest. Snuffling loudly, it nosed toward the meat, locating
it by smell since its eyes were blindfolded.

"That's it," Jakim said softly, and the tiger's ears flicked.

It prowled forward a step, which was as far as its harness allowed,
and tore into the meat. Since the one attendant had been attacked, they
had taken to leaving the tiger in its traces, never bothering to unhook it
from its chariot, despite the sores developing around the leather straps.
Since the only time Nahrog paid attention to the creature was when he
was lashing it to cart him here or there, Jakim guessed he either didn't
notice the state of his beast or just didn't care.

But Jakim could smell the sourness coming off one of the sores, and
when the creature finally relaxed enough to crouch over its meal, he
inched forward.

Its head came up, teeth exposed in a muted snarl.

"It's just me," he said in that same calm voice. The stone-eye
thrashed its tail but gradually returned to its meal, and Jakim eased
in from the side. The beast was much bigger than it seemed from a

distance. Stopping even with its ribs, Jakim reached out gingerly and touched it.

Thick coarse hair parted under his fingertips, and Jakim slid his palm flat, feeling the ropey mass of muscle and of scars beneath its striped coat. He let out a breath in a puff, and the creature halted its meal, stiffening. But Jakim had started sneaking it food days ago. He tossed it scraps in passing and then watched from a safe distance as the tiger nosed for them. When one of his throws had accidentally fallen short, Jakim had crept over to tip the food closer, and the tiger's blindfolded gaze had settled on him.

Directly on him, as if it could see him.

That had been so unnerving that he had retreated at once. Only to come back the next night, and the next, and now, Aodh have mercy, he was touching the beast.

More than that, he meant to treat its wounds. He dug out the rags and ointment he had borrowed from Ineth. Working gently, he dabbed the ointment on half a dozen weeping sores before he found the infected one high on the stone-eye's side, where the collar of the harness pressed against the point of its shoulder. It had scabbed over, but trails of stiff hair showed where it had wept, and when Jakim pressed the rag against the wound, a thick, yellowish pus oozed out at once.

He nearly gagged at the foul, sickly stench.

The tiger snarled suddenly and pushed into a crouch. It growled, extending its head so that all its teeth were on display. Jakim froze, even as his wiser instincts screamed for him to run. Then a rumbling voice barked out a command, and Jakim realized that the tiger wasn't reacting to him at all. Still snarling quietly, the tiger sank low until it was almost cowering before the priest who stalked up, whip coiled at his side.

Nahrog eyed Jakim. "Shouldn't you be off deciphering embroidery?"

He had been off *deciphering embroidery* for quite a long time today, until all the colored threads seemed to melt together like paint in a puddle, and he'd found nothing. Which made sense. If anyone was going to solve it, it would be the engineer. He had the mind for it. It was frustration, as well as righteous anger, that made Jakim square off with the priest rather than back down. "Shouldn't you take better care of your tiger?"

The priest scowled and stepped nearer, and the tiger hissed. "Quiet." He smacked the coiled whip against the chariot shaft, startling the beast into silence. "Koata needs only a firm hand to guide her."

Koata. So the tiger had a name.

He hadn't had a chance to fully treat her infected sore, but with the priest there, she was much too agitated to risk getting close.

"You are from Eliam, are you not?" Nahrog asked suddenly.

The priest had never so much as looked at him like he was a real person before, so the question startled Jakim enough that he answered immediately. "I am Eliamite, yes, from one of the exiled tribes. But I have been . . . away for many years."

"But with your tribe, you lived in the wastelands?"

"My tribe was nomadic. We lived many places."

"What about a place called the Center of the World?"

That phrase tugged a cord in Jakim's memory. Words his father had spoken, long ago, referring to their hallowed ancestral city as *the tree rooted at the center of the earth.*" Words Jakim had half forgotten over the drift of years since, dismissing them as the sort of nonsense his father was known to mutter, when his fits took him. "Do you mean the City?" he asked Nahrog.

"I was not aware your people built cities."

"Not cities. The City. In Broken-Eliam. It is a sacred place to my people, though few have seen it since the exile. But once it was beautiful, or so the taleweavers say."

Nahrog eyed him shrewdly. "You have seen this city? You know where it is?"

No, though that was the lie that had landed him here.

Jakim darted a glance beyond the priest as a roar of laughter rose from the fires scattered across the hollow where they had set up camp for the night, close to the border of Gimleal. He didn't want to leave without treating the tiger, but the priest's questions struck him suddenly as unnerving. "I have never been. But it may not be what you seek. I was very young when I left."

"Your people have many prophets, do they not?"

"Prophets?" Jakim's throat tightened. "What makes you say that?" Oh, Aodh, he was sweating now, all too cognizant that the priest would no doubt be highly interested to know that his own sister, Siba, was his tribe's Wise Woman, and had spoken a prophecy about *him*. One that might well prove concerning to the empire of Nadaar.

The tiger could wait. He took a step back. "I should really be going."

But Nahrog unfurled the whip with a flick of his wrist, sending it snaking across his path, and Jakim stopped, remembering the hiss and crack and bite of another whip in another hand tearing into his flesh.

"Why the sudden interest in Eliamites, priest?" Ineth. Jakim had never been so glad to see her. She stood only a tiger's leap away, carrying a small steaming cup. "I thought the empire had forgotten about them as soon as their homeland was destroyed."

Nahrog grumbled something unintelligible in response.

She turned from him to Jakim. "Ondri's sons caught fish from the Tain. We'll be entering Craddock's territory tomorrow, so this is the last fire we'll risk for a while. You should enjoy the warm meal while you can."

"I will. Thank you," Jakim said, truly grateful for her arrival.

He was even more grateful when the priest stalked off, and Ineth lingered, allowing him to finish cleaning the tiger's wound. Her meal ended, Koata groomed her paws, working down around each curved claw. She didn't seem to mind as he pressed gently on the scab until no more pus came out. He would have liked to be able to rinse the wound with water, but he settled for spreading Ineth's ointment over the sore, then picked a few burs from Koata's matted coat.

When he was finished, tufts of hair clung to his sticky fingers, and that faintly sickly scent wasn't likely to wash off anytime soon.

He found his conversation with the priest far more disturbing.

THIRTY-SEVEN: CERIDWEN

The earthhewn's great strength is also its weakness.
Once it reaches full tilt, an earthhewn cannot easily counteract
its own momentum without time and space to slow.
- Wisdom of the Horsemasters

C eridwen dreamed she burned from the inside out. She opened her mouth to scream but only flames poured from her throat, engulfing everyone and everything she held close. Her friends. Her kingdom. Her fireborn too.

Mindar's shriek rang and rang and rang in her ears.

She jolted awake, gasping, to a low rumble of unfamiliar voices and the dull roar of crashing water, and found her body wrapped in a net that swung from the rafters of a strange, rounded ceiling. She tried to jerk free of its encroaching folds and felt it buck and twist beneath her, dumping her out onto the ground. Woven rugs rumpled beneath her fingers. Bandages were wound around her hands, her wrists, her left forearm. She lifted her head.

It brushed against something swaying above. Not a net, but a cloth sling that draped from the ceiling. Three others drooped at intervals around the small, circular space. All empty.

No sign of Liam. No sign of anyone.

She rose, swayed, and clutched the sling. Outside, the voices became more distinct—two of them, both speaking Nadaarian. Coming closer. Likely foes.

"Told you I heard movement," said the first.

"You did." The second, deeper voice rounded the woven wood

structure. "Didn't think she'd be up yet, though, not with that dose she got."

Chills slithered through her. Had she been drugged? Maybe that was why she had no chains. They assumed she was already contained.

Off to her left, a shadow fell across a colorfully woven curtain, and a hand shoved one side of it open. She staggered to the opposite side of the curtain as a big man carrying a steaming bowl stooped through, and she slipped out past him into a cacophony of sights and sounds that assaulted her senses. Mist on her face. Cries—animal and human— echoing off the rock walls of a cavern. Water and sunlight mingling in a thunderous deluge that tumbled through a hole in the ceiling above and through another hole above that, and down through a third hole in the rock beneath her feet. She reeled from it all and turned sharply into a shorter, younger man with a bush of dark, curly hair, and a wide, curious expression.

"Whoa, steady." His hands clutched her elbows.

Her muscles reacted on instinct. She lashed out, pushing him away so hard he tottered toward the curtain, hitting the big man, who was coming back through, still holding the bowl.

Crockery shattered, hot soup splattered, and she took off at a sprint, ignoring the shouts that rang out behind her. "Hoy. Hoy! Stop!"

Only with the sting of her bare feet upon rough stone did she realize that her boots were missing. Her leathers too. She wore strange, unfamiliar clothes—a formfitting sleeveless tunic and loose trousers that billowed around her legs as she ran. She made it only a dozen steps before catching sight of a handful of warriors with spears slung over their shoulders walking along the rim of the waterfall toward her. Hearing the shouts, they pointed and jogged forward. She spun the other way, shoving through a startled knot of people carrying baskets, but the big man loomed before her, hands raised, lips forming words she couldn't hear over the high-pitched whine in her ears.

He stepped toward her, and she sidestepped out onto the brink overlooking the cavern below and the water that pooled at the base of the fall. It was a drop of maybe thirty feet. But she could sense the net of people closing in around her, and she would not be taken again. She didn't pause to think.

Without a backward look, she threw herself over the edge.

The pool rushed toward her, deep and black and glistening with the churn of the cascade and with swirls of luminous strands. She hit it with a dizzying shock and felt she would sink forever down, down, down into the cold and empty dark.

Then her feet struck stone, propelling her back to the surface.

Gasping, she emerged from the shallows, slipping on moss-slick stone, and flung herself through the mouth of the cavern. Out into a wild, verdant space where the walls of a gorge reared toward a ribbon of blue sky above, where trees and plants in every rich, vibrant hue imaginable burst from every hollow and crevice. To her right, workers pounded poles into the earth and wove canes between them, enlarging a fenced enclosure. Over the top of the fence, inquisitive ears, wispy forelocks, and deep, dark eyes met hers.

Those were solborn.

She pulled up sharply, staring at the steeds packed within. Seabloods. Riveren. Shadowers. Earthhewn. So many of them, here, in Nadaar. How?

Out of their midst sounded a familiar nicker. Mindar.

It struck her like a blow. She'd been so desperate to escape, so determined not to be caught and caged again, she'd nearly forgotten about her fireborn. And Liam. Her knees buckled, and she sat down hard. Some of the workers eyed her curiously, others as if they questioned her sanity.

What in flames was wrong with her?

One man, tall with dark hair that brushed his shoulders, traded an armload of poles for a waterskin. Slightly crooked grin, freshly scabbed cut on his brown cheek—it was the searider, Rafi. "Here." He held the waterskin out to her. "You look like you could use some of this. Want some food too? Moc was supposed to bring something up, but we could stop by the kitchens. Saffa's always got something simmering."

Metal bit into wood with a *thwack*. Ceridwen braced for an attack.

But it was just the other man she had met in the temple, Nef, holding a pole he'd apparently split in two, using the wide, curved blade he'd fought with at her side. "Rafi thinks everything can be fixed with food."

Rafi shot him an amused look. "Not with any food, Nef. Saffa's food. Her saga crisps especially. I'm pretty sure she could stop wars with those."

"That's the problem. Some of us want to win the war, not stop it."

Ceridwen shook her head, trying to gather her scattered thoughts. Questions swarmed within her, but she brushed them and the waterskin aside. First things first. "Liam. Where is he?"

Ceridwen lifted a damp strand of hair from Liam's forehead. His skin felt cool, clammy beneath her fingertips, and shivers racked his body beneath the clean sheets.

"One hour ago, he was burning up," the white-haired healer said from the low stool where he sat beside Liam's cot in one of the back rooms of his hut. He pushed the damp cloth he'd removed from Liam's forehead into the bowl of water on his lap, then wrung it out. On entering, she had noted his missing limb and the crutch propped against the wall behind him. Noted too the strength of his arms and his keen-eyed gaze.

"So his fever has broken? That's good, isn't it?

"More like a momentary respite, I'd say."

Shivering aside, Liam lay completely still. It reminded her of when she'd first met him mid-battle, trapped by a stone-eye. She'd saved him, and he'd gone on to save her, too, awakening something inside her she'd thought lost with Bair. She listened intently as the healer explained the extent of Liam's injuries, using terms that Finnian would surely have understood but which only left her with a growing frustration that this was an enemy she couldn't help fight against.

Or could she? "Did you dose him to make him sleep, like you did me?"

The healer raised an eyebrow. "I gave him a tincture to help him rest, yes, but you can thank Nef for treating you. You were, apparently, quite a handful. And since this lot"—he raised his voice to be heard by the others in the front room—"managed to turn a sneak raid into an utter disaster by attacking that temple while the emperor of Nadaar was in it, they needed to get you back here quietly before the entire jungle was flooded with imperial guards."

Someone—possibly Nef, possibly Rafi—coughed at that. On their trek up the slat-and-rope staircase, which had left Ceridwen shockingly weak with exhaustion, they had met the big man, Moc, rushing down. Moc had apparently been convinced he was about to fish her corpse out of their drinking supply. Instead, he'd ended up tagging along, and was now regaling the others with the tale of her break for freedom.

"Jumped into the waterfall! Who does that?"

"She's a fighter." Nef's voice. "Shows spirit. Unlike Rafi here, who lazed in his hammock, whining for Umut for a week."

"I'd have stopped after day one if you'd let me see him."

"Trust me, cousins." That was Moc. "She's mad."

Ceridwen drew back to the doorway where she could see them lurking in the dim light of the larger space. Both Moc and Rafi were stooped to avoid the bundles of herbs drying from the ceiling, Moc's clothes still damp with the soup he'd been bringing her, Rafi idly tossing a jar of salve from hand to hand. Nef glowered from the shadows.

She stepped forward. "Aye, she is mad," she said, "and since clearly none of you are in charge, she wants to speak with whoever is. Who is Umut? Your leader?"

Moc barked a laugh, and Rafi spun the jar up with a flick of his wrist, caught it near his chin, and nodded behind her. Toward the healer sitting on his stool, gnarled fingers now working a mortar and pestle, grinding some sort of a yellow paste.

He didn't look up from his work. "You want to speak? Speak."

This man was their leader?

She raised her chin. "Who are you? What is this place?"

"You mean individually or collectively? I am Umut of the Hanonque, healer, elder, and chief resident of this hut. We are the Que Revolution, and this cavern, such as it is, is our base of operations. Our shelter against the storm of imperial oppression, if you will." His gaze flicked up. "You know something about that, don't you? Ceridwen, Fireborn of Soldonia?"

Her throat felt suddenly dry. "You know who I am."

It made sense that he did. Of course Nadaar would have spread the news of her capture far and wide, reveling in their victory to stifle resistance wherever it might rise. "Then you must know what I want. I am queen of a nation at war. I must return to my people." Whether they would still accept her rule or whether she would find another crowned in her place didn't matter. She had been their Fireborn before their queen, and who was she now if not that?

Only the tainted fruit of a poisonous vine, as Glyndwr had said.

Umut resumed his grinding, pounding the pestle down and twisting it with a deft flick of his wrist. "We too are at war. Over a hundred years, we've been crushed under the paw of the imperial beast—"

"Which is trying to crush my nation as we speak—"

He raised the pestle, pointing the paste-coated end at her. "And finally, we're about to be able to strike back with real teeth. That's my only concern right now. That, and we just staged a costly and highly visible assault that left me with wounded aplenty to tend, even without reckless stunts from you or your friend, and who knows what storm of consequences building over us even as we speak."

She was suddenly conscious of the state she was in, soaked from the waterfall, barefoot and clad in strange clothes, without blade or steed at her side, or anything to barter or bargain with. And she was exhausted. She sank down onto the edge of the cot and clasped her bandaged hands on her knees. "All I need is passage home."

"The only ships departing Nadaar for Soldonia these days are troop transports. Doubt you'll be wanting to hitch a ride on one of them." Some of the grit washed out of Umut's voice. "Much less with the Emperor's Stone-eye launching an empire-wide hunt for you, which he's bound to do. You might be able to get passage elsewhere, like Canthor or Slyrchar, but you'd be stuck at sea for months while the war unfolds without you."

His words cast a chill over her.

In her mind's eye, she sailed back to a kingdom smothered in ash, the war-chiefs fallen, her friends gone before she could reach them. Like Bair.

"Way I see it, the beast has you pinned too." He set down the mortar and pestle to retrieve his crutch, then stood. "Might as well stick a blade in his chest while you're in striking reach."

"You want me to fight for you," she said slowly.

"No, I want you to fight for you. For your kingdom. Every soldier tied up stamping out rebellion here is one less soldier on those troop transports to Soldonia. If that means you fight for us, too, well, you won't find me arguing against it." He winked but his tone was sincere. Of course, Glyndwr had seemed sincere before he betrayed her.

"What if I want to leave? Am I a prisoner?"

Umut's gaze dropped to her hands. "You're not wearing any chains, are you?"

"That's not an answer."

He laughed a short, throaty laugh. "I suppose not. But if I tell you not to leave, I'm fairly sure you'll see that as a challenge, and your friend is in no condition to be moved. He needs rest and care if he's going to recover." He pulled a wad of bandages from his pocket and lobbed it to her. She caught it against her chest. "Change that wet bandage on your arm. And use some of that salve Rafi's playing with if you want to keep the wound from souring," he added over his shoulder, then exited with Nef.

Crushing the bandages in her grip, Ceridwen thudded her hand onto the cot, which made Liam's fingers twitch in his sleep. But he did not stir, and he did not speak. She stared up at the high, rounded ceiling, at the blue moss creeping through gaps in the weave.

Just one more reminder of how far she was from home.

Until a scuffed footfall beside her told her that at least she wasn't alone. She found Rafi standing at her elbow, a hint of sympathy, but thankfully not pity, in his eyes. "Come with me."

THIRTY-EIGHT: RAFI

As salve to a wound and balm to a burn is soup to the soul.
- Mahque saying

Sweet, tangy scents rolled off the steaming surface of the rich, orange soup. Chunks of root vegetables floated among leafy greens and bushka beans. Saffa had even gone so far as to top it with crumbled cala root crackers. Rafi savored the aroma as he slid the bowl, a spoon, and the salve he'd borrowed across the table toward Ceridwen. "One bowl of soup and no sleeping draughts. Promise."

Her gaze flicked to the bowl, then did a quick scan of the kitchen. Somehow, he got the sense that she wasn't scoping out the flatbread baking on hot stones in the oven or the bean cakes Jasri was crisping in a pan. No, her gaze snagged on the many knives spread out across the workspace—and on the solitary exit and the spear Saffa kept tucked in the corner with the brooms.

No wonder Nef approved of her.

Saffa appeared at his elbow, the little graybeard monkey perched on her shoulder. She held a plate of cala root crackers, and concern pinched her forehead. Nothing worried her more than uneaten food. Rafi took the plate with a smile and set it in the center of the table before settling onto a stool between Moc and Iakki. Both eagerly helped themselves, Iakki crunching loudly. Rafi hadn't even seen the boy since getting back, but he had characteristically emerged from the weeds as soon as there was food for the taking.

"So," Iakki said, eying Ceridwen. "Moc said you're called the Fireborn?" She nodded warily. "Kind of a funny name. Got another one?"

"I am called Ceridwen tal Desmond tor Nimid."

"What? All of them? That's a lot of names. Really long, too."

She almost smiled at that. "You may call me Ceridwen."

Iakki scrunched his nose. "Got a shorter one? Like Iakki—that's me. Or Rafi—but he used to be Nahiki. Or Kaya. Or Moc?"

She shook her head. "Just Ceridwen."

Moc reached for another cracker. "Do all you Soldonians have such complicated names? What do you do with them all?"

"Our names tell the story of our ancestry. Desmond was my father's name. Nimid my mother's." Something in her gaze receded then, and a hollowness that Rafi knew all too well surged to the forefront. Her fingers rose to the raised scar on her forehead. It looked like some sort of symbol, a brand, maybe?

Iakki fidgeted on his stool. "We could come up with a shorter name for you. What about Ceri . . . or Wen?"

"No." Her answer came swiftly. "Not that."

"Say, Iakki," Rafi interjected before he could press her further, "you know who'd love some of these crackers? Ghost. Why don't you bring him some? Then maybe you and I can go for a ride later."

Iakki's eyes gleamed. "Sev would hate that."

Which made him seem to relish the idea even more. "Sev's already had his turn. You could ask him about it. I bet he'd be—"

"What? Sev rode Ghost? Not fair!" Iakki snatched the rest of the crackers and took off, barely avoiding Saffa, who carried a bowl of fresh snap peas and a plate of the bean cakes, still steaming hot, to the table. "Sorry!"

"Don't cause a riot!" Rafi called after him. Iakki paused just long enough to shoot him a mischievous grin before racing out.

He turned back to find Moc looking at him as though he'd just taken leave of his senses, and Ceridwen, who still hadn't touched a bite of food, seeming mildly curious. "Ghost is the sea-demon," he explained.

"Sea-demon?" Her eyes narrowed. "You mean the seablood?"

"Seablood? Is that what you call them?" He leaned in. "What about fire-demons, like yours? What do you call them?"

"Terrifying," Moc supplied, then appealed to Ceridwen. "I mean, you did burn a scadtha alive, right? Before Rafi, I hadn't heard of anyone surviving an encounter, let alone killing one. Two now, I guess."

Ceridwen regarded Rafi with an odd expression. "You've fought one before?"

Fought didn't really feel like the right word for how he'd faced down that first scadtha. It seemed to imply a level of intention, when really, he'd just annoyed the creature, then ran for his life, then used his harpoon to fend off its mandibles when it tried to eat him. "It was mostly an accident. The colt helped."

"Ghost," she said as if testing the name. "How did you get him? Where?"

"That was mostly an accident too." Rafi eyed the soup still sitting in front of Ceridwen. Maybe he shouldn't have made that jest about a sleeping draught. "Got himself trapped in a net on the beach. I saved him. He saved me. Twice. I wound up with a colt-shaped shadow."

"Just like that?"

"More or less."

She shook her head. "You can't have bonded him. It's not possible. Only a Soldonian can form the sol-breath. It's . . . just how it is."

He shrugged. "If you say so. I don't even know what that means." He glimpsed Saffa straining her neck to see the untouched dishes, and leaned in. "I do know that Saffa is going to keep bringing over food until she finds something you'll eat. She's persistent that way. You want to maybe try something before the table collapses?"

Only then did Ceridwen seem to notice the assortment that had accumulated before her. Rafi dragged first the soup bowl then spoon over and helped himself to a mouthful. More tepid than cold, but still flavorful. "See?"

"See what? That you ate my soup?"

"Yes, and I'm still alive. Not poisoned."

"You ate my soup," she repeated.

"I tasted your soup. One of us had to. It's too good to waste."

She reached out her bandaged hand and took the bowl. "What about the other steeds? Where did you get them?" she asked, scooping a vegetable-laden spoonful into her mouth. She paused, then immediately took another.

Rafi grinned. "Good, right? No one cooks like Saffa." Over by the ovens, the old woman was back at work, content now that order had been restored to her kitchens. "So, you want to know about the demon-steeds?"

"Solborn," she corrected, selecting a bean cake from the plate.

"Solborn," Rafi assented, and with Moc occasionally chiming in, told her the whole story. Or well, most of it, leaving out a few minor details like his personal history and royal heritage—neither of which could help his argument, since she had good reason to distrust anyone with ties to the Nadaarian throne. He started with the ship theft and wreck, continued with their race to reclaim the runaway solborn steeds and the tragic conclusion to his meeting with Sahak, then ended with the raid on the temple.

"You know the rest," he said.

"I recall only smoke after the fire. How did I get out?"

Moc intervened before Rafi could answer, slinging a heavy arm over his shoulders. "Rafi got you out. And when we were about to have the entire force of the imperial guards and the emperor's charioteers descending around our ears, he summoned a flood and swept the bridge away, cutting off our pursuit."

Rafi squirmed. "Really, it was mostly—"

"An accident?" Ceridwen offered.

"See? You know this story already."

"Perhaps. Shall I take a stab at guessing the rest of it?" Steel shone suddenly in her eyes.

"Sure." Rafi spread his arms. "Stab away."

"How's this? You think those steeds would make a fine weapon in the hand of your grand revolution, but you don't know how. You haven't the faintest idea where to start. Supposing you did indeed bond that *sea-demon*, what do you know of the other demon-steeds, of mounted combat and tactics? So . . . it isn't me Umut wants but my knowledge. He doesn't want me to fight for his revolution. He wants me to train riders."

Rafi exchanged a look with Moc, who shrugged. "So, will you?"

"No," she said, ruthlessly cutting their hopes down.

"You don't want to, maybe, sleep on it?" Moc asked.

"I don't need to. Sahak wanted such information too. He didn't get it. Call yourselves enemies of the empire all you will, you're still a part of it. Our steeds are the beating heart and thrumming soul of our nation. I won't betray that. I cannot."

"Look," Rafi said carefully. "I've seen what those steeds can do—"

"You haven't. You've barely scratched the surface."

"That's why we need your help. Sure, we're part of the empire, because we're fighting it from within." Rafi avoided meeting Ceridwen's eyes. Definitely not the time to unveil his full story. If she was reluctant to cooperate with rebels, knowing he was a Tetrani prince was unlikely to help his case.

Still, he pressed on. "We're the enduring resistance, but we won't endure or resist long enough to make an impact without some sort of edge. We need you and you need us—unless you want to take on Sahak and the imperial army alone."

Ches-Shu, he should probably leave the recruiting speeches to Umut and stick to what he was good at, like juggling. "But Moc's right," he added. "No need to decide now. Why don't you come down to the steeds with me? Ghost loves cala root crackers. We could bring some to your fire-demon . . ."

"Mindar." She stood, plucked the jar of salve from the table, and started away. "I should be with Liam." Moc moved to follow, and she forestalled him with a raised hand. "No need. I know the way."

Moc looked to Rafi, who just lifted his shoulder. Umut had said she wasn't a prisoner. More or less. He pretended not to notice the knife she stole on her way out.

THIRTY-NINE: CERIDWEN & RAFI

*Seariders are equipped with formfitting clothing for underwater dives
and trimmed-down saddles crafted from the hides of fallen seabloods,
capable of withstanding the harsh environs of the sea.*
- Wisdom of the Horsemasters

With a final twist of her wrist, Ceridwen peeled off the old bandages and discarded them on the floor. On the cot to her left, Liam shivered and twitched and mumbled in fevered dreams, despite the damp cloth she'd placed on his forehead. Sitting with her back to the wall, she rested her hands on her knees and surveyed them.

Raised burns oozed across both palms and fingers. Red and blistering in some places, brown and scabbed in others. But it was the shape of the marks more than their appearance that caused her to shudder. She bore no chains upon her wrists, but they were etched into her skin, seared by that deadly inferno she had unleashed in the temple. That scorching, starving, unstoppable blaze that had threatened to consume her.

If she closed her eyes, it would overtake her again.

She busied herself smearing the pungent salve on those burns and along the gash Rhodri's blade had torn into her left forearm. She cast a critical eye over the stitches, then tried not to think about how uneven and jagged they seemed compared to the painstakingly small and neat stitches with which Finnian had once sewn her wounds closed. Her movements felt awkward and clumsy as she wrapped the fresh bandages over her hands and arm, and her frustration at the resultant creasing and rumpling only made it worse.

Wrestling with the bandages, using her teeth to tie off the knots, her hair fell lank before her eyes, the ends brittle and singed by that blaze. She reeked of burning. Without pausing to think, she seized the knife she'd stolen from the kitchen, grasped a tangle of hair, and cut off a chunk. It didn't slice neatly, all in one go. She had to saw at it, until bit by bit, it came loose in her hand. She dropped it, seized another handful, and took off a little more this time. Then another.

Sawing. Scraping. Tearing. Cutting.

Until the rug was littered with broken strands, and her hair, which before had reached far down her back, hung only a handsbreadth past her collarbones. Casting the knife aside, she sank back against Liam's cot. How long she sat there, she did not know, but when the reek of fever sweat and soured wounds finally drove her out of the suffocating room, and out of Umut's silent hut, night had fallen over the caverns.

She looked out past the waterfall, which shimmered in the moonlight like an icy rain, toward the enormous cavelike window that overlooked the gorge. Down there, Mindar and the other steeds were trapped in the enclosure. She should go down to them. But merely thinking of the steeds made her blood boil at this new depth of Rhodri and Astra's betrayal, for she had no doubt that they had sent the shipload of solborn to Sahak, just as they had sent her.

The slat-and-wood staircase that led to the lowest cavern and the one that led to the highest lay on opposite sides of the natural bridge that formed the outer edge of the middle cavern. She saw at once the strategic value of this design. If the caverns were attacked from below or above, and one or the other should fall, the attackers would have to cross that narrow bridge, fighting every step of the way, to reach the next staircase.

Down was closer, but her feet carried her up.

Up away from the steed she wasn't yet ready to face. Up away from the warm glow of candles spilling from the beehive-shaped huts and of sparks dancing over communal cookfires. Up away from the sounds of laughter and chatter and music. Up into the highest cavern, past an open grassy stretch that extended along the side of the gorge where she'd seen warriors sparring earlier, out across the higher bridge and up one final weaving staircase, until she emerged onto the outer rim of the chasm through which the waterfall tumbled.

Its tumultuous roar drew her to the edge to look down into the frothing white pool at its end.

Up here, a cool wind stirred the strands of hair that clung to her neck, flinging brittle, singed wisps in front of her eyes. She swiped them back from her face, kept one bandaged hand pressed to her head, and breathed deeply. She had missed the wind, though she had not known it, until she felt it again. It was a constant in Soldonia, where it danced over the rugged terrain with a ceaseless sighing, raked fingers through the long golden grasses, and often threatened to scour bark from trees and flesh from bones with its furious, frenzied gusts. This wind was far more gentle and damp, and she closed her eyes, relishing the feel of its touch on her cheeks, on her eyelids.

"You know," a nasally voice said behind, causing her to reach for her sabre, though she had lost it, "there are easier ways to kill yourself, if that's what you've come up to do."

Rafi plunged his face into the stream, let its coolness erase the burn of the cut on his cheek. The chatter of the rippling current drowned out everything, save the echoes of the ringing scream that had filled his ears when the scadtha's claw slammed into him and sent him and Ghost tumbling.

No words. Just a scream.

Agonized. Enraged. Human.

He knew that voice. He *knew* that voice.

Delmar, he thought toward the ghost who had deserted him. *Can you hear me?* It felt ridiculous to be flinging his thoughts out into the void, expecting his long-dead brother to respond. Whatever he'd thought he heard before was probably the result of too many head blows and never enough sleep, but still, he couldn't shake this feeling.

It towed him down, ripped at his insides, made him want to weep, because if that truly was Delmar screaming, then surely he'd died as Sahak had claimed. Tortured, suffering and railing with his final breath against the worthless younger brother who'd been only a burden.

Something prodded his leg.

Rafi jerked his head up to see Umut withdrawing the crutch he'd used to poke him. The rebel leader stood just upstream of the half-submerged rock where Rafi knelt, his back to the waterfall. The plunge pool provided a source of fresh water for the camp, but the overflow downstream could be used for washing or swimming or the occasional late-night attempted conversation with a ghost.

"How long were you standing there?" he asked.

"Moc said you'd be down with the steeds. Just happened to see you as I passed." Umut paused. "I was beginning to think you'd fallen asleep in there."

"Sleep? Sleep is for mortals," Rafi said, then bit his tongue.

"Ah, and you aren't? The arrogance of royals."

"It's . . . just something my brother used to say."

Rafi had stayed on in the kitchen after Ceridwen left, helping Saffa and Jasri clean up, but even those familiar, calming tasks hadn't been able to quiet his restlessness for long. Nor had visiting the circle of huts that Umut had allotted to the freed villagers—refugees now, all of them—a place to regroup until they decided what to do next. Returning to Zorrad was out of the question, and the village itself would doubtless be burned to deter other Alonque from choosing the rebel path.

He didn't know what it said about the revolution that there were always vacant huts to spare, whether it was the steady ebb and flow of refugees coming and staying or coming and moving on, or whether it simply reflected the high costs of taking up arms against the empire.

But he'd seen Sev sitting with his arms around Kaya, her head resting on his chest, while Aruk serenaded the fisherfolk on his panpipe, Gordu rocked a grandchild, and old Hanu cheered on Iakki and the rebel children he'd befriended as they taught his Alonque cousins a new game. Surely the cost was worth it if it meant creating a place where people could be safe from the likes of Sahak. It was what Delmar would have done, if he'd lived.

Rafi stepped ashore, shaking the water from his trousers. "So, Moc told you I was down here? Were you looking for me then? Curious to know where we stand with the demon-steeds? About this high with the taller ones—"

Umut pulled an object wrapped in a stained cloth from his pocket, and Rafi's stomach twisted. "Wait, is that—"

"Oh, yes. Scadtha claw. Found it in one of the boy's wounds." He regarded Rafi closely. "Just like yours when you got here."

"Is that what's wrong with him? Why his fever is so high?"

Umut shook his head. "Only wound he had that wasn't turning sour."

He didn't add the comparison again, because he didn't need to. It was already echoing through Rafi's head. *Just like yours.* Without thinking, he reached out to touch the curved claw tip with its mottled bluish black chitin, but Umut drew it back. "I wouldn't. Yath Ha'Nor, that informant you pulled out, he claims Sahak is conducting some kind of twisted experiments in that temple."

Rafi withdrew his hand, skin prickling. What did *that* mean? "Some kind? So he doesn't know what Sahak is doing?"

"Overheard rumors. Scraps of muttered conversation from the guards, that sort of thing. If he knows more, he's not saying, though he did let slip that he was on the trail of some missing Eliamites when he was captured." Umut's expression was shrewd. "He'll be sticking around for a bit, though, so you might be able to get more out of him."

"Me? Why would he talk to me?"

"You set him free, didn't you?"

"I only unlocked a door."

"Unlock a door, unlock the chains from a man's wrists, you unlock something inside of him too. There's a power in that, a power that your cousin, for all his cruelty and all his cunning, will never understand."

"This the part where I'm supposed to remember or forget that you're the one who freed me and my brother all those years ago?"

"Me?" Umut's eyes gleamed. "Riku unlocked the door."

Rafi laughed. "I thought you'd come to tell me that Sahak had burned down a village. Or, I don't know, the whole jungle."

"Well, not tonight," Umut said and rapped his knuckles on his crutch.

Still, the more Rafi thought of it, the more certain he was that consequences smelled like smoke, and he could smell it drifting toward them even now.

Nef emerged from the shadows to her right, dark hair slicked back with sweat, his wide blade resting atop his shoulder. Ceridwen watched warily as he crossed behind her to come up on her left—an action that felt at once oddly unsettling and familiar, until she recognized it as a move Markham often used to counteract his limited field of vision.

"I came up to feel the wind," she said, and though it may not have been why she had come, it was why she'd stayed.

His smile was edged like a blade. "Sure you did."

She stiffened at his disbelief, and the arrogance it revealed. Who was he to think he knew her? "And why did you come up here?"

"You don't post watch over your war-camps in Soldonia?"

His tone seemed a clear deflection, so she countered in kind, nodding at his weapon. "You usually train while posted on watch?" He grunted, which could have been yes or no or neither, so she just nodded again at his blade. "What do you call that?"

"This? It's a *chet*. We of the Mahque use it."

"May I?" She held out her hand, then added as he drew back. "I'm not going to stab you with it. There are easier ways to kill you too."

His laugh was as nasal as his voice, yet there was something unrestrained about it. "*Chets* are not made for stabbing."

"Clearly not. A wide, heavy blade like that? Only good for hacking. Chopping, not slicing. Useful for lopping off the occasional limb—"

He raised an eyebrow.

"Trees and bushes, of course."

With a faintly amused snort, he spun the *chet* from his shoulder and set the wooden hilt in her hand. It was heavier than she expected, considering how much shorter it was than her sabre, but the heft felt good. She let the balance of the *chet* carry her arm through a series of swings. Single-edged with a unique upswept curve on the dull edge of the blade, it was wider at the tip, the weight channeling force through her strike.

Oh, *flames*, the thrum of a blade in her hand, this, too, she had missed.

She pivoted sharply and slashed the *chet* at an angle through the top of a lanky bush. Caught by the wind, the decapitated top sailed out over the waterfall before dropping and vanishing into the churning flow.

"Right," Nef said. "Bushes."

But she barely heard him, for in wielding the blade, she'd rounded the waterfall onto the opposite rim and looked out over a dark and tumbling drop, overgrown with jungle thickness. The silken moonlight seeping through shredded clouds was too soft and silver to reveal much more below than a sense of denseness and vastness, and still, she caught her breath at the sight of it.

She had never been so far and so utterly cut off from home.

"It's quiet up here." Nef stepped up beside her. "Peaceful. I don't notice it"—he gestured vaguely at his eye—"so much in the dark."

She heard the newness of his loss in his voice and considered telling him of Markham, the finest man and the greatest warrior she knew. But she held her tongue. Wounds of the flesh needed skilled tending. How much more so wounds that cut so deeply into the soul?

Nef shoved his fists into his pockets. "You should come up here sometime just before sunrise. It's worth the climb to watch the sun come up over the ocean to the east, see it catch alight the mist on the jungle and burn it away." His voice bore a hint of awe. This, too, seemed a revelation, a glimpse at the heart beating beneath his armored hide.

"I will." Rotating the *chet* so the blade ran parallel to her forearm, she turned and held it out to him.

He pressed it back toward her. "Keep it, Red. Rafi already owes me one anyway. Might as well make him pay up."

Such a simple gesture to make her throat swell. She ran her thumb over the carved wooden grip, over the blocky shapes that seemed to reflect the outlines of rivers, trees, and leaves, and she could not help but think of Finnian, and of the fireborn steed that he had whittled for her.

Below, the scream of a seablood suddenly spiraled up from the gorge, and with it, a familiar tangy smoke filled the wind.

She spun toward the descent. "Mindar."

She should have gone to him sooner. Guilt impelled her down through all three caverns, with Nef loping grim-faced at her side. She slowed as she neared the enclosure, where steeds shifted and churned in a mass of tossing heads, all wreathed in smoke. Rafi was astride the woven fence, calling out in a gentle, shushing voice that reminded her of the wash of the sea.

"Shh," he sang out to them. "Shh, shh, shh."

Ghost, the seablood, swung at once toward his voice, but Rafi's attempts to calm the rest were thwarted by the onlookers crowding around, and by the thickening fumes emitted by Mindar.

"Nef," she said instantly, "move them back."

Without a word, he swung around and chased off the crowd with a few barked orders. She strode on toward the enclosure, more sure on her feet with the *chet* in her hand and a task before her. Rafi met her at the gate and swung it open. Clearly, he meant to enter with her. She pressed the blade into his hands instead and slipped in alone.

Hands raised, she eased into the midst of the uneasy throng of steeds. Skirting wide around one, sliding close beside another, dodging as teeth clacked. The shadower beside her squealed, causing a spurt of rushed movement that nearly crushed her between two earthhewn. Still, she followed the current until she reached the smoky center and beheld her smoldering fireborn standing in the eye of the maelstrom.

"Easy, boy," she whispered in Soldonian. "Easy."

Emberlike eyes flicked toward her, beneath a tangled forelock, and reflected in the gaze were flames unending. The blaze that had ended her brother. That had nearly ended her.

Then he nickered, and she saw only Mindar.

She gripped his halter and guided him out past the parting steeds, past Rafi at the gate, past the onlookers who shied away, and over to Umut. "You need more than one enclosure for this many steeds. Not all the breeds get along. You need to be able to separate them, otherwise you'll have more trouble like this."

His mouth twitched. "Trouble? We certainly don't want that."

He glanced to Mindar, to the smoke still rising from his nostrils and the wisps of flame still curling off his mane. Gently, she ran her knuckles down the white streak that zigzagged down Mindar's nose. He snorted out a final puff of smoke and sparks before lowering his head.

"How did you do that?" Voice full of wonder, Rafi was at her elbow, holding out the *chet*, though his focus was fixed on the enclosure where the steeds were gradually calming. "Ches-Shu, but we could have used you aboard the ship. Don't you see? We need you. What say you, Ceridwen? Will you help?"

His eyes were bright, his expression eager.

Of course, he could not understand.

She looked from him to Umut. "Do you know what it is you ask of me? Were I to reveal our secrets, I would be a traitor to my people."

More so even than Rhodri or Astra, for the steeds they had sent were as wild as the day they were born, delivered to the Nadaari untamed and untrained for war.

But if she were to tame them, and if she could train riders . . .

If. It seemed the world itself hinged on that impossibility. On Rafi, this searider who was not a Soldonian and therefore defied everything she had been taught. On the chance that he was not a fluke but the first, and these steeds were only the beginning. That single ship, a pledge.

How far might the Dominion of Murloch spread if it no longer marched forth at the speed of men but was borne aloft on wings, sped along on hooves, and raced through every ocean and stream of the world?

Prepare yourself, woman, for the falling of all nations.

"But perhaps also their deliverer," Umut said, his eyes fixed on her. "Is that a risk you are willing to take? A sacrifice you can make to save them?"

What other option did she have? She was under no illusions about this man. He did not care for Soldonia. He had told her as much. She was a weapon to him as much as the steeds were, but perhaps his forces could be her weapons too. If there was a way to fight for her people here and now, she must take it.

Surely, this was what it meant to be their Fireborn.

She spoke again. "Should I agree, I will have conditions. You doubtless have plans in place, some idea of how you think four dozen riders can overthrow the empire on its own soil, when ten thousand times that number cannot force the invaders from my homeland." Umut's face yielded nothing to scrutiny, so she continued, "I don't just want details, I want a voice in the war-meet over tactics and strategy."

"That's a bit irregular," Umut began, but she went on.

"And I will need your solemn oath that once the steeds are trained, and Liam can travel safely, you will help me return home to Soldonia."

Umut sounded sincere enough when he promised to consider, and a faint tinge of amusement crept into his voice when she suggested renewing the discussion on her return. "Oh, are you going somewhere?"

"To the coast, if Rafi will guide me."

There was something she needed to see for herself.

FORTY: RAFI

Trust is the root of all bonds, and of all bonds, the sol-breath is the most sacred.
- Soldonian saying

Rafi felt like he was flying as Ghost skimmed along the surface of the ocean. Spray on his face, salt on his tongue, waves tugging at his legs, and Ceridwen, the Fireborn of Soldonia, sitting behind him. She wore Nef's *chet* belted at her side, which struck Rafi as odd, considering Nef was the most suspicious person he knew. Combined with the knife she'd stolen from the kitchen, she was amassing quite the armory, though she had, fortunately, left her fire-demon back at the rebel camp.

Fireborn, he corrected himself.

While she'd been fairly quiet at first, eventually his charm and humor had worn her down enough that she had shared the correct terminology for the various solborn steeds. Or, rather, he'd persistently used the wrong words until she had grown annoyed and corrected him.

Out of the corner of his eye, he glimpsed wisps of red hair dancing in the wind, and he grinned. Cut Ghost left, then right, and then dove. Her grip on his upper arms tightened as they plunged swiftly downward, arced back up, and surged out of the water. Dove again, arced up again, out again, higher. Once more, deeper, faster through the turn, and this time, Ghost soared into a flying leap.

Spray sparkled around them like falling stars.

Rafi flung his head back and whooped before they hurtled back into the sea. So, maybe he was showing off a little bit. But that was what this was about, wasn't it? Ceridwen had been vague on the details, but he gathered she wanted proof that he and Ghost truly were . . . whatever it was they were, since, apparently, taking on a scadtha wasn't convincing enough.

Of course, she was the Fireborn of Soldonia.

She probably ate scadtha for breakfast. Well roasted.

Hence, showing off. He dipped Ghost deeper still, straight through a mass of silvery fish that scattered before them, then around a rock spur covered in fluttering yellow and pink anemones. He tucked Ghost into another spin, dancing through the rays of shifting sunlight, then urged him forward. Ghost lunged into every stride, neck bobbing as he rapidly picked up speed.

Rafi felt the sea pulse as Ghost thrust his head forward and screamed. So focused on catching that moment when his sensation of the water shifted from a rushing in his face to a current swept up in the colt's wake, his awareness of all else faded until Ceridwen abruptly made a grab for the reins. No, for his rein arm. Seizing his wrist, she spun them off course.

Startled, he looked back to see panic in her eyes.

Oh, Ches-Shu, Cael, and Cihana Three, he was an idiot. She needed air. He sent Ghost racing for the surface. They burst out into the sunlight, and Ceridwen sagged against his back, gasping in long breaths. He held very still, and Ghost tilted his head back to eye him curiously. The colt nickered low in his throat, then shook himself violently.

Rafi turned to offer Ceridwen an apologetic grin and found that she had slid back almost onto Ghost's haunches, leaving a gap between them again. "So I take it you still need to . . ."

"Breathe? Aye, of course. You're not immune to flame, are you?"

"I don't know." Could he be? Was she? "Odd as it may sound, it hadn't actually occurred to me to stick my hand in a torch."

"You're not, so I wouldn't recommend it."

"You're the one who brought it up."

"I was making a point. Poorly, it seems. I've never had to explain any of this before." Strands of hair that had worked free of her braid clung to her face, and Rafi resisted the urge to brush them away. "With the sol-breath, seariders like you are inured to underwater pressures, granted increased lung capacity, capable of sensing currents, that sort of thing."

Most of that he'd guessed already, or at least experienced.

"But you're not," he acknowledged. "So it has something to do with the steed you ride? Let me guess: You could stick your hand in a torch?" Only after he saw the catch in her throat did he recall the burns he'd seen when he'd pried the chains from her hands after fishing her out of the canal. "Oh, Ches-Shu, I'm sorry, that was—"

She waved him off. "Yes, fireriders are less susceptible to smoke or heat or flame. But we're not invulnerable. Just like you still need to surface for air eventually, we rely on treated gear. Speaking of which, you don't happen to know what became of mine, do you?"

Rafi shook his head. "Umut might know. One of his healers tended your wounds. I can ask when we get back, but it wasn't in the best shape when we pulled you out." Waves lapped up over his knees and a whisk of breeze stirred his hair, and he couldn't restrain his curiosity any longer. "So, what exactly is the sol-breath? Come on," he added. "You got your proof, didn't you? Ghost and I are a team? What's the harm in telling me now?"

Conflict waged in her eyes as she searched his expression, and he tried to overlay a shade of Delmar's confidence atop his own grin. Seemed to work, too, because she actually answered.

"It's not a thing you explain. It's something you see. Something you feel and experience."

"But where does it come from? How does it happen?"

"Where does the wind come from? How does it blow?"

He squinted an eye at her. "You mean Soldonians have been bonding steeds for centuries without developing any sort of stories or explanations for how it works?"

"Of course there are stories—"

"So tell me those."

"I am not a storyteller."

No, she was the substance stories were made of—raw heart, aching soul, and gritty bone. "Don't be so hard on yourself," he said. "I'm sure you're not that bad."

She blinked, then laughed. "Some say that the final breath of every fallen warrior is transformed into a blessing that may be bestowed upon a worthy rider by the spirits of ancient heroes."

"Your face says you disagree."

"My face says nothing."

"It does. It practically screams."

"I've met too many 'unworthy' riders to believe it."

Ghost jerked his head up with a muffled snort and drifted sideways on the waves. Rafi patted his slick neck to calm him. "How many too many? One too many? Two? Three? I'm trying to figure out if you really have met others or just me."

"Others"—a subtle emphasis on the word implied a dual meaning— "believe that the power resides solely within the steed to give or not as they will."

"You still disagree?"

She shrugged. "You asked for stories; I'm giving you stories. But I did say it's a thing to experience, not explain, so you know what I—" Ghost's squeal drowned out her voice, and her gaze slipped past Rafi and widened.

Rafi twisted to see, and there, floating before them, was a dusky gray seablood. Coiled neck, dark eyes peering out beneath a shockingly white forelock, nostrils flared, it snorted out a damp, snuffling breath. Ghost tossed his head, but his ears were pricked. Curious, not angry.

Splashes sounded to the right, then the left.

Two more seabloods emerged alongside, one an opalescent white, the other a deeply dappled gray. Ceridwen tapped his shoulder and pointed down to the stream of shimmering shapes drifting past below Ghost's gently churning hooves.

"*Shades*," she whispered in awe. "It's a whole pod of them."

"Uh huh, and the odds they're here to eat us . . .?"

Ghost shrieked suddenly and struck out with his forelegs. With echoing shrieks and a crash of water, the three seabloods whirled away, drawing the coursing mass below in their wake. Stretching out his neck, Ghost keened after them, and Rafi watched their diminishing shapes with an odd ache in his throat that vanished when Ceridwen gripped his shoulders.

"Go on. Chase them!"

"Chase them?" he repeated. "Why?"

There was a fierce light in her eyes. "For the thrill of it. Go!"

Obligingly, he gave Ghost slack, and away they sprang, bounding over the waves. Ceridwen threw back her head and loosed a wild cry that sent a shiver down Rafi's spine. Forget before—now they were truly flying. Rafi thought they could have gone even faster if they were fully immersed—if they were both seariders—but as it was, they would have to rise too often for Ceridwen to breathe for it to make a difference.

So, they sped along the surface while their quarry raced below, until Rafi could hardly breathe for the slap of the wind in his face or see for the sting of the spray in his eyes. The pod gradually began to pull away, but Ghost sped on, until Rafi finally drew him to a stop.

Chest heaving from exhilaration, Rafi sank forward over Ghost's neck. Oh, Ches-Shu, that had been freedom. He closed his eyes, savoring the gentle rocking of the colt upon the wash of the sea.

Ceridwen spoke softly behind him. "Others say that trust is the root of all bonds, including the sol-breath. She called it an echo of the bond Aodh shares with mankind."

"She?" Rafi asked, straightening. "You said 'others' first and then 'she.' Who is she?"

"My mother." Her voice grew softer still. "She always clung doggedly to the belief that whatever wounds life dealt her, Aodh bore them upon his skin and would one day remake them into something new." She faltered. "In that, she was as much a mystery to me as the sol-breath."

Aodh. Bearer of the Eternal Scars.

Rafi absently rubbed his thumb over the rough scar on his left palm. "I know what you mean. There was this fisherman who took me in when I had no one. Torva. He offered me a home and called me his son. I'd never thought much about gods or deities before, Aodh or Murloch or the Sisters Three, but his trust in Aodh was like breathing, right up until he jumped in front of a stone-eye tiger to save me."

"What happened to him?"

She asked it as if she knew the answer.

"He died." If there was power in unlocking a man's chains, there was power in taking his scars on yourself, too, and it wasn't the kind of power Sahak sought. It was something older and deeper and freer than that. Something that flipped the whole world on end, like staring at the horizon where sky met sea and sea met sky and the line between the two was indistinguishable.

You wanted to talk about mystery? How about a power that looked like weakness, and weakness that looked like strength? Maybe Sahak would never understand that, but maybe Rafi could. Comprehension still felt beyond reach, but of one thing Rafi was certain. He wanted to understand, maybe more than anything.

He craned his head around to Ceridwen and found her looking off eastward over the sea, cheeks still flushed from the race, sadness in her eyes.

"It's out there," she said, and he knew she meant Soldonia. Her home.

He had fled from the palace without a backward glance, for home had been the brother running at his side, and he had raced off into the jungle after Torva died, for home had been the old fisherman and not his hut. But there was longing in her voice, and loss, too, though whether for people or place he wouldn't ask.

She shook her head. "So far away, and still I can't help thinking that if I just strain my eyes enough, I'll be able to see it, them, waiting for me."

Or both people and place, a devastating combination.

Rafi shaded his eyes with his hand, then risked a bit of humor. "So, that's what this was. You were trying to trick me into ferrying you all the way to Soldonia, weren't you? You do know that would take days—weeks, even—and I'd be sure to notice eventually? Maybe not right away, but by the third or fourth, surely."

She visibly rallied herself. "Day or week?"

"Somewhere in between, I think." If he looked back to his right, he would see the jungle-carpeted mountains forever encroaching on the white coastline, but ahead, there was nothing but sea and sky stretching unknown and empty before them. That endless horizon kept drawing his eye. "Would it be possible though?" he found himself asking. "Could a searider make the crossing between here and . . . anywhere?"

"Seabloods do it. Clearly. But no, I've never heard of a searider making the journey without an accompanying vessel, and it certainly couldn't be attempted by anyone who isn't. Seabloods sink when sleeping, keeping only their nostrils above the surface, which would leave a rider submerged or stranded to stay afloat on their own."

Rafi cocked his head at her. "So the odds of you stealing the colt and breaking for home, which truth be told, I hadn't even considered until now, are slim? Well, that's a relief. For me, anyway. So, what now? Do we race our shadows to the horizon? Seek out a scadtha to slay? Juggle moonbeams and chase starlight on the open waves?" He should net his tongue, but drifting here beneath the endless expanse of sea and sky, he felt unbelievably alive.

Ceridwen took a deep breath, then drew on his arm to turn Ghost about, until they faced the rumpled shoulders of the mountains, now blanketed in shadow and rimmed by the setting sun with fire. "Now, we have steeds to tame."

FORTY-ONE: JAKIM

The vows of a Scroll are binding. As the ink seeps beneath your skin,
let the truths it contains seep indelibly into your soul.
- Traditional words spoken at the inking ceremony

Rhodri scrutinized the embroidered cloth as Jakim and Khilamook stood nearby. The war-chief sat on a rock, gloves discarded and the lacings of his jerkin undone, exposing a sweat-stained tunic beneath and the strange dark dawnling relic resting on a chain about his neck. But it was the unsheathed sabre beside him that held Jakim's attention.

He scratched the back of his neck, which made grime flake away under his fingertips. They were all of them dirt crusted and weary after a long day of toiling across Gimleal, ever alert, ever ready to take cover to avoid being seen trespassing on another war-chief's territory. At least they were back to traveling during the day. After crossing over at the streams of Soltain, through a lush green valley where seven springs flowed together to form the River Tain, they had found a richly cultivated country, strewn with farms and villages. For those first few days, they had traveled only at night, lighting no fires and cooking no meals—which had sparked more than a few complaints—and swung wide to avoid roaming herds of pastured solborn.

But now that the green had given way to a far more rugged, far less inhabited terrain, they were back to day travel, and Jakim was glad of it. Khilamook seemed to thrive on an upended sleep schedule, but he had never been able to sleep past dawn.

Rhodri flicked his gaze up. "Have you uncovered the map yet? Either of you?"

For a split second, Jakim considered lying. But that wasn't who Aodh had called him to be. "No," he said.

Khilamook shifted beside him, and Jakim steeled himself for the announcement. It seemed every time he'd seen the man lately, he'd been scrutinizing the cloth, muttering constantly to himself. Jakim could scarcely believe it when Khilamook dipped his head and offered an apologetic sounding, "Not yet."

Rhodri's eyes narrowed, and he laid the silk square aside. "I offered life to the one who succeeds first, but should you both fail me, you should know that I'm not in the habit of making idle threats." He looked past them, and Jakim turned to see Arlen and Brawly marching Finnian up, one on each arm. His hair was standing on end, his arm had slipped out of its sling, and a cut had opened on his right cheekbone—clearly, there had been a scuffle, and clearly, he had lost.

Hands bound, two against one, the odds were stacked against him.

His dark eyes caught Jakim's for a moment as the brothers bore him down, resisting, to kneel before Rhodri, who shifted the sabre so it rested across his knees.

"You seem to be recovering, te Donal. That's good. There's nothing more wretched than a warrior ruined at their peak." Rhodri flexed his grip on the sabre.

Finnian said nothing, only stared straight ahead.

"You were close to Ceridwen and to that old wolf, Markham. You sat in on their war-meets, heard their strategies. I know Ceridwen, and I know that she would not ride out after me without organizing the defense of the kingdom in her absence. You will tell me what she planned."

A muscle twitched faintly in Finnian's jaw.

Rhodri's expression tightened and he nodded. Brawly let fly a punch that knocked Finnian's head sideways, then another that split his lip.

Finnian spat out blood and sat back on his heels.

"What will Markham do next?"

Finnian deliberately turned away from Rhodri. "Still feeling that arrow wound, Brawly? Pretty sure Madden hits harder than you. You should have invited him to help. Or no, I forgot, they all went off and ordered you to stay behind, didn't they?"

Indeed, the rest of Ondri's sons had ridden off soon after they made camp, and the shouting match that had broken out between Cormag and Brawly before they left might have alerted all of Gimleal, if Ineth hadn't put a stop to it.

"You like taking orders from Cormag, Brawly? Who died and made him chieftain?"

Brawly seized Finnian by the tunic and smashed a fist into his jaw, rocking his head back.

"Oh, he is good," Khilamook murmured. "Nearly got his knife."

Who? Finnian? Jakim eyed him, but he just looked dazed.

Brawly hauled back his fist again, but Rhodri stood abruptly, slicing his sabre down at his side with the lethal grace of a stone-eye. "Not his face. His arm."

Arlen seized Finnian's right arm and wrenched up on the elbow. Finnian let out a gasp as the strain caused his injured shoulder to shift visibly in its socket.

"One word from me, te Donal, and you will never wield a bow again." This threat seemed to strike the mark. Jakim saw the catch in Finnian's throat as he swallowed. Then Arlen yanked up sharper, and Finnian collapsed forward with a groan.

"She is not queen anymore, te Donal," Rhodri snarled. "Your loyalty to her is misplaced. What kind of queen would forsake her kingdom for the sake of a single life?"

Hunched over his knees, Finnian lifted his chin. "Ceridwen would."

A furious flush darkened Rhodri's face and the leather grip of his sabre creaked as his fingers tightened around the hilt. Shouts spread through the camp, but he did not seem to notice. He flicked his wrist, slashing at Finnian's exposed neck. The blade sliced through the sling hanging loose over his chest, and the cloth fell beside him.

Jakim felt his knees go weak.

"My lord!" Ineth came hurrying up. "We have a problem."

She nodded grimly as the three other sons of Ondri swept past with wineskins swinging from their saddlebows, along with what appeared to be an entire meal stolen straight off the table. Madden carried a whole side of venison, roasted, and still on the spit. They were followed by a crowd of warriors on foot, who clustered around them as the brothers slowed and began to pass out food.

"Eat up!" Cormag shouted, pulling out small round loaves of brown bread from his saddlebags and tossing them to eager hands. "It's still hot, all of it!"

It smelled good too. So good, Jakim couldn't keep his stomach from growling as Rhodri halted on the edge of the clamoring crowd, which did not part before him. Ineth reached in and snatched a war-horn from the warrior before her and blew a sharp blast. Only then did the crowd notice their war-chief, and they instantly fell silent—all save Ondri's sons.

"Te Oengus!" The bald brother threw up both hands, causing the jugs he held to slosh liquid over the sides and onto his steed.

"What do you think you're doing?" Rhodri demanded.

Cormag shrugged. "You forbade lighting fires, so we found one that was already lit for us, didn't we, Moray?" The bald brother grinned.

Khilamook made an odd snorting sound, and Jakim glanced over and saw undisguised merriment in the engineer's eyes.

"You're enjoying this?" Jakim asked.

"Immensely," Khilamook said. "You are a Scroll, though, so I suppose I cannot expect you to grasp how entertaining it can be to simply sit back and watch the ants run. But it is. Very."

Rhodri focused on the gathered warriors. "Leave us," he said quietly. The warriors obeyed and dispersed with only a few muttered complaints. He strode over to the still-mounted brothers, stopping beside Madden, who still held the stag, dripping, on its spit. "Were you seen?"

Madden glanced uncertainly at Cormag. "It was . . . only a small holding."

Rhodri muttered an oath beneath his breath, then addressed Ineth without turning to face her. "You know what must be done?"

She stiffened. "My lord . . . I . . ."

"There were only a few people," Cormag insisted. "Old ones and young ones alike."

"One voice is all it takes, te Ondri. One voice carrying word to Craddock that we are here and that we are few, and this mission ends in ruin. You think that with Ceridwen gone, he will not see a clear path to the throne by my death? No, I will not let you destroy this." He glanced briefly over his shoulder. "So, Ineth," he said again, "you know what must be done?"

That couldn't mean what Jakim thought it did.

But the tension on Ineth's face seemed to confirm it. For an instant, he thought she would refuse. But she pursed her lips then nodded. "Aye, lord, I know what must be done."

"Then see to it, and take these fools with you."

Jakim awoke as the first brush of dawn streaked the sky, so he saw Ineth's return. She dropped from the saddle, then stood still a long moment before slumping with her forehead resting on her steed's neck. He lay where he was, wrestling inwardly, then finally got up.

She spun at his approach, the reek of smoke wafting off her clothes. There was a smear of blood on her cheek. She did not speak and neither did he. He fetched the small waterskin she kept with her healing satchel and held it out for her.

Her hands shook slightly as she gripped it but did not lift it from his grasp. "Sometimes, we do what we must, Scroll. But I do not expect you to understand that."

The truth was that he didn't, not if she had done what he thought she had. But maybe he didn't have to understand her actions so long as he knew the guilt she felt. He took a breath. "I was not supposed to leave the Sanctuary in Kerrikar. The Scrollmaster thought my vows too newly sworn, my faith too fresh, to trust to such a difficult journey. They were sending out a mission, you see, to Broken-Eliam, to the City, but I wanted to go home, so I told the Scrollmaster that I could guide them to the City, because I had been there before."

She took the waterskin then. "You lied."

"I lied. Then our ship was sunk, and I was made a captive, and I thought that Aodh was punishing me as my lie deserved because it made me unworthy to be his Scroll."

"Aodh is just," Ineth offered with a tinge of scorn.

"He is, and he is merciful," Jakim said. "It is one of the paradoxes, the paired truths that seem to contradict one another because they are too complex for us to grasp—"

"I know what the paradoxes are. Why are you telling me this?"

He looked earnestly into her eyes. "Because I believe that the place where Aodh's justice and mercy meet is in his scars. He bears the wounds of the world, after all, even our unworthiness."

Ineth stoppered the waterskin and tossed it roughly back to him. "Spare your breath, Scroll. I have heard it all a hundred times before." She turned to her steed and loosened her cinch but did not unsaddle.

Soon, they would be moving out for the day. Jakim should go rummage up some food for himself, or maybe check on Koata the tiger. Instead, he found his tongue running away with him again. "Why are you loyal to someone who makes you do such things? Who treats you like a tool to be used and discarded?"

Ineth rounded on him. "I am not the one being used and discarded. You should be glad you never reached the City on your mission. There is only death there. Or did you never stop to wonder why none of the missions ever return?"

She was actually shaking.

"What do you mean? Only the last mission, ten years ago, did not return."

The bitterness in her laugh sent a chill down his spine. "Is that what they told you? Then you are not the only one who lied, young Scroll. You should question everything they ever told you, because even if you believe that Aodh is true, his servants are not."

FORTY-TWO: CERIDWEN

The gear of a firerider consists of a hooded leather jerkin and chaps,
tall boots, gloves, and half mask, all routinely treated with skivva oil.
Harvested from plants that grow only in the scorching conditions found
among the craters of Gauroth, skivva oil provides flame resistance
and prevents leather from cracking.
- Wisdom of the Horsemasters

Rafi was already waiting, perched atop the fence overlooking the steeds when Ceridwen reached the enclosure the next morning, though it was so early the songbirds had scarcely begun singing and a misty coolness still draped the dewed gorge and clung to her skin. She read exhaustion in his slumped shoulders, and when her spurs clinked faintly, bringing his head up, his bleary eyes confirmed it. Had he even slept?

They'd returned late last night from the coast, and after negotiating the final details of her agreement with Umut, she'd collapsed into her hammock, half afraid to sleep, lest sensations of drowning taint her dreams. When she finally succumbed, it was the first unbroken sleep she could recall since her capture, and she had not dreamed of anything.

"Morning." Rafi's smile shed any trace of weariness as he held up two steaming bowl-like cups. "Saffa already had water boiling, so I was able to steep us some tea."

She accepted a cup, catching a whiff of an oddly floral scent. "You ready for this?"

"I'm always ready for . . . whatever it is we're doing today." He took a long sip. "Want me to taste yours again, or do you believe me when I say it's not poisoned?" He kept a straight face, but she caught the spark in his eye.

Was he baiting her? There could be only one response to that.

Ceridwen tipped the cup back and drained it in a gulp. It was hot, of course, but she scarcely noticed that, for it was also unbelievably bitter. Water sprang to her eyes, and she swallowed several times, trying to dispel the cloyingly sweet aftertaste. "What was that?"

"Same thing I'm drinking: rassa leaf tea." His lips twitched. "It's better savored." He dropped beside her. "Did you find your gear?"

"I did." She gestured at the boots she'd pulled on over her trousers— her own trousers, freshly washed and free of the stink of the ship and captivity. She had found them bundled with her leathers and tucked just inside the curtain of her hut when she awoke, though there'd been no sign of her old tunic. No doubt that had been far too tattered and bloodstained for salvaging, so she still wore her borrowed sleeveless green shirt. "That was you?"

He nodded. "Just boots? Was the rest too far gone?"

"I won't need the rest today." Which would hopefully prove true enough, even if it wasn't the full truth. "Do you have the ropes?"

He stacked the cups carefully and nodded toward a basket waiting at the base of the fence. "Ropes I've got. Along with brushes, rags, cala root crackers, and not the faintest clue what exactly we're going to be doing."

She plucked a coil of rope from the basket and, with a few deft twists, knotted it into a slip-on halter. "We are gentling the steeds before allowing anyone else near them. Usually, riders start their own steeds, and the rigors of the process strengthen their bond, but since none of our potential riders will have any experience, I thought it best to ease them in."

"You mean, they'll miss out on all the falling and flying through the air? That hardly seems fair."

"Oh, trust me, there will be falling aplenty." Slinging the halter over her shoulder, she moved toward the gate, rounding the stacks of poles and materials the rebels were collecting to build additional pens, like the smaller one off to her left where Mindar had been separated out from the others. His ears flicked at their approach, and he thrust his head over the side, nickering. Smoke puffed from his nostrils, and steam drifted off his hide like a cloud.

She paused, then softly clucked her tongue at him.

Ghost shoved his nose over the fence, too, pink-tinged nostrils snuffling, forelock draped messily over one eye. Why was he in there too? Rafi tugged a handful of crackers out of his pocket and fed one to Ghost, who jostled close beside Mindar with a brazen carelessness that usually would have summoned sparks from her volatile steed. Today, the fireborn merely pinned back his ears and tossed his head before also taking a cracker from Rafi's hand.

Ceridwen stalled midstep. "*Blazes.*"

Rafi fed Mindar another. "His breath really is warm."

"It could sear the flesh from your bones."

Rafi looked at her in confusion.

"You can't hand-feed fireborn," she said. "They usually scorch their food before eating it. You're lucky you still have a hand."

"Scorch it? Really?" He took a step back. "Sad waste of food. You think it's because they've completely seared their taste buds?"

She stared at him. "Do you take anything seriously?"

"I take food seriously. Humor too."

"You take humor seriously?"

"If I don't, who will?"

She was dimly aware that the caverns had come awake, and a steady stream of workers passed on their way to the fields. She stepped up to Rafi and looked him in the eye. "Starting now, solborn are on that list. Do you have any idea how many riders have died taming steeds? Soldonian riders with stories and legends and experience to guide them, and still they died, and my brother among them. So no jests, no jokes, and no feeding my steed."

It was harsh, too harsh, and she knew it. Must she always be as quick to flame as her fireborn?

She flung open the gate to the main enclosure and waded into the reeking mess within. Muck, churned by far too many hooves confined far too closely, clung to her boots as she caught a dun riveren and a blue roan earthhewn with a head and legs so dark they were nearly black. Rafi opened the gate for her, standing with his hand out until she draped the riveren's lead across it.

"I'm sorry about your brother," he said. "I didn't know."

"You couldn't have. Besides, it's been three years. I should—"

"Move on?" His lips pressed thin. "It's been six years since my brother died, and I spent far too much of that time trying to escape his memory, and now, it's like the whole world has forgotten he ever existed. He deserved more than that. A lot more."

That raw scrape of pain and regret in his voice—Ceridwen knew it well, though she never would have expected to find it buried beneath Rafi's veneer of humor. Which returned in an instant, as his lips curved into a grin. "There, I've gone and dragged us down. You see what happens when you put a ban on jokes?"

Ceridwen's plan for the steeds was simple. Once they set up in another, unfinished pen, they began with grooming and moved on to simple ground maneuvers, embedding responses for leg and rein pressure. She sank quickly into the familiar flow and was able to keep a thoughtful eye on Rafi as he worked. Singing softly, he glided around the riveren, moving with a natural fluidity and ease, and she found herself marveling. If he lacked the finesse that her horsemasters had drilled into her, he more than made up for it in instinct and innate skill.

It no doubt helped that this particular riveren was about as threatening as a songbird. She had chosen well for him, if not for herself. The beastly earthhewn had a neck like a tree and a head like a mallet, and though it was clearly too young to have sprouted a horn yet, she imagined that it was simply worn down from bashing its skull against rocks. It kept flicking its tail at her in annoyance, as if she were no more than an irritating fly, and it moved with a sluggishness that was exasperating.

She considered moving on. Working with another steed and coming back when her head was clearer, her temper in check. But stopping tasted like defeat, and she had drained enough of that bitter brew to last a lifetime. So she stifled her mounting frustration until Nef showed up to deliver the bridles Umut had commissioned at her request. Then she threw caution to the wind, coaxed the bit into the beast's mouth, and swung onto its back.

It stood stock-still at first, then slowly lumbered forward.

She had forgotten how sitting astride an earthhewn could feel like straddling a moving landmass, and yet, there was something undeniably intoxicating about the sensation of power that came atop a creature so massive. It resisted her rein, drifting sideways. Heel pressure swung it around, and it picked up speed, enormous hooves pounding the ground.

One full circuit of the pen it loped, then a second. Earthhewn were hardier than stone and capable of great endurance. If she were back in Soldonia, she would have ventured out onto the plains and let it run clear across Lochrann until it was finally exhausted. Only as she urged the steed into a seventh circuit, then an eighth, did she consider the impossibility of achieving that same end by going round and round in circles. She would weary before it did.

Gathering the reins tight, she drew back.

The beast plunged on, tugging against her pull. She had not fully reckoned with its strength or with the weakness of her wounded arm. Pain shot through her grip as the earthhewn bounded across the pen, fighting her attempts to slow it. It crashed sideways through the fence, poles snapping under its weight, and then careened on without slackening its pace.

Toward the main enclosure crowded with steeds.

Ceridwen hauled its nose toward her right knee, locking her fist against her thigh and forcing it into a turn that spun its bulk just shy of demolishing the enclosure. One crisis averted. But with her left grip failing and no stirrups to brace against, she couldn't apply even pressure to the reins. So the earthhewn spun like a cyclone, whirling across the path, scattering workers on their way to the fields, crashing through foliage, until finally fetching up with its hindquarters pinned against a clump of trees.

She wasn't sure which one of them was breathing harder.

Some part of her expected to see Finnian rushing over and to hear the concern even thicker than exasperation on his tongue. *"Shades, Ceridwen, must you always bite off more than you can chew?"*

Her chest tightened. Then the earthhewn stamped, and the ground shuddered, cracks crawled out from beneath its hooves, and the trees creaked and groaned as their roots shifted. Ceridwen was once more a thousand miles from home, and Finnian was . . . gone. She slid down the earthhewn's side and pressed her forehead against its ribcage, breathing in the slightly musty scent of its coat.

In. Out. In again.

"Ches-Shu." Rafi's voice. "You weren't joking when you said to take this seriously, were you?" He drew up alongside on the riveren mare, scratching her neck as she shyly dipped her head.

Straightening, Ceridwen spat out the wisps of hair that had blown into her mouth and flexed her aching arm. She winced as she surveyed the swath of destruction she had left behind: trampled crops, broken fences, workers staring from the fields, and all before the sun had spilled over the edges of the gorge, which was a new level of overachievement, even for her.

"You think anyone noticed?"

"She jokes! Careful. I have it on good authority that isn't allowed."

And there must have been balm in Rafi's smile, because Ceridwen found herself giving a half breath of a laugh, and the cavity in her chest ached just a little bit less.

"Off to a rampaging start, eh, Red?" Nef strolled up, gaze sweeping to take it all in. He dispatched workers back to their tasks with a sharp jerk of his head. "You got a plan for selecting riders and steeds yet?"

Rafi answered for her. "Sure we do. Came up with a list of qualifications too—really tough stuff to weed out the, well, weeds—such as bringing us food, not trying to kill us, supplying a steady stream of Ceridwen's favorite rassa leaf tea, that sort of thing."

Nef ignored him. "Where do I sign up, Red?"

"You want to ride?" Ceridwen gestured at the settling dust. "After this?"

"Not just ride. I want to ride that one." He indicated the puffing earthhewn. "We want to topple an empire, don't we? Seems a little destruction is just what we need."

In the ring of his voice, Ceridwen could hear the collapse of Sahak's temple, the fall of Sahak himself, the ruin of the great palace in Cetmur, surrounded by its thousand waterfalls, and she nodded. But as she guided the earthhewn back to the wrecked pen, a voice inside her wondered if even that would be destruction enough to give her rest on the other side. Or would there be yet another battle to fight? Another war to be won?

These questions lingered the rest of the day as she and Rafi each traded one steed for the next in a steady stream until shadows again blanketed the gorge. With Rafi focusing mainly on the waterborn steeds, Ceridwen had an abundance of earthhewn, shadowers, and stormers to gentle. Each time she mounted the first, she thought of her father and the poisonous secrets he had withheld; and each time the second, she pictured Finnian lying dead and forgotten on some desolate hillside in Ardon; and each the third, it was Iona she saw falling from the sky over and over again.

Once these creatures had been beautiful to her, but now all that color seemed stricken from the world, buried beneath a layer of ash.

Shutting the gate behind the feathered tail of a stormer, Ceridwen double-checked the latch while Rafi gathered up their supplies. She'd been so focused, she hadn't even noticed the onset of twilight until the workers started trooping past on their way to the caverns. But now the scents of cookfires, of roasting meat and vegetables, were wafting down the gorge, and she sensed Rafi's eagerness to be done in his increasingly frequent guesses as to what was being prepared. "Smells like someone's cooking goat meat . . . frying up parsnips . . . that there, bushka bean soup . . ."

Ceridwen slung the bridles over her shoulder. "And we're done."

"Really?" Rafi stretched out his shoulders. "No need to stop on my account. I can still feel my legs, so clearly, I can keep going." He grinned, dirt streaking his face, bits of grass sprinkled over his dark hair. "Not bad for a first day? Three for you, seven for me." Seeing her confusion, he clarified. "That's the number of falls we each took."

"I had no idea you were keeping count."

"Oh, not me, Iakki. He's helpful like that, the little sea urchin." He hefted the basket of supplies. "Wouldn't be surprised if he and Moc were taking wagers. Not a half bad idea, really. Especially if we were to get in on it. What do you say? Willing to take an extra fall or two for coin?"

"Pretend to be less? Never."

"Can't fault a man for trying."

"Oh, but I can."

She halted before the smaller pen, where his seablood and her fireborn were crunching away at piles of roughage—Mindar's charred black and crisp. Wisdom said that seabloods and fireborn should not get along, yet here they grazed side by side, muscles relaxed, ears flicking lazily. Content. "Tell me something: Why did you put Ghost in with Mindar?"

Rafi lifted a shoulder. "He seemed lonely."

His tone held no censure, but she felt guilt all the same. Of course Mindar was lonely. She had been neglecting him—Liam too.

Rafi gestured to the caverns. "You coming? I smell saga crisps, I'm sure of it."

"You go on ahead. I'll follow."

She watched his limping trek up the path into the caverns, then she entered the pen. Mindar's eyes glowed molten in the fading light, and she took a deep breath before she crossed to him and scratched at his whiskered chin. Simply pulling her boots on this morning had instantly made her feel more like herself, bones settling into well-worn grooves, spurs a familiar clank, even the way the weight of the undercut heels changed her gait. But whatever comfort that brought had vanished when she splayed her leathers out on the floor, overcome with dismay at how pitted, scarred, and stiff they had become.

Gloves missing, her left vambrace, too, half the straps worn so thin she feared they would snap when she tugged on them.

No saddle. No saddle bags. No skivva oil.

How many more blazes could her gear endure before it succumbed to the heat? And without treated gear, how many more could she?

Mindar's warm breath puffed over her, though it did nothing to alleviate the chill within. She faced it defiantly, called it by name. Fear.

She, Ceridwen tal Desmond, the Fireborn of Soldonia, was afraid of her own pit-spawned steed. Of the inferno that raged so fiercely within him, within herself. Of its reckless, clawing nature, desperate to be unleashed.

Of her own inability to contain it.

She drew his head up to hers, stood directly in the path of his flame, and felt the fear slithering up inside her. And then she stamped it out. "We do not back down, Mindar. We do not give up. We do not fear the flame, and if we do, we brave it anyway."

FORTY-THREE: RAFI

He who sees a monsoon in every sun shower will never venture far from shore.
- Alonque proverb

Rafi shuffled clumsily down the slat-and-wood staircase, muscles protesting each downward step. Four days of relentless riding, of being tossed, thrown, and trampled into the dirt more times than he could count, and still he'd had to chase down sleep last night and wrestle it into submission, only to wake up still fogged with exhaustion. Not to mention waking up late—a quick glance showed that the basket of riding supplies, which was usually stashed by the entrance to the lowest cavern, was missing.

Today, however, would be different.

Today, they moved on to the second phase of training: not just steeds, but riders. Assuming, of course, that anyone showed up.

Umut, however, was nothing if not skilled at recruiting warriors to desperate causes, as the strength of the Que Revolution proved, and there was a mass of rebels gathered around the solborn pen. Most stood a respectful, even fearful, distance away, but Nef leaned against the woven fence, arms knotted over his chest, basket of supplies at his feet. Of Ceridwen, Rafi saw no sign.

"Cousin!" Moc bellowed and waved as Rafi hobbled up.

"Moc, you're back! How was the raid?"

"Ah, cousin, it was so boring."

"So, a success then?"

Moc gave a shrug as he peeled a simba. "Ran a few errands for

Umut, checked in on outposts, stole some water buffalo hides from a tanner—for what, I have no idea."

"Ceridwen gave Umut a list of supplies. She wants to have tack made for the riders, gear for the steeds, that sort of thing." Rafi eyed the fence, decided climbing would take too much effort, and collapsed onto a stack of poles instead. He bit back a groan as he landed on his already-bruised tailbone.

"You look terrible," Moc observed around a bite of fruit. "I've been gone, what, a week? You look like you've aged a decade."

"Really? Only a decade? Guess I look better than I feel."

He felt like he'd aged two or three. At least. His skin was a net stretched too tight over aching bones, and his muscles were strings plucked taut and fraying. Of course, the stiffer he got, the slower he was to react, and the more likely to wind up eating dirt after a fall, which contrary to Ceridwen's assertions, did not taste like the mumagung bean tea he'd brought her yesterday.

Mumagung bean tea was far, far worse.

Though he would never admit that to her. It had been worth choking down his cup after she spat her sip out, just to see the shocked disbelief on her face. He'd meant to bring her pale rainflower tea today, to make up for it.

Moc held out a simba ring. "Here. Eat this. You look like you need it."

"Can't. I'm too tired to eat."

Someone snorted behind him. "Too tired for eating? You?"

"Sev?" Rafi tried to turn his head, but the cramp that shot down his neck warned that his body, apparently, no longer worked that way.

Sev came into view, fists shoved into pockets. "You seen Iakki?"

"I haven't, but I bet he's close." Probably perched somewhere that afforded him a clear view of the pen and any riders who went flying.

"Can't seem to pin that boy down. I think . . . I think he's avoiding me." Sev looked gutted by the admission. Or maybe just reluctant to make it to him.

They hadn't exchanged words since the raid.

"He was watching from there yesterday, if that helps." Rafi pointed out a cluster of thickset trees with a sprawling tangle of branches.

"I'll check. Thanks."

But Sev lingered as if he wanted to say more, and Rafi ached that things had become so painful and uncertain between them. "How is Kaya?"

Sev seized on the topic. "Settling in. Seems we'll be here a while. Your rebels aren't keen on us leaving with Sahak on the hunt, and we have nowhere to go, so we might as well make ourselves at home." He scratched at his jaw. "She convinced me to come down here. She would have you join us for a meal, and I think it might help . . . with Iakki. Maybe tomorrow?"

"Really?" That was more than Rafi could have hoped for. "I'd love to."

Sev seemed to relax. "She'll be pleased. Me too."

It began as a sound like distant heartbeats that brought Rafi to his feet and quieted the murmuring crowd. It grew into a rumble like soft thunder as Ceridwen swept into view, racing down the gorge toward them atop her fireborn. Mindar was stretched out long and low, and with each stride, white smoke puffed from his nostrils. He maintained his pace as he neared, and Ceridwen did not slow him, though the rebels shifted like a shoal of fish, until at the last instant, Mindar sank back onto his haunches and slid.

Sparks and dust flew out from his hooves, spraying the onlookers as he came to a halt less than a spear-length away. Ceridwen, sitting deep on his spine, stayed still, though such a maneuver would no doubt have flung Rafi over the fireborn's head.

That was skill, and Rafi gaped in awe of it.

"So," Moc said knowingly to Rafi, "what do you think of your Fireborn?"

"She's not mine, Moc, or even ours." She was Soldonia's. Or just her own. Still, try as he might, he couldn't tear his gaze away. She had a pull to her, like an eddy. Delmar had been like that too. "Reminds me of my brother."

Sev snorted. "Really, Rafi, your *brother*?"

"Yeah, she has that same . . ." He struggled to explain. Confidence? Command? Sense of innate certainty? Moc and Sev exchanged amused looks.

"Face?"

"Hair?"

"Ah, it's the—"

"She's relentless," he said, watching as Ceridwen twisted Mindar into a dizzying spin, his forelegs dancing one over the other. Slowly, at first, then swiftly and smoothly as a waterspout coiling in the wind. Steam curled up from his mane, but no sparks or flames like Rafi'd seen before.

However much she had demanded of him these past few days, she had demanded even more of herself. That, too, was like Delmar.

Moc sighed. "Ah, cousin, you are hopeless."

Ceridwen whirled to a halt, and Rafi met her eyes through Mindar's pricked ears. Her nod spurred him into motion. He dug out a rope and bridle and painfully jogged to retrieve the first steed, a shadower with a coat the muted brown of neefwa bark, save for a single creamy patch that spilled from its mane down its shoulder. Nostrils flared, it shied away, but he brushed his fingertips over its silky coat, and his soft singing settled it enough that he was able to guide it over to the repaired training pen as Ceridwen addressed the rebels behind him.

"Before I was queen of Soldonia or war-chief of Lochrann, I was an Outrider. Warriors who wish to join their honored ranks must ride the gauntlet, facing down a host of flashing hooves and scabbarded sabres, striving to emerge from the melee still mounted. You will not become Outriders, but if you have the mettle, you will become solborn riders. It will demand courage, tenacity, and heart, and today, you must prove all three. Today, you must ride for it."

Ches-Shu, the way she spoke, Rafi was ready to spring up and dare the gauntlet himself. But while the would-be riders formed a line and Ceridwen went over some of the basics of sitting and steering and staying calm, he guided the steed in a wide loop instead, felt its body bending away, away, away, and then toward him, drawn by his own movements, as if in a dance.

Moc and Sev watched him over the fence.

"Not planning on riding?" he asked.

Moc snorted. "Who, me? Ches-Shu gave me two good feet of my own, and I wouldn't want to appear ungrateful. No, I'm just here to watch Lowen ride."

"Lowen is here?" Rafi twisted as Ceridwen opened the gate atop her steed, to see Nef swagger in to cheers, hoots, and howls. No surprise that Nef would insist on going first. The line behind him, however, left Rafi amazed. It bunched in twos and threes and wrapped all the way around the enclosure. He spied Lowen's dark curly hair toward the middle. "Might want to get comfortable, Moc. We'll be here a while."

"You didn't expect a turnout like this?" Sev asked.

"Honestly?" Rafi gestured at his bruises. "I thought I was a walking, limping deterrent. Come, ride steeds, look like me, it'll be fun!"

Nef marched right up to the shadower. "That's because you lack conviction. Not everyone is so concerned about their own skin, Tetrani."

Tetrani. Rafi darted a glance at Ceridwen, who was observing from beyond the fence. No doubt to avoid unsettling the shadower with her fireborn. One knee slung across Mindar's withers, elbow resting on it, she looked at ease. Nef's voice must not have reached her.

Ordinarily, Rafi would shrug off such insults, particularly since Nef's tone suggested a jab to the ribs not a stab to the back, but there was too much at stake. "Enough, Nef. The name is Rafi. Only Rafi."

"Oh?" Nef's eyes narrowed. "Since when?"

"Since I didn't betray the revolution under torture. Now come on."

He cupped his hands for Nef's foot and hoisted him onto the shadower. The steed shifted, and Nef snatched the reins and drew them taut toward his chin, which made the shadower toss its head and drift sideways.

Rafi caught up and towed Nef's hands down. "Easy. Try to relax."

"Shut it," Nef snapped and spun the shadower away so quickly he nearly slid off the side. Sighing, Rafi raised his hands in surrender—and to fend off the steed if it tried to trample him—and retreated to the fence.

"You never learn, do you, *Nahiki*?"

Rafi turned to find Sev scowling. "What?"

"I saw the look on your face. You don't want her to know who you are. You would hide behind Rafi the rebel, just like you did Nahiki and Talik before that."

Nef rode past, spine stiff as an iron rod, and dirt flew up from the shadower's hooves, spattering the fence.

"Come on, Sev, it's not like—"

"Oh?" Sev thrust his jaw forward. "What is it then, *Only Rafi*? Every time I think maybe you've changed, or maybe I know you again, you fall back into the old pattern. It's like you've been lying so long, you don't even know yourself anymore. So, fine. Don't tell her who you are. Keep juggling your lies. Just don't expect anyone to stay through the mess when you drop them."

Sev stalked away just as there was a startled grunt from Nef. The shadower, thoroughly exasperated, finally kicked up its heels and sent him sailing. He soared awkwardly and crashed into the soil, but managed to turn his tumble into a controlled roll.

He was up again in an instant, expression dark. Cursing under his breath, he slapped the dirt from his trousers and turned to leave the pen.

Ceridwen's voice halted him. "Ride again."

"Why? I tried, I failed, I'm done."

"This is the first lesson every rider must learn: falling is not failing. Riding is getting up again. Again and again. So, Nef, would you be a rider?"

Nef worked his jaw, then gave a sharp nod.

"Then rise and ride again."

FORTY-FOUR: RAFI

Cihana laughs and grass sprouts, crops flourish, and flowers blossom.
She groans and the earth splits asunder.
- Mahque teaching

Training riders proved no less exhausting than taming steeds, though fortunately, it did involve less faceplanting into the dirt. It still left Rafi coated in a thin layer of grime from jogging back and forth across the pen, chasing steeds all morning. Which made the water he guzzled taste like grit, and when he swiped his lips, left a smear of mud on his forearm.

He sagged against the ribbed trunk of a chuchoco tree, grateful for the speckled shade cast by its elongated yellow leaves, and raised the waterskin to pour a stream over his head.

A shovel hit the ground inches from his feet.

Nef plucked the waterskin from him and took a long swallow. "You know, when Red said we would be riders, I thought we'd be doing more riding and less—*that.*"

His tipped head indicated the main enclosure where Rafi had set the newly selected riders to work, grooming steeds and shoveling manure into piles, while Ceridwen continued to sift through the catch of recruits they'd netted. She dismissed any who balked on their first attempt, as well as any who refused to ride again after a fall. Ruthless? Maybe. Or maybe just driven by the same urgency Rafi felt whenever he thought of Sahak.

Right now, though, he wasn't thinking of that. "You call her *Red*?"

Nef scowled. "No." He tossed his head back and drained the entire skin in a series of long gulps, then shoved it toward Rafi. "So when do I get that earthhewn? I didn't sign up to shovel dung. Quicker we finish, quicker I get back to the fight."

"It takes time and effort. You'll have to be patient."

"You learned. How hard can it be?" Nef's stance seemed to dare a fight, but he broke into a laugh and clipped Rafi's shoulder. "Relax, Tet–Rafi, I'm just ribbing you."

Oddly enough, he actually seemed to think he was.

He had even stopped himself from saying Tetrani. That was a first.

Could this be Nef's way of trying to extend the hand of friendship? Not just fellows-in-arms or partners on a raid, but friends, like Nef was with Moc? Rafi wasn't sure what he thought of that. He got the sense that Nef, like a python, was better kept at spear's length.

Nef abruptly straightened, standing at attention. When Rafi didn't react quickly enough, Nef slapped his chest with the back of his hand and nodded toward the gorge path, where Umut was approaching, feathered cloak draped loosely around his shoulders, beaked crown sitting low on his weathered forehead. Beneath, he still wore his old, ragged tunic and a belt fitted with pouches for medicinal supplies, both of which seemed better suited to the man Rafi had come to know.

On one side of Umut paced a compact, dark-skinned woman, all wiry muscles and ropey scars, with hair cropped close to her skull, save for a single knot behind her ear that held an Alonque bead strand. On the other marched a thickset, bearded man with a forehead like a cliff and shoulders like a plateau, and a scowl like a cleft between the two.

Rafi spared them only a glance, for behind, clad in a colorful coat still unmuted by the dust of the road, strolled the taleweaver Eshur.

What in Ches-Shu's everlasting, watery embrace was he doing here?

Seeing Rafi, Eshur broke into a warm smile. "Ah, it's the juggler. I suppose it's safe to assume that you're not here to kill me this time either?"

Rafi shook his proffered hand. "I had no idea you were a rebel."

"It tends to be safer that way."

Umut's keen gaze slid between them, but he merely addressed the two newcomers. "Owga, Clae, this is the one I told you about before."

The woman regarded Rafi with interest, but the man's focus was on the steeds. "He's working to ready our team of riders."

There was an implied "or he should be" in Umut's tone.

"Water break." Rafi raised the empty skin, and it flopped in his hands. "Or, well, it was. Now, I guess we're water *broke* and—"

"We should get back," Nef interrupted, nodding respectfully toward the others. "You know how it is: war rests for none, and we can rest when it's won."

"Well said," the bearded man grunted. "And you are?"

"Nef, sir, and proud to fight for the Mah."

"Then why aren't you out there already, fighting with me?" He looked Nef over. "Any time you feel like trading this sideshow for the front lines, you know who to ask for."

Umut coughed and pressed on, beckoning the others toward the caverns. Once they were out of earshot, Nef rounded on Rafi. "Do you know who that was?"

"Eshur?" He shrugged. "Sure, we've juggled together."

Nef scoffed. "No, Clae of the Mahque. He's a legend. Mahque head on the revolutionary council. One of our most effective war leaders. His forces wage a constant fight with the Nadaarian garrisons on the westward fringes of the Mah. They pose such a threat that the Nadaari started burning villages at random to tempt the tribes to turn against them." His smile sharpened. "But every time the oppressor flexes his claws, more join our ranks."

This Clae sounded like the kind of rebel leader that Torva had always frowned upon. One who brought just as much devastation to his people as the Nadaari.

Consequences, hissed a voice in the back of Rafi's mind.

"Who was the woman?" he asked.

"That was Owga, head of the Alonque insurgence. Used to be a tiger fighter in the Chiznowith arenas." Nef said it dismissively, though Rafi found that far more interesting than anything he'd relayed about Clae.

"Tiger fighter? Like stone-eyes?"

"You know another kind?"

Rafi had seen a tiger fight once long ago. His uncle had taken both him and Delmar, under the guise of teaching them the art of charioteering. In the traditional Choth sport, warriors battled a single stone-eye in pairs, one blindfolded and armed with a spear, the other seeing, but armed only with a net that had iron claws instead of weights attached to the edges. The stone-eyes wore no blindfolds.

But the arena they had visited had hosted a variety of fights, from one warrior versus one tiger—both or neither blindfolded—to ten warriors facing off in a melee against ten raging beasts. Rafi had shut his eyes but not his ears, and the sounds were enough to know that the fights tended to be short and bloody for both beast and man.

"Don't you see it?" Nef demanded. "If the three heads of the council are meeting now, then we are on the verge of everything we've been striving for. Outright war to win our freedom. Can't you taste it on the air? Victory?"

His fervor made Rafi uneasy. "Only if victory tastes like dirt."

"Yes. Yes! Like dirt and blood and sweat, and when all is done—"

"Don't tell me. Saga crisps?"

"Freedom."

Nef didn't say it the way Rafi felt it, rich with hope and desperate with longing. Or the way Delmar had, as a fearsome shout of determination. No, on Nef's tongue, it was a final gasp, an agonized groan, a parched plea for a drop—just a drop—of water.

Nef tilted his head, and his one eye burned. "Tides shift, cousin."

Then he retrieved his shovel and walked back toward the steeds.

By the time the sun sank behind the edge of the gorge, and rebels and refugees drifted back toward the caverns, Rafi was mentally counting the steps that it would take to reach his hammock and calculating whether or not it was worth detouring past the kitchens. It wasn't much of a detour—the staircase from the lowest cavern let out on the kitchen side of the natural bridge, while the staircase to the next began across it—so really, it was less about the distance and more about optimism and the hope that tonight, maybe, he'd be tired enough to sink effortlessly into slumber, rather than stare at the ceiling.

Ghost's nicker recalled him before he took two steps, and he swung back, digging in his pockets for crackers. He'd barely seen the colt today. He let Ghost's whiskery lips thump up the crumbs from his palm, while he scratched the soft patch of scales in the hollow of his throat.

Smoke coiled toward him as Mindar stretched out his head, nostrils suffused with a warm, red glow. Without thinking, Rafi reached for another cracker.

"Flames," Ceridwen warned.

Ches-Shu! His pulse ricocheted.

He hadn't even seen her there, sitting with her back to the fence. Startled reflexes made him drop the cracker, and Mindar seared it with a burst of fire that left sparks dancing across his vision.

Ceridwen raised an eyebrow.

"I know," he said, sparing her the trouble. "You told me so."

She went back to gently massaging her left forearm while opening and closing her fist. Soiled bandages cast off in a pile allowed him to see the healing marks on her palms and the closed and slightly puckered wound on her arm.

"How did it happen? Your arm?"

"What happened to your hand?" she countered.

"My cousin." His throat tightened around the confession. Earlier, Sev had accused him of juggling lies. But was it a lie if he just didn't want to admit that he was a Tetrani like Sahak? Why must he be bound to the crimes others had committed against Ceridwen's people?

"Do you have a lot of those?" she asked curiously. "It seems everyone around here claims everyone as their cousin."

He grinned. "We're not actually all related. Or well, we all were once, all the Que tribes. But now, we call each other 'cousin' to remember our shared heritage. You get used to it."

"You sound as if you speak from experience."

"I'm, uh, only half Alonque. My father was Nadaari."

The truth pooled on the tip of his tongue now, flooding his mouth with a sour taste. But he'd been imprisoned, hunted, and tortured for his name, and he'd seen how quickly it could turn people against him. Was it truly so wrong to want to be just Rafi the rebel around her?

He was, after all, good at juggling.

Seeking a distraction, Rafi noticed loose papers scattered over her knees, a discarded charcoal by the toe of her boot. "Were you working on something?"

"Just making notes before we're back at it tomorrow."

He dropped on her left and stretched out his legs. "What kind of notes?"

"The strategic kind. Riders typically have years to hone their skills before they seek to bond their first steed, but we're trying to create a combat-ready force with no time to spare, which means we must remove every obstacle we can."

"Such as?" he prompted, digging out another cala root cracker.

"Steeds and riders are said to bond more quickly when they share certain aspects of temperament, so if we intentionally pair them, it might move things along."

"Really? What do Ghost and I have in common?" Snuffling breaths suddenly ruffled his hair. Without bothering to look, he raised the cracker and let Ghost steal it from his fingers.

Ceridwen eyed him wryly. "I'll let you figure that one out."

"Okay." Rafi made a grab for her notes, reaching across his body. She reacted swiftly, thrusting his arm aside. Distracted, exactly as he'd hoped, by the obvious movement of his left hand, which concealed the subtler shift of his right hand palming the papers.

He sat back, grinning, to shuffle through the stolen pages.

The hilt of her *chet* jabbed into his ribs, and he looked up to find her glaring at him, chin raised like her fiery steed when he was about to flame. She held out her hand. Rafi rapidly scanned the first page and let out a snort of disbelief.

She had written her notes in *Soldonian*.

He flicked his glance up to catch a defiant smile on her lips. He could no more read Soldonian than he could speak it, as she'd clearly surmised. But he could parse out the names of the rebels on her list, and from there, it wasn't such a great leap to hazard a guess.

"Lowen and the silver-winged stormer, huh? Good choice."

Ceridwen merely raised an eyebrow. "*Obvious* choice. He jumped up eager to fly even after being thrown across the pen. You'll have to do better than that."

Rafi flipped the papers toward her hand. "Or you could just translate."

She regarded him with a long, scrutinizing look, and Rafi couldn't help himself. He unleashed his mother's crooked smile. Ceridwen rolled her eyes but took the pages back and abruptly began relaying her notes. Yath, who had surprised Rafi by showing up to ride, had been assigned a riveren. The Eliamite had displayed an unexpected ease around the steeds, despite looking just as awkwardly lanky mounted as standing. But the true natural had been Jasri, who'd come from the kitchens with the scent of roasted garlic in her hair to become the only rider who hadn't been thrown, or even forced into a hasty dismount. Ceridwen intended to let her choose her own steed, which made sense, but had also granted Nef the earthhewn he'd requested.

Rafi snorted. "Nef riding an earthquake monster? What could go wrong?"

"So many things, and not just with Nef." Ceridwen sighed. "This may all be for naught. We have no proof anyone else will be able to bond a steed. You could be an anomaly. No offense."

"Offense greatly taken, I'll have you know. What about Aruk?"

"Too cautious. He rounded that riveren five times before he got on."

"He did get off to a rocky start with a shadower a few weeks back, but I've seen him slipping it treats more than once. They might make a good match." He stopped her as she flipped past the next sheet, which bore only a half smudged-out drawing. "What's that?"

Ceridwen tucked it away. "Nothing. Just proof I can't draw."

"That depends. Is it a drawing of an oddly shaped fungus?"

"It's a saddle. For riding. Umut's craftsmen were able to fashion bits and bridles from a description, but saddles are more complex, and no one here but me has ever seen one up close, hence the very poor drawing."

"Wait, there's something you can't do? Tell me more."

She set her notes down, her shoulders suddenly taut beside him. "You want to know what else I can't do? I can't figure out how Umut thinks any of this will matter. Less than fifty steeds against the might of the empire? Not with a thousand times that number could we make a difference. Not in Soldonia, and certainly not here. I would gladly die to draw the fight away from my people, but what does that gain Umut? Or the revolution?"

"But no one could touch us at the temple. Or on the coast." He'd told her about taking on the longboat with Ghost, while stealing the ship.

"Those were surprise attacks where your steed was in his element. You've been either extremely lucky or extremely clever about when and where you fight."

"Thank you . . . I think."

"But you can't control every battlefield. That's the nature of war. It only takes one spear thrust to bring down a fireborn. One volley loosed at the right angle at the right time, and your friends are tumbling from the sky." She'd gone completely rigid.

This was what it had meant for her to become Soldonia's Fireborn. Fighting to defend her nation, seeing friends fall. "So, why did you agree to help?"

"I could not do otherwise. I could not sit idle while my kingdom burns. Not when I myself am the spark." Her voice dropped. "Markham warned me. He warned me there would be no one to rule in my stead and unite the war-chiefs, that the loss of another monarch would splinter the nation beyond repair, and now I'm a thousand miles away, and . . . *flames . . .*"

She straightened. "I know what he's planning."

Scrambling to her feet, she took off toward the cavern, leaving Rafi to gather the papers and chase after her. "What, Ceridwen? What who's planning?"

"I need to find Umut," she called back.

She quickened her pace as they reached the caverns and scaled the staircase to track down Umut. He was not in his hut but sequestered for a meeting in a strange triangular building that was, apparently, the council hall. Ceridwen seized the latches of the doors in both hands and shoved them open. She halted at the foot of a low table filled with dozens of dishes from Saffa's kitchens and looked directly at Umut, who sat at the head.

"You're planning to assassinate the emperor."

Rafi nearly stumbled over the threshold, but Umut just cocked his weathered head and studied Ceridwen through narrowed eyes. "Shut the door, Rafi, and the two of you take a seat."

FORTY-FIVE: JAKIM

Aodh's hand is the hand of a gardener, planting, uprooting, and bringing growth.
- The truths of Aodh

Ineth was avoiding him. She had been, ever since their early morning conversation—more like confrontation—about the City and truth and lies. Her words were like a cactus spine lodged under his skin. Too irritating and aggravating to ignore. Too thin and flimsy for him to really sink between his teeth and pull out.

So, he was stuck, worrying it over in his mind, because any time he tried to raise the subject or ask questions, she evaded them, just as she avoided him—which was truly quite impressive, considering he spent all day riding directly behind her.

All day, every day, in silence, as they wound ever deeper into a rugged, rocky country, with steep dives and even steeper climbs, and hills dotted with occasional mines and towering spires of rock like stony scadtha rearing toward the sky, shaped no doubt by the wind forever howling and whistling among them.

Ineth rode with her head down, and Jakim wondered if she had nodded off, especially as the line ahead slowed while her earthhewn kept drifting, nudging past a shadower and easing up behind Rhodri. Despite the narrowness of the path, Rhodri's fireborn kept pace beside Nahrog and his chariot, though most of the other steeds seemed to give the tiger a wide berth, and their voices could just be heard over the rattle of tack and wheels.

"He is not pleased, son of Soldonia," came Nahrog's rumble. "This is taking far longer than expected."

"So is your army." That was Rhodri.

Ineth wasn't asleep. She was eavesdropping.

"I am not my betrothed, priest. No dawnling will leave these shores until the army you promised me has arrived. I suggest you use your arts to tell your master that."

"The Voice does not serve me. I serve the Voice."

Ahead, Finnian toiled up the climbing path beside his steed, which limped after the riverrider who held its reins. Finnian's hands were bound and fastened to a rope trailing from his saddlebow, and Jakim wondered if he had been forced to dismount or had chosen to so Sif could rest.

Finnian's keeper stopped suddenly, leaning over in the saddle, forcing the rest of the column to an abrupt halt. Rhodri's fireborn flung up its head to avoid running up against an earthhewn's stony hindquarters, and Nahrog cursed as Koata's slashing claws carved the air only inches from the steed's tail.

Nahrog carelessly clipped the tiger's ears with the whip, then continued in a sullen voice. "Besides, son of Soldonia, his attention is focused elsewhere. It would seem she has escaped."

Rhodri seemed suddenly taut as a rope plucked by the wind.

"Escaped and is running rampant with the Que rebels."

She? Ceridwen? Jakim leaned in, which unfortunately alerted Ineth to the fact that he, too, was listening in. She coughed loudly and shifted in the saddle, then, muttering something about finding out why they were stopped, urged her steed forward. As they edged past, he caught the war-chief's terse response. "You cannot possibly blame me for your own failure to keep Ceridwen tal Desmond contained."

Wings overhead drowned out the priest's reply. Jakim had been in Soldonia long enough now that he looked instinctively for a stormer patrol swooping in from above, but the thing that dropped like a stone out of the sky was much, much bigger. It fell in a howling whirlwind of russet feathers, black beak, and extended talons, and struck the halted riverrider from above with a force that slammed both steed and rider to the ground.

Finnian fell back, half dragged by his skittering steed as it found its reins suddenly trailing, knocked free from his keeper's grip.

With a piercing shriek, the massive raptor spread its wings, casting a shadow that swallowed the struggling pair trapped in its talons, then it shot up again, lifting both steed and rider straight off the ground. Swinging up onto his plunging steed, Finnian made a grasp for the captive rider, but the rope tethering his hands to the saddlebow restrained his reach.

Climbing aloft with thunderous wingbeats, the monstrous raptor vanished behind shredded clouds, carrying both rider and steed with it. Gone in an instant.

Not a single archer had managed to get off so much as a shot, and Rhodri had no stormriders to give chase. Finnian sat staring after it, fingers twitching, as if longing to nock an arrow to his string and let it loose.

Ineth shoved back the visor of her helm. "We are cursed. All of us."

Jakim found Finnian when they halted at a stream to water their steeds. He was sitting on the bank, cupping water in his bound hands and splashing it, gingerly, onto his right shoulder.

"Did you hurt it again?" Jakim asked, crouching beside him.

Finnian let the scooped water trickle through his fingers. "Strained it. The real damage came the other day, from Arlen." His eyes darted darkly toward the archer, who stood back a few paces, keeping watch, while Cormag and Moray sprawled on the bank as their steeds drank, and Brawly and Madden splashed into the water.

How could they be so relaxed? It had been long enough since the attack that Jakim's pulse had stopped thrashing, but he still flinched at every flash of movement or shadow racing across the ground.

"What was that thing?" he asked Finnian.

"The roc? They're rare here. Mostly found in Mabassi, even as far north as Rhiakkor. I've never heard of one in Gimleal before."

"Ineth thinks we're cursed somehow."

"For hunting a dawnling?" Finnian's lips twitched. "Didn't work out so well for old Harrigan, did it?" Then, at Jakim's confusion, he clarified, "Old song. Ceridwen hated it."

Ceridwen. Oh, Aodh have mercy.

The attack had driven all else from his mind. He seized Finnian's arm, ignoring the shadowrider's wince. "There's something you need to know."

By the time it had all spilled out of him, Finnian looked to have aged ten years. He sat there on the bank, motionless, as the stream lapped at his toes. "You're sure?"

"That's what the priest said."

"Then, *shades*, not only is she alive, but she's free! Just trapped there in Nadaar. I've got to get out of here, get to Markham, and—" He broke off, eying Jakim. "I need to know, once and for all, which side you're on."

Jakim shifted uncomfortably. "I am on Aodh's side. But I helped Ceridwen once before, and I want to help you if I can."

Finnian nodded. "Right then. Stay here." Gripping Jakim's elbow with his bound hands, he levered himself up and splashed downstream. Toward Ondri's sons.

Was he going to do something right now?

"You've figured it out, haven't you?" Khilamook said behind him.

Just the sound of the man's voice made Jakim's skin crawl, not to mention the fact that Khilamook had chosen to speak in Canthorian, which never boded well. Jakim turned to face the engineer, who was standing in the middle of the stream, the tails of his high-collared robe blooming out in the flowing water. Droplets trickled down his golden head and fell from the tips of his fingers.

"The map? No, I haven't."

"No, not that. Clearly not that. Don't be a fool. This crew, this motley troop we find ourselves a part of, it's like one of my poison spheres. Each element on its own, seemingly harmless. Crack just the outer shell, and you'll get a small dusting of powder. But jostle it hard enough to shatter the cylinder inside, and suddenly the elements react to devastating effect. This camp is full of such elements: the priest, the traitor, the archer, the old woman."

"I don't understand what you're saying."

"Isn't it obvious? I want us to work together."

Jakim blinked at the engineer, unable to credit his ears.

"You and I can be helpful to one another. They want a map? We can give them one, then while they chase a false trail, we could take the dawnling for ourselves and give it to the emperor of Canthor, and then you could be free, and I could go home."

Something in the way he said those last words rang with a note of truth. Jakim recognized the longing in the engineer's voice because he had felt it himself.

"I can't, you know," continued Khilamook. "Go home, that is. Even if I were free. My brother, Carpaartan, denounced me to the Supreme Chancellor, who erased me from the scholarly records. But with such a gift for the emperor, he would have no choice but to restore me, and then I would be grateful. To you."

That seemed to ring slightly less true.

But that odd churning inside him, was that pity for Khilamook? It was a disorienting sensation, and Jakim was almost grateful when raised voices and the thuds of a scuffle startled his focus downstream to see Brawly tackling Finnian into the water.

Khilamook sighed. "You see what I mean? Elements. Reacting. Think on what I said . . . Jakim."

There was an almost wistful air to his tone, and Jakim couldn't quite dismiss it from his mind as he jogged over to haul Finnian, gasping, out of the water—once Cormag convinced Brawly to stop strangling him. Finnian collapsed onto the bank, his nose bleeding. Water and mud streamed from his dark hair, but he flashed a grin, and when Jakim caught the glint of the knife disappearing up his sleeve, he couldn't help grinning inside too.

"When?" he whispered furtively.

"Soon as Sif has recovered enough to run and we have a new moon to darken our path."

Your path, Jakim thought, but didn't bother correcting him yet. He would help Finnian escape, but he would not abandon the new path that Aodh had set before his feet, no matter where it might lead.

FORTY-SIX: RAFI & CERIDWEN

Fear not the stone-eye you see but the one you do not.
- Choth axiom

"Who told you?" Umut demanded, fixing his keen gaze on Ceridwen as she took the open space beside Eshur, across from Owga and Clae.

Ches-Shu, that wasn't what Rafi had been expecting.

Still holding Ceridwen's papers, he mechanically shut the doors, then lowered himself into a seat. He felt dizzied and slightly nauseous, senses overwhelmed by the mingling aromas of food that had been sitting out for too long, by exhaustion, or maybe by something deeper. They were speaking of assassinating the usurper of Nadaar. Old habits drilled into him by Delmar made it impossible to think of his uncle as anything else, but still just the idea of participating in such a plot rattled him.

"You told me yourself," Ceridwen said. "You invited me to stick a blade in his chest while I'm close enough to strike."

"That was a metaphor."

"But also the truth, unless I'm mistaken."

She wasn't mistaken. Rafi could see it in Umut's face. "Ches-Shu, you actually mean to do it. You're going to assassinate him."

"So?" Clae growled, plucking chunks of meat and root vegetables off a skewer with blunt fingers and tossing them into his mouth. "You got a problem with that?" His mud-like eyes glinted with a hostility Rafi knew well.

Clearly, he knew all that Rafi was and hated him for it.

Rafi's mouth went dry. "No, it's just that . . ."

That poisons in the night, knives in the throat—those were Sahak's methods. The sort Delmar had always believed had claimed their parents, despite the official proclamation that attributed their deaths to illness.

It felt wrong for the revolution to be involved in the same.

But whatever concerns he raised would no doubt be tainted in Clae's mind by the fact that he was a Tetrani. Only, how did Clae know? His thoughts felt as thick and murky as Saffa's bushka-bean stew, but he could have sworn the introductions Umut had just made hadn't identified him as anything other than "Rafi." So if Clae knew, Umut must have told him beforehand. Likely Owga as well, which would leave only Ceridwen in the dark.

He was an idiot. He should have told her before and risked the consequences. Too late now, unless he could navigate this conversation without forcing a revelation, which would be tricky, to say the least.

"It's just," Rafi continued, "once he's dead, then what?"

"Then the Que will have won their freedom, what else?" Clae arched a thick eyebrow. "Why? You want to take his place? Sit enthroned at the Center of the World?"

"No. Never." Rarely had Rafi felt words so strongly.

The force in his voice seemed to take Clae aback. But even if he had sworn to aid the revolution, even if he would take up his brother's mantle to win this fight, even if he must own his own name to do it, still, he had no intention of making a claim for his father's throne. That had been Delmar's burden to bear, not his. Never his.

"It's not, actually." Eshur spoke up, drawing a confused scowl from Clae. "Cetmur. It's not the Center of the World. That's just Nadaarian myth."

Clae flicked the comment away and leaned toward Rafi. "You seem to have a lot of objections. Having second thoughts?" Up close, his snarl drew attention to the sharp twist in his nose and the scar that bisected his bottom lip. "Well? Tiger got your tongue?"

Owga shot him a disdainful glance over the rim of her teacup.

Seaweed tea, by the scent of it. Just one whiff made Rafi breathe easier. It tethered him to the Rafi who had been resurrected on the beach, rather than the one who had spent four years buried in a cell, mourning his lost family.

"Nope," he said, dropping Ceridwen's papers onto his knees. "Just trying to wrap my mind around what this means for us. What's the point of having a squad of demon-steeds and riders out there, wreaking havoc and providing a focal point for imperial wrath, if you're plotting to assassinate the emperor? Wouldn't you want to avoid attention? Lull the empire into a false sense of security before you strike, so there's no warning?"

Just like there had been no warning before his parents died, before he and Delmar were hauled off and entombed in stone.

"It's a little late for that, don't you think?" One corner of Owga's mouth curved upward. She had a warm, deep voice with a distinctive rasp to it. "If you wanted to avoid attention, you would not have attacked that temple while the emperor was inside."

He tried not to react. "You know about that?"

Clae snorted. "Pity you missed your shot."

"There was no shot."

"Whatever you say."

So Nef now had competition for being the most suspicious person Rafi had ever met. Great. He turned to Umut. "Has Sahak retaliated?"

"Not Sahak, no. But the emperor has. We've received multiple reports that two full legions of imperial guards have marched into the Mah with orders to sweep the jungle for insurgents."

Rafi's gut clenched. "That's . . . that's two thousand soldiers." Did the revolution even have that many? He felt a fool for not knowing. That seemed the sort of all-important question Delmar would undoubtedly have asked before committing to a cause.

"A crude display of force." Clae shrugged dismissively. "But they don't know the Mah as we do. They'll crash through the brush with their clinking mail and their rattling spears and their clunky formations, and we'll melt into the thick before them and emerge behind them, harass and harry them, until they fall back to lick their wounds as they've done a dozen times before."

Only Rafi hadn't been here then. How far would the soldiers go now that his uncle had seen him alive and clearly a threat to the throne? It was as if they were all racing to stay ahead of a massive storm surge that hissed and tugged at their heels—one he had unleashed by announcing his survival.

"Regardless," Umut said, "this isn't the response we were anticipating from the Emperor's Stone-eye. He is far too cunning for such blatant moves."

Owga grunted her agreement. "Stone-eyes stalk their prey by slinking unseen through the tall grass until they're close enough to pounce. It is not the stone-eye you see that you should fear, but the one you do not."

The scars that stretched from her collarbones down her bare arms gave a sobering weight to her words.

Ceridwen spoke up then. "I, for one, am glad you attacked the temple, Rafi. They should be, too, if they understand their own stratagems. They don't want to avoid attention because they need it. This isn't a coup. They're not trying to replace the emperor but to collapse his empire, which requires destabilizing it first. Uprooting its structures and sowing chaos that will rage on after the emperor falls. That's why they need us."

"Well reasoned," Umut said. "You have a keen eye."

"Only because I have seen firsthand the devastating effects the sudden loss of a ruler can have upon an already unstable nation." Her voice hardened. "What I still fail to see is how four dozen steeds can accomplish so much."

"Pardon me for saying so," Eshur interrupted, "but what you fail to see is the power of legend. Yours and his." With a nod of his head, he indicated both Ceridwen and Rafi. "You arrived on these shores as a prisoner of war, destined for death, and instead, you arose from the very ashes of defeat, threw off your chains, and now threaten ruin to those who captured you. Can you not see the poetic irony? The symbolism your tale offers all the nations chained to the empire against their will? Whereas Rafi—"

"Has a reputation for being notoriously hard to kill," Rafi cut in, supplying an explanation sprinkled with enough truth that he hoped Eshur wouldn't feel the need to say more.

Eshur seemed to accept it. "Over the years, I have woven a complex tapestry of fellow taleweavers and informants across the empire. With your tale spread among them, we would show all the territories that chafe under imperial rule the possibility of resistance. Undermine the empire's grip upon them so that the Que need not fight alone. Did you know that since the invasion of Soldonia began months ago, Nadaar has doubled their demands for both taxes and soldiers levied from the territories? When the wood is dry and rife with kindling, all you need is a spark."

Ceridwen's eyes narrowed. "Sparks die out, and even wildfires take time to spread. Reaching other territories could take years. Years Soldonia doesn't have."

"Years?" Clae snorted. "Don't you know how Nadaar stocks its armies?" The only one still eating, he reached for another meat-and-vegetable skewer. "Conquered territories supply soldiers to serve as tribute, and the empire ships them off to foreign soil, whether that's somewhere in Nadaar or on whatever battlefront is chewing up their ranks currently. More than half the garrisons in Nadaar are made up of tributes from Slyrchar, Esgurd, Choth, you name it."

He spread his hands wide, which exposed the scadtha-shaped sigil inked across his bicep. It was old and faded now, the lines distorted, but still clearly recognizable as the mark of a conscripted Nadaarian soldier. Clae spoke from experience, it seemed.

"The other territories are within reach because Nadaar put them there. Not that we need them," he added. "Que blood has brought us this far. Que blood should see us through."

Owga sharply set her cup down, annoyance thick in her voice. "Ches-Shu, Clae, we're not rehashing that old argument again. The council voted. It's done."

"Sure, it's done, and now look at us." He jutted his bearded chin at the table. "Eliamite. Soldonian. Nadaarian. We used to be the *Que Revolution*."

Of course he would be the one Nef looked up to.

"Speaking of Nadaar," Umut cut in, seizing the reins of the conversation again, "we've made some inroads there, too, thanks to Eshur. His skill as a taleweaver has gained him access to the imperial court, where he's identified several officials who may be of use to us."

"Identified?" Owga repeated. "How?"

Eshur smiled. "Let's just say they've been vocal in their displeasure with the current regime, both at the time of the coup and since."

Who? The question sprang to Rafi's lips, but he did not ask. It made sense for Rafi Tetrani to wonder which courtiers had resisted the usurper, but Rafi the rebel could not ask without steering the conversation into even more dangerous waters.

Umut's sea-blue eyes settled on him. "Several have made inquiries about you. Seeing you in action might just give them cause to finally set their teeth behind their complaints, so the sooner we can get you in the field the better." His gaze swung toward Ceridwen. "So you see? Your riders and steeds are only one strand in the net, if an integral one. How soon can they be ready?"

Ceridwen darted a glance from Rafi to Umut. But true to nature, she focused first on the steeds. "How soon? One ride does not a rider make, and most of them spent more time in the dirt than on their steeds. I could train them for a year and not teach them half of what a Soldonian learns before bonding a solborn." Her eyes flickered as if in calculation. "Give me a month, let them live, breathe, eat, and sleep with the steeds, and I'll get them riding."

"Good." Umut thumped his palms on the table. "You two focus on the steeds and riders, and leave the emperor to us. We do this right, we'll send up such a flare of smoke from every corner of Nadaar, he won't be able to see us coming."

Ceridwen gave a sharp nod. "Smoke we can give you, right, Rafi?"

He shook off a sense of numbness to the realization that all eyes had turned to him. "Smoke? Sure. Or between the two of us, at least steam."

Ceridwen stepped out into soft night air, thickened by a gentle mist blowing off the waterfall. It felt oddly refreshing. Her mind hummed with all that had been said and all that she must do to forge the steeds and riders into an effective tool to deflect Nadaarian attention away from Soldonia.

One month. *Blazes*, what had possessed her to say that?

It wasn't nearly enough time to train a war-host. It was also far, far too much time, considering how long she had already been away. Senses fogged with fever and pain, she'd lost track of time on the ship and in captivity, but since awaking here in the rebel camp, she had felt the passing of each day like an iron manacle constricting her chest.

She shifted her focus to training instead. Being on the move always helped her think, so she pushed herself forward, focusing on the solid thump of her boots, the faint chime of her spurs, the scuff of footsteps coming up behind.

Ceridwen spun, hand to her *chet*, to see a man jogging toward her. Rafi lurched to a halt. "It's just me. You forgot these." He drew nearer. Though darkness blanketed the caverns, the full moon was visible through the opening that overlooked the gorge, and enough light reached them to reveal that he had something in his right hand.

She regarded it warily. "What is it?"

"It's your notes and your drawing that's not an oddly shaped fungus."

She took the papers. "Thanks."

He lingered, and she could sense his agitation in the hand he raised to the back of his neck. "One month, huh?" Something in his tone told her that wasn't what he'd set out to say. "On a scale of crazy from charging a scadtha to jumping into a waterfall, where would you say trying to train a squad of riders and steeds in a month ranks?"

"Depends on which end of the scale is which."

"Waterfall, scadtha. You have to ask?"

"Well, since I've survived both . . ."

"Oh, it's like that, is it? You should know I've ridden a waterfall down myself."

"Really? Was it mostly an accident?"

He hesitated, then gave a short laugh. "Yes, actually, it was."

"I can't help wondering exactly how you've survived this long."

That seemed to sober him, though she'd said it in jest. He took a step nearer, until she could smell the horse sweat clinging to his skin along with a faint hint of something tangy like the sea. "Ceridwen, there's something—"

The tap of a crutch on stone marked Umut's approach. "There you are. I'd hoped to find you still nearby. One of my healers just brought me the news. Your friend is—"

Liam. Ceridwen didn't wait to hear more. She sprinted around the rim of the cavern. Reaching Umut's hut, she flung herself through the dimly lit, herbal-scented space to the curtain covering the sickroom doorway.

Her fingers trembled as they touched the cloth.

"My lady?" a voice called weakly in Soldonian from within. "Is that you?"

She pressed the curtain aside to see Liam propped up on his cot with his back to the wall, smiling wanly at her. His skin looked ashen, and his hair clung like straw to his damp forehead, but *blazes*, he was alive, and he was awake.

With a lump in her throat, she dropped to her knees beside him and caught him to her heart. Pain she could endure, sorrow was a thing to be expected, and disappointment no longer bore the sting of surprise, but a breath of goodness breaking through all the grief and woundedness of the world, that could bow her to her knees in sheer gratitude and wonder.

"My lady . . . are you all right?"

She drew back, smiling through a haze of tears. "Oh, for flames' sake, Liam, what do I always tell you?"

"To . . . keep my helmet on?" His voice was frail, but he managed a grin.

"Aye, and . . . "

"And to call you tor Nimid or tal Desmond or anything other than 'my lady,' which you know I can't do, now that you're queen." His gaze dropped, and he lifted a crumpled sheet of paper. "What's this? Funny-looking saddle, isn't it?"

Or rather, a funny-looking sketch of a saddle.

She must have scattered her papers over his cot when she hugged him. "It is, unfortunately, my best attempt. How are you at sketching?"

"I'm not one to sing my own praises"—considering he'd once practically begged Nold to compose a song about his stone-eye kill, that was categorically untrue—"but it's been said I've a good eye and a true hand. Why do you ask?"

She had been half joking, but the light that sprang to his eyes caused her to reconsider. "I might have a task for you, once you're up to it."

"Up to it? Of course, my lady."

Shadows darkened the room as Rafi stooped through the doorway, and when he saw her and Liam, he sagged against the door frame in apparent weariness and relief.

Creaking from the cot alerted her to Liam's movement.

He was sitting bolt upright, a cold fury in his eyes, not directed toward her but toward Rafi. It was such an unnerving expression coming from him that a chill crept down her arms, and she reached for him.

"Liam? What is it? What's wrong?"

Then he shivered, and it was gone, replaced by bewilderment.

"Do . . . do I know you?" he asked Rafi, who looked no less confused.

Rafi gave his head a shake as if disoriented and pressed one hand to his temple. *Shades*, he looked utterly exhausted. He doubtless hadn't even understood the question, since Liam had spoken in Soldonian.

"It's a long story," she told Liam, then switched to Nadaarian to address Rafi. "You should rest. You look like you need it. Back at it early tomorrow."

He swiped a hand over his face. "Right. Rest. Tomorrow."

Still, he hesitated, head tilted to one side, like a man straining to catch the fading strains of an echo, then he shook himself again and walked stiffly off. The curtain fell closed with a swish behind him. Ceridwen turned back to find Liam surveying his surroundings intently. Cot, walls, ceiling. Those creeping fringes of soft blue moss.

His eyes came back to her, bearing a hint of fear. "This . . . isn't Soldonia, is it?"

Rafi knew hatred when he saw it. He was well acquainted with its many forms, from initial exposure to full-on infection. How it so often corrupted the corners of the eyes first, so you caught only the glint of it in passing, like light glancing off a shard of metal. There one second, gone when you looked for it the next. He'd seen it that way in the eyes of Sahak long ago before the world spun on end, tumbling him from palace to dungeon, though he hadn't known what to call it. Only later, as Sahak stalked outside their cell, recounting their family's death with a cold smile upon his lips, had Rafi begun to understand.

That unsettling glint of hatred was the same look he had just seen lurking behind Liam's unnerving stare. Though why, he couldn't imagine, unless the boy somehow knew who he was. Knew what he was.

Maybe he was telling Ceridwen right now.

What Rafi wouldn't give to be able to speak Soldonian. Delmar had been tutored in foreign tongues as part of his princely education, before they were locked away. Yet even with all those hours of boredom in the cell, he hadn't bothered to teach Rafi anything useful. Just juggling. Maybe he'd known Rafi wasn't fit for such things. Wasn't fit for anything but running.

Even now, reeling from fatigue as he was, his limbs itched to sprint. Shouldering the door open, he burst out into the night, feet aimed away from his hammock, down into the gorge where he could run until he reached the point of collapse and the mind-numbing relief beyond it.

"You said you were in, Rafi. Fully."

Umut stepped into the glow of the lamp hanging beside the door.

Rafi stifled his jolt of alarm. "You say that like it's in question."

"Would you say I imagined your hesitancy tonight?" Umut pressed toward him, crutch striking with a ring against stone.

"You just told me you mean to assassinate my uncle. I happen to have had some up-close and personal experience with such things, so it caught me off guard. Can you blame me for that?"

"So you admit to having second thoughts?"

"Oh, no, I'm way past that. More like fourth or fifth thoughts now."

Half of him rebelled against the idea of resorting to such means, while the other half forced him to consider which was more unsavory, the death of one tyrant or the murder of countless Que villagers each time the empire decided to impose its will.

His admission seemed to blunt the tension. Maybe Umut appreciated his honesty, if not his sense of humor.

"Not about the cause," Rafi clarified. "I hold to my oath. I just can't help wondering what you still need me for. You have the Fireborn of Soldonia. What's the point in resurrecting a long-dead prince?"

"You mean other than driving a wedge through the imperial court, granting us an ear among the Nadaari, and scattering the sparks of rebellion beyond the Que territories?" Umut planted his crutch and rested both hands on its padding. "Freedom is never won without cost."

"Saw that up close and personal too," Rafi said, thinking of a cliff's edge, a drop into darkness, and his brother's dying scream.

"Yes," Umut said softly. "You did. Because your brother valued your life worth the cost of his own. Is being known as a Tetrani too high a cost for the lives of your mother's people?"

It wasn't what had happened, of course.

Delmar hadn't traded his life for Rafi. He had died because Rafi slowed him down. Because Rafi hadn't been strong enough to keep up. Still, there was only one response to such a question. "Of course not."

Umut squeezed his shoulder. "Good. Learned anything from Yath yet?"

"Yath?" Rafi blinked. Ches-Shu, his mind was churning sluggishly. It took him far too long to latch onto the recollection of their conversation about scadtha claws and Yath's warning that Sahak was conducting unusual experiments in his temple. "No, not yet. Been a little swamped with training. But I will."

"Oh? And when was the last time you got a full night's sleep?"

Rafi backed away with a quick grin. "You know what Nef says. We can rest when the war's won." His muscles were afire now with the need to run, to stretch beyond the limits of his capacity, to prove that if he had the chance to do it over, he would not fail Delmar again, so without waiting for a reply, he took off toward the staircase and the moonlit gorge below.

FORTY-SEVEN: CERIDWEN

Quilted gambesons and fur-lined hoods offer warmth for the high-soaring stormrider, while boiled leather harnesses clip onto rings in the saddle to provide security while diving into the buffeting wind.
- Wisdom of the Horsemasters

J asri was the first to take to the sky. She had chosen a stormer mare with dark gray wings, or perhaps the mare had chosen her, for Ceridwen had seen the shift in the creature's ears, felt the openness in its stance as Jasri wandered among the steeds on their second day of riding.

Only days after that, she was soaring through an azure sky, dipping and wheeling in complex spirals and spins that rivaled the songbirds of the caverns. Others quickly followed. Some took to the earth and some to the rivers, and though some, like Nef, grew more sullen with each day that passed without bonding their steeds, Ceridwen imagined that Markham would be proud of what they were accomplishing, even if these riders were not Soldonians.

Or perhaps because of it. This was, after all, a monumental task. She and Rafi had begun by teaching the riders in rotations—some riding, some caring for their steeds, and some working them on the ground—but eventually, that training had to narrow to mastering the unique skills of each steed. Ceridwen was bone-tired from the time she rolled out of her bedroll at the first gleam of dawn to down a cup of yet another bitter tea Rafi insisted she try, to the time she rolled back in with her boots still on, after a hasty dinner scarfed down after dark.

But it was a good tired, and if she thought of Markham often these days, it was because his sardonic voice guided every decision she made, his teachings informed the exercises she chose, and his gritted determination drove her onward whenever her strength flagged. His wisdom steered her when she saw the depth of longing in Lowen's eyes as he watched Jasri take flight again, the way he stalled with his brush to his stormer's silvery coat and twisted to keep her in view.

"You must tend to your own steed," she admonished.

Lowen started, and his eyes dropped to the saddle slung on her hip, the woven blanket rolled and tucked under her arm. With Liam's sketches to guide them, Umut's craftsmen were working nonstop to create the tack she had requested, though she still barely had enough to outfit even the fully bonded riders.

His head bobbed, and he resumed brushing with a vigor that caused the stormer to lash her tail and sent the brush spinning out of his hand. Ceridwen stopped it with her boot, then bent to retrieve it.

He was eager, this one, if a little clumsy around his steed.

"Steady," she said, passing him the brush. "It's not a race."

He took it, somewhat sheepishly. "Sure feels like one."

"It's not." She paused as Nef trotted past atop his steed, spine stiff and muscles taut, wrestling the reins for control. "Easy," she called. Maybe Rafi had been right to question that pairing, though Nef certainly matched his earthhewn in sheer willpower, which was, perhaps, the problem.

She couldn't ask Rafi now. He had taken the sea- and riverriders on a quick trek downriver to the coast to train in their natural element. So she turned back to Lowen. "You'll soar in your own time, so long as you fix your sight on your own horizon and not Jasri's. Otherwise, you'll never get off the ground."

"Makes sense, I suppose. Just wish it wasn't so hard."

Neither jealousy nor bitterness marked his voice, merely an earnest yearning to fly. Ceridwen knew that feeling, though her soul had called her to smoke and flame not wings and sky. She set the saddle at his feet, then unrolled the blanket, revealing a full stormrider harness made to wrap around his shoulders and fasten over his chest then clip to rings in the saddle's frame.

Unlike the saddles of her people, these were no works of art with ornate tooling and engraved metal embellishments, but they were sturdy and should enable the riders to be more effective in a fight.

In the end, that was all that mattered.

"It's yours," she said, holding it out. "Ride ready to soar, and you will soon enough."

His eyes widened as he took it, and he was still running a hand over the dark, textured leather when Ceridwen moved off to distribute the other saddles the craftsmen had delivered. One, she gave to Aruk, and another to Flick, a soft-spoken, young Hanonque with a wide smile. Flick had bonded his horned bay earthhewn with an ease that only made Nef's continued struggle more apparent.

What, she wondered, would Markham say to Nef?

Standing with her back to the fence, she felt someone lean against the opposite side—too heavy for Iakki, though he was constantly crouching underfoot or dangling overhead, determined to get as close to the steeds as possible. Out of the corner of her eye, she caught a glimpse of dark, wavy hair and eyes scored by constant smiling.

It was Eshur, the taleweaver.

"You are a hard person to pin down, Fireborn of Soldonia."

She had evaded him the last two times he'd come to the training grounds simply by focusing relentlessly on her work. "You may call me tal Desmond. And if you've come to see the Fireborn in action, I'm afraid you're wasting your time."

"Isn't this you? Aren't you in action?"

"I mean if you've come for flames, you won't get them."

"What need have I for flames when I have a thousand stories to keep me warm?" He spread his arms, allowing his coat to flare behind him, unveiling dozens of hidden panels of color. Those, Aruk had told her with a tinge of awe in his voice, each represented a story Eshur was capable of telling.

She knew little of Eliamite culture and even less of taleweavers, but there was one question that had been bothering her since she and Eshur met.

"Why are you here?"

"Not to see the Fireborn in action, it would seem."

"Here with the rebels, I mean. What is your stake in their fight?"

"Ah," he said, "I'm here to collect stories, not tell them. This time."

Eshur's gentle tone softened the refusal, but Ceridwen could not be dissuaded so easily. She tried to recall lessons from long ago on Nadaar's early conquests, which included Eliam. Her father had insisted she and Bair fully understand the threat they would face, should Murlochian Dominion ever overshadow their shores. Which it had.

"Your people are exiles, are they not?" she said. "Cast out by the empire centuries ago? Would you tear the empire down to return them home?"

"The breaking of Eliam left us no home to return to."

"So you would risk your life merely to see the Que win their freedom?"

He smiled at her skepticism. "Why should I not care for the freedom of the Que? Or for the wellbeing of every person to cross my path. Our stories are intertwined after all, as densely and thickly as the wildest patch of jungle in the deepest part of the Mah. You understand this. How else would you explain the tale of a queen who offered her life for the sake of a lowly rider?"

She felt a sudden chill. "You have been talking to Liam. How?"

"He has a good ear for a story, that one," Eshur said in passable Soldonian, "and a tongue skilled to tell it."

"Aye, and he's lonely, too, which makes him easy prey for you." She thought guiltily of Liam enduring the slow drift of hours alone, with only the occasional visit or sketching task to keep him preoccupied until he regained enough strength to use the crutches Umut had set aside for him.

"He spoke of your exploits of his own accord, with only the barest prompting from me," Eshur replied placidly. "And yes, of course, I prompted. I'm off tomorrow, after all, to weave the tale of the Fireborn of Soldonia and the Sea-Demon of Zorrad. Would you have it be a threadbare one?"

"You can make up whatever tale you like."

"But it is the truth in a tale that matters. One false thread and the whole thing unravels, no more enduring than an idle thought."

She bit back her reply as Jasri suddenly swooped low through the gorge in a screaming dive, then bounded upward again through the clouds as though she were crashing in and out of waves. Ceridwen could almost imagine herself atop Ghost again, racing after the pod of seabloods, wind in her teeth, spray on her cheeks, Rafi's laugh ringing in her ears.

The Sea-Demon of Zorrad? It suited him.

"You don't want me telling your tale. Why?"

Eshur's question rooted her. Why indeed? She had longed to earn glory undying in the songs and legends of her people. And here, across the ocean, in the stronghold of their greatest foe, she had the opportunity to do just that, whether or not she deserved it. She reached to unearth the answer, but old reflexes drove her away from the pain it held before she'd fully grasped it.

"You didn't answer my question," she said, "and I asked it first."

"No, I suppose I didn't. Though I can't help wondering if you've asked Yath the same questions. He is an Eliamite, too, after all."

In truth, she hadn't considered it. "He was imprisoned by Sahak. Revenge can be a powerful motivator."

"Revenge? Perhaps. Though not so powerful as a longing for redemption, I daresay." He fell silent then continued, "Would you believe that I've committed to this cause because of a story? If all our stories are tangled together like the Mah, this other story is woven deeper still, a root system entwined through the very fabric of the earth, occasionally sending up tendrils here and there, in the most unlikely places. Chasing those threads, untangling them, seeking to understand the image they create—that's what I'm here to do."

He raised one eyebrow expectantly.

Her turn. She had asked and he had answered, and if his answer only surfaced more questions, that didn't negate the bargain. "Maybe I simply can't imagine my story would be of any interest. There's not much to it. Only failure."

Only defeat.

Eshur's brow creased, but before he could speak, Nef's curse and the heavy thudding of hooves startled her. His earthhewn careened across the pen, scattering steeds and riders. His face was carved into a scowl, but it was fear she read in his taut expression, and that fear spurred her into action.

She could hear Eshur calling after her but could not make out the words as she caught the steed's left rein in both hands and tucked her body into a sharp leftward turn. She did not set her heels, so her scrambling feet kicked up a dust storm, but the addition of her weight to Nef's strength dragged the earthhewn's head around, forcing it to slow, then stop.

Its neck, pressed against her arm, was slick with sweat. It puffed out rapid breaths, rocking Nef roughly in his seat on its back. With a strangled curse, he dropped the reins, flung himself over the side, then stalked away.

Ceridwen did not call him back.

"Never a dull moment around here, I see," Eshur remarked, meeting her farther down the fence as she guided the earthhewn over to a trough.

Only then, as it lowered its lathered muzzle to the water and began to suck in noisy gulps, did she finally release the reins. Strands of dark mane clung to her fingers, and her left arm tingled as she flexed her grip.

A reminder of weakness. Of battles forever lost.

Eshur's voice softened. "Don't negate your own tale, tal Desmond. Stories have a way of getting beneath the skin. Even if they are only the ones we tell ourselves." His fingers tapped out a fluttering rhythm against the fence, then he pushed off it and added before he turned away, "Never underestimate their power."

Eshur's words had a way of getting beneath the skin, too, it seemed. Ceridwen couldn't shake free of them, even hours later as she sat removed from the small group of riders gathered around the outdoor cookfire in the waning light of evening. Both soup pot and bowls had long since been emptied, and the riders listened, rapt, as Jasri described soaring at heights where trees looked like moss and rivers like snakes and her sol-breath-enhanced vision could still make out the shape of a graybeard monkey leaping from one branch to another.

Lowen shook his head in wonder. "I can't imagine it."

"You don't have to," Jasri said, patting his arm. "You'll see it for yourself soon enough, cousin. I have faith in you."

Ceridwen sighed and rubbed grit from her eyes, oddly restless as the aquatic riders, freshly returned from their excursion to the coast, chimed in with talk of the wonders they had seen on seafloor and riverbed. She was supposed to be dreaming up ways to modify the various challenges she recalled being given by both her horsemasters and Markham, to help transform this team into a battle-ready unit. It would have been easy to blame her distraction on the noise of their conversation, or on the lingering effects of Eshur's words, or even on Rafi's nearby attempts to teach Iakki to juggle, which seemed as much an exercise in patience for him as for the boy in agility, but the truth ran much deeper.

Shades, she wished Markham were here.

No, she wished she were there. To be Soldonia's Fireborn once again. She told herself to strive for that single-minded focus she had relied upon so many times before, but she already felt herself fraying at the edges, like a stirrup leather worn thin, groaning under each new twist of pressure.

How long until she snapped?

Something thumped against the toe of her boot and rolled away. She caught sight of a fist-sized leather ball that came to rest just within reach. Rafi waved as he jogged up to retrieve it, while Iakki seemed suddenly very interested in the sky, in anything but looking directly at her.

"Sorry about that," Rafi said, stooping down to grab it. "One of the many hazards of juggling, I'm afraid." Before his fingers could close around the ball, Ceridwen reached out and snatched it away.

"Many hazards?" she repeated, holding the ball up.

Rafi rocked back on his heels, looking amused. "Sure. Usual stuff, you know. Sprained wrists, rolled ankles, damaged pride, oh, and thieves too." He grinned as she tossed the ball at him. Though, as he twisted and caught it easily behind his back, she was half tempted to snatch it from the air again.

Once, she had enjoyed such mischief with Bair. With Rhodri, too, truth be told. But she was a thousand sorrows and a thousand miles away from that wild-haired child who had planted manure in Rhodri's boots, slicked Bair's stirrups with oil before he attempted to mount, and collapsed helplessly in laughter when they paid her back in kind. Her tears, she knew, had been spent with Bair.

She had never considered when her laughter had faded.

Oblivious to the turn her thoughts had taken, Rafi bounced the ball from hand to hand. "Nice, isn't it? It's Eshur's. Was Eshur's. He gave me his set. It's been a while since I juggled anything other than odds and ends."

"And here Lowen told me you liked juggling knives."

"Oh, he did, did he? Must be confusing me with my cousin—with Nef I mean. Seems the type to try something like that, doesn't he?"

He did. Of all the riders, Nef reminded her most of herself. Stubborn as a sand-blasted earthhewn, as Markham had put it. Desperate to be in the thick of it, as Finnian had. Which should qualify her to root out his challenges, one would think. *Should.*

"Nahiki!" Iakki shouted, drawing Rafi's attention before she could mention what had happened with Nef earlier. "Come on."

"And . . . duty calls." Rafi started to jog off, then turned around instead. "You know Iakki thinks you're working too hard."

"Oh, Iakki does, does he?"

Iakki's jaw dropped. "I do not."

"He does. He thought you might care to juggle with us."

"I did not. You take that back, Nahiki."

Rafi's smile grew wider. "He said you weren't the sort to blink at a challenge."

The boy's voice rose. "You know I said no such thing!"

Probably not, but Iakki *had* said something interesting, and she had nearly missed it. "Tell me, Rafi, did he also say why he calls you Nahiki?"

His gaze darted away from hers, and she sensed that whatever came out of his mouth next would be an evasion, only Iakki chose that moment to fling a juggling ball at the back of his head. Rafi sidestepped without even looking and snatched it out of the air. He gave an impish smirk right before Iakki crashed into the back of his knees, tackling him to the ground.

"Ches-Shu," he gasped, mouth pressed into the dirt.

Iakki scrambled onto his shoulders, crowing loudly, while Rafi pushed himself up. With a sharp twist of his spine, he tried to fling the boy off. Unfortunately, Iakki had locked his hands and ankles, so the force of the throw only made Rafi lurch sideways and collapse onto one elbow, while the boy clung on, laughing.

If Rafi rolled onto his back or got a foot under him, he could regain control quickly enough, but either he didn't have the muscle memory drilled into him or—

Shades, she had not been so long at war, had she?

This wasn't a match. He was playing along for Iakki's sake.

With a whoop, Lowen detached himself from the fireside group and loped over, followed by a quietly smiling Flick. Lowen called out a count until Rafi sagged flat in surrender, and they all laughed. But Ceridwen stood and went in search of Nef. She found him atop the highest bridge overlooking the three caverns, slumped on a boulder misted with spray blowing off the waterfall, a new *chet* resting on his knees. He heard her coming and tugged the patch down over his missing eye, but not before she glimpsed reddened, swollen flesh.

"What are you doing up here?" he demanded, turning his face away. His fingers tightened on the hilt of his *chet*. The edge was freshly chipped and scored, and white scars marred the rocks where he had apparently unleashed his anger.

He was fortunate he hadn't snapped the blade.

"I wanted to see if it was worth the climb to see the sun set as well as rise."

His only response was a grunt. She walked past him to the outward-facing edge so she could look out over the gorge, and over the tumbling thickness of the jungle on the slopes of the mountains. It sprawled in all directions, so different from the forest she had fought in on the border with Rhiakkor, with its towering straight pines and needle-carpeted floors, free of undergrowth.

Westward, dark clouds streaked the sky, and the sun burned through rents in the shroud, reminiscent of the fiery streams that crisscrossed the crater of Koltar. Closing her eyes did not banish the image, for she still tasted ash on her tongue, and summoning her voice took effort. "I did not set out to claim a steed when I bonded Mindar, but to kill one."

She could hear him shift on the boulder, but he did not speak. "I sought to claim vengeance for the death of my brother. I failed in that, just as I had failed to save him, and when my catch-rope finally settled around the neck of a fireborn, it was not the blood-red stallion I sought, but a copper-colored colt with embers for eyes and fire beneath its skin. Mindar."

Flung face-to-face, they had frozen. She, braced against the rope, her sabre at his neck. He, coiled to flame, an inferno blossoming in his throat.

One breath more should have meant immolation. She slashing, he flaming, both perishing together in that ashen wasteland. But instead, she had lowered her blade, and he had swallowed his blaze, and that, Ceridwen told Nef, was her first taste of the changes wrought by the sol-breath.

Nef shifted his gaze away. "There some point to this story, Red?"

She had told this tale only once before, to Markham. It had been raw then, and though it was less raw now, still his tone stung. "You're treating all of this—bonding your steed, training—like a fight, Nef, and it isn't."

"Life is a fight. Just a nonstop, blood-on-your-teeth and scrapes-on-your-knuckles, struggle from the day you're born until you die. Don't believe me? Ask the dead of my village that the Nadaari left to rot in the jungle."

"Save the fight for the Nadaari, then. You're not at war with your steed. You can't force the bond. You have to earn it, and you can't do that by trying to out-stubborn an earthhewn."

"Can't I?" he shot back.

"No," she said evenly. "You can't."

That finally seemed to reach him, for he straightened and eyed her warily. "Can't because it won't work? Or can't because you won't let me ride?"

"Both. We ride to war as a fighting unit, Nef, and each rider must be able to trust their own steed as well as the steeds of their companions."

Gripping his *chet* tighter, he leaned forward, his eye glittering with anger. "What about you, Fireborn? Do you trust your steed?"

Blazes, he knew.

How, she couldn't comprehend. Could he have overheard the words she had whispered to Mindar alone that night in the darkness? But no, she had spoken in her own tongue then . . . hadn't she? She couldn't recall. She sensed the satisfaction radiating off him, at having sniffed out a weakness.

Her instinct, as always when threatened, was to flame.

"Mindar and I have scorched armies, slain a scadtha, and battled four shadower assassins in the dead of night. We have weathered infernos you cannot imagine. I trust him as I trust myself." So why did her voice crack as she said it? Why, flames take her, did she turn to leave?

"You don't understand." Nef's voice halted her descent. "I need the fight. It's . . . it's all I am."

She did understand. More than she cared to admit to him.

FORTY-EIGHT: RAFI

Rivers, roots, and rock, these are the things that bind us all together.
- Mahque saying

Rafi did not move a muscle. Sweat beaded on his forehead as a mosquito whined hungrily, but he did not flinch. He was being hunted today. Not for the first time, of course, but even Sahak, with his uncanny ability to detect a trail in a broken twig and sniff out a path over bare rock, did not have the unnervingly sharp eyesight of his current pursuers.

Yath shifted in his saddle. "How long will we—"

"Hush," Nef growled. "He's coming."

Crouched low over Ghost's neck, Rafi watched through a break in the foliage as a shadow raced across the surface of the stream, followed by a silver-winged stormer, flying just above the treetops. Lowen stood in his stirrups, scanning both banks, not just for them but for signs of their passing. His steed beat its wings thrice, then glided, dipped, and beat its wings again, until it rounded the curve of the stream and disappeared from view.

"He's gone," Nef said, his earthhewn giving an impatient stamp. "You're up, herder."

Yath nudged his riveren forward, then abruptly pulled up. "Wait."

Rafi scanned the sky but saw nothing. "What are we waiting for?" That drew a snort of disapproval from Nef. No doubt because Rafi was supposed to be in charge—Ceridwen's idea, not his. She claimed the others needed to grow accustomed to seeing him lead in the field. He just didn't think leading and asking questions were mutually exclusive.

"There's another stormrider. Circling high."

Squinting, Rafi caught a flicker of movement. He let his eyes lose focus slightly, then finally spied the stormrider gliding high above, its dusky-gray hide and the light underside of its wings blending into the cloud. If he hadn't glimpsed that flash of darker color as its wings flapped, he would have missed it. "Ches-Shu, Yath. How did you see that?"

Yath shrugged one shoulder, a smile tugging at the corner of his mouth. "I've always been good at spotting patterns. Who is it, do you think? Timre? Kotal?" Both Hanonque whose affinity for heights had made them natural stormriders.

"Jasri." Rafi recognized both the steed and her perch in the saddle, even the two long braids she had started wearing to keep her hair pulled back from her face. Once she never would have dared expose her scars so, but since taking to the skies, she seemed different. More confident. Daring even.

"It is clever," Nef admitted grudgingly. "One comes in low to flush us out. The other circles above, where we're less likely to hear them."

Yath's thick eyebrows rose. "You think she saw us?"

Rafi watched Jasri circle slowly upstream. "I don't think so." If she had, she would have altered course or tried to signal one of the other seven stormriders currently in the air. Today's trial was for them, designed so they could practice locating foes moving through the jungle toward an undisclosed location, then coordinate a force to intercept them.

Once the sky was clear, Yath urged his dun mare down into the stream, which swirled around her knees. His lanky legs hung down so far on her sides that it flowed over the tops of his feet too. The mare lowered her head as if to drink, and a low, throaty humming filled Rafi's ears.

Nef fidgeted, and so did his steed. "This is taking too long. We could have just charged across the stream and been well on our way to our target by now."

"Sure, we could, muddying the water and leaving a trail so obvious the next stormrider who flies over can't help but find it."

"We move fast enough, and it won't matter."

"That would be missing the point."

"Thought the point was to win."

Rafi's fault, no doubt, for suggesting Saffa offer saga crisps to the winning team. High incentive, that. Out in the stream, the flow shifted sluggishly, and he felt a thrill of pride for Yath as the water backed up before the riveren and drained from the bed below, creating a dry pathway across, strewn with limp riverweeds and still-twitching angling vines thick as his wrist. "The point is to use our steeds' abilities until it's just second nature to us."

Nef scowled. "Got any hillsides you want crushed?" He clucked his tongue, and the earthhewn lurched forward, its massive hooves gouging deep skid lines in the soggy bank.

Stealth never had been Nef's thing, even before the earthhewn.

Sighing, Rafi adjusted the heft of the short spear he carried and followed. Once they were across, Yath spun his mare after them, releasing the pent-up stream in a surge that temporarily flooded the banks, washing out their hoofmarks. He rejoined them in a rush of scattered droplets, smiling wider than Rafi had ever seen him smile before.

Nef grunted as he rejoined them. "Took you long enough, herder."

Yath's smile evaporated. "Just because I am an Eliamite, I must keep sheep?"

"I don't care what you keep, so long as you keep up." Clucking sharply to his steed, Nef plunged ahead, under the cover of a cluster of neefwa trees that curved over the stream and through a dense patch of ferns.

Yath muttered in his own tongue as he fell in behind Rafi.

"It's not you," Rafi said, slowing Ghost slightly to let Nef pass out of earshot. "Nef can be a bit prickly—in the way that a kaava can be a bit thorny or the sea can be a tad wet."

"He's not wrong though." Yath's mouth pressed thin. His thick eyebrows sat low over his eyes in a way that usually struck Rafi as pensive but now seemed almost sorrowful. "My brothers keep sheep. I did, too, once." His voice grew fainter, nearly swallowed by the swishing of their steeds through the ferns. "I turned my back on my past a long time ago."

Clearly, this was a sore point. Nef had a knack for rooting out such raw places and digging his thumb into the wound. Rafi changed the subject. "So tell me, Yath, what caused you to switch from spying on the empire to riding to battle against it?"

"You free me twice and you have to ask?"

"You're saying you're bad at stealth missions?"

"Well, not as bad as Nef." Yath gave a small smile. "But I am clearly an Eliamite"—he indicated his distinctive combination of curly brown hair and ruddy brown skin—"and that, apparently, is no longer a safe thing to be in some corners of Nadaar. Particularly where Sahak Tetrani is concerned."

"Sahak is rounding up Eliamites? Why?"

"I don't know. But I think he took one of my brothers. Iben went missing months ago. When I went looking, I discovered others, dozens, that have vanished over the years. We are a scattered people since the breaking, one tribe cut off from another—but I saw the pattern. Unraveling it led me to Sahak, but not to answers. Just more questions. And a cell." Yath rubbed absently at a woven cuff knotted around his wrist. It was made up of threads of red, orange, green, and yellow. "Whatever Sahak is up to, I won't uncover it through stealth or spying alone. But if these steeds truly can give us the strength to fight back, maybe we can stop him, together."

There was a mission Rafi could undertake without a second thought. "You think it has anything to do with those experiments Sahak is conducting?"

"Why would you ask that?"

Both Yath's tone and his face seemed carefully blank.

Rafi drew Ghost to a halt and swung to face Yath head-on. "Because this whole time, I've been waiting. Waiting for Sahak to make a move, to exact retribution for the ship, the steeds, the temple. The more time that passes, the more I'm convinced the only reason he hasn't is because he's preoccupied doing something much, much worse."

Yath's right eye twitched, and he looked away.

"You want to stop Sahak together? Tell me what you saw."

"It wasn't something I saw. It was something I heard." Yath dragged his gaze back to Rafi, then, with a twitch of his reins, brought his riveren closer and continued in a low voice. "When I was first locked up, there was an elderly Eliamite man in the opposite cell. He was lost in his head. He paced day and night, muttering mangled scraps of the holy writ in Eliami, and even I could barely understand him. He didn't speak a word of Nadaarian. Not when the guards beat him senseless, not when they withheld his food, and not when they hauled him off."

Yath hesitated briefly. "Not until the guards dragged me past the heart of the temple later that day, and I heard his voice within, railing about war and sacrifice and death."

"That's . . . strange."

"No, what's strange is that he was speaking Nadaarian. Perfectly." Yath fixed him with a stare, and Rafi could think up a dozen possible explanations for what he had overheard, but less for the flicker of unease still lurking in his eyes. "That's not all. I heard another voice—"

A sharp whistle cut across his words.

Rafi jerked his head over to see Nef scowling at them from twenty strides ahead. Nef threw up his hands impatiently, then tugged his steed about, clearly expecting them to follow. Rafi twisted back to find Yath gathering up his reins, preparing to ride on.

"What about the other voice? What did it say?"

Yath swallowed. "It told Sahak to come. To the Center of the World."

Considering Rafi had spent several months convinced he could hear, even communicate with, his dead brother—and often still caught himself pausing in anticipation of the occasional ghostly, sarcastic remark—he'd thought himself prepared for whatever Yath might say.

But Ches-Shu, he couldn't make head or tails of it.

He pondered it as Ghost jogged to keep up with the blistering pace Nef was setting, crashing on, heedless of the swath they cleaved through the jungle. Before, when they had spoken of such things, Yath had been insistent that Cetmur was not the Center of the World. Eshur too. Clearly, the phrase meant something else to an Eliamite. If Sahak had gone to Cetmur, or wherever the Center of the World might be, perhaps that explained his disquieting lack of response to the raid. But what to make of the rest of it?

Ghost stopped abruptly, nose to the earthhewn's tail.

Nef had come to a halt, fist upraised. Instinct drove Rafi's gaze up, through the dense weave of branches draped with mollusk moss, orchids, and dangling vines, to the sky. He didn't see any stormriders. A tug on the reins drew his focus, as the colt tucked his head, nibbling at . . .

Oh, Ches-Shu, the earthhewn's tail?

The tail lashed out, startling an angry squeal from Ghost.

Wings whirring, a flock of birds burst from the canopy to their left in a riot of color and scattered in all directions. Rafi winced. Great. If Ghost's squeal hadn't alerted the stormriders, that certainly had. But when Ghost swung his head up, ears pricked, it wasn't toward the sky but toward the trees where the birds had startled. A soldier stood there, clad in muddy armor, helmet hanging from a clasp on his belt. He stared at them, frozen in apparent shock.

Rafi stared back. A Nadaarian soldier. Here.

Granted, that wasn't as geographically astounding as, say, the presence of three riders on solborn steeds, but rebel scouts were constantly monitoring the two legions of Nadaari currently sweeping the Mah. The latest report had them angling on a westward track that would leave nearly forty miles of thick jungle between them and the concealed rebel camp. That was why Umut, who wouldn't sanction raids within a day's hike of the gorge, had agreed to today's trial.

Either this soldier was very, very lost, or the scouts had been very, very wrong, and the camp was in serious danger. Regardless, they would need to capture him. Alive.

Rafi snapped his spear up. "Yield or—"

Nef's wordless cry drowned out the rest as he barreled past, *chet* drawn. For a fleeting heartbeat, Rafi thought the soldier was just going to stand there, waiting for Nef to crash into him, but then he spun around and fled. Four other shapes detached from trees and raced away.

Ches-Shu, there were more of them.

Rafi tore after them, Ghost bounding through the knee-high ferns as though they were waves. The soldiers couldn't be allowed to escape, couldn't carry back tidings of a demon-steed sighting, or the Nadaari would flood this corner of the jungle with so many troops that the gorge, and all the rebels and refugees who called it home, would never be safe again.

He ducked under a looped vine, veered to avoid a kaava's blood-red thorns, and raked the skin from the knuckles of his spear hand, all in the span of a dozen strides. Such dense undergrowth favored runners over steeds, for runners could duck and dodge and double back easily. If these soldiers had been Mah born and bred, they would have lost them in less than a minute. As it was, Rafi's band caught up to them just as quickly.

Nef closed in first, hurtling into and over the rearmost soldier. The next soldier glanced back, the whites of his eyes flashing, dodged as the earthhewn bore down on him, and spun, swinging the haft of his spear like a club. It cracked against Nef's back as he barreled past.

There was no time to see if Nef was hurt, for Ghost angled left, then right, tracking a soldier on the edge of the pack, just as he did when chasing fish beneath the waves. Rafi overran the soldier, splitting him off from the others, then wheeled to close in. The soldier planted his feet and thrust out with his spear.

Ghost skittered to the side, the blade narrowly missing his chest.

His momentum rammed him against a second soldier, who'd been darting up to attack him on his left. Rafi lashed out, first to one side, then the other with his own short spear. Sharp, downward strikes. The first glanced off steel. The second didn't. But it did lodge fast, wrenching from Rafi's grip as he spun Ghost to avoid another spear thrust from the first soldier.

It tore a gash across the colt's neck, and the soldier lunged again, forcing them into a sidestepping rush. Weaponless now, without sea or current to aid him, Rafi bent low over Ghost's neck and hummed a cue. Shaking droplets of silvery blood from his mane, Ghost reared back his head and shrieked.

The cry of a seablood up close was an unearthly thing.

It made Rafi's skin crawl and the blood surge to his ears, even though he was accustomed to it, for the sound had haunted his nightmares for years. It struck the soldier much harder, made him falter, hindered him from seeing the riveren gliding up behind until Yath leaped off the mare's back and buried his knife in the back of the soldier's neck, toppling him to the ground. Paces away, Nef's opponent crashed into a tree and crumpled at its base, breastplate caved in by an earthhewn hoof strike.

Rafi did a quick count. Four down. Where was the—

Rapid footsteps marked the final soldier making a break for it.

"Rafi!" Nef shouted, angling off to the right. "Ring him in!"

Ghost was lathered with sweat now and still bleeding, but when Rafi called for speed, he sprang away. Then, with a *crack* like a bolt of lightning, Jasri plummeted through the canopy and landed with a sharp flare of her stormer's wings in front of the fleeing soldier. He nearly fell over himself in his haste to stop, then seeing Rafi, he tore off, scrambling, toward the right.

He did not make it far.

Nef emerged from the thicket before him, earthhewn rearing up, sinking back on its hindquarters, forelegs bent and hovering. It descended with a thud that rattled the soldier's armor and sent a tremor through the earth. Falling to his knees on the quaking soil, the soldier raised his hands in surrender, and Yath loped up a moment later to take him captive.

Rafi slid off Ghost's side. He tugged off his shirt, then wadded it up against the gash on Ghost's neck. The colt flinched, but Rafi sang softly to him until he calmed, though it wasn't until Ghost nuzzled at his pockets, searching for cala root crackers, that Rafi felt the knot in his stomach relax. Sagging against the colt's shoulder, he gave a lopsided grin as Nef trotted over on the earthhewn. "One hillside demolished."

"And one crisis averted."

Watching Nef scratch the earthhewn's lathered hide, a grin pulling at his lips, Rafi wondered if he meant the soldiers, or the fact that he had, apparently, finally bonded his steed. "Unless the rest of the legions are waiting for us around the next rise. We weren't exactly quiet."

Nef rolled his eye. "Scouts, Rafi. Light armor. Not heavy infantry."

"One thing's certain," Jasri said, casting a critical eye over the scene. "You lot won't be winning saga crisps for stealth tonight."

"No one will," Nef said. "With scouts sighted this close to camp, Umut's going to impose a fire ban until he's sure we're in the clear. You mark my words."

FORTY-NINE: CERIDWEN

Riverriders prefer streamlined raiment, typically patterned in dappled shades of blue, green, and brown to blend with the riverbed. While the use of breathing masks is still rare, such devices are increasingly gaining traction.
- Wisdom of the Horsemasters

The muster for battle came without fanfare or war horns, without brazen shouts or the clatter of spear on shield. It came without any words at all, with the sudden appearance of Umut at the solborn pens, waiting as Ceridwen and Rafi trooped back up the gorge at the head of a straggling line of riders all leading their steeds by hand, cooling them off after an evening of drills.

One look, and she saw it in his eyes, and she felt nothing at all.

Not eagerness, not nervousness, not dread, or even relief.

Mindar's reins slung over her shoulder, she split off from the riders and greeted Umut. "When?" she asked, watching his gaze follow the movements of her mud-spattered and saddle-sore crew, as they untacked their steeds and released them for the night.

Umut didn't seem to have heard her. "You Soldonians always chew up your trainees and spit them out?"

"It'd be odd if they didn't," Rafi remarked as he came over after releasing Ghost. Since he still rode bareback, untacking for him consisted of unbridling, a quick rub down, and a scrub of the colt's wound. "Swallowing one's trainees would seem counterproductive."

The run-in with the scouts out in the jungle a few days ago had compelled them to confine their training sessions to the gorge, which meant more early mornings and late nights to avoid trampling field workers. It had also underscored the reality of their situation and caused the riders to embrace their training with renewed vigor.

"They'll thank me when battle comes and they're ready," Ceridwen said. "Which I gather will be sooner than expected, so I repeat the question: when?"

Umut's gaze twitched to meet hers. "Tomorrow too soon?"

"Too soon for what? Too soon for battle?" Rafi inquired. "I think we need a week's notice for something like that—two, if it involves actual fighting and not just spear waving."

"You have a target in mind?" Ceridwen asked.

Umut nodded. "One I wager you'll like. It means striking directly at the empire's oppression of my people and indirectly at their ability to wage war against yours."

Rafi cocked his head. "Did something change? Or did we just look bored to you and that's why you decided to move the timeline up on us?"

Someone nearby chuckled at that. Ceridwen turned to see Eshur sitting at the base of the chuchoco tree, one wrist resting on his upraised knee. Clad in a loose tunic and trousers, not his colorful coat, he lifted a lazy hand in greeting.

"Eshur's back," Umut said offhandedly. "And no, that's not what's changed. It's the Nadaarian legions. Both had been combing westward, but they've suddenly shifted their focus inward. Started soon after you took out the scouts."

Rafi looked serious now. "But we got all five of them."

"Their movement suggests otherwise."

"What did the captive say?"

"Nothing of use. Clae has dispatched several raiding parties to harass them, try to draw their attention away, but so far it hasn't worked, which means it's time for something a little more . . ."

"Drastic," Ceridwen finished for him. It suited her well enough, after all. She who had been called volatile and destructive all her life.

Umut lifted a brow. "I was going to say distracting. You won't be attacking them directly, just drawing their focus away."

Rafi sighed. "Should have brushed up on my juggling skills." His gaze suddenly darted downward, and a knot formed in his brow. "Um, Ceridwen, is the grass supposed to be on fire?"

Startled, Ceridwen looked to find Mindar dozing on his feet, his head drooping low. Dark smoke drifted from his nostrils and coils of flame dripped from his mane, feeding a small fire which had sprung up around his smoldering hooves. She drew his head up and hastily stomped out the twists of flame, kicking up a flare of sparks that quickly winked out.

"Well, that's certainly distracting," Rafi said with a shrug.

"Which brings us to why I'm here." Eshur rose. "One of my contacts within the imperial court wants to meet with you, Rafi, and I think this raid provides the perfect opportunity to set it up. Show you in action. What do you say?"

Rafi shifted uncomfortably. "Sure, I guess."

Ceridwen was only half listening. She felt strangely winded, almost breathless, as she tentatively pressed her palm against Mindar's neck. Reflexes caused her to flinch back from the heat boiling off his skin. *Shades*, she needed to cool him down before he combusted and set the entire gorge aflame.

Gathering up her reins, she turned to Umut. "Tomorrow. We'll be ready." And she hoped, by all the seas and floods and skies above, that she spoke true, especially when it came to her and Mindar.

She hoped it still the next morning as she saddled Mindar in the pale flush of dawn, then drew on her leathers. First chaps, then hooded jerkin, wincing at each creak and groan of the stiff and brittle material. At her request, Umut's craftsmen had repaired a few damaged sections and replaced the worst of the laces, lessening the odds that her gear would simply fall off, though how long it might withstand the heat of fireborn combat remained to be seen.

What she wouldn't give for a pot of skivva oil.

It was all in desperate need of oiling, but those new, untreated additions concerned her the most, both in her gear and Mindar's. She put the gloves on last, flexing her fingers to get the feel of the newly worked leather, then for the first time in far too long, she lowered her hand to the soft patch of skin between Mindar's nostrils and scratched at his muzzle.

"We can do this, can't we?" she whispered.

He dipped his head into her hand, snuffling for . . . treats?

Someone coughed behind her.

"No tea today, Rafi." Sliding her *chet* into her belt, she turned around. "Have you been giving Mindar crackers after I told—"

Liam stood behind her on crutches, a smile on his face as he addressed her in their native tongue. "Would you believe I understood nearly three words you said? Something about Mindar and Rafi and crackers? I daresay my Nadaarian is improving nearly as rapidly as my leg." He gestured at the bandaged limb. "Possibly more, so long as we restrict the conversation to food."

She blinked. "Liam . . . you're up?"

He dipped his head. "I've been up for days now, my lady."

Which she would have known had she visited, had she not buried herself so completely in her work. She had failed him again. *Flames*, she should be stronger than this. Capable of bearing up both herself and others, not stumbling, trying to find her own footing.

His gaze swept slowly over the riders saddling, watering, and forming up their steeds for the march. "So, you're riding out now? Don't suppose there's a steed for me, is there?" Wistfulness tinged his voice.

"Not this time, I'm afraid."

"But . . . but who will ride at your back?"

The question rattled the shield she'd placed over her heart, and she swung abruptly into the saddle, checking Mindar before he could start after Ghost who jogged past, carrying Rafi to the head of the column. "I must go, Liam."

He stepped nearer, looking up. "But you will come back, my lady?"

However much she had lost, he had lost more. Wounded, cut off from everyone he loved, forced to grieve alone, now about to be forsaken by one of the only people who spoke his tongue in a country far from his home.

Should she fall in battle, what would become of him?

She leaned down and clasped his shoulder tightly. "Of course I will, and what's more, I will get us home. I swear this." Still holding his gaze, she slid her hand to her *chet*, marking the first blade oath she had sworn on Nadaarian soil.

Then under the expectant gaze of all the rebels and refugees of the caverns, with Umut's blessing to spur them forward, they moved out in single file. With scouts ranging ahead and Moc leading a squad after on foot, to erase all traces of their passage, the wild expanse of the Mah swallowed them.

The jungle seemed a beast alive to Ceridwen, one made uneasy by the unexpected presence of the so-called demon-steeds sheltering beneath its wings. She sensed it in the stark silence that swept over the canopy, in the sudden snap and crack of distant branches as creatures skittered and swung and darted away, in the slither racing through the grass before the hooves of her fireborn.

It moved. It bristled. It even seemed to breathe.

Concealed now atop her steed behind a cluster of enormous shieldlike leaves, Ceridwen hoped the jungle would not betray them to their quarry. But the Nadaari were not a people of the earth, and if the jungle whispered warnings to their convoy, they fell on heedless ears. With a stone-eye chariot in the lead and two dozen soldiers escorting a cart laden with coin, collected to satisfy the emperor's high war-time tax to the nearby fortified Nadaarian town of Sabee-Saador, it should have been a difficult target to take. But the convoy was straggling now that dusk was near, and their destination was almost within reach.

Relaxed. Unfocused. Oblivious.

Or so her scouts had reported, and the soldiers certainly seemed unaware of the threat as the chariot rattled into the open jaws of the ambush.

On the far end of their position, Ceridwen smothered an errant spark that winked alight on Mindar's neck. "Steady," she whispered.

This was it—their true test. For some of her warriors, their first battle.

One restless steed, one impetuous rebel, one fumble of weapon or reins, and the trap would spring too soon, exposing her force. She had only a dozen riders and steeds concealed in the trees on either side of the path, now that Eshur had split off with Rafi and Yath and the rest had gone ahead with Moc. But if the warrior spirits were kind, and if this dozen remained firm, that was all she would need.

The final soldier entered the strike zone.

The familiar thrum of anticipation ignited Ceridwen's blood. Drawing her blade, she emerged from the jungle and rode out into the center of the path. Summoning Mindar's flame, she faced the oncoming convoy.

Not even the power of a stone-eye's gaze could penetrate such a blaze.

It poured from his throat in a roiling stream that caused the tiger to rear in its traces, brought both cart and chariot grinding to a halt, and beat back the lead soldiers. It roared so loudly it nearly drowned out the twin crashes of the trees that toppled behind the convoy to block their retreat, felled by hoof strikes from Nef's and Flick's earthhewn. Feeling the warmth spreading up Mindar's ribcage, Ceridwen cut off his flame after only a few seconds, allowing the two waiting rebels to roll out from beneath the bushes bordering the path and plunge their spears deep into the tiger's sides.

Before the soldiers could level their own weapons, her riders crashed through the dissipating smoke and surrounded them, menacing the Nadaari with spears and blades and the flashing teeth of their steeds.

Ceridwen closed in on the enraged charioteer, advancing until the wisp of smoke rising from Mindar's nostrils curled around his face. "Surrender," she demanded, and saw his eyes shift to the steeds jostling around his men. For all he knew, every one of those steeds might be a fireborn, every swinging head and gaping maw an avenue for an agonizing death.

Sweat dripped down the charioteer's face, and he nodded, then barked a command that sent spears to the ground and his soldiers to their knees.

The rebels burst into a cheer that Nef silenced with a slashing hand.

"Now," Ceridwen called out, switching to Nadaarian. "Who among you are the swiftest runners? I have a message for you to carry to Sabee-Saador."

FIFTY: RAFI & CERIDWEN

The river is never lost.
- Mahque saying

The signal, when it came, was not at all what Rafi had expected. Signals were supposed to be subtle things. A nod, a wave, a darting glance. Certainly nothing so blatant as juggling flaming torches. Eshur stood on the stern of a barge moored to the wharf, where the slow-moving Eecoolie River curved around the walled town of Sabee-Saador. Crouched beneath brush cover on the opposite bank, Rafi watched in awe as the burning brands spun through the air, hafts seeming to rest only briefly in Eshur's hands before flipping up again in a dizzying display.

Yath nudged him. "Can you do that?"

"Sure. In my sleep." As long as he was dreaming.

He shifted in the muck, feet itching to take off, but unsure if he should commit. For a man who wove stories for a living, Eshur could be surprisingly closemouthed, not to mention vague on the details. Minor things, like what the signal would be, or who they were going to meet.

One of the torches suddenly shot higher than the others, arcing out over the side of the barge, where it plunged into the river and extinguished with a hiss. Well, it couldn't get more blatant than that. Rafi clapped Yath on the shoulder, and they slipped into the river where his riveren waited. Ceridwen had warned Rafi about pushing Ghost too far upstream from the ocean, where the lack of salinity in the water could be sickening to seabloods, though only after prolonged exposure. Rather than risk it, he had left the colt behind in the jungle and opted to catch a ride with Yath.

Gliding smoothly through darting fish, skirting the writhing tendrils of angling vines, they slowed alongside the barge. With the aid of a subtle swell that lifted Yath's steed without forcing it above the water, Rafi caught the tall stern of the barge and hauled himself, dripping, onto the rocking deck.

What he could see of the vessel was empty, though his view of the elongated prow where rowers would sit was blocked by the cabin that sat atop the center of the barge like a hut. Voices rumbled within, and as Rafi crept closer, a damp breeze caused the silk hangings over the entrance to gust outward.

"Ah, that would be him now." Eshur's voice.

The hangings swept open, and the taleweaver ushered Rafi into a richly draped and carpeted space, thick with the spicy scent of incense. Coils of it hung from the ceiling, emitting thin wisps of smoke that stung his eyes. He had to duck under them, which drew an amused sniff from the cabin's occupant, a woman clad in robes of embroidered silk, who reclined on an ornately cushioned couch in the center of the room.

"Silent One Alive, he's completely drenched," she said in the cultured drawl affected by those from Cetmur. "You might have mentioned that you were dredging him up from the riverbed, Eshur."

"And ruin such an entrance? No taleweaver worth his salt reveals all his secrets." Eshur swept a low bow, colorful coat flaring wide around him, and the woman shook her head with a suffering mien, then fixed her gaze on Rafi.

"Well, don't just stand there dripping on my carpet. Come in, so I can have a good look at the one who claims to be Nement's son."

She spoke with such an air of authority that Rafi found himself obeying reflexively. He could see now that she was older than the dark hair piled atop her head had led him to expect and thin almost to the point of gauntness. There was a sort of fevered brightness to her eyes that nearly outshone the cascade of gold necklaces draped down to her waist. "Eshur told me your story. Quite the riveting tale, full of wicked plots and the most inventive twists, but then he is a taleweaver, so of course, I would expect nothing less."

Rafi tipped his head. "So pleased my misfortunes didn't disappoint, *alasha*." It was a Nadaarian honorific for a woman of high rank, which she clearly was, and in lieu of a formal introduction, it would have to suffice, even as an afterthought.

She pressed her lips together. "Oh, I didn't say that. But it is why I wish to hear from you now, and not our silk-tongued friend. Tell me, O prince, did you eat with your family the night they fell ill?"

"If you mean the night they were poisoned, then yes."

She smiled, as if that was exactly what she had expected him to say. "And how, if they were poisoned, can you explain your survival?"

"I can't." Though he and Delmar had speculated about it often. "Maybe they ate something I didn't."

"Such as?"

Rafi bit back the first words that sprang to his lips, an admittedly insolent suggestion that she ask the poisoner rather than the victim. "I don't know. I wasn't paying attention to the food on every plate."

She narrowed her eyes. "And why, O prince, if your uncle truly did scheme his way to the imperial seat, did he leave you alive?"

"Overconfidence in the architects of his dungeons?"

"But to take such an easily avoidable risk . . ."

"Tell you what, O *alasha*, I'll be sure to ask next time I see him. Now that he knows I'm alive, he's bound to welcome me back with open arms—all the easier to stick a knife between my ribs."

She rose abruptly with the aid of a gilded cane. Standing, her head barely reached his shoulders, but there was an aura of gravity and regality to her that he had recognized in Delmar, and had seen in Ceridwen, and that he lacked. Ches-Shu, must he always play the fool? He was supposed to convince this woman that he was truly a prince, but rather than maintaining his brother's noble bearing, he allowed her to needle him into acting like, well, like himself.

"It's not, actually," she said.

He cocked his head at her, puzzled.

"Open arms don't make it easier to stick a knife between your ribs. That only invites you close enough to do the same. Far better to strike from a distance, with cunning, such that you never see it coming."

"I'll keep that in mind."

"You should, if you ever wish to sit upon your father's throne, Crown Prince Rafi Tetrani, son of Nement, heir of House Korringar."

His mouth went dry. "So you believe me? You don't want me to share details only I could know to prove that I'm me?"

Her lips twitched. "If only you could know them, I would be unable to corroborate them, wouldn't I? No, I knew you as soon as you began to speak. You have the look of your father about you."

That took Rafi aback. "I do? But everyone always said Delmar looked like him."

"He did, and so do you. More so now than your brother did then, I would say. Oh, you have your mother's spark of wit, I'll grant you, but that belligerent stone in your eyes is your father's."

Where before she had irritated old wounds, now she no doubt meant to salve them. His father's face had long since faded in his mind's eye, and Rafi feared that Delmar's would soon follow, but if the face he offered the world was not his alone, maybe they need not be lost to him forever.

"You must have known them well," he said.

"Well enough. We have met before, you know."

No, he didn't. Really, couldn't Eshur have prepared him?

His struggle to recall must have shown on his face, for she gave a sharp, dry laugh and squeezed his hand in her own small yet wiry grip. "I am not offended you do not remember, my prince. You were but a cub then, though you still had that unseemly and incorrigible sense of humor. I am Imbé Tisani, and I am your father's third cousin, once removed. Under your father, I administered foreign trade for the empire. Under Lykier, I am but a glorified tax collector."

"Speaking of taxes," Eshur spoke up, parting the silk hangings so he could look out. "I have more for you to see, Imbé."

"More? I ask for proof, and you bring the crown prince himself. What more could you possibly show me?"

Gongs crashed high upon the walls of Sabee-Saador, and there was a grim satisfaction in Eshur's voice as he flung the hangings open wide. "Proof that he can indeed bring Lykier to his knees."

Imbé exited with deliberate steps that masked her limp, and Rafi trailed after, knowing already what she would see. From the stern of the barge, they had a clear vantage of the roadway that snaked from the jungle toward Sabee-Saador. And of the three soldiers that scrambled from the trees and raced down it, chased by a handful of Moc's rebels on foot, voicing war cries and shaking their spears.

"Silent One Alive," Imbé murmured. "The convoy."

One soldier fell and was dragged back toward the jungle. The other two stumbled and staggered on, rebels howling at their heels.

Then the gates of Sabee-Saador, bolted in anticipation of nightfall, groaned open, and out poured a squadron of soldiers. The thud of their booted feet and the clank of their armor carried over the water as they rushed the rebels, who abandoned their pursuit and jostled one another in their haste to retreat.

Rafi fidgeted, suddenly wishing he were out there with them, and Eshur shot him a steadying look. This was the trickiest moment. If the garrison recalled their troops now, satisfied with driving off a few rebels, there was nothing gained by the ploy. But if they tried to recover the convoy . . .

"They will," Ceridwen had insisted. *"They will envision either a slow-moving cart or a handful of rebels making off on foot, burdened with sacks of coins. Trust me. They won't be able to resist."*

Without slackening pace, the squadron plunged after the rebels into the Mah.

Imbé did not speak, but stood, watching. For a moment, all was silent. Then the very trees seemed to shake as a rumbling tore through them, and cries of alarm rang out and were cut off. Soldiers spilled back onto the roadway like a flock of birds startled from the canopy, fleeing the onrushing tide of demon-steeds and the blazing figure at their head.

Ceridwen tore after the fleeing Nadaari and felt Mindar's strides quicken, until the wind of his speed seemed to lift every burden from her shoulders. Until there was only the rush of the chase, the thrill of this glorious ride. Few could withstand the shock of a fireborn descending upon them in fume or flame, and these soldiers, stunned at the sight of solborn on their soil, did not have the war-hardened discipline of those who had invaded Soldonia.

So they fled before her, but there was no escape.

Jasri's stormers, who had been soaring high above, dropped in a howling dive, then, skimming low over the roadway, charged the soldiers head-on. Catching the horn strung about her neck, Ceridwen blew a long blast, and with a low rumbling of hooves, the rest of her forces broke from concealment bordering the roadway and crashed into the soldiers' flank.

Upon the walls, the gongs continued clashing, and a small squadron of archers raised bows skyward and loosed a haphazard hail of arrows that whistled and thwacked among both steeds and soldiers. One glanced off Ceridwen's upraised blade, but the gates did not reopen. No more of the garrison marched to relieve their beleaguered companions.

She had chosen to attack within sight of the wall, so that the legend of the demon-steeds might spread through the heart of Nadaar. Her riders lacked the honed finesse of Soldonian warriors, but Ceridwen wielded them like a cudgel, trusting in momentum and shock to do the trick. The result was a chaotic, teeming mass of whirling steeds and scattering soldiers, pouring out over the roadway. In some places, clusters of Nadaari put up a stronger resistance, and it was there that Ceridwen focused her effort, crashing into their midst and lashing out with both *chet* and steed until their defense shattered.

Some fled and had to be chased down.

Some threw down their arms in surrender.

One mass broke off, retreating into the trees, and with shouts of triumph, dozens of her riders poured after them. Ceridwen shifted her blade into her rein hand, then, seizing her horn, blew three sharp blasts to call off the pursuit. Though some checked their steeds, most hurtled on, unheeding, into the woods that would favor their enemies. Cursing their lack of restraint, Ceridwen shot a glance over the field, then tore off at an angle she hoped would intercept the reckless pursuit before disaster overtook them.

She passed Flick loping back on his earthhewn, one of the few who had obeyed her signal. "With me," she called, and he wheeled the horned beast and fell in behind her.

Mindar surged into his stride, sparks flying from the whipping ends of his mane. She urged him on, aware of the perilous line she trod. She needed speed, but not too much heat, lest she lose control of both, and perish in her own blaze, as even Glyndwr–faithless, treacherous Glyndwr–had warned. She whispered to her fireborn and kept a gentle restraint on his reins, until she spied steel gleaming through the trunks ahead.

She sang out the Outrider war cry, and Mindar sped faster in response, leaving Flick behind, as first his mane, then his tail, then his hooves caught alight.

Rivulets of flame crawled across his hide, and within a dozen strides, both her saddle and leathers were smoking. Without skivva oil, neither would resist for long. But she was so close now. She could not slow, and she would not turn back. Only one choice remained. Gritting her teeth, she slashed her *chet* across the waterskin she had tied to the front of her saddlebow in anticipation of such a failure, and the hide burst, dousing Mindar's flames in an instant.

The shock of it caused Mindar to stumble.

He shuddered, smoke puffing to white, then dissipating entirely. That glint of steel resolved into helmets, and she drove Mindar out after the soldiers. Only, they weren't fleeing anymore. She came to a plunging halt, facing a tight formation bristling with spears and arrows.

Her senses sharpened to a heightened awareness.

Bow strings creaked. Hooves raced up behind as her rebels charged forward, unaware of the danger. Instinctively, she called for flame, for with a concentrated burst, a fireborn could destroy arrows before they struck, but Mindar had none.

She had quenched Mindar's reserves, and now, she could not save her warriors. She could not even save herself.

Strings twanged and the arrows flew.

And with a roar, Flick–sweet Flick, with the wide smile and the big ears and the hands so gentle upon the reins–spurred into their path before her. The volley struck. Her ears filled with the *thwack* and *snap* of arrows. She envisioned Flick toppling before the onslaught, but it must have been aimed for her steed, rather than for her, for most of the shafts splintered off the earthhewn's broad chest as it rammed into the formation.

Most, but not all. Flick grunted in pain, and Mindar jolted as an arrow tore through the tip of his right ear. But she was completely unscathed. She flung herself furiously into the fray, cutting down an archer as his shot whizzed past her, knocking aside a spear thrust with her backswing. Wheeling Mindar in their midst, she sensed the resistance failing, even before the other rebels tore up to join the fight.

For a firerider, battles were measured in strides, in smoke, and in firestorms, but this one was over before Mindar's flames even rekindled.

Steed circling restlessly, Flick grimaced, gripping an arrow that stuck from his thigh. His knuckles tightened, readying to yank it out, but Nef, already dismounted, caught his wrist.

"Don't be an idiot. Do you want to do more damage?" Scowling, he tugged a cloth from his belt pouch, wrapped it around the shaft and folded Flick's hand around it, then seized the earthhewn's reins and started to lead him away.

Ceridwen cut them off. "What were you thinking?" she demanded of Flick. "Your steed may be immune to arrows, but you are not. You're not invincible." She raised her voice. "None of you are. So when I call the halt, you will heed my word, or you'll find yourself grounded for the duration of the fight. By blood and blade, I swear it."

Nef sniffed as she spun Mindar away.

He had probably been at the lead of those who had ignored her command to halt. She would address him alone later.

But now, with the reek of her own failure rising from the dampened ash still clinging to the hide of her steed as she rode to regroup with the others, she could not bring herself to care.

FIFTY-ONE: JAKIM

Aodh's hand is the hand of a shepherd, guiding, shielding, protecting.
- The truths of Aodh

The dark of a new moon might not be much of a hindrance for a shadowrider, since they could apparently see in the dark, but Jakim couldn't. Gripping the stolen knife tightly, he sawed through Finnian's bonds by feel, then held out the knife, and felt calloused fingers take it.

"Give me five minutes," he whispered before turning to sneak away.

Finnian's hand found his shoulder. "You're a good man, Jakim Ha'Nor."

Then with no more indication of his movement than a faint shift in the breeze, Finnian was gone, off to fetch his steed. But Jakim's part in this escape was not yet done. He could not move with Finnian's easy grace and silence, but he did his best to tiptoe and creep his way through the web of sleeping riders and hobbled steeds. On dry nights like this one, most slept out under the stars, not bothering to string up their makeshift oilskin tents, which added to the challenge of trying to pick his way through, but he had marked out his path beforehand and reached the priest's chariot without problem.

Faint rustling indicated Koata was awake, then she chuffed softly to greet him, recognizing his scent. "That's it, Koata," he whispered. "It's just me." Hand outstretched, he slowly felt his way to her side, and she leaned into his touch, using it to scratch her neck.

Her coat felt less coarse and matted under his fingers. He had taken to brushing it out almost every night, using a brush borrowed from Ineth.

Not tonight though. Taking a deep breath, he felt along her harness for the straps that bound her to the chariot where she slept, ate, lived, and breathed, and he began to work the buckles loose. The leather was stiff, but he pried first one, then a second and third free, and was tackling the fourth when a low, rumbling growl sounded deep in Koata's throat.

He stilled with his fingers on the buckle.

The tiger had not growled at him in days. What if she turned on him? She was still blindfolded, so at least he'd have a chance to run before she caught and ate him.

But they needed a distraction to give Finnian a head start, otherwise every shadowrider in the camp would be on him at once. Sif might have recovered from her injury, but Jakim questioned her odds in an immediate chase.

Yanking up on the final buckle, he released Koata.

She stood still a moment, braced as if in anticipation of pain, then padded hesitantly forward. Settling into a stalking crouch, she crept toward the sprawl of sleeping warriors.

This wasn't how he'd imagined it happening.

In his mind, there had been a lot more roaring, which led to screaming, which woke the camp and kept everyone preoccupied running around after Koata and oblivious to the fact that Finnian was slipping away.

What if the tiger ate someone? Or got shot by an overzealous archer?

Clearly, he hadn't thought this through. He wavered, no longer able to distinguish the tiger's slinking form in the darkness, then shouted, "Tiger! Tiger's loose!" in both Soldonian and Nadaarian, to be sure everyone was on alert.

It was also probably a clear indication of who was responsible.

He turned, and his pulse rocketed at the sight of a dark figure directly behind him. "Oh, Finnian. Shouldn't you be off on your steed, riding away?"

"Scroll?" That wasn't Finnian's voice. "What are you doing? Did you just free that beast?" The metallic hiss of a blade being drawn made the hair rise on Jakim's arms.

He backed away and ran up against the chariot, his heel striking the rock used to chock the wheel. Before he could break off in another direction, his attacker moved without a sound, only a sense of looming darkness closing in, then the cold prick of a blade at Jakim's throat.

Something crashed into his attacker from the side, tackling him to the ground.

Stifled grunts, muted thumps, and ragged, strained breathing filled his ears. A foot careened into Jakim's ankle, knocking him to one knee. He felt for the rock that braced the wheel and tugged it loose, arming himself, then crouched there, straining to see.

Guttering light suddenly flared behind Jakim, revealing Finnian locked in a savage hold with another shadowrider on the ground. Finnian strained against the grip on his wrist, then with a powerful thrust, he brought his knife down.

Leaving Arlen te Ondri gasping, knife in his heart.

Finnian rolled free and tried awkwardly to get his legs under him, but sank onto his back, cupping a hand around the hilt of a blade jutting from his gut.

Oh, Aodh, he'd been stabbed too.

Jakim was about to rush to his side when the light swayed, coming nearer, and Khilamook rounded the side of the chariot. The engineer halted at the scene. Robes disheveled, hair unkempt, clutching the green silk cloth in one hand and a small torch in the other, he seemed disoriented at first, as always when life conspired to drag him out of the deep focus that consumed him in his work. Then he greedily drank it all in, and the thin smile that crawled across his face was as cruel and as smug as ever.

He opened his mouth. To speak? To shout?

Jakim didn't wait to find out. Still grasping the rock, he shot up to his feet and smashed it against the side of the engineer's head. Khilamook staggered and dropped the torch, then collapsed beside it, the embroidered cloth still clutched in his hand.

The rock dropped from Jakim's fingers.

Prickling heat swept over him, and a roaring noise filled his ears. He grounded himself in the truths of Aodh, mentally repeating the familiar words—Aodh is true, Aodh is compassionate, Aodh is merciful—until the dizziness receded. Off in the night, shouts and the clatter of running feet seemed to indicate that Koata's distraction had been effective.

Hopefully, it would last long enough.

Finnian let out a hiss of pain, and Jakim sprang back into action. Snatching the cloth from the engineer's limp hand, he hurried over as Finnian let the blade drop beside him.

Blood was already spilling down his side.

Jakim pressed the cloth against the wound. "Can you hold it?" Finnian nodded and clamped a trembling hand over the wound, freeing Jakim to haul him to his feet. "Where's Sif?"

"Hold on." Shivering, Finnian struggled to purse his lips to whistle but stopped as Sif suddenly loomed beside them. The shadowrider was taller than Jakim by a head, and both the weakened shoulder and stab wound robbed Finnian of his dexterity, but Jakim managed to push and shove him up onto his mount.

Finnian took up his reins, then kicked his left foot free of the stirrup. "He saw you." No doubt about who *he* was. "And you didn't hit him hard enough to kill him."

"I wasn't trying to. I don't want to kill anyone."

"You stay here, they will kill you. Come on, Scroll, let someone help you for once."

Jakim lingered, torn between his desire to stay and find the dawnling and his certainty that Finnian was right—staying would mean dying, and what good could come of that? Then he nodded and scrambled up onto the shadower and held on tight as they sped away into the night, leaving Khilamook unconscious and Arlen dead behind them.

FIFTY-TWO: RAFI & CERIDWEN

The trees speak wisdom to the one who will listen.
- Mahque proverb

With only the moon and the stars to light his path, Rafi ran. He abandoned his usual route on the gorge floor, flanked by the cultivated fruit trees and rows of crops that formed a dam against the continual creeping of the jungle, and let his feet carry him upward. Up past the caverns and out onto the rim of the gorge itself. It was a night for daring, and his pulse already raced from the brazen theft of the object now tucked away in his pocket.

But no sentries halted him or made themselves known. So, with nothing but sky above him and darkness below, he defied the heights and continued to sprint into the night.

His head pounded in time with his stride. His thoughts too.

Umut had counted their first raid a rousing success. Not only had they lightened the imperial coffer and soundly defeated a Nadaarian garrison, they had also diverted the attention of the two legions scouring the jungle away from the gorge. Which meant that they had been greeted upon their return by the rich scent of Saffa's cooking. On top of all that, as a parting salvo to Sabee-Saador, Ceridwen had sent the stormers aloft, high above bowshot, to rain a portion of their captured coins down upon the town. Certainly the most memorable way to make use of it. Rafi suspected the townsfolk would be crawling over rooftops, pulling coins out of the thatching for weeks, and thus, the legend would spread.

Of the Fireborn of Soldonia and the Crown Prince of Nadaar.

He ran faster, but there was no escaping the guilt that panted and howled at his heels. As the last echoes of the demon-steeds' hooves had died away, Imbé had sunk into a deep bow before him, called him her prince and her liege, and vowed to rally the other loyalists to his cause and see him enthroned, as his father had been, upon the Center of the World.

Never mind that he did not desire such a thing.

Never mind that the true crown prince had died because of him.

So he flung himself onward, feet crunching leaf, scattering loam, until his legs flew out from under him, and he fell, scraping as he hit the ground. Wincing and winded, he picked himself up and felt his pockets—still there—then pulled it out, and gingerly unwrapped it.

It lay shriveled and twisted atop the cloth draped over his hand.

Hooked like a talon, sharp as a kaava's thorns, dark as a bruise, a scadtha's claw. Or the very tip of one, at least. Rafi had been pierced by dozens of such claws before when fighting the beast that had tried to eat Ghost, for the claws grew from the ends of the numerous legs that sprouted along a scadtha's sinuous form. He had been stabbed by one, too, and Umut had found it and removed it, just as he had this one, from Liam.

His breath hitched as he looked at it. He touched it lightly, his fingertips catching on the slightly rough, almost sandpapery, and brittle surface. And . . . nothing. He felt nothing, sensed nothing, heard nothing, neither from the ghost nor from that thunderous voice that had invaded his mind when the priest Cortovah first scratched his forehead. *Scratched.*

His palms were scraped from the fall, laced with tiny, bleeding cuts. He didn't give himself time to reconsider. He took hold of the claw and tightened his hand.

Flame suddenly erupted below, its red-gold flare searing his vision. Startled, he dropped the claw back into its wrappings. Shoving it into his pocket, he scrambled to his feet, gaze drawn to the throbbing glow and the dark figure he could see at its core. Ceridwen.

Waves of heat washed over Ceridwen's skin as Mindar spun, forelegs crossing, hooves tossing up clods of charred earth. He burned brightly in the night, and she burned with him. She could feel the blaze in each scar that marked her skin, from the *kasar* brand to the burn from the stallion who had slain her brother, to all the various injuries she had received in combat, culminating in the scarcely healed wound on her left forearm. Each throbbed with its own molten pulse, as though the heat had seeped in through the cracks and now sought to consume her from the inside out.

She had survived each one.

Why should they threaten to undo her now?

Grinding her teeth, she endured it as long as she dared, then drew Mindar out of the spin and twitched her reins, cuing him to stop. For one agonizingly protracted breath, he burned on, and she reached for her *chet*, readying to unleash the waterskin again. Then his fires finally dwindled, and Ceridwen planted a gloved hand on his warm neck to steady herself.

To try and tame her own erratically racing heart.

Bending his neck, Mindar snuffled at the toe of her boot, quivering, though his eyes had faded to the mellow red of a sunset rather than the radiant glow of smelted iron. This wasn't his fault. He wasn't trying to harm her. Dragged across the sea to this strange country where monsters boiled from the deep and pythons coiled in the trees and he had been mistreated by Sahak, was it any wonder that he raged now against the uncertainty of this new world in the only way he could? Or that her own distress only fanned his flame?

But what was she to do? What could she do?

Rise and ride again—that was the way of the Outriders.

She had heard those words often enough from Markham, a rallying cry, a command, a bludgeon to goad her to pick herself up and push herself onward again. But what happened when sheer grit wasn't enough? How could one rise and ride again after falling so often? Failing so drastically?

Ceridwen gathered up her reins, blew out a short breath, and urged Mindar back into a *firestorm*, defying the heat again. She had to, for this was who she was.

Soldonia's Fireborn was nothing without flame.

Up close, the heat of the blaze made Rafi's eyes sting, and he ducked behind the slightly scorched trunk of a neefwa tree, wincing as a muscle in his thigh spasmed. He must have cramped it on his way down. Rather than retrace his steps to the staircases in the caverns, he'd used the scouts' ladder, which consisted of a terrifying sequence of nets strung across sheer sections of the gorge wall connected by trails so steep and narrow they were better suited for goats.

It made for a fast, if harrying, descent. Particularly if you weren't fond of heights.

Whirling within that vortex of flame, Ceridwen seemed as much a thing of fire as her steed. She moved like fire itself, swiftly, with a fierce, darting intensity, as she spun Mindar, head aimed aloft so his flame streamed harmlessly into the air, then slowed him, quieted him until the glow faded, before spinning him back into a blaze again.

And again. And again.

But it wasn't the radiance of the coiling flames that stopped Rafi in his tracks, but the look upon Ceridwen's face. Of an ache that cut far deeper than blade could bite. She looked the way he felt when memories dragged him out of sleep, caused him to fling himself out into the teeth of the night.

Ches-Shu, he shouldn't be here, intruding upon this.

Rafi turned to leave, and a twig snapped under his foot. He sensed the crackle of heat as Mindar swung toward him, poised to flame. Metal whipped through the air, and in an instant, Ceridwen's blade hovered at his throat. Her leathers were charred, and her eyes above the half mask that shielded her lower face were red from the heat.

Slowly, Rafi raised his hands. "It's me. Rafi."

She was breathing raggedly, and she held herself stiffly, chin raised like a demon-steed waiting for a fight. Her blade arm sank slowly to her side, and even more slowly, the blaze in Mindar's eyes died. "I thought myself alone," she said warily.

"I was just out for a run. I didn't mean to startle you." Rafi glanced at the wisp of smoke curling off the shriveled left sleeve of her jerkin. "Your sleeve is smoldering."

She dropped the *chet* and slung herself over the side of her steed. She thwacked at her arm with a gloved hand to smother the latent sparks, and her sleeve hitched up, exposing red and blistered skin beneath.

Rafi started. "You're hurt. Is that a burn?"

"It's fine." But she winced as she tugged down her sleeve. "It's only a small one."

"But your gear is supposed to protect you, isn't it?"

"It would, if I could treat it." Bitterness tinged her voice. "Only skivva oil can keep firerider gear from cracking or drying out, and skivva oil is extracted from plants that only grow in the fiery craters of Soldonia. So I've no way to get it without sailing home and no way to sail home without committing myself flesh and bone to this fight."

In an eyeblink, he could see the compounding nature of the challenge. Each blaze might bring her closer to gaining passage home, but each one also threatened to undermine her ability to keep fighting. "Then what were you doing just now? Why would you risk such a thing?"

"It's called training."

"Sure, or just sheer insanity."

"Flick was injured on our raid, Rafi. Because of me. I have failed my kingdom, my warriors, my brother, and my friends. I will not fail at this too. I cannot. Umut made a deal with the Fireborn of Soldonia, and Mindar and I will be ready for the next fight, come floods, come rain, and yes, come flame."

She shrugged out of the jerkin, careless of her injury—though Rafi winced for her as the sleeve scraped her arm—then slung it over her shoulder, snatched up her blade, and stalked back toward Mindar. Was she planning to ride again? Without her gear?

"I failed my brother too."

Ceridwen ground to a halt, her back toward him.

Rafi swallowed, aware that he strayed on the edge of a precipice with this truth. "We were on the run. Six years ago. Chased by Sahak and his soldiers. Delmar could have gotten away, but I slowed him down. I couldn't keep up. Couldn't run another step. I gave up, Ceridwen, but he wouldn't leave me. He covered for me even as he died because of me, and I can't . . . I can't imagine why, because he was everything that I am not."

Sea-demons screaming.

Cold stone digging into his cheek.

Gasped breath from Delmar's lips, just before he fell.

Rafi shook free from the memory's grip and found Ceridwen facing him, her eyes no longer burning but softened. He took a breath and continued. "I run at night when the memories won't let me sleep, because I don't know how to face the fact that my brother was always enough to save me, but at that moment when he needed me most, I couldn't be enough for him. I know failure, too, Ceridwen."

She was quiet, then said, "Your brother's name was Delmar?"

His stomach knotted. Had he given himself away? He had tried to tread lightly with the details of his story, and it wasn't a wholly uncommon name. "Yes."

"My brother's name was Bair. We can remember their names together." She said this as though bestowing a great honor, and maybe among her people, it was. She sank to the ground, cradling her burned arm against her knees, and Rafi crouched beside her, digging out the salve he had been carrying in his pocket since Ghost was injured. His fingers brushed against the wrapped scadtha claw as he drew the salve out, but he ignored it.

"I have not burned like this since the day my brother died," she said, watching him closely as he scooped up a glob of the pungent salve and spread it over her burned skin. He worked as gently as he could, and she did not flinch, but his hands felt clumsy and thick. "My father was forever testing us, pitting us against each other, and against his . . . ward. And I was desperate to prove myself, to earn his respect, so I challenged my brother to the Sol-Donair. It is an ancient contest, a race to bond a wildborn steed, and he would have been content with a lesser beast, a stormer or a riveren. But I would have nothing less than a fireborn."

The tale that unfolded from her then was not what Rafi had expected.

She told him of finding the wildborn herd, of the stallion who had torn free of her catch-rope, and of how she had been unable to save her brother, though she had carried his body home. She told him, too, the meaning of the brand on her forehead, seared there by her father's own hand, forever declaring her an outcast, and how the taint of that brand had followed her as an Outrider, as a war-chief, and now as queen.

How it had led to her betrayal and capture in the end.

With each word, she seemed to expect him to pull away, for she did not spare herself in the telling, her tone at times as harsh as the voice in Rafi's own head could be. But by the way she spoke of the brand becoming all that people could see, he wondered if maybe she might understand what life was like for him, as a reluctant Tetrani.

Capping the pot of salve, he leaned in and listened and saw the guardedness and defensiveness that steeled and hardened her gradually melt away. Whenever Ghost leaped upon the crest of a wave, there was this moment where Rafi hung suspended, weightless, soaring over the frothing surface of the sea. Where the concerns of the world faded. Where he felt truly and completely free. Free to be himself, whoever that might be.

He felt that now in this moment of shared pain and grief.

Go on, a voice inside him cried. *Just tell her.*

Who he was. What he was. This, if ever, was his chance.

Then Mindar snorted noisily, and like the crash of seawater that followed Ghost's leap, it dashed Rafi back to his senses. Ceridwen was speaking about how the war-chief who had betrayed her had believed her tainted not only by her own deeds but by the deeds of her father and how she couldn't help but wonder if he was right.

"You keep expecting the tide to shift, convincing yourself that something will change eventually, that you cannot keep failing endlessly. But when the failures just keep piling up, one after another, surely it's clear that the problem isn't the tides, it's you."

It was a manner of speech, of course. She was referring to herself, not him.

But Rafi swallowed and pulled back anyway, then pasted on a grin. "That's what everyone keeps telling me." Because if she thought herself tainted by the deeds of her father, then there was no way she would think any differently of him. Pocketing the salve, he stood and dusted himself off. "You hungry? Because I'm starving. What do you say we swing up to the kitchens? Grab something to eat, maybe even steep a pot of your favorite mumagung bean tea?"

She eyed him curiously at the abrupt shift in conversation, then seized her discarded jerkin and shoved up to her feet. "Oh, *flames*, anything but mumagung bean tea."

Ceridwen stared into the cup that Rafi had pushed into her hands. Pale green liquid swirled inside, throwing off a warm, salty tang. She set it down on the table. "When you spoke of swinging up to the kitchens, I didn't think you meant cooking an entire meal."

"Why not?" He dumped an armload of supplies on the table, then made a grab for a squash that tried to dive over the edge. Mostly root and vine vegetables, shelled peas, a variety of bundled greens—all of which he had assured her Saffa had given him free rein to use. "Cooking a good meal to eat is half the fun." He rapidly gathered spices, bowls, and knives, moving through the kitchen with the same fluid grace with which he handled his steed.

Meanwhile, she stood uncertainly in her soot-stained gear, holding her battered jerkin, feeling drained after the night's revelations—and more than a little useless.

She set the jerkin down. "I've been out on patrol with the Outriders eating travel rations for the past three years. Mostly dried things— meats, fruits."

"Not tonight." He hauled a cauldron over to the table. "Tonight we feast." He took up a knife and started dicing onions. "You can sit if you want. This will take a bit."

"*Flames*, no. Give me something to do."

Rafi slid another knife toward her, then abruptly retracted it, eyes narrowing. "You seem entirely too excited about the prospect of chopping vegetables. You're not planning on stealing this knife, too, are you? Because Saffa is very fond of her knives."

She had nearly forgotten about the knife she had stolen on her first day. How had Rafi found out about it? "Just give me the knife and tell me what we're making."

He grinned, relinquishing the blade. "Soup."

Of course it would be soup. Lining up the root vegetables, she began slicing them into thick chunks. She relished the satisfying clunk of the knife almost as much as seeing the mound of uncut vegetables diminish. Here, at last, was a task she could accomplish. The accompanying sound of Rafi's knife stopped, and she found him watching her with a curious smile. He pushed the squash he had been cutting over to her, then hooked the cauldron onto the hearth's swinging arm and shoved it over the flames. He hung a smaller pot of water beside it.

Ceridwen focused on her task and, moments later, set her knife down. "Done."

Rafi looked up from stirring the vegetables. "Already?" Trading his spoon for a bowl, he transferred the chopped squash to the smaller pot, then collected the knives, pausing beside her with one in each hand. "You planning to try that seaweed tea? I swear you'll like it."

"Don't swear with a blade in hand."

He looked at her strangely. "Why not?"

"Because that's a blade oath. It's a sacred thing in Soldonia." She folded her fingers around the *chet* at her side. "Swear an oath on a blade, and it will bind you to your death."

Rafi made a show of setting the knives down. "I swear you'll like it."

Blade oaths were a solemn matter, yet Ceridwen found herself joking along. "It's too late, I'm afraid. You've taken a rash oath. It would be far too risky for me to taste the tea now, lest it be the end of you." And she couldn't help smiling when he shrugged and downed the tea himself. He had a disarming air about him that set her at ease in a way she had rarely experienced with anyone since Bair, but if she had learned anything about Rafi tonight, it was that there was pain beneath his humor.

Yet what about anger? What drove him to fight, if not that?

She asked him, as he mashed the squash and stirred it in to thicken the soup, "Why do you fight for the revolution, Rafi?"

"Well . . ." He clanged the spoon on the cauldron. "The food is really good." She gave him a flat stare, and a grin pulled at his lips.

"It happened mostly by accident. I didn't exactly set out to fight for anything. That was more my brother's calling than mine. I spent most of my life running. I suppose I wanted to do something to make him proud of me. But once you start running, it's hard to stop. In some ways, I still am. Running, that is. I—"

He broke off as a bootstep scuffed the entrance.

Moc shuffled in, yawning. "Is that midnight soup cooking?" He was trailed by Yath, Lowen, and Taka, a shadowrider with a crinkling smile and hands as weathered and strong as the wood he had once worked with as a boatbuilder. "Smells almost good enough to eat."

"That's the idea. Come on in." Rafi swept the table clear, and Yath pulled out bowls while Moc dragged stools over. Ceridwen ladled out servings, then settled in beside Taka, who somehow always smelled comfortingly of wood shavings.

The soup was rich and spicy, sweet and savory, all at once.

Ceridwen had not realized how hungry she was until she began eating. Though the others talked, Moc and Lowen ribbing one another while Taka and Yath seemed intensely engaged in a conversation about wood beetles, she did not look up until her bowl was empty.

Rafi quirked an eyebrow at her. "Better than Outrider travel rations?"

"Ha!" Lowen snapped his fingers. "That's what we need."

"What?" Yath asked. "Travel rations?"

"No, we need a name to call ourselves, like the Outriders."

They all looked at once to Rafi, who rocked back on his stool, eyes gleaming, a troublesome smirk on his lips. "How about . . . the Out*raiders*. Since we're out there, raiding."

Moc looked confused, and Yath snorted, but Lowen grinned. "I like it."

Ceridwen stood and gathered up empty bowls, shaking her head. "Oh, please, anything but that."

"Why?" Rafi's lips twitched. "Because it's . . . outrageous?"

She rolled her eyes and dropped the bowls in the wash basin. But even with the sting of the burn on her arm and the residual ache of the memories that this night had dredged up, she found herself smiling.

FIFTY-THREE: JAKIM

Aodh's hand is the hand of a healer, comforting,
tending, and binding up broken bones.
- The truths of Aodh

Jakim should have guessed that Finnian would be just stubborn enough to sit there, suffering in tight-lipped silence while he bled to death without so much as saying a word. As it was, he barely kept Finnian from toppling from the saddle. One moment, they were riding along, maintaining a swift lope and a steady course toward Rysinger. Jakim's mind was back on the search for the dawnling and those strange words from the holy writ inscribed on his arm, and on Koata, too, hoping his actions hadn't gotten her or anyone else killed.

The next, Finnian swayed and started to tilt sideways.

Jakim grabbed hold of his arm—the injured one, it turned out. The pain seemed to shock Finnian back to his senses, for he lurched upright again and shook himself.

"Should we, maybe, stop for a rest?" Jakim asked.

Finnian gave a coughing grunt and urged his shadower on. "I'm fine."

He didn't look or sound fine. They had been riding for hours now, well into daylight, desperate to outpace the pursuit. Jakim had gotten a crick in his neck watching the sky, until Finnian reminded him that Rhodri had no stormriders with him. So far the lean shadower mare had maintained her pace well, despite carrying two instead of one, but even Jakim could tell that it was beginning to wear on her as the hitch in her stride, which had been slight when they set out, gradually became more pronounced.

"You might be, but what about Sif?"

They came to a halt then, saddle creaking faintly to the rhythm of Sif's labored breathing. Finnian nodded. "Quick rest. For Sif."

Jakim dropped to the ground. It felt so good to stand, to stretch. He glanced up at Finnian, who had not moved. "Are you coming?"

Finnian hesitated. "I don't know if I'll be able to get back on. I know a thing or two about wounds . . ." He trailed off, looking away.

The way he said it, it didn't seem a good thing.

Jakim squelched a tremor of panic and modeled his tone after Ineth. "Good. You can tell me what to do. Now come down before you fall down."

"You're pushy for a Scroll, you know that?"

That made Jakim grin. No one had ever called him pushy before, but he'd always been stronger than he looked. He stepped up even with Finnian's stirrup and, catching the archer's weight on his shoulder, managed to swing him to the ground, where he sank back with a groan, leaving Jakim's hands wet with blood.

Not good. The cloth, strapped to the wound with Jakim's own belt, was soaked through. "Okay . . . more bandages . . ." He cast about uselessly, then reached for the neck of his tunic.

Finnian's voice stopped him. "In my saddlebags."

Jakim fetched them, and Finnian dug through them ruefully. "Usually, I'm the one doing the patching up. Ceridwen, mostly. I swear, sometimes, it seems like she sees getting out of a battle unscathed as proof she wasn't fighting hard enough." Finnian tossed first bandages, then a small metal flask, then a kit with needle and thread to Jakim. "You sure you're up for this?"

Jakim fumbled the flask to catch the kit. "My sister Siba was a healer. She practically raised me after our mother died, and I used to help her gather medicinal herbs and watch her brew tinctures. She taught me everything I know—which, granted, isn't much, since our lessons ended when I was ten."

Finnian's voice gentled. "I'm sorry. It must have been hard to lose her."

It took Jakim a moment to realize his mistake. He had spoken about Siba in the past tense. But then, everything he knew about her belonged to the past, even if he hoped it might belong to the future, too, someday. "It's not what you think. I was lost, not her. Carried off by slavers and sold far from my home. But I still remember her as the kindest and most compassionate person I have ever known."

Finnian nodded slowly. "So, you get it from her, then? Your compulsion to help everyone?"

"Maybe." He liked that idea. "Speaking of helping everyone, you seem pretty desperate to get to Ceridwen."

"I am her back-rider. It is my sworn duty." His tone implied a *but*.

"Only . . ."

"She doesn't want help. Or maybe just not help from me." Finnian shoved his hair back, leaving a smear of blood on his forehead. "There was almost . . . something . . . between us. But I gave fear rein over my tongue. Balked when I should have leaped." He worked his jaw. "Markham was right. My judgment was clouded, or I never would have let her send me away. I should have been there. Could have . . ."

"Stopped her?" Jakim asked, skeptically.

Finnian shook his head ruefully. "Never. I've tried. She can be a firestorm sometimes. You'd have better luck bridling the wind than bringing her under control. And why would you want to? Until she off and does something utterly reckless and terrifying. But I should have been there. I failed her, as her back-rider, and I need to make things right."

"And you will." Jakim held up the bandage roll. "Once we patch you up."

"That's it? No words of wisdom, Scroll?"

His tone made it a jest, not mockery, so Jakim responded in kind. "How about 'much talk leads to much delay.'"

"That from the holy writ?"

"Something Scrollmaster Gedron used to say. Seemed to fit." Because it did feel like Finnian was delaying for some reason. "Ready?" he asked, reaching to undo the belt, and Finnian released a breath, and nodded. The wadded-up silk cloth squelched under Jakim's fingers as he peeled it back, then he stilled.

"What? What is it?" Finnian bent his head to see.

"It's . . ." Jakim swallowed, unable to believe his eyes, let alone put it into words. "I don't wish to alarm you, but your wound . . . it's glowing."

"What?" Finnian plucked the cloth away, exposing the wound on his abdomen, a deep blade-shaped cut barely longer than the pad of Jakim's thumb. "I don't see any glowing."

Not on the wound. The cloth.

Jakim took the silk square and spread it out on the ground, revealing the intricate embroidered design he had spent so many hours studying. The vibrant colors were stained with blood, the image itself rendered nearly unintelligible, but that didn't matter, for cutting across the stitched mountains and flowering fields and canals of Canthor was another design.

A map, sewn in an unbroken line of golden, glowing thread.

"Aodh have mercy, it's real." Jakim hesitantly touched the glowing strand, and his fingers tingled at its soft warmth. What could cause something like that? The radiant light that had bathed his dreams lately suddenly filled his mind. The dawnling. It had to be. "Some of these landmarks . . . do they look familiar to you?"

"Jakim," Finnian said quietly.

He looked up to find Finnian staring at the blood seeping through the fingers he'd pressed to his wound. The look on his face, the way he'd said those words earlier—oh, Aodh, it suddenly made sense.

Finnian's pale, cracked lips drew tight. "We should hurry."

Jakim tucked the cloth into his belt and sorted through the supplies Finnian had pulled out for him. Flask. Bandages. Needle and thread. "How far is Rysinger?"

"Four days' ride." Finnian's voice wavered faintly.

"What if we went to Lord Craddock?"

"No. Craddock is no friend of ours. We need Markham."

But four days? "Will you . . .?"

"I'll be fine. Flask first, then needle and thread."

FIFTY-FOUR: CERIDWEN

*Earthriders typically utilize saddles with high pommels and cantles
and reinforced straps, as well as heavy stirrups for bracing against
the brunt of impact, while cloth cowls filter out the dust of a quake
and visored helmets deflect flying shards.*
- Wisdom of the Horsemasters

The river smelled like death today.

Ceridwen could taste the reek through the half mask she wore over her nose and mouth. Husks of empty armor lined both shores, mounted on stakes or strung from banyan trees. Those were not the cause of the stench. There were no bleached skulls or decaying bones housed within, yet the effect of those jumbled pieces of armor—strung together like twisted limbs, topped with lopsided helmets that seemed to leer at those passing—was distinctly unnerving.

The root of the smell was something far more subtle. So when the flotilla of five Nadaarian riverboats rounded the bend and cries of alarm drowned out the chant that the rowers used to keep pace, she gave a grim smile of satisfaction. So long as the Nadaari focused on the trees, they would miss the true threat closing in below. Just as they had the last three times the rebels used this strategy.

The Langee River offered the swiftest trade route through the Mah, across the rich lowlands beyond, and on to Cetmur, capital of Nadaar, which meant there was never a lack of prey to hunt.

"It's okay to savor it, Fireborn." Owga slid alongside Ceridwen. With five riverboats for the taking today, Owga's rebels were a welcome addition to their war-host—if twoscore riders could be called such a thing. Ceridwen missed the days when a single note from her war horn scrambled three hundred warriors to her heels, with the rest of the Outriders only a swift flight or a whistling signal arrow away.

Owga's sudden appearance drew a shiver of alarm from Mindar. Ceridwen calmed him with a touch and eyed the compact woman, who crouched with a spear in hand, radiating an air of coiled tension like the stone-eye tigers she had been trained to fight.

"I certainly do." Owga nodded toward the flotilla, lip curling into a sneer. "Just look at them. All of them plump with the spoils of the Mah, with food plucked from the mouths of our children to feed the beast of war."

The beast of war currently raging across Soldonia.

Of all the raids Ceridwen had helped mastermind and execute over the past few weeks since the riders had been unleashed, this offered the most direct opportunity to thwart Nadaar's efforts to conquer her nation. The flotilla carried supplies bound for the army's staging ground outside Cetmur, where it awaited orders to depart for Soldonia to restock the invasion force. More than ten thousand soldiers cooled their heels there, despite scout reports that the transport fleet had been ready to depart for weeks now.

She dared claim some responsibility for the delay. Surely the emperor feared committing so many soldiers to a distant fight when upheaval surged near at hand. She might not be able to sail home yet herself, but she would fight for her people here, with every warrior, weapon, and tool she had in her arsenal. And *flames*, it seemed to be working.

Whips cracked, and with a thud and thump of oars and oarlocks, the riverboats lurched forward again.

Owga cocked her head, listening. "Ches-Shu smiles upon us." Then, at Ceridwen's questioning glance, she added, "The chant, Fireborn. Can't you hear what they're saying?"

It had started up again.

Louder this time. Sharper. Almost defiant.

But with Mindar only a spark or two from bursting into flame, Ceridwen had paid no heed to the words that the rowers—Que most likely, either too poor to pay taxes or suspected of rebel leanings and pressed into service—shouted back and forth.

"They call for you, Fireborn, and for the Sea-Demon of Zorrad, to cast off their bonds and free them." Owga raised an eyebrow. "It seems our taleweaver has done his work. The legend spreads."

As if on cue, Ghost emerged from the middle of the river.

Or rather, the river level dropped, revealing Ghost standing flatfooted on the bottom, with Rafi on his back, directly in the path of the flotilla. His seablood was not the cause of the sudden shift, though the boatmen would not know it. Raising his spear, Rafi threw his head back, voicing an echoing shout, and as if at his command, the lead riverboat ran aground, the jolt tumbling rowers from their benches and propelling an overseer up against the rail.

The other four veered to avoid the unseen danger, only to find themselves also scraping to a stop, stuck in foul-smelling muck, exposed as the river drained away beneath them. Ceridwen had never before wished to be a stormrider, but she longed for their enhanced vision in that moment, to see the shock on the faces of all on board.

Ceridwen blew a blast on her war horn, and Owga's rebels sprang to the attack with hoots and shouts and warbling cries. Charging through the knee-deep water, they swarmed the boats, backed by shadowriders and seariders, while stormriders screamed past overhead and earthriders formed a wall on the inner bank. Earthhewn were too heavy for such uncertain footing, and simply setting hoof in that watery sludge would deprive her steed of fire, so Ceridwen forced herself to stay in reserve, too, on the outer bank, in case flames were needed.

That was unlikely, however. Most of this was just for show, a display of force meant to overwhelm the boatmen into a swift surrender, for she had far too few riveren stationed upstream to delay even a portion of the river's flow for long. Rivers were wild and untamable creatures, akin to fireborn in their resistance to restraint, and the longer they sought to hold it back, the more likely it would come crashing through with the rampaging strength of a flood. They needed to strike swiftly and seize control of the riverboats before that happened.

Rebels flung hooks on ropes and began to scale the riverboats. But they were not met by a handful of boatmen, but by soldiers. Soldiers who boiled from the holds to repel them from the decks.

Shades. It was a trap. Owga had been right. The legend was spreading, and the Nadaari were striking back.

Ceridwen shot up in her stirrups, and Mindar tensed, readying to surge into the fray, when a familiar metallic cranking caught her ear. She had heard it often in war in Soldonia. It was the sound of a ballista being loaded with a spear-like bolt, of the string being drawn back to fire. She searched out the device and spied it, mounted on the deck of the rearmost riverboat. Soldiers swung it around, bringing it to bear, not upon the rebels or the steeds, but upon—Rafi.

He was perched unexpectedly on the prow of the lead boat, where the boatmen and overseers were still slowly clambering back to their feet. Why was he up there?

She could imagine him greeting them in his mildly humorous manner, making some inane comment about the perils of river travel these days, followed by an invitation to surrender.

The ballista twanged.

"Rafi," she shouted. "Run!"

He wheeled to face her, and the overseer he'd been talking with collapsed with a bolt through the chest. Rafi reached as if to catch the man, then ducked belatedly behind the rail as the ballista crank sounded out again. The second shot flew astray as the rearmost boat abruptly shifted. Of the five in the flotilla, it had shuddered to a stop closest to the inside curve of the bend, where the river cut deepest, and its rowers still groaned against the oars, lashed relentlessly by their overseers.

The flow of the river suddenly increased, slipping from her riverriders' control. The other four riverboats only rocked slightly, but the rearmost boat lurched forward, closing in on the one where Rafi was now hurrying among the rowers, freeing them from their bonds.

A third bolt splintered the rail inches from his ducked head.

He flinched, but pressed on, and Ceridwen couldn't restrain herself any longer. She charged Mindar in a skidding run down the muddy outer bank, foregoing fire, as his hooves plunged with a hiss into the river, for the sake of action. He hesitated when the spray struck his ribcage, and Ceridwen urged him on, though without flame, she didn't know what she intended to do. Crossing the width of the river, she closed in as the attacking riverboat hugged the curve. A fourth bolt pounded Rafi's boat, a

fifth chased Jasri's stormer from the sky. A sixth splintered off the chest of
Nef's earthhewn as he launched off the high inner bank in a soaring leap.

He landed on the deck of the advancing riverboat with a resounding
crack, as the earthhewn's massive hooves crunched the ballista into
matchwood.

Upstream, a horn blared a warning.

The river had broken fully free.

Ceridwen slung Mindar toward the bank, catching up her own war
horn and repeating the warning. Rebels and riders alike scattered.
Owga's fighters had control of three riverboats, and Rafi, along with his
freed rowers, had the fourth. They would ride out the surging current
aboard. On the deck of the fifth, Nef lashed out with his spear, kicked
out with one foot, and swung his steed, until the earthhewn's churning
hindquarters cleared a space amongst the soldiers.

Defiantly meeting her gaze as the flood tore around the bend, he drew
his steed up into a *sundering* stance, one of the classic earthhewn battle
forms, and crashed its forehooves onto the deck.

Ceridwen felt the ominous rumble, as hooves that could demolish
even mountain-root splintered wood and caused the planks in the
hull to crack.

Just before the flood struck and sent the riverboat spinning away with
Nef and his earthhewn still on board.

"No telling what shocked the Nadaari more," Lowen said with a grin,
scooping a bite of the spicy bean paste Rafi had made onto a cala root
cracker. "The river disappearing beneath them, or Nef's impression of a
sea eagle." He mimed a swooping dive, which earned a round of snorts
and laughter from the riders seated around the cookfire.

Ceridwen had cued Mindar to light it when they made camp for the
night, and though she sat on the outskirts of the gathering, the familiar
hiss and crackle of flames was comforting.

"If you wanted to fly, Nef," Jasri said, "you should have joined the
stormriders."

Nef just grunted, hunched over his knees, his wrinkled vest open over his bare chest. After the flood, both he and his earthhewn had washed up on the bank downstream, soaked but none the worse for their dousing, unlike the riverboat, which had turned up in pieces. A loss Ceridwen had accepted willingly. They had claimed three for the Que Revolution after giving the fourth to the freed rowers to sell or use to rebuild their lives. Something Rafi had insisted upon.

"And lose the chance to grind Sahak's bones under the hooves of my steed?" Nef snorted. "Think I'll pass."

"Ah, but you could catch him in a lightning strike." Lowen dug in with another cracker. "Like we unleashed on the beaters."

It was what they had taken to calling the force of Nadaari who were sweeping the Mah for them, like hunters trying to flush game. But as far as lightning strikes went, the one Lowen spoke of had been more shocking than damaging. Combat lightning was one of the most challenging bonded skills to master. Still, combined with the thunder of an earthhewn charge, it had distracted the war-camp, allowing her force to tear through, felling soldiers in their tents, destroying supplies, and generally wreaking havoc, then vanishing into the Mah before the soldiers managed to regroup. Since then, the Nadaari had slowed their march to fortify their position each night.

Ceridwen counted that a victory, albeit a small one.

"Can't do anything if we're too busy chasing down convoys instead of taking our enemy out. That's the kind of thing that would make a tale actually worth telling, taleweaver." Nef shot a glance toward Eshur, who lounged with his back to a tree, colorful coat rolled up behind his head, listening with an expression of amused interest.

"Oh, if you want tales worth telling, you should ask Moc about his ground crew." Grabbing the whole bowl of bean paste, Lowen settled back with a fistful of crackers and a cheeky grin. "Scattering manure piles, erasing hoofmarks—real exciting stuff."

Moc shoved his brother's head down and stole one of his crackers. "But not nearly so exciting as that false alarm you saved us from last week—mistaking a rock for a stone-eye chariot. Such a relief to know we are safe with you on the lookout, little brother."

That unleashed a clamor, which quieted only when Rafi launched into a humorous retelling of the story. Eshur's eyes twinkled in the firelight as he soaked it all up.

Ceridwen felt his gaze fall on her more than once as she dug the tip of her dagger into the charred sleeve of her leather jerkin and twisted it, widening the hole so she could run a string through, securing the patch. The blade was of Nadaarian make—forged steel, not Que iron—stolen off a corpse a few days back. It was still a poor tool for such work, and she a poor workman, though her solo patrolling days had forced her to learn the basics of repair.

The evening had begun simply enough, with Rafi regaling the riders, while he cooked, with the tale of the time he'd survived waking up snared in the coils of a python. That prompted the others to tell of their own close encounters with the many deadly creatures and treacherous fauna that populated the Que territories. All of which made Ceridwen long for Soldonia, where there were no fist-sized wasps or carnivorous vines, and nothing was so deadly as the riders and their steeds. Then Yath and Taka the boatbuilder had taken turns identifying the stars by name in their own tongues, and telling the tales of their constellations, which tended tragic among the Eliamites and humorous among the Alonque. The rebels had already been in storytelling mode when Eshur's unexpected arrival had shifted the focus to their rebellious efforts instead, to their raids upon convoys, attacks on Nadaarian garrisons within the Mah, and command of the river trade routes.

More threads for the legends Eshur would weave.

These, too, it seemed, were proving effective, for though the tribesmen they occasionally encountered had at first seemed wary of the "demon-steeds" and their riders, now they were greeted with cheers whenever they passed Que on the trail or in their villages. More than that, Eshur insisted that the tales were spreading through the territories, too, and that both Slyrchar and Esgurd had shortchanged the empire on their tributes that month.

Hardly a precursor to outright revolt.

But the rebels whooped and hollered at the tidings as though they were barely one stride away from casting the emperor from his throne, so Ceridwen held her tongue. Nef, however, did not.

"So what?" he demanded, spitting into the fire.

"It's an auspicious sign," Eshur replied with a shrug.

"It's a distraction. We have the demon-steeds. What are we waiting for? We could achieve so much more. When are we going to advance this fight beyond Que borders and water Nadaarian soil with blood, instead of tainting our own jungle loam?"

His raw frustration grated upon Ceridwen. But he could not know how much she longed to fling herself headlong into the fight, and how it was only thought of Liam and the promise she had made to him that restrained her. She could not spend herself or these twoscore riders recklessly, not if she wished to get Liam home. And to ensure there was still a home to return to.

"We will ride out when the time is right," she said.

"I did not think Soldonia's Fireborn was one to shrink from a challenge."

Ceridwen returned Nef's hard stare. "Soldonia's Fireborn has seen more warriors die in a single battle than your rebels can summon to fight their war. Unless you wish to all fall scattered across the grasslands of Nadaar, we ride out when I say."

But her words only fueled the discussion, rather than quelling it, causing some to murmur in concern and some to mutter their assent with Nef. Even steady, unflappable Flick spoke up. "I have no wish to die, Fireborn, but I became a rider to make an impact—"

"Good thing you chose an earthhewn then, and not a shadower," Rafi said absently. Sprawled on his back, he tossed a juggling ball up with a lazy flip of his wrist and caught it just as smoothly, seeming unbothered by the tension around him. "Wouldn't you say, Moc?"

Moc grunted. "Suppose that's true enough."

"Of course," Rafi added musingly, "shadowers aren't completely trace free. If they could just make their manure vanish with them . . ."

Moc broke into a grin. "Oh, believe me, shadower manure isn't the problem. What do you feed that rock beast, Flick? Boulders?"

Chuckles broke out, and just like that, the tension dissipated. Rafi could set the riders at ease as effortlessly as he did the steeds, and soon they were once more laughing and joking by the fireside. With the strangeness of her surroundings shrouded in darkness and the cadence of voices drowning out the jungle noise, Ceridwen could almost imagine that she sat with her own riders once more.

With Nold and Kassa. With Finnian and Iona. As though she had never failed them.

Trying to ignore the ache that thought reawakened, she knotted off the string and tugged the patch to test it. Which proved a pit-spawned idea, for the new string tore through the weakened sleeve, leaving the jerkin more damaged than when she'd started. She muttered a curse, tossing down her tools, and felt their eyes settle on her. Lowen raised a cracker invitingly, welcoming her to join them.

But something held her back. Something always did.

Gathering up her gear, she shoved to her feet and off into the night. To work, since she could not rest.

"Watch out for pythons," Rafi called after her, and the others chimed in with warnings about stone-eye tigers and howling spiders, all of which made the Mah jungle—so vibrant and entrancing during the day with its rambling canopy and bursts of colorful flowers sprouting on vines—seem equally grasping, claustrophobic, and simmering with threats after dark.

She checked on the picketed steeds, then ventured farther out to the sentries, where she found Owga with a torch, receiving reports from a pair of scouts. Owga's forces would move out in the morning, one group to conceal the three remaining riverboats up some small tributary of the Langee, the other group to cart their stolen supplies back to the gorge. The compact woman acknowledged Ceridwen's arrival with a nod, dismissing the scouts, who bent to lift something lying before them. A body.

Suddenly, that aura of threat seemed real and imminent. Ceridwen reached for her war horn. "Who is that? What happened?"

"It's nothing," Owga said. "He's not one of ours."

Burdened with the body, the scouts started to shuffle away, but Ceridwen barred their path and looked to Owga again. Sighing, Owga motioned for them to set down their load. "The scouts brought him in. He wears the garb of an Alonque fisherman, but they found him strung up outside the smoldering husk of another Mahque village."

The scouts stepped back from the body, and the dead man's features fell into torchlight. High cheekbones, wry lips, raw scar carved below one eye, and an inked placard pinned to his chest with a knife. One look at the wording, and her blood ran cold.

Owga's reluctant nod told her she was not mistaken.

She needed to speak to Rafi. Now.

FIFTY-FIVE: JAKIM

Aodh's hand never lets go.
- The truths of Aodh

Finnian offered no argument when Jakim insisted they stop and rest after only a few hours of travel the next day. That seemed a bad sign. So did the sheen of fever in his eyes and the tremors that racked his body. He slept fitfully, wrapped in his cloak, until Jakim shook him awake again.

"I would make a request of you." Finnian's voice was weak, and he swayed as they plodded along. There was something in the way he said the word "request" that gave Jakim pause. It sounded like it should have the word "dying" in front of it. Such requests were sacred among the Scrolls.

He held his tongue and waited for Finnian to speak again.

"Word that Ceridwen is alive and fighting must reach Markham. He is the only one who can convince the war-chiefs to do something about it. To save her. If I fall, swear that you will ride on to—"

"Me? Ride on? I'm no rider."

"But you are a survivor. You'll make it."

The assurance in Finnian's voice warmed Jakim through. He *was* a survivor. He had endured his brothers' hatred, seven years enslaved, and captivity under first the Nadaari and then Khilamook's cruel thumb.

But he was not a slave nor a captive anymore. He was here for a purpose.

"No," he said, and the word felt stranger and more foreign on his tongue than any of the many languages he had picked up over the years. He repeated it in every one of them. At Finnian's baffled look, he tugged out the embroidered map. "*You'll* make it. You are not going to die, because we know where to find a dawnling."

Finnian shook his head slowly. "It's not that simple."

But Jakim felt that it was. The words, the dreams, the map, the need—all coming together—and the dawnling was the key. "Perhaps not. But do you want to live to make amends with Ceridwen yourself? Or would you have me tell her that you died from sheer stubbornness?"

That brought a faint chuckle from Finnian. "She might just believe you."

"Of course she would. She knows you." Jakim pushed the cloth toward Finnian, who looked at him, then took it and studied the route in silence.

He altered their course accordingly. Not retracing their steps but cutting northward on a diagonal. Lacking the concealed map to guide him, Rhodri had strayed too far eastward over their last few days of travel. But with the glowing thread on the map to light the way, Finnian said they could reach the last known location of the dawnling herd by the next midday. Maybe it was Jakim's imagination, or just hopeful thinking, but Finnian seemed to sit straighter in the saddle than before, and he urged Sif on at a quicker pace, and the leagues seemed to pass swiftly as the sun slid past its zenith and began its creeping descent.

"It's hair."

Jakim blinked alert to find that they had slowed to a walk again, winding through a copse of short, scrubby trees, with wind-warped branches and spines like tiger teeth. Though fallen leaves littered the ground, Sif's hooves made no sound. "What is?"

"The glowing strand that makes the map. It's a tail hair."

"Solborn tail hair? From a dawnling?"

"It could be—" Finnian broke off and pulled Sif up sharply. "Smoke."

Jakim tensed, though he did not grasp the danger until Rhodri te Oengus emerged from the trees ahead on his fireborn. Finnian uttered a curse and tried to spin Sif around, but they were already surrounded. Shadowers swarmed around them, melting from the trees, emerging from the shadows, and crushing in on all sides with a rattling of spears and creaking of bows.

They were outnumbered and completely cut off.

Rough hands seized them and dragged them to the ground. Jakim heard Finnian give a sharp gasp in pain and struggled to reach him but was hauled forward and shoved onto his knees before Rhodri's fireborn, Vakhar. Finnian was tossed beside him, collapsing onto the loam. Jakim reached out to help him, and Vakhar snorted a stinging burst of sparks into their faces. A warning.

He stilled, wary of flame, and spied Ineth beside Rhodri. She met his gaze and looked away. No help there.

Rhodri's reins creaked under his grip. "Kill them."

"With pleasure," growled Cormag. He forced his way to the front of the crowd, followed by his brothers, all of them furious and fixated on Finnian.

Brawly already had an arrow nocked. He raised his bow and deliberately sighted down the shaft, aiming the cruel barbed tip directly at Finnian's face as he shakingly pushed himself up until he slumped on his knees. His hand was pressed to his wound, a scrap of green cloth visible through his fingers.

The map.

"No!" Jakim cried out. "I solved it!"

Brawly's bow creaked but he did not fire. Yet.

"You can't kill us. I solved the map. I solved it!" Jakim looked to Rhodri, but it was not the war-chief who answered him.

"Too late, boy." Khilamook stepped around Vakhar, sporting a pristinely bandaged head and a glare that made Jakim shiver. "Why do you think we're here? I solved it first."

"Really?" Finnian countered, voice rasping. "So you figured out how to make it glow too?"

It was a bluff, of course, but like an arrow shot by an expert archer, his words struck their mark. Rhodri swung out of the saddle, landing with a clank of spurs, and Nahrog, the priest, stepped eagerly up beside him. Jakim saw no sign of the chariot or of Koata, the stone-eye tiger.

"It glows, you say? You must show us," the priest demanded, eyes glittering.

Jakim kept his attention away from the scrap of cloth in Finnian's hand. "We will, once you swear to release both of us."

"He slew our brother!"

"We will have retribution!"

The shouts of outrage burst from Cormag and Moray, while Brawly took a step nearer, arm straining with holding his shot. One slip of the fingers, one twitch of the muscles, and the broadhead arrow would take Finnian in the eye, and Rhodri would not try to stop it.

Desperate now, Jakim struggled for something to say.

Ineth cleared her throat. "If it is retribution you want, have you considered that a slow death can be far more satisfying? Have you ever seen a man die from a soured gut wound before? It is quite agonizing and always fatal. I mean, look at him. He can barely stay upright, and the pain will only get worse before the end."

Was that true? Jakim glanced at Finnian, who was hunched over his knees, sweat trickling down his brow, breathing shallowly, concentrated on that arrow.

"Our brother deserves to be honored," muttered Moray.

"And he will be," Rhodri said. "You will avenge your brother, but fast or slow should make no difference to him, so you will wait until after we have our goal." He turned from their anger and towered over Jakim. "And you will not try my patience. You will show me now, or I will kill both of you and find it upon your corpses."

He would too. Jakim could see it in his eyes.

So he held out his hand, and Finnian gave him the cloth, and he spread it on the ground before Rhodri. It was dusk now, and the glowing thread threw off rays of such a warm and brilliant golden light, it cast an almost healthy flush over Finnian's fevered pallor. Rhodri stood transfixed, staring at it in awe, until Jakim folded it up and tucked it away again.

Then he rounded on Khilamook. "You said nothing of this, engineer."

For once, Khilamook seemed utterly speechless. Jakim could have sworn the man had never seen the glowing map before. Had he truly solved it on his own, without the aid of the glowing thread? Or had he lied and just made a lucky guess?

Rhodri shifted his stance and drove his sabre hilt down. "Tomorrow, you will lead us to the dawnling herd, all three of you." He made no vocal threat, but the atmosphere bristled with it. With orders to see them secured as the force made camp, he strode off, and Ineth followed him.

Jakim didn't see her again until later that night. He and Finnian had been trussed hand and foot and anchored to a tree with the engineer across from them. Steeds had been untacked, bedrolls unslung, and the few lit fires burned down low. Finnian was already twitching in a fevered sleep, and the warmth radiating off his skin was as unsettling as the warmth of the cloth Jakim clutched in his hand was soothing.

Jakim looked up and found Ineth standing stiffly over him.

"Ineth." He straightened instantly and tucked the cloth into Finnian's hand which was pressed against the wound on his side. "Thank you for what you said."

"What I said? That your friend was going to die slowly and painfully? You shouldn't thank me for that." Her tone was at once harsh and stinging. "Besides, I didn't say it for you, or for te Donal. Ondri's sons are headstrong beasts, and they need reining in now and then, lest they run wild."

And yet, she was here, wasn't she? Checking on him?

She looked away. "Why didn't you keep running?"

"I had to come back. I had to find the dawnling."

"Then you are a fool like the rest of them, Jakim Ha'Nor."

"No, you don't understand," he insisted. "I think that's why I'm here. I think Aodh wants me to find the dawnling." It was the first time he had tried to put it into words, and it sounded as uncertain and implausible as he had feared.

"Aodh?" Her laugh was jagged. "Aodh doesn't want anything. Aodh is *dead*."

He recoiled from her words.

That only seemed to cast fuel upon her tongue. "Dead. And you want to know how I know? Because I went on a mission to Broken-Eliam too. The last mission. I traversed those dead and twisted wastes, and I ventured into the tainted City, and there on the walls, within the sacred words themselves, I found the truth."

She seized her left sleeve and yanked it up above the elbow, exposing a forearm covered as Jakim had guessed in the familiar scrawl of blued lines that represented the foundational truths of Aodh. But they were all of them blotted out. Slashed through. Covered by ragged scars, carved by a knife to form the words she had spoken: *Aodh is dead.*

Jakim felt cold.

Her voice was bitter. "The one. Final. Deplorable truth. That cancels out all the rest of them. Look at it, Scroll. Look at it and see. This is the answer to all the questions."

He licked cracked lips. "It can't be."

"But it is, and your Scrolls know it, and they lied. And who can blame them, because if Aodh is dead, then what does it matter?"

Jakim didn't know what to say as she tugged her sleeve down and walked off, but her words whispered in his ears all the restless night. Her words were the undercurrent of fear humming in his chest the next morning, too, as he was shoved out in front of the column to march on foot alongside Khilamook. Finnian's hands were tied to a tether behind Cormag's steed, and he was forced to keep up or be dragged. It was the engineer's presence that finally allowed Jakim to overcome the uncertainty Ineth's words had awakened inside him and focus only on the map. On the locations recorded in glowing thread and on their destination.

His steps quickened as they toiled up a rugged path toward the base of a towering hill, which seemed to be one of the last locations marked on the map. Soon, he would know. Soon, he would see. He threw himself forward, outpacing even Khilamook, who was panting in his high-collared robe, skin reddening in the heat, when the golden thread suddenly flared with a brightness so intense Jakim flinched from it as if it were the sun.

Then the glow flickered and went out.

FIFTY-SIX: RAFI

What is the jungle without the seed, the leaf, the twig, the log, and the loam?
Remove but one, and the jungle itself will be no more.
- Mahque saying

Rafi had been many things in life—a prince, a fugitive, a fisherman, a soil-tender—but he had never been a legend before. It was decidedly unnerving. He scooted away from the fireside gathering with a few cala root crackers that he'd managed to extricate from Lowen for Ghost. The colt nickered at his approach and greedily lipped up the crumbs from his hands, while Rafi gently ran his fingers over the scar on Ghost's neck. Soft white hairs were starting to grow back in from the edges. Soon, the wound would be covered, but not forgotten. Scars, even the unseen ones, left their marks.

He could see it in Ceridwen. He felt it in himself.

It had forged a bond between them that night in the gorge. Was that what he found so appealing about the whispers of Aodh, the deity who carried all the wounds of the world in himself? It was comforting to know that even in pain, you need not be alone.

Beside Ghost, Mindar snorted and raised his head, eyes aglow in the darkness, but it was the scuff of a footstep behind that made Rafi turn. He expected to see Ceridwen, but it was Eshur who stood there, coat slung over one shoulder.

"Imbé Tisani wants to meet."

Rafi dusted off his hands. "So gathering stories . . .?"

"Is not the primary reason I'm here. Though that one you shared about the python was certainly a delightful bonus." Eshur shifted his stance, winced, and pressed a hand to his side.

"You're hurt?"

"Only slightly. No cause for alarm. This isn't the first time someone has tried to kill me, and I doubt it will be the last."

Suddenly Eshur's assumption at their first meeting that Rafi was there to kill him made sense. "I had no idea taleweaving could be so dangerous—unless this has to do with your rebellious leanings instead."

"So far as I know, my 'leanings' remain largely unknown. But taleweaving can be dangerous if you tug the right threads. Usually, I'm better at dodging, though I'm nowhere near as skilled as you, prince, at evading death. Speaking of which . . ."

Rafi sighed. "The meeting. When is it?"

"Tomorrow, not four leagues from here. Imbé has convinced a number of those discontented with the current regime to gather, and she hopes to unveil you as their not-quite-so-dead-as-assumed prince to convince them to commit to the cause."

"And how am I supposed to do that?"

"By being yourself, I would imagine."

"I don't know, Eshur. Seems a lot to ask," Rafi observed with a slight smile.

The taleweaver dipped his head. "You know, the wise among the Mahque have a saying: 'What is the jungle without the seed, the leaf, the twig, the log, and the loam? Remove but one, and the jungle itself will be no more.'"

"And what does that mean?"

"Just as it would prove foolish to debate the importance of seed over loam for the existence of the jungle, so we cannot compare the value of any soul among us. It means that you, Rafi Tetrani, have as integral a role to fill in this life as leaf or twig or log in the Mah."

Rafi shifted uncomfortably, sticking his hands into his pockets and finding the cloth-wrapped scadtha claw he'd neglected to return to Umut. "What about thorns? Angling vines? Those are a part of the jungle too. Where do they fit in?"

Something thudded to the ground behind him, and it was not Eshur who answered, but Ceridwen. "Poisonous thorns certainly would be a more apt comparison for one of your birth, wouldn't they, Rafi *Tetrani*?"

Her voice was sharp and tinged with scorn no less corrosive than the toxin she described.

Ches-Shu, Cael, and Cihana Three, she knew.

Rafi turned to find her standing over a body she had apparently just dumped at his feet. It was a young Alonque man with cut bonds unraveling on wrists and ankles and a noose around his bruised neck—so, not slain by the *chet* she gripped at her side, knuckles whitening.

Could they be under attack? "Ceridwen . . . I . . . what is this?"

"Oh, come, don't tell me you don't see the resemblance."

Resemblance? Rafi didn't even recognize the man.

"I don't understand," he began, then broke off, as Ceridwen tossed a wooden placard and then a blade onto the man's chest. There, carved into the placard and inked with blood in bold, blocklike Nadaarian letters, were the words:

DEATH TO THE PRETENDER
RAFI TETRANI
SO-CALLED SON OF NEMENT
AND CROWN PRINCE OF NADAAR

Suddenly he did see the resemblance, though not in the man's features but in the wounds carved into his flesh. His hand. His thigh. The mark below his right eye. Each a match to the scars Rafi now bore. Only one person in all the world could have recreated those marks with such sadistic accuracy: Sahak.

Rafi's first instinct was to run.

His second, drilled into him by a month of training and weeks of raiding, was to reach for his steed and *then* run. His gaze darted from the body to the encircling closeness of the jungle, which suddenly seemed bent on caging him in. "We need to go. We need to—"

"So it is true." Ceridwen's voice cut across his own like a knife. "Owga told me it was, but I wanted to see the truth in your eyes."

Ches-Shu, this wasn't the time.

"I meant to tell—"

"Meant to? When, exactly? When did you mean to tell me that you are kin to the emperor whose lust for conquest has drenched my kingdom in blood?" Only the corpse parted them now, and he could have sworn her eyes burned with flames all their own. "Clearly not until after you made me a traitor to my people by betraying the secrets of our steeds to our sworn enemy. To a Tetrani."

"I'm not like them."

It sounded a pitiful excuse, but it was true. He wasn't like Sahak, who, if this corpse was truly his handiwork, might be lurking nearby even now, readying to attack. "Look, you don't understand. We need to move out now. Sahak could be closing in as we speak."

"Sahak isn't here."

"How could you know—"

"Owga's scouts brought the body in. They found it strung outside a charred Mahque town miles away." She regarded him distastefully. "Sahak would be . . . what to you? A cousin? You know he tried to uncover those same secrets you did. How do I know you're not in league with him?"

Rafi found his temper fraying. He rubbed at his face in exasperation. "You mean aside from the fact that I broke into his temple and rescued you? Or that, clearly, he still wants me dead?" He gestured at the corpse. "He always has. We were on the run from him the night that Delmar died, and I have been hunted every day of my life since then because of who I was born to be. So forgive me, Ceridwen, if I didn't want to tell you that I was related to the monster who'd tried to kill us both. Ches-Shu, it's not as if we're on speaking terms!"

His laugh broke hoarse and ragged across the silence.

Her voice when she spoke was rigid. "I have told you truths about me and my brother that I have shared with few others. I told you of my brand and of my father's betrayal, and all the while, you withheld this? You think I do not know fear? Shame? They are predators, Rafi, like your stone-eyes, and you do not run from such things, for that only gives them power."

Stepping over the corpse, she shoved past him to reach her fireborn. She saddled swiftly, fastening straps and buckles with a force that drew sparks to the curling tips of Mindar's mane, and she was done before Rafi managed to untie his tongue.

"So, that's it then? You're leaving us?"

"You have your riders, Rafi. Your legend, your steeds, your war with the empire. What more need have you for me?"

Because she was everything he was not. Just like Delmar.

But the words came to him too slowly, and she had already set foot to stirrup. He stepped up to her. "Just tell me this: Would you have agreed to help if you'd known the truth of my identity?" She swung astride Mindar. "You wouldn't," he said resolutely. "You know it. I did what I had to."

She wheeled Mindar to face him, and the fireborn snorted, choking Rafi with the noxious fumes that blasted from its nostrils. Crimson flames ignited at the back of Mindar's throat, danced across his mane, and coiled down his legs to kindle the burning embers of his hooves, and the heat of it forced Rafi to pull back.

He held out his hands. "Can't you see I'm not your enemy?"

"I'd hoped you might be a friend," she replied, and for an instant, he thought he saw a softening in her eyes, but it dissipated as swiftly as a wisp of smoke. "But trust is the root of all bonds, Rafi, and without it, there are no riders and steeds, and there is nothing between us at all. You saved my life. You may keep yours. But now leave me to mine."

With that, Mindar sprang away. Rafi shouted after Ceridwen, but the jungle only echoed his own voice mockingly back at him.

"Not going to try and stop her?" Eshur asked mildly beside him, startling Rafi, who had forgotten that he wasn't alone.

"I'm fairly certain Ceridwen would defy the winds and the waves if they tried to stand in her way." She was like Delmar in that, too, practically a force of nature in and of herself. And as with Delmar, he had failed her.

"You know where she is headed then?"

"If we're lucky, to burn down the emperor's palace." Which would be quite the feat, considering how it was situated amongst the thousand waterfalls of Cetmur, though he wouldn't have put it past Ceridwen to try.

"Why leave it to luck?" Nef shoved through the thin tangle of undergrowth that separated the steeds from the fireside gathering, carrying a glowing brand. "I'm in."

"I was joking," Rafi said shortly.

Nef's eye gleamed. "I wasn't."

Rafi didn't doubt that. Or that the sudden hush that had fallen over the group by the fire meant the rest of the riders were listening, attention drawn by his shouts.

Nef ground his heel against a spark that still smoldered in a twist of leaves where Mindar's hooves had tossed it. "We have the steeds. The training. Why waste our efforts on supply convoys bound for Soldonia when we could be laying waste to the Nadaarian countryside? Burning their villages and stringing their cousins up on trees."

Rafi tracked his nod to the body, and he couldn't help wondering what ill winds had blown the slain man into Sahak's path. He had been distracted before by the all-too-familiar wounds to catch more than a vague sense of rounded features, but now the glow of the brand fell full on the man's face as Nef leaned over to inspect him, and Rafi's stomach twisted.

"He looks even younger than the others," Nef remarked.

More boy than man, Rafi thought with a pang. Then his brain snagged on that one word: *others*. He raised his head slowly, senses coming wholly alert. "What do you mean 'others?'"

"The other bodies."

Bodies. Plural. "How many?"

"Five so far. Same wounds. Same words. Scouts have been reporting the sightings across the Mah for weeks." Nef eyed him. "That shocked look on your face is surprisingly convincing. You really didn't know?" He picked up the placard, flipping it around in his hands to scan the writing. "Didn't think Umut had it in him to keep it from you."

That was even more staggering.

Rafi stood stunned in disbelief. He had known there would be consequences for the choice he had made to emerge from the shadows and own his true name. But this? "You mean Sahak has been going about murdering Alonque at random, to get someone to turn me in?" He looked to Eshur, who appeared as disturbed as he felt, then back to Nef. "And Umut kept it from me? Why?"

"Why do you think?" Nef scoffed. "Obviously to keep you from running off to turn yourself in to spare them and spoiling all his plans."

Rafi swallowed. "And you decided to tell me now because . . .?"

"Because I know you, Tetrani." Though Nef called Rafi by his Nadaarian surname, there was no bite of scorn in his tone. "And I think you deserve to know. Because from what I've seen, you can't look on what the empire is doing to your cousins in your name and not want them to pay. And if that convinces you to burn the imperial palace down rather than netting yourself to these so-called loyalist noble friends, so much the better."

With that, Nef shoved the placard at Rafi and walked off. Rafi held it numbly, fixated on the question Umut's concerns forced him to confront. Would he have done it?

Could he have turned himself in? Ches-Shu, he didn't know.

Just the thought of it now raised a cold sweat on his brow. Made his feet yearn to run. But did it matter? Even if Umut had been right to question his resolve, to not be told, to not even be given that choice—

Choice? Like you denied Ceridwen?

It was his own voice that whispered it, and it stopped him fast. Sickened at the realization of what he'd done, he gripped the placard until its splinters bit into his fingers.

"That one is a tangled thread and no mistake." Eshur nodded toward the fading glint of Nef's light wending deeper into the jungle, toward the sentries. "Speaking of those 'loyalist noble friends,' we should bring that sign with us to the meeting. They wanted proof that you are a threat? Sahak has given it to us."

"How? He called me a pretender."

"He addressed your claim head-on, and in so doing, he acknowledged it, which gives it credence. Ignore a tale and it dies. Try to kill it, on the other hand, and it sprouts like a weed."

"A weed," Rafi repeated dully. "Yeah, that's me."

Not leaf or log or even thorn. Just a weed. Unwanted, and a pain to kill.

Ever perceptive, Eshur laid a hand on his back. "Take heart. Sahak, in his cruelty and his cleverness, has overplayed his hand. When the net layer stumbles into his own net, all the world breathes in relief."

Maybe, Rafi thought later as he crashed into his hammock, Eshur was right. Maybe it need not all turn to rot and ruin in one night. Maybe this was just the proof he needed to convince Imbé's nobles that he was the changing tide that could sweep Lykier from his throne. And yes, Sahak had given it to him. He could find satisfaction in that, couldn't he?

Couldn't he?

FIFTY-SEVEN: JAKIM

On that day, the ancient ruins will be rebuilt,
and the broken dwellings restored.
- Scroll Thirty-One of the Holy Writ, Kerrikar Sanctuary

Jakim stared at the embroidered cloth where the glowing map had just gone dark, vanishing from view amongst the blood-soaked stitches that formed the landscape: the mountains, the fields, the dawnling steed in the foreground. Oh, Aodh, where had the light gone? He couldn't even make out the golden thread anymore. Without that radiant glow to set it apart, it was lost amidst a sea of a thousand other strands.

"Why did you stop?" Khilamook plodded up. His gaze fell on the darkened cloth and narrowed. "Where did it go? Is this another trick? Because I will not die today."

A blast of heated air struck their backs, and the engineer stiffened.

"What is this?" Rhodri demanded, pressing closer on his menacing steed. For all its smoke and spark, there was something oddly cold and distant about the creature. It didn't have the sheer passion Jakim had seen in Ceridwen's fireborn. "Why have you stopped moving?"

Jakim tried to find the words to explain.

"We're here," Khilamook said, then muttered, "more or less."

"Here? Then where—" A strange keening hum rose in the air. It was oddly high-pitched and deeply resonant at the same time, like tinkling glass and vibrating stone, emanating from somewhere among them. Rhodri stiffened and drew out the relic on its chain about his neck.

The noise was coming from it.

Nahrog stumped up, puffing for breath, his robes dusty from the trek, and Jakim couldn't deny a twinge of satisfaction at seeing him forced to blister his own feet, without his chariot or tiger. Before he could speak, Rhodri spun his steed and loped down the line. He returned a moment later, with Cormag on his shadower, still dragging Finnian along behind. Swaying and weaving, Finnian looked on the verge of collapse.

"It weakened for a moment back there," Rhodri said, holding the relic out, "but it's growing stronger again. Can you hear it?"

Khilamook spoke up. "Perhaps you should follow it? See where it leads?" He nodded at Cormag. "Wasn't he the one who said it's supposed to react when other dawnlings are near?"

"That was my brother, Arlen," Cormag growled.

"Oh, right, the one *he* killed." Khilamook tipped his head toward Finnian. His tone was all innocence, but the look on his face told Jakim he knew exactly what he was doing.

What was it he had said the other day? Elements . . . reacting?

Rhodri urged Vakhar forward, Ineth on his heels, and the rest fell in behind, continuing around the curve of the hill. No longer needed in the lead, Jakim seemed to have been forgotten for the moment. So he waited until Cormag jolted past, then slipped in beside Finnian and tried to steady him as the tether tugged him along.

"Let me help," Jakim whispered.

Finnian flicked him a glance, eyes glassy and unfocused, but some of his weight came to rest on Jakim. Something clipped Jakim's ear, and he saw the tip of Brawly's bow withdrawing, while the rest of Ondri's sons formed a scowling knot around them as on they trudged, rounding the base of the hill.

Jakim could no longer hear the humming of the relic, but it must have continued, for when they came to a cleft in the rock formation, Rhodri turned in without hesitation, and in twos and threes, pressing through the tight squeeze, the rest followed. Sound echoed eerily as Jakim ducked through, Finnian's weight sinking heavier on his shoulder. When he craned his neck back, he found the walls bowed so close above that only a thin sliver of blue sky was visible.

They emerged into a soft, green valley filled with the music of trickling water, spilling mistily over the rock face to their left and wandering away before their feet.

Jakim lurched to a stop, startling a groan from Finnian. There, standing just across the stream, was a creature that could only be a dawnling. It was tall and sleek with a delicate neck and legs that seemed too long and fragile for its body. Its pearlescent-gold coat gleamed with a metallic sheen, and there on its forehead, growing like a horn from an earthhewn, was a dark stone like the relic Rhodri held, only this one was pierced through with light. It blazed through the honeycombed rock or bone, or whatever it was, and that light seemed to ripple down its mane, beneath its coat, and along its tail, until the entire creature was glowing.

Like the thread. Like flames reflected on water. Like the sun itself.

Rhodri dismounted slowly, then deliberately dropped his reins and stepped away from Vakhar toward the edge of the stream. Jakim could have sworn the war-chief's eyes glistened with tears. Ineth and Nahrog joined him.

"*Sky's blood*," Ineth murmured, "it's real."

"Silent One Alive," Nahrog breathed.

Rhodri pivoted to face him. "Tell him, priest. Tell your Voice we have the dawnling. Tell him I want my army waiting in Ardon when I return." He strode back to Vakhar and, with a few sharp flicks of his wrist, undid the straps holding a looped rope to his saddle. "Move in"—he raised his voice to reach his warriors—"and surround it!"

The priest stiffened, and suddenly his eyes seemed to stare at nothing at all, as he murmured words so low they were unintelligible. Time seemed to slow.

Finnian's knees sagged, driving his weight against Jakim's shoulder, reminding him of the urgent reason they had come, as ahead, the dawnling's light flared brighter still, then pulsed, throwing off dazzling rays. The humming strengthened until it reverberated on the air, not just coming from the relic, but from the steed too. Jakim felt a sharp tugging sensation in his chest. They needed to get closer. Pulled forward, Jakim seized the tether attached to Finnian's wrists and yanked it from Cormag's distracted grip.

"Come on," he yelled in Finnian's ear. "We need to get closer!"

And together, staggering, and nearly falling, they moved toward the light. Jakim's lungs were heaving as he half dragged Finnian with each step, focused on one thing and one thing alone: reaching the dawnling.

Then the light erupted, bursting outward in a shining sphere that rushed across the stream toward Ineth and Nahrog. It flashed over them, crackling and radiant, and Ineth crumpled, trembling, to her knees, while Nahrog cried out and stumbled back.

But Jakim flung himself forward as the light rippled across the grass, fading now, dissipating fast. He was still five strides away when it puffed out and vanished. The humming and the ringing it produced in his ears went with it.

The dawnling's lightless head drooped, and it sank toward the ground.

It fell slowly, heavily, like a tree whose roots slipped through wet earth. Once down, it did not move.

"No . . ." Jakim whispered desperately.

Finnian swayed and lurched a step, then collapsed. His limp weight towed them both to the ground, Jakim catching himself with one arm. His wrist twinged as he rolled Finnian over.

Still breathing, but unconscious, with blood seeping again from his bandaged wound.

Jakim sank back as riders splashed across the stream to check on the fallen steed. He squeezed the sides of his head. He just couldn't make sense of it.

He had done it. He had found the dawnling. But too late for Finnian.

Could this truly be what Aodh had intended? Or had he just fabricated the sense that Aodh was guiding him because he was desperate for it all to mean something?

Ineth couldn't be right, could she? Aodh couldn't be dead.

Rhodri stood still as a statue, his catch-rope uncoiling from his hand. Ineth had not moved since the light crashed over her. She still knelt, palms up, staring down at her arms. And Nahrog—

Her arms.

Jakim looked down at his own hands, at the silk cloth crumpled in his fist, and though the threads still did not glow, he could almost swear he felt a residual warmth coming from it. Moving as if his hands were not his own, he pressed the cloth against Finnian's wound and used his belt to tie it in place again.

Thick hands seized his tunic and wrenched him to his feet. "What did you do?" Nahrog snarled. "Bring it back."

"Bring what? The light? I don't know how."

"Not the light," Nahrog spat out. "The Voice. It's gone." Suddenly the priest's thick hands were wrapped around his throat. "Bring it back!"

Bright specks bloomed before his eyes.

Jakim kicked and thrashed and clawed at the man's knotted hands, but the priest far outweighed him and had the iron grip of a charioteer. *Oh, Aodh, please!*

Close by, a guttural snarl sounded out.

The priest's eyes widened as, with a roar and a blur of orange, Koata sprang at him.

FIFTY-EIGHT: RAFI

It is arrogant indeed to scar the world in order to leave your mark upon it.
- Mahque saying

Satisfaction was not at all what Rafi felt as Imbé Tisani presented him before the officials. He held the bloodstained placard, a strange and morbid proof of his claim, and was clad in the garb of royalty—vibrant silks, a richly armored belt, heavy gold collar, and vambraces, all embossed with the tiger sigil of House Korringar. These had been supplied by Imbé, who apparently hadn't trusted him not to show up covered in river sludge, so he could look the prince she titled him.

Rafi Tetrani. Son of Nement. Crown Prince of Nadaar.

But he felt the pretender that placard proclaimed, for in his mind it was not he who stood regal before their devouring gaze, but Delmar. It was the only way he could keep from flinching (or fidgeting with the scadtha claw he had impulsively shoved into his new pockets) throughout Imbé's speech. Or afterward, as she towed him through the throng to meet them one by one, with Eshur repeating names and titles in his ear.

Odd that these were supposed to be his father's most loyal supporters, and he couldn't have picked one of them out. They were nobles, officials, satraps, and merchants. How Imbé had begged, bribed, or dragged them all out here—to this dilapidated upper room of a ramshackle tavern, in a backwater town on the outskirts of the jungle, so far from the city that declared itself the Center of the World—just to meet him, he couldn't imagine.

Where were they when his family was murdered? When he and Delmar spent three years buried in a cell?

He could not understand it. At least not until he caught the glint of greed in every eye, the avarice that varnished each welcoming grin, and the smoothly spoken hopes for his reign that boiled down to a long list of demands, for everything from titles granted to lands bestowed to edicts enacted.

Rafi had seen a man eaten alive by a swarm of boura. The tiny, copper-colored eels infested the shallows of the Alon coast and seemed completely harmless, up until the moment they tasted blood in the water and transformed into a ferocious, seething, carnivorous mass that could strip flesh from bones in minutes. He couldn't shake that image now, convinced that the officials sensed his weakness and would devour him just as eagerly as they vowed both wealth and sword to uphold his claim.

It had been years since Rafi had been tutored on matters of imperial governance, but he felt fairly certain that if he honored even half the demands he had received, the empire would splinter into a dozen pieces.

Which was, ironically, exactly what the Que wanted. An empire so destabilized, it could hold them captive no longer.

Rafi shifted uncomfortably and twisted his left vambrace, which kept sliding around cumbersomely on his arm. Ches-Shu, but he would give anything to trade places with Nef and Aruk, keeping watch in the tavern below. Or to be back at the riders' jungle camp with Jasri and the others. Or, better yet, racing after Ceridwen to apologize.

Imbé pinched his wrist. "Relax."

He flexed his hand. Felt the vambrace slide again. "I'm not good at this."

She raised one eyebrow. "Did you expect to be without practice? You will learn. And excuses are unbecoming for one of your station. 'Not good at it' indeed."

Sighing, Rafi turned to the next official, an old man with more gold bangles stacked beneath the wide sleeves of his deep purple tunic than hairs upon his head, and pasted on a smile. "Let me guess: You'll want my firstborn child?"

The old man's eyes darted to Imbé. "Is that . . ."

"Our prince's famed sense of humor? Indeed." She shot Rafi an annoyed look, though he'd have sworn the old man seemed crestfallen as she drew him away.

Eshur coughed slightly behind him.

"What?" Rafi muttered without turning. "You told me to be myself."

"And that requires offering up your unborn children as bribes?"

"Only in jest." Bitter jest to offset the cloying sweetness of the nobles' promises. But not even humor could make every situation palatable, and it was getting harder and harder to swallow this one. Nef had warned him against being netted, and Rafi could practically feel the cords enmeshing his limbs. He was clearly just an excuse for these nobles to make a bid to control the throne. A throne he still intended to topple, not sit upon. Maybe he hadn't told Ceridwen the full truth of who he was, but he hadn't told them either.

Be yourself, Eshur had said.

But left to himself, he would never choose to be here, to do this. Was this what it meant to be Rafi Tetrani then? Only ever a pretender, even to himself?

Imbé beckoned to him with her cane from across the room, where she had cornered an official so tall he must be of Choth heritage. Her eyes were alight with the same intensity he had seen when she remarked on his likeness to his father. Oh, Ches-Shu. Rafi abruptly wheeled away. Long strides ushered him out onto the dim stairwell that descended round a corner into the tavern below. He clattered down to the landing before sagging with his back to the wall.

"What are you doing?" Eshur stopped halfway down the stairs.

He was running. It was what he did. Sometimes, he managed to do it in the right direction. He raised his head to see Imbé pass Eshur and rest on her cane two steps above him. She pressed her lips into a stern, thin line, her expression demanding an explanation.

But how to even begin? "I'm sorry. I just can't do this."

"This," she said crisply, "is how thrones are won. And you must face that reality, Rafi Tetrani, however uncomfortable it may seem. Keep them," she added as he reflexively started to unfasten the vambraces. "You will need them again, soon. Our plans mean nothing once the empress births an heir, and my sources in the palace warn that time is not on our side. I can make your excuses tonight, but we must be ready to coordinate our move."

With that ominous note, Imbé returned above. Rafi let his head sag, then pushed off the wall, only to find his path blocked by Eshur, who swung off his colored coat and held it out. Rafi took it and shrugged it on over his silks. Much as he wished to exchange them for the worn shirt and trousers he'd stuffed into Eshur's pack, he wanted to be out of this suffocating place as soon as possible. Back to the Mah.

Back to Ghost, where he could at least pretend to be free.

Exiting the stairwell into the smoky haze and rowdy din of the tavern below, crowded with Nadaarian boatmen and only the occasional Que tribesman, Rafi easily spied Aruk, seated at a rickety table in a corner with a clear vantage of the door, and shouldered his way over.

"How did it go?" Aruk slid a cup of saga wine toward him.

"Oh, I all but promised away my firstborn child, so you know, about as expected." Rafi ignored the wine and shoved his hands into the coat pockets, which were stuffed with a variety of unusual odds and ends— juggling balls, twists of thread, seashells—drawing it even more tightly closed over the Nadaarian finery. "We should go. Where's Nef?"

"Out." Aruk sniffed. "Hopefully cooling off."

"Why? What happened?"

"Beats me. Just up and stalked out."

"You didn't ask where he was going?"

"Of course I did. He grunted. You know how he is."

Unfortunately, Rafi did. Which was why he'd dragged Nef along in the first place, despite knowing how much forging such an agreement would infuriate him. No doubt Nef was also still angry that Rafi had placed Jasri—and not him—in command of the riders' camp. But with Ceridwen gone, and Nadaarian patrols in the area making it too risky to bring all the riders along, Rafi had needed to leave someone in charge, and of the two, Nef certainly had the twitchier hand on the reins. Still, angry or not, it wasn't like Nef to shirk duty.

Eshur leaned in. "A word of caution: that coat draws eyes, and unless you wish to deliver a dramatized reenactment of the escape of Vorgis the One-Handed from the angry mob of Ubeezi, we should be on our way. Nef will know to meet us at the steeds if he finds us gone."

Sure enough, curious faces were turning toward them, and several voices called out for a tale. They beat a hasty retreat out of the tavern, into the night, and out of the town, until it was just a grimy stain on the riverbank behind them. They slipped into the hollow nestled between the towering roots and sprawling crown of the banyan tree where they had concealed their steeds. Steel struck flint, and the muted flare of Aruk's torch showed all three steeds still hobbled within.

Seablood. Shadower. Earthhewn.

And still, no sign of Nef.

Rafi's skin prickled. "I don't like this. Something's wrong. We should go back." He shrugged out of the coat and slung it to Eshur, then undid the gilded clasps of the silk tunic. It gaped open to his ribcage, and he started to tug it up before realizing that Eshur had not moved. "Toss me the pack, won't you? I'll need my things."

"You cannot go back."

Rafi released the tunic. "Why not?"

"Because those nobles committed to treason tonight, and you with them," Eshur said patiently. "Going back risks drawing attention that could expose everything. Simply waiting here is dangerous enough."

"Dangerous? Says the man with assassins on his trail?"

"You know what they say—it takes one to know one."

Humor and logic combined made for a persuasive argument. "Fine then. We'll wait. But I won't leave without him." Nef was often a thorn beneath his skin, but over these past months, they'd become almost friends. "We don't leave anyone behind."

The sound of slow clapping mocked his words.

Rafi lunged for Ghost, but dark shapes unfolded from the many root pillars of the banyan tree, and glinting spear tips and bared blades ringed them in.

Not Sahak. Not now.

But it was not Sahak who spoke.

"I'm touched, Rafi," Nef said, stepping into the glow of the torch, spear slung casually over one shoulder. "Really."

"Nef? What is this?"

"What's it look like?" a rough voice asked behind him, and the burly shape of Clae of the Mahque swaggered up out of the dark, *chet* in hand. "Just a chat among friends."

Yes, because that was what this looked like. A friendly ambush.

Rafi tested forward a step, and the circle closed in. Mahque warriors, all of them, bearing stern expressions.

"Don't mind them," Clae said curtly, though he did not call his fighters off. "Can't blame them for being wary when you flaunt the enemy's silks and sigils."

"It's called a disguise," Eshur observed. "And this is a council-approved mission."

"Don't lecture me about the council, taleweaver. The others might suffer your meddling, but we of the Mahque don't lose sight of the jungle for its leaves. You think I don't know all about your little mission here?"

Rafi exchanged a glance with Aruk, who shifted nervously, falling momentarily into shadow and nearly disappearing from view. "So it's not just coincidence then, running into us here?"

Nef snorted. "Hardly. I brought him here to give you the good news." With a flick of his wrist, the spear spun from his shoulder and planted in a root by his foot—because who didn't like their good news delivered at spearpoint? "We found Sahak."

"What? Where?"

"Back at the temple. Confirmed by multiple sightings. Which makes now the time to attack before he disappears again."

Rafi lifted a brow. "So, after all this time, Sahak just shows up again? Doesn't that seem too easy?"

"Easy?" Clae spat. "Trust me. It was anything but."

"But taking him will be." Nef leaned on the spear. "We already know the layout of the temple. Sure, there's been some uptick in sentries and patrols, but between Clae's fighters and our riders, we can strike hard and fast and raze it to the ground. Bury Sahak and his schemes, once and for all. What say you . . . cousin?"

It struck Rafi as an earnest question. Unlike the many times he'd witnessed Nef offering a choice with one hand and a threat with the other. But if Rafi had learned one thing, it was to never underestimate Sahak. "Sahak is many things but not a fool. We took him unawares at the temple once. There's no way it will work again."

Nef opened his mouth to object, but Clae clapped his shoulder, cutting him off. "You heard him, Nef. He's made up his mind. Now don't you have somewhere else to be?" His tone was friendly, but his eyes were flat. Nef hesitated only a second before pivoting toward his earthhewn, checking bridle and cinch, then mounting and wheeling around.

Gripping the leads for the other steeds too.

Rafi felt a pang pass through him. "Nef? What—"

"Do yourself a favor, for once, Rafi," he said sharply, "and listen." Then, ducking under a branch, he urged his steed to speed and thundered away, taking Ghost and Aruk's shadower with him.

Rafi rounded on Clae. "Where is he—"

Clae's calloused hand clamped onto the back of his neck. Rafi caught only a glimpse of the fighters hemming Eshur and Aruk in with spears and *chets* before he was steered out from under the banyan tree and shoved back up the path the way they had come.

"So," Rafi gasped out, propelled awkwardly over the uneven surface. "No more friendly chat, huh?"

Clae grunted. "Nef was convinced you could be persuaded to be useful."

Considering what Nef had watched him endure from Sahak only a few months back, that stung. "I'm a gull for saga crisps," he quipped, but that only earned him sore ribs as the Mahque leader slammed him up against a tree. He straightened, winded. "Did Nef also tell you I withstood all Sahak's methods of persuasion? So we can skip past the knives and the tigers, because I'm not going to lead my riders into a trap, and trust me, if you saw Sahak, it's only because he wanted you to."

"Trust you?" Clae shoved in close, and Rafi flinched from the man's rank breath. "Trust you while you tell us to wait? While you throw away chances to strike against our oppressors because they are your own blood? While you curry favor and amass support for your claim to a throne you expect us to believe you don't intend to keep?"

"I don't. I swear it."

"You could swear until your dying breath, Tetrani, and still I wouldn't trust you. I have clawed for every ounce of power I now possess to free my people and exact retribution upon our foes. I will not believe that any man given a crown could simply throw it away." Clae shifted pointedly to look past the tree, and Rafi turned his head to see.

Beyond the looping vines and the dangling tendrils of mollusk moss, a garish red glow painted the town where it squatted on the riverbank. It was the glow of fire, the glare of destruction, and though they were upwind of the smoke, Rafi thought he could hear screams.

"Better to carve out the temptation at its root," Clae growled.

"Ches-Shu," Rafi whispered. "What did you do?"

"One spark, a few bolted doors, and the tavern went up like a torch, taking dozens of Nadaarian officials with it."

Officials. *Imbé.*

Bile burned the back of his throat.

Clae's voice was laced with satisfaction. "I did exactly what we have been aiming for. I struck a blow to destabilize the empire, and it didn't require propping up yet another Tetrani to sit on the—" He broke off, distracted by a muted *thump* that sounded from the direction of the banyan tree.

Muffled shouts rang out after it, and Rafi seized his chance. He'd left his spear beside Ghost, and his belt knife was bundled with his clothes in the taleweaver's pack, which left him no weapon but surprise—and the juggling balls he'd filched from Eshur's coat.

Dropping low, he flung all his weight against Clae, who stumbled back. Rafi bolted through the opening, but Clae latched onto his arm. Reacting on instinct, Rafi pivoted and lashed out repeatedly with his fist. Solid hits that split skin over bone and reverberated up his arm.

Clae shook off the blows, then unleashed a howling strike of his own. Rafi dodged it, and stepped straight into a gut punch that missed his armored belt and snapped against his ribs. Winded, he didn't even see the next hit coming.

It cracked against the side of his jaw.

Rafi's vision spun, and he hit the earth. Spittle turned to mud on his lips. He pushed up onto hands and knees, but Clae kicked out, forcing him back down, *chet* at his throat.

He spat out dirt. "So, what now? You going to kill me?"

"You ever heard of baiting a stone-eye with dead meat? No, Tetrani,

Sahak wants you alive, which means so do I. Just long enough to draw him out, and then—"

A meaty *thwack* drowned out the rest of Clae's speech. He toppled to the side, and Rafi tried to fight off dizziness.

"Rafi, get up!" Aruk. Close beside him, and utterly unseen.

Sturdy hands tugged him to his feet as Clae groaned and struggled to rise. Shoulder under his arm, Aruk hurried Rafi into the bordering jungle, and they took cover in the ferns. Just in time to avoid the cluster of rebels who pounded down the path from the banyan and halted by their leader. Clae's hoarse shouts scattered them into the trees, where the initial crunching of leaves and beating of underbrush rapidly dwindled into a much more unsettling quiet.

Just a rustling here, or a creaking there.

A soft warbling cry off to the left.

No strangers to the jungle were these, but Mahque warriors, attuned to the language of earth, vine, and tree. Rafi hunkered down in the ferns, wanting to wait for them to pass, but Aruk pulled him on, breathing in his ear, "We need to move while there's still a gap."

If there was a gap, Rafi couldn't see it. But then, he wasn't a shadowrider, endowed with night vision and soundless movement—a fact that became doubly apparent as he crept after Aruk. Despite his best efforts, he felt an earthhewn in comparison, as they darted and ducked and finally collapsed behind a vine-heaped fallen neefwa whose roots had pulled free of the sodden riverbank.

Water rippled softly only a few feet away. It called to him, as the jungle did to the Mahque. They could cross it to safety.

Rafi gripped Aruk's arm. "Eshur. Where is he?"

Aruk shook his head helplessly. "He was the distraction. I was the rescue. But then that commotion broke out, and I don't—" Insect noises stopped abruptly nearby, and the metallic *ting* of a spear blade catching on a twig warned Rafi of the pursuit closing in. It was too late now to attempt a crossing, even if he were willing to leave Eshur behind. But he would not be caught and dragged before Sahak again, not while he still had a trick up his sleeve.

Or juggling balls in his pocket.

Clutching the three balls, he drew back his arm and flung them out over the water. They struck with a series of faint splashes, which to Rafi sounded more like fish jumping than two fugitives trying to make an aquatic escape, but scattered footsteps tore off downstream. Chortling cries mimicking bird calls rang out, then all was silent.

Gradually, the insect song sprang up again.

"Come on," Aruk breathed. "It's clear."

They crept cautiously back toward the banyan tree, occasionally calling out for Eshur in hoarse whispers. Rafi had nearly given up hope when he heard a weak "Here."

Sweeping aside a thicket of ferns, Rafi uncovered Eshur lying with his pack upended beside him, trying to staunch the blood flowing from a wound on his thigh. *No.* Rafi knelt and pressed both hands against the already-soaked cloth, while Aruk hastily rifled through the scattered supplies. Rafi heard ripping and bade his old, worn clothes a silent farewell.

He shook his head at the taleweaver. "Thought you said you were usually better at dodging."

Eshur gave a shaky laugh. "*Usually* being the operative word, I'm afraid. I seem to be . . . off my stride . . . lately."

"Got it," Aruk said, and Rafi made space for him to press a fresh wad of cloth over Eshur's wound, then bind the dressing securely in place with Rafi's old belt.

The knife Aruk dropped beside Rafi, still sheathed.

Once Eshur's breathing slowly steadied, Rafi sank back on his heels, muscles weak as the survival rush faded. His fingers were stiff and sticky and trembled slightly as he fastened the knife onto the wide armored belt Imbé had given him.

Before she died—no, was murdered.

He swiped the back of his hand across his mouth. "Ches-Shu, aren't we all on the same side? What's it all for if it comes to this?"

Plans ruined. Steeds stolen. Ghost gone.

Now they were stranded afoot far from the gorge, while Clae's forces careened toward a massacre. And maybe not just Clae's forces. As if spun ashore by the shifting tide, understanding lodged in Rafi's mind.

He pushed to his feet. "Our steeds. Nef took them. Why?"

"To make it harder for us to escape," Aruk said.

"No," Eshur interjected, voice weak. "Nef went for the steeds at the start. It was a part of the plan, perhaps as proof for Sahak?"

"Not Sahak. Jasri." Too restless to stand still, Rafi paced as he continued. "You heard Nef. He didn't just want me as bait for Sahak, he wanted to use the steeds to destroy the temple. If he shows up back at our camp with our steeds and *without* us, he might just be able to wrest control of the riders from Jasri, and then it won't just be Clae and his rebels who run headlong into Sahak's trap . . ."

It would be all his riders and all their steeds.

"Aodh have mercy," Eshur breathed, and Rafi echoed it silently.

He turned and found them both looking to him expectantly. The same way he had once looked to Delmar.

Ches-Shu, had his brother ever felt this lost?

"I can't let him get away with it," he said, and his resolve solidified as he spoke. "I won't let him get them all killed." Him. Not Clae. But Nef. Nef who had betrayed and then saved him. Nef whom he had unbelievably come to think of as a friend. Nef who was even now readying to lead his riders to their death. "Aruk," he began, but the Alonque was already nodding.

"I'll look after Eshur. Go, Rafi. Run."

And with those words echoing with the cry of his brother so many years before, Rafi ran.

FIFTY-NINE: RAFI & CERIDWEN

Run, Rafi.

Rafi flung himself into the night. Strides sure and quick, he ran, and once the first thousand footfalls were behind him, he sensed the aches from the fight fading and the fog of weariness dissipating before the clarity which propelled him forward. Over log and under bough, across gullies and alongside sluggish streams teeming with angling vines. He could not hope to beat Nef's head start. Across broken ground and thick underbrush, one man alone might outstrip most demon-steeds, but earthhewn could trample their own path through the densest thicket, if their riders disregarded stealth, and subtlety was not in Nef's nature.

No, Rafi wouldn't arrive first, but he'd settle for arriving before they all left.

So he ran on, and he found that his limbs remained strong, until the sky gleamed a sickly gray above him, and he finally burst out of the brush and came to a breathless halt over the scattered ashes of the campfire. The same campfire where he had laughed and traded jokes with Moc and Flick, where Ceridwen had uncovered the truth, and where Jasri and the other riders should have been waiting for him.

It was deserted.

Nef had already gotten to them.

"No." Rafi folded over his knees, over legs limp as riverweed, as the fatigue he'd been resisting crashed into him. His eyes prickled, and frustration boiled in his throat. He dug his fingers into the dirt, clenching it in his fist.

Deep hoofmarks discolored the soil before him.

Nef may have ridden in with only three steeds, but he had clearly left with many more. The trail carved off through the trees, secrecy abandoned for reckless speed. Nef rode as if to escape the ending of the world. Or maybe, to unleash it.

Don't stop, Rafi. Run.

Before his mind's eye, Delmar slumped, bowed by the certainty of defeat, and then, unbelievably, he straightened. Stood up tall. Set his jaw and stared down the miles ahead. And without even thinking about it, Rafi felt himself do the same. His legs shook, and he groaned, but he broke into a jog. Dug deep. Pressed into a run. Maybe continuing the chase didn't make sense anymore, but the voice that whispered inside him—a voice that might have been his own and might have been the ghost's—would not let him give up.

He was weary, yes, but he had run weary before. Not only as a fugitive, but many a haunted, sleepless night on the Alon shore. And his feet might be aching now, but they weren't weeping blood or oozing pus from infected cuts. And when the rumble of thunder swelled to a roar that released a downpour, it was cold and wet, but he had been colder and wetter every time he dove into the sea.

Raising one arm to deflect the sheeting rain, feet slipping over the hoof-pocked and water-slicked ground, Rafi ran on. The trail before his feet was clear, and it led to Dagmur.

Ceridwen blew into the gorge on the winds of a storm, and for once, she did not resent the rain or its effects on her steed. Though his ears were pinned back atop his head and his mane fell in sodden strands, there was no hint of spark or ember about him, save for the occasional irritated tossing of his head or swish of his tail. Which was a wonder, for her own temper raged on unabated. Even after two full days on the move, sometimes loping, sometimes walking, occasionally laying false trails and looping back—the meandering route the riders always took to protect the gorge—her anger had not cooled.

Rafi Tetrani had lied to her, like her father, and had made a traitor of her. Like her father. What had she been thinking in agreeing to train riders and steeds for the rebellion? To tear down the empire from within? She should have fought hoof and blade for the chance to sail home at the first sign that Liam was recovering, and now, flames take her, she would.

Soaked hood to boot, she dropped from the saddle into squelching mud. She did not untack. She did not plan to be here long. But she did lead Mindar past the empty solborn enclosure and hitched him beneath a sprawling banyan close to the cavern mouth. She ran up the shuddering slat-and-wood stairs and across the bridge, the ring of her boots and spurs drawing startled glances. Then she burst into Umut's hut, fierce and streaming water on the threshold.

Umut broke off speaking but continued stirring the pot that simmered atop his stone oven. Sleeves rolled up past his elbows, gray hair loose and wet across his shoulders, he looked even more disheveled than usual. "You made quick time," he said by way of greeting, nodding curtly toward the sickrooms, as if that was where he expected her to go. He turned back to the two scouts who stood by the stove—both as soaked as she was and neither familiar to her—and the knot of concern on his brow as they resumed speaking tempered her fury.

Something was amiss.

Entering more slowly, she found the air thick with the reek of illness. She passed a low table cluttered with healing supplies—uncovered pots of tinctures, piles of crushed leaves, and what appeared to be a bowl of fermenting slugs.

Umut shuffled back a step, making space for her to join him. It took her a moment to untangle the thread of the scouts' report—or rather, their lack of one. They had been stationed as part of a relay tracking the movements of the Nadaari, and the reports from the scouts downstream, closest to the enemy, were now days overdue.

On top of that, Clae's forces, which had been positioned as the first line of defense, had gone to ground, and none knew where to roust them.

"And the Nadaari?" Ceridwen asked, feeling chilled.

"Moved on, with nary a sign left in earth, leaf, or twig." Umut nodded at the scouts. "Go. Double the runners. We need to find them. Cael knows, when there's a tiger on the prowl, you want to know where it is."

The scouts dashed off before Ceridwen could offer to dispatch stormriders to try to pick up the trail from above. Though if the jungle was thick, runners would be more effective. And in any case, she had no stormriders to send. Not since Mindar spat flames at Rafi's feet, and she rode away into the night, away from him and his falsehoods. This news didn't change anything. She was here to demand that Umut honor his oath to send her home, where she might breathe a spark back into the ashes of her reign. And if he would not, she knew the countryside well enough now that she would take Liam to the coast and steal a ship on her own and attempt the crossing herself.

"Come on then," Umut said, banging the spoon against the pot before shifting the concoction from the heat, then shuffling off toward the inner rooms. "He's right through here."

"He?" Ceridwen hesitated. "Who?"

"You didn't get my message? That's not why you're here?"

War horns sounded the alarm in her head. "What message?" She started to press forward, but Umut forestalled her, using his crutch to push the curtain back from the doorway of the closest sickroom.

On the cot inside was Liam.

She shoved to his side, shucking off her waterlogged gloves to lay a hand on his arm. Her fingers were wrinkled from long exposure to the rain, and still, his skin felt strangely clammy and cold to her touch. Her quick scan revealed no obvious injury, but wide strips of cloth bound him to the cot.

She rounded on Umut. "Why is he restrained?"

"Because he's delirious and keeps trying to walk off, despite swallowing enough sibesium to sedate a stone-eye, and he's in no shape to repeat your waterfall stunt."

"Sedated?" She glanced back at Liam, whose eyes were tightly shut yet moving beneath the lids as his head twitched. "So, he's sleeping now?"

"More or less."

"What does that mean? Do you know what's wrong with him?"

The harsh lines around Umut's eyes softened. "If it's a fever, it's like none I've seen before. Seems he was up atop the waterfall with Iakki when the fit struck him. Iakki came running, yelling for me, but when we got back, your friend was gone. Took half a day before scouts happened across him in the jungle, just wandering and muttering to himself with that glassy look of fever in his eyes. Only the odd thing is, his skin is—"

"Cold," Ceridwen supplied, feeling a shiver whisk across her own skin.

Umut pressed her shoulder reassuringly. Unlike Markham's firm shoulder clasps that somehow demanded one stand up straighter, whether one willed to or not, Umut's was a gentle grip that conveyed only warmth and compassion, and she sensed her defenses failing before it. Could simple kindness undo her, when all the forces of war and destruction could not?

She did not flinch from heat or from battle, but she drew back from the comfort Umut offered and clenched the hilt of her *chet* instead. "What can I do?"

"You can wait and watch . . . and hope."

"Hope," she repeated flatly.

"Yes, hope." His voice took on a tinge of the sternness she was so accustomed to. "It is not a thing to be disdained. Hope is the power that reshapes worlds. It is what has allowed the revolution to defy all odds and remain standing, and it is what gives your friend the strength that will carry him through this."

But hope had betrayed her when her brother died, when Iona fell from the sky, when the ship bore her away from Soldonia, and when she discovered that she had betrayed her people's secrets to the blood of their greatest foe, earning at last the brand forced upon her so long ago.

Umut shuffled to the doorway, then turned. "If it wasn't my message that brought you, then why did you come? Is all well with Rafi and your team?"

Here was her opening. The words lay like unlit coals upon her tongue. But the anger she had relied upon to ignite them had burned out and shriveled up. Without it to fuel her, she had not the energy to confront Umut tonight.

"I came for Liam," she said simply, and he did not press her for more.

Clae's eyes stared sightlessly at the sky, rain striking his waxen face. His wounds were numerous and deep and no longer bled, and still Rafi crouched beside him to feel for a pulse. Nothing. He bent his head, then drew Clae's eyes closed. Only yesterday, this man had beaten him flat on the jungle floor, and now, he was dead, and countless others with him.

Shaking with exhaustion, Rafi sank back on his heels, ignoring the floodwaters lapping around his knees. The last few hours of the run had been the worst as his last embers of energy faded, until there was nothing to carry him on but endurance, and that relentless whisper inside him, constantly demanding more, more, more. Stumbling, falling, staggering doggedly onward—

Only to find Dagmur in ruins.

One half of the temple was gone, caved in. Chunks of rubble choked the stream, causing it to overflow its banks, welling up around the ornate stone structure, which looked like it had been crushed, as if by some mighty fist.

Given enough steeds and riders reckless enough to attempt it, Ceridwen had hinted that earthhewn were capable of causing the earth to shudder and break. Nef was certainly reckless, but there were only eight earthriders in the whole unit.

Could so few unleash such destruction?

Rafi sidestepped a fallen soldier and slogged across the stream. Seeing the destruction from a distance, he had scanned first for the victors, whether rebel or Nadaari. Seeing none, he looked now for survivors, while the rain continued to fall, pinging off the gilded armor of scattered Nadaari, thudding off the boiled leathers of slain Mahque warriors, and drumming against the swollen flanks of lifeless solborn steeds and their riders.

Here, a shadower pierced through with spears, fallen atop its rider. There, a stormer shot from the sky and draped across the thorny crown of a saga tree, its rider sprawled broken at the base. Here, a face he knew well. There, a friend. He waded on, abandoned by hope, surrounded by death, until he reached the epicenter of the ruin at the temple's mouth. And there he found Nef.

Crushed under a mound of collapsed stone, only Nef's head and chest were visible. His skin was ashen, and rock shards dusted his hair, but as Rafi veered around a hoof so massive it could only belong to a buried earthhewn, he saw a flicker of movement. Nef was still breathing.

"Nef? Can you hear me?"

No response.

"Hold on, Nef. I'm going to get you out." He attacked the rubble, clawing at the earth with his bare hands, until he uncovered the massive slab pinning Nef from the waist down. He tried to move it, to no avail. Hunted out a spear and positioned a rock to create a fulcrum and lever, then seized the *chet* he found by Nef and tried to first carve out the rubble from beneath him. But the blade struck a buried rock and snapped.

Rafi flung down the broken pieces and twisted away, wrapping his hands behind his neck as if that might tamp down the sickening fury that seethed beneath his skin.

It wasn't supposed to end this way.

"Looks like . . . you owe me another *chet* . . . cousin."

"Nef!" Rafi spun back to the Mahque rebel, whose eye was fluttering open. "Never thought I'd say this, but it is good to see your scowling face."

Nef took a shuddering breath. "You were right." He coughed weakly.

Blood came to his lips. Rafi planted one hand to steady himself. His fingers sank into the soil he had dug out from beneath Nef. It was sodden and warm, but not with rain, with blood. The sol-breath was supposed to strengthen the bones of earthriders, endow them with an inhuman resilience, but could anyone survive this?

He offered Nef a smile. "Never thought *you'd* say that, cousin."

"It was a trap, just like you said." Nef spoke unevenly, gasping. "They were waiting for us to begin our assault . . . and then the earth upended." A trickle of blood touched his chin. His teeth were chattering now, and there was a tinge of panic in his eye. "I'm sorry . . . about before. I hoped . . . hoped you would agree . . . and then Clae . . ."

Rafi laid a hand on Nef's arm. "Never mind that. Did anyone get out? Anyone at all?"

"Sahak. You . . . you need to go . . . now."

"Why? What about Sahak? Is he still here?"

"Not here. Rafi . . . he's at the gorge."

Saltwater sluiced through Rafi's veins. "He knows about the gorge?" Nef's eyelid fluttered and his head began to sag, but Rafi gripped his arm tighter. "Nef! You have to tell me! When did he leave? How long has he been gone?"

"Didn't leave. He was . . . already gone." Nef's voice trailed so faint that Rafi had to strain to hear. "You understand . . . cousin? He already . . . knew."

SIXTY: CERIDWEN & RAFI

To avoid breaking the silence of their ghosted steeds, shadowriders
rely upon cloaks patterned in varying muted hues.
They wear soft-soled boots, tie straps rather than buckle,
and keep their tack oiled soft and supple to forestall creaking.
- Wisdom of the Horsemasters

Ceridwen was not made for the agony of waiting. Were it Finnian in her place, she knew he would sit and watch sleepless by Liam's cot all the hours of the night. But she must be moving. Onward, ever onward. She returned below to untack Mindar and scraped the damp from his coat with the flat of her *chet* while he ate. Shedding her sodden leathers, she bundled them and her saddle off to Umut's craftsmen for repair. They were singed and frail, splintered with cracks like the ones inside her. And like her, in danger of coming wholly undone.

Her feet carried her to the kitchen alcove next, though she was not hungry. Saffa took one look at her, then pressed a cup of tangy seaweed tea into her hands and pointed her to a knife and a mound of vegetables. One whiff of the tea made her think of Rafi. She set the cup down as if it had scalded her and took up the knife instead. Each clunk of the blade on the board formed a rhythm for her thoughts as she quartered and diced and dissected her anger.

At Rafi. At Umut.

But at herself most of all for failing to see the truth of Rafi beyond his smokescreen of likeability and self-deprecating humor. Something nudged her ankle. Then again, harder. She peered under the table and found Iakki scowling up at her beneath dark eyebrows.

"Shh." He motioned. "I'm hiding."

"Hiding? From who?"

"Who do you think? Sev."

Sev was, of course, nowhere to be seen.

Ceridwen resumed chopping, ignoring when Iakki tapped her ankle, prodded her foot, then brought his fist down with a thump on the toe of her boot. That did it. She lowered her head, face inches from his. "What?"

"Nahiki come back with you?"

Nahiki. *Rafi.* "No. He didn't."

"Oh." He looked completely crestfallen.

"Why do you call him that? Nahiki?"

"Because he was Nahiki for a long time. Before I knew he was Rafi." She couldn't help herself. "So, he lied to you, too, about who he was."

Iakki wriggled until he could hug one knee to his chest. "I guess. I mean, sure, maybe he lied about his name, but that's different than lying about who you are underneath. He's not just his name, is he? Nahiki. Rafi. He's still him. Not like Sev." He frowned, then his eyes took on a mischievous gleam. "You gonna drink that seaweed tea? Or you gonna let me have it?"

He's not just his name, is he? He's still him.

Those words seeped through the cracks inside her, and hours later, sprawled on a bedroll beside Liam's cot, she considered them. Having borne the shame of her branding as a traitor and kinslayer, she could understand better than most the gulf that could exist between who you were declared to be and who you truly were.

But then who was Rafi really?

If it were his actions that should exonerate or condemn him, then how could she, who had received atonement upon the sacrifices of her friends, weigh one deed against another?

Eventually, she found herself clawing free from the grasp of a suffocating slumber with the mumbling that had saturated her dreams still echoing in her ears.

It was Liam she heard, twitching in fevered sleep. He muttered words she couldn't comprehend, and then, suddenly, one she did. Rafi.

That one proved the key to the rest, and the words seemed to unravel in her head, drawing her up to Liam's cot.

It was not Soldonian he spoke, but Nadaarian.

"Run, Rafi, run. He's coming. Run. *Run.*"

When last she rode out from the gorge, Liam's Nadaarian had still been limited to a few poorly pronounced words, forcing him to use signs and pantomime to make himself understood. She heard no such struggle in his speech now.

"He's coming, Rafi. Run."

"It's me, Liam," she whispered in their own tongue, to no effect. She gently shook his shoulder. "Can you hear me? It's me. Ceridwen."

He did not stir, but his murmuring continued.

She rose slowly, suddenly aware of the cold prickle of sweat upon her forehead, and reached for the *chet* at her waist. She switched to Nadaarian instead. "Who, Liam? Who's coming?"

"Not coming." His eyes shot open, staring unseeing at the mossy ceiling. "*Here.*"

Ceridwen was a creature of instinct and impulse. It was the dual edge that had kept her alive through many a peril. She could not say which guided her now, but she did not question it. She acted. Whipping out the *chet*, she sliced the cloth strips that bound Liam to the cot, and dragged him up, arm slung over her shoulder.

They made it to the door as the first screams sounded in the cavern above.

Rafi knelt in the rain amidst the ruin of the temple and sang the sorrowing song of the sea over the corpse of his friend. He sang the melancholy lullaby his mother had sung to him, until his voice went hoarse from exhaustion. And from despair. He had run on as hard and as fast as he could—as he wished he had years ago, when a fugitive with Delmar—and it still hadn't mattered. He had still been too slow to make a difference.

You understand, cousin? He already knew.

Sahak. But of course Sahak knew. He was not the emperor's infamous assassin for nothing. He was always at least ten steps ahead. Rafi wouldn't have been shocked to learn that Sahak had been lurking in the shadows all along, allowing them to do the work of training the demon-steeds, biding his time, until he was ready to pounce and cage the rebels, the cousin he had betrayed, and Soldonia's queen. And not only them, but every tribesman and woman who had carved out a new life in the gorge: Saffa and Sev, Kaya and Iakki, and all the villagers of Zorrad.

Sahak would kill them all, and he was helpless to save them.

Rafi ground his fists into the blood-soaked mud and let his head tilt back toward the weeping sky. It was not to Ches-Shu that he cried or to Cael or Cihana that he poured out the unspeakable ache of his heart, but to the unknown, and yet still he hoped knowable, Bearer of the Eternal Scars, Aodh.

He cried out and waited, as he had waited so often lately for his brother's voice, but all that broke the agonizing quiet was a familiar, damp snort.

"Ghost?" Rafi twisted to see the colt slogging toward him, trailing a broken branch from his reins. It snarled and snagged on the fragmented ground, tugging his head sideways. Rafi scrambled over and caught up the reins to ease the strain, then flung his arms around the colt's neck.

He'd thought Ghost lost for good. Claimed by Sahak, along with everyone else.

Yet by some unearthly shift in tide or fortune, the colt was here, free. Shaking his head, Rafi allowed Ghost to nuzzle at his hands while he reeled in the branch. He felt at the sticky tear where it had been ripped from a tree and tried to envision Sahak trusting such an anchor. Odds were Nef was the one he had to thank for that. Or, possibly, Aodh.

With that thought came a thrill of awe and a crisp breath of hope. Every fiber of his being wanted to collapse onto the rain-soaked ground and into sleep. He had failed every race he had attempted so far. He would likely fail again. But he was not alone or unhorsed or helpless anymore, and if there was even a chance that he could change the tides and warn the rebel camp in time to save them from Sahak, he would try.

He would rise, as Ceridwen put it, and ride again.

He unknotted the reins from the branch, then slung himself onto Ghost's back. Ghost tossed his head, mane flying like the spray upon a cresting wave, and his muscles tensed, readying to spring. The colt still had some run left in him, and so, Rafi found, did he.

"Run, Ghost," Rafi breathed, and Ghost ran.

SIXTY-ONE: JAKIM

Aodh's hand mends all things.
- The truths of Aodh

Both priest and tiger crashed to the ground. Jakim staggered back, gasping from the chokehold. He didn't know where Koata had come from, but she crouched over the priest with a snarl. Nahrog lay completely still. Unnaturally so. Trapped by her stone eyes.

Somehow, Koata had clawed off her blindfold.

Teeth flashing, she lunged for the priest's throat, but a series of sickening thumps shook her. Arrows sprouted from her neck and chest. She snarled and shook her head, snapping the spell, then collapsed on top of the priest.

"Oh, friend," Jakim whispered. "I am sorry."

The priest groaned beneath the tiger's fallen bulk. But no one moved to help him. Order seemed to have completely disintegrated in the wake of the pulsing light and the unexpected tiger assault, and Rhodri made no move to restore it. Voices shouted, steeds scattered, and stalking through the chaos like predators themselves, Jakim saw Cormag and Moray riding toward him, bows raised.

No, not toward him. Toward Finnian.

The shadowrider still lay sprawled where Jakim had dropped him, unconscious. In the confusion, the sons of Ondri were going to seize their chance to strike.

Jakim rushed over to Finnian and, grabbing him under the arms, dragged him backward as fast as he could. Cormag and Moray kicked into a lope, closing in, but they did not fire. Maybe because they knew there was nowhere for him to go. The ground suddenly dropped under his heels, and he and Finnian slid down into the stream, an arrow thrumming past his head.

He splashed across and lost one of Finnian's boots when the heel snagged on a root as he dragged him up the opposite bank alongside the fallen dawnling. He had some vague idea of taking shelter behind the creature's bulk.

With a yell, Moray launched his shadower over the stream, bowstring drawn back and ready to fire. But he jolted as a pair of arrows pierced his chest and toppled from the saddle a split second before the deep notes of a dozen war horns flooded the valley. Cormag skidded to a halt and whirled his steed around as a host of strange warriors flying banners the hue of red earth poured from the cleft.

Jakim did not recognize the banner, but Rhodri's forces rapidly regrouped and clashed with the newcomers in a tempest of darting steeds and flashing blades. Cormag tore off to join them.

"So, Craddock has come," remarked a familiar voice.

Jakim eased Finnian to the ground, the shadowrider's eyelids flickering as he did so, then turned. Khilamook stood over the prone dawnling, one foot braced on its neck, sawing at a chunk of pale gold mane with a knife. It came loose in his grip and the strands draped long from his hand. He nodded in satisfaction and tied the shorn strands into a knot, then slid it into his pocket.

"What are you doing?"

"What does it look like?" Khilamook attacked another clump of mane.

The rest of the dawnling's coat no longer gleamed with that dazzling metallic sheen. It had turned an odd dingy gray speckled over a rosy pink, as if it had been singed somehow by the release of the energy burst. Jakim could see all its ribs, jutting beneath its skin.

"Those fools can fight it out if they want," Khilamook continued, "but the prize is here, ripe for the taking, and I don't mean to go empty-handed. If I can't give the emperor a live dawnling, then I shall bring him its heart. Or whatever I can get." Pocketing a second knot of mane, he eyed the dark stone honeycombed with gold growing from the dawnling's forehead. "That should do nicely." He raised the knife.

Jakim felt sick. Then he realized the dawnling's ribcage was moving. "It's not dead."

"No, oddly enough, it doesn't appear to be. Not yet." Khilamook set the blade against the ridge of stone.

Jakim had no weapon, nor skills for a fight, but he lashed out with a kick, striking the engineer's wrist, sending the knife flying.

Khilamook shot him a withering look. "I'm beginning to think I've let you live long enough." He sprang, snatched up the knife, and lunged for Jakim before he could react.

The blade stopped inches away.

Khilamook gasped raggedly and looked down at his chest, as if expecting to see something there, then pitched forward, revealing the arrow stabbed in his back. Finnian stood behind him, hand still raised from the blow.

Jakim gaped at him, then Finnian swayed, and instinct drove him to help. Instead, the shadowrider yanked him abruptly to the ground.

An arrow whisked past, exactly where he'd been standing.

"Te Donal!" roared Brawly, across the stream. He tossed down his bow and drew a sword, then urged his steed to cross. "Te Donal, I'm coming for you!"

Coughing out a groan, Finnian rolled onto his side. "Come on." He crawled to Moray's corpse, which had fallen on their side of the stream, and, taking hold of the man's fallen bow, used it to lever himself to his feet. Several arrows had spilled from Moray's quiver, but Finnian ignored them. "He wants me. Stay back. Once the fight starts, you might be able to get clear."

Jakim hesitated. "Shouldn't you grab some arrows?"

"Don't need them. Can't shoot."

Brawly charged up out of the stream and rushed straight at them. Finnian held the bow low in his left hand and waited until the shadower was only two strides away. Brawly reared his arm back to strike, and Finnian spun to the side, lashing out with the bow as if it were a staff. It slammed up into the elbow of Brawly's descending sword arm, causing his arm to fall limp at his side as his steed charged past.

He did not drop his sword. Wheeling around, he advanced again, more slowly. That allowed him to match Finnian's attempt to dodge him, then slash down at his neck. Finnian raised the bow in both hands, blocking the strike.

It cleaved through the bow, and narrowly missed cleaving through Finnian too. He staggered back, clutching one half in each hand, and Jakim steadied him once more.

"You were supposed to run, Scroll," Finnian grated out.

Too late for that. Brawly swung again, sword flashing for their heads. But a bristling gray blur shot up and caught his wrist in its jaws, wrenching his stroke off target. A thrown spear took him in the side, and he toppled from his steed, dragged by the snarling wolfhound.

The shadowrider who loped across the stream then was unfamiliar to Jakim. Grizzled hair stuck out around his head, and he had only one arm and one eye. His reins hung loose upon his steed's neck, until he took them up at the last second and drew to a ragged, skittering stop before them.

Finnian sank to his knees, and tipping his head back, he laughed. "Oh, Markham, you old wolf. You have no idea how glad I am to see you."

"Not half so glad as I am, considering you left me with only Fool Beast and Cù for company." Words notwithstanding, the grizzled warrior slapped his shadower's neck before dismounting, then swaggered forward and seized Finnian in a hug.

Finnian let out a groan, and Markham released him.

"You hurt? You look half dead."

"Only half. What are you doing here?"

Markham snorted. "Not looking to find you. I came north to convince Craddock to stop sitting on the fence and commit to defending the kingdom. Was in the middle of my finely pointed argument, when we received word of a stone-eye tiger in the area and came to investigate. Thought we'd stumble across a Nadaarian incursion. Not Rhodri-flaming-te-Oengus himself. Speaking of which, I could ask you the same question. But I imagine that's an explanation best received over a pipe and a flask."

"Aye, best." Finnian quirked a smile. "What of Rhodri?"

"Routed. Fled. We'll get him another—" Markham broke off as his shadower snuffled at his neck, whiskers scraping over his skin. "Steady there, Fool Beast. What are you on about . . . oh." His gaze latched onto something beyond Jakim.

Jakim turned and came face-to-face with the dawnling. Coat still a dingy gray, it extended its nose curiously toward him, puffing out soft, warm breaths that bore the faint aroma of dewed grasses basking in a summer sunrise. Its eyes were a deep liquid amber. Slowly, gingerly, he reached out and let the dawnling breathe on his palm, then lifted his fingertips to the dark stone on its forehead. A jolt of energy shot through him, and the familiar stir of warmth in his chest could only be one thing. Aodh's hand, guiding him still.

He looked back to find Finnian grinning.

"So much for not being a rider. Looks like you're stuck now."

Khilamook shuddered where he lay in a tangle of limbs. He was not where Jakim had expected to find him. He must have picked himself up after Finnian stabbed him and staggered out across the battlefield, only to be trampled in the melee. Jakim doubted even the most skilled Canthorian surgeon could save him now. Certainly not a battlefield healer out in the wilds of Soldonia. Stooping, Jakim lowered a waterskin to the engineer's bloodstained lips.

Khilamook blinked then focused on him, and a thin, disdainful smile stretched across his face. "It seems I won't be getting revenge on my brothers after all." His words came faint and slurred. "Still, it may be years before tidings reach them, and the thought that they will continue to rest uneasy is some comfort, I suppose, here at the end." He swallowed thickly. "What of you, Scroll? You never did tell me what you wanted from your brothers, if not revenge."

Jakim met his eyes. "To tell them I forgive them, as Aodh forgives."

Khilamook tried to lift a hand. "And have you forgiven them? Could you forgive me? Would you use the power of that steed to heal me?" His gaze flicked to the dawnling, which had drifted over and was nuzzling gently at Jakim's ear.

It looked a ragged, half-starved creature. Nothing like the iridescent beauty he had seen on their arrival in the valley. If it still had any power, Jakim didn't know how to access it.

"I don't know how to heal you," he said honestly, "but if I could, I would." And it was surprising to realize he meant it. The other questions he found harder to answer. He forced down the lump in his throat. "And Aodh help me, I will forgive you."

"Then . . . you are as great a fool as ever, Jakim Ha'Nor."

The engineer's eyes closed, and a tear slipped down his cheek. Then, because Jakim was a great fool, or perhaps only a great dreamer, he held the engineer's hand and whispered the truths of Aodh over him as he died.

SIXTY-TWO: RAFI

He who plants a saga cannot expect a neefwa to grow.
- Mahque saying

"Whoa, Ghost," Rafi whispered, and Ghost came to a shambling halt, sides heaving. Only twice on their trek had he stopped to let Ghost rest and graze, while he flung himself wearily on the sodden ground. He hadn't dared close his eyes, though, for fear he would oversleep, and now his lids seemed lined with sand.

The second time, Ghost had just stood there as he did now, head drooping, lower lip dangling, not even bothering to shake off the flies that swarmed the scrapes on his legs. Over the intervening hours, his gait had grown shorter and his pace uneven, his spurts of speed petering out until Rafi stirred from his own weary haze to urge him on again.

Now, with dawn breaking and the gorge just ahead, they found the jungle entrance blocked by a force of Nadaarian soldiers.

Despite Ghost's desperate efforts, Sahak had arrived before them.

Splashes of orange and scarlet and gilded steel pierced the dense foliage as the soldiers fell into ranks but did not advance down the gorge. Perhaps they were only the reserve, for the wind was already laden with the clangor of distant battle. The rebels would not fall quietly, but Ches-Shu, without help, they would fall.

Rafi braced one hand against Ghost's hot dry neck. Something about those sensations nagged at him, but he couldn't tear his mind away from the refugee-packed caverns at the end of the gorge and the slaughter Sahak was already unleashing among them.

Ghost stirred and nickered weakly toward the thicket on their left.

A dappled gray stormer stood motionless in its shadow, dark wings flared, and on its back—

"Jasri?" Rafi croaked, disbelieving. "How—?"

"I could ask the same of you." She cued her steed to relax its wings, exposing her ready bow and nocked arrow, though it wasn't pointing at him. "Nef told us you were dead."

Rafi slid down Ghost's side and was immediately seized and pounded in a massive hug that could only come from one person. "Moc?" he gasped. "You didn't go with Nef?"

"Convinced the rest of us not to go either," Jasri said. "He wouldn't believe you were dead, even after Nef showed up with Ghost."

Moc released him with another stout thump to the shoulder. "Who could believe you dead, cousin, without seeing a body? Even then, I would think you were faking it." Which made sense, since he had seen Rafi fake his death once before, when Nef had tried to murder him. Moc had lifted his voice then but not a finger to help him. There had always been something unnamed that bound him to Nef, some debt owed.

For Moc to have refused him now . . .

"I've known Nef long enough to know when he is lying," Moc said. "But you have Ghost, so you must have seen him. Tell me: did his plan succeed?"

Tavern burning. Eshur wounded. The temple in ruins.

Dead eyes staring up at a gray sky.

Sahak here.

Rafi shook his head. "I'm sorry, Moc." He would say more later, but he had not raced all this way to be distracted now. Two demon-riders and a single rebel might not be enough to turn the tides against the host besetting the gorge, but together, they must try. He turned to Jasri. "You said 'the rest of us'? How many?"

He trailed off as another arm slung over his shoulder, and bristly black curls brushed the side of his face. Lowen. Rustling boughs and the muted stamp of hooves sounded out as riders and steeds closed in on all sides. So many more than he would have dared hope. There was Yath on his riveren, Flick on his earthhewn, and nearly all the aquatic riders he had trained. Most of the shadowriders, too, and six of Jasri's stormriders. He noted several missing faces as well—mostly those who had been the most vocal about their hatred of the empire and their desire to see it burn.

"All but nine," Jasri said, confirming his count. "With both you and Ceridwen gone, we came back for orders, only to find the caverns under attack."

Not through the gorge, as Rafi had expected, where the rebels might barricade themselves within the caverns and hold them off, but from above. Sahak's soldiers had come over the mountains and were now fighting their way down through the stacked caverns. Suddenly, Rafi understood the purpose of this force at the end of the gorge. It was stationed here to close the net, so none could escape the slaughter.

But Sahak wouldn't be content with that.

"You send any scouts aloft?" he asked.

Jasri rubbed her thumb along the fletching of her arrow. "I went myself. It was still dark, but I could see them—archers all along the rim. No one can get out. And we can't get in."

Never one to miss a cruel trick, Sahak.

But Rafi wasn't about to accept defeat. Iakki was in those caverns. Sev and Kaya, too, even Gordu, and they were there because of him. "No. Only we can get in. Think about it. What does Sahak want more than the rebels?"

"You?" Jasri arced a brow.

"A knock on the head?" Moc grunted.

"The demon-steeds," Flick said quietly, meeting his gaze.

"Yes. He wants the demon-steeds. Alive. To use to his own ends. Which means his archers can't simply mow us down, making us the only ones who *can* enter that gorge."

Most of the riders didn't appear convinced. Yath looked pale. Jasri dropped her gaze to the ground, and Taka shuffled uncomfortably, his outline fuzzing in and out of shadow.

Moc voiced their concern, his gaze fixed on Lowen. "But what if you are wrong, cousin? What if Sahak wants you dead more than he wants the steeds? One volley from above could kill us all."

"Even supposing we do break through, what then?" Yath spoke up.

"We ride in there, we'll be trapped like all the rest. Those archers won't simply let us ride out again."

Murmurs of agreement met his words.

And Rafi couldn't deny it. Wouldn't lie about the risk.

Then Moc shifted uneasily and folded his arms across his chest. "Maybe . . . they won't have a choice. There is more than one way out of those caverns, a secret exit of sorts." His eyes darted to Rafi, and for the first time in days, Rafi felt a touch of hope. Of course. He had used it himself. More than once. It was accessible down the tunnel that carried the drainage stream away from the waterfall and out, down a steep plunge, through a hole into a cave that let out toward the sea.

Moc went on. "I don't know if the steeds could navigate it—"

"Not on the way in," Rafi said, thinking of the flimsy rope ladder that hung beside the cascading stream. "But Ghost and I got out." The drop might prove a challenge for those without waterborn steeds, but they could deal with that when the time came. "It might be the way in for your team, though, Moc. We'd just leave you behind in a charge up the gorge, but you could go the long way around, secure the tunnel from the far end, then meet us on the inside."

"Then why not leave the steeds, cousin, and all go together?"

"Because it'll take more than three dozen spears to help our friends inside, but with the steeds, we can give them a chance."

Ghost's breathing seemed suddenly painfully loud. Or maybe the atmosphere was just painfully silent as the riders considered his words. Rafi turned to the colt and, scratching at the scales that speckled his throat, found his own throat unexpectedly tight.

"Why do you fight for the revolution?" he asked quietly, without turning from Ghost. "Do you know? Ceridwen asked me that recently, and I said something about making my brother proud of me. Maybe that was true once, but it's about so much more than that now. I fight because this place, this sanctuary for the Que, where Iakki can chase goats and Saffa can cook, where the hunted of all the tribes can live free, it's a beautiful thing. I fight because the empire has stolen my family and my home from me, and every time I've dared to think I could build a family or a home somewhere else, they've come to claim that too.

"I fight because when the world you love is in danger of drowning, you don't stand by to watch. You dive in to save it. I know I'm asking a lot of you—Ches-Shu, I know it." He turned and faced them. "But I am asking. Will you ride in, my friends, and change the tides with me?"

It was not the speech Delmar would have given. But they were the truest words Rafi had ever spoken, and as he gazed at each of the riders in turn, he saw his determination reflected in their eyes. Murmurs rustled through them, like leaves in the wind, but no one left.

No one left.

Rafi felt the thrill of that knowledge as he mounted once more, and it resonated on in his chest as the riders he had trained and the steeds he had tamed fell in around him. To death or captivity, perhaps, they would ride, and they would not flee.

They would run to face it together.

He raised his borrowed spear. "Change the tides," he cried, and with every rider echoing the shout, they broke from the thicket and crashed hoof-first into Sahak's soldiers.

SIXTY-THREE: CERIDWEN

Catch the shadower upon a sunlit plain on a cloudless day.
Without shadows or cover, the shadower will be unveiled
and unable to ghost from sight.
- Wisdom of the Horsemasters

Ceridwen flicked her head, dashing blood from the cut on her cheek, torn by a spear thrust over the rebels' shield wall. She flung her weight behind her retaliatory strike, catching the screaming soldier beneath the chin and throwing him back into the onslaught of Nadaari. The move nearly wrenched the spear from her exhausted grip, and she stumbled against the line of rebels who crouched, bracing the overlapping shields. Muscles taut, mouths opened in a wordless roar, the shield bearers defied the flood of soldiers ramming against them, trying to claim the narrow bridge and the central cavern with it.

The uppermost cavern was lost.

It had been lost, even before Ceridwen managed to pass the delirious Liam off to a family fleeing to the deepest cavern, freeing her to fight. Every blade was sorely needed, for most of the fighters had been housed above, closest to the scout outposts and the training ground. Their resistance had raised the alarm, but many had died or been cut off in the downward retreat.

Spears clacked and rattled in darting thrusts. Sweat and blood flew.

Ceridwen stabbed out again and again with the spear she had stolen off a slain rebel. Shoved chest to back and packed shoulder to shoulder, she had quickly realized that reach was needed most and traded her *chet* for the longer weapon. And still, they were losing ground, being shoved relentlessly backward by that unyielding advance. To her right, a rebel stumbled back too far and fell off the bridge, screaming a high thin wail that was swiftly lost in the roar of combat and waterfall. The shield line started to bow inward.

"Hold the line!" came the cry behind.

Setting her teeth, Ceridwen threw herself into the gap. This was a warfare wholly unfamiliar to her. She was accustomed to the shock of the *firestorm*, to the twisting, wheeling, constantly lashing furor of mounted combat, not this unrelenting grind. It wore upon the rebels as well, who were given to rapid raids and equally rapid retreats. They did not know formation fighting, whereas the Nadaari had perfected it.

And on the Nadaari came, unwearied and unstoppable.

Her heel brushed the edge. Waterfall spray misted the back of her neck. She caught and bound a thrust with her spear and strained to hold it, even as she felt her foot slipping backward. Then Owga shoved through the press with a fresh team of shield bearers to reinforce the fraying front, and the pressure eased, allowing Ceridwen to regain her footing and catch her breath.

Resting on her spear, she wiped the blood from her cheek with the crook of her arm. Once, Finnian had told her of the Nadaarian tide that had swept over the white stone city of Tel Renaair on the coast of Cenyon. Now, at last, Ceridwen felt she understood what he meant. No more than three soldiers abreast could descend the slat-and-rope staircase that switchbacked down the wall of the cavern, and since the rebels had initially formed up where the steps met the natural bridge, it should have created a deadly funnel. But the soldiers poured down with such momentum that they had seized half the bridge already.

"What I wouldn't give to have that fire-demon of yours up here." Owga fell back beside her, winding a bandage tight over a deep gash on her forearm and using her teeth to tie it off.

Ceridwen just nodded. With Mindar, she could have held the bridge alone. For a time, at least. Until his flames ran out, or the blaze overcame her. But he was below, and she doubted he could scale the narrow, snaking staircase without his blood boiling hot enough to set the entire construction alight, cutting off their escape.

Still, the Nadaari would have to claim the rest of the bridge if they wanted access to the lowest cavern. The steps down were already choked with tribesmen, women, and children, clutching what belongings they could carry, for the caverns were home to far more than rebel fighters. She glimpsed cooks emerging from the kitchen alcove carrying stuffed food baskets, followed by Saffa with her monkey perched on her shoulder. The old woman ushered them on ahead, then glanced back at the kitchens before shuffling down the steps.

That sight rekindled the dwindling fire in Ceridwen's chest, and she threw herself back into the fray beside Owga. For a moment, it seemed the rebels were finally succeeding, holding their ground, defying every Nadaarian attempt to beat them back. Then Ceridwen broke out of the fighting onto the inner edge of the bridge and saw the true reason for the shift. With the bridgehead won, their foes were splitting in two, with the greater force seeking to avoid the crossing by advancing around the circumference of the cavern. It was a much longer route, but they would eventually be able to fall upon the rebels from the rear or simply claim the staircase outright.

Owga nodded grimly when Ceridwen seized her arm to point out the maneuver. "We'll hold out as long as we can."

There was nothing else they could do, for they had too few fighters to split their own force. But so long as they held the bridge, those below could escape the slaughter for at least a little while more.

But it wasn't long before arrows suddenly pelted their unprotected flank and rear, felling the rebels like wheat before a scythe. One toppled against Ceridwen with a thick shaft in his neck. She faltered under his weight as arrows hissed on all sides. He was dead to a second arrow in an instant, and she let him fall.

Through the gaps suddenly opening in their ranks, she spied the archers. They stood on a ledge on the side of the gorge above, which had formed the rebels' training ground and was accessible from the uppermost cavern. Staggered in rows, they fired in unrelenting waves that would decimate the thinly armored defenders in minutes, if the rebels didn't break first. Ceridwen felt it coming, felt the shift in the fighters like the shiver that shot through Mindar when he tasted rain upon the wind, and she stood to rally them to hold fast.

Owga called the retreat instead, and the rebels tore for the stairs.

Everything within Ceridwen burned to fight, and for a breath, she stood motionless as rebels streamed past and arrows whisked by. Owga seized her and towed her along. This was no measured withdrawal so much as a mad rush to the end of the bridge, where the curve of the cavern offered some protection, and then down the staircase. Ceridwen gripped the guard-rope as the slat-and-wood structure swayed under hundreds of pounding feet.

She had seen no Nadaarian archers on the bridge itself, and no volleys struck them now as they made their scrambled descent. Above, the shield bearers formed up for one final, desperate stand, and Ceridwen hesitated, heedless of the rebels pushing past her. If she could have battled her way against the tide pouring down the stairs, she would have joined them. But a familiar keening neigh echoed through the cavern, drawing her gaze down.

Refugees clustered along the walls, while all who could wield arms were massed before the opening that led out into the gorge. And there, in the midst of it all, in a gap wreathed in smoke and flame, was her fireborn. Sparks shot from his hooves as he let out his high shrilling call again, tossing his head while Iakki clung stubbornly to his reins.

But it was not fear for the boy that propelled Ceridwen down the final steps—through the tide of descending rebels and the force Owga was trying to muster at the base—but hope.

Straight to Mindar she raced, and snatching the reins, she spun her steed around. "Clear the way!"

Roiling smoke shot black from Mindar's nostrils, more compelling than her command, and rebels and tribesmen alike scattered as she ran her steed back to the steps. The Nadaari had cut through the shield bearers and were now fighting their way downward. With each clang of steel, the heat rolled more thickly in waves off Mindar's quivering skin.

"Steady," Ceridwen whispered, stroking his neck though she wore no protective gear. "Steady, boy." She held him back until the first soldier broke through, shoving away the man he had just killed. She waited until he saw them, then she aimed Mindar's head high, and with a snap of her reins, unleashed his fire.

Rope and wood went up in a blaze beneath the soldier's feet. The flames raced upward, coiling along the structure and climbing swiftly, until, with an ominous creaking and twanging, the lowest section of the staircase dropped into the cavern. That left the survivors scrambling for surer footing, chased from below by howls and thrown spears that clattered off the walls. A single twitch of the reins quieted Mindar's blaze, but while the Nadaari were still reeling, Owga sent Hanonque climbers to scale the rock face and cut the ropes securing the unburned upper sections of the staircase.

The staircase fell with a clatter that rang through the cavern, and in the wake of its fall, a few raised thin cheers at their victory, small though it was. But this, Ceridwen knew, was not the end.

Turning with Mindar puffing smoke at her heels, she met Umut's eyes over by the opening to the gorge and saw that he knew it too. He summoned her with a jerk of his head. She wanted to check on Liam, make sure that he had made it safely down, but the defense was more pressing, so she joined Umut in the shadowed entrance. Strands of white hair clinging to the raw scrape on his forehead, he stared down the gorge.

Several bodies sprawled out on the path, slain while trying to flee. With archers gathered thickly above, there would be no retreat this way for the masses in the cavern.

"You need to see this." Umut waved her forward, and she came cautiously, wary of the archers. "Can you stop them?"

"What is it? Another wave of soldiers?" Already?

"Cihana," muttered a rebel. "They'll be slaughtered."

"Not soldiers," Umut began, but she had already dropped her reins and was hurrying up the slight slope that led out of the cavern so she could see out into the gorge. For here, with the roar of the waterfall diminished behind her, a far more familiar rumble caught her ears.

It was the sound of hooves.

SIXTY-FOUR: JAKIM

In Aodh's hand, there is rest.
- The truths of Aodh

Finnian was not dying. Not as fast as he should have been. That was the general consensus of the various healers and warriors alike who lifted the embroidered silk dressing to poke and prod at the wound in his abdomen, which, despite its apparent severity, had not soured and no longer appeared inflamed. It had not healed yet, either, so Finnian endured the scrutiny with an air of wry sufferance, stretched out on a bedroll with his back propped against his saddle, pinned by the ragged wolfhound who lay, panting, across his legs.

"He'll keep you from doing any fool thing, like rising," Markham remarked with a glimmer of amusement in his eye as the healers and gawkers trailed away, leaving them alone with Craddock, and Nahrog, who had been bound with his own chains.

The priest stared bleakly ahead and spoke only when questioned.

"You say the light never reached te Donal?" Markham fixed Jakim with his piercing gaze and scratched at his ragged beard. "Odd that, wouldn't you say, Craddock?"

Craddock tilted his head to also regard Jakim. "Maybe. Maybe not." Craddock was a bit of an enigma to Jakim. He had charged into the thick of the battle on his earthhewn, and his mail shirt could still be seen beneath the wide sleeves and neck of his brocaded surcoat, yet he lounged now upon a cushioned stool beneath a fringed shade that his warriors had set up for him. "There hasn't been a dawnrider in my family in centuries, though not for lack of trying . . ."

There was bemused resignation in his tone, but it didn't lessen the sense of thrill Jakim felt at the title. *Dawnrider.* It felt right somehow. Even if he didn't yet know how to ride.

Craddock yawned. "Still, some things persist in the lore. There wouldn't be dawnling hair in the stitching of that cloth, would there?"

Jakim shot Finnian a startled glance. "Yes, actually, we think so."

"It was glowing earlier," Finnian added, "so it seems probable."

"Well, there you have it. A few aged strands won't be potent enough to heal that wound outright but they could keep te Donal here from dying long enough for his body to do the rest." Craddock chuckled. "I doubt the Canthorians have discovered its usefulness as bandaging material, though, or they'd be less inclined to waste it disguising messages for their emissaries. This isn't the first time we've found such things. It's clever, certainly, but not foolproof, since the hair starts glowing on its own, following the cycle of the steed it was harvested from. Predictable, once you know the pattern. Not exactly secure enough for state secrets."

Given what Khilamook had said about the emperor, Jakim wasn't convinced that the Canthorians were ignorant of its healing properties. "Wouldn't you just sew dawnling hair into all your clothes then?"

Craddock cocked an eyebrow. "If not harvested at just the right time, it is inert, and even if it does retain some potency, it loses it over time. Besides, dawnlings are indeed rare creatures. They have been hunted to near extinction, and my line has sworn to protect them from the rest of the greedy world." Finnian snorted at that. "Yes, yes, I know how that sounds, given what is said of me and my appreciation for fine things. How ironic. But it's true, and riding around in clothing that occasionally glows would undermine that sacred charge."

Jakim's gaze drifted to the dawnling grazing beside the stream, its soft gold forelock falling over its eyes. "What did you mean by the cycle of the steed?"

"Once a dawnling's light reaches its zenith and is expelled, like you saw today, it might take days or weeks, depending on the steed, before light accumulates beneath its skin again."

"So its light will return?"

"Oh, yes. No telling when yet, but yes."

"And then it will be able to heal again?"

Craddock eyed him resignedly. "Once its light again reaches its zenith."

Finnian cleared his throat, and his eyes flicked to Markham. "Now that we've established that I'm not dying, what say we move on to important matters, like Glyndwr and Ceridwen?"

Markham was silent. He had received the news of both Glyndwr's betrayal and of Ceridwen's capture and escape in Nadaar with no outward sign of emotion. In turn, he'd told them that with Eagan's aid, Telweg had retaken large portions of Cenyon, though the Nadaarian fleet continued to ravage the coast. A steely hardness entered his eye as he informed them that Glyndwr had been reinstated as regent of Soldonia. It seemed the war-chief had returned with tales of devastation, claiming Ceridwen's recklessness had sparked a full-scale conflict that had forced him to pull back when her forces were overwhelmed and scattered.

The other war-chiefs had believed him.

Craddock sniffed. "Never could stand that old bear. Wouldn't have pegged him for a coward though. Or a traitor."

Markham uncorked his flask. "Glyndwr, we can deal with. I'll see him in flames for doing this to her, if I have to hurl him into Koltar myself." He threw back a swallow. "But Ceridwen . . ."

"She's alive, Markham, and she's free," Finnian said. "You heard the priest."

They had spent over an hour questioning Nahrog about the dawnling and about Rhodri's plans. Nahrog seemed to consider their defeat a foregone conclusion and answered them willingly enough, if somewhat sullenly. He had even told them that the Voice had confirmed that the promised army was setting sail—the last words he had heard before the light struck him and his connection had been severed.

"Free?" Markham repeated. "She's stranded across the sea in the heart of the empire, and there's pit-spawned little we can do about it. I might hate it, and you might hate me for saying it, but her fate was sealed the moment she surrendered to Rhodri."

"I don't believe that. I don't think you do either."

Markham dropped the flask with a clank. "*Shades*, te Donal, even if I don't, what resources do you think we have? We're stretched thin, fighting Rhodri, Ormond, now maybe Glyndwr? Now, on top of civil war, we learned there's about to be another army crawling like ticks across our land, and we can't even drive off the ones we've already got."

Finnian pushed up with a wince, dislodging the wolfhound, and met the older man's gaze. "That's why we need her. I'm going, Markham."

Markham regarded him stiffly, a muscle quivering below his eye. Then he sniffed and shook his head, clearing his throat loudly. "Of course you are. Should have known she'd be a bad influence on you, te Donal. But where in flames do you suppose you're going to get a ship to carry you across a sea infested with the Nadaarian fleet?"

Clinking chains drew Jakim's focus to Nahrog. He straightened his shoulders and indicated the priest. "He was going to take the dawnling to Nadaar. Why don't we ask him?"

Jakim followed Aodh's hand through the purpling dusk of the valley, the dawnling ambling along at his heels. She didn't seem comfortable away from his side for long. He would have to get used to constantly being tailed, or maybe just resign himself to riding everywhere he went from now on.

He found Ineth among the other Ardon warriors Craddock's forces had captured. She saw him coming and pointedly turned away. But he strolled right up to her, then slid a knife from his sleeve.

"That's a stupid way to carry a knife, Scroll."

He smiled and crouched before her. "You may not feel the hand of Aodh right now, Ineth, but I do. I do, and I have a lot of questions, but I know that Aodh is drawing me across the sea to Nadaar. Maybe to my home, maybe to somewhere else. Somehow, someday, I think I'm going to wind up at the City. I have a feeling I'll find out as I go. But wherever he leads me, I'm going to follow, and I'd like you to come too."

"Why?" Skepticism filled her tone. "Why would you want that?"

He shrugged. "I think you'd get along with my sister, Siba."

Her eyes narrowed. "I won't go back to the City, if that's what you want. Won't tell you how to get there either. Believe me, you don't want to go."

"Maybe we start with just getting you out of these ropes?"

She huffed a disbelieving breath, but raised her hands, and he sliced through the ropes. Once freed, she rubbed at her wrists, then hesitated. She slowly drew back her sleeve, showing him first her left forearm, then her right.

Her skin no longer bore the sharp, twisting scars. No longer the gouges of pain. No longer even the faded blue script of the Scrolls.

It was fresh and new and smooth.

"Aodh have mercy," Jakim whispered, and the dawnling nickered softly, easing alongside him. He reached up to brush her silky neck and his fingers snarled in the shorn tufts of her mane, cut by the engineer's knife. And there, peeking out from amidst the ordinary, lusterless locks, was a single glowing, golden strand.

SIXTY-FIVE: RAFI & CERIDWEN

Cage a songbird and its melody dies.
- Hanonque saying

Scattering soldiers like leaves before a monsoon wind, Flick and the other two remaining earthriders burst through the rear of the unsuspecting formation, and Rafi charged at their heels. He could feel Ghost trembling with each plunging stride. The colt was on the final dregs of his strength, just like he was. It was all he could do to hold his spear poised to strike, but he didn't have to use it, for they were out and racing up the gorge before the soldiers could regroup. Out beyond the shelter of the cultivated trees, where they had a clear view of the caverns before them and the gorge rim above.

It was bristling with archers.

Rafi's muscles twitched involuntarily at the sight, survival instincts warning him to turn back. To run. But the archers wouldn't fire—Sahak wanted the steeds alive. He told himself that with each hoofbeat, and he almost believed it.

Until the volley fell, whistling viciously around them.

Flick jerked in the saddle, arrows sprouting in his shoulder and thigh, and still more splintering off his steed's hide. Ghost stumbled, and Rafi caught at the colt's withers to steady himself. Cries rose behind him, and a riderless shadower bolted past, kicking up its heels, hindquarters riddled with arrows. It didn't matter that the dark shadows of Jasri's stormers were now sweeping in from where they'd been gliding high above to target the archers and divert their focus. Because Rafi had been wrong, terribly wrong.

Then a sharp, clear shout echoed over the gorge, and the volley abruptly ceased, freeing them to hurtle on toward the lowest cavern.

Ceridwen met them as they poured through the opening and drew their steeds to a halt. She seized the reins that draped loose around the neck of Flick's lathered earthhewn, and Rafi was off Ghost and catching Flick before he could tumble from the saddle. He miscalculated his own failing strength, and Flick's limp weight nearly brought him down.

Strong hands braced his shoulders from behind, while Ceridwen steadied his elbow. "Flames take you, Rafi," she snapped as she gestured for a pair of rebels to take Flick to the healers. "Don't you know you've run to your death?"

One look at her, with blood smearing her face from a cut on her cheekbone, soot streaking her skin, and flakes of ash in her hair, quelled the desperate apology he'd toiled over. One look, and he was struck dumb, unable to express the rush of relief he felt at seeing her again, still alive, and still vibrantly aflame.

"Ceridwen, I . . ."

"Of course he knows," came Sev's voice near his ear, and the grip on his shoulders tightened briefly before releasing. "And of course he came back anyway, because that's who he is. It's who he's always been." Sev retrieved the spear Rafi had dropped in his haste and held it out toward him. "Own it, cousin."

His lips twitched into a grin, and Rafi felt his own do the same, seeing the gesture for what it truly was. Reconciliation.

Then Ghost coughed behind him.

It was a ragged, wet sound, and Rafi turned to see the colt shifting on his forelegs, nostrils flaring with each puffing breath. Ceridwen was already inspecting him, pinching the skin at the point of his shoulder and running her hands under his shuddering girth and down his legs.

"You've run him near to death too," she said shortly. "He's overheated. We need to cool him down, replenish his salt. But not you," she added, casting a critical eye over him too. "You look half dead yourself."

She led Ghost over to the pool, and Rafi turned to his riders. Most were dismounted and tending to their own steeds. Only two besides Flick had taken arrows and needed to be helped over to the healers, where

Saffa and her crew were pitching in, along with several of the fisher tribe, Kaya and Iakki among them.

Iakki spied him and waved wildly. Then, making sure Rafi was watching, he started juggling rolls of bandages. Two, then three, then four at once. He almost managed five, but a missed throw thwacked Gordu in the face, and Kaya took the bandages away.

Completely unchastened, the boy shot Rafi a cheeky grin.

Oh, Ches-Shu, that boy would be the death of him someday, but come sun, come storm, Rafi would see him survive to master that five-ball sequence, and for that, he needed to find Umut.

"I thought you were all of you dead for sure," the rebel leader declared in disbelief, when Rafi finally tracked him down. He was not in the center of the action or tending to the wounded but standing with his back pressed to the cavern wall and his crutch braced against his chest. His voice creaked like splintering wood, and he looked even more worn than he sounded, with his shirt hanging limp, the front streaked with blood.

Rafi opened his mouth, but Umut shushed him as the cries of the songbirds, ever a constant in the caverns, suddenly rose to a frantic pitch. His blunt fingers stabbed upward, directing Rafi's gaze to the opening in the ceiling, where garish torchlights could be seen roving through the caverns above. "Torching the nests, Cael smite them."

The songbirds were sacred to the Hanonque, which made torching their nests just the sort of thing Sahak would order his soldiers to do.

"Over a century this cavern has been shelter and stronghold and sanctuary alike for the Que Revolution. That it should fall . . ." Umut's eyes were mere slits of blue as he regarded Rafi. "I hope you've come to do more here than die with the rest of us?"

"Oh, trust me, I've no aim to die," Rafi countered with a tired grin. "With the rest of you or otherwise. We're here to cover for the evacuation, while you lead these people to safety. We were always meant to be a distraction, sir, and that's just what we mean to do."

"This . . . is far more than I asked of you."

"Maybe, but it's why we've come."

Umut pushed off the wall. He swayed slightly, and Rafi caught him. But the rebel leader pressed him back with a firm hand. "Come then. We'll see the Que Revolution survive one more day."

Ceridwen had spent most of her life living toward the next challenge, the next test of skill, the next battle. First as her father's twin-born daughter and potential heir to not only his chiefdom but the throne of Soldonia, then under Markham's relentless tutelage, and then as an Outrider dispatched alone to the farthest wilds of the kingdom where one misstep could mean death.

It was Finnian who had first dared her to look beyond the clash of combat, to long to live for more.

But this was not a fight she expected to survive.

It began with a hail of arrows that dropped like sheeting rain from the opening in the ceiling. Most spat harmlessly into the waterfall pool or splintered on stone, but some struck flesh, and cries echoed throughout the hollow space as both riders and rebels spun apart. She had ordered the riders to rest in shifts while the others milled about on their steeds alongside the rebel fighters, to distract from the stream of refugees quietly slipping down the escape tunnel.

That had been Rafi's idea—an attempt to forestall the deadly attack Sahak would unleash to keep his prey from eluding his trap.

Now, that attack had come, and not one of the steeds had been struck— or even targeted. Even now, Sahak sought first to take them alive. She would make him rue that choice, ere the day was done, for she had not been trained to warfare since she could first sit on a saddle to now miss so obvious a feint.

So it was not to the caverns above that Ceridwen looked.

"'Ware the gorge," she called, cinching her right vambrace down tight. She wove gloved fingers through Mindar's mane and swung up onto his back, feeling the ridge of his spine beneath her, for she rode bareback today. Her saddle had been dismantled for repairs and forgotten when the craftsmen fled, but one had thought to grab her leathers. Still unrepaired, but she was grateful to have any gear for the coming fight.

Shouts traveled from the cavern mouth. "Soldiers marching down the gorge!"

"Steady," Ceridwen warned, hearing the creak of shifting saddles, the jingle of shaken tack, the stamp of a nervous hoof. This was a far cry from the strategic raids the riders had been on so far, and they had always been more Rafi's team than hers, yet she found on their faces the same taut determination she would have expected to find on her Outriders. "Wait until their shadows reach the entrance."

Then the front ranks wouldn't have time to flee before the hooves of their steeds crashed into them. Her words met with nods and fists tightening on spear hafts.

And then she saw Rafi.

He was helping with the evacuation. He had a little boy on his shoulders and an old man gripping his arm for support, and as he turned to watch the riders, Ceridwen read the pain on his face at being grounded while his warriors rode to the fight. She had told him that Ghost was far too drained to be risked in battle yet. He had not spared his steed in his race to save the rebels. He had not spared himself either.

Yet his was the blood of tyrants.

Of course, she had yet to meet the would-be tyrant who, denied the honor and glory of the fight, would defy his own exhaustion and throw himself wholeheartedly into helping noncombatants escape. Who, with his one free arm, would laughingly sweep the basket from an overladen mother and cradle it against his side. Who would offer a shoulder to a wounded rebel, carry a stretcher, and spur on the evacuees with a smile and a well-placed jest.

These were not the actions of the invaders of her kingdom.

Ceridwen tugged up her half mask and set her face forward in time to see the first shadows darken the entrance and the first soldiers come into view behind them. Mindar sprang, anticipating her move, as she brought her *chet* down sharply to signal the attack. His eager flames blasted the front ranks as her riders surged seven abreast from the cavern's mouth and thundered into the Nadaari.

Slashing right, then left, Ceridwen tore like a flaming arrow through the first ten rows. With howls and shouts, the riders raced after her, and she felt the battle cry of the Outriders rising up her throat. Rarely had she dared ride her fireborn bareback. Only once into battle, and that had been during her escape from Sahak's temple. Her hooded jerkin was still battered, and her chaps were worn thin, but she rode out to battle upon her own bonded steed, and what more could a warrior of Soldonia ask for? Save to die on her own soil with her own blade in hand?

So much more, the ache in her heart whispered.

High above, the throb of stormers' wings marked the entrance of Jasri's cloud into the fight. Switching her reins to her blade hand, Ceridwen caught up her war horn and blew a single blast: the signal to fall back. Checking Mindar, she wheeled to the left, and the riders behind did the same. It was a tricky maneuver that required those on the inside of the turn to slow more than those on the outside, but they had drilled it before, and it was an exhilarated, breathless group that poured back into the cavern, leaving the front of the Nadaarian column crushed behind them.

"Reform," Ceridwen called, swinging Mindar sharply about to face the smoke-ridden haze outside, and the riders and steeds veered back into place. Without numbers or terrain to use to her advantage, using rapid, demoralizing sorties was the only strategy that offered hope. She must strike hard and fast as the soldiers started to recover, then pound them into the dust, until even their discipline failed them. None knew better than she how hard it could be to claw your way up out of the ash only to be struck down over and over again.

So she raised her *chet* and brought it down. "Onward!"

One step. One step. Just one step more.

The chant formed an endless refrain in Rafi's mind as he headed back toward the cavern after his fifth trip to the escape shaft. Slogging up the stream to avoid the crowded footpaths, he was dimly aware that the fatigue was getting to him.

Had gotten to him. He was nearly delirious with it.

It took him far too long to recognize that the distant murmur racing up the dimly lit tunnel and swelling as it neared was panic. It overtook the evacuees like a flood and swept them up into its rush. Suddenly, Rafi was staring down a mass of people running, shoving, slipping, and stumbling up the stream toward him.

He stopped, swaying, mesmerized by the sight.

Until now, the evacuation had moved steadily, almost fluidly, with refugees draining down the tunnel to the circular chamber at the end. There, Moc oversaw the descent with his crew, guiding them through the drop on makeshift rope ladders, then downstream out of the cave below, and out into the flush of jungle that bordered the Alon Coast. But now, pounding footsteps and smothered cries echoed harshly in the confined space, and beyond it, the dull roar of battle. That shocked Rafi back into motion.

He fought against the current, struggling alone upstream through the onslaught, until he broke free of the fleeing mob and out into the cavern.

Clusters of soldiers and rebels clashed across the open space surrounding the waterfall pool. Some soldiers streamed in through the gorge entrance, where the riders were visible beyond only as whirling shapes lost in a dense cloud of smoke. Others dropped by rope from the cavern above—tall soldiers in burnished armor capable of shattering spears and blunting *chets*.

They were the famed Choth warriors, sent in only to crush and quell and destroy, and they wielded their curved battle axes to deadly effect.

His spear. He needed his spear. And Ghost.

Rafi staggered blindly forward. Compared to the sea Sahak had amassed outside, only a trickle had broken through so far, and yet even a small leak could sink a boat. His foot struck something weighted and soft, and instinct drove him to reel back even before he saw the body.

Umut's body.

The rebel leader slumped beside the tunnel entrance, fallen where he had chosen to stand so he could look the fleeing Que in the eye, to show them that hope was not lost. A dark, wet trail down the rock face marked where he had slid down to land as if sitting, shirt soaked through with blood, eyes staring upward.

Oh. Ches-Shu. Rafi sagged, numb.

"He's gone, Sea-Demon, isn't he?"

He managed to nod. He slowly lifted his head to see Owga a few paces away, clenching a broken spear. Most of the noncombatants were disappearing down the tunnel, leaving the two of them in a rapidly clearing pocket behind a thin shield of rebels drawn up to guard the escape route. Owga shifted into a defensive stance, facing the cavern. She watched the ebb and flow of combat with an intensity that made him believe every wild tale Moc and Lowen had ever spun about her arena fights.

"Yes," he said. "He's gone."

"Cael take him." She muttered it as if it were a curse, but a son of the Hanonque had no truer hope in death but that Cael might sing him to sleep.

Whatever else she might have said was drowned out in the clatter of hooves as the riders spilled back into the cavern. Even from a distance, Rafi could see that several steeds were limping, and few riders were unscathed. Three were missing. Still, at Ceridwen's command, half rode on, cutting down the soldiers who had managed to slip past them, while the rest wheeled to face the mouth again, forming up in a mass of lathered hides and heaving ribcages.

Ches-Shu, how much more could they endure?

"We cannot hold out much longer," Owga said, as though he had spoken the question aloud. "Dead rebels cannot win freedom for the Que. Or vengeance. The final civilians are clearing out now. I will order my fighters to begin to withdraw down the tunnel." She glanced at him briefly. "You should do the same."

Time for the final stage of the evacuation, then.

Somehow, he expected he would have to convince Ceridwen to agree. Weary, Rafi just nodded and watched Owga stride away, issuing commands for the retreat. Splashing his face with water from the stream, he whispered farewell to Umut, then stood shakily to retrieve both his spear and his steed.

It was time he and Ghost rejoined the others.

He called for Ceridwen as he neared, and the teeming throng of steeds unfolded. She emerged on her fireborn, escorting a battered stormer mare trailing a mangled silver wing, Lowen slumping dazed in the saddle. Ceridwen drew the stormer clear of the cavern mouth, then swung down to inspect the stormer's wing, which hung awkwardly, feathers broken and torn.

"I didn't even see it coming." Lowen clutched his right shoulder. "Those archers dropped a stone on us from the rim. Must've clipped her wing. We smashed up against the gorge wall on the way down. How bad is it, Fireborn? Will she fly again?"

From the press of Ceridwen's lips as she felt along the joints of the wing, Rafi didn't hold out much hope. "Not in this fight, she won't," she said at last. "That wing won't get her aloft. You're fortunate she landed without sending you both into a tumble." She gripped his forearm, then gathered up Mindar's reins, leaving Lowen fumbling helplessly with the fused straps of his harness until Rafi took the knife from his belt and sliced him free.

Ceridwen called out for the others to regroup, and the weary, sweaty, blood-streaked steeds melted back into a column.

Rafi pitched his voice to reach her. "Owga's withdrawing."

She stilled with one hand gripping Mindar's mane, one step from swinging up onto his back, and bowed her head.

Quieter, he added, "I'm not much of a tactician, Ceridwen, but even I know that means we're about to be overrun."

Smoke coiled languidly around her. Around them both.

Her head came up. "Ride with us. One final charge out into the gorge." She pivoted to face him, and he knew already the look he would find in her eyes, for he had seen it before in Delmar, in the colt, and in Nef, there at the end. It was the look of one who sensed death's fetid breath on their neck and who would not shrink from it. "I would die with the sun on my face, not trapped in a cave like a beast brought to bay. What say you, Rafi Tetrani? Will you ride into battle by my side, one last time?"

It was both challenge and peace offering.

Over her shoulder, he could see the riders shifting anxiously on their steeds, could sense the dread under their determination, and he understood it, because he felt it too.

He had led them into this. He had to try to lead them out again.

"What do I say?" Rafi met her fierce, proud gaze with a wan smile. "I say, why settle for one last ride, Ceridwen? I'll gladly ride out to battle with you a hundred more times, until we break the empire's grip on the Que and on Soldonia. But first we have to get out of here. Alive."

Her eyes went to the hand he'd planted on the head of his spear, marking it a blade oath, like she'd shown him.

"Will you trust me?" he asked.

Her jaw tightened, turmoil afire in her eyes. "Flames take me, Rafi, but I do. What do you have in mind?"

SIXTY-SIX: CERIDWEN & RAFI

*Seabloods cannot long endure extensive submersion in freshwater,
while riveren suffer in the tang of the sea, but those frequently exposed
to both gain some resistance to ill effects.*
- Wisdom of the Horsemasters

"Burn brightly, Ceridwen."

Those were the final words Rafi had uttered as he took off down the tunnel on Ghost, with her war horn and three riverriders at his side, and her solemn oath to order the retreat upon his signal. She had told him that she trusted him, and against her judgment, she did. So she would hold off Sahak until the horn call came, then yes, she would command the riders to fall back down the tunnel.

Until then, she *would* burn.

Mindar snorted out a blast of sparks as they reached the front of the column, facing the cavern mouth. She was glad to find his fires stoked hot, for the delay had cost them, and the Nadaari had seized a foothold. Soldiers with shields and spears formed a bristling line inside the entrance and were advancing further, step by chanted step. She called Mindar to flame as she charged the line, felt the rush of warmth through his ribcage, and drew his head down at the last moment so the blazing torrent swept under the shields and engulfed the soldiers' legs.

The first three rows melted back before her.

She shot into the gap and swung Mindar in an arc, skimming his flames across the cavern floor. She was the tip of the wedge, the iron head of the ram, so she drove herself deeper and deeper still, opening the path for those at her heels. Until the charge caught up to her, and she checked her steed and his flame and took to her blade instead. Out, they tore, until the sun struck their faces, until their hooves drummed on packed earth, on broken spears, on fallen foes. Then they turned and swept back into the cavern again.

"Reform!"

They wheeled to face the gorge mouth.

Ceridwen ignored the press of steeds jostling, heedless of Mindar's heat, into position around him. He flicked an apathetic ear toward them, which would have worried her, had the situation in the cavern not claimed her attention. Owga's forces were withdrawing far more rapidly than she had expected. So rapidly that the collapse of their defensive line toward the tunnel had ceded much of the cavern to the soldiers they had been opposing, and more and more were dropping in on ropes every moment.

Soon the weight of soldiers behind would present too grave a danger for her riders to continue forcing the Nadaari back down the gorge, even if she didn't have to worry about guarding their exit down the tunnel. She swung back to the gorge where the gleam of spears shredded the haze of smoke as the broken column regrouped and marched on again.

Split her forces? No, they were too few.

"Fall back," she called, and her voice cracked upon the words. "Fall back to the tunnel. On me."

Now she wished for her war horn, but several riders echoed the cry, and with the mass flaring around her like wings, she swept in to cover the rebels' fraying rearguard as it retreated down the tunnel. The shock of their arrival drove the attacking soldiers back, creating space for her force to form a defensive arc, several riders deep, and claim a moment to breathe. To tie off bandages, drink from the stream, adjust tack, and flex aching hands. All in a haunted silence she doubted even Rafi could have relieved.

She did not try. Her tongue was more likely to scald than sway.

She barely had time to peel away the charred remnant of her gloves before the Nadaari started streaming in from the gorge.

Ceridwen sprang into their midst in a shock of flame. She cut off the blaze swiftly, though she could not extinguish the fires that whipped along Mindar's crest as she spun and twisted through the soldiers. Solborn were made for the blinding impact of a charge, the wildly roving conflict, and the extended chase that could turn an orderly retreat into a deadly flight. They were not made for holding ground. Guarding the tunnel against such overwhelming odds left her forces vulnerable. In close quarters, even a ghosted shadower could be caged and stabbed and a fireborn engulfed in flame could be gutted from the flank. If the soldiers had not been ordered to take the steeds alive, their slaughter would have been swift. As it was, the soldiers who advanced now came with nets, ropes, and spears to pen them in.

Ceridwen struck out with her blade again and again, until her wrist and fingers were numb. She sought to reserve Mindar's flame and brought him rearing up and plunging down instead, knocking spears from hands and soldiers to the ground. And still the Nadaari came. Out of the corner of her eye, she saw a riveren netted and a rider brought down by spears. She cut away a thrusting blade and rammed the hilt of her *chet* against a threatening face.

But hoof and blade were not enough. She needed flame.

Already, the residual heat wafting off Mindar's skin was enough to make her eyes sting, but she called for more, and fire ripped from his throat. Streams of it swept across his skin and licked at hers, and just before the roar of it engulfed her, there came resonating from beneath the earth behind her, a horn call.

Rafi. Not a moment too soon.

She spun Mindar to the side, directing the violent torrent of his flame into the stream. Thick, roiling steam billowed up, enveloping steeds and soldiers alike, shrouding her forces as they broke off the fight and raced down the tunnel. One hand raised to shield her face, Ceridwen backed Mindar after them, maintaining his blaze, teeth gritted against the riotous assault upon her senses, until someone pounded on her shoulder and a muffled shout invaded her ears. She blinked alert to the barely visible shadowrider at her elbow.

Taka. The boatbuilder.

His words took on form. "Fireborn, it's done!"

She twitched her reins, and blessedly, Mindar's flame cut off. Shivers raked her skin in its absence, but Taka looked relieved when she nodded for him to go. Then something flashed in her peripheral vision, and Taka faltered, blood spilling across his neck. He toppled from the saddle, arm slipping from her instinctive grab.

That futile attempt saved her.

Stinging pain clipped her ear. A knife clanged off the cavern wall behind her. She looked back over her shoulder. Out of the thick swirl of smog, an enormous stone-eye tiger stalked forward on massive, padded paws, drawing a war-chariot behind it. Standing beside the charioteer, with fists braced against the rail, bloodstained blades glistening on the baldric slung across his chest, was the emperor's infamous assassin, Sahak.

Rafi stood beside Ghost over a drop into roaring darkness, and for once, the specters of the past held no power over him, for he could still feel the warmth Ceridwen's words had ignited in his chest. Here, at the end of everything, she trusted him.

And trust was a powerful thing.

It was, she had told him once, the root of all bonds between rider and steed, and of the sol-breath. But never had that truth been more apparent to Rafi than now, as riders and steeds broke into the circular chamber at the end of the tunnel and surged toward the escape shaft, where the stream poured over the edge of a gaping hole.

When Rafi had made that plunge himself on Ghost, it had been a complete accident. He had stumbled across it and barely snatched a glimpse of his surroundings, before the colt had caught a whiff of sea tang down the shaft and, quite literally, dragged him into it.

Then, it had seemed a fathomless descent into a raging torrent of inky black night. Now, a scattering of torches ringed the hole above and below, and if the drop was not quite what Rafi would have sworn it had been, it was still daunting enough that any sane rider might balk at it.

Not to mention any earthbound steed.

Rafi didn't give them time to think. On his mark, Yath swept in from the side on his riveren to take the lead, and the riders tore down the waterway after him. Hooves churning up a misty spray, the demon-steeds flowed in a tossing, tumultuous stream over the edge. Some flung themselves forward like a shot from a bow. Some came with throats shrilling, steps short and staccato. Others did try to bolt to the side, only to ram up against the earthhewn Rafi had positioned flanking the stream.

But down they dove, and a deep vibratory hum arose from the riveren stationed below, wielding the river to cushion their drop. It caught them up, and swept them gently downstream, out where the refugees and the rebels had already gone. Out where Sahak, with his heavily armored soldiers and massive army, would be sore pressed to follow with any speed. What Rafi wouldn't give to see Sahak's face when he realized they had all slipped his net.

Ghost sidled toward the drop, nostrils flared, legs buckling for a jump.

"No, you don't." Rafi backed Ghost swiftly away, then swung the colt around in an attempt to break his fixation on the sea air he'd caught drifting up the shaft.

From this vantage, Rafi could see a gap in the line of steeds and a final knot of riders charging up the tunnel behind. This was it, then. In his exhaustion, it took two tries to muscle onto Ghost's back and snatch up his spear, and by then the final four riders were sweeping past him. Three shadowriders, one riverrider. He peered down the tunnel but saw no more coming.

No riders. No soldiers either.

And no Ceridwen. Not yet.

Uncertainty formed a cold lump in his gut. He looked to see the last steed poised on the brink, haunches quivering as it readied to jump. "Wait!" The word snapped from his lips with a ring of authority, and the rider checked his steed.

It was Yon, Rafi realized, recognizing the Hanonque man's thin and scrubby frame. "How many more are coming?" he asked him.

"There are no more," Yon said. "We are the last."

"The last?" Rafi stared at the man. "Shouldn't there be an army howling at your heels?" Suddenly, it seemed painfully clear. "She's back there, isn't she? Holding the tunnel?"

Yon met his eyes. "She's giving us our escape."

Ceridwen. Ches-Shu.

Rafi pivoted toward the empty tunnel, Yon's voice continuing behind him, sounding dimmer with each word. "It's too late. She'll have been overrun by chariots by now. You can't do anything. We should go while we have the chance. We should run."

Run, Rafi. *Run.*

"No."

Usually, his anger was a simmering thing, but in that moment, it boiled. His blood turned scalding. His voice too. "No. I'm done running."

SIXTY-SEVEN: CERIDWEN

Of all firerider contests, the Sol-Fiere is the greatest,
pitting fireborn against fireborn upon a battleground bordered
by water in a test of flame, skill, and endurance.
- Wisdom of the Horsemasters

Only the force of the mightiest blaze could diminish the power of a stone-eye's gaze, and Mindar burned fiercely. Ceridwen swung him in a tight turn, blasting a torrent of fire toward both chariot and tiger. This was not the whirlwind of the *firestorm*, which burned out hot and swiftly. No, this was a slow pivot and heavy blaze, meant to match pace with the stone-eye as it prowled a sauntering circle around them.

Just beyond reach of the flames.

Something hissed toward her.

She slashed her *chet* before her, felt the *clang* that sent the knife zinging away. But she sucked in a breath as another sliced across her ribcage, easily splitting the weakened leathers. Sahak was only taunting her, for he could have commanded his archers to open fire. She would have been unable to fend off both the tiger and a volley of arrows. The fact that he had not, seemed to indicate that he still wished to take her alive, though she could sense his irritation growing as they circled again, parted by the pulsing waves of heat. Nearly at an impasse.

He could not close in to strike, and she could not allow Mindar's flare to so much as flicker, or they would be trapped by the stone-eye. This was not the fight she would have chosen. Initially, she had tried to flank Sahak and attack the chariot from the rear, but Sahak was far too skilled to be outmaneuvered so easily. The tiger had matched her, turn for turn, demanding all her focus, which allowed the soldiers, braced with heavy shields dampened against combustion and slicked with freshly skinned goat hides, to close in behind.

Until she had found herself surrounded, forced into this deadly, protracted standoff that favored Sahak. He need only wait for her steed to tire, or her will to give out first.

Mindar was already bleeding, shoulder torn open by a raking spear, dark blood spattering the stone beneath his hooves. But he was not yet favoring his leg.

She doubted he had even felt it in the rush of his inferno. He was fire incarnate, and she was smoke upon his back. She rode with no saddle, no gloves, no shielding from his flame save the sol-breath, and despite its power, she could feel the outline of each of his bones like coals beneath his skin. She fought to keep his flames steady, to hold back the searing torrent, lest they climb too high and consume her. Lest his flames become her funeral pyre, the roar of his breath the only song raised at her passing, the tale of her deeds summed up in a pile of blackened bones on the cavern floor.

She fought desperately. But it was not enough.

Strands of fire crawled up her legs, wound around her torso, cinched her chest tight. The stench of singed leather and burning cloth filled her nostrils, and she knew the blaze would claim her in the end, as it had claimed Bair, unless she quenched her steed and let the stone-eye take her. But she was a firerider. She was supposed to be stronger than this. More than this.

She was the Fireborn.

Shutting her eyes against the sting of blistering tears, Ceridwen screamed her defiance into the scorching flames.

And felt their strength diminish.

Mindar, her volatile, wildborn steed, who had ever before been inflamed by her agitation, shuddered, reacting instinctively to her pain. Not with more flame, or a renewed blaze, but with less. And in that breath, as his focus shifted to her, and his flare dimmed to save her, the stone-eye had them.

Ceridwen felt Mindar stiffen, his neck remaining extended and taut, and the jet he had loosed before was nothing compared to the explosion that roared from his throat now. Snared while flaming by the stone-eye tiger's paralyzing gaze, he was completely immobilized to do anything else.

He could not stop, and she could not help him.

His mane burst into a crown of grasping flames. As did his hide.

The shining copper sheen of his coat, the deep umber of his mane, and the patch of speckled white that dusted his withers were engulfed in racing rivulets of fire. And Ceridwen, who had knelt upon the ash-choked heart of the crater of Koltar, who had stood over streams of molten firerock that burned with the strength of a hundred pyres, who had caught the focused blast of a fireborn upon her arm and borne the agony of the brand searing into her forehead, had never before endured such a savage and incinerating heat as the flash that seared her lungs and bathed each breath in white-hot shards.

Mindar burned, and she burned with him.

All the world was fire and ash and scorching smoke.

Then a spray of salt and of damp sea air burst through the suffocating fume, and the keening shriek of a seablood filled her ears as a wave rose and towered overhead, then fell upon her, dousing her and her steed in a single stroke.

SIXTY-EIGHT: RAFI

Change the tides.

G host hurtled down in the wake of the descending wave into a
cloud of roiling steam. He stumbled, dropping on one knee, but
recovered his balance and shied in a circle, splashing through the
puddles their arrival had deposited on the hot stone.

Up close, the residual heat seemed a physical force, beating against
Rafi's face, tightening around his throat, until everything within him
screamed to retreat. He pried his fingers from Ghost's mane, which
he had held in a death grip as they exploded from the tunnel upon the
towering flood and soared out over the cavern, over the soldiers, over
Sahak, as if on wings of water. He raised his hand to shield his eyes
from the stinging smog.

Mindar coughed sporadically a few paces away, forelegs splayed,
trembling. White ash coated his hide, and Ceridwen, too, who was
draped across his neck like a dead thing.

The *chet* dropped from her hand.

"Ceridwen?"

His voice sounded hollow in the deadening silence that had fallen
in the aftermath of both fire and wave. Flakes of ash drifted over him,
over the soldiers strewn beyond, like refuse across a beach, and the
ones who stood stunned behind them. Over the chariot and tiger,
which had been swept backward and overturned by the cataclysm of
his arrival. There was a body pinned beneath the wheel, but it wasn't
Sahak. For as he watched, Sahak's head then shoulders appeared as his

cousin pulled himself out from beneath the upended frame. They were running out of time before the shock broke and another attack came.

"Flames take you, Rafi."

He turned to see Ceridwen braced against Mindar's quivering neck, staring out over the devastation. Her eyes were dark as the soot-stained water streaming down her face. "Flames take you," she repeated, her voice a harsh rasp. "Why did you come back for me?"

"Sorry, Ceridwen, but this isn't your sacrifice to make."

Her jaw tensed as she looked out over the rows upon rows of soldiers drawing back into formation. Not attacking yet—wave and flame had left them wary—but cutting them off from the tunnel, from the gorge, from any chance of escape, but one. Though, judging by the look on Ceridwen's face, not the one she was thinking of.

She fumbled for her reins, as though her fireborn wasn't still quenched, as though his flames hadn't just nearly killed her, as though she did not feel the pain of the burns he could see blistering beneath the coating of ash.

Maybe she didn't, but she would soon enough.

"You should have let me burn. I won't be taken alive, Rafi. I won't."

She had already been burning when he reached the mouth of the tunnel. Burning unreservedly, like a spark in dry thatching. He had barely been able to see her through the raging inferno pulsing outward from her steed, but the fire's glow had shown Sahak's face clearly, and with one glimpse of the pleased curl of his lip and the cruel gleam in his eyes, any shred of uncertainty or fear in Rafi had vanished.

He had known then what he would do.

Had known, perhaps, even before he left the escape shaft, because the seeds had been sown in him six years ago, even if he had not understood the truth until now. Delmar hadn't died because of him. He had died *for* him. It was a choice he had made at the end, to stand in the gap, to take Rafi's scars on himself. The choice Torva had made.

The choice Rafi was making now.

"No, Ceridwen, you won't. You'll live."

"I can't, Rafi." She met his eyes. "I cannot fail again."

He saw her fear then, and he understood it, for he had felt it himself. "Of course you can. You'll fall, and you'll fail, and you'll get back up

and ride again. You'll live, Ceridwen. For Soldonia. For Liam. For you."
He grinned wryly. "For saga crisps."

She shook her head again, but it was in anguish, not refusal.
"Flames take you."

Ghost quivered beneath him, and Rafi smiled. "No, not flames.
Water."

His gaze dropped, and hers followed, to the miniature waves already
churning and reforming in the water pooling around Ghost's hooves,
as the colt strove to maintain the invisible tether that had granted him
control over the stream. It earned Rafi the undeniable pleasure of
seeing shock blossom on Ceridwen's face for a split second before he
tossed her his spear as the first soldiers charged up. Then he whirled
Ghost around and plunged into the waterfall pool. Down, they dove,
beneath the frothing churn where the currents were strongest, where
Ghost strained with the effort of corralling them, a shriek building
in his throat. Then they spun and shot back up, dragging the pool
with them.

Shrilling his wild scream, Ghost sprang onto the bank, and Rafi
braced against his withers as the shriek was drowned out by the roar
of the massive wave rushing past them. Without the long run the tunnel
had offered, the wave wasn't high enough to soar upon, just powerful
enough to wield like a battering ram.

It shot along the streambed, scattering the knot of soldiers Ceridwen
was fending off with the spear, then swept her and Mindar up with it.
Down the tunnel to freedom.

SIXTY-NINE: RAFI

Water wills and even stone gives way.
- Hanonque proverb

The roar of the wave died away, and Rafi slumped over Ghost's neck, completely drained. He tried not to think of the thousands of soldiers surrounding him, or of Sahak closing in, or even of the awful rasp that punctuated each of Ghost's heaving breaths. Clearly, between the desperate race to reach the gorge and then the demand to command a freshwater stream from a steed meant for the sea, Rafi had asked far too much.

"Shh, shh," he murmured, stroking Ghost's neck. "We're done. It's over." No more running. No more striving. He wished only that he could have freed Ghost before his capture.

Ghost swayed and wobbled forward a step. Then one leg buckled, and he dropped like a stone.

It happened too fast for Rafi to react, either to brace himself or to jump free. He went down with his steed, flung sideways, and the colt's weight came down on his right leg.

He cried out and tried to roll free, but the sharp rods of pain that shot through his knee stopped him. Shoving out instinctively, he felt Ghost's neck draped over his thigh, stiff and unresponsive, Ghost's ribcage crushing his knee.

"Ghost?" he choked out, but the colt did not stir. "Ghost?"

Oh, Ches-Shu, oh *flames*, not Ghost.

He fell back, gasping, and he almost just stayed there, staring up through the slow drift of ash, waiting for Sahak to seize him again.

Almost. With a groan, he shoved himself up, teeth gritted against the pain, and he twisted and pulled and dragged his body until he could cradle the seablood's rigid head in his lap.

Ghost's blue eyes, so like Delmar's, stared vacantly.

Ceridwen had warned him that freshwater wielding could be dangerous for a seablood. Warned him that he had already run Ghost near to death.

"I'm sorry," Rafi whispered, eyes burning, and though clanking armor and approaching bootsteps told him that the soldiers were closing in, he didn't bother lifting his head. Flakes of ash clung to the colt's thick, white lashes. Rafi brushed them away, then traced his fingers over the speckling of blue scales that trailed around Ghost's eyes, down his jaw, down his throat. His knuckles grazed the underside of his steed's jaw, and felt a slow, throbbing tremor there.

Rafi drew in a quick breath.

The stone-eye. Ghost wasn't dead. Just caught under its spell.

But before he could try to break the tiger's line of sight and hopefully snap Ghost free, the cold bite of a spear tip forced his chin up. Sahak leered down the shaft at him, grin bloodstained from a split in his lip. "Rafi. Cousin. Ever a disappointment."

"Sahak. *Cousin.* Come to kill me again?"

"Kill you?" Sahak's eyes gleamed, and he limped a step closer, driving the spear tip up against Rafi's windpipe. "No, cousin, I'm here to take you home."

SEVENTY: CERIDWEN

Rise and ride again.
- Code of the Outriders

Ceridwen drifted in an endless haze over a blazing sea.
It seethed and simmered beneath her and threw up coiling wisps of fire that tried to latch on and tow her down. But she knew there was pain there, unbearable pain. Once, she had thought herself forged of fire and ash, but she was only smoke. And like smoke, she could hover upon the wind.

Untouched. Untethered.

Until some distant, physical sensation—drops of water falling agonizingly on her lips, cool compresses laid like shards of glass across blistered skin, or astringent scents that burned her lungs with each breath—shattered her focus, sending her crashing down into that engulfing sea of pain until she could tear herself free and float upward again. Voices murmured at a distance, here and then gone, but there was one that stayed, speaking soft and low like the wash of waves, or the rippling course of a river, telling her a story.

It felt like a voice she should know, and a story she should remember, but comprehension was a thing of that blazing sea below, and she sought to float above it.

"*Shades*, how long has she been like this?"

That too was a familiar voice, and at the sound, a coil of fire wrapped around her, tugging her down. She fought it, fought it even as molten tears dropped on her face from above. And as the voice urged her to hold on, that familiar blend of frustration and concern caused comprehension to spring to life within her, forming his name on the tip of her tongue.

She gasped and let go, and the sea rushed up at her.

She sank into a shining expanse, and she could not feel pain from wounds or burns. She could not feel her body at all or see anything but light welling around her.

A soft, warm light. A light that did not burn.

It stooped and kissed the scar branded on her forehead, and for an instant, she saw a face, shining and weathered and kind, bearing the same scar, the same brand, seared upon its skin.

Then the light fell away, and she jolted awake, swathed in stained bandages and lying on a bedroll on the floor of a hut. She felt no pain, only a faint warmth still humming through her.

Still pressed against her forehead.

She lifted a bandaged hand and found that the tips of her fingers were not blackened as she feared, or even blistered, but *whole*. Through the open doorway, against a backdrop of white sands and green jungle, she glimpsed a shining golden steed, then she was caught up in arms that carried the scent of saddle oil and beeswax and the wilds of Soldonia, arms that felt like home.

"*Shades*, Ceridwen. Just . . . *shades*."

Her forehead still pulsed with warmth.

She reached to touch it, and Finnian sensed her movement and pulled back slightly, allowing her to see his soft smile and dark eyes shining with unshed tears. "It's gone, Ceridwen. The *kasar* . . . it's gone."

"It was Aodh's hand that led us here," the Scroll, Jakim, said, drawing a snort from the thin, weathered woman, Ineth, who sat in the sand across from him. "We were bound for Cetmur, when we were swept off course by a storm and carried here."

And here they were indeed, though Ceridwen could scarcely believe it.

Here, being a cluster of abandoned huts nestled in a sandy cove somewhere on the Alon Coast, where smugglers were apparently known to shelter from Nadaarian warships. They, being her warriors, all that Finnian had been able to muster on short notice after her defeat scattered them. Together with seariders sent by Lady Telweg, they had crossed the sea to find her.

She sat now with the core members of her patrol, and also of Rafi's team, out on the beach, while the rest of her warriors disembarked steeds and assembled makeshift shelters, since the smuggler's camp was already bursting at the seams with refugees from the gorge. Nold and Kassa were there with Liam pressed between them, looking better than he had in months. Hab, too, casting the occasional wistful glance toward the open-air firepit where Saffa's crew was cooking up a feast for their unexpected guests.

Ceridwen caught a whiff of frying saga crisps and thought of Rafi.

"It was just a storm, Ha'Nor, that blew us off course," Ineth said.

Jakim just smiled. "Exactly where we wished to go? Aodh's hand can guide the wind and the waves. What is a storm to him? You saw how the dawnling's light returned as we sailed. If we had arrived even a few hours later, we would have missed its zenith and the dawnling's opportunity to heal. I cannot help but see Aodh's hand in that."

He seemed different, somehow, than Ceridwen recalled, and it was more than the dark hair covering his formerly shaved head or the fact that he had bonded one of Soldonia's most sacred solborn, and was now, apparently, a dawnrider. It was the way he carried himself. Steadier and more assured. Peaceful.

Her gaze went to the dawnling dozing behind him, nose drooping until it almost rested on his shoulder. The steed did not glow now. Its light, apparently, had been expended to heal her.

Her burns were gone, both old and new, healed across her entire body. She felt no residual pain, no aches, no tenderness even, though from the look on Finnian's face when she mentioned that, she could only imagine how gravely wounded she had been. She had no memory of what had happened after she had been swept from the cavern by Rafi's wave.

Her old battle scars remained—all save the *kasar*.

She kept wanting to reach up and feel for the waxy lines of the brand that had declared her a traitor, to reassure herself it was truly gone.

She shivered slightly, and Finnian's hand tightened on hers.

He looked different too. His tunic hung loose over a frame that seemed far too thin. Though he had not died as she had feared, he had been wounded and was still recovering. He insisted it was nothing serious, but the lines of his face seemed drawn more deeply than before.

"You worried about the army sailing for Soldonia?" he asked.

Owga had stopped by earlier, only briefly, to check on the new arrivals. It was the first time Ceridwen had seen her since the battle. With both Clae and Umut fallen, Owga was now the sole leader of the Que Revolution, or what was left of it, and even their short conversation had been interrupted constantly with requests. She had remained long enough to tell Ceridwen that the army encamped outside of Cetmur had set sail the morning after the attack.

Which was now over two weeks ago.

Soon, ten thousand more soldiers would land in Soldonia.

"Markham knows they're coming," Finnian said, shifting to look out over the sea, eastward toward home. "We'll be ready for them. He's convinced Craddock to stand with us. They mean to force Glyndwr out of the regency, maybe out of his seat, too, if they can do it without sparking civil war. When we get back . . ."

He kept on like that, filling the space between them with words, which was unlike him. But then, they all kept doing it. Nold. Kassa. Even Liam.

Desperate to know that she was all right.

That she was still their Fireborn, even though they had seen her burn.

They did not know that there was something missing. *Someone* missing. Unable to sit still any longer, she stood abruptly and brushed off the sand. Finnian made to follow, wincing as he pushed up, but she waved him off, and he sank back down again. She was grateful for time alone, though a part of her missed the Finnian from before, who would never have yielded so easily.

Mindar was grazing just within the Mah, hobbled to keep him from wandering too deep. She paused, watching as, with a tiny spurt of flame, he crisped a vine before eating it. The flame sputtered out quickly, and the smoke that curled up from his nostrils was a dingy gray. He had burned while trapped in the stone-eye's gaze, yet he bore no outward scars. Not like she had before the dawnling restored her. Still, he seemed hollowed out, somehow. Brittle as dead coals.

She did not fear his flame anymore. Back in the cavern, before the stone-eye wielded Mindar's flame against them, he had sensed that she was hurting and tried to diminish his blaze on his own for her. Whispering softly, she stepped up beside him and ran her bare hand down his shoulder. His ears flicked, and he raised his head, snuffling.

"He's still alive."

She stilled and closed her eyes a moment, then turned to face Eshur as he limped toward her, leaning on a staff to support his wounded leg.

"Or he was a few days ago. Spotted nearing Cetmur in Sahak's entourage. But there's been no tidings since." Eshur planted his staff before him, cupping his hands on the top. "It's possible the emperor plans to sweep it all under the loam. Having a nephew in the rebels doesn't build confidence in his throne."

"Either way you get your tale, don't you?" She couldn't disguise her disdain.

Her rancor did not seem to bother him. "Perhaps. Perhaps not. That's the thing about the tales we're living. It's hard to tell when they're ending or just beginning. You see tragedy here, failure and defeat, and it's right to grieve, but that doesn't mean this is the end. I look out there at the rebels camped upon the beach, and I see courage and hope. I look here"—he inclined his head toward her—"and I see an ember waiting for a breath to stir it alight."

She raised her chin. "Or blow it out."

It was meant to be a dismissal, so she turned to release her steed from his hobbles, but when she straightened, she found Eshur standing directly behind her, a kindly look on his face.

"If I may offer a word of caution?" He did not wait for her response. "Tales can be treacherous things if we try to live up to them, instead of just living. You are not the Fireborn of Soldonia, Ceridwen tal Desmond."

Those words burned in her chest, and she opened her mouth.

"You are not the Fireborn," he repeated, cutting her off.

"Then who am I?" she demanded. "Tal Desmond? Tor Nimid?"

He smiled and reached out and tapped a finger on her forehead, where the scar had once been. Where it was no more. "The Fireborn is *you*. And I do believe there is an ember in you yet." With that, he turned in a swirl of colors and limped away.

He was nearly gone when she called after him. "Someone sat with me while I was unconscious and told me stories." Stories about her and her friends. "Was it you?"

His smile crinkled his eyes. "Young Liam. I do believe he could make a great taleweaver someday."

Ceridwen walked along the shore, boots in hand, watching the water pool in the prints her bare feet left in the damp sand. Mindar trailed on a loose rein just behind her, shying slightly to the side each time a wave came in, dancing to keep his hooves out of the frothing water. The fact that he hadn't yet tried to set the entire ocean ablaze seemed an improvement.

"Markham would have come if he could," Finnian said behind her.

She startled, unnerved still, after all this time, then turned to see him on his shadower, one knee thrown casually across his saddlebow. "Markham has a kingdom to save."

The kingdom she had failed as queen and as their Fireborn.

"So do you," Finnian said and swung down. He caught himself clumsily and straightened with a wince, then removed the oilskin-wrapped bundle fastened behind his saddle. Spreading it out on the sand, he revealed a folded set of firerider leathers—jerkin, chaps, half mask, and gloves—and a pot of skivva oil. "From Markham. Says he won't have you flaming off at the empire, or some other fool thing, without the proper gear. His words, not mine."

The richness of the leather, so dark and oiled and fresh. Unscarred. Ceridwen knelt and brushed her fingers across the jerkin, breathing in the deep, earthy scent.

"This too." Finnian pulled out a sabre. At first, she thought it was hers, and her pulse quickened at the thought of fighting with her own weapon again. But this blade was slightly wider, and the pommel was an oddly misshapen wolf's head that looked like it had been used to knock in more than a few teeth. More than a few enemy helmets too.

This was Markham's own blade.

She did not take it. She couldn't. She did not deserve it. With the unfamiliar sting of tears in her eyes, she sank down in the sand and turned to face the sea. Finnian eased beside her a moment later, laying the sabre across his knees.

"I fell off the first three times I tried the gauntlet," he said. "I know you made it through without falling on your first attempt—Markham won't let me forget—but have you ever fallen off so hard and so often that you couldn't for the life of you pick yourself up again?"

She could not bring herself to speak.

"That's how I felt then—twelve years old and thin as a stick, wishing the ground would swallow me so I didn't have to try again. But Markham wouldn't leave me there. He stuck out his hand and hauled me up, threw me onto my steed, and then he rode through the gauntlet with me." He faced her, and there were tears shimmering at the corners of his eyes. "There's no shame in having someone haul you back to your feet again, Ceridwen. That's what we do. We rise and ride again, but we don't have to do it alone."

Lifting the sabre from his knees, he held it out to her, and this time, she took it. And as she stood and belted it around her waist, she breathed easier than she had in weeks. Months even.

He smiled a little sadly. "We're not going back yet, are we?"

So well he knew her still.

"There's something I have to do first."

"You mean 'we,' I hope. What exactly will we be doing?"

Ceridwen took a deep breath, then swung atop Mindar. "Burning down the empire." And rescuing a friend. "What say you, te Donal? Are you still in?"

His smile widened. "Wouldn't miss it for the world, tal Desmond."

EPILOGUE: SAHAK

Sahak Tetrani had been to the Center of the World, and the grand city of Cetmur—crown of the empire with its thousand singing waterfalls and colossal wall—seemed pale and weak in comparison to the marvels he had seen there. And to the mysteries he would yet unlock.

That didn't mean he couldn't enjoy the view.

He sharply twitched his reins, and Raas, his stone-eye tiger, brought the war-chariot to a rocking halt on the rumpled slope overlooking the approach to Cetmur's jungle gate. Firecrackers exploded in starbursts of scarlet and orange over the palace, arenas, military complex, and city center, catching alight the dusky sky and illuminating the streamered banners flying from every rooftop and turret. It seemed word of his victory had traveled ahead of him. As well it should, considering he had dispatched runners to carry the news to every Que village they passed on their trek southward from the bloodbath in the gorge.

The Fireborn and some of the rabble might have escaped, but he would see that the only tidings that reached the tribes were those of defeat. And of death.

Culminating in the execution of their beloved Sea-Demon.

Chains clinked faintly, and he turned to view the ragged figure that had slumped down, exhaustedly, behind the chariot, head bowed in the red dust of the road. Sahak had set a blistering pace today, and more than once had heard the chain snap taut as Rafi tripped and was dragged before he managed to clamber upright again. Seeing him kneeling now, Sahak's fingers twitched toward his knives. One throw would sting Rafi back to his feet. But no, there would be time enough for that later.

The chariot rocked again as he sprang down and summoned runners to attend him with a sharp jerk of his head. Moments later, they were loping the three leagues toward the jungle gate to ensure the city and its emperor were prepared to receive him with the triumphant procession his victory had earned. In the meantime, his army washed down the dust with a drink and a bite to eat, and he contented himself with pacing, working out the twinges that a day of rattling and jostling had left in his injured ankle.

His neck prickled, alerting him to the presence behind.

He glimpsed bright embroidered robes out of the corner of his eye as the Canthorian scholar stepped up beside him. Vishna had flung open the high collar of his robes, and though it was twilight, a slave held a fringed shade over his shaved skull to protect his pale skin.

"What of the sea-demon?" Sahak asked, quelling his disdain for the man.

"I believe the correct term is seablood." Vishna's eyes flicked down, focusing on the knife Sahak had slipped from his baldric and was now making dance across his fingers. "Still alive. For now. It recovered slightly once we let it drink from the sea, though we nearly lost control of it, and it took ten guards to drag it out of the waves." He cleared his throat as Sahak let the knife spin faster, over and around his wrist now, catching it before it fell each time. "Fortunately a consistent diet of seaweed seems to result in the same effect, so we need not risk losing it again."

Sahak nodded. "Indeed. Fortunate."

He sheathed the knife with a *snick*.

Vishna went on, warming up to his topic, but Sahak had stopped listening, watching as a tall figure in ashen robes drifted toward them. Soldiers fell silent, priests rattled the chains of their office in respect, and more than a few faces turned ashen as they fell under the stare of the gilded mask beneath the hood. Even from a distance, Sahak could taste the power emanating off the figure, and it tasted of chilled salt springs, sharp copper, and the rich, red draught of utter domination.

Without slackening pace, the figure glided past Rafi, who sat now with his back to the chariot wheel, swollen knee stretched out before him. Sahak abruptly left Vishna rambling to greet the figure, but sharp cries forestalled him, heralding the return of his runners.

So soon? That boded ill.

For the first time again since the band of riders had raced up the gorge, willfully flinging themselves into the heart of his trap, Sahak felt a twinge of uncertainty. He arrived at the robed figure's side and let the intoxicating sensation of power sweep over him, steeling his hands against straying toward his knives as his runners trooped toward him. They were escorted by a full company of gold-plumed imperial guards.

Somehow, he doubted they'd come to honor his victory.

Before he could speak, an officer bearing a transverse crest on his helm stepped forward and declared in an exaggerated Cetmurian drawl, "By order of His Imperial Majesty, Emperor Lykier, the priest Sahak and all his force are denied entrance to the city this night. You may stage your camp no closer than five leagues from the gate and await the emperor's good pleasure."

Sahak clenched his twitching fingers before they could betray him and bury a knife, or a pair of knives, in the officer's arrogant face. He knew Cetmurers like this one well, born of old Nadaarian stock, secure in their untainted blood, disdainful of any with even a trace of the territories about them. "Oh, we may, may we? And what excuse does my father give this time, for overlooking this momentous victory?"

"The emperor," the officer corrected stiffly, "in his magnificent beneficence commands that you feast tonight upon the riches of his own table." He flicked a hand toward the road where a convoy of carts was rattling toward them.

Truly, his father's beneficence knew no bounds.

"And I am to be satisfied with this paltry offering?"

A tinge of insolence crept into the officer's smile. "This offering is not for you. It is to celebrate the birth of the emperor's son and heir, Nikam Tetrani, of House Korringar, Crown Prince of Nadaar. Hear the words of your emperor and rejoice." With that revelation, wielded like an expert dagger thrust between the ribs, the officer grounded his spear twice, and the company marched off.

Sahak stared after them, a tempest stirring to life in his chest.

"Out with the old, in with the new, eh, cousin?"

He looked down to find Rafi with his head tipped back, bleeding from a cut on his chin, skin peeling from the still-healing steam burns, smiling wanly up at him, and a jolt of fury shot through him. The masked figure at his side swung swiftly toward Rafi, caught him by the throat, and slammed him against the chariot. The sharp motion made the figure's ashen hood fall back, exposing the gilded scadtha-skull mask affixed to his face, hooked under his jaw with barbs embedded in the skin.

Rafi let out a strangled gasp, and Sahak knew it had nothing to do with the gruesome mask, and everything to do with the eyes behind it. Blue as the Alonque blood that ran in Rafi's veins. And in the veins of his brother.

"Del . . ." Rafi choked out. "How . . .?"

The figure did not relinquish his grip.

Coldly, dispassionately, strangling the life out of him.

Sahak watched as Rafi pried vainly at the hands clamped around his throat, as his strained pleadings trailed off, as his eyes started to roll back, then he stepped forward. The figure instantly released his grip. Rafi dropped to the ground, coughing and wheezing. Head dangling, he pushed himself up again, speaking in gasps as soon as he could breathe.

"It's . . . me, Del. It's . . . Rafi. I know . . . it's you."

"Not quite, I'm afraid." Sahak crouched over Rafi, aware of the flutter of ashen robes moving into place behind him, of a masked face staring off into distances unknown. "He isn't your brother anymore, Rafi. Or at least, not the brother you thought you knew. You should kneel, cousin, and show deference to the Voice of Murloch."

THE STORY CONTINUES IN

THE FIREBORN EPIC BOOK 3:
OF DAWN AND EMBERS

ACKNOWLEDGMENTS

Of all the books I have written so far, this one put up the fiercest resistance. Every day that I sat down to write felt like picking myself up out of the dust after a breathtaking fall. So crafting this book from start to finish felt like rising and riding again day by day, and as Finnian himself points out, I was so grateful to discover that I didn't have to do it alone.

Mom and Dad, I truly cannot thank you enough for your unwearying encouragement, championing of my work, and steadfast belief in the stories I write and my ability to write them. Maris, thank you so much for coffee shop hopping with me during edits. Ryan, if you read this, this is not the book where your promised character appears. Lydia, this *is* the book with the Iakki moment inspired by the "untouched paint" incident. Have you found it yet?

Brynne and Bryan, thank you for giving me a beautiful quiet place to write when I desperately needed it, for mountain adventures and drinks by the fire. It's true, Brynne, that I have always looked up to you like Rafi looks up to Delmar, and because of that, I truly cannot express how much it meant to me to have you read this book first. I certainly would not have had the courage to declare it finished without you.

Inkwell crew (Claire, Amy, Katie, Emily, and Mollie), our group is such a bright spot on the internet! Thank you for the brainstorming help—especially with the dawnling hunt—and for all the writing sprints, prayers, and check-ins. I'm so grateful we all found each other!

Mollie Reeder, thank you for endlessly cheering me on, for offering feedback and encouragement in turn, and for helping me to stop overthinking every tiny detail.

Steve Laube, thank you for showing me what true grace looks like. Your patience and graciousness during the writing process was the light that kept me typing. Lisa Laube, thank you for tackling this wild manuscript with me, for not being daunted by the word count, and for wielding your expert red pen to help rein it in.

Sarah Grimm, thank you for working your copyediting wonders on this book. Trissina, you make marketing so much more fun, and I'm so thankful for your creativity and expertise. Jamie Foley, your design work is flawless, and I couldn't be more thrilled to get to work with you again on this project. Lindsay Franklin, thank you for brilliantly managing behind the scenes, and Katie S. Williams, I'm so grateful to have had your sharp eyes proofreading this massive tome. And to the entire Enclave crew and author family, you each make the world a more beautiful place, and I'm so thankful for all of you.

Darko Tomic, yet again, you've created a masterpiece of a cover! Thank you for taking my wild ideas and transforming them into something beautiful.

Gerralt Landman, this map! I didn't think anything could be more beautiful than the map you created for Soldonia, but you proved me wrong. Thank you for bringing such incredible skill and artistry to every aspect of the map and chapter illustrations.

Outrider Street Team, you are all of you amazing! Thank you for sharing your love for this story with the world!

To the One who reframes stories, thank you for reframing mine, and for leading me onward one step, one day, one story at a time.

Finally, to all of you faithful readers who have been waiting so expectantly to ride onward with Ceridwen, Rafi, and Jakim—and all the rest—your love and support for this story means the world to me. I write every day with you in mind.

Until next time, rise and ride again, my friends!

ABOUT THE AUTHOR

G illian Bronte Adams writes epic fantasy novels, including the award-winning *Of Fire and Ash* and The Songkeeper Chronicles. She loves strong coffee, desert hikes, and trying out new soup recipes on crisp fall nights. Her favorite books are the ones that make your heart ache and soar in turn. Over the years, her work has taken her from the riding arena as a youth camp equestrian director (where she also served on a rural volunteer fire department) to the recording booth as an audiobook narrator, all of which now provide fodder for the thing she loves most: creating vibrant new worlds and dreaming up stories that ring with the echoes of eternity. At the end of the day, she can be found off chasing sunsets with her horse or her dog, Took. Connect with her online at GillianBronteAdams.com or @gillianbronteadams.